A TIME OF WAR

The Transgressors

A lorry full of cheering soldiers swerved around the border gate. A tank ran through it and wood and splinters flew in every direction. A rifle shot rang out from the customs building and the tank stopped. The turret revolved and the stubby thirty-seven millimetre gun fired. A gout of flame and smoke blew out a wall.

The sky exploded with sound at the same moment and a flight of Stukas tore the heavens apart. There were four in spread formation at not more than two hundred metres altitude streaking into Poland. Another four followed and another until the sky snarled with aircraft engines. Ahead were the flat, clean fields of Poland, all the way to the Vistula.

Also by Joe Poyer in Sphere Books:

THE CHINESE AGENDA
THE CONTRACT
THE DAY OF RECKONING
OPERATION MALACCA
THE BALKAN ASSIGNMENT
NORTH CAPE
HELL SHOT
VENGEANCE 10
TUNNEL WAR

A Time Of War

Volume 1
The Transgressors

JOE POYER

SPHERE BOOKS LIMITED
30-32 Gray's Inn Road, London WC1X 8JL

First published in Great Britain by Sphere Books Ltd 1983
Copyright © Joe Poyer 1983

TRADE
MARK

This book is sold subject to the condition that it shall not, by way of trade or
otherwise, be lent, re-sold, hired out or otherwise circulated without the
publisher's prior consent in any form of binding or cover other than that in
which it is published and without a similar condition including this condition
being imposed on the subsequent purchaser

Phototypeset in Linotron Palatino

Reproduced, printed and bound in Great Britain by
Hazell Watson & Viney Ltd,
Member of the BPCC Group,
Aylesbury, Bucks

For those who sacrificed,
from one who benefited.

To every thing there is a season, and a time to every
purpose under heaven:
A time to be born, and a time to die; a time to plant,
and a time to pluck up that which is planted;
A time to kill, and a time to heal; a time to mourn
and a time to dance;
A time to cast away stones, and a time to gather stones
together; a time to embrace and a time to refrain from
embracing;
A time to get, and a time to lose; a time to keep, and a
time to cast away;
A time to rend, and a time to sew; a time to keep silence,
and a time to speak;
A time to love, and a time to hate; a time of war, and a
time of peace.
Ecclesiastes 3:1

Main and Secondary Characters

Torsten Fredriksson	Swedish journalist and narrator
Jeanette Rodale	French artist, heiress and his lover
Keith Thorne	American pilot
Jacob Yitzak	Polish musician
David Yitzak	Polish army officer
Deborah Yitzak	Wife of David and then Keith
Shirley Case	Keith's fiancée
Keith Thorne Senior	His father
Charlotte Simpson	His lover
Friedrich Prager	German Panzer officer
Sonia Vishenka	His wife
Joachim Brenner	Army officer and boyhood friend
Erwin Rommel	Commander Seventh Panzer Division in France
Charles Atkins	British attaché and tank officer
Johan Erko	Finnish staff assistant to Marshall Carl von Mannerheim
Erika Brotherus	*Lotta Svard* Volunteer
Lers Radikko	Finnish army officer
Timothy O'Brien	Sergeant-Major, Royal New Zealand Army
Wendy Hiller	Yorkshire librarian
Rand Dobson	Officer, Royal Australian Navy
John Peters	Commander, HMS *Adelaide*, Royal Navy
Sir Martin Dunbar-Naismith	Admiral Commanding, Western Approaches

Alfredo Marchetti	Officer, Italian Army
Giulo Maroni	Captain, Italian Army
Vincente Osano	Colonel, Italian Army
Mikhail Gregor Dogorov	Officer, Red Army
Olga Semonova Dogorova	His mother
Alexander Prokovitch Braun	Sergeant, Red Army
Saburo Takeda	Officer, Sixth Sasebo Special Landing Landing Force

FOREWORD

The idea for a book that would tell the story of the Second World War from all sides first occurred to me twenty years ago when I was employed by an American aerospace firm. Such organizations are true 'melting pots' of modern technological man and thus I met people who had served in every Allied and Axis army involved in the Second World War.

It was then fifteen years after the end of the War and many with whom I talked were beginning to reflect on what had happened to them between 1939-1945 and to ask if any of it had been worth while. My conversations with many of these people have continued over the years, with certain points becoming increasingly clear.

First, the vast majority of those who served were apolitical – apolitical in the sense that they did not understand the ramifications of total war nor their government's participation, but served simply because an enemy had been defined and they were expected to help defend their nation. Not one single individual ever expressed the opinion that he or she had participated solely because they feared punishment. Their reasons were of course quite complex, but chief among them was patriotism – a concept that had rather a different meaning in 1939 than today.

Secondly, most were only a very small part of a monstrously huge machine. In common, they were bored, frightened, exhausted, hungry and homesick, all of which left little time for the greater ramifications of the world struggle.

Third, fully 25 per cent of my confidants admitted to knowing of, and 10 per cent to having committed an atrocity. These divided roughly into two types – deliberate and, what I choose to call, conditional.

Deliberate atrocities were matters of policy, written or unwritten and included the killing of prisoners, the operation of concentration and death camps (three of those with whom I spoke at length had served as concentration camp guards – two on one side, one on another), and the harsh and often murderous treatment of civilian populations in occupied areas in retaliation for resistance efforts. Reasons for committing atrocities seemed a curious mixture of hatred induced by their government, fear for themselves if they did not obey, and reaction against what they were doing which generated a terrible self-loathing, which in turn increased the harsh treatment of their charges.

'Conditional' atrocities were by and large limited to the battlefield and not all were perceived, then or now, as 'atrocities' even though they might be so considered by the perpetrator under 'peace-time' conditions. They often involved the kind of incident that could occur under the terrible stress of fear and imminent death. But no matter the national or moral backgrounds of the individuals involved it seemed that remorse was greater in the latter category than among those involved in government-sanctioned atrocities.

As one ex-soldier pointed out to me; why speak of atrocities when the war was an atrocity from start to finish. When I ventured the opinion that wars must be fought by rules if the participants are to remain civilized, he smiled as one who had been there.

Numerous other impressions were gained which I have tried to distil into *A Time of War* by creating eight characters – British, German, Italian, American, Japanese, Australian, Russian and one neutral, a Swedish journalist. All eight are simply human beings thrown into the abnormal situation of war. They are neither heroes nor cowards, fools nor geniuses and none has a measurable effect on great events. They live and die as no more than they are. Some will participate in the great known battles, some in the great unknown battles, others in actions long-forgotten except by the survivors. But in the end, the reader hopefully will have witnessed the full sweep of the Second World War.

Many post-war events had their beginnings in the War and certain of these trends are identified and followed. Many wartime resistance movements evolved into national independence movements after 1945 which disavowed and then ejected colonial masters. Others became powerful political organizations that changed post-war governmental systems, some by democratic means and others by force.

The Second World War was largely a struggle for survival between the great industrial nations. Ideology, forms of government and the rescue of defeated peoples were all secondary to the need to obtain and/or maintain control of such vital resources as oil, rubber, certain minerals and agricultural land. A comparison of maps showing the distribution of natural resources in the eastern hemisphere with the thrust and direction of challenging Axis armies in 1939-1942 will bear this statement out. It was not by accident that these territories were controlled by nations who were to become known as the Allies, nor that the Axis powers were industrial nations who had developed too late to participate effectively in the establishment of colonial empires.

A word of caution: I have made every effort to eliminate forty plus years of hindsight and present the incidents of war as the characters involved would have experienced them. If a character's perceptions seem limited, that is because the combat soldier always knows less than anyone else.

Finally, the reader will find no 'good-guy versus bad-guy' character treatment in *A Time of War*. Such simplistic concepts existed only in the imaginations of the propagandists and rarely in the perceptions of the man at the 'sharp end'.

Prologue

Berlin 29 August 1946

Torsten Fredriksson watched the four men pause on the steps below. They exchanged handshakes that seemed just a bit too perfunctory, then separated and hurried away into the night. Four men. Four survivors. Four professionals. He closed the curtains and turned back into a room suddenly empty and cheerless. There had been seven of them including himself at that Embassy party in Warsaw seven years before. Three had been killed in the war and the survivors had changed beyond recognition, physically and mentally.

The contrast between then and their behaviour tonight had been striking. Granted they were strangers to one another, having met only that one time in 1939. But then, he remembered, there had been the sense of comradeship that came from a shared profession. New factors acted as barriers now, even to individuals whose nations were supposedly allied. Tonight, there had been no talk of the future, while the talk that night in August 1939 had been about little else. Or were the spectres of the past years still hovering, the pain, disappointment, death and horror? Whatever, it had not been the reunion he expected.

He began to clear away the dinner dishes but a sudden restlessness stopped him. Instead, he sat down at the battered portable typewriter that had served him all over the world and rolled a fresh sheet of paper into the carriage. It was the need all writers experience, the need to describe some great complexity, to break it down and examine each component.

How? There was too much to tell, too much to understand in six years of total war.

Novels and non-fiction books describing the war were proliferating around the world and he had read many, but they seemed incomplete; not in the literary sense but in the sense of the complete story of what had happened to mankind since 1939. Nowhere was there a human life that had not been affected by the war.

As a neutral journalist and a Swedish citizen, he had been allowed access to all sides and so perhaps had gained a better appreciation of the war's effects than most. He had met, in fact had sought out each of those men as often as possible in the cauldron of horror, questioning, listening, comforting until he knew their stories by heart. And in doing so, he was certain that he had come to know more about the war in total than they did, even though each had been engaged from the beginning.

He thought he knew these men, and the three who had been killed, well enough to know that they, like most of the professional soldiers and, later, the majority of conscripts and volunteers, had not been especially concerned with the political aims of their respective governments, except perhaps to pay them lip service. Nor with the grand designs of global strategy nor were they the confidants of that handful of men who had set the course of the war. They were soldiers, like the millions who came after them, shorn of individuality and compressed into a coherent mass whose task was the murder of their fellow man. They did what they were told to do because it was expected of them.

In his experience, only a handful of people in the very top echelons of government – whether democracy or dictatorship – had even the haziest idea of the political and economic goals for which they, with the complicity of those they governed, had sent forty-three million people to their deaths, damaged and maimed countless millions more and forever changed the history of man.

The question of *how* was intimately connected with *why*. Why had the British bomber pilot over Dresden like the German Panzer officer in the Crimea or the Japanese sailor in the Slot or the American marine at Iwo Jima done as he was ordered, even though the result was likely to be as horrible a death for themselves as for the enemy?

Had that question always been in his mind during the years he trudged battlefields, waited at aerodromes, and walked up gangways to talk with the people going out to kill and die? *Why* were they doing it? Because they had been told to and the penalty was prison or the executioner's bullet? That was a factor of course, but it had to be something deeper even than fear and the propagandist's persuasion.

Fredriksson paused and thought about the way the survivors of that Warsaw dinner party had walked softly about one another, measuring, remembering. Did it still make a difference that one of them had been the enemy of the other four? He didn't think so. Not any longer.

He began to type the story, from the beginning. There was no need to do an outline as it was all in his memory – the central event of his life.

. . . sie macht sich nur durch
Blut und Eisen

Otto von Bismarck

Warsaw, Poland 27 August 1939

The summer fields had already been stripped of their harvest, Torsten Fredriksson noted while the Berlin–Warsaw Express snorted impatiently on the siding while one goods wagon after another, filled with laughing soldiers waving at the side-tracked passenger train, rumbled past. After the troop train had come another, carrying canvas-shrouded bundles that even to the untrained eye were the *panzerkampfwagons*, the powerful tanks of the German army.

At the border, the train paused to exchange crews. The banter between the German and Polish customs officials seemed normal enough and when the train ran into Poland there was no diminution of service and politeness. Were the Germans so confident they dared move troops and equipment openly to the border? Were the Poles so blind to German preparations, or did they think they could negotiate a way out of this latest crisis or, failing that, stop the German armies on the battlefield?

The concise, well-tended German fields gave way to the sprawling, untidy Polish farms. Stands of forest were scattered about the countryside and homes and buildings were tucked away in the folds of rolling land. A village flicked past, sleepy in the afternoon heat, no one to be seen. The previous year, Fredriksson had attended a military demonstration in the Kummersdorf suburb of Berlin. There, great, growling juggernauts of devastation had crashed through brick buildings, climbed rock walls and spat thirty-seven millimetre high-explosive shells at simulated enemy vehicles and trenches. He had seen no evidence of cardboard cutouts mounted on old motor cars that Germany's enemies liked to pretend still existed. The metal monsters were real and they were terrifying in their destructive power. These farmlands would become race courses for German Panzer tanks.

Fredriksson had ridden this train many times. One could go from London – via the Dover–Ostend packet – to Moscow. The train ran through water-logged Flanders into the wooded hills of the Ardennes, then down onto the great Rhineland plateau. The land rose again in central and northern Germany and the train raced through the well-tended suburbs of Berlin and from there into the richest agricultural land on the continent, eastern Germany and Poland, across the vast marshes of the Pripet and onto the plains of Russia. Beyond lay Siberia, so carefully hidden from the world by Tsar and Commissar.

He liked the alliteration of that phrase. It read well in both Swedish and English and he had to be aware of both languages in composing his syndicated column – 'From Across the World'. He lit a cigarette, thinking about the Soviet-German Non-Aggression Pact signed four days earlier. It certainly was a coup of the first magnitude for Herr Hitler. And it made war a certainty in the spring. Or even sooner. Perhaps in October. Germany could not be planning another great bluff on the scale of Czechoslovakia because not even Chamberlain would be taken in this time. It would be war for certain because the Poles would not back down, as the Czechs had.

Poland had been a gleeful party to that nation's dismemberment and now it was their turn. Poetic justice?

Torsten Fredriksson stood to one side of the arched ballroom entrance the following night and watched the diplomats and their wives dancing the intricate pavane of alliances and understandings, spoken and unspoken. For once, he was enjoying himself. Usually, he found these affairs a boring waste of time but tonight was different. Perhaps the staff of the American Embassy knew it might be the last such party and were determined to make it an affair to remember.

The Russian Ambassador and his dour wife were deep in conversation with the German Ambassador, their backs rigidly turned to the British Ambassador and his wife who were pointedly ignoring them anyway. Only two weeks before, the Russian and British Ambassadors had fawned over one another.

Fredriksson took another glass of champagne and thought about the blonde secretary who had checked his engraved invitation. Had she smiled at him out of politeness or interest? He had decided to stroll into the foyer and find out when a young man in an American suit, well-tailored for all that, appeared and stared about the room with that tentative, half-smile people adopt when they don't know a soul in the place. The man looked vaguely familiar and Fredriksson riffled through his prodigious memory for a name.

New York, a year or more ago; of course. There had been a society scandal of the type that only the Americans, with their penchant for public puritanism, could devise. A young woman, pregnant, an accusation in court and a hearing that ended abruptly when the defence was able to demonstrate that the young woman in question was not really pregnant after all. The press had enjoyed the dénouement and thousands of words of useless drivel had been written in which, something . . . Thorne, was pictured first as a blackguard with a great deal of money, and little sense and then as the victim of a scheming Jezebel.

Longish brown hair fell over his forehead and Fredriksson recalled that that signified education at a certain type of American private school. He was of medium height, well-built and handsome in a way that would especially appeal to older women. He also possessed an air of indolence and fashionable cynicism that prevailed among upper class young all over the world, insulated by money and privilege from the ravages of the Depression.

Thorne turned to him when he noticed that Fredriksson was studying him and, unembarrassed, the journalist strolled over.

'You are an American, are you not?'

The young man nodded. 'Yes. Are you German?'

Fredriksson smiled. 'Thank God, no. I'm Swedish. I am also a journalist, of the type the British call a freelance. A strange term as it makes me sound like a mercenary soldier. My name is Torsten Fredriksson.'

'Keith Thorne.' They shook hands and the American thought for a moment. 'A "free lance" was originally a knight or soldier for hire. You are a journalist for hire and isn't the pen mightier than the sword?'

Fredriksson laughed, appreciating his quickness.

'Speaking of soldiers,' the American went on, 'there seem to be a lot of them here tonight.'

'Rumours of war,' Fredriksson responded. 'Before the autumn is over, they will be killing one another. Why are you in Warsaw at such a time, if you don't mind?'

Thorne shrugged. 'I was sent by my publishing company to negotiate a contract with the famous violinist Jacob Yitzak, for his autobiography.'

'Ah yes, that Thorne. I thought I recognized your name. Your family owns Thorne, Dorsten and Winslow Press, I believe.'

'My father is chairman of the board, president and chief editor. I'm merely a flunky.'

He turned to survey the crowded room and to break the uncomfortable silence, Fredriksson asked, 'Then you are a guest of the American Ambassador?'

Thorne's expression was cool, as if he were deciding whether or not to answer and Fredriksson said quickly, 'Please, I do not mean to pry. Journalistic instinct only. I believe others refer to it as snooping.'

Thorne laughed suddenly. 'No, I am not a guest of the Ambassador – different political party. I was invited here tonight by an old school friend, Jim Howell who, it seems, is not here.' He regarded

Fredriksson. 'Now it's my turn. What are you doing in Warsaw at a time like this?'

A waiter offered a tray of fresh cocktails and they both took one. Fredriksson lifted his in mock salute and Thorne responded, 'Skol.'

'Ah no. One only "skol"s the ladies, and then the hostess first.' Fredriksson sipped his drink. 'I am here because there will be war before long. A tremendous war that will begin here in Poland.'

Thorne snorted. 'I've been hearing that since 1936. Every time Hitler threatens to gobble up another country, the British and French rant and do nothing. Hell, they couldn't even force Mussolini out of Abyssinia. The colonial powers have had it. Their so-called empires have sucked them dry.'

'Ah yes, the American view.' He smiled to rob the remark of its sting. 'Perhaps you are right but I think the turning point came with the signing of the Nazi–Soviet pact. The British had hoped to win the Russians for themselves – at arm's length, of course. Hitler beat them to it and now his back door is secure. Needless to say, there was profound shock in London.'

Fredriksson nodded to the cluster of uniforms. 'If you need more proof, look at them. They aren't vultures gathered to the feast, but eagles. The one in the fancy dress uniform is Herr Hauptmann Friedrich Prager of the German Army. I met him two years ago in Berlin. Prager was assigned here to the German Embassy in June. Since then, he has travelled extensively throughout the central and southwestern sections of Poland. The Panzer corps must have excellent route maps to Warsaw by now.'

'Do you mean he's a spy?'

'Not at all. He is a military attaché – although there are those who question the distinction. The man he is speaking to is his opposite number, so to speak, in the British Army – Captain Charles Atkins of the 4th Hussars, one of the British military attachés to the Polish government. No doubt, they are exchanging views on the most efficient use of their toys. The Oriental gentleman in naval whites is Lieutenant Saburo Takeda of Japan's Imperial Navy. He arrived in Poland several days ago with a Japanese delegation. The rumours have it that they are seeking an alliance with Poland against the Russians.'

'Whatever in the world for?'

'A very logical move. Russia is understandably nervous over Japanese moves in Manchuria and China. You may not know this but Russia and Japan are fighting an undeclared war in Manchuria at this very moment. So far, I have only the barest details. The Japanese are seeking a mutual defence treaty in case their little war should widen. This might explain in some way why Moscow was in such haste to sign the Nazi–Soviet pact.

'Now those two gentlemen engaged in a side conversation are the Soviet and Italian military attachés. The taller man is Lieutenant Mikhail Dogorov and the shorter is Lieutenant Alfredo Marchetti.'

'If you are correct,' Thorne observed, 'these people, with the exception of the Jap, constitute the warring, or soon to be warring, powers.'

'You discount the Japanese?' Fredriksson regarded him with interest. 'Do most Americans? Even in the face of evidence to the contrary.'

'What evidence is that?' But Fredriksson did not have the opportunity to answer as the German officer, Prager, noticing Fredriksson at that moment, excused himself and hurried towards them.

'My dear Torsten, I did not know you were coming tonight,' he said in German.

'Friedrich, allow me to introduce a new acquaintance, Mr Keith Thorne. Mr Thorne is an American and a publisher's representative in Warsaw on business. Mr Thorne, may I present Captain Friedrich Prager.' Fredriksson had spoken slowly in German and the meaning was clear enough to Thorne.

They shook hands and Prager switched to heavily accented English. 'Welcome to Warsaw, Mr Thorne. I hope you are. . .' he paused, searching for the word.

'I do speak French,' Thorne said and Prager smiled in relief. 'So do I, Mr Thorne. I hope you are enjoying your trip.'

They made small talk for a moment before Prager turned to Fredriksson and said, still in French, 'Torsten, several of us are getting up a supper party. Can we persuade you, and Mr Thorne, to join us?'

'I would be delighted! Mr Thorne?'

Thorne hesitated. Suddenly, he was aware of how much he had missed such dinners over the past two years. 'I'd like to tag along if your friends wouldn't mind.'

The conversation flowed easily and Thorne found himself marvelling at the way they could discuss military tactics and weaponry with never a thought to the fact that they might soon be using them on one another. But then he remembered his days as an army officer when he had done the same. They were all professionals and as such were concerned with the technique of their profession and not the end use to which higher authority might see fit to put them. He had no sympathy for the German or Italian governments, political methods or objectives, merely the interest of an ex-army officer in their military abilities.

A servant appeared at that moment with a note for Prager. He frowned and tore open the envelope while the others watched. Thorne was aware of a sudden tension.

Prager muttered to himself and shook his head. 'Gentlemen, I am afraid I must return to the Embassy. Nothing serious. My relief has taken to his bed with a severe cold. Please do not let my absence affect your supper plans. Mr Thorne,' he shook hands, 'I am honoured to have met you.'

His new companions deferred to Fredriksson when it came time to choose a restaurant. The Swede thought for a moment and snapped his fingers. 'Palaccio's!'

The others seemed to know the name and agreed instantly. A taxi was summoned, Fredriksson gave the taxi driver instructions and the ageing Chevrolet swerved off through the crowded streets. Thorne knew it was *de rigueur* for travellers to report cab drivers in whichever city they visited last to be the absolute worst but those who had ridden the Warsaw cabs knew better.

The restaurant Fredriksson had selected was on Weilka Street, on the verge of the old Jewish Quarter. The evening was warm and entire families walked in the fresh air. There was a rich smell of cooking, spices and sauces and something else which took him a bit longer to identify – the odour of too-crowded humanity. He had noticed it in New York, in the Harlem area, in Hell's Kitchen, up and down the Lower East Side and along Tenth Avenue.

Palaccio's was anything but Italian, both to Thorne's and Lieutenant Marchetti's surprise; it was, in fact, a kosher version of a French restaurant. The food and service were superb.

Fredriksson told the others of Thorne's purpose in Warsaw and he in turn found himself confiding that he had served in the American Army Air Corps until retiring after a flying accident two years before. He was instantly accepted as a member of the club and the conversation moved swiftly to military matters again. There was little discussion of specifics, Thorne was not surprised to discover, but a great deal of argument over tactics and their applications in the broadest sense.

Coffee followed and his companions settled back loosening Sam Browne belts. The restaurant was crowded but Thorne realized that no new patrons had entered in some time. Apparently the doors were shut when capacity was reached so as not to rush those with the good sense to arrive early.

With the brandy, all traces of formality disappeared and the talk became more specific. Lieutenant Takeda began with questions to the British army officer, Atkins, about his government's intentions now that Germany and the Soviet Union had signed their non-aggression pact. Thorne mentally braced himself for an explosion

11

but instead, a serious discussion of British alternatives resulted. Thorne stole a glance at the Russian officer, Dogorov, but found him listening impassively. The general consensus was that while Germany held the upper hand at the moment, she still had to reckon with France and Britain.

'No one outside Germany,' Atkins told them, 'considers that Germany would dare take on France and Britain together – again. Moscow apparently thinks as we do, but it is doubtful if Berlin does. In 1914, Germany came near to accomplishing her goals. If those 160 divisions required on the Eastern Front could have been used in France,' he shrugged, 'we all know how close she came in the spring of 1918.

'Hitler has proved himself a shrewd strategist. He has shielded his eastern borders from attack and left himself a free hand in the west. Does your government not agree, Lieutenant Marchetti?'

The young Italian officer shrugged. 'But of course. Both the Duce and Hitler have demonstrated the hollow policies of your democracies. In the world today a strong, stable government free to hew to a single course year after year, will certainly triumph over wrangling democracies which veer with each wind.'

The journalist turned to Thorne. 'And where does America stand in all this?'

As an ex-Army officer, Thorne could take an intellectual interest in the conversation, but as an American citizen, he felt no emotional need to defend one side or another. This was strictly a European squabble and he said as much.

'We discovered after we entered the last war that America had made a serious mistake. A hundred and fifty years of consistent foreign policy were thrown out overnight. Our refusal to join the League of Nations afterward suggests how severe was the national rejection of European alliances. We prefer not to bother anyone and not be bothered ourselves.'

There was a sharp intake of breath from the Japanese officer. 'Do you disagree, Lieutenant Takeda?' Fredriksson asked with a bland smile.

Saburo Takeda shook his head. 'I find your remarks at odds with the facts, Mr Thorne,' he said quietly. 'America has claimed for itself the entire Pacific Ocean and seeks to control all nations bordering it. That, my dear Mr Thorne, is seen as the height of arrogance in Japan, at all levels of society.'

Thorne was plainly quite puzzled. 'I . . . I'm not quite certain what you mean, Lieutenant. It would seem to me that your government's actions in China are more disturbing to your neighbours than anything the United States might have done.'

'No, Mr Thorne. Japan is a very small nation with few natural resources. China is a very large and an inefficiently run nation. For many years, Japan tried to reach an accommodation with her regarding the use of certain of those resources, as well as lands to the north which are sparsely settled. China, supported by America as well as the British and Dutch colonial empires, has refused our approaches with insults, thus leaving us no other alternative.'

'I don't believe that one nation's lack of resources ever justifies aggression against another nation. . . .'

The Japanese officer smiled at him. 'No, Mr Thorne, I would not expect you to understand what I am certain is unintentional hypocrisy on your part. America has ever been hostile to the Asian; your own history supports this contention. Your Immigration Act of 1924 barring all orientals was an insult to everyone of my race. Even today. Asians are allowed only the most menial jobs and, like your Negroes, hounded into the most squalid sections of your cities where they are easy prey to the worst elements of white society.

'Today, your nation, a land rich, perhaps too rich, in natural resources and living space not only refuses to understand our position, but seeks to inhibit Japan's own growth on the Asian mainland and in the Pacific. America has become greedier than the colonialist powers whose actions are at least understandable as they depend upon the resources of their colonies to survive. But America has no such excuse. Your natural wealth is a source of envy around the world. The restrictions you have illegally placed on our trade are reminiscent of those saddled upon your thirteen colonies in the eighteenth century by England. War was the inevitable result then; without a change in your Government's attitude, it may well be again.

'There is a saying in my language, Mr Thorne. It translates as "who must do harsh things? He who can." The entire Japanese nation is ready, Mr Thorne.'

Thorne bristled at Saburo Takeda's remark but before he could retort, the Russian Lieutenant, Mikhail Gregorvitch Dogorov laughed and slapped his huge hands on the table.

'Gentlemen, gentlemen, enough politics, please! I should like to recall my last night in Warsaw with fondness and not least for the company I am keeping.'

'Last night?' the others echoed.

'My last night,' he repeated with regret. 'I have been recalled for reassignment.'

The attachés exchanged uneasy glances and Fredriksson thought to himself that a summons to Moscow these days could as readily mean trial and execution as reassignment or promotion. But Dogorov did not seem in the least worried, in fact he interpreted their worried expressions.

'I am to be given command of an artillery battery. While I enjoy the loose life of a diplomat, I am most happy to be returning to the discipline of a line unit.'

That was obvious, Thorne thought. Dogorov was turned out in dress uniform on which the brass and braid gleamed in the candle light. He was a big man, well over six feet tall, Thorne guessed, and with the square, heavy browed head unique to the Slavic race. His hair was cropped very short and the bluish shadow across his chin suggested a heavy beard. His uniform fitted well over a broad chest and broader shoulders. Thorne suspected that, if the Russians used recruiting posters for their Army, Dogorov would make the perfect model.

'In that case,' Fredriksson picked up his glass, 'I propose a toast. To Mikhail Gregorvitch Dogorov, Lieutenant of Artillery. Long life, good health and the love of beautiful women everywhere!'

Fredriksson leaned on the balcony railing to watch the peaceful city wake. A thin mist mixed with summer haze had infiltrated Warsaw's streets and it was still too early for the harsh blend of traffic noises. He sipped his coffee and thought about the column he was writing.

In contrast to warlike preparations along the border, neither Berlin nor Warsaw seemed to take the war threat seriously. No rigorous air raid precautions had been taken and mobilization was desultory at best in Poland.

He sat down at the breakfast table on which he had placed his portable typewriter, moved the coffee pot and rolled a fresh sheet of paper into the carriage. He hesitated, fingers poised, then began to type his impressions of the two cities and the previous night's dinner into one of the 'From Across the World' columns for which he was becoming well known, detailing the contrasts between the soldier's frank reality and the never-never land of Government pronouncements. He ended with two paragraphs that had probably been written a thousand times during the past week:

> It does not require prescience to realize that before the year is out, these six men, and others like them, will be killing each other. Not until there are surrender documents to be signed will they sit together again at the same table. For surely this next war, when it comes, will be far too desperate a struggle to end in an armistice.
>
> There are few national leaders today who will not admit the mistakes of 1914 and 1918, but none appear to have the cour- age to stop the inexorable slide into chaos. Only one question now remains. When will it begin?

14

Poland 1 September 1939

Captain Friedrich Prager had driven all night from Berlin to join forward elements of Hoeppner's XVI Corp south of Kreuzeberg and within sight of the Polish border. Prager had not expected the summons from Warsaw until the end of the month at the earliest, before the Poles completed mobilization and after Germany had tested the border defences. General staff planning had anticipated that *Fall Weiss*, the attack on Poland, would take place in the usual abominable autumn weather of persistent rain and mud. Apparently, someone had decided that the fine, dry weather of late summer might hold just long enough to complete the campaign.

Whatever the reason, he had been summoned from Warsaw three days before to a meeting with General Hoeppner's staff and then ordered straight to the frontier. Strangely enough, he felt no weariness but rather a great exultation that the waiting time was almost over. In the quiet dawn, Prager turned slowly to survey the goblin shapes of Panzer II and III tanks stretching into the dark mist before glancing again at his watch, 0550. The attack was set for exactly 0600, summer time.

A great deal had happened to Friedrich Prager since that day in 1928 at the gates of the Gross-Lichterfielde Cadet School near Berlin. He had shaken hands with his father and Abraham Meyer, his father's old friend, had turned his wheel-chair towards the gate. Characteristically, the old man had gone without a word. His mother had died when he was very young and there had grown up between him and this hard, disciplined old man a love and respect that was as close as it was unexpected. His father had been a non-commissioned officer in the Imperial Army before the Great War, had fought and been wounded on the Eastern Front and had imbued his son with all the traits and beliefs of a professional soldier. Having escaped from the factory and the grinding boredom of industrial work – even in the benevolent social regime of Bismarck's Germany – by enlisting in the army, his father had come to see military service as the highest profession to which a man could aspire. And, ever since he could remember, Prager had wanted nothing more than to be a soldier.

As he grew older, Prager realized that his father, like so many of Germany's other professional soldiers, had been betrayed by Germany's surrender in 1918. 'Armistice' had merely been a face-saving device forced on the army by traitorous politicians. The unendurable had been made worse by the Allied Occupation and the troubles of the early 1920s and then, when it seemed that better days were ahead, a worldwide depression had begun the cycle all over again.

By the time the younger Prager passed out of the cadet school four years later, he had been moulded into an unbending copy of his father; as narrow minded and as certain that Germany had been betrayed and would be avenged. Seven years in the army as an officer had moderated a few of his ideas but like many of his brother officers, most of them the sons of World War veterans, he had dedicated his life to restoring Germany's greatness. The political unrest of the 1920s and the ever-present menace of communism convinced them of the need for a strong, authoritarian government and, when the Nazi Party came to power, its one redeeming feature in the eyes of the officer corps was the fanatical dedication to wiping out the shame of Versailles.

The memories of discussions with his father over this very matter were strong and he always associated them with the smell of old books, for his father had made a fetish of education. He could clearly recall the shape and texture of the room and his father's crippled figure becoming smaller and more shrunken as the years fled, his voice losing that booming bass note that carried command so easily until it had become an old man's querulous whine protesting against a world changed past understanding.

'Work with this Hitler fellow,' his father had said, 'but do not trust him. Support his policies while they support Germany, but not an instant longer.' And he remembered the last discussion, the one in which they had discussed the Fuehrer oath at great length.

'No!' his father had shouted with a distant semblance of his old fire. 'You must tell them no! The oath can only be taken to support the Fatherland, not a leader. In the old army we did not swear to support the Kaiser, but Germany. It would have been dangerous to do otherwise. The army acts as a brake on the leader. It has always been that way.'

Prager, concealing his few qualms, had laughed at the old man's fears. 'But this is not the old army,' he persisted, 'and this is not the Kaiser's Germany and so the old remedies no longer hold. New and bolder measures are called for today. Our enemies surround us and they can only be beaten by cunning and dedication. The Fuehrer knows what must be done. And besides, the Army will retain control, as always. How can it be otherwise? We hold the guns!'

'An oath is sacred, boy,' his father had warned. 'Hitler asks *you* for an oath to *him*. Even if he chooses to style himself *der Fuehrer und Oberst Befehlshaber der Wehrmacht des Grossdeutshen Reichs*, remember that he is only an Austrian corporal and not the Fatherland!'

16

Prager noticed that the old man's head was nodding with fatigue and he had tucked the lap rug more closely about him. The Kaiser moustache still bristled but the cancer had melted the flesh from his face, leaving a caricature of the man who glared from the mantelpiece photograph.

Prager had picked it up. The man – boy really – pictured there was barely twenty and had already been a soldier for six years. His unit was on manoeuvres somewhere in Germany, well before the turn of the century. The young man stood proudly against a background of forest, tents and soldiers and one or two officers. His Guards uniform and *pickelhaube* were the old style worn years before the simpler *feldgrau* of 1910 had become regulation. Represented in that photograph was everything the old man had known and loved of Germany; discipline, elegance, purpose. All gone now, wiped away by the disaster of the Great War and the traitors who had sold out the nation in 1918. The Nazi Party, much as he disliked some of their policies, at least understood that, had at least the will to organize the home front in such a manner as it would never happen again. There were compromises to be made, he knew, as in everything.

A whistle shrilled in the dawn and the sound of engines coughing to life broke his reverie. He had never seen the old man again. The cancer had killed his father a week after his return to Berlin. That was five years ago and he was no longer the idealistic young officer he had been at the time. But on the other hand, he was not a seasoned veteran either. Prager felt a surge of excitement mingled with apprehension; that was about to change.

The sweep second hand of his watch moved towards the top of the dial. The ragged noise of the tank engines had settled into a steady roar. Across the frontier, he saw a door open and a figure step outside to listen. The sky was full of dawn and mist streamed along the ground. A rocket arced against scattered clouds to burst in a shower of green sparks and the tanks surged forward. A single organism, they moved steadily across the farm fields towards the border. His own car was bumping after the tanks, now gathering speed to pass them and reach the road first. Behind, he heard a rifle cocked and the snick of the safety.

The car struck a pothole and slewed but the driver fought the wheel. Prager hung on as best he could. The jouncing was painful and his teeth came down on the edge of his tongue and he swore under his breath. The driver spared him a glance and grinned; and suddenly, the pain was gone, the apprehension disappeared and in its place a feeling of well-being and anticipation welled up.

The driver swung the staff car onto the paved surface and they

17

shot ahead, aiming to be the first to reach the single candy-striped pole and gate – there was no fence on either side, only the gate – marking the border. A Polish guard stood in the road, holding his rifle foolishly as he gaped at the line of approaching tanks. Prager could almost read the thoughts running through the man's mind as he brought his rifle up, aimed, then threw it down and jumped for the verge.

A lorry full of cheering soldiers swerved around the border gate first but Prager's car was close behind. A tank ran through it and wood and splinters flew in every direction. A rifle shot rang out from the customs building and the tank stopped. Looking back, Prager could see its commander standing in the turret, speaking carefully into his microphone. The turret revolved and the stubby thirty-seven millimetre gun fired. A gout of flame and smoke blew out a wall.

The sky exploded with sound at the same moment and a flight of Stukas tore the heavens apart. There were four in spread formation at not more than two hundred metres altitude streaking into Poland. Another four followed and another until the sky snarled with aircraft engines. The road went over a hill then and he lost sight of the action. Ahead were the flat, clean fields of Poland, all the way to the Vistula.

They stopped at noon, having come some ten kilometres without resistance other than a few scattered Polish units which were taken by surprise. A single burst of machine-gun fire was enough to convince most to surrender at once. The sight of tanks rattling over the fields in a steady wave had unnerved every Pole they had met, civilian or soldier.

Prager tucked the map back into his briefcase. So far there had been no need for the battalion commander to request his assistance as roads were well-marked this close to Germany.

A ripple of engines grinding into life went along the line and the air was suddenly shimmering with exhaust heat. They had stopped below the crest of a long hill to rest the infantry and allow the fitters to see to the tanks. A shallow valley spread before them in the mellow sunlight of early afternoon and a small stream meandered in the distance. Near the base of the hill, some three hundred metres distant, a small stand of forest, separated from a large wood by an open, park-like area through which the stream ran, occupied the left side of the road. Except for the Walther pistol at his side, he might have been on a picnic.

As the line moved ahead, a motorcyclist shot away down the road, riding easily on the paved surface, his mate in the side car, both obviously enjoying the ride. The noise of the cycle's exhaust fell away and Prager went back to making notes on the small pad he habitually carried in his breast pocket.

The driver's sharp intake of breath caused him to look up. The motorcycle had swerved off the road as it approached the stand of trees and was bumping over the fields. Spurts of dirt followed it and Prager realized that the cyclists were under fire. The machine's driver threw up his hands and fell forward across the handlebars; the cycle cartwheeled, throwing the passenger from the side car. The man hit, bounced and lay still, arms and legs akimbo so that he resembled a discarded doll. Prager found that he was clutching the top of the windscreen. The driver yanked him down and shouted something about Poles.

They were less than a hundred metres from the trees when the steady tacking of a machine gun began again. The driver turned off the road and they banged into the field and stopped in a slight depression that provided a modicum of cover. There was silence for an instant – he could hear a bird call and the summery sound of a cicada nearby – before it was shattered by tank engines moving at high speed. He vaulted from the car in his excitement and raced to the top of the bank.

Through field glasses, he saw khaki Polish uniforms edging out of the woods on horseback. A cavalry unit, he thought. Surely, they won't be foolish enough to send horses against tanks! Four tanks had been detached from the unit and they swung into line abreast on the slope. Exhausts spouting, they ground towards the patch of woods. The machine gun began again and Prager heard the sharp whine of bullets glancing from armour. A flash and a bang and a gout of earth spurted up near one of the tanks. They turned outwards then, opening the line to make it harder for the enemy gunners. The horsemen had formed up on the edge of the woods, two slim lines holding in spirited horses. On either flank, riflemen were taking cover.

The tanks opened fire and the woods whirled into flame and smoke. Round after round of thirty-seven millimetre high-explosive shell crashed among the trees, tearing jagged splinters that transfixed men and horses alike. The neat double line of cavalry disappeared and the riflemen that survived staggered back into the trees. The tanks had stopped at less than fifty metres distant and were firing in rapid succession. The single howitzer fired one more shot before an explosion shook the woods and smoke cascaded over the trees. A lucky shot must have struck the ammunition limber, Prager thought.

The tanks stopped firing and waited, seeming to crouch like huge cats. But only the crackle of flames and screams of wounded men or horses, Prager could not tell which, came from the trees.

The column was formed up again leaving a single armoured car to keep watch from the hillside on the patch of woods until a mechanized infantry unit appeared to clean it out.

Warsaw 31 August – 5 September 1939

Keith Thorne checked the address on the slip of paper against the street sign fastened high on the corner of a building. The elderly cab driver, who still wore his taxi licence on a chain at the back of his neck, as in Tsarist times, had stopped here and with gestures made him understand that he would go no further. He kept pointing down the tree-shaded street of the former Jewish Quarter running at right angles to Mila Avenue and muttering something incomprehensible. Since the man knew neither English nor French, it had done no good to argue with him and Thorne had counted out the proper amount of the strange looking bills called *zloties* and added two more for a tip. The driver counted the money carefully and drove off after giving Thorne the same puzzled look he had received from the desk clerk when he asked him to write out instructions for the driver.

The mid-afternoon sun was hot and the street narrow. Both sides were closely lined with old brick and stone two- and three-storey buildings crowded one against another. Every square inch of land was in use. Even the trees that curved above the patched pavement seemed to have been begrudged the few square feet they required, so closely had the pavement been fitted about their trunks.

He walked along the narrow sidewalk searching the building fronts for numbers. The close-fitting rows gave the impression of huddling together for mutual protection and comfort, much as settlers hid behind stockades of North American frontier forts. Yet the area was not completely lifeless; a rooster crowed and from somewhere came the sound of a woman shouting.

Number fifty-seven seemed little different from its neighbours. Three storeys high, its frontage could not have spanned more than thirty feet. An imposing doorway was flanked by two windows. A flight of concrete steps scrubbed to glistening in the sun led up to the door and he cranked the bellpull.

The afternoon was unusually hot and he had shed his coat and loosened his tie. He used his reflection in the door glass to adjust his tie and saw a pair of large, dark eyes watching him. Surprised, he straightened as the door opened. The young woman was in her early twenties. A mass of dark curls framed an oval face and a small, thin nose that was slightly tilted. She wore a grey dress that drew in to emphasize a narrow waist and high, proud bust. Aware that he was staring, Thorne flushed and handed her his business card, printed in English and Polish.

'How do you do, Mr Thorne. Won't you please come in. My father-in-law is waiting for you in the garden.' Her English was only slightly accented and her voice was delightfully low. Thorne found himself grinning like a schoolboy as he stepped past her into the cool interior. She shut the door carefully and turned the lock before extending a slender hand. 'I'm Deborah Yitzak. Please come this way.'

The girl led him through a silent house smelling of flowers. The rooms seen through open doors were filled with comfortable furniture and framed photographs and mementoes. The house proved to be narrow but exceptionally long. All rooms opened to the left off this narrow corridor and at the end, seen as if in a glowing vision, was a greenish blur of trees. Thorne hesitated on the steps leading down into a yard as long and narrow as the house. Here, near the door, the yard was shaded by an oak tree while further on the sun poured down on an intricate series of paths that wound in and out among dozens of rose bushes, all in bloom.

An elderly man worked with vigour on a new flower bed. He had just finished spading the ground and was attacking the clods with the shovel. The girl motioned Thorne to follow and ran ahead, calling to the old man. Thorne did not understand her Polish – or was it Yiddish – but guessed she was reproaching him for working so hard in the heat.

The old man kissed her cheek in answer and Thorne halted midway along the path. The old man wiped his forehead with his gloves, stuffed them into a pocket and came to meet him.

'Ah, Mr Keith Thorne.' They shook hands. 'I hope you had a pleasant journey. Come, come, sit down, here in the shade.' He indicated a table and chairs beneath the oak and the girl hurried up the path to the house.

The old man peered at him through pince-nez glasses which he took from a shirt pocket. 'I am Jacob Yitzak,' he introduced himself. 'I am pleased to meet you after our correspondence, although your journey has been for nothing. As I told you in our last exchange of letters, I. . . .'

He broke off as the girl reappeared with a tray bearing two bottles of beer, one showing a delicate frosted surface and the other dry, and two tall, conical beer glasses.

'I learned, Mr Thorne, in my visits to your country that

Americans take their beer cold. So I asked Deborah to place a few bottles in the ice chest. I hope it is to your liking.'

The girl poured and stepped back as Yitzak lifted his in toast. 'I hope you have a pleasant stay in Poland, my new young friend. Long life to you.'

The beer was delightfully cold and Thorne finished half in one long pull. Yitzak laughed and sent the girl for another. 'Good, heh? The best beer in the world is brewed right here in Warsaw.'

They talked for a few minutes about inconsequential topics until Deborah returned to refill his glass. There must have been a signal that Thorne missed for the girl curtsied and left. When he turned back to the table it was to see the old musician regarding him with some amusement.

'I beg your pardon . . . ,' Thorne began, thinking that he had committed some breach of etiquette but the old man only waved a hand. 'You Americans! Everything must be done now. If it cannot be, you find a way to do it anyhow. And if you are told no, you are convinced that a personal appeal will win.'

'I don't quite understand. . . .'

Yitzak smiled again and traced a pattern in the moisture from Thorne's glass that had dripped onto the table. 'While I am flattered that you consider me important enough to travel all the way from New York, I do not change my mind. I am not interested in writing my autobiography, either here or in New York. I am retired and there are not many years left to me. I intend to enjoy them surrounded by my family. For a man who has had only one son and then so late in his life the time for enjoyment flows past in moments,' he threw up a hand in a dismissive gesture. 'Let someone else write about me if they find me so interesting. I surely do not.'

Thorne had expected this reaction, had anticipated it from the gist of the old Jew's correspondence. He was familiar with Yitzak's career which had begun in 1891 and when he had announced his retirement two years before and virtually disappeared, it had been a surprise to the entire world. But in the years between, he had been something of a terror. On only two points did his critics agree; first, that he was the premier violinist of his time and second, that his ego was greater than that of any other ten artists. It was through his ego that Thorne had carefully planned his attack. He leaned forward and stared at the wispy haired old man, noting the smooth, unlined face marred by a stubble of day-old beard and perspiration.

'Mr Yitzak, you are the greatest violinist of your time and probably the greatest Polish musician since Chopin. You have a duty to share your greatness. . . .'

'Bullshit.'

Yitzak pronounced the American vulgarity calmly enough and

then laughed at Thorne's astonished expression. 'You see, Mr Thorne, my time in your country was not totally wasted. I learned a few of your slang profanities. Is that the right word, profanities?'

Thorne nodded dumbly.

'I am also aware that I was portrayed as a very egotistical man, always demanding this, that and the other thing. But as you can see, I am not! It was a façade. To have such a reputation saved me untold annoyance as people were afraid to pester me. So, you must save your breath. I am too old to care what the world thinks of me now or when I am dead.'

Thorne drank a bit more of the beer to gain time to organize his thoughts but the old man was not finished.

'Perhaps when I am too old to work in my garden I might undertake an autobiography. Perhaps your father will still be interested. If not,' he shrugged, 'the world will have lost nothing.'

Thorne knew it was time to fall back on his last line of attack.

'Look here, Mr Yitzak,' he said quietly, unconsciously dropping the formal pose he had adopted, 'the political situation is very unsettled. Germany has turned the border into an armed camp. Even your government expects war in the spring. Wouldn't it be an excellent idea to take your daughter-in-law and son out of the country, to the United States?'

The old man nodded. 'Yes, an excellent idea. However, Mr Thorne, have you forgotten that we are Jews? And that your government has imposed a quota for Jews entering the United States of America? It would be impossible.'

Thorne leaned over the table. 'But not for you, sir. You are a distinguished musician. My father has contacts in the State Department. Visas could be arranged with little trouble.'

'No, Mr Thorne,' Yitzak said firmly. 'I stay here, in Poland, in my home in Warsaw, where I belong.'

The old man had said goodbye to him in the garden and the daughter-in-law had seen him out with a reserved smile and closed the door firmly, as if glad to see the last of him.

Damned Jews, he muttered to himself as he sat in the hotel bar that evening. Stubborn, obstinate, egotistical. Old Yitzak reminded him of the orthodox Jews in New York. In addition to their funny clothes and ear locks or whatever they were called, they were pushy and loud and now he knew where that kind of behaviour came from.

The hall porter knocked softly, opened the door, slipped into the room and deposited the tray of coffee and rolls next to the bed. Thorne woke easily as the curtains were drawn and morning sunshine flooded the room. The windows were open wide and the fresh air was like a tonic.

His travelling clock showed just after six-thirty. Thorne had always been an early riser; something to do with his metabolism which often seemed to him to be twice the normal. As a child, he had been considered loud, abrasive, full of energy and poor at school simply because he hated wasting the time involved in studying. From the moment he had become aware of his parents' wealth, he had decided that academic pursuits were unnecessary. By the time he was old enough to realize how fallacious that decision had been, it was almost too late. As a freshman at Harvard – only by virtue of his father's position on the Board of Governors – he had discovered flying. His civilian pilot's licence had come easily enough but his heart was set on the United States Army Air Corps and the fast, powerful aircraft that flew from Logan Field near Boston. But he was failing all his classes and the Air Corps officer who had conducted the interview had been impressed neither with his civilian licence nor his father's wealth and position as chairman of the board of one of the nation's largest publishing houses.

'Forget that nonsense, Thorne,' the officer had snapped. 'It doesn't count. What does is intelligence and self-discipline. Your school transcripts are a disaster. We aren't running a social club.'

The following day had begun with a physics lecture and he had slipped into the lecture hall even later than usual. The instructor, who had long since given up on him, ignored the disturbance.

Thorne settled into his seat, prepared to resume his interupted sleep. He had a bad hangover and was in a foul mood. Only gradually did the text of the lecture penetrate.

' . . . lifting force on an airplane wing varies with the angle of attack. Generally, the lifting force increases as the angle of attack increases, but if that angle becomes too great the air no longer flows smoothly over the cambered surface but begins to break up, to roll or burble. Bernoulli's principle no longer applies, and the lifting force decreases rapidly. When that happens, the aircraft is said to stall.'

Thorne found himself visualizing the flow of air over a wing and for the first time in his life, an academic lecture had become meaningful. Afterward, Thorne raced back to his room and searched the closet for his physics text, pulled the chair over to the window and began to read. He was still reading when the dinner gong sounded.

That single lecture convinced Thorne of what he had already begun to suspect. Charm, and Daddy's money were sufficient to see him through life but only as a parasitical playboy. He was discovering that the people that mattered, that could award or deny him privileges – like the Army officer – managed to see through his façade of charm and easy good looks in a very short while. Those that didn't matter, didn't care. As a result of that Army officer's contemptuous dismissal and a half-heard lecture, the remainder of his college career was aggravating, difficult and rewarding. He graduated well below the middle of his class but with a degree nevertheless and a coveted commission in the United States Army Air Corps – to the horror of his friends and family.

His reverie was broken by an unfamiliar wailing noise that blanketed the city. He walked out onto the balcony to see people scurrying from the streets. The hall porter hurried onto the balcony beside him, glanced at the sky and rattled something in excited Polish. Thorne grinned and shrugged and the porter, collecting himself with a visible effort, said in poor French, 'That is the air raid siren, Monsieur. We must take cover in the basement.'

Thorne stared at him in astonishment. Air raid siren! How foolish to conduct a test so early in the morning. As if sensing his thoughts, the porter shook his head.

'It is not a practice, *Pan* Thorne.'

Scenes from films of devastated cities in Spain and China went through his mind as he dressed quickly, heedless of the fact that the porter had left the door open. He grabbed his briefcase and dashed out. The porter was pushing people towards the stairs and Thorne hurried down, pressed from behind by a heavyset man in pyjamas and robe. They were still on the stairs when the explosions began.

The bombing was unendurable in the so-called shelter. The building shook violently and the air was full of fine powder that made breathing agony. Worst of all was the darkness. Thorne found an unexpected irony in the situation; for two years he had practised dropping bombs with little thought to the fact that the targets would be mainly civilians. In all those months, the make-believe buildings destroyed and armies scattered had never included civilians and not even the paintings and photographs of Guernica and Chunking had been real – until now.

The shelter was a portion of the basement, an old storage room hastily cleared in response to the Government's half-hearted legislation. Since no one believed the German air force capable of bombing Warsaw, the hotel staff had done little but sweep the floor. There was no drinking water, no sanitary facilities, and little fresh air. No provision had been made for small children and they cried and screamed incessantly, infecting one another with terror.

They could not hear the all-clear signal and it was left to an elderly porter to hobble down to tell them that the Germans had gone. They came out into the warm, bright sunshine like prisoners reprieved from death. Through the shattered glass of the lobby doors, Thorne caught a glimpse of a stretcher being loaded aboard a truck pressed into emergency service as an ambulance.

The manager shouted from a step-ladder to make himself heard but no one paid any attention. Thorne was still unable to absorb the fact that the much-anticipated war had actually begun. He went up to his room to find the door still wide open and the bed rumpled. Everything was as he had left it and not until he moved to the window and could look down on the city and see the fires raging along Krakowskie Przedmiescie and east to the Vistula where whole blocks of buildings looked like mouths full of rotted teeth, did the reaction set in. He closed the door and sat down on the bed, shivering.

He sensed fear emanating from the closed and shuttered houses lining the narrow streets in the old Jewish quarter. The ghettoes had gone with independence from Russia but many Jewish families remained in the old quarter to the west of the Krasinki Palace and Gardens. Thorne climbed the steps and rang the bell. He could hear it echoing through the house and turned away, certain the family had already left. He was half-way down the steps when the door opened.

He took off his hat and bowed to the daughter-in-law, Deborah – was that her name?

'I wish to see Mr Yitzak,' he said. The girl hesitated then beckoned him in. The entrance hall was gloomy and all the doors had been shut and the curtains drawn over the windows at both ends. The smell of floor polish and scented oil was stronger than ever.

Yitzak appeared, shook hands then solemnly ushered Thorne into his study. He whispered to Deborah; the girl hesitated, then went out.

The room belonged to a musician without doubt. Framed sheet music and phonograph records hung on the wall with dozens of photographs of Yitzak and other famous personalities. Antique musical instruments were displayed in specially built glass cases and a grand piano occupied one corner, a magnificent instrument of polished ebony that dominated the room.

'My dear Mr Thorne,' Yitzak smiled. 'I see that you are safe.'

Thorne had decided on a direct, no-nonsense approach but Deborah spoiled it by returning with a tray on which were three glasses of wine. She placed the tray on a small table and sat down, smoothing her skirt over slender, silk-stockinged legs and watched as Yitzak handed the glasses around and murmured a toast.

'Now, Mr Thorne. . . .?'

'Germany has declared war on Poland, as you are no doubt aware.'

'Of course. We heard the news on the wireless, and the bombs. I understand that little damage was done as the bombs were mainly directed onto Okecie Airfield. The news reports speak of a number of German bomber planes shot down.'

Thorne snorted at that. The bombs had certainly fallen onto the city and he doubted if many German planes had been shot down. He had wrestled with his conscience all morning over whether or not to make one more appeal to Yitzak. But no matter the outcome, he intended to go from here to the American Embassy and out of the country as fast as possible. This war was no business of his.

'Then, sir, you must realize how dangerous it is to remain in Warsaw, to remain in Poland at all.' Thorne leaned forward attempting to put every bit of persuasion possible into his words. 'You must leave Poland immediately. Yours is too great a talent. . . .'

Yitzak clapped his hands on his knees and sat back to chuckle. 'You were right, my dear,' he said to Deborah. 'She said,' addressing Thorne, 'that you would make one more attempt to persuade me to go.' He shook his head. 'I am afraid my answer is still no. Now more than ever, I cannot leave my home.' He raised a hand to forestall Thorne's objection. 'You must not be afraid for our safety. The German may have attacked Poland but he must first reckon with our good Polish army.'

'Mr Yitzak . . . the German army has barely begun the campaign. Neutral military observers have told me that the Polish army does not stand the slightest chance. You must have heard the stories about how Jews are treated in Germany? Can you possibly believe that will not happen here as well. You must . . .'

'I have heard all these arguments before and I did not change my mind then nor will I now.'

The distant wail of air raid sirens began again and Deborah hurried to the window. The old man watched her for a moment, then called her back. 'There are no targets of military or industrial significance nearby, my dear. We are safe enough here.'

Thorne stood, angry at the old man and at himself. 'You are risking your daughter-in-law's life just as you are risking your own. And your life belongs to the world,' he tried one last time.

Thorne saw the old man's anger then and understood why he had been considered a terror in his younger days.

'You have no right to bring my daughter-in-law into this matter. You do not have a visa for her or any other member of my family. You know as well as I that your country will not admit her, or my son because we are Jews. I will not leave them, or my nation. I may be too old to be a soldier but if my fame is even half what you claim, I can do more good by remaining. *Do widzenia*, Mr Thorne.'

Poles jammed the streets around the American Embassy in spite of the air raids. The snarling drone of aircraft and the peculiar hollow sound of airborne machine guns supplemented by the distant cracking of large calibre anti-aircraft guns predominated. Thorne pushed through the crowd to the gate and waved his passport at a perspiring guard. The marine corporal let him in, shouting imprecations and thrusting back those who tried to follow.

'Fucking god-damned bastards,' he muttered to Thorne. 'Wait 'til the last god-damned minute.'

Inside, the scene was just as chaotic. Two lines of haggard, frightened people besieged the visa desk. A harried clerk found himself dealing with two and sometimes three shouting people at a time. A single guard moved up and down the lines trying to keep order.

James Howell looked up from his desk and an expression of exasperated relief swept over his face. He yanked his spectacles off and wiped his neck with a large handkerchief and thrust the other hand out to Thorne.

'Damned glad to see you Thorne! Been trying to telephone your hotel all morning. Damned Poles. Go to pieces whenever there's a crisis. You don't seem hurt. A drink?' It all came out in a rush and Thorne grinned as Howell locked his door before producing a bottle of rye from his desk.

'Not supposed to drink in the building. First Secretary's a regular puritan.' He poured the whiskey into paper cups and handed one to Thorne.

'Sit down, sit down. I expect you want to get out of this madhouse as quickly as possible. I've had a wire from your father about you. I'll send an answer through the Embassy, of course. Save you having to go along to the cable office which I imagine is *hors de combat* at the moment.'

Thorne nodded, irritated that his father should have sent a cable so quickly. He checked his watch. Hell, he thought, it was four in the afternoon here. That meant it was ten in the morning in New York. His father must have sent the wire at the first newscast.

'No trouble getting you out, of course. The Ambassador's reserved air transport to Stockholm for tomorrow morning. Best bet of course. I'm afraid now that we won't be able to accommodate your Jews. Only American citizens with valid passports allowed at the moment. Could change though in a few days when the Poles dig in and give the Germans hell, so I don't see any real problem.'

Howell's assumption that he was only concerned with escape

annoyed Thorne and that, coupled with his father's cable, aroused his stubbornness. 'No thanks, Jimmy, I'm staying a while longer yet.'

Thorne was gratified at Howell's disbelief. Even as classmates at Andover, he had always had a desire to tell him to go to hell.

'Whatever in the world for, Keith? Things are going to become . . .'

'Probably. But I still haven't finished my business and besides, how often do you see a war in the beginning stages?'

'Not often, thank God,' Howell told him with asperity. 'But then I forgot you were once in the Army. You like this sort of thing.'

Modlin Front 6 September 1939

The days that followed saw Polish hopes decline even as Great Britain and France duly declared war on Germany on September third. Poland waited for the great Allied aerial bombing they imagined would be unleashed on the German homeland and for the masses of khaki-clad tommies and poilus they expected would swarm across the Rhine. Instead, British troops crossed the Channel to Flanders and dug in as they had done in 1914 and French troops reinforced the Maginot Line and extended north towards the Belgian border. Offensively, a few leaflets cluttered the skies over Berlin; nothing more.

German armour rolled to Poland's historic if meagre barrier against invasion from the west, the Vistula River. But it proved this time to be no more than a momentary check to their engineering battalions and the Panzers were across within hours.

Prager, dirty and unshaven, bent over the route map, painstakingly copying a dirt road he had marked on his Michelin auto route map the month before. He hadn't had more than a few hours' sleep in the seven days since the campaign had begun; hadn't changed his uniform once. He had lost two automobiles and drivers to breakdowns and exhaustion.

'That's the one.' He capped his fountain pen and handed the copy to the young lieutenant. 'Watch for the landmarks and you will go directly to the bridge. It's small, meant for farm vehicles but should bear the weight of one Panzer III at a time.'

When the tank crews had gone, Prager allowed himself to slump in the seat of his newly requisitioned motor car, an elderly Panhard with a folding top. He tilted his cap down and let himself drift.

The hot sun and sultry air, the exhaustion that made him feel as if his mind were slipping away from his body, the tick of the hot engine, all served to lull him to sleep.

The sudden scream and crack of high explosive blasted him awake. The stench of cordite and dust, the horrifying paralysis of fear, the utter darkness all froze him into immobility as lines of flame, reds and greens, arced towards him through the night. Air-tearing noise seared, great annihilating waves of concussion slapped him and, confused and disoriented, Prager floundered out of the car and down the slope, searching blindly for cover. Dirt and stone splattered his back and the noise made coherent thought impossible.

He pressed against the damp black earth, conscious of every square inch of his flesh, imagining his unprotected back penetrated by a sharp-pointed shell that would explode him into atoms of blood, muscle and gristle. 'Dear God,' he begged, 'don't let me die.' Over and over the soldier's litany ran through his mind as the world erupted in madness.

The bombardment lasted ten minutes, an eternity of fear and anxiety, then the explosions ceased as suddenly as they had begun. After a moment, Prager raised his head. In the darkness, he could hear others moving. A sudden scream brought a flurry of shouts for a stretcher bearer. Some distance away, the firing began again, loud crashes and blinding glare through which he caught sight of the river's sheen and he felt a sickening sense of relief that the renewed bombardment involved someone else. He climbed back up the slope to the motor car.

A voice shouted and a shielded torch bounced crazily towards him. Panicked, he drew his Walther pistol but the torch veered away as someone shouted again – in German. Tank engines boomed to life and Prager sank down on the running board of the Panhard, shaking with delayed shock, then staggered away from the car to vomit. Afterward, he rinsed his mouth and cursed again the loss of his toothbrush. In seven days, this was the closest he had been to death.

At dawn, the armoured column moved again. The engineers had completed the pontoon bridge and tanks clattered across and up the far bank past the wreckage of the Polish field guns that had done so much damage. Six tanks destroyed and fifty-three men killed before Panzers, using Prager's map, had flanked the Polish strongpoint. Point-blank fire had destroyed the four guns but it had been a Pyrrhic victory at best. Prager stared at the bodies of the Polish gunners as his car went past and felt nothing. Maybe, he decided, he was becoming a seasoned combat veteran. He had certainly seen enough dead Poles by now.

Warsaw 7 – 12 September 1939

Now that he had made the decision to remain in Poland just to demonstrate his independence, Thorne felt obliged to justify his action. Twice more, he tried to persuade Yitzak to leave Poland and each time he was met with increasingly stubborn refusal.

By the end of the first week, German bombing raids on Warsaw had become a regular feature of the city's life. On Friday afternoon, he hired a *droshki* driver and set off for Yitzak's house and his fourth visit. A raid forced them to take shelter in a city park and it was late afternoon before he arrived to find Yitzak arguing with three elderly men in the front hall. The argument stopped abruptly as Thorne peered in through the half-opened door. Reluctantly, Yitzak invited him in and introduced him. Immediately, the old men descended on Thorne waving photographs and documents under his nose, all talking at once in Yiddish before Yitzak restored order. Thorne's stomach lurched at one of the photographs. In it, a dozen bodies, necks distended, hung from a gallows. In the background could be seen grinning, helmeted soldiers in German uniforms.

'What the hell is this?' he demanded.

Yitzak looked uncomfortable. 'We believe it to be a photograph of executions in the village of Modice, near the German border.'

'But why?'

Yitzak shrugged. 'We do not know.'

One of the old men must have understood Yitzak's reply because he protested vigorously, yanking the photograph from Thorne's hand and pointing first to one of the bodies and then to the hair falling in curls before his own ears.

'What's he trying to tell me?'

Yitzak gave the man an exasperated glance. 'He thinks they were executed because they were Jews. He is telling you that they are Orthodox Jews and identifiable as all of the bodies have earlocks, as he does.'

Thorne saw Deborah pale visibly. 'But that's ridiculous . . . why should. . . .'

'Because, Mr Thorne, the Nazis as you may know, are violently anti-Semitic. But I do not believe that is the reason these people were executed. Modice is in the area known in Tsarist times as the "Jewish Pale". Even today, the population there is ninety per cent Jewish. We have known for several days that the Germans are taking reprisals on local populations for acts of sabotage. Perhaps that is what happened here. If so, then it would not be unusual for the executed men to be Jewish.'

Deborah closed the door and Yitzak mumbled an apology and hurried after her. Thorne and the three old men stared at one another uncomfortably. After a moment, the man with the photograph tucked it into Thorne's jacket pocket, brushing away his protests. He waved a hand in a half circle and mimed showing the photograph.

Yitzak came back at that moment and spoke angrily to the three men who nodded in distress and left, the one who had given him the photograph turning back to nod solemnly to Thorne.

'I am sorry you were subjected to this in my house. I asked them to leave . . . my daughter-in-law.' He waved a hand vaguely, indicating his distress. 'Please, may I offer you refreshment?'

Thorne refused but the old man insisted and drew him into the parlour. He took a deep breath when the old man bustled out, surprised at how badly the photograph had shocked him. Sunlight streaming through the curtained windows touched the polished furnishings and in this warm, comfortable home he found it hard to credit that people were executed simply for their religion. Such things just did not happen in civilized nations. He had seen similar atrocity pictures from China, but the Oriental had a different concept of life. The individual was of little importance to them. His reverie was interrupted as Yitzak returned with a tray bearing glasses of beer.

Thorne drank gratefully and Yitzak refilled his glass. After a few moments, he said: 'The photograph bothered me as well. I find it hard to believe that Germans could do such things. I remember Allied propaganda during the Great War . . . Belgian babies spitted on German bayonets, French nuns raped, whole villages murdered. It was shown to be false after the war and so I must question the validity of that photograph. And too, Poland, which was under foreign rule for 350 years until 1919, has a history of anti-Semitism that was instigated and encouraged by the Tsars.'

Thorne nodded, not knowing what to say. He was uncomfortably aware that he was not involved in this war. He had paid little attention to the political analyses in the *New York Times*. Hitler's march through Europe had begun about the time of the aircraft crash, so to him it was academic who won this war. If pressed, he would have admitted favouring Germany. After all, hadn't Poland shown her true colours when she took part in the dismemberment of Czechoslovakia? Wasn't she now reaping the results of that action?

Yitzak took a deep breath. 'I will write the book your father wishes me to write.'

Thorne sat up, surprised. 'Why that's wonderful. . . .'

Yitzak held up a hand. 'There are conditions.'

'I am certain they can be worked out. If it's a matter of more money. . . .'

The old man scowled at him. 'It is not. I wish for your father to see that my daughter-in-law and son are admitted to the United States. *When* that has been accomplished, I will begin work. I myself will remain in Poland.'

Thorne took a deep breath. He was certain that his father could organize sufficient pressure to have the old man admitted to the United States – but his son and daughter as well?

He looked up at the old man standing anxiously before him. 'I cannot promise. I will have to cable my father.' He stared at Yitzak, wondering if the photograph had affected him more than he wanted to admit.

'Perhaps if we went to the American Embassy and you explained.'

'Look here, why now? You yourself said you did not believe that Germany would do . . . that you had anything to fear because of your religion.'

Yitzak frowned. 'You are an American and therefore cannot understand. The American brand of anti-Semitism does not run to such depths as it does in Central Europe, except perhaps in some of your southern states. Perhaps you can understand better if you think of me as a Negro.'

'A Negro?'

'The Jew in Central Europe is a pariah, an outcast. The origins of such feelings are lost in time but have to do with economics, religion and the fact that many of us preserve our old customs. To a gentile, we eat strange foods, practise different religious rites and generally consider ourselves the chosen of God, although why he should have selected such a cantankerous race I will never understand. Because we are different the Jew has served as a convenient scapegoat, just as your Negro does because he is also different.' The old man shrugged. 'It is differences that cause dislike. There are many Jews who dislike gentiles because *they* are different.

'As in your country, such feelings run deep, beyond logic. We Jews have known for some time now of the persecutions that are taking place in Germany. Confinement in special camps, beatings and even murders. I am very much afraid that if all they say, if even half of what they say, is true, that Polish Jews are in grave

33

danger. I wish to see my son and daughter out of Poland, out of Europe even, as some day soon Germany will march across this entire continent.'

'But that can't happen,' Thorne protested. 'Great Britain and France have declared war on Germany. She can't stand up to the French army. Even Hitler admits they are the strongest in the world.'

Yitzak dismissed the Allies with a wave. 'They have not come yet, nor will they. And how would they reach Poland? By airplane? There is no place to refuel and German airplanes would shoot them down. By ship? German submarines would sink them. The Polish army is being beaten. You have only to listen to the wireless to know that. It will soon be over and who knows then what will happen?'

'Surely, you're exaggerating,' Thorne began, then stopped as caution asserted itself. For the first time, Yitzak had agreed to write the autobiography; he would be a damned fool to argue him out of it. 'All right, I'll see what I can do at the Embassy and at the same time I will cable my father.'

He left thinking that, unwittingly, the old man had provided him with the lever to force him out of Poland – his family. If they were allowed out, he would make it conditional on Jacob Yitzak's agreement to go as well.

Thorne began to detect subtle changes in his opinion of the Poles as the siege of the city intensified. Before, he had seen them as inhabitants of a comic opera country where the soldiers wore shiny breastplates, carried lances and sang over wine. In reality, Poland was a country of poor peasants, of wrangling, opportunistic politicians and one or two great musicians and writers such as Jacob Yitzak – no better and certainly no worse than any other nation of Central Europe.

It was clear enough from news reports emanating from neutral Swedish, Finnish and Romanian radio stations, that the Poles were fighting a tenacious battle. Wandering the streets, Thorne saw thousands of civilians constructing barricades and tank traps, filling sandbags and fighting fires, rescuing trapped people and clearing the streets of debris. And it was done with a purpose that proved the Poles were truly a nation.

As he expected, his attempt to obtain visas through the Embassy were rebuffed. His father's attempts in Washington must have trod on sensitive toes because Thorne was given a severe dressing down at the Embassy for trying to circumvent government policy – this last pronounced in capital letters – regarding refugees and especially refugee Jews. His own departure from Poland was scheduled for September seventeenth and he was given strict orders to be at the Embassy no later than nine o'clock that morning.

A telephone message from Yitzak asked Thorne to call a few days later, at his convenience – a visit he had been hoping to avoid. When he rang the bell, Yitzak himself answered the door and courteous as ever, ushered him into the library.

'Is there word from your Embassy concerning the visas?'

Thorne had been dreading this moment. 'The State Department will make an exception for you as your application was filed before the war started, but not for members of your family. They will have to wait their turns.'

Jacob Yitzak took the news with only a flicker of disappointment, as if he had expected nothing more. 'You must realize that I cannot leave my family behind.'

Thorne nodded. He was saved a fumbled apology when the door opened and tall, dark-haired young man in a Polish officer's uniform stepped in. Deborah followed. 'You must be the American,' he said in French and Thorne nodded and stood to shake the offered hand. 'I am David Yitzak.'

Thorne was surprised by the man's broad-shouldered good looks, never having associated good physical condition with Jews before.

'Your Embassy will issue the visas for my wife and father?'

'For your father only. Of course, he refuses to leave without you and your wife.'

David Yitzak spoke angrily in Polish to the old man who shook his head wearily. 'I told him,' David Yitzak translated for Thorne's benefit, 'that he must go. From the United States, a man of his stature, coupled with your father's influence, could procure a visa for my wife, Deborah.'

Thorne wasn't certain why he was unhappy to hear David Yitzak refer to Deborah as his wife, but he was. For a moment, the argument flowed past him and he had to grope for the sense of the discussion.

'Of course, he must leave Poland. But,' he added, 'I can certainly understand his refusal.' He was aware of Deborah staring at him then and the younger Yitzak turning away in disgust.

'Of course,' the man snapped. 'Very chivalrous. But I am concerned with getting my wife out of Poland as quickly as possible. The Germans will beat us before winter. I have seen what . . .' Words failed him and Thorne examined him closely for the first time.

David Yitzak was wearing a clean uniform on which a lieutenant's insignia gleamed, but his boots were broken and covered with dirt. He was freshly shaven, however, and the dark patches of exhaustion beneath his eyes more noticeable as a result. Seeing that Thorne was staring at him, he nodded.

'I have just come from the Vistula front. The Nazis crossed the river two days ago. The city will be surrounded by the end of the week. I've been transferred to the south. A clean uniform is my excuse for seeing my wife and father.'

Thorne nodded. 'I am sorry,' he began, 'but we've tried everything.'

'I know,' David Yitzak interrupted, half-angrily, half in resignation. 'I know,' he repeated in a softer voice. He turned to look at Deborah on the sofa and Thorne felt suddenly that he was an interloper.

There seemed to be nothing further to say and he moved to the door. 'I am sorry,' he repeated. 'Of course, we will keep trying, but I am afraid there is not much hope.' He looked at the three people facing him. There were so many questions he wanted to ask but this was not the time. There probably never would be, he thought.

Deborah rose quickly. 'I will see you out, Mr Thorne.' At the door he fumbled for words but she held up a warning hand.

'Please Mr Thorne. Do not come again.' She closed the door quickly and through the dark glass he glimpsed her walk away without a backward glance.

Thorne sat in the Lasienski Park, ignoring the wailing air-raid sirens. He was partly concealed by a lilac bush from the street where an air-raid warden was marshalling people into a basement shelter. The last traces of the purple flowers had long ago faded but he could still detect his favourite fragrance and it brought back memories of his mother years ago and a summer picnic in a meadow, now gone forever – except in memory. His mother, a different person then, had always worn lilac except on the most formal occasions.

The park was undamaged as was the Belvedere Palace beyond, the former residence of the Russian Governor General. There was little to attract the Stukas in this part of the city but even so there was no one to be seen, leaving him with the irrational feeling that he was completely alone.

The bombing began as a dull crumping sound in the distance, probably the industrial eastern suburbs, he thought. The reports came in measured series at first but gained in volume and ferocity until the sound was one long roll of 250 and 500 kilogram bombs. He knew if he turned in that direction he would see the first clouds of black smoke rising above the trees and buildings.

He was still puzzled by his reaction to Deborah's husband. He certainly looked capable and strong and not very Jewish; the type of man who would draw women with ease. He wrenched his mind away. This was stupid, he thought, sitting in a park in the midst of an air-raid thinking about two Jews. But he did not move. The photograph the old man had given him was troubling. Twice, he had started to throw it away. He took it out now, a simple snapshot, three by five inches in size. The border was cut irregularly and the image had a thin brown cast as if the film had been developed too hastily. The executed prisoners were all men, all dressed in dark suits. What was their crime? Sabotage as Yitzak had suggested? Or being in the wrong place at the wrong time? He peered more closely. Yes, several wore their hair curled before their ears. Jews? Probably. All of them? It was impossible to tell.

The Poles were retreating on every front. The radio broadcast continuous appeals for soldiers to move here, civilians to report there. The British and French did nothing as another country was gobbled up, another ally betrayed. Not a French or British aircraft was seen in Polish skies, nor in German either, for that matter. Yet the exhortations to Poland from both allies were to *hold, hold, hold*! People were beginning to ask each other. 'Hold with what, for what?'

No, Poland was alone and she would lose. Even the national government and the *Sejm*, the parliament, abandoned Warsaw while the people laughed in scorn. The same government that had dragged them into the war scuttled out of town in the dead of night, leaving the mayor to organize the defence and relief efforts.

Rumours had reached epidemic proportions, but one predominated; while gentile soldiers were being put into prison camps, Jewish soldiers were shot. Thorne did not know what to believe. He put the photograph away.

The droning aircraft were closer now and he looked up to see tiny black specks moving eastwards across the patch of pale sky framed between buildings. Several specks detached themselves from the swarm and turned away. Thorne, as an ex-army pilot, knew they were dive bombers, Stukas beginning their descent. He watched as they drew into near-vertical dives – as much as seventy degrees – much steeper than any American aircraft could achieve. When they reached three thousand feet the angle of their dive decreased and sirens attached to their landing gear came to him as a thin banshee wail. Bombs arced away to crash with astonishing fury and, in moments, the entire swarm was lost to sight and silence fell about him once more.

From Across the World Torsten Fredriksson, Warsaw, 12

September 1939 – For immediate release: Since the final occupation of Czechoslovakia earlier this year, few have doubted that Poland's turn would follow. Since the western powers dithered away at Munich any chance of peacefully convincing Adolph Hitler to mend his aggressive ways, it has become increasingly evident that nothing less than all Europe under the Swastika will suit him.

All during the long summer months the western press has predicted with confidence that Germany would meet her match if it came to a showdown with Poland. But no one thought the real fighting would be done by the Poles; they were only expected to conduct a holding campaign while the great French army mobilized.

But now, as German tanks draw a strangling cord about Warsaw, the French remain behind their Maginot line, fooled by their own propaganda into believing that not only are they impregnable but the Germans hiding behind their own Siegfried Line, are as well. Land and air fighting *is* being done by the Poles after all and they lack everything a modern army requires. Only the Polish air force is equipped with a surprisingly modern fighter aircraft in their single-engined low-winged monoplane, the PZL-P.23 B and the twin-engined PZL-P.37. These have given an excellent account of themselves in the first week of battle – those that escaped destruction on the ground – but there are simply not enough of them. Even so, time after time they climb up from their hidden aerodromes, one or two at a time to attack the swarms of Stuka dive bombers that fill the Polish skies. And they die, one or two at a time, in flaming wrecks pursued by half-a-dozen or more enemy. Their bravery is incredible.

But it is these swarms of aircraft which appear to be working closely with mechanized ground units which have brought a new element to warfare and have banished the spectre of the trench from this war. Stukas range far ahead of the advancing tanks and lorries serving as airborne artillery to destroy the Poles whenever they show themselves. That, coupled with the fact that the Poles have few mechanized units and fewer tanks that can match the Nazi monsters, and the nation's impossible borders and few natural obstacles to slow down an advancing army, would appear to make their defeat inevitable.

Lublin Front 14 – 17 September 1939

Lieutenant David Yitzak stepped to the side of the road and watched his weary half-company file past. The men were exhausted and filthy and he could smell them, their acrid odour compounded of sweat and fear. They had marched ninety kilometres from Warsaw in two days.

He thought again of that last meeting at his divisional headquarters where he and other junior field officers had stood at parade rest in the broiling square while the senior officers argued and fought among themselves as to the course to take. After an hour, a mud-spattered armoured car drove into the courtyard and a tall officer stepped out and started for the administrative offices. Noticing the men standing at attention, he veered towards them. A staff colonel who had hurried out when the car arrived, tried to intercept him but the newcomer – a general, he saw – waved him back with an impatient gesture. As he approached, David Yitzak recognized him as Lt General Wladyslaw Anders, commanding the Nowogrodek Cavalry Brigade.

'Why are these officers standing in the sun?' he demanded. The staff officer tried to tell him that the other generals were waiting for him but Anders repeated the question.

'Why, General, they are waiting for orders. If you. . . .'

'And who ordered them to stand here, in the sun?' Yitzak caught the edge to Anders' voice but the staff officer obviously did not.

'I did, General, of course. They are. . . .'

'Gentlemen, dismiss! Fall out to the officers' club, immediately.' Anders then rounded on the fat, unctuous colonel. 'You sir, will be personally responsible for their mess bills. One word of argument and I will have you at the front, as a private! Now show me into the conference.'

When they were assembled again on the parade ground, dusk had fallen and a cooling breeze stirred the sun-baked surface. The General's automobile had gone and another officer came out to read orders directing them into a shortened defensive line east of the Vistula and south towards Lublin. Then they were dismissed to find their own way to the assembly points.

Yitzak had been hungry and thirsty and the thought of the ten-kilometre walk to where the twenty-four men of his attenuated half-company were encamped was discouraging. As a Jew, he was not welcome in the officers' club and so had spent the afternoon dozing in the shade of the long brick wall between German bomb attacks. He had spent the intervening time thinking about Deborah.

They had been married three months before his promotion to

officer's rank – an unheard of honour for a Jew and one which his father's fame had surely influenced. The government's belated and cynical attempt to show Poland's Jewry that all were Poles together had not gone much further.

His father's house was four kilometres across the city from the barracks, in the opposite direction. But there was a chance that he could find someone with a motor car to drive him tomorrow. Yitzak shrugged. The hell with it. He was going home to his wife for at least one night.

Standing beside the dusty road ninety kilometres to the south, he could still remember the love that rushed across her face when she opened the door, could still feel her arms about his neck and her firm breasts against his chest, healing the despair that gripped him, the weakness, the cowardice, that made him want to run and hide from the horrible endless treadmill of killing and maiming that had convulsed Poland.

The old man had gone out, to the synagogue, and she had helped him upstairs to his old room, now hers, and undressed him quickly, brushing away his protests that he should bathe first. She had slipped out of her own dress and underthings and was in his arms so quickly that it seemed all a dream. He had hesitated at first, running his hard hands over her body. She was so delicate, so slim and he was so big but she had pulled him down onto her, wrapping her arms about his back and clenching them with all her might. . . .

Yitzak was jolted rudely back to the present when his sergeant nudged his arm.

'We'll have trouble with some of the men before long, *Pan* Lieutenant.' He ruminated a moment. 'Particularly those two.'

The sergeant, a heavyset Gallician with immensely long and powerful arms, nodded at two soldiers trudging past. Their bearing was anything but soldierly and one glared at him. He wasn't surprised.

'They or someone else, sergeant. Neither of us are very popular at the moment.'

The sergeant nodded and hesitated as if he wanted to say something more. 'Be careful, sir. We . . . we don't have many good officers left.' He glanced back the way he had come, then swung into step with the half-company trudging past.

Yitzak waited for the tail end of the column and fell in behind. Later, he would step up his pace until he was at its head again; a favourite trick to show the men that whatever they could do, he could do better.

For the sergeant to even consider warning him must mean he was badly worried. That he had done so in full view and hearing of the men, indicated that Yitzak could trust him as an ally. That might be important very soon, he thought. Then, as if from long habit, he touched his holster, conscious of the comforting bulk of the heavy Radom pistol. After a while, thoughts of plots were obscured by the monotony of the march and the hot sun pouring down on his head. For the moment, the war seemed a million kilometres away and there was only the leaden air and the dull hum of insects and heat. Scorched fields stretched under the relentless sun on either side and dust coated the dried weeds lining the road. The drainage ditches were bone dry and the flies bothered him with their persistent buzzing. Ahead, a small stand of trees edged the road; he'd call a short halt there. A shadow slid past and he realized suddenly that the humming did not come from insects.

'Aircraft!' he shouted. 'Take cover!'

Yitzak threw himself against the man beside him and they sprawled together into the ditch under the steady yammering of machine guns. Yitzak saw a triple line of spurting dirt race along the road. Behind, one body lay in the dust, legs twisted at a curious angle. Then it pulled up into a steep climb, twisted at the top and flashed around to attack again. For a moment, the Stuka was parallel to and fifty metres above and he could see the pilot peering down at them.

'Into the trees,' he shouted. The sergeant was already pushing men up the bank and into the field and Yitzak hauled the young soldier he had knocked down to his feet. The boy seemed dazed and he pushed him towards the trees. Yitzak ran along the line, one eye on the Stuka as it banked and tipped its nose down. The men had not scattered but huddled together for reassurance and he ran towards them, yelling, waving them apart but it was too late and the Stuka's machine guns blasted grass and dirt and copper-tipped bullets among them.

The trees were a hundred metres away. He raced across the iron-hard surface, enveloped in the scent of dried grass and baked earth and waiting for a bullet's smashing blow. The sound of the engine was right on top of him, the pilot questing from side to side, fastening his sight on his back. He ran.

The ear-splitting roar of the aircraft passed with the intensity of a slow-motion nightmare. Men stumbled about him; he glimpsed faces contorted in terror. Then, as if the film had jerked into fast speed once more, the aircraft was bearing down on them again. He saw a body jack-knife and tumble head over heels, like a rag doll thrown aside by a spoiled child. The trees were ahead; bullets snicked across the grass, cracked branches away and churned the leaves before the dark shadow enclosed them.

Yitzak collapsed onto his back and through the treetops, a glint of silver arrowed. They were safe, he exulted. But the sergeant was still shouting at them, still kicking men to their feet, pointing deeper into the woods. Yitzak did not comprehend what he was trying to tell them . . . The verge exploded into dust that swirled in the sunlight and clipped branches and clouts of dirt and falling, twisting bodies. The Stuka pilot had made one final pass, he realized, as he ran in terror. He was machine gunning the edge of the woods, suspecting that they would stop running. Only the old sergeant had guessed . . . and he paid for it with his life. They found his body afterwards, the head almost severed from the shoulders.

After a while, Yitzak went back to the road where he found the bodies of four more men. Five dead. Not a bad return for a few minutes' work, he thought. The pilot had butchered them. His mind was filled with the stories he had heard of the first war, when Germans had occupied Poland. There had been such stories then of German cruelty but he had never quite believed them, believed instead in all the children's stories that wars were fought by honourable men and that soldiering was a noble profession. Even the hard fighting around Modlin had not suggested the savageness of the Stuka pilot. He was suddenly afraid, for Deborah, for himself, for Poland.

They dug a single shallow grave and buried the men side by side. Yitzak put their paybooks into his field pack, wiped his face on his sleeve and ordered the march resumed. The men went, sullenly.

At sunset, Yitzak chose an open field through which a drought-stricken stream seeped. The survivors ate their meagre rations in silence and spread blanket rolls. Yitzak took the first sentry-go but when he named the others to follow him, he thought for a moment they might mutiny. They quieted instantly when he selected a rifle from the stack.

Within minutes, the field was silent and darkness slipped across the countryside. Vivid stars blazed and the new moon would not appear until dawn. Yitzak found it difficult to remain awake and after a while, he paused beside the road and leaned on an ancient rail fence.

He thought about Deborah and cursed the stupidity of the government that had trapped them into this mess, the French and the British who had betrayed them and the Germans who were threatening his wife and father with their stupid bombing. And he was here, forcing dispirited men who hated him because he was an officer and a Jew, to march on and on until they were all killed. God, how he wanted to go back to Deborah.

What was he doing here when the real danger was in Warsaw? They would never hold the Germans. A counter-attack might produce a favourable armistice they had been told. He chuckled in the darkness. A fool's hope. Not only were the Huns not about to allow them the time to organize such a move but the British and French weren't coming to their aid as they had promised. They had egged Poland into this war in the hope that she would beat Germany alone and they would not have to fight. But now they were in it and it would be a fight to the death.

David Yitzak had no illusions that the Polish army could yet rally and win. They were done for. The real war would go on after the government surrendered, as it had in 1918 and 1919 against the Germans and then the Russians. Resistance groups would form; it was inevitable and in a moment of clairvoyance, he saw nothing but misery and slaughter for Poland. But he had not yet reached that point of complete hopelessness when a professional soldier shrugs off the habit of obedience.

Lieutenant David Yitzak could see the hopelessness growing as they struggled on for the third day under the pitiless sun. Where were the rains that always turned September fields and roads to quagmires? Hour after hour, they searched the sky for the least sign of clouds but, as the sun climbed towards its Zenith, the sullen, brassy colour only deepened. And out of it came Stukas to harry them. Two more men were killed and the fourteen who survived hated him more than the Germans – he represented everything that had brought them to this pass – the government, the mythical Jewish bankers, the army.

They stopped that evening along the dried mud banks of a small stream full of brackish water and Yitzak's orders to boil drinking water were received in sullen silence. Ignoring them all, he built a small cookfire and filled his canteen from the stream and suspended it over the fire on green sticks. He squatted in the shade of a dusty tree to wait and smoked.

The overweight soldier the sergeant had pointed out as the likeliest of the trouble-makers that first day south of Warsaw got up and ambled towards Yitzak's fire. He looked at it then laughed and kicked the canteen over. As he turned towards Yitzak, a huge grin on his face, he was cocking his rifle. Yitzak shot him through the chest with his service pistol.

The others sprang up, insolent expressions disappearing abruptly. Yitzak ignored everyone but the man's ferret-faced friend who dropped to his knees beside the body. With a scream of rage, the man snatched the rifle up and Yitzak shot him before he could bring the weapon to his shoulder. Only then did he see the young soldier whom he had knocked away from the Stuka's machine gun bullets standing to one side, rifle menacing the others. They all stared at Yitzak in stunned silence and he realized that while they may have grumbled, they were not part of a plot to murder him – yet.

He ejected the Radom's magazine and slipped two new cartridges into the clip, nodded his thanks to the young soldier who ducked his head uneasily. Three men moved reluctantly to drag the bodies away and the rest scattered to hunt for firewood.

That night, three soldiers deserted, leaving their weapons behind. Yitzak guessed they were making for Warsaw and home. He weighed the advantages and disadvantages of trying to recapture them but decided that if he did catch them, he could never bring himself to hang them for desertion, as an example to the others. But to let them go would only encourage the others to do the same. Time and weariness forced the decision in the end and they went on.

In mid-afternoon, they spotted a dust cloud in the distance. Yitzak divided the men into two squads and placed them on either side of the road where it made a shallow bend to the left and entered a grove of pines. The dry drainage ditches offered meagre enough cover but would have to suffice.

Ten minutes later, Yitzak made out a line of horsemen in double column through his field glasses. He breathed a bit easier; they could handle cavalry but tanks would have been out of the question. Perhaps with trained, steady troops, but not these ill-trained conscripts.

'Horsemen,' he said quietly as he moved along the road. 'Don't open fire unless I signal.'

He watched the horsemen approach, polished equipment glinting and jangling. In the alternating sun and shadow of the pine grove they were full of menace until he saw the lances. He waited a moment longer to make certain then passed the word. 'Polish cavalry. Hold your positions.'

When they were fifty metres away, he stood up carefully, hands well away from his sides and walked towards them. The officer whistled and the horsemen wheeled to deploy. Yitzak waited while the officer cantered towards him. Except for a faint coating of road dust, the lancers looked fresh enough and they were not even wearing steel battle helmets. The young captain's face was even freshly shaven, Yitzak noted with a flash of anger. The man curbed his horse and Yitzak saluted.

'Lieutenant David Yitzak,' he introduced himself.

The cavalry officer, a captain by the three silver stars on shoulder straps and square *czapka*, sketched a half-hearted salute in return.

'Yitzak?' he repeated.

David nodded. The harsh, ammoniac smell of the horse reminded him of summer afternoons spent on his grandparents' estate near Brest-Litovsk when he was a child.

'What's the road like ahead?' Yitzak asked but the officer continued to stare about him. Finally, he rose in the saddle and started to motion his squad back onto the road.

'I asked what the road is like ahead,' Yitzak repeated with a hard edge to his voice.

The cavalry officer glanced down at him, an amused smile on his lips. 'I don't speak to Jews,' he sneered.

Yitzak chuckled at this rear-area dandy. 'But you will make an exception this time, won't you?'

The cavalry officer looked down again to see Yitzak's pistol pointing at his belly. Yitzak had stepped just enough to the left that he was out of view of the cavalry detachment. With his left hand, he held the bridle short, forcing the horse to stand still.

'My men are tired, thirsty and hungry. We've been marching for three days and before that we were in the line north of Modlin. We've had nine killed by Stukas and I have personally shot two of my own men for mutiny. One rear-area coward of a lancer captain won't make the slightest difference to me.'

The captain tried to speak but the words stuttered out and Yitzak laughed at his fear. The man swallowed twice and finally forced the words out.

'The Hun has occupied Kock, twenty kilometres southwest. You are cut-off from Lublin.'

Suddenly, it was no longer a game between them. 'You bastard,' Yitzak hissed. 'You would have let us march right to them.'

The captain squirmed in his saddle, but never took his eyes from the pistol. 'If you shoot me,' he whispered, 'my soldiers will hang you.'

'Look again, Captain,' Yitzak waved a hand at the ditches on either side of the road and his men stood slowly, weapons ready.

'You will have plenty of company before they've gone two metres. Now order your men to split their rations with us and get the hell out of here.'

'Split our rations? What will we eat?' the captain protested.

'Shit for all I care. My men need that food to fight the Germans. Since you don't intend to fight, you needn't eat.'

The captain gave the orders and Yitzak sent two men to gather them up. As the cavalry troop clattered past, he received their salutes while holding the pistol behind his back.

After the lancers had disappeared up the road, Yitzak quickly marched the men into the forest and called a halt. While they ate and discussed the lancer captain's news among themselves, Yitzak dug out his tattered map to study the area about Kock. With Nazi tanks less than twenty kilometres distant, they had to leave the area quickly. Tanks could cover twenty kilometres in two hours or less as he had discovered north of the Vistula. But there were two questions to be answered first. Was it worth while going on, and if so, would the nine men follow him? His fear that the night would bring more desertions was answer enough to the second question. To answer the first, he had only to look at the map. They could turn east, circle the Nazi thrust and march to Lublin. But to what end? They would only bottle themselves up with the rest of the army.

A shadow fell across the map and he looked up to see the young soldier. The boy – man, damn it, he thought – saluted and fumbled for words.

'Permission to speak, *Pan* Lieutenant?'

'Of course. Your name is Oroski, isn't it? I haven't thanked you yet for backing me yesterday.'

Oroski hesitated, expression grim, then squatted down. '*Pan* Lieutenant, I . . . we . . . heard what the cavalry officer said. There isn't any hope now, is there?'

Yitzak noted the intelligence in the boy's eyes and his own expression softened.

'It is beginning to appear not. If it's true that there are tanks between us and Lublin. . . .' He let the sentence trail away but the boy finished it for him.

' . . . we would be wasting time and our lives by going on to Lublin, even though we were ordered to do so.'

Yitzak raised an eyebrow, wondering what he was driving at. 'Continue,' he encouraged.

The boy looked abashed. 'Well, *Pan* Lieutenant, it . . . that is, I think that . . . well, wouldn't we be better off by leaving Poland?' He looked anxiously at Yitzak as if he were afraid he might be accused of treason and hurried on. 'I mean, *Pan* Lieutenant, there are bound to be a great many other Polish soldiers escaping over the border. We could join them and form a . . . a . . . ,' he fumbled for the word and Yitzak supplied it,

'A partisan group.'

'Yes, that's what I meant to say. We could continue to fight against the Germans that way.'

'The thought had occurred to me. But I am afraid that you and I would go alone.'

The boy glanced over his shoulder at the rest of men. 'Maybe, *Pan* Lieutenant. But they really aren't such a bad lot. We were all called up in the third week of August. We did not have much training and well. . . .'

Yitzak nodded. 'Perhaps. But what about the two men I shot? Were they part of the "not such a bad lot"?'

'Oh no, *Pan* Lieutenant. They weren't from our village. They came from Modicew.'

'You think then that your comrades would follow us to Romania?'

The boy looked at him sharply and Yitzak was surprised at the flash of suspicion in his eyes.

'Not Romania, *Pan* Lieutenant. That's too far away and the Nazis will have occupied much of the country we would have to pass. But Russia is only a week's march east. And there are no Germans that way. We could surrender at a border post.'

'Russia!' Yitzak exclaimed. 'For God's sake, they would throw us back to the Germans. They have a non-aggression pact, or hadn't you heard.'

The boy shook his head doggedly. 'No, *Pan* Lieutenant, if you will permit me. The Soviet Government did what it had to. They know they must fight the Germans eventually as Communism and Fascism can never co-exist. You see, they are only buying time. They will welcome us as fighting proletariat, as allies. It is only a matter of time.'

Yitzak understood then that the boy was a communist. He shook his head in exasperation but the movement was misinterpreted as a denial.

'I am sorry, *Pan* Lieutenant, but we have already decided.' Oroski spoke softly and did not take his eyes from Yitzak's face. An insolent smile curled about his lips and it seemed to Yitzak that he was suddenly harder, more mature.

'We would like you to come with us, Yitzak. You are a good officer and a brave man – for a Jew.' He did not miss the fact that Oroski had dropped the honorific in advance of the calculated insult.

'And if I refuse?'

Oroski stood slowly. 'I am afraid we would have to leave you behind,' he said dramatically.

That night, they camped on the banks of a small river that wound east towards the Bug. Oroski selected the spot and Yitzak agreed casually enough, as if he were in the habit of taking advice from a common soldier every day. Yitzak was still in command but only nominally, he knew.

He had just found a quiet place under a tree and had sat down to write a letter to Deborah when Oroski shouted at him to gather

47

firewood. Thoughtfully, Yitzak put away his pen and paper and walked to where the little private was squatting on his heels studying Yitzak's map. He bent and with one quick, fluid motion, yanked him straight off the ground. Yitzak waited just long enough for the boy's astonishment to turn to fear, then carried him to the river, feet churning air, and pitched him in.

Oroski described a cartwheel and landed half in the water, half on a mudbank where he thrashed and floundered to his feet. The river was low because of the drought and he had to wade through a metre or more of smelly mud, stirring up great gaseous bubbles that burst with nauseating plops. The others shouted with laughter as Oroski gained the bank and stood shaking with anger. Yitzak stepped towards Oroski and had the satisfaction of seeing him stumble back.

'Even in the Red Army,' Yitzak growled, 'respect for an officer is required.'

Without waiting for an answer, he shouldered his way through the grinning soldiers and went back to his tree, knowing that he had made a deadly enemy; Oroski was an insignificant little man who, through force of circumstance, had suddenly found himself in a position of some authority. But the exercise of authority depends on respect, and that Yitzak had taken away when he threw him in the river. There was only one way for Oroski to regain that respect and that was to kill him – which, of course, he had intended to do in any event. He was, after all, an officer and Oroski would have to present some kind of credential to the Soviet authorities.

Yitzak left at midnight after slipping his officer's paybook into the field pack of a sleeping soldier. He moved so quietly that the dozing sentry did not hear him go.

Just after dawn, he removed his officer's insignia, sorted through the paybooks to find the dead sergeant's and buried the rest. After resting for a while and studying the map one more time, he struck off towards the north across the fields.

Eastern Poland 17 – 23 September 1939

The traffic jam of men, horses and machines stretched back for kilometres from the River Bug somewhere northwest of Sokal under the blazing September sun. The enthusiasm and laughter which had characterised the operation during the cooler morning had begun to evaporate in the heat and tempers were becoming short.

Already there had been several arrests by harassed military police whose justice was swift and simple. The arrestee was hauled out of line, beaten mercilessly with boots and rifle butts, then bound and hauled back along the line to a detention centre somewhere in the rear.

Lieutenant Mikhail Gregorvitch Dogorov slouched as comfortably as he could on the caisson of his lead artillery piece, an elderly Model 1902/30 76.2 millimetre Field Gun, a standard Model 1902 modernized in 1930 by rebarrelling for a more powerful shell, and watched it all with stolid indifference. His woollen uniform buttoned to the neck was soaked with sweat but he never thought to unbutton or even remove it. It was forbidden. Likewise the heavy steel helmet remained on his head because regulations required it. But if Dogorov was indifferent to his physical discomfort, he was still alert and aware of what was going on around him. At intervals, he sat up to see that his unit was alert even though they had been on the move since midnight.

The line jerked forward again and he nodded to his sergeant to get the men back into position. Again, they trundled ahead, leaving behind the cool patch of woods that had screened the river. It lay before them now, a broad stream flowing north to join the Vistula near Warsaw. Two pontoon bridges had been thrown across to supplement the single, ramshackle ferry that in normal times handled the meagre traffic between the two hereditary enemies, Poland and Russia. The bridges were crammed to capacity with vehicles, both motor and horse drawn, the latter predominating. The far bank resembled a disturbed ant hill but like an ant hill, and the simile was apt, Dogorov thought, the activity was purposeful and every man knew and did his job. Shirkers were not tolerated in the Red Army.

His driver dismounted to tie canvas hoods over the horses' heads so that they would not panic on the bridge. The remains of several vehicles and drowned horses in the river testified to the treachery of the bridges. They swayed as traffic trundled across and horses snorted and danced as drivers dodged and soothed, hampered by the narrowness of the bridge. One horse, half rearing as the bridge dipped alarmingly, flicked its handler over the side as neatly as a spun coin. The man hit the water with arms and legs flailing and shouts of laughter roared from either bank. The frightened horse was brought under control while the driver floated downstream, waving his cap as a picket boat started out to him. Dogorov did not see the outcome as his unit edged gingerly onto the bridge. He stood up on the caisson, as much to encourage as to threaten the drivers.

On the far bank, the drivers whipped the canvas hoods off and the horses, reacting to the welcome feel of solid ground, plunged up the steep slope with a will. An exasperated military policeman waved them on to a dirt road which, after the long jam-up behind, seemed almost empty. The choking dust was less ubiquitous here and they bowled along at a good clip, paralleling the main route of march.

Dogorov had a chance to look about now. He still found it difficult to believe that only three weeks ago he had been in Warsaw as the assistant military attaché, had lunched with Polish army officers and attended manoeuvres at their invitation. Today, they were the enemy – no, not actually the enemy, rather a stubborn people who were allowing a thousand years of history to misguide them into thinking the Soviet Union was still their enemy. No matter how they had tried to deny it, the fates of Russia and Poland were irretrievably intertwined. He remembered the staff lecture in which the political officer had pointed out that if the Polish government had only allowed Soviet troops to be stationed in Poland to protect both Russian and Polish borders, the Germans would never have dared attack. Now the Poles were paying the price for their shortsightedness.

They made good time on the secondary road and Dogorov could sit back on the caisson and review his orders and anticipate events as a good officer should. But, as the afternoon wore on, his mind began to slide away to memories of his leave which had ended so abruptly two days before.

His mother had met him at the Kursk railroad station in Moscow. She had obtained reservations at Emile's for dinner that evening and the fact that the waiters had been polite was due to her position in the government and not his uniform, he was certain. The sterlet caviar and the roast duck baked in rice confirmed it.

He hadn't seen his mother for nearly a year. She was fifty-two but looked forty or less, and was still quite stunning in the black silk evening dress and thin strand of pearls she had saved from pre-revolutionary days. She had laughed and flirted with him and that eased the contrast between grey Moscow and gay Warsaw. They had danced to the orchestra and she had been full of questions about his months in Warsaw.

He had been lucky in his choice of parents; the revolutionary backgrounds of both were impeccable. His father had been a Petrograd munitions worker and a member of the Bolshevik Party long before the revolution. He had served on the Petrograd Soviet from the beginning in February, 1917, had thrown his support to Lenin from the moment of his arrival in April of that fateful year, had been nominated to Lenin's Military Revolutionary Committee and had taken part in the capture of the Fortress of Peter and Paul.

Dogorov barely recalled his father; he had been captured and hanged by Denekin's counter-revolutionary bandits, while leading a red Militia brigade in the Ukraine in 1918. Mikhail was only five at the time. His mother had assumed her husband's duties in the New Red government's innumerable committees and by the time he was old enough to attend school, he was passed immediately into the best academies for the children of party members, his place secured by his father's standing in the pantheon of minor communist martyrs.

His mother surprised him the next morning with the announcement that she had not only arranged several days off, but had secured the ministry's summer dacha for the week. They travelled to Borodino that afternoon and disdaining the rickety bus, had walked the five kilometres to the log cabin in the golden sunlight of the September afternoon. This was his first visit in several years but it was just as he remembered – a low cabin of vertical logs covered by a peat roof, hidden in the same trees that concealed a jewel of a lake. Even the dilapidated rowing boat moored to the rickety dock was as he remembered it.

His mother, Olga Semonova Dogorova, was widely acknowledged as a beautiful woman. She had been an actress and in 1917 had served with his father on the barricades about the Telephone and Telegraph Exchange in October of that year when the Bolsheviks turned out that last vestige of capitalist rule, the Constituent Assembly. She was tall and lithe with the typical White Russian facial structure which he had inherited; high cheek bones and straight nose over rounded, firm lips.

They had changed into bathing suits and had a swim in the sun-warmed waters of the lake. His mother's suit was form-fitting in the latest style and once wet did not conceal the slightest curve or dimple. To distract himself, he talked at length about the progress the Germans were making in Poland.

'But,' he had predicted, 'don't count the Poles short. Just as I was leaving, there were rumours that the Polish general staff was disengaging along the Vistula and pulling back into the southern mountains. The rains can't hold off much longer and, if the army can concentrate about Lublin, the Germans will have to hold and consolidate. Their tank divisions seemed to have run wild and in many places are so far ahead of their infantry support that a determined counter-attack could wipe them out to a man. So far, the Nazis have had it all their way because the roads are dry and the country is flat and perfect for their tanks. But when they get into the Carpathians and the rains turn everything to a quagmire, they'll stop quickly enough.'

Later, over a light supper, his mother had reminded him that his three-month assignment in Warsaw as military attaché was a mark of the high esteem in which the government held the family. He grinned at her across the supper table. Her concern for her standing in the government was obsessive, and with good reason, he admitted. More than a few of her friends had disappeared during the past few years. Yet in thinking back, they all had in common an unreliable political background. All had been SRs, Social Revolutionaries, or Mensheviks and, in a few cases, rightists who had changed their politics after 1918.

To take her mind away from such matters, he described his interview with Vlachislav Molotov himself, his cordial – for him – greeting and hard handshake. 'He even asked if I remembered my father, and,' he grinned slyly at his mother, 'he asked about you, by name.'

A look of pleased surprise overcame her apprehensive expression. 'Oh, he certainly did not!' she protested.

'But he did. He said to me, and these were his exact words, "How is your dear mother, Olga Semonova? Please convey my respects to her." '

The line came to an abrupt halt and angry at himself for being caught day-dreaming, Dogorov shouted for his sergeant. Simultaneously, Dogorov heard the distant boom of cannon.

The sergeant saluted. 'Polish guns ahead, Comrade Lieutenant. They are reported to be well dug in. Infantry have been sent ahead to engage them.'

'Infantry!' Dogorov exploded. 'Who would send infantry against prepared artillery positions? We'll be here the rest of the day. Asimov!' he snapped.

A small, wizened man in a dusty uniform hurried up to the caisson and saluted. Asimov was his forward fire observer and could be trusted to return concise, accurate information no matter the situation.

'Asimov, there is a Polish gun position a kilometre and a half ahead.'

'More like two kilometres, Comrade Lieutenant,' Asimov murmured, not at all abashed.

'Have it your way.' Dogorov had learned long ago not to argue with him. If he said two kilometres, Dogorov could depend on it. 'Go forward. I will give you ten minutes.'

'*No s' bogom*, God go with us,' the irrepressible Asimov muttered and hurried away, shouting at his telephonist. Two reels of wire were piled onto the backboard and the telephonist trotted off after him, unreeling the wire as he went. Dogorov nodded to his sergeant who began to bellow orders.

The horses dragged the medium field gun into position, then were unhooked and led aside. Away from the flash area, the ammunition was unloaded and laid in two piles; the main supply was stacked near the caisson and a canvas cover thrown over it. The ready supply was stacked near the gun within reach of the loaders and covered in a similar manner. The sergeant set up the field telephone nearby, clipped the two wires in place and waited with the handset pressed to his ear.

The sound of firing was steadier now and he could see the bursts some distance ahead. There seemed to be two guns from the rapidity of their fire and when he climbed onto the caisson and searched the fields to the west, the noise settled down to a steady rumble. Three guns, he decided.

South of where they waited, a kilometre or more away, he could see the main convoy had stalled. Shells were bursting among the baggage train and tiny figures scurried into the fields. The explosions marched along the road until the sky was filled with seething brown clouds of dirt and dust.

The sergeant shouted that contact had been made and Dogorov snatched the handset up. Asimov's unhurried voice came through, reporting that the infantry had been held up by well-concealed Polish machine guns. There were three cannon some fifty metres apart and protected by small hills. He proposed a walking burst north to south. Dogorov agreed and Asimov fed him the first set of coordinates. The ungainly cannon barrel rose and humped slightly to the right. A shell was snatched up and sent home, the breech closed and the lock spun down.

'Fire,' Dogorov shouted and the muzzle concussion lashed them like a whip. Stepping aside, Dogorov caught a glimpse of the shell in flight. Asimov's unhurried voice came through the buzzing line, a drop of two degrees and one left. Dogorov relayed the instructions and the gun fired again. This time, only a minor correction was called back and anticipating Asimov's skill, Dogorov ordered rapid fire, moving laterally a quarter of a degree at a time.

Asimov reported all shells falling on target about the first gun and he gave instructions for the second and third guns in his section to open fire. The sixth shot was a direct hit and he was fed new coordinates to shift to the second Polish gun. The change was made without pause and the firing continued until, on the fourth shot, that gun too took a direct hit. Through his field glasses, Dogorov could see that explosions among the main convoy had stopped. The surviving Polish gun had decamped. Dogorov gave the order to cease fire.

He turned away from his grinning artillerymen, struggling hard to suppress his own laughter. Someone shouted for a cheer and he scowled but the men were waving their helmets as they cheered themselves as much as him. He could not contain his excitement any longer. Laughing, he swept his own helmet off and made a low bow. He had fired his guns in war for the first time.

Just before sunset, they were directed into an artillery park established on the outskirts of a small village. Dogorov dismounted stiffly from the caisson and nodded to the sergeant who began to shout a flurry of orders to the drivers and gunners in the company. Dogorov stretched to work out the kinks then strolled over to the company that had arrived ahead of them anxious to see what the others thought of his shooting. He knew the lieutenant, Shuslov, having attended a gunnery school with him at Sheremkvo two years before, where he had been known as a *zubrilos*, a greasy grind. Nevertheless, Shuslov's company had been with the main column, had endured the shelling on the road and he was quite envious of Dogorov's showing in putting the Polish guns out of action.

Dogorov carried out his usual inspection and dismissed the section for dinner. He took his tray to his tent and ignoring the taste of the questionable meat and too-soft potatoes, ate and studied the orders for the next day's advance. Just as he was finishing, a policeman loomed out of the gathering darkness.

'Lieutenant Mikhail Gregorvitch Dogorov?'

'Yes, corporal?' Dogorov had been half-expecting this summons.

'I am instructed to escort you to regimental headquarters immediately. Please come with me.'

The corporal left him at a two-storey, whitewashed building that had formerly been the village hall and now served as regimental headquarters. It stood on a rise of ground beyond the village proper. Several more two-storey buildings fronted on a dirt road, among them a school and a post office. Several shops stood side by side, already emptied of course. Poland was a capitalist tool of England and so, he guessed, they were privately owned, like so many shops in Warsaw. A strange concept, he thought, and wondered why the people permitted it. He stepped into the foyer.

A guard summoned an orderly who took his name and went into another room. The building was crowded with staff officers rushing about or shouting into field telephones. He leaned against the wall, wishing he dared smoke and waited. The doors and windows were all tightly shut and the building had retained the heat of the day. Trickles of sweat made their itchy way down his back and ribs and his head was soon swimming from lack of oxygen. He thought to step outside and wait but noticed that the guard watched him closely when he straightened from the wall. Dogorov sighed and endured.

The orderly returned twenty minutes later and beckoned him through the swinging doors. Dogorov, grateful for any relief, followed with alacrity, even though a prison sentence might be waiting for him inside.

The crowd had thinned and the windows were open in here. Dogorov took a deep breath to clear away the muzziness as the orderly led him to a table where three high-ranking officers were studying a map. Dogorov came to attention; his years in the Soviet Army had taught him that patience was indeed a virtue.

He looked around the room without moving his head. The walls were panelled in a dark wood that reached halfway to the ceiling and were covered with maps, and even a poster exhorting greater effort for Russia as well as one cautioning against foreign spies and influences. The colonel commanding the regiment pounded the table and shouted angrily.

'I do not care what it costs, the position will be taken before the Germans do so. I am giving you all direct orders to that effect and Commissar Antov will bear witness, if need be.'

Antov was the tall, good-looking man in a major's uniform who turned a baleful eye on the others. There wasn't even a trace of humour in the commissar's face. 'He's memorized the book,' Dogorov thought. If Antov intervened in his case, he'd be sentenced to a labour camp for certain.

The colonel straightened, dusting his hands and turned towards him. 'You are Dogorov?'

'Yes sir.'

'You destroyed two Polish guns today?'

'Yes sir.' Dogorov edged a glance at the political commissar to find him watching closely. His nervousness increased.

'Who gave you orders to fire?'

'No one, sir.'

'You took it upon yourself to do so without orders of any kind?'

'Yes sir.'

'I see.' The colonel looked at the commissar who nodded slightly. Dogorov went cold.

'Explain.'

He swallowed and cleared his throat, struggling to organize his thoughts and described how his section was placed at an angle to the column, with a clear field of fire to the Polish position.

'I felt I was in perfect position to relieve the column, sir. In my judgement, the Polish fire was accurate and rapid enough that to have sent for permission would have endangered the column's objective.'

The colonel turned away in thought and the tension built in Dogorov to an unbearable peak.

'Lieutenant, I will overlook your action this one time as it produced a desirable result. However, should you ever take such independent action again, I will have you court-martialled. Do you understand? Good! Then dismiss!' The commissar nodded at Dogorov's salute and he beat a hasty retreat.

Only when he was well away from the building did he pause to light a cigarette. His hands were still shaking and he looked around for some place to sit down and compose himself. He found it in a bench beneath a tree facing the road.

That had been close. Today's unauthorized action could have ruined his career. The colonel, like most officers these days, operated by the book. And why not? You stayed out of trouble that way – unless they changed the book, he thought drily. Thousands had been purged in the past few years and all had been guilty of deviant behaviour. Ranking officers tended to be timorous, plodding and inexperienced. Three years ago, he might have been decorated for his prompt action; today, he could have as easily earned a tenner, a ten-year sentence to a labour camp. He smoked and stared moodily into the darkness until disturbed by the sound of an engine labouring up the hill.

Turning in that direction, he saw a canvas-covered lorry stop before the school building. Several uniformed men jumped down, unslung submachine guns and formed a line to the door. An officer went inside and a moment later, ten or eleven men and a woman were hustled out to the truck. The NKVD men climbed in after them and the officer fastened the canvas curtain, climbed into the cab and the lorry rattled away.

He lit a fresh cigarette and started back to the artillery park. The night was peaceful. Stars blazed in a cloudless sky and he traced the great spill of the Milky Way from horizon to horizon. Astronomy had been a boyhood hobby and he had hoped to study physics at Moscow University. But his ability with mathematics was needed by the State for other purposes and he had given up the idea years before, even ending his participation in the amateur astronomy league at school. Dogorov oriented himself on Sirius and began to pick out the major and minor stars, scorning the use of the constellations as markers. The low grinding of a lorry engine sounded briefly in the distance. He had just found Arcturus when he heard the distant shots like tiny pops. Dogorov drew on his cigarette and waited. A few moments later there were four distinct pistol shots. The people from the school, he thought; the NKVD had again dealt efficiently with anti-Soviet elements.

The battery commissar had discussed fifth column activities in

Spain where Soviet forces had supported the Socialist cause and their application to Poland.

'We discovered quickly that the fascist mentality does not permit humanitarian considerations. Intellectuals never take part in violent operations yet are responsible for their planning and for the selection and training of those who do. The obvious way to end sabotage therefore is to neutralize all intellectuals. Without a brain, the organism cannot function and many innocent lives will thus be saved.'

On September 21st, the city of Lwow surrendered to the German XVIII Corps and German troops moved into position along the far bank of the Bug. The following morning, a headquarters orderly found Dogorov studying disposition orders in his tent and handed him a mimeographed sheet of paper.

Full dress uniform, he read with surprise. Perhaps they had decided to court-martial him after all. But no, that could not be. A court-martial notice was always delivered by another officer. He rummaged through his duffle bag and found a limp, wrinkled mess and bellowed for his sergeant.

'Get those pressed,' Dogorov nodded at the dress pants and tunic. 'I'll give you fifteen minutes. And send someone to clean my boots. I'm going for a bath.'

He stripped and wound a towel around his waist and went out across the field. Dust kicked up by hooves and feet formed a choking haze through which the already scorching sun blazed. The stubble hurt his feet and a few soldiers greeted him with catcalls, not realizing he was an officer. He ignored them and joined others who apparently had the same idea. No one had bathed since the day before they moved across the border.

The Bug was broad and placid at this point and the usually muddy banks had dried to fine dust. Dogorov stalked along the bank in ill-humour, ignoring the German sentries watching from the other side. After five days of constant marching and countermarching, he had been looking forward to at least one day of light duty and much needed maintenance.

He found a spot where the bank dipped towards the river and was shaded by a huge oak and the air still held the morning coolness. Willows dipped to the water and the river flowed quietly between the widely-spaced banks with little trace of current except for an eddy or two in the shallows. Throwing off the towel, Dogorov waded in and wonderfully cool liquid began to dissolve sticky sweat and dirt. He took a deep breath and slid under the surface and swam well out into the river.

He floated on his back, entranced with the contrast between the river and the icy spring water of the lake at Borodino or the warmish, crowded municipal baths in Moscow. This was altogether different, more like the Black Sea, where he had once gone to bathe while a cadet on manoeuvres. He and three others had sneaked away one night from the guarded training camp.

With powerful strokes, he swam back to the bank, soaped himself quickly, ducked to rinse and waded out. He found his towel and started back, towelling his hair dry. Someone shouted and he peered from beneath the towel to see an ample young woman, hands on her hips, laughing at him and he discovered that he had walked right into her vegetable patch.

Dogorov whipped the towel about his middle and backed away trying to apologize but he knew no Polish and if the girl spoke Russian, she was laughing too hard to understand him. She kept motioning for him to drop the towel as she flipped the hem of her dress. Blushing furiously, he fled.

His dress uniform had been steamed and ironed into a semblance of presentability when he reached his tent. The sergeant had even had water heated for shaving but Dogorov's embarrassment was turning to anger and he snapped at the soldier to get out.

On the way to regimental headquarters, he began to grin. He supposed he had looked ridiculous striding naked across the field, head wrapped in a scrap of towel. The girl certainly was attractive enough but her ribaldry had shocked him as had her open invitation to sex. It fitted, of course, with all he had been taught about the Poles.

For most of his life, Dogorov had lived in male-dominated academies in which the students had been rigidly segregated by sex, or in the army. His only sexual experience had occurred once in Kiev when, egged on by a drunken friend, he had bought the services of a prostitute on payday. It was over before he knew what was happening and for weeks afterwards he had worried about venereal disease.

The only woman he knew well was his mother and they had, of course, never discussed the subject of sex. She was so attractive that, for some reason, he felt inhibited. He remembered how she moved about the flat in nightgown and robe or the summer cabin in bathing costume. She had never lacked for male attention. Tall and with an ample figure, she . . . he yanked his mind away when the tumescence began. He threw the cigarette in the dust and stalked on across the field.

The regimental headquarters had been established on a rise to catch the slightest breeze. It seemed that every officer in the regiment had been summoned. A harassed aide motioned him into line just as the band crashed out. Dogorov winced. He was tone deaf and music was just so much noise to him, noise made more unbearable since others seemed to take great delight in what to him were cacophonic grumblings and squeals. Only the drums had any meaning and here his innate mathematical talent reinforced a meagre sense of rhythm.

From his vantage point, he could see several boats crossing the river. Uniformed figures stepped out, salutes were exchanged and he realized that the German commander and his staff were paying a courtesy call.

As the officers trudged up the rise from the river, Dogorov experienced a sense of anticipation. He had met German officers in Warsaw, but this was different. These were veterans of war. The double line of Russian officers came to attention. The German commander touched his hat brim in salute and the colonel replied. The German commander – a colonel he suspected although he was not certain what rank the man's shoulder braids signified – wheeled and strode along the line, peering closely at tanned faces beneath steel helmets. He reached the end of the line and exchanging remarks in Russian with his host, continued to the buffet table set out under an awning. An aide gave the command to rest.

Dogorov stood in the broiling sun while the two colonels and their staff officers conversed and toasted one another with glasses of iced tea and vodka. Sweat poured from him under the dress tunic and he thought longingly of the river and, for a moment, of the Polish woman.

The German officer's Russian was quite good and Dogorov thought he heard him say that he had trained in Russia in the mid-1920s. How could that be? he wondered. They talked about their respective campaigns and there were several remarks about the fine, dry summer weather so late in the season.

'Hitler weather,' the German colonel boomed, pointing out it had been the same when they had marched into the Rhineland and Czechoslovakia.

'And when you march into France,' Dogorov's colonel observed slyly. The German guffawed and slapped his knee and presumably repeated the remark to his officers in German as they also laughed.

A thin haze began to move in from the east to mitigate the worst of the heat but the humidity grew worse. Perhaps the late summer heat wave was breaking, he thought and smiled. Now that Poland had paid the price for her arrogance and Soviet borders were once again secure, autumn and her rains would be welcome.

The heat was killing. Thorne lifted his pick with a grunt, caught it on the back swing and threw his weight forward as it reached the top of its arc. On the descent, the handle wobbled and the pickhead struck a jarring blow. Swearing dully, he leaned on the handle. Every muscle in his body screamed with overexertion.

This was his fifth day on the tank traps and it might well be his last. Heat prostration or a heart attack had begun to seem an attractive alternative. He glanced at the brassy sky smudged with smoke. He had lost count of the days the city had been under aerial and artillery siege but in the past day or so, it had become even more vicious than before so that the caruump of German cannon and bombs had become as much a part of the unpleasant background as the heat, dust and stench.

Along the rim of the trench he was helping to dig, he could see others in the same crew, two young women in overalls, three men in their fifties or sixties and numerous teenagers who came and went as it suited them. They looked on the war as a great lark; their elders knew better but had given up admonishing them. It was not unusual to see a civilian carrying a paper bag containing a meagre lunch and a hunting rifle on the tram, going out to the front lines to snipe at German soldiers.

Since the beginning, he had bitterly regretted the impulse that had brought him to the suburb of Wola on the crowded tram. Why the devil he had not got out of Warsaw before the city was surrounded and the trains and airplanes stopped, he did not know. A combination of procrastination, stubbornness and anger and, perhaps, the hope that he might yet persuade Yitzak, or possibly even a sneaking admiration for the Polish people who had reacted to the succession of German ultimatums with defiance and tank traps. He didn't know and no longer cared. The whole world had become the shovel and the dark earth of the trench.

The work was killing in the heat; no one asked his name or paid him much attention other than a young woman, a girl named Maria. He had come at first out of curiosity, he told himself. Digging tank traps would make a hell of a story back in the States. He hadn't intended to stay that first day past noon and would not have except for the elderly woman who sat beside him on the tram.

She wore expensive shoes and an expensive Paris dress and she carried baskets of earth away without complaint or regard for her clothes. At noon, when they stopped to eat, she sat nearby, back as straight as a ramrod even though fatigue was etched in her face.

Then she had closed her eyes and slumped sideways. A stroke, the ambulance attendant said.

A flurry of dirt caused him to look around. Maria stood up, grinning as she dusted off the seat of her overalls. She was short and plump with a hoydenish face and an ever-ready smile. A factory worker released for civil duty, he supposed, she seemed to be making the most of her freedom.

Maria mimed wiping perspiration from her brow and unbuttoned her overalls still further, flapping the collar against her neck, then pulled off her bandana and used it to wipe her face. She grinned at Thorne as she slipped the bandana inside the suit and he laughed in appreciation when she bent to roll up a pant leg and he was allowed a view of two large, well-shaped breasts. She straightened, tugging the front of her overalls together in mock modesty and plunked herself down in the shade cast by the side of the trench and patted the ground beside her. Thorne tossed the pick aside and joined her.

He lit cigarettes for them both and leaned back, cooling his blistered hands against the damp earth. His eyes shut of their own accord and he felt he could sleep forever. It was still mid-afternoon and there was at least two more hours to go. Maria smiled and shyly covered his hand with hers.

My God, he thought, a week ago he wouldn't have given this sweaty, uneducated foreigner a second glance. Today, he was enjoying her company and fearing the moment when it would end. A comparison of Maria in her sweaty overalls and his fiancée, Shirley Case, tall and elegant in a cocktail gown, impeccably groomed and trailing the scent of Chanel, slipped into his mind. The contrast was so ludicrous that he nearly laughed.

Artillery shells fell not far away and the earth shuddered against their backs. Secondary explosions went off and the smell of escaping gas, sewer damp, dead flesh and the acrid odour of burning buildings filtered into the trench. Both cursed in their respective languages and returned to work.

An hour later, a stone smacked his leg and he paused in mid-stroke and looked around to see Maria climbing up the side of the trench. She called to him but he could not hear. As she gained the top, she hesitated, staring at something he could not see. The sound of an aircraft engine and machine guns startled him and it was over before he could move. The Stuka had come in low over the shattered buildings and its machine gun bullets tore two long furrows of dust and swirling dirt and deluged Thorne with sand and stones.

Maria lay in the mud at the bottom of the trench. He scrambled to her, shouting for help. Her eyes were wide open in shock; one

61

arm had been torn nearly away. Blood welled from a second wound in her chest and he covered it with his hand, somehow convinced that he could stop the blood. Her eyes began to film. She screamed as the pain struck and twisted from side to side in agony as he struggled to maintain the pressure on the wound. Someone thrust him aside and he saw a Red Cross brassard. A short man with a fierce moustache tore away the overalls to expose the wound and Thorne gasped.

A bloody gash ran from breast to shoulder. The bullet must have struck there and angled down, glancing off bone to exit from her chest. The Red Cross man shook his head, tore a paper wrapping from a bandage pad and pushed it against the wound where it turned red immediately. He muttered something in Polish and hurried on along the trench to the next victim.

Thorne cradled Maria's head against his chest, hoping to stop her screams. His mind was a conflict of horror, hatred and disgust at the blood, the dirt and her agony. Her eyes were tightly closed and she was as far beyond reason as she was help. He could do nothing but hold her tightly while she bled to death.

Thorne stumbled through the gathering dusk to the tram stop, oblivious to the blood crusting on his clothing. He was not aware of the stares, the comments exchanged behind hands as people made way for him. He only knew that he had found, blessedly enough, a seat on the tram. The ride was a nightmare of exhaustion coupled with images of the dying girl, thrashing and screaming in his arms as she grew weaker and weaker. He had torn his jacket to shreds for bandages but the bleeding did not stop until she was dead. He did not know how long it was before a burial detail had arrived. Gently, they had pried his arms away and covered her body with a blanket while a policeman urged him to his feet. Unable to communicate with him, the policeman appealed to the others who made him understand that Thorne was an American who spoke no Polish. The policeman singled out a reluctant teen-aged boy to take him back to his hotel but the boy had disappeared when the tram appeared.

The tram came to an abrupt halt. Someone shouted and the tram emptied abruptly. His mind was clearing of shock and Thorne stumbled after them. Apparently, there had been another massive air-raid. An entire city block was in flames. Firemen and rescue workers were two-dimensional figures against the raving fury. Blast-furnace heat swirled about him and the air was starved of oxygen. The crowd did not need the air-raid warden's urging to move back. Thorne leaned against rough brick gasping for breath. Everything about him was drenched in reddish light and for an instant, he was hallucinating and the scarlet light was Maria's blood. He choked back a scream and began to run along the empty street, not knowing where he was going, only that he must get away from the blood-light and the sound of the fire.

Thorne never knew how long he ran or how he stumbled into the intersection where Braca ran into Wiejska Street. He stopped beside a fountain that continued to splash in the midst of the devastation and scooped water over his face. Steadier now that he knew where he was, he rested beside the bank before continuing on up Nowy Swiat towards the Hotel Bristol. He pushed into the empty lobby as air-raid sirens wailed and in the distance he heard the crump of bombs. Someone shouted as he went behind the counter for his key, then headed for the steps. A clerk ran into the foyer and called after him but he waved the man off and trudged up the curving marble stairs.

He was gasping for breath when he reached his floor. The porter's desk was empty and he knew that everyone was in the bomb shelters. The hotel had been hit twice in the second week and several people killed. After that the hotel staff had no more trouble getting the guests down to the shelters. Thorne did not care. He slammed his door and shot the bolt to keep the staff out. The water was not running and he swore dully and went back to the bedroom and shoved open the french doors to the balcony.

Anti-aircraft guns threw curving lines of fire into the sky and lights criss-crossed in vain search for enemy bombers. Over all was the mixed thunder of exploding bombs, wailing sirens and the sharper bark of anti-aircraft guns while beneath him, the city seemed a continuous sea of fire. In an instant, it all rushed together, the bombing, the lights, the girl's death and he began to rave and curse at the utter waste and futility of it all.

Incessant banging on the door woke him, the noise penetrating the horrible dream in which he was running and running from some unseen menace that screamed like a Stuka dive bomber as it pursued him across the rubbled wasteland of Warsaw. Thorne sat up abruptly, disorientated, uncertain of where he was. The bedsheets, unchanged since the third day of the war, were soaked with his sweat and his watch read four-thirty, obviously quite ridiculous since it was daylight. Then he remembered. It had been broken the day before, in the air attack that had killed the Polish girl. The pounding resumed and a muffled voice shouted his name.

Swearing dully, he opened the door and Howell charged in, berating him for not staying in touch with the Embassy. He stopped abruptly when he saw Thorne's filthy clothes and stubbled, exhausted face. The deadly rhythm of the artillery bombardment was still going on, dull thumps in the distance interspersed with the sharper cracks of exploding shells as the German guns shifted targets at random. In the distance, an airraid siren began to wail and both men fell silent without noticing, intent upon the direction of the sirens. As soon as it became clear that the warning was meant for the southern district and not the city centre, they both relaxed.

'Damn it, Keith, what have you been up to?' Howell began. 'No, there isn't time. Get your things together and be at the Embassy by ten o'clock. Didn't you receive the letter?'

'Ten, why?' Thorne was still not awake. Without thinking, he started for the bathroom to see if the water had been turned back on.

Howell caught his arm. 'Look here, Keith, the mayor's office has warned all the neutral embassies that the city will surrender sometime within the next thirty-six hours. Now that the Russians have occupied the eastern sections of the country and have refused to assist the Polish army, there seems to be no sense in holding out any longer. The Germans have agreed to a two-hour cease-fire today to allow all neutrals to evacuate and the Ambassador has ordered all Americans out of Warsaw. Promise me you will be at the Embassy by ten?'

Thorne hesitated. There was no longer anything to be gained by remaining, he saw. He had made his childish point. The events of yesterday and Maria's death had brought home to him just how futile it was to continue resisting. The citizens of Warsaw may have had the will, but they did not have the means. Hunting rifles were no good against tanks. What's more, it wasn't his fight . . . .

'Damn it, Keith,' Howell snapped. 'This is not the time to imagine yourself a hero. Any foreigners left in Warsaw when the Germans take over will probably be treated as spies, neutrals or not.'

He paused at the door and Thorne, awake now, saw how his face had grown increasingly haggard. 'I'm not certain of the exact arrangements,' Howell said. 'The Red Cross is handling it and there's been some talk of Sweden. Just be there, for your own sake.'

The Hotel Bristol had made a valiant effort to provide their accustomed services in spite of the difficulties raised by the aerial and artillery siege. Thorne obtained a cup of weak tea and a stale croissant served by an elderly waiter in an immaculate tuxedo and Thorne wondered how he kept it clean. The sky was filled with dust and when he stepped outside, the morning sun was a copper ball. The doorman saluted and handed him an envelope.

'A message for you, *Pan* Thorne. Delivered a few minutes ago.'

He tore open the envelope as he walked and extracted the single sheet of folded notepaper. It was a request in Jacob Yitzak's spidery handwriting to call as soon as convenient. Thorne swore to himself. What the hell did that stubborn old bastard want now? He hadn't seen him for more than a week, since Deborah had asked him not to return. He tossed the note away and walked on, one ear cocked for airraid sirens or the peculiar whistling note of a German artillery shell, wondering if he could get a decent cup of coffee at the Embassy. Halfway there, he stopped. Damn it all, he thought, angry at himself. Why jeopardize your own safety for a hopeless . . . There was no chance of finding a cab or a droshky but there was sufficient time to walk, if he hurried.

The old Jewish quarter had suffered extensively from the shelling. Entire blocks were nothing more than mounds of rubble and he saw burial parties everywhere carrying bodies to the trenches that had been dug to stop tanks and were now being used to bury the dead. The few anti-aircraft guns that had been stationed in the area had been destroyed. One, placed in the courtyard of a building, was buried in rubble so that all that remained visible was the twisted barrel.

Jacob Yitzak had been watching for him and opened the door as Thorne reached the steps. The house was pocked with splinter holes and the taped windows had shattered and been replaced with pieces of cardboard or wood. One corner of the roof had been smashed and brick and slate shingles had cascaded into the street.

They went directly into the library where Deborah was huddled in a chair, a yellow message form clutched in her hand. She was staring straight ahead and although her face was expressionless, her eyes were haunted and filled with pain and grief.

'You must help. In return, I will promise the autobiography . . .'

'Help, how?' Thorne broke in. 'What the hell can I do? I'm leaving Warsaw today.' He glanced at the girl but she did not acknowledge his presence.

'Yes, yes, I know. The last neutral convoy. Last night, we received word that my . . . my son has been killed.' The old man's eyes filled with tears but his voice remained steady and his grip on Thorne's arm firm. 'His body was found near the River Bug, close to the Russian lines.'

Thorne stood mute, at a loss for something to say. He recalled a tall, sunburned officer sitting in this same room a week ago.

'My daughter-in-law is all that I have left and I love her as if she were my own child. Take her out of Poland, as your wife.'

'As my wife! That's ridiculous!' Thorne protested but Yitzak's grip tightened.

'Deborah is pregnant with my grandchild. She must get out of Poland. I will begin work on my autobiography immediately. It will sell tremendously well because I am writing it as the German. . . .'

'But that's ridiculous. . . .' he repeated lamely. The girl appeared not to have heard a word that was said. Christ, he thought, saddle myself with a zombie? Who the hell would believe that he would marry a Jewess?

'The ceremony has been arranged. A protestant minister, a Dane, will come shortly.'

'My God, I can't just marry someone like that. It's not the way . . . damn it, it's not right.'

'Not even to save a life?' the old man countered. 'When you reach your country, you will, of course, have the marriage dissolved. By then it will be too late for your government to force Deborah to return.'

'Jesus,' Thorne muttered. He would still have to persuade the Embassy that the marriage was legal.

'You can't believe for one minute that we could get away with this, this charade, do you?' Thorne protested but Yitzak did not miss the *we*.

'I have looked into the American law. If the marriage is legal, the authorities have no choice. Americans, like the British, honour the form if not the actuality. Please . . . the autobiography. Help us and you will have accomplished what you came for.'

'God damn it to hell,' Thorne raged. 'If I do, it won't be because of that damned book!' He looked again at the girl, seeing her quiet, self-contained beauty. There was no doubt about it, even with huge black shadows beneath her eyes and her hair uncombed, she was damned attractive. But that sure as hell was not reason enough to risk his own life. Then he remembered the Polish girl crumpled on the ground as her blood pumped away. The metallic odour was still strong in his memory.

'All right,' he said quietly and was as surprised as the old man that he had agreed.

The Embassy grounds were crowded with people and their belongings. Outside the iron fence, the endless line of petitioners clung to the hope that an exception would be made and they would be allowed into the United States. Inside, their travelling companions – a priest, four nuns, two businessmen and four college boys with filthy hands and clothes – sat on their suitcases and waited in what shade the dying shrubbery offered.

Deborah had remained silent during the brief ceremony in the Yitzak study. She had nodded in response to the nervous minister's questions and signed the register when the old man had guided her hand to the book. Only when Jacob kissed her goodbye did she show any animation. Her eyes glistened and she clung to Yitzak. Thorne looked away, struggling for self-control. His own handshake had been perfunctory and then they were hurrying down the steps. The minister had a car and offered them a ride to the Embassy. As they drove away, Thorne looked back to see the old man standing with head bowed in prayer. He did not wave.

At the Embassy, the marine guard had been suspicious until Howell appeared. Inside, the marriage licence was examined thoroughly. Thorne was on the verge of exploding when Howell interceded with the First Secretary and Deborah's name was added to his passport as his wife. They were processed quickly after that and sent out onto the lawn to wait for the convoy that was making the rounds of the neutral embassies.

Thorne tried to ease Deborah's despair – his wife, he thought in surprise, no matter how briefly the marriage was destined to last. When she did not respond, he gave up. The death of her husband had driven her into deep shock and she neither seemed to understand nor care what was going on about her.

The two-hour armistice was scheduled to begin at one o'clock but the trucks did not roll into the Embassy grounds until twenty minutes past – dangerously late. They were old transport lorries, commandeered by the city government and turned over to the Red Cross. The wagon beds were covered with straw and huge red crosses had been painted on the cab doors and roof. A perspiring Swiss official jumped down from the lead truck even before it stopped, to shout orders. Burdened with their suitcases, Thorne staggered to the nearest truck. A sweating marine pitched the bags into the back and swung the girl up. A familiar face caught Deborah and grinned down at him.

'Putting things a bit late, aren't you?'

Thorne sought for the man's name . . . Fredriksson, something Fredriksson, the Swedish journalist who had introduced him to Prager. Before he could answer, the marine banged the tailgate closed and slid the pin home.

Jim Howell shouted his name and as he turned, Howell lofted a paper-wrapped parcel over the tailgate. The package gurgled as he caught it and Thorne laughed when he looked inside. Scotch whisky! The truck jerked into motion and Thorne nearly lost his balance as he flourished the package in farewell. Maybe old Howell wasn't so bad after all.

He took a deep breath. He was going home, dammit. He turned

to see Deborah slumped against the side railing with Fredriksson regarding her curiously and some of his euphoria evaporated to be replaced with a mixture of annoyance and apprehension.

The trucks ran through the devastated streets on a pre-arranged route to the airport. Thorne removed his jacket and folded it into a cushion for Deborah and seated her against the cab wall. He leaned on the railing, watching the city pass. The damage wrought by German bombers and artillery was incredible. Apparently the Germans did not themselves realize how much or they would never have allowed the convoy to follow this route. Certain areas had received concentrated bombing and shelling but not even the streets where the foreign embassies were clustered had been spared. In places, the city looked like photographs of Belgian and French towns during the Great War and only the spidery remains of walls still stood. Houses with roofs torn off and walls stripped away to expose naked rooms were on every side and the stench of gas, sewer damp, dead flesh, high-explosive fumes and dust were all-pervasive. Especially the dust. He would remember the Warsaw dust for the rest of his life.

Fredriksson sat down beside him and sighed. 'It is incredible how much damage can be done, yet life goes on,' he remarked, nodding at the crowds of people going about their usual business in spite of the streets filled with the rubble of demolished buildings.

Thorne grunted.

'I'd have thought you would have left long before this?' Fredriksson waited for an answer and when Thorne did not respond, went on. 'It seems I may have seen the young lady before.' He had not but it was a good gambit. 'I assume she is travelling with you?'

'Jesus!' Thorne exploded. 'Don't you ever quit?'

Fredriksson laughed. 'Of course not. What kind of a journalist would I be then?' His good humour was so apparent that Thorne had to grin as well. In apology, he opened the bottle of Scotch whisky and offered it to the Swede.

'My God,' he breathed with reverence, 'Johnny Walker Black Label! Your friend must be a man of immense power!'

'I'm beginning to think so myself.'

'So then why are you still in Warsaw?' Fredriksson handed the bottle back, reluctantly.

Thorne shrugged. 'Stupidity, I suppose.' He thought for a moment. 'No, not really. At first, I wanted to see how the Poles were going to react to aggression directed at them. After a while, I began to admire the way they were standing up to the Germans. I don't think I ever seriously considered what it might mean if the Germans capture the entire country.'

Fredriksson glanced at the girl, but wisely refrained from asking about her again. Fifteen years as a journalist had taught him when to ask questions and when to wait for the information to be volunteered.

Thorne leaned over to check on Deborah. She gave him a wan smile when he touched her shoulder but said nothing. He sat back with a troubled expression.

'You know, there is a good human interest story for you. Do you know who her father is? Jacob Yitzak, the concert violinist,' he answered his own question. 'She just learned yesterday that her husband was killed. He was an infantry officer.'

Fredriksson grimaced and started to say something to her, but Thorne stopped him. 'Easier if you just let her be.' He hesitated, decided to keep the fact of their marriage to himself then abruptly changed his mind. 'Her father-in-law wants her out of Poland before the Germans take over. But Jews can't get visas, so we were married this morning. She's an American citizen by marriage so the government can't keep her out.'

He saw the sceptical look on Fredriksson's face. 'I know what you're thinking,' he said. 'I used to feel the same way.' Thorne had leaned back so that Deborah could not hear. 'But I've begun to wonder in the past few days. Look at this.'

Thorne drew the photograph from his wallet and handed it to Fredriksson, noticing as he did so that the man barely reacted to the image of the hanged men.

'Notice that all of them are Jews.'

Fredriksson peered at the photograph. 'Why do you say that?''

'Every one is an Orthodox Jew. Look at their hair, especially the ear locks.'

Fredriksson studied the photograph, scepticism conflicting with anger and more than a little fear. In spite of the years he had spent as a military correspondent, the sight of such needless cruelty never failed to anger him. It was as useless as it was senseless and he had long ago formed the opinion, from first-hand observation, that such atrocities were the result of people indulging themselves in man's basest instinct, no matter how they tried to justify it. There certainly had been plenty of propaganda from the Polish, British and French governments concerning German atrocities, as there had been in the Great War, most of which had been proven false. But this was the first time he had seen photographic evidence involving Jews. Was it real, a coincidence or. . . .

'Where did you get this photograph?'

'A friend of Jacob Yitzak. . . .'

'A Jew?'

'Yes, but that doesn't change the fact that those men were all Jews and they were hanged in reprisal for some act committed

against the German army, in wartime. The Geneva Convention.
. . .'

'Has relatively little to say and less authority to enforce what it does say. As you observed this is wartime, and terrible things happen in war.' Fredriksson had hoped he was onto something; perhaps the first documented report of an actual atrocity. But the photograph had come from a Jew. For all he knew, the scene could have been staged by a Zionist organization or even by the Polish government. Their propaganda department had been excellent, enough to make the world forget that, until recently, the Polish government had aided and abetted Hitler with a great deal of enthusiasm.

He handed the photograph back and began, skilfully, to draw Thorne out. The convoy wound along a pre-determined route through the suburbs as Thorne described his experiences during the past three weeks – the bomb shelters, the damaged transportation system and his work digging tank traps on the city outskirts. Fredriksson made careful notes as he talked about the Polish girl, Maria, and her death from a Stuka's machine gun bullet, recognizing in its basic simplicity a story that could be shaped into the classic struggle between innocence and overwhelming evil.

After an hour, the convoy broke out of the depressing ruins into more open suburbs. Even here, the ravages of the shelling were apparent. They passed through an area of semi-detached houses and block after block of workers' flats. In one, a single house remained standing, shattered windows staring at the convoy picking its way between mounds of rubble and impromptu barricades of timbers and walls; in the next block, only one house had been hit and it had collapsed to cascade brick and broken concrete into the street. A dead horse lay near a curb, raw wounds festering with flies to show where starving people had hacked meat away. A water main spouted a cooling spray glistening with diamond points of light and Thorne found himself cursing its inappropriate beauty.

Someone pointed out that it was two-forty, and only twenty minutes of the cease-fire remained. Apparently the Red Cross official was worried as well. Thorne could see him standing on the running board of the lead truck waving frantically at the driver ahead to step up his speed.

At two-fifty, the convoy gained the main highway and the speed crept up as homes and buildings gave way to empty fields. The drivers had to contend now only with shell holes in the pavement and a last Polish barricade which they roared past as haggard soldiers stared after them and Thorne told himself angrily that even though it wasn't his concern, he had still done something to help. Even so, he could not entirely suppress an irrational feeling of guilt.

At three o'clock exactly, Okecie airport appeared; first a distant fence, then wrecked, humped-roof buildings among scattered trees. Two transport aircraft waited, Fokker trimotors with Swedish markings which Fredriksson saluted with a cheer. The convoy turned onto the access road and churned through columns of dust towards the runway. The other trucks were already clustered about the aircraft, unloading their charges.

People swarmed across the grass and the Swiss officials gave up any pretence of order and shouted them on. Their truck braked to a halt a hundred yards short and the college boys were first out. A sense of panic had infected them all. The priest started to run and the nuns followed. One of the businessmen cursed his suitcase wedged against the side wall, then abandoned it and raced towards the aircraft. Fredriksson helped lift Deborah down, grabbed their suitcases and followed the businessman's example.

A familiar snarl hammered across the field. A woman screamed and a shadow flashed. Thorne ran with Deborah towards the nearest aircraft. Dirt and dust fountained across the field as bombs smashed the runway and whipped them with concussion. Polish anti-aircraft guns blasted streams of fire into the sunny afternoon sky. They were half-way to the plane when the sound of its engines changed pitch and the Fokker turned away and began to taxi towards the runway. The aircraft had been painted with white neutral crosses but machine-gun fire from German aircraft spattered the ground about it. Fredriksson, standing in the doorway, shouted at them and waved, then ducked inside. He raced up the aisle, cursing and shoving people aside, to the cockpit, but the door was locked. The Fokker gained speed and the wheels broke free. The German pilot saw the crosses at last and pulled up in a tight, climbing turn.

Thorne stopped running and cursed the pilot. Around them, firing raged as German aircraft dove in fresh attacks. Fifty yards away was a low mound of earth; enough, he thought, and began to run. Thorne never heard the explosion that tossed him away like a scrap of paper just as he pushed Deborah over the mound.

He regained consciousness in a dingy room filled with wounded and dying people. At first, there was only a single Polish doctor with the glazed expression of a man not far from physical collapse. He examined Thorne perfunctorily, handed him a single aspirin tablet and shook his head to questions about Deborah.

A raw abrasion covered half his forehead. Blood had matted in his hair so that it was difficult to tell the severity of any wounds. His ribs and back hurt whenever he moved but he concluded that the pain was due to bruising and wrenched muscles and not broken bones. He choked down the aspirin without water and lay back. The room was a cacophony of moans and the stench and heat were unbearable.

When he woke the second time, the room was quiet. A single, unshaded bulb flickered like a candle. The room seemed emptier and the air was decidedly better. A German officer appeared in the doorway and Thorne fell asleep again.

The next time he woke, it was morning and men in civilian clothing moved about the make-shift hospital ward, examining the tags attached to each cot. Occasionally, one motioned and orderlies shifted the patient to a stretcher and carried him out. When they stopped beside his cot, he tried to tell them that he was a neutral, an American. One man glanced at him, nodded and motioned for him to be removed. He relaxed as the cot was lifted, thinking that at least now they would take him to a decent hospital.

They came out into brilliant sunlight and Thorne squinted against the harsh glare. The end of the stretcher was raised abruptly and he clutched the sides to keep from sliding out. Someone laughed and the stretcher was dropped to the floor of a truck. Doors slammed and the engine started. The truck was completely enclosed with only a single row of angled slits near the ceiling, presumably for ventilation. When his eyes stopped tearing, he saw a soldier seated at the back with a rifle. The truck had been designed to carry wounded. Rows of shelves built against the sides were filled with stretchers. Could all of these people be neutrals wounded at the airfield?

All but he and Deborah had made it to the aircraft. He could remember Fredriksson shouting at them from the doorway as the plane wheeled away. He pushed himself up and tried to speak to the soldier, first in French and then English. The man spat deliberately on the floor and motioned for him to lie back. Suddenly apprehensive, Thorne did so.

The truck stopped and the doors were thrown open. Ragged civilians swarmed in to bring the stretchers out. The two who carried his stretcher trotted down a wide corridor. A long stairway and more guards waited at the far end. A red-faced NCO shouted and they turned towards the steps. At the next landing, another NCO consulted a clipboard and directed them in Polish to a desk where they left him. The NCO kicked the stretcher and shouted in Polish but his meaning was clear enough. He was to stand up.

'I am an American,' he protested, again in English, then in French but the NCO kicked the stretcher, harder.

'American . . . yankee, you son-of-a-bitch,' Thorne shouted at him. He reached for his passport and fear jolted through him. It had been in his jacket which he had used to make a cushion for Deborah . . . and it had been left in the truck at the airfield.

The NCO grabbed the stretcher and tipped him out, then laughing, kicked him until Thorne pulled himself to his feet. He was half-dragged, half-carried along the corridor to an iron-bound door. A scrawny man ran up and unlocked the door and Thorne was shoved into a prison cell.

The cell was jammed far beyond capacity and there were angry shouts. Bodies were pressed against one another so closely there was no room to sit or lie down. The atmosphere was sweltering, as if all the oxygen had been used up and they were now to suffocate in their own carbon dioxide exhalations. A tall man wearing the blouse and trousers of a Polish officer spoke to him in Polish.

'*Nie rozumien Poliski,*' he croaked and repeated in English, 'I don't speak Polish.'

The officer studied him with renewed interest. '*Angelski?*'

Thorne shook his head. 'No, American. United States.'

The man stared at Thorne in disbelief, then snorted, obviously thinking him to be a police spy. Why else would an American be in a Nazi prison? Thorne was too weak to convince him otherwise.

As the hours passed with agonizing slowness Thorne retreated more and more from reality. His world narrowed to a very dark, very narrow tunnel at the end of which was a blur of light. The airlessness of the metal box had ceased to affect him and the crush of bodies had become a blessing as he no longer possessed the strength to support himself. The Army officer had organized a rota system and cleared a space beside the door in which the prisoners took turns sitting to relieve tortured leg and back muscles. But new prisoners had been jammed in so that even that tiny space disappeared before Thorne's turn came.

He was in the B-17 bomber struggling to maintain altitude on two engines while the oil pressure on the port outboard motor slipped inexorably towards zero. His co-pilot, on his first flight since training school, watched him and tried to hide his shaking hands. Beneath, the broad Kansas fields were dun coloured in the late afternoon sun, mile on mile of rolling prairie that seemed so smooth and flat but was, in fact, only an illusion. Their altitude was less than one thousand feet now. He concentrated on keeping the nose up; he was certain he could bring the aircraft down in one piece if he could reach that county airfield. A road came into view and he altered course, easing the aircraft around so as not to lose more precious altitude than necessary.

They were below five hundred feet now, low enough that the land was beginning to take on three-dimensional relief. The wheat fields, flattened by heavy rains, were far too soft and muddy. He considered the road, eased the wheel back and banked slightly. Telephone poles on one side, barbed wire fence on the other. The airfield appeared ahead and the altimeter read three hundred feet . . . the temperature gauge on number three climbed into the red. He felt the first cylinder miss and swore. He flicked a quick glance at the airspeed indicator. No more time.

He lost his balance and fell. Pain slashed through his back and shoulder and he huddled into himself, fighting the tearing sensation that threatened to reduce him to gibbering madness. Gradually the pain subsided and he realized that he was lying at full length on the wet concrete floor.

Hauptmann Friedrich Prager strode along Aleja Szucha, staring with satisfaction at laughing Army troops standing about, weapons slung. Warsaw had surrendered almost a week before and the remnants of the beaten Polish forces in the area were straggling in to surrender. Only a few hours earlier, it had been announced that the last Polish forces still fighting had surrendered at Luck. In all, more than 700,000 Polish soldiers had been taken prisoner and more than forty thousand killed or wounded in four weeks of war. The much vaunted resistance movement had never appeared. He snorted. They were a thoroughly beaten crew, these Poles with their nineteenth-century cavalry and tactics. There had been some resistance in the areas to the west which had been occupied from the first days – a few civilians with rifles – but speedy courts-martial and speedier hangings had put an end to that and undoubtedly saved a good many lives, Polish as well as German.

As he came in sight of the modern building, his good humour evaporated. He was far from pleased with his present assignment – to assist in the transfer of authority from the Army to the new occupation government. His specific duties had to do with turning over police duties to the *Schutzstaffel*. And he despised the SS, the military arm of the Nazi party. They insisted on aping the Army, yet maintained their independence from military authority. He was required to salute superior SS officers but such courtesies were not always returned. During the past few days, he had come to know their 'pacification' techniques first hand and his disgust had only deepened.

There was no denying the fact that most Poles hated the very existence of Germany. An understandable, if misguided reaction, under the circumstances. The Fuehrer had been correct when he said that one had either to crush one's enemies entirely or treat them with fairness and concern. While it would be infinitely less expensive in the long run to show concern and fairness, the SS seemed determined to take the expensive path and crush the Polish spirit to dust.

The weather had turned colder in the past few days as if autumn had decided that Germany's task was finished and she could now get on with the business of the approaching winter. He hesitated on the steps of the former Ministry of Education building which had been acquired by the SS security services, the Gestapo and the *Sicherheitsdienst* – the latter best known by its initials, SD – as headquarters. He took a deep breath and returned the careless salute of a non-commissioned officer hurrying down the steps to a waiting lorry packed with SS troops. Another foray after disaffected elements. He went on reluctantly, knowing it would again be a busy day.

Inside, a clerk hurried forward with Gruppenfuehrer Erich Gorman's compliments. Hauptmann Prager was wanted as quickly as possible in the Gruppenfuehrer's office.

'Gruppenfuehrer,' he snorted, as he climbed the broad marble stairs to the first floor. The SS rank was equivalent to General-lieutenant yet the man was only a jumped-up accounting clerk. His only qualification for the job of rooting out spies and saboteurs lay in the fact that he had joined the Party in 1925 and had taken part in every SS brawl since its inception.

Gruppenfuehrer Gorman was now so fat that he had continually to gasp for air, even when half-recumbent, as now. He glared at Prager from the depths of his overstuffed chair and flourished a piece of paper.

'I have here your transfer, Hauptmann Prager!' In spite of his ponderous size, his voice was high-pitched and squeaked, like that of an eunuch – which had given rise to much speculation. The supposed sophistication of his Cologne accent only increased his air of precious fussiness.

'I must refuse to grant it, Captain,' Gorman puffed. 'You went over my head to arrange this transfer. . . .' Lack of oxygen forced a pause and Prager grabbed the opportunity.

'I beg the Gruppenfuehrer's pardon,' he broke in, using the formal third person because it annoyed Gorman, 'but I did inform him and in writing before doing so.' And he had, sending the note to Gorman's chief of staff, a notoriously lazy and useless appendage. 'My request is based on the fact that I am a soldier and not a policeman.'

Be careful, he cautioned himself. 'I am certain that I would be more valuable to the war effort serving in my capacity. . . .'

'Silence!' The Gruppenfuehrer struggled up. He glared at Prager. 'Do you suppose that you, a mere captain, are better qualified to know where best to serve than I?' He paused for breath and Prager noticed with satisfaction that his face was turning purple. Prager had never actively hated any single individual in his life as he hated this obese excuse for a man. He wondered for the dozenth time if it was possible to push him into apoplexy.

But Gorman surprised him by subsiding into the chair like a blob of jelly. 'All right,' he panted. 'These orders were signed in Berlin and I can do little to have them changed.' It was unlike Gorman to admit defeat and Prager watched him closely. Gorman's cunning had seen him through Byzantine layers of party and SS for nearly twenty years. Prager did not for a moment underrate him as an enemy. He had hoped to be out of Poland before the paperwork found its way to Gorman's desk.

The General threw the paper across the desk to Prager. 'I will not forget this insult, Captain, rest assured of that,' he grunted.

Only when he was in the corridor did Prager read his new orders. He had been assigned, effective 10 October 1939, to Oberkommando des Wehrmacht, the high command of the armed forces, to Section One, Supply and Administration – planning again!

His disappointment at not receiving a field command again was somewhat mitigated by the fact that he would soon be out from under the thumb of SS Gruppenfuehrer Gorman.

The door slammed back and an SS guard stamped into the cell. He carried a rifle slung over his back and his boots were polished to mirror brightness. He spotted Thorne, compared his face to a photograph in his hand and shouted, '*Raus.*' He kicked Thorne twice as an effective means of translation.

He was marched back along the same corridor but, this time, was pushed into another hall and herded up two flights of stairs. A greyish sky was visible through a wire-grated window and Thorne thought he saw rain falling. The guard snarled and shoved him through a partly opened door.

A man in civilian clothing was hunched over a desk, reading a file. His lips formed each word and he traced the line with a manicured fingernail. When the man did not look up, Thorne cleared his throat. The man glanced at him with an expression so malevolent, that Thorne backed away in astonishment. Without a word, the man dropped his eyes to the file and resumed reading.

It took him, Thorne estimated, all of fifteen minutes to read two typed pages of information. When he finished, the man fitted them into the crease of a buff folder and with one pale hand, closed the cover.

'You claim to be an American citizen, one Keith Thorne. You state that you arrived in Warsaw on 25 August 1939, on business.' It was not a question but a statement and Thorne remained silent.

'You did not leave the city when the war began nor did you take advantage of means made available to neutrals to do so.' Again, they were not questions, but statements.

'What in hell are you trying. . . .'

The man held up a hand. 'You will speak only when told to do so. You will answer my questions truthfully and completely. Do you understand?'

'Like hell! Now you listen to me. I'm an American. . . .'

The man pressed a button on the desk twice and the door opened behind Thorne. Before he could turn, a rifle butt smashed against his ribs, his legs were kicked away and he fell heavily. He tried to get up, so frightened by the sudden violence that his fingers scrabbled on the bare floor. The guard kicked him again and air seared out of his lungs and he collapsed, his diaphragm paralysed, unable to breathe. After a while, he was aware that the guard had gone out. He dragged himself up and leaned against the wall. A tearing pain was constant in his side and he could feel blood soaking his shirt again. Every breath was so painful he thought the guard's boot must have broken ribs. The civilian had turned his attention back to the file and it was several minutes more before he spoke again.

'If you do not do exactly as you are told, I will have you beaten again. Now, we know that you are not an American. I wish to know your name and nationality?'

'How do you know . . . ,' Thorne had to grit his teeth to keep the pain in bounds and his words had an angry pitch '. . . I am not an American?'

The man pursed his lips. 'We know exactly who you are. You are an intelligence agent in the employ of MI6.'

Thorne absorbed the information and waited for more. When it wasn't forthcoming, he shook his head. 'What is MI6?'

The little man smiled. 'I shall summon the guard once more if you persist.'

'No, really,' Thorne protested as the little man reached for the button. 'It's easy enough to verify my story.'

The hand moved away from the button and Thorne took a deep breath, wishing to God that he had never heard of Poland. What in the name of God had possessed him to. . . .

'I really am an American and my name is Keith Thorne. My

father is Chairman of Thorne, Dorsten and Winslow Press in New York City. I came to Warsaw to negotiate a contract with Jacob Yitzak, for his autobiography.'

'Yitzak, the concert violinist?'

'Yes, exactly. Do you know of him?'

'He is considered one of the world's greatest violinists.'

'That's correct,' Thorne said with a sigh. At last he seemed to be making headway.

'He is also a Jew.'

There was no inflection in the man's voice. He might have been commenting on the weather.

Thorne stared at him nonplussed.

'We are well aware of your affiliation with the Jew, Yitzak. You have been observed in frequent visits to his residence. The Jew Yitzak is known to be an ardent Zionist, an agent of the British Government and the father of the known terrorist, David Yitzak. This was found in your personal effects.' He flicked a small rectangle of paper onto the desk and Thorne saw that it was the photograph of the hanged men.

He slumped against the wall, trying to absorb it all. Zionists, terrorists, agents of the British Government, it made no sense. 'His son is an army officer,' he protested. 'He was killed a few days before Warsaw surrendered. He. . . .'

'Is a terrorist,' the civilian replied in a calm voice. 'Was a terrorist rather. He was captured near the River Bug. After an interrogation, he was tried, convicted and hanged in company with eleven other terrorists. As a matter of course, all family members of convicted terrorists are subject to the same penalties. When the house of the Jew, Yitzak, was searched, other photographs, like the one found in your suitcase, were discovered. The possession of such photographs is forbidden and is punishable by death.'

'This . . . this is monstrous. Yitzak is the world's most respected violinist. How can you even. . . .'

'Maxim Gorky was a great writer, but he was also a Communist.'

In spite of his fear, Thorne could only gape at the juxtaposition. 'I don't understand what. . . .'

The man slapped the desk with the folder. 'It makes no difference what you understand. You are here to confess to crimes against the German people!'

'This is Poland,' Thorne exclaimed. Then suddenly intensely angry, 'Any crimes committed in the past month were by the German people against the Poles!'

The door swung open again and the guard rushed in. This time, he tried to defend himself but he was too weak and the guard beat him savagely. When he regained consciousness, the civilian was again reading the file. Thorne struggled to prop himself into a sitting position against the wall.

'Stand up.'

Thorne shook his head, not able to speak. The door opened again and the guard came in to kick him to his feet. The interrogator resumed his reading and Thorne had no idea how long he remained standing before the desk, determined that he would not collapse.

'Tell me the name of your superior officer.' The voice floated towards him from a great distance. 'I wish to know the nature of your contact with the Polish Intelligence Second Bureau.'

He shook his head. 'I've . . . told you . . . don't know what you're talking about. I'm an American . . . my name is Keith Thorne. You can check . . . with the American Embassy.'

'The Embassy is closed. Give me the name of your superior officer.'

Thorne tried to think but nothing made sense . . . Fredriksson . . . he could identify him.

'Look . . . there is someone, a citizen of a . . . neutral country, a Swedish . . . journalist . . .' he found that he was speaking so fast he had begun to flounder. 'He can . . . vouch for me. He would be in Stockholm now . . .'

The interrogator swore and stabbed the button.

Hours later it seemed he was being dragged along a dark hall. His hands were tied together behind his back with wire. He was taken up another flight of stairs and thrust into a narrow room that had been walled off from the hall with plywood panels. A cot, stripped of bedding and mattress, stood against one wall. A dresser had been turned to face a window. Two women in uniform were seated at separate desks, typing. They glanced at Thorne and went on with their work.

Without warning, the guards tripped him to the floor and tore off his shoes, pants and underwear, then ripped his shirt loose and folded it back under his bound arms. One of the girls giggled and said something that made the guards laugh. A tall, dark-haired officer stalked in as he stood shivering against the wall. The officer did not look at Thorne but took the buff folder offered him by one of the typists and skimmed the pages quickly.

'American, heh?'

For a moment, Thorne could not absorb the fact that the officer had spoken in English. 'Yes,' his reply was eager. 'Thank God, someone finally. . . .'

'Where from?'

'New York, Long Island.'

'Harvard?'

'Yes, class of '33. I. . . .'

'Damned liar. I spent two years at the University of Michigan. You are no more an American than I am.' He got up from the desk and sauntered over to Thorne. 'Now you listen to me. I haven't the time to play games. I want a full rundown on your operation. Give it to me now and it'll be a hell of a lot easier for both of us. If you don't,' he shrugged. 'I'll make you regret you were ever born.'

He paused and when Thorne, too confused to understand what was happening, did not reply, he grinned. 'Okay, buddy. How about a bath?'

He motioned and the two guards grabbed Thorne at knees and shoulders, lifted him from the floor and rushed through a door into a bathroom. They flipped him over so that he was looking down into a dirty bathtub filled with water in which large chunks of ice floated.

'Wait!' he screamed but the guards thrust him into the tub, face down. The icy water seared his skin like a torch and in a single convulsive heave, he thrashed free of their hands and spun over, spitting and choking. Before he could draw a breath, he was shoved under and water cascaded into his mouth and throat. He was dragged up for an instant to hear laughter before a guard planted a boot on his chest and pushed him under for a third time. The guard held him down and with his hands wired behind his back it was impossible to gain purchase on the smooth porcelain. The ice-water burned his body and a terrible vice-like pain clamped his chest as the water filled his lungs. Through the wavering surface film he could see the guards grinning at him. A woman's face, distorted with laughter, appeared between their shoulders.

Water trickled from his mouth and he retched. Someone rolled him over and his eyes began to focus. They were all watching him, including the typists. The officer spoke but the words were a meaningless jumble of noise. Thorne shook his head. His lungs and throat were raw and it was impossible to speak. His hearing began to return and music came from somewhere.

He could only shake his head when the officer spoke to him. The guards picked him up and before he could begin to struggle, he was dropped into the tub again. The water burned his body even more brutally this time and the guard heaved on his chest. Water tortured his mouth and throat and the grinning gargoyle faces distorted by the water floated above him before he passed out.

Twice more, he was revived. The last time, he was conscious only of the horrible pain in his chest. He almost welcomed the last immersion and opened his mouth wide, praying for the courage to

gulp the water into his lungs and kill himself but the officer saw
and they dragged him out quickly. The pain, the faces and the
dingy bathroom were already receding into darkness. With his last
conscious thought, he knew he was dying and damned them all.

Thorne knew only that he was freezing to death and that his chest
felt as if it had been torn open. Only gradually did the semi-twilight
resolve into a floor and walls of greyish stone. When he was finally
able to sit up, he was wearing only a torn shirt, still damp. His
pants were wadded next to him but he did not have the strength
to untangle and put them on. How long he sat like that, leaning
against the wall, he had no idea. He thought he might have slept
until the door was opened and a figure stumbled in to collapse on
the far side of the cell.

The shape did not move and Thorne regarded it without curiosity; he could summon neither pity nor concern. When he woke
again, he felt somewhat better. The pain in his chest had subsided
until it was bearable and he could breathe a bit easier. He was stiff
with cold and remembered his pants. Like his shirt, they were
quite dry. How long have I been here? he wondered.

It took forever to untangle and pull them on but the measure of
warmth they provided proved worth the effort. After a while, he
felt well enough to crawl to the shapeless bundle of clothing and
turn it over.

It was Jacob Yitzak. Thorne stared in shock at the badly bruised
face beneath the several days' growth of whiskers. His lips moved
faintly, the only sign of life. He chaffed the old man's hands and
bare feet and after a while, Yitzak moved his head. His lips worked
as if he wanted to say something. Thorne dragged the old man into
a sitting position against the wall and took the unresisting body in
his arms and tried to warm him with his own body.

Yitzak woke him. 'Are you all right, my boy, are you all right?'
he kept repeating over and over.

Actually, Thorne felt worse, if anything. His body was stiff with
cold and every breath seared his chest. His skin burned and he
was deathly ill.

'Why are you here?' he whispered. 'Why would they arrest you?
What have they done. . . .'

'Ah, because my son is an army officer . . . and because I am a
Jew. As to what they have done to me . . . it is best we not speak
of it.'

He took a shaky breath. 'Perhaps you will tell me what has
happened to my daughter-in-law and why you are here and not
safely in the United States of America?'

'I don't know. The convoy was late. We reached the airfield just

81

as the time limit expired. We were running towards the airplane and Stukas began to bomb and strafe the field. I had her hand . . . I remember waking in a hospital, if that's what it was. I was brought here . . . I . . . I just don't know.'

Yitzak sat rigidly against the wall for a long time, lips moving as if in prayer and Thorne fell asleep again. When he woke, Yitzak was gone.

'Gruppenfuehrer Gorman requests that you come to the courtyard, immediately.'

Prager returned the SS messenger's disdainful salute and dismissed the man. He sat for several moments at his desk, wondering whether to go or not. He was damned if he wanted to participate in that SS farce, yet until he stepped aboard the train, he was still Gorman's subordinate. As distasteful as it might be, he had no other choice. He glanced once more around his desk, seeking anything that might offer the slightest delay, but there was nothing. He had already cleared away all pressing matters.

Prager strode through long corridors lined with frightened people huddled against the walls under the watchful eyes of armed guards. There had been too many rumours of bestial goings-on, he thought, and these people were proof of how wide-spread they were. Unless Reichsminister Himmler clamped down on his subordinates soon, there was going to be hell to pay. He knew from first-hand experience that too many Army officers were outraged that the Wehrmacht might be blamed for these excesses.

Gruppenfuehrer Gorman and two other SS officers, a Sturmbannfuehrer, a rank equivalent to Major, and an Oberfuehrer – for which there was no equivalent Wehrmacht rank but was somewhere between a full Colonel and a Generalmajor – were seated at a table in the garden. Each was resplendent in full dress uniform, although who they hoped to impress besides each other was not clear. Certainly not the poor fools brought before them.

Gorman turned as he stepped into the courtyard and smiled broadly. 'Ah Captain Prager. So glad you could spare a few moments from your busy schedule.

'Since this is your last afternoon on my staff, I thought I would do you the honour of asking you to participate in these proceedings. I realize you. have been exceedingly busy but the orders do specify that a *regular* military officer be a part of these courts-martial proceedings.' Gorman made a small moue and winked at the others.

Prager bowed stiffly and took his seat at the end of the table. Gorman snapped his fingers and his aide stepped forward with a file. A gate in a wall to their left opened and a guard prodded a man, dressed in what had once been an expensively tailored business suit, into the garden. He stumbled to the table where he endeavoured to stand straight. He was unable, however, to conceal his trembling.

Gorman pretended to study his file in some detail, conferring with the aide in whispered asides. After a few moments during which the man's trembling grew more evident, Gorman slapped the file closed and tossed it carelessly onto the pile.

'You owned a small factory that produced wireless valves?' he demanded.

The man nodded, as if he did not trust himself to speak. The guard immediately slammed his rifle butt into the man's back, knocking him to his knees. Prager started to protest, but held himself in check. To do so would only make Gorman the more determined to show him up.

'Yes, Excellency,' the man whispered in excellent German.

Gorman peered at him suspiciously. 'You are not German?'

'No, Excellency. I was born in Krakow.' The man coughed nervously and flinched as the guard lifted his rifle butt. 'I . . . have relatives in Berlin, *Pan* General. German citizens . . . I . . . attended university in Stuttgart. . . .'

'Enough,' Gorman snapped. 'I did not ask for an autobiography. You are accused of anti-German propaganda. You are further accused of promoting terror by virtue of your position as owner of a wireless valve factory. Many of your instruments were found in the hands of terrorists after they were captured by German forces.'

'But, Excellency, I manufactured wireless valves for the Polish Army. Many of my wireless valves would of course. . . .'

'The sentence passed,' Gorman intoned as if the man had not spoken, 'by this court in accordance with the laws of occupying authority, is death. Are there any objections?'

The other two SS officers answered in the negative but Prager raised a hand. 'Gruppenfuehrer, I think it. . . .'

'Sentence is confirmed by unanimous vote and will be carried out immediately.' He waved a hand in dismissal and the guard dragged the unresisting man to another gate in the opposite wall.

Furious, Prager turned on Gorman. 'I object, Gruppenfuehrer! The man was clearly not guilty. If we are to execute everyone who manufactures wireless valves or has anything to do with goods that might be used by a resistance force, we will have to execute the whole of the Polish population!'

Gorman leaned as far back in his chair as his corpulence allowed and smiled nastily. 'You see, my dear colleagues,' he gestured at

Prager, 'why the SS was given the task of cleaning up the dregs of Poland. The Army is far too soft.'

A ragged volley of rifle shots punctuated his words and he chuckled. 'When dealing with vermin, one must do so quickly and with harshness. That swine was not only of little account to the Reich Government, but was careless enough to allow his wireless valves to fall into the wrong hands. He was as guilty as the man who throws a bomb. He was also a Jew and that in itself is sufficient reason to shoot him. As for executing the whole of Poland,' he leaned forward, and regarded Prager grimly. 'If necessary, it will be done.'

Gorman straightened and snapped his fingers. 'Next case!'

The afternoon dragged. Person after person was summoned before Gruppenfuehrer Gorman and his two henchmen, examined briefly, often inanely, and sentenced to death. The crackling of rifle fire became as constant as a metronome's tick. Several times, Prager tried to intervene but was ignored or, if he persisted, shouted down by Gorman.

After his last attempt to intervene in the case of a young woman, who had clearly been in the wrong place at the wrong time, failed, Prager began to register a negative vote. The clerk looked up in surprise but Gorman waved a hand and the clerk bent again to the record book. Prager knew that his vote would be recorded in line with the rest of the tribunal but at least he had the satisfaction of knowing he was following the orders he had been given by the army, to exercise his judgement independently of the SS.

Where the corridors intersected, the guard pushed him in a new direction. It made little difference to Thorne. No matter what they had planned next, it could not be worse than the tub. He stumbled under the guard's repeated prods and once had to lean against the wall to catch his breath. His body belonged to someone else and at times his mind tended to float so that he was watching every-thing from a great distance.

A short hall led to a sun-filled vista in the midst of which was huddled a line of ragged, battered people. The vivid greens of the garden were in such startling contrast to the drab walls around him that Thorne could not absorb it at first. Irritably, the guard pushed him into line.

The line had shortened considerably and he was nearing a gate before which stood an SS guard with a rifle and bayonet. A hand tugged at the remains of his shirt. Jacob Yitzak smiled at him, in spite of the bruises that disfigured his features.

'Bad?' Yitzak whispered.

He nodded dumbly and broke into a fit of painful coughing.

Yitzak propped him up. The guard stepped towards them and Thorne shrank away; he caught himself whimpering and clamped his teeth together, muttering obscenities at the people who had done this to him.

'It will soon be over, my friend,' Yitzak whispered. 'Change places with me. I tell them again you are an American. Who knows?'

Thorne was too dazed to understand what the old man was saying as he sidled past Thorne. The guard yanked a woman towards the gate, striking at her head with his rifle as she began to scream. When she continued, he swung the rifle in a vicious circle that knocked her flat. Thorne watched without curiosity, as if it had nothing to do with him. The guard hit her twice more and the woman collapsed, unconscious. The guard did not hesitate but grabbed Yitzak and pushed him through. The old man had only time to call out, *'Dowidzenia,'* good luck, to Thorne.

Only then did the significance of the periodic gunshots register.

Prager watched the elderly man shuffle down the flagstone path to the table. His shoulders were back and his head held high in a pathetic attempt to salvage pride. He lit a fresh cigarette. This affair was becoming more and more distasteful all the time.

Gruppenfuehrer Gorman looked up in mock surprise as the elderly man stopped before the table. Like so many other of the Poles who had faced them that long afternoon, he did not bow or plead, only stared at them with an expression of disdain.

'So! We have a celebrity before us,' Gorman crowed. 'We are honoured.'

The man replied in excellent German. 'You will forgive me if I say I do not share the feeling.'

Gorman laughed. 'Gentlemen,' he said expansively, 'May I present Jacob Yitzak, the world's greatest violinist – if you believe his press agents.'

He tapped the folder and his expression became severe. 'You are the father of one David Yitzak, an officer in the former Polish Army and now a terrorist. I beg your pardon. I should say former terrorist, as he was hanged several days ago.'

Yitzak tried to shrug but it was obvious that his arms and shoulders pained him too much to do so. 'My son, David, was an officer in the Army of Poland. There is nothing else to tell.'

Gorman waved a hand in disbelief. 'Be that as it may, for yourself, your career ends today.'

Yitzak smiled. 'You are too late, General. I retired a year ago. However, there is a young gentleman following me. He is an American named Keith Thorne. Your thugs do not seem to understand that he found himself in your prison by mistake. They think he is a British spy.'

Gorman, who had already picked up the next folder, hesitated. 'A British spy is he?'

Yitzak rolled his eyes, as if despairing of the man's stupidity. 'No. He is not a spy. Keith Thorne is an American and the son of an influential New York publisher.'

The name struck a familiar note, Prager thought. Thorne?

Gorman shook his head in exasperation. 'The sentence is death by firing party, to be executed immediately. The Reich has no need of Jew fiddle players.'

Yitzak turned away before the guard could touch him and walked to the other gate. Prager watched him, wondering how a man could go so calmly to his death, concerned more about another man's fate than his own.

The next prisoner was being led along the path. He seemed only partially conscious and stumbled in bare feet on the flagstones. His trousers were tattered and his shirt was in shreds. A livid scar ran across his ribs and his face had been battered into a rainbow of bruises. The guard stopped him before the table and the man rocked on unsteady legs. The old man had called him Thorne. Prager leaned to look at the man's file just as the rifle volley crashed out.

Thorne jerked about to stare at the wall, then shouted an obvious obscenity in English and spat at Gorman. A mixture of blood and saliva spattered the SS general's uniform tunic and he erupted from his chair faster than Prager would have believed possible, screaming with rage.

'Hold him,' Gorman bellowed and drew his own pistol. Prager lunged along the table and knocked the weapon away.

'Stop, you damned fool! Get hold of yourself!' he shouted. Prager shoved Gorman back and went around the table to kneel beside the American who had fallen as the soldier jumped away at the sight of Gorman waving a pistol.

'Gruppenfuehrer Gorman,' he snapped. 'The Army has just done you a favour, one for which you should be grateful for the rest of your life.'

Gorman's sense of survival had been finely honed in the medieval ambience of the SS and he spluttered into silence, sensing that Prager would never have had the courage to challenge him unless he knew for certain he was right.

'This man *is* an American. His name is Keith Thorne, as the

86

Jewish musician whom you just executed tried to tell you. His father is a powerful publisher in New York, one with sufficient wealth to launch an inquiry into the whereabouts of his son, even here. I would suggest, Gruppenfuehrer, that if anything happens to this man, you will find yourself standing before one of your own firing squads. And I have no doubt there will be no end of volunteers for the task.'

Prager had the American taken directly to the officers' lounge. Gruppenfuehrer Gorman, puffing along behind, cleared the room instantly and sent his aide running for a doctor. Thorne's dry, pasty complexion was evidence of deep shock.

The resident SS doctor was out of the building and the aide telephoned for an army surgeon and Gorman paced the room until he arrived. Twice he asked Prager if he was certain of the man's identity. Prager repeated what he knew of Thorne's background and told of meeting him at a cocktail party given by the American Embassy. Gorman gave him a bleak stare and suddenly Prager knew he was calculating the chances of concealing his mistake.

When the doctor arrived, Prager slipped up to his office and telephoned Army headquarters. He explained what had happened and requested an ambulance and an escort. It would be a question, he knew, of advertising Gorman's mistake as widely as possible if he was to survive. If he had only kept his mouth shut – but then he remembered that all the court-martial votes had been recorded as positive – his as well.

' . . . to a hospital as soon as possible,' the doctor was saying when he reentered the lounge. 'His lungs are very bad but how much damage has been done will not be clear until I can examine X-rays.'

Gorman nodded ponderously. 'I will make arrangements for him to have the best care at an SS medical centre.' Prager could see that the Gruppenfuehrer was already regaining his balance. Prager intervened smoothly.

'No need, Gruppenfuehrer Gorman. It would be best if your name was kept entirely out of this affair. I have arranged for an ambulance to take him to an Army hospital.' Gorman reddened with anger and Prager lowered his voice and turned so that the doctor could not hear.

'After he receives proper care,' he said quickly, 'it should prove easy enough to convince the American that he was tortured by the Poles. Then he can be returned to America and thus you will avoid a scandal over his treatment. He, for his part, will remember the SS as his rescuers. The Reich will be grateful to you for such a propaganda coup. And please remember that his father is an influential American publisher.'

He watched Gorman's anger fade and a cunning look slide across his face as he weighed the alternatives. The telling point was the fact that an Army ambulance and escort was on the way. It would be very difficult to conceal the affair unless he followed Prager's lead. There were too many enemies waiting for him to make a mistake. He nodded abruptly and stalked from the room.

'Herr Thorne?' The man's face was familiar somehow, Thorne thought.

'My name is Prager, Captain Friedrich Prager. We met a month ago, at an American Embassy party.'

Why wasn't his mind functioning properly? Thorne wondered. His vision tended to fade in and out. The voice was difficult to understand . . . where was he? Where was Jacob? Hadn't he just been talking to him, or was it all a nightmare?

'You were captured by Polish bandits who took you for a German. But you have been rescued by the German army. This man here,' he gestured to someone outside his narrow arc of vision, 'is a doctor. You will be taken to a hospital and as soon as you are well enough to travel, sent home to the United States. Do you understand?'

Thorne closed his eyes, not quite certain why he felt so relieved. Poles had tortured him the officer had said. But it wasn't true!

He opened his eyes. 'Please notify . . . American . . .' he had to stop until the pain eased. He could see a hand with a syringe moving towards him. Were they going to kill him with poison? 'Notify American . . . Embassy . . . safe.'

Prager nodded. 'It will be done immediately. Now, you must rest. The doctor will give you something to help you sleep.'

Thorne tried to shake his head. 'My wife . . . find my wife . . . notify the Embassy.' The doctor wiped his forearm with alcohol and he was surprised that he could feel the tiny bite of the needle among all the other pain. Thorne struggled to find the words to make the German officer understand.

'Deborah . . . separated at the airport. Attacked by aircraft. My wife . . . an American citizen.'

'Oh Christ!' Prager muttered but there wasn't time to think then as the door flew open and two medical orderlies followed by two soldiers in motorcycle helmets and carrying machine pistols hurried in. Two more soldiers argued with SS guards in the hall.

The American was eased onto the stretcher. Thorne clutched his hand and tried to speak but the morphine was beginning to work. Prager bent close.

' . . . must find her. Maiden name is Yitzak . . . has an American passport. . . .'

Prager disengaged his hand and the stretcher was taken out to the waiting ambulance. He noted with satisfaction that there was someone at headquarters with brains, or else with sufficient dislike of the SS to see that an entire squad of combat infantry had been dispatched in addition to the four men of the motorcycle escort. The lieutenant in command had deployed the men in a defensive ring about the ambulance, weapons ready. The young officer saw him as he left the building and came running. He wore the Iron Cross first class ribbon on his tunic and Prager thought it went well with his hard face.

'Everything all right, sir?'

'It is now, Lieutenant. I want you to see this man immediately to whatever medical facility the major,' he indicated the doctor, 'directs.'

'Are you staying here, sir?'

'For the moment. Our SS comrades have made a mess of things. They tortured and nearly shot an American citizen. And his wife is missing.' No harm in spreading the story as far as possible, he thought. 'There is a bit of cleaning up to be done.'

'Jesus!' the lieutenant exclaimed then caught himself. 'I'll leave a few men then, sir.'

'No, thank you, Lieutenant. That will not be necessary. Please inform the chief of staff that I remained behind to tidy up.'

The lieutenant saluted although his expression was plainly dubious and hurried down the steps, shouting orders to his men. As they formed up to board the truck, SS troopers watched with puzzled expressions. Prager took a deep breath and went back inside.

The bed was unbelievably soft and the injection had forced the pain to the furthest removes of his consciousness. He knew he was lying on a cot in a ward beneath a row of high windows through which afternoon sunlight touched everything with gold. There was a pleasant humming in his ears through which meaningless words in German filtered at odd moments.

A different doctor appeared, drew a blood sample and left, leaving behind a smiling nurse. The woman was the hearty Central European type; pretty and plump with a daunting bosom. Her hair was done in two spiral braids about her ears. After a while, she went away and he slept.

*

'Keith? Can you hear me?' Thorne recognized James Howell's voice as he emerged from an endless drug-induced sleep.

'Of course,' he mumbled in irritation. ' . . . thought you left . . . evacuated.'

'We were allowed back a few days ago. Christ, we've been searching high and low for you. When you did not arrive in Sweden, your father. . . .'

'Depend on him to. . . .' He fell silent, struggling for breath.

'Keith, the Chargé wants you out of Poland as soon as possible as it seems there is still some trouble with the SS. But the doctors think it best that you stay here a few more days.'

'Where is Deborah?' He began to cough and it felt as if his lungs were being torn apart. He couldn't stop coughing. His throat fluttered and he flailed about until a mask was slipped over his nose and mouth and a mist flowed in that calmed his lungs. When the spasm ended, he tried to tear it away, to make Howell understand, but hands held it firmly and he slipped into blackness again.

'I am sorry, Mr Howell,' the doctor told him. 'I can give you no more time. We fear he may develop pneumonia.'

Prager, who had been standing to one side, nodded at Howell and they left the ward. Outside, Howell drew a deep breath and fumbled for his cigarettes. He offered one to the German officer and they walked to the main lobby and stepped outside. Light rain was falling and the night air had turned quite cold. Howell buttoned his overcoat but Prager seemed oblivious to the temperature.

'I leave Poland tonight,' Prager said suddenly. 'You will do what you can for him?'

'Yes, of course,' Howell replied in surprise.

Prager regarded the shorter man with misgivings. 'You will not allow yourself to be bullied by the SS?'

Howell ground his cigarette beneath his heel. 'Not a fucking chance.'

The slang term escaped him but he understood the anger and determination in Howell's voice.

'You know something,' Howell said, glancing along the empty street. 'You people had better bring the SS under control or they will ruin you. Some of the things I've seen since returning to Warsaw.' He shook his head. 'You have support in the United States. Most Americans would even be satisfied to let you settle with the Jews, but only if you observe the proprieties. This killing business has got to stop. . . .'

'What foolish nonsense!'

'Damn it, Captain, don't try and tell me it isn't happening. What the hell happened to Jacob Yitzak, one of the most famous musicians of the twentieth century? Yesterday, I received a list from

ASCAP, the American Society of Composers, Authors and Publishers, a damned influential group in my country. Yitzak's name was on it and so were forty-six others. I was asked to establish their whereabouts and verify their safety. When I tried to do so, I was told by the SS to mind my own business!'

Howell took a deep breath. 'One government does not tell the diplomatic representative of another country to mind his own business, especially when that diplomat was able to verify from other sources that at least eighteen of the names on that list were Jews and that each has been executed. Not killed in the bombing or the fighting, but executed. There is no excuse for that sort of thing. Germany is bound to lose every bit of support she has in the United States if this keeps up.'

Prager heard him out without comment. The American diplomat was correct in his appraisal but there was little he could do about it. He had already risked his own neck to rescue one American – who was probably going to die anyway. Thank God he was leaving tonight. A Jewish wife, for God's sake, and married the day before the city surrendered!

But he could not just let Howell's patronizing comments pass. 'Mr Howell, I fully understand what is at stake. You are an American, safe in a country protected by oceans and which dominates not only your own continent but your entire hemisphere. You are rich in resources and are entirely self-sustaining in food production. Therefore, do not lecture me or my country, sir. We do not have your advantages and do what we must to survive. We are surrounded by proven enemies; we are barely self-sufficient in food and, other than coal and iron ore, Germany has few natural resources. Nor do we have millions of kilometres of empty land for expansion and farming. That we, you and I, stand here tonight in Warsaw, protected by the German army, only serves to illustrate the rightness of our course.

'I am well aware that there are fanatics in my government, just as there are in yours. But as all Americans are not like your gangsters or your Ku Klux Klan, neither are all Germans like the SS, and not all SS men are like the ones you have encountered. Many are decent, honest men who want only the best for our nation. If this were not true, your friend would now be dead.'

Prager broke off when he saw the scepticism in Howell's eyes. He was wasting his time. Howell was at best a minor functionary and even if he weren't, the Americans had no experience on which to base an understanding of Germany and German motives. By tomorrow noon, he would be in Berlin, thank God. He bowed quickly.

'Good night, Mr Howell.'

'For a man who was damned near dead a week ago, you look lively enough,' Howell observed as he guided Thorne's arm into a sleeve.

'It's just the thought of leaving this damned country.'

'I dare say,' Howell muttered and followed Thorne along the aisle.

'Not one of these bastards would even speak to me,' Thorne indicated the beds of convalescent soldiers on either side.

'Fucking master race! They tried to make me believe I was tortured by Poles. Can you believe that? They must think everyone is as stupid as they are. Then when I wouldn't play ball, they simply stopped speaking to me. Staff as well.'

Howell had obtained an Embassy staff car and he drove through streets empty of all traffic except for a few German military trucks or the Mercedes limousines favoured by the Gestapo. Thorne watched the rain-wet streets pass; there were few pedestrians about and most were well-dressed – Germans or German-Poles, he thought. The very few Poles among them could be distinguished by their ragged clothes and furtive air. In one month, Warsaw had been transformed from one of the cleanest and gayest capitals in Europe to a wasteland of ruin and human despair. Polish stupidity and German greed were responsible.

Howell maintained a small flat in the south-western suburbs which had been relatively untouched by the bombing and artillery barrages. He let them in and immediately opened a window. The two rooms were musty from disuse.

'I've only been here twice since we were allowed to return.' Howell shook his head at the dust and grime that had penetrated windows warped from their frames by concussions. 'Had a near miss two houses along. Damned strange. The front of the house looks fine but the entire back is gone.' He rummaged through drawers until he found a half-empty bottle of bourbon.

'Look here, old man,' he said as he poured the whisky into paper cups, 'the Chargé expects you to remain here until it's time for the train this evening. Just in case the SS has second thoughts about letting you go.'

Thorne gulped his drink and his face reflected a curiously lost expression. Perhaps he still hasn't recovered from the shock, Howell thought. He remembered the X-rays that showed two cracked ribs. And his face was still badly bruised.

Howell laughed nervously and refilled the paper cups. 'Look here, I forgot in all the hurry. Your wife is safe!'

Thorne took a deep breath and Howell had to put the bottle down to steady him.

'Safe?'

He nodded. 'She was separated from you on the airfield. A Polish anti-aircraft gun crew brought her to relatives who hid her. When the Embassy was reopened, she followed me here to find out what had happened to you. I smuggled her into the Embassy that night. Two days later, we were notified that you were in a German military hospital, under the protection of the army.'

Howell made him drink the whisky. 'My God,' he whispered. 'I was certain she was dead.'

'Deborah is safe,' Howell repeated. 'She will be brought to the railroad station tonight.'

'Damnit! Bring her here, now. I want to see my wife.' His vehemence surprised him as much as it did Howell.

'I thought you married her only to get her into the States?'

Thorne looked away to the streaked window where rain lashed the leafless trees. 'So did I,' he mumbled.

Surprised by Thorne's ambivalence, Howell answered briskly. 'I'm afraid that would be impossible, and dangerous. The SS has already requested our cooperation in locating her and their fifth column people, the *Auslands-Organization*, are still very active. She will be brought, under escort, to the station. The train is under the protection of neutral Romania and once aboard, you both will be safe.'

Rain pelted the Embassy car as they drove to Warsaw's Kovel Station. Armed troops were everywhere and barriers were manned by SS soldiers who painstakingly examined all travel permits and identification documents with maddening absorption. The huge building was curiously muted. Trains rattled in and out, whistles shrieked and the tannoy system provided frequent announcements in German and Russian only. Their driver, a US Marine sergeant in full dress uniform accompanied them to the platform where Howell ignored the checkpoint. An officer shouted and a soldier ran after them. The marine blocked his way and the soldier stopped in confusion. The officer hurried up, shouting until Howell snapped at him in German and the man shut up abruptly.

A line had formed on platform four behind a German officer who wore the uniform and lightning flashes of the SS. Howell felt Thorne stiffen and rested a warning hand on his arm. The officer was busy questioning a poorly dressed little man whose hands shook badly as he clutched his papers. Howell pushed between them and motioned Thorne onto the train.

The stunned SS officer grabbed Howell's arm and immediately

his face twisted in pain as the marine gripped his left elbow joint hard and drawled in a deep Texas accent, 'Take your fuckin' hand off, boy.'

His meaning was clear enough and the German released Howell.

'What do you think you are doing?' Howell attacked in German as he waved his identification papers under the officer's nose. 'You have no right to question these people. This is a neutral train, guaranteed by the German Army as such. Is it your intent to commit aggression against citizens and diplomatic representatives under the protection of the sovereign nation of Romania as well?'

The confused SS officer stammered and impatiently Howell told the sergeant to find the military official in charge. Howell then turned to the man the SS officer had pulled out of line and told him in Polish to step aboard the train. Thorne understood just enough to realize that Howell was telling him that he had nothing to fear and a murmur rose along the line.

'You have to treat these bastards like naughty children,' Howell said easily in English to Thorne, glaring at the German all the while.

The marine came striding back across the concourse with a senior SS officer almost running beside him in an effort to keep up. Howell took him aside and Thorne, suddenly exhausted, leaned against the side of the filthy coach. The senior SS officer listened respectfully after examining Howell's credentials. His expression slowly changed to anger and twice he tried to interrupt. Howell persisted until the officer broke away and shouted at his bewildered junior, then hurried off. Howell, looking pleased with himself, motioned the line of people aboard.

Thorne had always thought of Howell as a weedy, rather annoying young man from too good a family and too full of that knowledge. He was the last person in the world Thorne would have expected to stand up to an SS officer.

Howell must have sensed the direction of his thoughts for he glanced away, as if suddenly embarrassed. 'They might have made trouble for your wife if we had let them go on.'

'We?' Thorne grinned for the first time since the truck had left the Embassy grounds an eon ago. 'Jimmy Howell, giant killer in action. Wait until I get back to the States.'

Howell was definitely embarrassed now but the appearance of another marine escorting Deborah Yitzak saved him.

Thorne laughed in relief and Deborah smiled at him nervously. A Romanian official materialized and was introduced by Howell as the member of the Romanian Foreign Ministry who would serve as the official escort for the train.

'You haven't a thing to worry about,' the Romanian assured

them in French. 'You are now under the protection of the Romanian Government. We shall cross the border into Romania in a few hours.'

Thorne shook hands with Howell, unable to find words to express his appreciation. Howell spoke softly.

'I'm supposed to tell you not to talk about your experiences to the press. The State Department feels it would be bad for our relations with Germany.' He paused a moment, then grinned. 'Hell, Keith, you do what you think best. We'll be dragged into this war, sooner or later.'

Thorne helped Deborah into the car and they found two seats in a crowded compartment. Howell stood on the platform and waved as the train jerked into motion. An overwhelming feeling of relief swept over Thorne; they were now beyond reach of the Nazi authorities. The lights of the station disappeared as the train swept into the maze of tracks and wires and signals of the switch yard.

Deborah's skin gleamed like damp marble under the compartment's single fluorescent fixture. A thousand questions were ready to burst from him but she turned her head away and closed her eyes, as silent as a Madonna. The compartment was jammed to capacity but Thorne was at least fortunate to have the wall against his left side. His throat was raw and rasping with the first signs of his old childhood affliction, trachial bronchitis. The German doctors had feared pneumonia; instead it was to be bronchitis. One always paid, he thought; it was an immutable law of the universe.

Deborah's last clear memory was of her husband standing in the doorway that day in mid-September. Her father-in-law had been away at the Synagogue and she remembered the feel and smell of David's heavy body as she half-supported him up the stairs into his old room. He had stood with his shoulders slumped. Only with her, she knew, could he ever let down his guard and display emotion. He turned, staring at the furnishings as if checking his memory's inventory. The crystal radio set built as a young boy, old school books neatly racked beside the dresser and the picture of the American hero, Buffalo Bill, pasted to the wall. His eyes fastened on the familiar objects with a longing so intense that it made her horribly angry. God only knew what had happened to him, what he had seen and endured these past two weeks.

She took his rifle and leaned it in a corner. Firearms frightened her and she had to force herself to touch it. Deborah undid the buckles on the harness he wore to support his equipment, pulled the shoulder straps away and staggered under its weight. How had he ever carried it all? she marvelled.

Deborah wrinkled her nose as he turned and the odour of sweat and dirt came to her. She thought to make a joke but his haggard expression stopped her. He stood helpless, shirt partially unbuttoned, eyes staring sightlessly at something she could not see and that look told her he was still somewhere on the dusty plain to the north west. She brushed his fingers away and undid his shirt. The ragged undervest was soaked with perspiration. She pushed his arms up as if he were a child and pulled and the fabric disintegrated. She unfastened his trousers which were stiff with dirt and reddish brown stains which must be, she thought, dried blood. Not his, thank God.

Deborah unstrapped his huge boots and caked mud and bits of straw and grass fell off in clumps and she had a brief vision of sun-blistered fields. When the boots were off, she was appalled to see that his stockings had rotted on his blistered and calloused feet. As she stripped the loathsome mess away and wiped his feet, she wondered why in the name of God, he, or any man, would endure such suffering.

She bent to kiss him and he forced a smile, but the blankness hurried back. Determined to hold it at bay, she unbuttoned the print house dress and removed it, took off her slip and unfastened and let the brassiere fall away. Deborah had small but well-shaped breasts, lightly tipped with pale nipples, and she was proud of her lean body and flat stomach that smoothed into shapely hips and thighs.

His eyes roamed her body hungrily and she slipped out of her tights. 'God', he choked and made to get up. 'A bath. Deborah, I'm filthy.'

'Later,' she whispered. 'Later. Make love to me, David.' He hesitated only a moment then gathered her into his arms, crushing her to him as if she were his very life. They wasted no time on preliminaries. His rough hand parted her thighs gently and he poised only a moment before entering her. Deborah felt the delicious shock as her body convulsed and she pressed her face into his shoulder unmindful of his dirt and odour.

A whistle startled her awake and she stared at the blackened window, streaked with ghostly trails of water. A wave of crushing disappointment flooded her as she realized that David was . . . she could not force herself to admit his death. The dream had been so real, so . . . she wrenched her mind away, retreating into the blankness she had so carefully schooled herself in these past weeks.

Thorne woke to find the girl's head cradled against his chest. Why do I persist in thinking of her as a girl? he wondered. He smiled to himself when he thought of the reception they would receive in New York – married to a Jewess! His arm was cramped and he eased it away. The sky had begun to lighten with approaching dawn but rain slanted heavily to obscure the landscape. They passed an endless train of flat cars carrying canvas-shrouded vehicles – tanks? A single rain-slickered soldier with a rifle crouched miserably at the front of each car as the train ran on across the rain-soaked plains.

The train jolted over badly set points, waking Deborah. She sat up with a start and only relaxed when she recognized him in the dim light.

'Hello,' he said quietly in English. Deborah's answer was lost in the screech of air brakes. The train lurched and began to slow. The others in the compartment woke and instantly the fear was palpable. A shape rushed by in the corridor.

The train rattled to a stop on the outskirts of a village. Houses with thatched roofs huddled together along a dirt road that ran at right angles to the tracks. German troops were everywhere.

Steel helmets gleamed in arc lights that supplemented the faint dawn. Sheltering beneath an umbrella was the Romanian, laughing with a German officer. An agreement was reached and they shook hands, then the officer turned to regard the train. As he did so, the death's head insignia beneath the stylized eagle gleamed for a moment on his cap.

Armed SS soldiers stamped through the train shouting at everyone to get out. The passengers stumbled out into the slanting rain and huddled in single file beside the cars. The officer walked along the line, looking intently at each face. Several times he nodded and a man or woman was hustled out of line, down the embankment and forced aboard an open truck.

When the officer came to Thorne, he smirked and held out a hand for his papers. A terrible fear growing within him, Thorne handed them over. The officer tapped the passport with a gloved finger, noting the green American cover and flipped it open. He motioned and a soldier stepped forward with a list.

'You are Mr Keith Thorne?' he asked in surprisingly good English.

'That's right. Why have you stopped this train? It's a neutral train.'

'Be quiet!'

All the experiences of the past six weeks, the fear, anger, pain and frustration he had suffered suddenly exploded from him. 'By God!' he raged and the officer started back in surprise. 'You don't talk to me like that! I'm an American and I have. . . .'

A soldier stepped in fast and rammed the edge of a bayonet against his throat. Without thinking, he stiff-armed the blade away but another soldier swung his rifle butt into his solar plexus and he collapsed, gasping for air.

'Ah, Mr Thorne,' the officer smirked down at him. 'Your papers show you to be an American but there seems to be some question of your neutrality. You were interrogated in Warsaw about your connections with the British and I believe you were tried as a spy and sentenced to be executed?'

The soldiers yanked him up and braced him against the train. He struggled for air and the officer waited patiently.

'That . . . that was a mistake,' he managed but the officer had turned to regard Deborah with interest. She stared blankly into the distance as if he did not exist.

'This is your wife, I believe? Was she too born in,' he glanced at the passport, 'White Plains, New York?' It was a rhetorical question which Thorne could not have answered if he wished. The officer spoke to the soldier with the bayonet who stepped back.

'Mr Thorne, I do not believe this woman is either an American or,' he paused and smiled, 'your wife.'

Thorne braced himself and pushed one of the soldiers away. 'I don't give a damn . . . what you believe,' he snarled. 'You can read the passport can't you? Her name is listed, as an American citizen.'

'Ah, yes, but passports can be counterfeited and since the bandit former Polish government attacked the German Reich, many have been.'

'Look here, whatever your rank is.' Thorne strove desperately to catch his breath and at the same time to keep the rising panic from his voice. 'I am an American citizen and a neutral. This woman is my wife and she is pregnant with our child. And her passport is valid and can be verified by a telephone call to the American Embassy in Warsaw. This is a neutral train operating with the permission of the military government in Warsaw and under the protection of the government of neutral Romania. How in the world do you dare. . . .'

The officer held up a hand. 'Please, Mr Thorne, this discussion is useless. The SS has overriding jurisdiction where matters of State security are involved. We will respect your position as a neutral as a matter of course, even though there is some question as to that. Polish Jews however are enemies of the State and cannot be allowed to leave the country.' He tapped a folded paper against his lip. 'We are searching for a woman who is the wife of a former army officer turned terrorist, also a Jew. This woman who claims to be your wife is that person.'

The sudden knowledge of what he knew was going to happen caused him to gasp and he began to cough. The spasm grew worse, wracking his throat and chest so that his entire trachea shuddered, leaving him fighting merely to breathe. The officer ignored him and glanced at the paper in his hand.

'This woman, one Deborah Yitzak, is the widow of the Jew, Yitzak,' he announced, 'claiming to be an officer in the former Polish army.'

Thorne could see Deborah through his tears the coughing had brought, standing quietly, face expressionless.

'All members of the family of anyone found guilty of terrorism are subject to immediate execution wherever arrested.' The SS officer stared at Thorne. 'Due to the unwarranted intervention of a German army officer and illegal interference by your own embassy staff, this woman has so far escaped retribution.'

'For Christ's sake,' Thorne whispered. 'You can't just murder one harmless woman, you lousy bastard. . . .'

The officer nodded and a soldier stepped in fast and swung his rifle butt into Thorne's solar plexus again. The blow smashed the air from his lungs for a second time and drove him to his knees. The pain was so intense that he could only lean forward until his forehead was touching the ground. He was vaguely aware of soldiers herding people back onto the train, of the smirking Romanian diplomatic official looking on, of Deborah being dragged down the embankment. He managed to get to his feet but a soldier barred his way. Thorne tried to push past but the man held him back, gently. His face was expressionless but he murmured softly in German to him.

A sergeant pushed Deborah to her knees and unholstered his pistol. The muzzle touched the back of her neck. Her eyes sought and fastened on Thorne's and the crack of the pistol was like a whip.

They tossed Thorne onto the bouncing steel plates between the cars as the train began to roll forward. Deborah's body, sodden with rain, lay huddled on the cinders. SS troops were climbing into trucks and the arc lights went out one by one. Over all, the rain slanted down in silver spears.

Qui desiderat pacem, praeparet Bellum
Vegetius Fourth – Fifth Century AD

Finland 2 – 28 November 1939

The sun was so bright when Captain Charles Atkins, Fourth Hussars, Royal Army came on deck that he stood blinking at the un-November-like quality to the atmosphere, then wandered to the stern rail, sipping tea from a paper cup, to enjoy the panorama of pellucid sky, azure water and brown-green islands.

The ferry ran east through the Åland Islands, the vast archipelago of thirty thousand bits of land celebrated in Sally Salminen's novel, *Katrina*. This was his first sight of them as he had fallen exhausted into a bunk the night before after boarding and had slept through the short call at the island capital, Mariehamn. The islands had once belonged to Sweden and, in fact, he had read somewhere that she and Finland had nearly gone to war over them in 1919.

The purser's assistant had awakened him twenty minutes earlier to announce their arrival at Turku at noon. He could not remember the last time he had slept past 0600.

A gull screamed and dipped closer and he watched the firm white body, marvelling at the way the bird rode the air currents as easily as a dolphin rode a bow wave. The bird spotted something of more immediate interest and with a last penetrating glance from its evil red eye, veered away and dipped towards the sea. Atkins shivered and pushed away from the railing. He did not like birds.

The harbour at Turku was filled with warships. A Russian destroyer was tied up to a berth just ahead of two Finnish motor patrol boats. Anchored in the harbour proper was a light cruiser flying the Swastika ensign of the German Navy. Atkins studied the German ship though his binoculars and cursed himself for not bringing his camera on deck. German sailors were visible as were several officers on the fighting bridge.

A porter directed him to the railroad terminus at the end of the dock and he stepped directly aboard the express for Helsinki that met every ferry. The train ran at a slow pace, as if reluctant to disturb the serenity of the city under the bright sun. An obsessive neatness – like Dutch villages – impressed him. So many Swedish acquaintances had commiserated when they found out he was being transferred to Finland that he had expected the country to be one vast slum.

Instead, as the train rolled through the city, he saw shops and offices of glass and shining chrome, and huge apartment buildings designed with a futuristic flair and recalled that the Finns had always been known for their bold designs and architecture. The city gave way to spacious suburbs and then to open countryside. Fields were carefully demarcated by trenches which formed an intricate drainage system across the flat countryside.

Helsinki came into view after dark. The train rounded a curve and the high-roofed car swayed to one side, rattling loudly. Lights shimmered in the distance, disappeared as the birches closed in, appeared again for a moment and were lost as the train dipped into a cut. Then the city was spread before him in a misty glimmer. To one side, a deeper, polished black glinted with tiny lights – the harbour, he suspected.

The railway station was awesome, he thought as he trudged along the platform towards the concourse. It was as ultramodern as anything seen in London, yet it had been designed and built in 1919, immediately after their war of independence from Russia. He left the station to meet a brisk wind smelling of salt and oil and assorted other harbour smells. The immense square was the equal of San Marco's in Venice or Cathedral Square in Mexico City. His preconceived notions of Finland were tumbling fast.

Reservations had been made for him at the Hotel Torni and his office mate in Stockholm, familiar with Helsinki, had told him to walk straight across the square to the largest building visible. He did and it was.

Since his escape from Poland, Captain Charles Atkins had spent the two previous months in Stockholm sitting behind a deal table day after day interviewing Polish military officers for those suitable for transfer to Britain. It never ceased to amaze him that so many had managed to cross the Baltic nor that the Swedes had not turned them away as so many other countries had done. German pressure on Sweden to return the Poles was very strong but the Swedes had continued to accept all who made it to their shores.

Atkins and his French colleague had stolen an automobile only the day before Warsaw surrendered, and broke through the German ring about the city that night. Twice, they had come under fire from marauding Stukas. Late the first afternoon, a group of Polish soldiers turned bandit tried to stop their car. The Frenchman shot one as Atkins swerved the heavy American Packard about, cursing the steering wheel on the wrong side, and sped back the way they had come. Several miles along the road, they stopped to assess damage – a shattered windscreen and a punctured petrol tank. As they were making repairs, a Pole wearing a uniform with lieutenant's rank emerged from the trees and offered to serve as guide and driver. He spoke only a little English but his French was fluent. His name was David Yitzak and he proved to be the son of the famous violinist. He would not tell them his destination, only that he had tried to reenter the city and failed. Atkins guessed that he had been attempting to reach some kind of assembly point for officers and men of the old regime.

They approached the road block carefully this time but the soldiers had gone, leaving the dead man, a sergeant, behind. Yitzak changed into the dead man's uniform, grumbling at its filthy state, poor quality and fit.

As they drove further away from Warsaw, Atkins had discovered a curious thing about mechanized warfare. Of course, it had been discussed in training classes at Sandhurst but he had never before realized the full extent of its implications.

The vaunted German army travelled mostly on foot or by horseback, once the thin screen of mechanized troops had passed by. Even though tanks had swept out of East Prussia into the northeastern sections of Poland there was hardly a German to be seen anywhere, other than roving patrols in lorries and armoured cars who kept to the main roads. The infantry occupied key road junctions and towns but had not yet spread into the countryside and all along the way, they saw furtive men in Polish army uniforms moving quickly through the forest fringes.

'The beginning of a new army,' Yitzak observed. 'The *Swazby* makes mistakes after all. By the time he is strong enough to stop us, it will be too late.'

They abandoned the car after it ran out of petrol and walked for miles in a thin rain. Once they heard a German patrol moving ahead and changed course. After a cold, uncomfortable night in a tumble-down shed, they swam the River Bug into Russian-occupied Poland and gave themselves up to the first Russian patrol they came across. As a Pole, Yitzak was led away quickly despite their protests and Atkins was separated from the French attaché. The next day, he had been driven to Smolensk where he spent an uncomfortable week in a dingy hotel room while a Russian guard kicked his heels against the floor to amuse himself.

At first he was told he would be surrendered to the German army and when he protested that the Geneva Convention required that he be returned to his own country, he was told that, instead, he would be interned for the duration of hostilities. No matter how often he demanded to be allowed to contact the British Embassy in Moscow his interrogator's expression never wavered, nor did he cease tapping the paper closely printed in Russian characters which he urged Atkins to sign. The Russian refused to translate the paper and Atkins refused to sign.

At the end of the week, Atkins tired of the game. He glared at the Russian sentry one morning, pushed him aside and stamped down to the hotel lobby. The guard hurried after him, gabbling in Russian and waving his rifle but Atkins ignored him. In a mixture of English, Polish, and German, he persuaded the nervous hotel manager to telephone the British Embassy in Moscow. Amazingly enough, the call went through directly and in less than five minutes, he was speaking to the chief military attaché.

'Ah there you are, Atkins. Beginning to wonder what happened to you. Everyone else got out safe and sound. I'll send someone down to collect you immediately.'

The chief military attaché was as good as his word and that evening, a Humber staff car picked him up and drove him back along the narrow, paved main road to Moscow. Two days later, he flew to Stockholm.

As he was registering at the Hotel Torni, a man in civilian clothing approached, removed his pipe and introduced himself as Steven Bennet, the commercial attaché at the British legation.

'Sorry I couldn't meet you at the station. Held up at a meeting.'

He told the clerk to have Atkins' luggage sent up to his room and led him into the bar. 'Realize you must be exhausted, but this is rather important,' he said. Bennet made practised small talk while a waitress with hair the colour of winter straw took their orders.

'I thought all Finns were dark?' Atkins asked when she left.

'Not at all. You are thinking of the Laplander.' He emptied his pipe with a small penknife, packed and relit it before going on.

'What do the Swedes think of the war?'

'Very apprehensive,' Atkins told him. 'Questions in their Parliament about the state of the army and civil defence, that sort of thing. They've designated bomb shelters and even put steel plates over the windows of public buildings for air-raid protection. The Stockholmers were appalled at what was done to Warsaw. A Swedish film crew stayed almost to the surrender and their films have been the talk of the country. People are stocking up on food and digging slit trenches in back gardens.'

'Just like at home,' Bennet murmured. 'The politicos always wait until the last minute and then blame everyone else for their lack of foresight. I understand you were in Warsaw during the siege. Almost captured weren't you?'

Atkins said quietly, 'I think I had better see some identification.'

Bennet smiled. 'Hoped you would get around to that.' He

showed Atkins a card with his photograph that identified him as a member of the British legation staff.

'You said you were the commercial attaché?'

'Something like that. The Minister is unavailable for a few days and so he deputized me to brief you.'

'Brief me?'

'Yes. The Nazi–Soviet pact has changed everything in the eastern Baltic. Now that Russia has, ah, persuaded shall we say Lithuania, Latvia and Estonia to allow Soviet troops in, they are making rather heavy demands on Finland. And with good reason. Leningrad is only sixteen or so miles from Finnish territory. Sooner or later, Stalin's unnatural love affair with Adolph must break up and without Finland as a buffer against Nazi tanks, the divorce may come even sooner. When the decree is finalized, we want to be on hand to catch poor old Joe on the rebound, so to speak. So, you must be nice to the Finns and do everything you can to persuade them to resist the Russians, keep the Germans out and invite us in.'

'If Russia should attack, what kind of defence could Finland put up?'

Bennet scratched his cheek with the pipestem. 'If Stalin decides to move, he'll take the country in a week. The Finnish army can't resist for more than a few days. The Russians have them outgunned and out-manned over ten to one. In tanks alone, they could form a line from Leningrad to Helsinki. They have three entire armies in position in Soviet Karelia; the Seventh and Eighth in the south, the Ninth in the centre and the Fourteenth at Murmansk, ready to move on Petsamo. Our best guess is they have a total of twenty-six divisions and against them the Finns can field nine divisions, perhaps ten, of less than 150,000 men. The Finns have a few old French tanks, some obsolete aircraft, damned little artillery and virtually no reserves.'

'I see,' Atkins nodded. 'Yet the idea is to persuade the Finns to stall the Russian demands. But wouldn't it be better if Russia did occupy Finland?'

Bennet shrugged. 'Whitehall seems more afraid of communists than fascists and the Finns are smart enough to see that. Until September third, the Finns were asking for Anglo-French guarantees like those given to Poland. They haven't asked since which very plainly suggests that they are going to follow an independent course.'

'Understandable,' Atkins observed and Bennet looked at him sharply.

'As I am certain you realize,' he replied in a frosty voice, 'there are other ways to win a war than pouring troops into battle.'

'Perhaps.' Atkins was noncommittal and Bennet sucked on his pipe, his expression a mixture of suspicion and thoughtfulness.

'In any event, you are to be encouraging if asked about troop support, weapons and supplies in the event of a Soviet attack, but no more. I wouldn't call it a strong fascist element in their government but the Finns have less distrust of Germany than Russia. They haven't forgotten that Germany helped them gain their independence from Russia twenty years ago.'

The following morning Atkins reported to the British legation which overlooked the harbour. His office was a tiny cubicle shared with the naval attaché, currently on leave in England. He found his desk piled high with paperwork as his predecessor had gone home in early July with a medical complaint and had only been replaced when someone remembered that Atkins was in Sweden.

He spent the first week sorting through piles of paperwork and when he had reduced them to manageable proportions, telephoned the French Embassy intending to introduce himself to his opposite number, only to be told their man had returned to France for consultations. He telephoned in turn to the neutral embassies and legations of Italy, the United States, Denmark, Norway, Sweden and Belgium before he finally was able to speak to an attaché. The Belgian attaché invited him to lunch – the following week. No one, it seemed, wanted to be too closely associated with the British after the Polish débâcle.

Atkins had never really been comfortable serving as an attaché. Although he had done so since 1935 he always felt somewhat at a loss when dealing with sophisticated diplomats. He was a product of the middle class and had little patience with the airs and graces of his supposed betters. His father had gone to France in 1916, had received a field commission and promotion to the rank of Captain before he was killed during the great German spring offensive in March, 1918. His mother had died in 1924 and an elderly aunt and uncle raised Atkins. His uncle wrote mystery novels and they lived on a small Oxfordshire estate purchased with the royalties from an unexpected bestseller. When Atkins was twelve, he was sent away to a small public school in Cornwall.

Perhaps it was the tales of his father's army service in the trenches described in detail in letters to his brother that persuaded Atkins to a military career. He applied for and received permission to sit for the Royal Military Academy examinations at Sandhurst. Eighteen months later, he passed out third and received a coveted posting to the Fourth Hussars.

An invitation to attend a cavalry field exercise arrived at the beginning of his third week in Finland and Atkins telephoned his acceptance. Finnish was a language more closely allied to Hungarian than any of the Scandinavian tongues but he was finding that many Finns spoke either English or German.

He found his way to the headquarters of the cavalry regiment some fifteen kilometres north of Helsinki on a cold, overcast day. No one seemed to notice his arrival and he wandered towards three large tents that had been set up in a clearing. Some officers were studying a map, heads bent, conversation intense and he hesitated to intrude. A soldier stepped from one of the tents, glanced in surprise at his uniform and ducked back inside. An officer wearing yellow collar patches with gilt metal rosettes hurried out, buckling on his pistol belt.

'You must be Captain Charles Atkins,' he said in strongly accented English. 'I am Captain Johan Erko and will serve as your guide today.' He nodded towards the officers still bent over the table. 'I will introduce you in a moment. Would you care for coffee?'

Inside the tent, a soldier manned a large wireless set, a German-made Telefunken, Atkins noted. When he had walked up the track from the headquarters building, he had been startled to see German uniforms. In fact they were Finnish – the differences were minor and had to do with colour. The Finnish uniform tunic was the same shade as the trousers and the cockade on the field cap was blue and white rather than black and red. Just how strong was the German influence? he wondered.

Atkins commented on his English and Erko smiled with pleasure. 'I was privileged to spend two years in England, to study at Cambridge.'

The Finn was a large, quite handsome man, a bit taller than Atkins at five feet eleven inches, and some fifteen to twenty pounds heavier. He was much broader across the shoulders and his uniform jacket fitted tightly over a frame that seemed exceptionally solid. They finished their coffee and Erko explained the objective of the field exercise.

'We will be attempting to use a squadron of cavalry to outflank a squadron of tanks and destroy them,' Erko indicated the three officers, still deep in conversation.

'Cavalry against tanks?' The question came out more sharply than he had meant it to. 'But the Polish experience shows that cavalry doesn't stand a chance against armour.'

Erko smiled. 'We have studied the German tactics in Poland most closely, I can assure you. We think we might have developed one or two techniques ourselves. I might add that the foreign military observer with the tank squadron is a German army officer.'

Atkins glanced up sharply but Erko grinned. 'If you wish to

protest, and even to withdraw, we will understand. This is an unfortunate mix-up. Each side is allowed to notify the Foreign Ministry if they will allow a foreign military observer to be present. Apparently, they did not realize when the requests came in that the units would be participating against one another. They are, after all, only civilians.'

'Damn!' Atkins thought. Strictly speaking, he should withdraw and the legation would make a formal protest. But he was curious to see just what the Finns might be up to. After having served as military attaché in Greece, Spain, Italy and Poland and attended numerous manoeuvres and field exercises, he prided himself on the fact that he could examine new techniques and equipment dispassionately.

'No,' he replied in a thoughtful voice, 'I would rather stay. Of course, I will not be able to meet or acknowledge the presence of the German officer.'

'Of course. I will make certain that you are not placed in such an embarrassing position.' Erko clapped him on the shoulder. 'I think we will get along fine. We Finns like a man who is willing to throw the book away, I think that is the proper expression. Do you ride a horse?'

'Yes, but not for some years.'

'Well, we shall have to use horses to reach the manoeuvring site. I have some clothes in the tent which may fit you. I phoned your legation this morning but you had already left. The gentleman I talked to, a man named Bennet, estimated your weight and size for me.'

At the mention of Bennet's name, Atkins glanced at the Finn but his expression was non-committal.

An hour later, wearing a Finnish Cavalry officer's yellow-striped trousers and field jacket, Atkins cantered behind Erko into a clearing in the birch forest where a squadron of cavalry had gathered. The men were standing beside their horses, drinking coffee and the heavy aroma in the cold air and the peppery tang of birch was exhilarating. The troopers greeted Erko with shouts and jokes and he replied in kind. The Finn slid from his horse and handed the reins to a young boy in a uniform a bit too big, greeted him by name and clapped him on the shoulder.

Leading Atkins to the fire, he chuckled. 'Not quite as formal as your army, I dare say.'

'No indeed. Not a bit.' But in spite of the informality, Atkins noted that every trooper's gear was carefully done up and the carbines, slung crosswise across their backs, gleamed with oil. Uniforms were spotless and carefully pressed and each man was freshly shaved and exuded an odour of soap that mingled pleasantly with that of horses, crisp air, coffee and gun oil.

'Our *Suomen Armeija* or regular army is very small. These men are reserves but they are professional soldiers in every sense. Their pay is usually just enough to cover transportation to and from their training barracks or to such manoeuvring grounds as these. But even so, we have no trouble in keeping the regiment up to strength. In fact, each has a long waiting list. Each man is responsible for his equipment. He takes his rifle home with him and is encouraged to use it for hunting and marksmanship practice and the government supplies all the ammunition he can use. In addition to the army is the *Suojeluskunta*, the Armed Civil Guard which is similar to your Territorial Army or the American's National Guard. So you see, we Finns take the defence of our homes most seriously.'

Two horsemen cantered into the clearing and were greeted with the same friendly banter, in spite of the fact they were high-ranking officers. Erko spoke to the senior of the two, a general by his insignia, then introduced Atkins to Major-General Wallenius.

'I have informed the General that you are the British observer for today's manoeuvres. General Wallenius extends a welcome and hopes you will enjoy yourself. The General has also invited you to ride with him, or you may stay with the squadron, as you prefer.'

Atkins hesitated; he would obtain a clearer overall picture if he remained with the general but he really wanted to see first-hand, how horsemen handled the tanks.

'Please thank the general for me but I would prefer to go with the squadron.'

Erko grinned in relief. 'I was hoping that would be your decision.' He translated and the general said something that drew a laugh from the troopers.

'The general understands and hopes you will not be too hard on his men.'

A few minutes later, they mounted and the squadron was split into two sections and filed off into the trees along paths invisible to Atkins. They rode in complete silence and Atkins was amazed at how quietly the horses travelled. Every piece of gear that could rattle or clank was tied in place or had been muffled with cloth. Each trooper carried a Finnish Model 1927 Carbine, a modification of the Russian Moisin-Nagant, and a holstered Model 1935 Lahti pistol. A short bayonet and musette bag of handgrenades completed their armament. In addition every trooper and officer carried a thin-bladed, guardless knife in a decorated sheath attached to his belt.

The squadron rode in single file for some twenty minutes before the colonel gave a hand signal. Erko pointed and Atkins followed as the squadron turned at right angles and moved into the trees. The birch had shed their leaves but Atkins was surprised to see how limited visibility remained. The entire forest seemed to have taken on the same chill grey as the overcast sky.

After a further fifteen minutes, the squadron stopped and dismounted. Each man unslung his carbine and knelt beside his horse. Atkins followed suit.

'The tanks have been reported moving along a forester's road a kilometre ahead. Scouts have gone to verify this,' Erko murmured.

Atkins was nearly frozen before a rider trotted in, dismounted and spoke to the squadron commander. Atkins saw him point to something on the map. A referee glanced at his watch. The Captain stood up and waved.

'Off we go, old boy,' Erko grinned. 'Now you will see what real cavalry can do.'

They trotted out of the clearing in a north-westerly direction and crossed a narrow space between the trees and, if he hadn't glimpsed the wheel ruts, he would never have noticed the forester's track. Hand signals turned them at right angles and they moved quickly onto higher ground and halted. Every third man led three horses to the rear while the remainder filtered into position on the slope. Atkins shook his head, thinking that if real bullets and shells were to be used, the Finns would be massacred.

'You do not think we are correct?' Erko asked.

Atkins waved at the line of dismounted troopers, some of whom had moved to within a few metres of the track before going to ground. 'The Germans sweep the roadsides with machinegun fire at the first sign of trouble. Your people will be cut to pieces.'

Erko chuckled and someone blew a single whistle blast. To Atkins, it seemed as if the forest froze into immobility; the troopers disappeared into the late autumn woods as if they had been Red Indians.

It was strange, he thought later, how different a tank sounded on the Aldershot manoeuvring grounds as compared to the suburbs of Warsaw or a forest track. He remembered his first encounter with an enemy tank, in a Warsaw street. The first shot from its stubby thirty-seven millimetre gun had smashed the barricade and killed four men. The second had completed the demolition and a third destroyed a motor lorry. The debris was too high for the tank to surmount and it had turned aside, sparing his life. He would never forget the insistent clatter of its treads slipping on smashed concrete and timber as it snuffled about the ruins like some monstrously evil predator. He had felt, in that instant, like a rabbit as the ferret slipped into its burrow.

The lead tank trundled into view, turret open, its commander scanning the woods on either side and Atkins nearly burst out laughing as he saw that they were ancient French Renault light tanks, relics of the Great War and a far cry from the snorting, powerful Panzer Mark IIIs or the British Matilda.

Erko nudged his arm. 'Watch! They will use highway flares and bottles of dye rather than explosives.'

A soldier on the far right of the skirmish line had wriggled forward until he was inches from the road. As the lead tank passed, he tore the cap from a flare and as it blazed in the waning afternoon, tossed it into the tracks. Immediately, a referee on the second tank blew his whistle and pointed. The startled lead commander brought his machine to an immediate halt, causing the second tank to slew out of line. At almost the same moment, Atkins saw another flare go off beside the last in line. The six tanks ground to a halt, their way blocked in both directions and bottles of dye rained onto them and a machine gun stuttered from the rise.

It was over in moments as referees from both units ran up and down the track, blowing whistles. Atkins gaped in astonishment.

Erko laughed as well. 'You see, Captain, how easy it is when your soldiers are well-trained.'

They rode down to the track where angry officers spattered with dye and wearing the black flashes of the tank regiment were arguing with the four referees. Atkins guided his horse along the line of grinning cavalrymen to examine the ambush site. Very clever, he thought. The muddy track ran between banks that were too high for the tanks to climb. By wrecking the treads of the first and last tank, the others were hemmed in. The cavalry troopers had then knocked each one out with explosives – simulated by the bottles of dye.

'Quite effective, hey?' Erko eased his horse alongside.

Atkins nodded. 'Yes, quite. But your hand grenades wouldn't be effective against modern tanks; in fact, they would barely suffice for these, and then only if you managed to get one inside.'

'Oh, those were not simulated hand grenades,' Erko laughed and pulled his horse away. As he started to follow, Atkins glimpsed the German officer staring thoughtfully at the line of dye-spattered tanks.

Atkins phrased his report carefully. He suspected that it would be widely read in the tank regiments and it was important that he offend no one if he wished it to be understood that the Finns were developing methods whereby the foot soldier could deal effectively with the tank. Two months previously, the entire military world had watched in astonishment as the Germans had hurled their mechanized divisions through the Polish army without serious resistance. If the Finns were correct and their lessons well-learned, no one would ever repeat that style of lightning war again, providing someone read his report and paid attention to its conclusions. He did not have high hopes that anyone would. He supposed that he was one of the few military observers outside of Germany who realized just how tenuous those lines of tanks and swift-moving infantry were, if the absence of German occupation troops in the Polish countryside had been any indication.

He reread the draft, added a line about the presence of a German tank officer at the exercise and wondered if he weren't being overly optimistic. No, he decided. The Finnish tactics were merely a logical development; every new weapon development carried the seeds of its own neutralization from the first moment of its use.

Atkins sat back in the chair. A bright sun filled the city with soft northern light and Helsinki harbour lay before him with its countless islands. To the left was the reddish grey mass of the Fortress of Suomelina, built by the Swedes in the mid-1700s to protect Finland against a Russian invasion. Two hundred years, he mused, and nothing had changed.

He gave the report to the typist and started for the door as the telephone rang. The temptation to ignore it was strong but discipline was stronger and he snatched the handset from the cradle.

'Is that Captain Atkins?' He recognized Captain Johan Erko's voice. 'Would it be convenient for you to pop around to headquarters this afternoon? A nuisance on such short notice, I'm sure but it is quite important. I'll be glad to give you lunch if you could come now.'

The number three tram took Atkins through streets cluttered with heavy trucks bustling back and forth to the new Olympic Stadium site. Now that the autumn leaves were gone, it was possible to just see the white spear of the stadium tower on Elaintarha. The amount of construction going on in Helsinki had never ceased to astonish him. New hotels sprouted along Mannerheiminite Boulevard like mushrooms. In spite of the rumours of war and the worsening situation with Russia, the city government confidently expected the Olympics to take place in 1940.

Captain Erko conducted Atkins to his office on the third floor and offered him a comfortable chair, a cigar and, early as it was, a brandy. Atkins had already discovered that the Finns were perhaps the world's greatest drinkers. Erko lifted the telephone receiver, spoke quickly, then beamed at Atkins.

'There is someone who wishes to speak to you. He will be along in a moment. Afterwards, we shall have lunch.' Then, without giving Atkins a chance to respond, he launched into small talk.

'How are you enjoying Helsinki? Have you seen much of the

city? There is a restaurant you must try, at the end of the Esplande, ah, I have forgotten its name! Sibelius's son-in-law conducts the orchestra. A very musical family. Anyone can tell you the name.'

Atkins sketched his sightseeing trips about the city and mentioned that his curiosity had been aroused by the fortress in the harbour.

'Ah, the Suomelina. Our ancient defence against the Russians.'

Erko's aide knocked and opened the door. A man of medium height stepped in and, as Atkins rose, he recognized Marshal Carl Gustaf Mannerheim, the commander of the Finnish armed forces. In the convoluted world of Finnish politics the Marshal was acknowledged a national hero by all factions except the communists. This affection stemmed from the 1918 Civil War when Mannerheim, then a lieutenant-general in the Imperial Russian Army, routed the Red Army from Finland. In twenty years, Finland had changed from an impoverished Russian province into a self-sufficient nation of nearly four million people.

Erko introduced Atkins in Finnish and Mannerheim took the seat offered and regarded Atkins with a guarded expression.

'The Marshal wishes to have your impressions of our cavalry exercise of last week.' Erko told him.

'Excellent discipline for a reserve unit,' Atkins said cautiously. The Marshal had a reputation for impatience with those who did not hold his views.

The Marshal's severe face creased in a slight smile.

'I was most impressed,' Atkins went on, his confidence increasing, 'by the manner in which the tanks were dealt with, but I wonder how effective that same technique would be against modern tanks?'

Mannerheim frowned at the question and said in excellent English, 'We may soon have the opportunity to find out.'

Surprised, Atkins glanced at Erko but the Marshal continued to speak.

'Our intelligence units report that Russian troops are massing along our Karelian border and in the north, opposite Petsamo. Massive quantities of bombs have been delivered to airfields near Leningrad. It has not yet been announced but Finland has agreed to the original Russian demands two days ago. But even so, the Russians have now presented new requirements and they are completely unacceptable. Perhaps they think that like the Baltic states, we will grovel in fear.'

'If you reject these demands, will it mean war?'

'Since 1920, the Soviets have worked to re-integrate Finland into the new "Russian Empire,"' he pronounced the phrase sarcastically, 'which they claim is Finland's historic destiny. After centuries as a vassal state of Sweden and then Russia, we freed ourselves in 1918 and will remain so at the cost of our lives. You may be assured that Finland is one in this matter.'

Atkins was not quite so certain, remembering a communist-sponsored demonstration the other day in the Market Square.

'How soon?' he asked, testing, and was surprised when the Marshal shrugged.

'In the spring, perhaps.'

Atkins was suddenly uneasy at the direction the conversation had taken. Why was the Marshal favouring him with this information? If he wished His Majesty's government to be so informed, surely he would do better to call in the British Minister. He hesitated a moment, then took a deep breath, conscious that he might well be gambling with his career.

'How can I be of service?'

All at once the atmosphere relaxed as Erko's face lit with delight and even the Marshal smiled.

'You see, it's like this,' Erko began. 'We have relayed this information to your Minister, of course. But we would be grateful if you would report separately to your own people, as if this were merely another briefing by the public information office. You may refer to this conversation with the Marshal, but only in the strictest confidence, you see?'

Good Lord! he thought. Erko is telling me that the Marshal does not trust our Foreign Office. What a bombshell that could turn out to be. And if the bomb went off, he could well become the first casualty! But then Atkins knew what happened when an inter-ministerial dispute had arisen over Poland; the Foreign Office had offered a blanket military assistance treaty while the Army was aghast at the sheer impossibility of all it implied.

And Bennet's cynical instructions that first night suggested it might be happening again. Atkins found himself faced with that crisis of conscience that all concerned diplomats are subjected to when forced to obey government policy though the result may be entirely inappropriate. It was clear now why he had been invited to the field exercises. Had the German officer been asked to make the same kind of report?

Seeing his hesitation, Mannerheim spoke again. 'We fully realize that your Government is preoccupied with the German menace to France and Belgium. We also realize that your first priorities for men and arms must go to your western front. But Finland is in great danger and we have only three choices. First, to meet the Russian demands. If we do, we will have taken our first step towards becoming a Russian province once again. Second, if we resist, the Russians will attack and we will become their satellite, in any event. Our third choice depends upon our friends. If Great Britain will assist us, the Russian bear must pause.' The Marshal's voice growled his last words. 'But whether you help or not, Finland will not again become a vassal state of Russia!'

Atkins decided to walk back to the British legation. There was a great deal to think about and the huge luncheon that followed the interview had left him groggy. Mannerheim had made it plain that if Britain did not offer assistance, Finland might turn to Germany. But the more he thought about that, the more he wondered how much of the threat was bluff. There was little enough for Germany to gain beyond tying down a few British troops in the north. He recalled the jitteriness he had left behind in Stockholm. The Swedes were so frightened they might become another Poland that it seemed at times as if they went out of their way to favour Germany.

In any event, the Marshal's request was consistent with his instructions to encourage – in any way that did not commit Great Britain – Finland to resist Russian demands.

Suomelina Fortress 30 November 1939

At 0630 on Thursday morning, 30 November 1939, his birthday, Atkins stamped up and down the Esplande as vendors set up stalls in the adjacent market square. There was a great deal of laughter as they worked in the icy wind. Two morose policemen stood watching, no happier about the below-freezing pre-dawn than Atkins. When Erko had telephoned the previous afternoon to invite him to see the Suomelina Fortress, he had been tempted to beg off. Now he wished to God he had done so, even though he was certain there was more to the appointment than a simple sightseeing tour.

South Harbour was as dark as the sky. A grey warship bulked against the overcast, steam wisping from its single stack. As he watched, a long rifle in the forward turret moved smoothly skyward.

'I hope I haven't kept you waiting long.' Captain Johan Erko, wrapped in a field-grey overcoat that made him look like a German officer, clapped him on the shoulder and steered him along the wharf. 'Bracing day!'

The nondescript ferry took them out of the sheltered anchorage into the teeth of a wind that knifed through his own overcoat as if it were tissue paper. In spite of the early hour, there were several other passengers including two young boys in naval officers' uniforms.

'Cadets,' Erko explained. 'Our naval training academy is on the island. The rest of the people are probably workers going to work or home.'

'Workers?'

'Yes. The island is large and quite a few people live there. It is especially attractive to those who do not like the city noise.'

The sky began to lighten with approaching dawn and tall cranes along the wharfs emerged from the gloom. The merchant ships of a dozen countries were in port, in spite of the war scare. There was even one ship defiantly flying the now-defunct merchant marine ensign of Poland. They passed small islands with houses and other buildings. On one, a house seemed to disappear into the island itself. A large red dome and siren were mounted on the roof.

'Harbour fire department,' Erko commented.

The Fortress of Suomelina was still hidden by the gloom when the ferry pointed its bow towards a rickety pier. They tied up alongside and the passengers disembarked quickly, anxious to get out of the wind. An elderly man unlocked a bicycle chained to a post and wobbled off along the narrow mud road. The two Naval cadets trudged off the pier and turned right towards a low brick building.

Erko glanced at his watch. 'I am afraid the café will not open for another thirty minutes. Shall we begin your tour of the Gibraltar of the North?' He took two deep breaths and strode briskly along the mud road towards a high, rather medieval wall. As they passed through the arched gate, Atkins saw the rusted tips of a spiked portcullis and was reminded of the entrance to Warwick Castle in England which he had often visited as a boy. They passed into an inner keep where the ground sloped away to the right. Ahead was another wall with a lower, smaller gate. Above he heard a baby crying and looked up to see a woman framed by a window cut into the wall as she bounced a baby. Smoke issued from a chimney beside the window. Parts of the wall, he was surprised to see, towered fifteen feet.

Erko chuckled at his expression. 'The walls are quite thick and formerly served as barracks for the garrison. Now they are used as low-rent flats for residents of the island, many of whom work in Helsinki.'

The inner gate opened onto an immense square. Buff brick buildings in the graceful style reminiscent of eighteenth-century Sweden surrounded it on three sides and had once served as administrative and officers' quarters, he surmised. In the centre of the square was a polished bronze monument of arms and armour.

'It was designed by Gustavus III,' Erko gestured, 'and is the grave of Marshal Count Ehrensvard who built the fortress in 1749.'

The fog had begun to clear in the time that they had crossed the island. In the east, towards Russia, a reddish hue signalled the sun's struggle to clear the endless pine and birch forest of Karelia. They climbed a bulwark that looked out over the Gulf of Finland twinkling with the firefly lights of thousands of homes scattered among the islands.

Erko slapped a huge, bottle-shaped cannon mounted on a rusted trunnion. The bronze gun had long ago turned as black as iron in the corrosive sea air and Atkins guessed that it had menaced shipping within its three-mile range since the time of the long-dead Count.

'This is my favourite place in all of Finland to watch the dawn. Here, I think one has a sense of the Finnish spirit of *sisu*. Many Finns will tell you that I am wrong, that the true spirit of Finland is deep in the forests and lakes. Perhaps. But here, on the coast, it reaches its fullest expression. Finns have been sailors as long as they have been woodsmen. The sea and the forest are very much alike, both enjoining silence and strength.

'We Finns are very isolated. To the west is our second oldest enemy, Sweden. In the north, a narrow bit of land owned by Norway separates us from the sea. In the east,' Erko paused to study the brightening horizon, 'is our greatest enemy, Russia. In fact, so great is our hatred of Russia that in 1904, Finns changed their last names to Finnish to protest against the suppression of our language and culture. Only *sisu* sustained us then and will sustain us in the future.'

Atkins had heard the term *sisu* before and knew it had to do with courage. But when he mentioned that, Erko shook his head.

'*Sisu* means a great deal more than that, my friend. It means self-discipline, stubbornness, and an innate sense of right and wrong. Our great composer, Sibelius, calls it a "metaphysical shot in the arm which makes a man do the impossible". It means that once a Finn decides on a correct course, he never deviates from it for one instant and so if there is a war with Russia we will not give up. The fighting will not cease until the Russians are vanquished or we are destroyed as a people.'

He faced Atkins. 'That is the reason for bringing you here today, not to show you a useless fort, built by one oppressor to stave off another.'

Atkins nodded. He would have been disappointed otherwise.

'We have now received an answer to the note handed to your

Minister by the President of Finland. I will not mince words. Your government has refused to help. There will be no aid and no soldiers. They will talk in the League of Nations, but nothing more.'

Atkins muttered a curse under his breath.

'The Russians, of course, will know the answer and will attack soon; perhaps by the end of December. We do not believe they will now wait for spring. Three days ago they cancelled the non-aggression pact. We then announced our intention to withdraw our troops to lines twenty-five kilometres from the border, but the Russians ignored the offer. They severed diplomatic relations last night and ordered our Ambassador to leave Moscow.'

Erko tried to gauge Atkins' expression. 'Germany has suggested a mutual aid pact.'

'Germany? That would be in direct violation of their non-aggression pact with the Soviet Union?'

Erko gave a bitter laugh. 'How?' he asked. 'They have not offered to fight Russia, only to supply us with the arms and material to use against an aggressor. Russia claims she is not an aggressor. Even so, the Germans know the time will come when they must fight the Russians again. Herr Hitler has made that clear in his own book, *Mein Kampf* – if you wish to understand Nazi Germany, I suggest you read it, terribly boring as it is. Russia wants our territory for military bases to protect herself against the Germans and, naturally, the Germans would prefer we not give in. So, we become a small battle in a larger war.'

'What do you wish from me?'

For a moment, Atkins thought Erko had blushed but decided it was only the dawn hue reflecting from his smooth-shaven face. 'The Marshal will meet with the British and French ministers today. But we already know what their answer will be. The Marshal requests that you again inform your War Ministry of Finland's position and intentions.'

Atkins was astounded at the audacity of the request. He found it difficult to believe that they would ask him to jeopardize his entire career. Good God, he thought, was this really a measure of their desperation? The Finns were exploring every possible avenue, leaving no measure, no matter how unlikely, untried. And this must be the least potentially productive of them all. What the devil did they expect that he, a mere Captain, could say to sway Whitehall?

He turned away, trying to reason it out. Bennet had told him in no uncertain terms that the Finns were to be encouraged in any way that aided, but did not commit, Great Britain. If Erko's assessment were correct, that Nazi support might cause the Russians to draw back, then Finland would be committed to support Germany when and if the Nazi war machine was unleashed on Russia. If so, might not British support accomplish the same objective? A blind man could see that Whitehall was only waiting for the Germans to attack Russia to offer her an alliance. Finland, as a British ally also, would then provide a position from which to attack Germany on her northern flank. Perhaps the gamble was worth it after all.

'I'll give it another try,' he said quietly.

Erko grasped his hand fervently and tried to speak. Atkins, always embarrassed by displays of sentiment, and particularly now when it was so undeserved, stamped his feet and looked away. 'My God, it's cold!' he exclaimed. 'Isn't that café open yet?'

They trudged across the snow-dusted lawn before the old officers' barracks. Ancient oaks towered about them, stark against the reddish sky as they walked into the square where buff- and blue-clad soldiers with heavy muskets and tri-cornered hats had paraded, and now schoolchildren ran and tumbled like brightly coloured leaves in warm snowsuits and red gumboots. The children clustered about the two soldiers, shouting questions and laughing. Erko made jokes and the children followed them in marching order, laughing and shouting, to the gate where a teacher smiled at the men and children in turn.

The café was open and the air was full of cooking odours, cloying after the sharpness of the winter morning. They shed overcoats and Erko ordered bacon and eggs and the waitress, a fresh-faced young girl with short blonde hair, brought them a pot of coffee and a plate piled high with toast.

'Enjoy the eggs. You will find them only in the bigger cities of the south. Chickens will not lay in our dark winter months and few wish to bother with them for the few weeks of summer. These were probably imported.'

The cold air had sharpened their appetites and they ate as fast as the waitress brought the dishes of food. She reappeared in time to refill their cups, slipped into a winter coat, picked up a school satchel and ran out.

Neither man said much as they ate; each occupied with his own thoughts. Atkins was thinking about the reception a second report that contradicted the Foreign Office would receive in London. He thought he had already detected a hint of coolness from the Minister and certain of the ranking staff members. An officer was expected to demonstrate sound judgement and the silence with which his previous report had been received made it clear that his opinions were not welcome. Yet the more he thought about it, the more certain he became that. . . .

A series of dull booms rolled across the harbour and Atkins put down his coffee cup. Erko turned just as a second set of explosions rattled the windows. Both men raced outside. The café faced the pier and the ferry had just tied up; Atkins caught a glimpse of their waitress staring across the harbour to where a column of black smoke rose. Without warning, the ragged scream of twin-engined bombers, flying very low, blasted across the water towards the city. The sun was well up now and he could see a second squadron of bombers in tight formation approaching. The red star insignia was plain on their wings and he heard Erko curse. As the airplanes crossed the city, dozens of black specks tumbled from each and cyclones of flame erupted in their wake.

Atkins shuddered, recalling the terror and stench of the bomb shelters in Warsaw. He glanced at his watch in reflex: 0812. War had come to Finland.

The bombing had ended by the time the ferry docked in South Harbour. Erko left him at the wharf with a mumbled apology and disappeared into the crowd. The ferry's whistle blasted sharply, ending the stunned silence. Curiously enough, neither the Market nor Suutori Squares had been hit by a single bomb. The slim girl in bronze at the west end of the market still gazed out towards the harbour, untroubled. Atkins wandered the length of the Esplande momentarily at a loss.

He had watched the bombing with Erko as the ferry waddled towards the white city and even though he had seen it all before in Warsaw, he was still struck with horror at the damage visible from the Esplande. To his left the sun struck gold from stone and brick shops across the boulevard and gilded the smoking pile of masonry that blocked one entire street; an office building blown inside out by a direct hit. As in Warsaw, he was angered at the obscene nakedness of a building thus exposed. A fire in the block behind shot up a thick pillar of black smoke. It was only later that Atkins heard that the fire departments had responded at the first air-raid alarms and fought the blazes all during the bombing.

The city began to wake from its shock. People appeared from doorways and buildings and a policeman shepherded them together, checking to see that no one was injured. It was the bombing without warning of a defenceless city that stunned one so, he thought. Nothing that happened to him in the war afterwards ever engendered such an intense feeling of anger as did the bombing of Helsinki.

Atkins sensed the feeling in people around him that he had first noted in Warsaw. The bombing did not demoralize the civilian population but, in fact, hardened their will to resist. Long after there was no further reason to do so, the citizens of Warsaw had fought on, driven only by their hatred.

He thought he saw that same resolve already appearing on faces he passed in the street. People hurried towards fires to help, not to gawk. Rescue parties formed spontaneously and taxis shut off their service lamps and served as emergency vehicles. Restaurants fed anyone who was hungry and people stopped one another on the streets to offer help. Would it last? he wondered. It had in Warsaw.

While Atkins worked well into the evening on the report, Russian bombers returned twice to bomb Helsinki. At six o'clock, he went down to the radio room where the rest of the staff had gathered to listen to the English language news broadcast from Moscow.

'Provocative attacks by Finnish infantry and artillery on Soviet border installations had been turned back at great cost to the invaders,' Moscow radio reported, 'and Finnish aircraft had attempted to bomb Leningrad. The Soviet Union had no other choice than to react against the bandit Finnish government.'

Also mentioned was Finland's rejection of a generous Soviet offer, designed expressly to avoid hostilities. The commentator's voice was full of sorrow as he noted that the Finns had chosen to give their answer in bandit attacks on peaceful Soviet villages. His voice harshened when he reported that the Red Army and Air Forces had pledged to wipe out this stain on Soviet honour, but would do so with restraint as they realized that the government of Finland did not represent the will of the Finnish people who desired only peace.

Atkins noted wryly that Russian restraint had not prevented bombs from falling on the peace-loving Finnish proletariat's collective heads.

On the BBC news at nine, it was reported that Foreign Minister Molotov had been asked by foreign correspondents to explain Russian bombing of open cities without a declaration of war. Molotov, never at a loss, had blandly replied that the Russian bombers were merely dropping food parcels to the starving cities. The following day, Finnish newpapers dubbed Russian bombs, 'Molotov Food Baskets'.

The evacuation of women and children to the countryside began the first day. In the noon raid, Soviet pilots concentrated on the Helsinki railway station and forty people were killed. The Technical Institute had been wrecked by a bomb and several people had died and apartment houses were demolished as the raids concentrated on the working-class districts. Incendiary bombs were scattered widely across Helsinki and the coastal cities of Viipuri and Turku were also bombed as was the power plant at Imatra – a former country retreat of Tsar Nicholas II – and the gas-mask factory at Lahti in the interior.

Lake Ladoga 15 – 20 December 1939

Two weeks to the day after the first bombing raid, Atkins received a telephone call asking him to come to the War Department. Snow had fallen that morning, the first really heavy snowfall of the winter, and the White City was shrouded by lowering grey clouds which were a more effective camouflage than man could devise, Atkins thought as the taxi edged through the streets. After the initial onslaught, the Russian bombing campaign had been slowed by poor weather. The Finns had managed to keep up with the damage and except for a building here or there showing a hole too large to be boarded up or a last pile of smashed stone and brick not yet carted away, there was little evidence to show what the city had endured.

An orderly conducted Atkins directly to Erko's office whom he had last seen striding off the wharf two weeks before. Erko smiled and stood to shake hands, strain showing in his drawn face.

'Ah, Captain Atkins. I trust the war has not caused you severe discomfort?'

'Not at all. But I think Finland has suffered a bit.'

Erko waved a hand in dismissal. 'Perhaps but, as you say, only a bit. Believe it or not, it is Russia who is being discomforted.' In spite of his obvious exhaustion, Erko was freshly shaved and his uniform pressed to knife-edge creases.

Atkins smiled politely.

'You don't believe me? How strange. Come, we will go down to the operations room.'

Surprised, Atkins followed Erko to the elevator. When the door opened, he saw a guard with a machine pistol watching them carefully.

The room was huge and the walls covered with maps. Erko led him to where a young woman in the blue uniform of the *Lotta Svard* was sticking pins into a map as she consulted a list. Erko greeted her in Finnish and she laughed and held up another black pin before inserting it into a map.

'This map shows the district around Lake Ladoga,' Erko explained. 'Blue pins are Finn, Red are the Soviets and the black signify a Soviet unit destroyed.' He said this last with such relish that Atkins grinned.

'In the first week, the Muscovites' Eighth Army of nine divisions, including one tank brigade, made a two-pronged attack towards Dtikaranta and Suojarvi, here above the lake.' He tapped an area where black pins clustered. 'We threw them back with two divisions and a regiment further north at Joensu. Soviet losses were heavy. They have attacked a number of times now but have got nowhere. They even dropped parachutists but we managed to kill most before they reached the ground.'

Erko did not fail to note Atkins' expression. 'They have invaded our country to kill our people,' he said in a grim voice. 'And they did so without a declaration of war. Even if the high command were inclined to order our soldiers not to fire on parachutists while in the air, they would not obey.'

Atkins remained silent. He would have expected the Nazis to shoot parachutists as a matter of course. Hadn't they dive-bombed and machine-gunned refugees to create panic and interfere with Polish army movements? But the Finns?

Guernica, Shanghai, Warsaw. The distinction was no longer made between soldier and non-combatant. Today, the individual was little more than a unit of production – and wasn't the objective of modern warfare to destroy the enemy's ability to produce and thus wage war? Therefore, it followed that one must destroy the enemy population to win. In such a context, the shooting of parachutists dangling helplessly beneath silk canopies made practical, if not moral, sense. Kill them before they reached the ground and killed you or your fellow countrymen. Silently he observed to himself that no matter how long one had been a soldier, the reality of war and death always came as a shock.

The story was the same on all fronts, from the Gulf of Finland north to Kuolojarvi. Only in the far north at Petsamo, had the Soviet Fourteenth Army of three divisions made any headway. They had captured the town, defended by a single battalion of Civic Guards who had burned it to the ground before retreating.

It dawned on Atkins as Erko talked that the Soviets had been stopped cold on the borders. Nowhere had they made a significant breakthrough. The meagre Finnish air force had even dealt a severe blow to the Russian bomber fleet and that, coupled with the bad weather, had drastically reduced the number of bombing sorties the Russians were able to fly.

From Petsamo in the Arctic to Viipuri on the Gulf of Finland, Russian losses must be staggering. Finnish casualties were reported to be exceptionally light and Atkins could not help the scepticism that crept into his expression.

Erko said nothing but traced the border with a finger and spoke with uncharacteristic animation. 'If we can hold them until the snows begin in earnest, we can hold through the winter. Then in the spring, after fearful losses, perhaps the Russian bear will be glad to negotiate. Until then, there is a Finnish word that best describes the tactics we use, *Moti*, which means a stack of wood, ready for chopping. That is how we see the Muscovites.'

This time Atkins' scepticism was evident. 'Captain, I realize that it is bad manners for a guest to disagree with his host but. . . .'

Erko held up a hand and grinned. 'Please. Perhaps I was carried away. But, it is true. We are doing more than holding our own. To convince you, I have obtained permission from the Marshal for you to visit the front and see for yourself. I myself returned from the Petsamo Front only two days ago.' He held out his hands and spread his fingers and Atkins saw the bluish bruises and patches of frostbite around the finger tips.

'I have been at a desk for so long that I grew a bit careless. Painful, but not serious.'

The offer took Atkins by surprise. Every military attaché in Helsinki was trying to obtain permission to go to the front. All had been routinely denied – a normal state of affairs at the start of any military engagement. The press had also been restricted and were becoming vociferous in their complaints.

'What is more,' Erko continued, 'you will be given carte-blanche to travel wherever you like and see whatever you wish, without interference, subject only to normal military security. How does that strike you?'

Shivering in a Finnish ski parka and white overalls, Atkins flogged his aching legs on as they made their way towards the front in the area to the north of Lake Laadogga. Snow drifted silently among the leafless birch and hardly a breath of wind disturbed the stillness. He was struck once more at how limited visibility was in the forest, even in winter. A Russian patrol could be lying less than fifty feet away, undetected until they opened fire.

His guide did not speak English and he was feeling isolated, sorry for himself and quite exhausted. They had been travelling since 0600 and his watch now showed 1300 hours. They had stopped once only to brew strong tea and eat a tasteless mixture of dried meat and berries. Atkins had learned to ski on winter holidays in the Swiss and Italian Alps, but this business of sliding through level forest for hours on skis so long and slender as to be almost unmanageable was exhausting. The handful of tasteless meat, suet and berries was almost an insult, even if the Finns did eat their ration stoically. Only after they were moving again did he feel the trickle of energy seep into his flagging body. The meat furnished protein, the fat carbohydrates and the dried fruit sugar.

The sky was visible above the bare birches but the snow and the heavy cloud rendered only an opalescent light that heightened the featurelessness of the woods. Without his compass, he would have been hopelessly lost as soon as the snorting post bus that had dropped them on the nearest road, twenty miles back, had disappeared. He noticed that even the woods-wise Finns depended on their compasses for direction. And, as the brief period of daylight waned, the light deepened, increasing the doom and sense of foreboding that was building in him and which he blamed on his Celtic ancestry.

Darkness came at 1500 hours but he was surprised to discover that sky glow reflecting from the new snow provided sufficient light to distinguish large objects.

Another hour brought them to a clearing. The sergeant held up a hand and whistled the first bars of *An American in Paris*. The answering whistle was from another Gershwin tune and a moment later, white-clad troopers materialized about them with startling suddenness and the march resumed. Ten minutes later, they reached a clearing around which squatted a series of huts looking for all the world like American pioneer cabins he had seen in pictures. Two men stood before one, talking, and they broke off to greet the newcomers. Both were officers and one, a tall, youthful looking man with a reddish beard, was introduced to him in Finnish by the sergeant.

'So, an English officer,' the Finn smiled. 'Sergeant Pulhamani tells me I am to show you anything you wish.' His English was quite good and Atkins was relieved that he no longer had to resort to a mixture of sign language and German.

'Right now, I prefer to see a stove,' Atkins muttered.

The translated remark drew a shout of laughter. 'They say,' the officer told Atkins, 'that the English aren't so foolish after all.'

He led the way into one of the cabins. The interior, fifteen feet on a side, was lined with triple-layered bunks. Near the huge fireplace in which, strangely enough, a sheet metal stove glowed, was a long table on which sat a wireless-transmitter.

'The wood burns better in the stove and there is much less smoke and so we are safe from Ivan's airplanes,' the Finn explained in one breath. 'You are hungry?'

An enlisted man brought them tin plates of stew and thick slices of fresh bread. A steaming mug of tea liberally laced with vodka was added. They found an unoccupied bunk on which to sit down and the officer introduced himself as Lieutenant Arvo Halkala, from the Petsamo district. 'I am regular army officer commanding the Sixth Company of the Twelfth Division,' he grinned, 'so they send me where they want. I am of more help in north, I think, but Marshal Mannerheim, he thinks differently. Now we eat, then sleep. Tomorrow early, we go on patrol. If you will like to come, I will give you rifle to protect yourself.'

Atkins remembered the Minister's frosty admonition as he left the legation. 'Do not allow yourself to be captured in a compro-

126

mising situation. Please remember that Great Britain is neutral, no matter how much you deplore that situation.' It was not, however, the possibility of being captured or killed that made him hesitate but the state of his leg muscles.

'Yes, of course I'll come. But without the rifle, thank you.'

A rough hand shook Atkins awake and a steaming mug of tea was thrust at him. When he swung his feet to the icy boards, he could not find his boots. Groaning, he knelt to peer under the bunk and a soldier laughed and pointed to a shelf above the fireplace where a dozen boots were neatly lined up. Atkins found and drew his on, certain that he had never felt anything so pleasurable in his life as the warmth flowed into his aching feet.

The patrol moved off through the trees at 0400 and the only sound was the thin whisper of metal-edged skis against crystalline snow. The moon was sinking fast in the west but there was still sufficient light to see by. Atkins knew generally that they were moving south towards Lake Laadogga. Erko had told him that in January when the lake was sufficiently frozen, it would offer a broad highway to Leningrad and so the original Russian demands had included sufficient land west of the lake to establish a wide frontier.

They were about five kilometres from the Russian frontier, Halkala had told him. The border itself was marked only by a few weatherbeaten signs in Finnish and Russian. Miles of forest on either side were as effective against the Russians but the Finns regarded the forest as an active ally. The forest and the cold – the thermometer at the camp had registered twenty degrees of frost.

They travelled fast and without rest for two hours. Atkins' leg muscles quivered with strain and his lungs ached with the icy, moistureless air. His body functioned by reflex and he was barely aware of light seeping through the forest and the darkness retreating sullenly beneath the trees.

When the light began to fade into winter twilight, Halkala called a halt. Six men were sent out in different directions to serve as sentries. The others began to clear spaces beneath fir trees, careful not to disturb the snow facing east. Halkala chose a large spruce whose branches brushed the snow. He thrust the lower ones aside and when Atkins crawled in after him, saw that the lower branches formed a loose roof. There wasn't room to stand but he could sit quite comfortably.

While Halkala and his sergeant studied a map, Atkins broke out the Primus stove he had bought in Stockholm. He loosened the fuel tank cap and tipped just enough white gas out to fill the depression about the top of the tank.

His stiff fingers gave him trouble lighting the stove but finally the gasoline flared then steadied to a blue flame. Atkins waited a moment, loosened the key with a gloved hand and was rewarded by the faint hiss of escaping vapour. A moment later, the stove caught and he put a canteen cup full of snow on to melt.

When they finished the tea, the sergeant crawled away to his own position. Halkala took a shelter-half from his pack, placed it on the snow, and lay down. Atkins followed suit and Halkala drew his shelter-half across their backs and swept snow over both of them. He then pushed his white rucksack into place to serve as a rest, laid the rifle on top and checked his sights. He cocked the bolt and set the safety and Atkins found the whispery snick of metal on metal unnerving.

'Now we wait,' Halkala muttered.

The clearing was silent. The snow had stopped and the forest brooded. The brief daylight of mid-winter seeped away. Atkins discovered that he was warmer than he had been on the march. The rubberized shelter half prevented the snow from melting into his winter clothing and the padded uniform and white snow smock insulated him from the chill. Halkala passed him half a ration of dried meat, suet and fruit. Atkins had quickly learned that keeping warm was as much a matter of energy levels as proper clothing, and needed no urging to eat.

It occurred to him to wonder why this particular clearing had been chosen for the ambush. As best he could determine, there was nothing to distinguish it from any other. Darkness had fallen before a shape materialized beside their tree and muttered in Finnish. Halkala's white teeth gleamed and he pointed. Atkins stared, then shifted his head so that he was looking at the area from the corner of his eye. Only then did he catch a hint of movement and a shock of fear surged through him, surprising in its intensity.

Shadows moved against the trees and for a moment, he thought his eyes must be playing tricks until one separated from a tree and moved towards them and Atkins saw the rifle across his back. As he drew closer, Atkins saw that he was also wearing a heavy, padded coat, ungainly felt boots wrapped round with yards of cloth in makeshift puttees and a fur cap. The Russian tramped forward, head down, his attitude a clear indication of his exhaustion. More figures took on substance and he felt a movement beside him as Halkala aimed his rifle.

The rifle shot shattered the stillness and instantly, a sheet of flame swept the Russians. Vague figures fell, others froze. A second volley smashed into them and they broke and ran. The shadows were full of howling, thrashing figures as another fusillade tore from the flank and muzzle flashes lit the clearing like summer sheet lightning. A few of the steadier Russian soldiers knelt and returned fire but were soon cut down by the repeated volleys. Halkala shouted at him to remain hidden and was gone. Muzzle flashes showed that the Finns were pursuing the fleeing Russians, worrying them from the flanks, herding them like cattle into a slaughter house, then the noise began to dwindle, indicating how hard the demoralized Russians were running. Atkins watched the clearing where he could see the dark shapes of several bodies, one or two of which still moved.

My God, he thought, they'll freeze to death. He got to his knees, undecided. He was unarmed and alone. He hesitated, castigating himself for his cowardice. Men were dying out there and it did no good to tell himself that was what war was about. A whistle blew in the distance and the gunfire died away.

He crouched beneath the tree branches, trying to see into the gloom and found that he was shaking. He gulped and struggled to keep from vomiting. He was afraid, almost sick with fear! Why? He had been under fire before, in Warsaw and Helsinki. Why hadn't he been afraid then? Because, his mind told him, artillery shells and bombs were entirely impersonal in their selection. Here it was different. These were armed men who would shoot him without a second thought. He was indistinguishable from a Finnish soldier and the random element was eliminated and that frightened him terribly.

Atkins lay sleepless a long time that night in his bunk, struggling to understand this new and unexpected facet of his character. To say that he was miserable was an understatement. He discovered that he was as frightened of being frightened as he was of being maimed or dying in action. Although he had served ten years in the British army, not once had he ever come under direct enemy fire. Traditionally, regular British officers received their initiation into combat on the North-west Frontier of India. But his baptism in 1935 had been denied when the army attaché to the British Embassy in Greece had gone sick as he reached Rome on his way to India.

Atkins had just been posted to the staff college at Quetta after which he had expected to join his own regiment, the Fourth Hussars, in Egypt. He was diverted instead to Greece, temporarily, but the posting became permanent when he was shifted to Spain and then Italy before being sent to Poland in early 1939.

After a while, the cabin began to give up its warmth. The door opened and closed quickly and a blast of frigid air swept the single room. Quiet words were exchanged and the door opened and closed again. Change of sentries, he thought. He could feel himself relaxing, the hard knot of fear in his stomach easing. It was over. Tomorrow or the next day, he would go back to Helsinki, back to where the only danger was from bombs that fell sporadically on the city. Back where luck could be supplemented by common sense and the danger of being killed or maimed by a bomb was less than that of crossing Trafalgar Square at rush hour.

'Saturday is bath day in Finland,' Lieutenant Halkala told him. 'But first, we must review yesterday's operation.' He gathered the members of the previous day's patrol about the table and gently kidded their only casualty, a soldier struck a glancing blow by a Russian grenade fragment.

They ran through the operation, identifying deficiencies as well as points of strength, much like a Rugby team studying their performance the day following a game. Between the bits and pieces of Finnish that Atkins had picked up and the Lieutenant's brief translations for his benefit, he got the idea that the Russians, stopped cold by strong Finnish positions along the Lake, had tried to infiltrate a battalion of infantry further north. He confirmed Atkins' suspicion that they had been well inside Russia when they had achieved complete surprise and routed a Russian force nearly a hundred times their size. They had killed, by actual count, an incredible 112 soldiers. Many more, wounded and unwounded, would die from exposure as they wandered through the wilderness of trees and frozen swamps.

'That is the Russian Army's greatest problem,' Halkala told him afterwards when they stepped out into the crisp morning air to smoke. Pale light filtered through the trees relieving the dour quality of the forest and snowflakes trickled from an empty sky. Atkins thought he was beginning to understand where the brooding quality in Sibelius's *Finlandia* derived.

'These Russians are not woodsmen. They are city people or collective farmers, which is to say not farmers at all, but workers whose factory happens to be a farm. The real Russian woodsmen, the people who could meet us on our own terms, live deep in Siberia and have no wish to fight or even to have much to do with their government.'

He extinguished the cigarette in the snow and dropped the soggy remains in a pocket. 'So many do not even know how to make a fire. A week ago, we came across a patrol of ten Ivans, all frozen to death. They were sitting about one soldier who had tried to light a fire of green wood.' Halkala shook his head. 'That is why we will win, even though there are so many of them. We only fear that we may run out of bullets first.'

Later, a soldier came to the desk where Atkins was drafting a report and gave him an uncharacteristically snappy salute.

The soldier held his nose and made a face. 'Sauna,' he pronounced carefully and looked at Atkins. The message was clear as he had not been out of his clothes since leaving Helsinki a week before.

He followed the soldier to a small shed further back in the trees. The snow was banked nearly to the roof but an entry way had been cleared to the door. Two soldiers waited for them outside. Atkins gaped. The temperature was below zero but both men were naked while even in his padded uniform, Atkins was shivering. Their only concession to the snow was to stand on their jackets. His guide began to undress and motioned for him to do so and the others waited patiently. The air whipped his bare skin and soldiers laughed at his expression. He was handed a fir branch and led inside.

The abrupt change in temperature of more than a hundred degrees left him gasping. The superheated air burned his nose and throat, seared his eyes and his skin reddened as blood pumped to the surface. A pine branch soaked in water smacked him across the backside. A soldier, grinning like a demon in the red glow, belaboured them all with the wet branches and to his surprise, he felt no pain, only an intense tingling.

Two levels of benches lined the heat-dark walls and the smell of birch was pungent and soothing. His guide indicated that he was to lie down, which he did gingerly. The hot wood stung for a moment and heat enclosed his head like a glove. A dipper of water was thrown onto heated rocks and steam exploded. His skin felt as if it were crackling.

The three Finns clambered onto the higher level and lay prone, then lifted their legs from the hips and hooked them over a wooden beam fitted below the ceiling. Atkins was persuaded to do the same and at once, scalding air seared his feet, blood rushed to his head and sweat popped on his skin. More water was thrown onto the stones and a fine steam suffused the air. Atkins was content to lie quietly; eyes closed to eliminate the ludicrous picture of four men hanging by their heels from a pole like so many sides of beef. His muscles grew limp and his troubles vanished.

He was almost asleep when someone shook his arm. Atkins sat up too quickly and vertigo made his head spin. A last cup of water fell on the hot stones and heat seared his skin. The door was thrown open, someone pushed him and before he knew what had happened, he flopped headlong into the powdery snow. But the excruciating shock never came. He sat up and ran a hand through the snow which he could feel as a substance, neither hot nor cold.

Instead, an electric tension crackled along his nerves, a pleasant sensation that filled him with a child's energy. With a whoop of laughter, he did another bellyflop.

Helsinki 5 – 7 January 1940

December faded into January as the sparse Christmas season rushed past. Atkins had written and submitted another thirty-page report on his experiences with the Finns but again no word had come from London praising or admonishing. He was certain that his previous report had a great deal to do with the frosty silence.

In the meantime, it was becoming clear that the Russians had taken on more than they had anticipated. They were being badly beaten by the tiny Finnish army on every one of the five fronts. The foreign press from Berlin to Sofia, from New York to Paris clamoured for help for the beleaguered Finns. Thousands of committees sprang up and gathered millions of pounds of aid.

Atkins wondered at the stubbornness of the men in London and Paris, Stockholm and Oslo who stood against military assistance to Finland even as the Soviet Union found herself isolated by world opinion. Even foreign communist parties, still in disarray from the shock of the Nazi–Soviet Pact of the past summer, were mute. Several regiments of the British army volunteered en masse to fight in Finland. Norwegian and Swedish volunteer units paid their own expenses to join the fighting in spite of orders from their governments to the contrary. Winston Churchill proposed that the British Government enter into negotiations with the Norwegians to use the North Sea coastal town of Narvik as a base for landing supplies to be sent overland into Finland.

But Atkins doubted the Norwegians would agree. Swedish iron ore shipments went through Narvik and down the coastal lanes in German merchant ships to the Skagerrak. If those shipments were endangered in any way, Germany had made it quite plain that she would take measures to protect them. Anything from a U-boat picket to invasion was possible.

The greatest demand for aid to Finland came from the United States and that surprised all of Europe. The Americans had resisted all blandishments to become involved in the struggle with Germany, but now the American press was indignant that Great Britain and France stood by while the Scandinavian countries blocked passage of so much as a single bullet in the face of clear aggression by the Soviet Union. Atkins tossed the papers down and paced the room. He felt confined, helpless to do anything, to get even the simplest message across. He knew that he was being punished for his earlier presumption but there was nothing he could do about it now but write more reports. At times, the urge to request that he be returned to his regiment was overwhelming; but the cold memory of his paralysing terror made him hesitate for fear that he would freeze in combat.

The invitation to attend a reception for a famous Finnish runner who had broken the world record for the 10,000 metre race only that past summer and who had distinguished himself at the front was for Friday evening. And so, clad in dress uniform, Atkins trudged up the steps of the massive Parliament building. At the top, he turned to look at the blacked-out city. Intermittent clouds scuttered across the full moon. Russian bombers would come tonight, he thought, as moonlight glinted on the Cathedral, surprisingly untouched. A limousine stopped below and a porter's electric torch flicked across a national pennant mounted on a mudguard – the Nazi swastika. Protocol required that diplomatic representatives of warring nations meeting accidentally on neutral ground ignore the other's presence in public. He turned abruptly and went inside.

The sudden change from frost and darkness to warmth and light as he stepped through the black-out curtains was startling. He stood blinking for a moment and a smiling young woman in the uniform of the *Lotta Svard* – the women's auxiliary of the Civic Guard – introduced herself with a firm handshake, as Erika Brotherus. She was to be his guide and interpreter for the evening. She seemed somewhat familiar, he thought as she noted the entry of the Germans, and steered him quickly into the reception hall.

The reception line moved quickly but still Atkins had a good look at the guest of honour. He was surprised at the young man's haggard expression and staring eyes, at the way his gaze continually flicked about the room as if expecting someone to jump at him. He had read that the Finn, now an army officer, was also an accomplished skier. Two weeks before, he had led a small patrol to ambush a Russian supply column. Eight tanks, twelve lorries and the lives of seventy-nine Russians had been forfeited at the cost of one Finnish soldier. Like the patrol in which he had participated, the action had taken place well behind Russian lines, east of Viipuri, and the survivors had travelled non-stop for three days to elude their Russian pursuers. The Finn acknowledged him with a glassy stare and, a moment later, Atkins found himself shaking hands with Marshal Mannerheim. The Marshal eyed him with only the barest trace of recognition and Erika Brotherus led him to the refreshment table.

'Please,' she smiled and offered him a glass of some deep red liquor, 'try this. It is a special Finnish drink called *Mesimarja*, which is distilled from bramble berries that grow where the forest has burned away in Lapland. It is said that the ash of the birch gives it a rich flavour.'

Atkins raised the glass in toast to the girl and she dimpled. He noticed how young and pretty she was as her eyes flashed with the excitement of attending the reception. The liquor was deep and sweet, perhaps too much so for his taste but he complimented her on the choice anyway.

'What do you do?' Atkins asked, indicating her uniform. 'I am a *Lotta Svard*,' she told him with pride. 'We are volunteers and serve in any capacity that will free a man to fight at the front. I drove a motor lorry before Captain Erko asked me to serve on the General Staff. Now I maintain the situation maps.'

Atkins remembered then where he had seen the girl before. He mentioned the fact that she had been tending the maps the day he had met with Marshal Mannerheim.

'Yes, I remember you,' she smiled. Then in a serious voice, 'You are perhaps the only foreigner who has seen those maps since the war began.'

Atkins had been keeping an eye on the three smartly clad German officers as they progressed through the line. One was large, extremely well built and his uniform with its exaggerated riding-style breeches set off his figure. He was an older man, probably in his fifties, Atkins thought, with artillery straps on his shoulders. The second man wore the blue Luftwaffe uniform and he was smaller and more compact. His high peaked cap was tucked under one arm and every few seconds, he fidgeted with it, either rubbing the glossy bill or shifting it about from one arm to the other. The last man was overweight and his white diplomatic uniform looked as if it were choking him. The purple shade that flowed upward from his tightly-encased neck darkened as he bowed to the Marshal.

Erika Brotherus noticed his expression but the French military attaché sidled up before she could say anything.

'Lovely sight aren't they,' he mumbled and nodded in their direction.

'Overdressed, I should think.' Atkins and the French military attaché, Major André Gide, had got to know one another quite well since his return from Paris. Gide tapped a cigarette on his thumbnail. 'You know, I often think we may be fighting the wrong enemy,' he said as he eyed Erika with appreciation. 'Perhaps we should conclude an alliance with the Boche and eliminate our Russian acquaintances. One day they will come pouring out of their swamps and forests and overrun us all.'

Atkins snorted. 'I don't see that ever happening.' It was on the tip of his tongue to say more but he wisely refrained. Except for Gide's propensity to view European power politics in terms of the 1840s – he claimed a great grandfather, an officer, killed assaulting the Parisian barricades in 1848 – Atkins had developed a great deal of respect for the Frenchman's ability to assess fact and fiction. But there was certainly nothing far-sighted about that analysis.

'If you could,' he told Gide sourly, 'arrange to shoot Adolf Hitler and Joseph Stalin, you might well go down in history as the man who single-handedly ended a war before it began.'

'Too late, I am afraid, Captain Atkins,' a voice intoned.

'Well, I'm damned,' Atkins laughed as he turned to see Torsten Fredriksson. 'When I saw you last, you were standing on a pile of rubble in Warsaw, watching us drive off to Russia.'

'And I see you made the journey without visible ill-effect.' Fredriksson turned expectantly to Erika Brotherus and smiled in anticipation. Atkins made the introductions and was pleased to note that the Swedish journalist received a decidedly cool reception from Erika. He then shook hands with the Frenchman and exchanged pleasantries.

The three German officers, also escorted by a young Finnish woman in *Lotta Svard* uniform, approached the refreshment table. Atkins and Gide pointedly turned their backs but Fredriksson bowed and stepped over to shake hands with the fat Colonel and was introduced to the other two officers.

'It would seem,' Gide murmured, 'that we French are well down on the list of possible allies. The British and the Boche have been awarded lovely young guides, while I must stumble about as best I can.' He gave Erika Brotherus a devastating smile.

The girl laughed. 'But Captain Gide,' she said in excellent French as she led them to a table, 'you do speak Finnish. But I must say, it was discussed. It was felt, however, that as you have such a reputation with the ladies, no woman, young or old, would be safe.'

'Me?' Gide exclaimed in mock astonishment.

'I believe I heard the English words, "lady-killer", used to describe you?'

'Good Lord,' Atkins exclaimed. 'Don't blame that American vulgarism on us.'

'Who could have told you such an obvious canard?' Gide protested.

'My cousin.'

'Ah, and who is this cousin who spreads slander about me?'

'André Brotherus. He is a member of the Foreign Ministry.'

Both men laughed. 'Well, then, it is probably true,' Gide admitted. 'Most regretfully, to use another Americanism, you have my number.'

Gide excused himself as a member of the Spanish military mission entered the hall. 'Must have a word with my colleague before our adversaries do. Fate of Europe, you know.'

'He is right,' Erika said cautiously when Gide had gone.

'I beg your pardon?'

'Your government has declared war on the wrong country.'

'Oh Lord,' he chuckled, 'have you been ordered to propagandize me as well.'

Erika's face reddened and she turned away, visibly angered.

'Look here,' he fumbled. 'I didn't mean. . . .'

After a moment, Erika took a deep breath. 'No, it is my fault. I should not have spoken. This is not my business.'

Atkins regarded the girl closely. She *was* quite pretty. A mass of blonde hair pulled severely back from her face only heightened the subtle curve of cheekbone and the uniform could do little to disguise an excellent figure. Her face was not beautiful; rather a photographer would have called it pert. Freckles dotted her nose and a bold brow was partly concealed by bangs brushed to one side. Her nose was short and turned up and her upper lip curled intriguingly to match. When she smiled, her face was engaging, when in repose, interesting and when angry, forbidding.

She was conscious of his scrutiny. To break the silence, he asked, 'Why do you say that? The war certainly concerns you as a Finn.'

'Yes, it does,' her answer was clipped. 'What does not concern me is what my superiors do or think. I had no business making such a statement.'

Before he could challenge her assumption, Fredriksson returned. 'What did you find out from your German friends?' Atkins demanded, nettled at the interruption.

Fredriksson smiled at him. 'They are no more my friends than you are. Neutrals cannot afford the luxury of friends – or enemies. Also, it would be silly of me to tell you, as I would have to rush back and tell them everything you and I talked about. I would soon be exhausted.'

'I was obliged to try.'

The journalist raised his glass in acknowledgement. It was clear that Erika was ignoring his presence. 'I understand,' he said to Atkins, 'that you were at the front. What did you think?'

Erika turned to him with surprise, 'Think of what?' he asked.

'Of Finnish tactics. I understand you accompanied a patrol across the border which routed an entire battalion.'

'I was merely an observer. And I didn't see all that much. Why don't. . . .'

Fredriksson cut him off. 'I was told by a reliable source that you had.'

'I am a military attaché of a neutral nation and as such am not allowed to participate in combat,' Atkins said, his voice formal. 'From my position, well to the rear, I was not allowed, nor did I see anything that would justify your characterization of my activities as. . . .'

'All right, Captain Atkins, have it your way.' Fredriksson stood up. 'Perhaps I may call on you at the legation?' Before Atkins could answer him, the Swede bowed to Erika Brotherus and went to the bar.

Erika shook her head angrily. 'I do not trust that man.'

'Fredriksson?' Atkins asked in surprise. 'Why not? I knew him in Warsaw. He's a good reporter. A bit pushy perhaps.'

'Perhaps. But he is also an opportunist. He is always nearby, trying to . . . I do not know what?'

'Snoop,' he offered and she nodded.

'I think so, yes. Does it mean to look for something you should not.'

Atkins chuckled. 'It does that. But isn't that his job?'

The reception line had ended and the athlete hero disappeared. Clusters of people moved slowly about the room, breaking up, revolving, recombining to create new groups by fission.

'We should join the others,' Erika began but Atkins shook his head.

'Not tonight, I'm afraid. I'm tired of explaining why the British government refuses to help when I don't understand it myself. I was in my office until two o'clock this morning, then back at seven. I would prefer to enjoy your company. Do you mind?'

The girl blushed and shook her head. 'You are the guest.'

'Precisely. Now, I apologize for my reaction a few moments ago. It was uncalled for.' Erika's expression brightened at the apology and her smile eliminated the last tinge of winter.

'Can we be friends now?'

She pretended to think a moment, then nodded. 'I would like that.'

Atkins was enchanted. 'All right then, tell me about yourself.'

'Please, how boring that would be. There is nothing that could interest you. Is it true that you were at the front?'

'Yes I was. It was cold and I was scared. And I am interested.'

Her eyes softened. 'Not many men would have the courage to say so.'

It was Atkins' turn to blush. 'Perhaps,' he mumbled, 'but everyone is, unless mentally deranged.' He wondered why he really did not believe that.

Erika gave him time to recover by talking about herself. She was born and had grown up in Alkvo, a small town on the Arctic Circle, and attended the University of Turku for two years. She had come to Helsinki on the second day of the war to join the *Lotta Svard*. When they discovered that she could drive she was made a lorry driver. A month ago, she had struck a lamp-post in the blackout. 'Well, the signs were confusing,' she protested when he chuckled. 'It was near the Olympic Stadium and between the bombing and the construction work, the road was in terrible shape and full of detour signs. I became confused trying to read them all. "Do not go here, do not go there. Stop, Go, detour".' She shrugged.

'My family was quite poor, in material things, like most Finns. But we never wanted for food and shelter. Father cut timber in the winter and farmed in the summer.' She shrugged. 'If you have lived on a farm, then you know how difficult that sort of life is. If you have not, well,' she shrugged again as if to say that he never would.

'How did you come to attend the University in Turku?'

'The government provides free scholarships for those who wish to continue their education. Even though we were poor, both mother and father saw to it that the house was filled with books from the travelling library. My father had also fought in the Civil War. Afterward, he travelled to many countries. He used to tell us stories of the cities and countries he had visited. He even went once to London and another time to Sheffield.' She paused here and looked at him as if to make certain he was still listening.

'But you haven't told me about the university,' he prompted.

'Perhaps between my father's stories and those I read in books, I wished to see for myself. I was very good at geography in my district school and won a prize. When I was offered the scholarship, I chose geography. It is that simple.'

'And now you know about the entire world but have never been outside Finland,' Atkins grinned. Erika looked down at the table and he put a hand over hers to apologize. 'Please, I didn't mean to make fun of you.'

She withdrew her hand, reluctantly it seemed to him, and smiled again. 'No, I know you did not, but it is strange isn't it. When this war is over, I will go back to my studies and then I will travel about the world.'

'I bet you will.'

'Well,' a voice startled them, 'so this is how you take care of our English guest.' Erika snatched her hand away and Atkins looked up, annoyed as Captain Johan Erko grinned at them.

'Go away.'

Erko shook his head and pulled out a chair. 'Sorry, old man. Erika, duty calls. You must excuse us.'

Before Atkins could object, she wished him a good night and hurried from the reception hall. Damn! he thought but the expression on Erko's face caused him to subside.

'What duty?'

'An Allied mission arrives in Helsinki in two weeks. It is no secret,' he said, glancing at the party of Germans exiting the hall.

Atkins nodded. 'So?'

'The Marshal asks that you go again to the front. Prepare another report on conditions there to show the mission when it arrives.'

Erko's matter-of-fact request chilled Atkins to the bone. 'You will visit a site on the Petsamo front,' he continued. 'The Russians plan a . . . what is the phrase, a decisive advance there soon. If we hold, the Russians will be forced to retreat from this single piece of Finnish territory. If they win, if they break through, there will be nothing to stop them until they reach the Gulf of Bothnia and they cut Finland in two.'

Atkins took a deep breath to steady himself. The first jolt of fear was subsiding. He drained the remaining vodka in his glass and lit a cigarette, striving all the time to give the impression that he was considering the proposal.

'When would I leave?' His voice sounded strained and he cursed his cowardice.

'In two days. You will travel by rail to Lahti where your interpreter and guide will board. Then on to Rovaniemi at the start of the Arctic Highway. You will change to a motor lorry there and continue to the front near the town of Nautsi. Everything you will need will be provided.'

Atkins nodded and Erko stood up. 'I am sorry to say that we have already been together too long a time. Until tomorrow.'

Atkins made himself smile and shook Erko's hand. When the Finn had gone, he made his way to the bar for another drink, then left the reception hall as inconspicuously as possible.

Outside, he hesitated as the wind tore past. The sky had cleared completely and the moon illuminated the city. The authorities had forbidden the clearing of snow and only the dark patches of trees or building walls relieved Helsinki's enchanted appearance. His watch glowed with greenish witch light and the hands pointed to nine-thirty. Still early for the Russian bombers to appear.

He walked down the steps trying not to think about the trip to the front or the two-mile walk ahead of him. A small black car was parked at the bottom and as he approached, a window rolled down and a feminine voice called to him. Startled, he peered into the car to see Erika Brotherus in the rear seat.

'May I offer you a ride, Captain Atkins?'

The interior was warm and they shared a car rug. Atkins was conscious of her leg touching his whenever the car turned. He was flattered that she had waited for him and when he glanced at her, the moonlight caught her smile and he was certain that she blushed. He tried to think of something to say as the car climbed the heights beyond the Olympic Stadium site. The city spread before them, shrouded in fairy moonlight.

'It's so beautiful,' Erika murmured.

'It's lucky for me you had the car,' Atkins said, finally thinking of something innocuous to say.

'Captain Erko asked that I drive you to your flat. It is too cold to walk.'

Silence fell between them again, growing more and more uncomfortable. 'I want to say. . . .'

'Captain Atkins . . .'

They began together, stopped and Atkins' sense of humour came to their rescue when he burst into laughter.

'This is foolish,' he managed at last. 'Here we are, two grown people, acting like children.' He turned. 'Look, I just want to say thank you for giving me a lift. It was quite thoughtful.'

Moonlight flooded the interior of the car as the driver turned off the main boulevard and began to climb a steep hill. Her pale hair glowed like molten silver and his breath caught in his throat. The air-raid sirens began at that moment and the driver swerved the car to the side of the road, careful not to skid into the snow banked along the verge. He slid back the panel and spoke to Erika in Finnish.

'We must get out,' she told Atkins, all efficiency and business. 'There!' she pointed across the top of the car. 'There is a park. Perhaps there will be a bomb shelter.' The car was already driving away and Atkins shouted at the driver but Erika grabbed his hand.

'The driver is only following his instructions. Automobiles are scarce and must be conserved. He will come afterwards if he can.'

In the moonlight, the wide-spaced houses with snow-covered lawns and trees resembled a Christmas card scene. Atkins found it hard to reconcile such beauty with the death-laden aircraft rushing towards Helsinki.

The tiny park was thick with tall firs and birch but there was no public shelter visible. Atkins hesitated.

'It will be safer in the trees,' he told her. 'They won't waste bombs on a park.'

Erika nodded and they struggled through knee-high snow into the trees which gave off an icy scent of pine and provided some protection from the wind. The trees ended abruptly at the crest of the hill and below them lay a ghost city. Not a light showed anywhere in the featureless plain of snow that ran down to the harbour, a darker mass splotched here and there with grey islands.

They huddled just inside the trees and Erika leaned against him for warmth. It seemed perfectly natural to put an arm about her waist, perfectly natural when her face tilted, lips parted and he kissed her, tentatively at first, then with firmness as a gloved hand circled his neck. She pulled away after a moment, grinning mischievously and kissed him again, lightly.

Atkins leaned back against the cold birch trunk and took a deep breath. The air-raid sirens had fallen silent and he could hear the sullen drone of approaching bombers. The moon was so bright it took only a moment to spot the aircraft, midway between horizon and zenith. They came relentlessly, a demonic swarm of insects. There were twenty-four in two echelons of twelve, one behind the other. Anti-aircraft fire marked their passage with dots of light and one plane blossomed, staggered and fell in a shroud of flame.

The bombers – SB-2 twin-engined craft with distinctively wide wings – were low, Atkins thought as they roared abreast seemingly only a few hundred feet higher than the hill from which they watched. The snow-camouflage had forced the Russian pilots to minimum altitude and the Finnish gunners were having a field day. As they watched, another airplane exploded.

The bombers turned inland; perhaps a navigator had spotted a landmark. The first squadron came on, turning more and more to the northwest until it seemed they were aiming at the park. Behind, a second squadron trailed them across the city speckled with bright flashes of light.

'Incendiary bombs,' Atkins muttered. The first squadron flew over them and looking up, they could see flaming exhausts and the silvery blurs of propellers.

An anti-aircraft cannon cracked with frightening suddenness a few yards away and smashed a staccato roar at a sky suddenly alive with hellish tracers. Erika screamed. The second echelon veered towards the strings of fire and Atkins had time to see ugly, fat cylinders dropping before he hurled Erika to the snow and fell on top of her.

The explosions began, lifting, jolting, slamming them with stunning concussions that tore at eardrums and skull, that dragged at flesh and burned their eyes and the membranes of their noses and mouths and plucked at their clothing. He had an impression of flame and smoke blasting skyward, as beneath him, Erika shuddered.

The bombing ended as suddenly as it had begun and he stared about, dazed. Except for loud ringing in his ears, everything was quiet. The little park seemed as silent and deserted as before. Atkins got up, stumbling twice. The dark smear beneath Erika's nose was blood and he fumbled for a handkerchief. At his touch, she opened her eyes wide and he thought she was going to scream. Instead, Erika controlled herself with a visible effort, took the handkerchief and held it against his nose. Only then was he aware that his own nose was bleeding and that he had bitten his inner lip badly. He spat an obscene globule of blood and they stumbled through the snow to the other edge of the park.

The Christmas card scene had been obliterated. Atkins knew he would never again look at one without seeing this night. There had been an anti-aircraft gun hidden in the trees. One bomb, a lucky bomb, had made a direct hit on the gun emplacement. The rest of the bombers had dropped their strings in long swathes through the residential district of pleasant, middle-class homes. In the light of the flames, he saw a body on the road and the moonlight made the wounds even more horrible. He turned Erika aside and drew her past the lop-sided head and the face that was less than blackish meat. The man in the aimer's seat had no head. His mate on the opposite side had no arms or legs, just a head and torso flung across the breech. The barrel of the cannon was bent, testifying to the force of the bomb. Atkins felt his own gorge rising and stepped back. Erika turned away, stumbled to her knees and vomited. Suddenly, Atkins felt out of place and time, an observer at a strange ritual he did not understand. Flames reached across the snow and he regarded them curiously.

Someone took his arm. It was all so unreal, he thought over and over. The beauty of the night contrasted so strongly with the macabre death he had just witnessed, the impersonal death of explosives dropped from aircraft. He knew that he was suffering from shock, that his shivering and confusion, his urge to weep, to bawl, to shout his hatred and confusion to the heavens was due to shock. He saw a hand, black with blood in the moonlight, held up and saw a strange face staring at him through the fingers. It was his blood on his hand.

Lips moved, eyes watched from a great distance. The tunnel began to close and the scene at the end seemed preternaturally sharp. He tried to find Erika before the light dwindled to nothing.

Atkins could not recall what had happened and an inexplicable terror filled him and he sat up with a shout. Immediately, warm hands pressed him back and a familiar voice murmured. He tried to move away but the hands were firm and reassuring. He lay back, gasping for air, aware of the room's closeness and the sweat that had burst on his skin.

Erika was beside him. 'You must be still,' she murmured. 'You are in an emergency clinic. Someone will come from your legation soon.' Beyond her, he could see dozens of people sitting or lying on rows of cots, some with bandages.

'The doctor said that you may have saved my life. If you had not covered me with your body when the bombs fell, I might have been killed. You nearly were. That was a brave thing to do. Very brave.'

Atkins stared at her, trying to make sense of what she was saying. His head was filled with confused thoughts and nothing made sense. What bombs? Brave? Someone stopped beside his cot; a voice spoke in Finnish and Erika leaned down and brushed his cheek with a kiss. 'The doctor said you are to sleep now.'

Atkins woke slowly, aware of a throbbing headache. It took him some time to realize that he was in his own flat. Someone had undressed him and piled several blankets on his bed. He lay quietly for a time, waiting for the headache to diminish and thought about Erika. He remembered what had happened now. Remembered waking in the clinic to find her beside him, then the driver from the legation helping him out to a motor car, how much later? It was the driver who had put him to bed. The bombing was the clearest of his memories. He could sense, almost feel the ear-shattering crack of the 20 millimetre Polsten anti-aircraft gun and the answering concussion of Russian bombs. How many had been killed? he wondered. Who had been so stupid as to site that gun in the centre of a residential area?

He remembered the feel of Erika's icy lips against his in the moments before the bombers came and strangely enough, he thought, he had not been afraid. There hadn't been time. She had waited for him to recover consciousness in the clinic. Did that mean that she was beginning to feel about him the way he did about her?

Atkins' experience with women was limited – as was common among many military men of his age group. Marriage was generally discouraged in the British forces for regular officers under forty. And, during adolescence he had had few opportunities for contact with the opposite sex other than the wives of school masters. Sandhurst had provided little opportunity for him to form more than passing acquaintance with females of any stripe. He had, it occurred to him, lived a singularly male existence in the company of males. His sexual needs were gratified through patronage of certain clubs in Chelsea that catered to the professional officer, or in similar institutions in the various capitals in which he was stationed. And those women were hardly the types who could instruct him in the virtues, possibilities and limitations of what he thought of as 'normal' women.

Erika was also quite different from the women he usually encountered in diplomatic circles. Most had been of two types – wives of civilian diplomats and officials, or young women in clerical positions too obviously searching for husbands. Then too, in pre-war days, what with constant pay cuts and poor allowances, military officers were not generally regarded as suitable mates, unless of course, they were fortunate enough to possess independent incomes. And Atkins did not. The sale of the estate after the death of his aunt and uncle had barely sufficed to pay off the mortgage and a few bills. Just how Erika was different he was at a loss to say exactly and in the moments before he drifted off again, he wondered if her attraction did not lie partly in the danger they had shared the night before.

Atkins was able to return to his office the following day. He was bothered by a persistent headache that no amount of aspirin powder would alleviate, but all that had no effect on the strange and buoyant sense of well-being that filled him. As the day progressed, he was able to think of little else but Erika and several times, had to restrain himself from phoning her at the War Ministry. Tonight would be soon enough, he promised himself. That afternoon, the phone rang and the clerk put his head in to announce that *Major* Erko was calling.

'Charles, how are you feeling today? Are you recovered yet?'

For just a moment, Atkins was tempted to beg off the trip to the front, but discipline carried him through. 'Yes, quite. A slight headache, but all proper in other respects. Have you been promoted? My clerk said a Major Erko was calling.'

'Yes, at long last. But never mind that now. Erika told me what happened and that you saved her life. And for that, I thank you. I would have been quite distraught if anything had happened to her.'

'I can well imagine.'

'Ah, can you, old boy? I don't think so. Erika and I are to be married in the spring. Her experience last night gave me quite a scare, forced me to do what I should have done a long time ago and propose to her. So you see there is more to it than the loss of an efficient assistant.'

Atkins was stunned; he managed to stutter something resembling congratulations and Erko went on to the details of his travel authorization.

'Your train leaves at 1900 hours, Charles. Are you quite certain you are up to it? The trip will be rough. We could wait a few more days, you know.'

'No, no,' he protested. 'I'll be fine. Just a spell of dizziness now and then.'

Erko rang off and Atkins sat staring through the window at the wrecked harbour and suddenly he began to laugh softly. How big a fool could one make of oneself?

Arctic Front 8 – 20 January 1940

No one saw him off at the railroad station. Air-raid sirens wailed across the city and anti-aircraft guns thundered as the crowd hurried along the platforms in the quiet, disciplined way that characterized the Finns and Atkins paused a moment to watch them. Twice now, he had watched a civilian population react under aerial bombardment, and twice had seen them rise to heroic levels. The morale effect of heavy bombing was vastly overrated, he decided. Either that or the Poles and the Finns were exceptional people.

The train reached Lahti at eleven p.m., having been forced to wait several times while priority military trains roared by in the night. A knock woke him and he opened the door to confront a stocky man in the white overalls of the Finnish army. Snow was melting from the brim of his fatigue cap in the overheated car.

'Captain Charles Atkins?' he asked in heavily accented English.

'Yes.'

'I am Lieutenant Lers Radikko. I am to be your guide. Is anything I can do for you tonight?'

Atkins shook his head. 'Not unless you can persuade the porter to turn down the heat.'

Radikko chuckled. 'Impossible. It is old Russian car. If vents are closed, all die from carbon monoxide – that is the correct pronounciation?'

Atkins told him it was and the man repeated it to make certain. 'The carbon monoxide will kill all inside.' He shrugged as if to say, what else could you expect from the Russians?

'If there is nothing more then, I will tell you good night. The porter will awaken you at six o'clock, just before we arrive at Rovaniemi.'

*

The porter knocked promptly at six a.m. startling Atkins from a light doze. Between the heat and intruding thoughts of Erika as well as apprehension over the coming patrol, he had slept little and that badly. He wished to God that he had found an excuse to beg off.

He washed in the hot water the porter brought and dressed in the winter officer's uniform and ski boots Erko had sent aboard. A white outer garment completed the uniform and he pulled high, waterproofed ski boots on over two pairs of wool stockings and tramped through the train in search of breakfast. He found that an unheated canteen car had been attached at the end. Two middle-aged women in heavy overcoats and Russian-style babushkas dispensed hot tea in chipped mugs and huge bowls of an oatmeal-like cereal.

He was finishing his second cup of tea when a bulky figure settled into the chair beside him. 'Good morning, Captain Atkins,' Lieutenant Radikko greeted him. 'I see you have eaten.' He raised a hand and one of the women brought him a bowl and a mug of tea.

'Now,' he said between rapid spoonfuls, 'we arrive shortly, a few minutes, I think. We will ski a bit to the road. Then we ride to Nautsi. Then we go to find some Russians. Okay?'

Atkins grinned uneasily, aware that Nautsi was almost two hundred miles north through a wilderness of forest and swamp. The hot tea and oatmeal had helped to dissipate some of his weariness and he obtained a second bowl.

It took them two days to make their way up the highway to the front that stretched in a wide semi-circle about the battered town of Nautsi. They followed a route cross-country to avoid Russian aircraft that appeared at odd intervals to strafe the road. They skied through endless miles of forest and rode for hours in the unheated backs of a succession of crowded motor lorries that had turned the frozen surface of the Arctic Highway to washboard.

At midafternoon of the second day, Radikko stopped. A cutting wind swirled fresh powder from the surface and mixed it with falling snow to form a haze impenetrable beyond a few feet. Radikko whistled loudly. An answering hail came from the blank whiteness and Radikko grinned in relief. Only then did Atkins realize that the Finn had been even more worried about their route than he. Armed men materialized and Radikko showed papers and, pointing to Atkins, spoke quickly. Someone slapped him on the shoulder in friendly greeting. They skied for another two miles at the end of which, Atkins remained on his feet only by exercising all his will-power.

146

The bunker was little more than a deep hole lined with split logs. Frost covered the walls an inch deep and behind their ski-masks, most of the Finnish faces were covered with frost blisters. All were haggard and their eyes were hard and glistening. Radikko introduced Atkins to the lieutenant commanding, a boy too young to have finished high school it seemed. They were served hot soup and dark bread, a measure of how the quality of Finnish rations had declined. Hungry as he was, Atkins was almost too exhausted to eat. They were shown to a pair of bunks and Atkins had the satisfaction of knowing that Radikko fell asleep first.

'A patrol is sent out every afternoon,' the young lieutenant explained in German. In the distance, he could hear Russian shells exploding as they pounded the devastated town of Nautsi. 'Russian lines are two kilometres from here. We have learned that a new artillery post is being established ten kilometres north, that will outflank and outrange our guns around Nautsi. We've been asked to see if they need our help.' He grinned wolfishly and Radikko laughed.

'You see, we Finns are neighbourly people. We like to award the "neighbours" the order of the wooden cross, second class, of course. You will come?'

Atkins ignored the levity and struggled to keep his fear hidden as he nodded.

This time he accepted the offered carbine. He checked the magazine and safety and slung a bandolier about his neck. Atkins had forced himself to choke down the usual iron ration of dried meat, fruit and suet and now, two hours later, as he knelt in the snow and readjusted his ski-bindings, snow drifted down slowly, undisturbed by wind. The heavy sound of the Russian guns was quite clear, often overriding the sharper bark of the lighter Finnish field pieces. The underbrush was both denser and higher in this area and protruded through the snow in places. Twice, he had fallen, the last time wrenching his ankle in spite of tightly-laced boots.

Radikko whispered, 'There, look.'

Atkins stared into the gloomy trees and gradually made out the outline of a lorry-drawn artillery piece canted steeply to one side. Apparently, the gun had slipped off the track and mired itself in the snow. A dozen Russian soldiers worked with picks and shovels to lower the track surface sufficiently for the gun to settle so that it could be towed out with the motor lorry. The sound of the picks on the frozen soil was curiously muffled by the trees. Atkins was aware of the Finns slipping into positions along the track and fought down a rising tension that threatened to gag him. Christ, he did not want to experience another rifle battle. The Russians must have felt safe enough several kilometres behind their lines as they had even built a fire for light and warmth and had posted only a single sentry.

Hand signals were passed and carbines and machine pistols slid forward. Two men, bombers, crept close to the road with their bags of hand grenades. When they were in position, the young lieutenant waved a hand and two grenades flew into the clearing. One landed under the lorry and the other bounced off the cannon's breech and exploded. A concerted volley of carbine fire slashed into the Russians. The survivors dove for cover but instead of running in panic as Atkins had expected, they returned fire.

Lieutenant Radikko was the first casualty. He had fired one shot when a bullet took him in the forehead. Atkins, crouching next to him, heard the distinct slap as the bullet struck. He stared at the smashed head for an endless moment, consumed by horror. His mind screamed at him to run, to run and hide somewhere away from the madness and the killing.

A bullet whined off a tree. They were shooting at him. He shrank below the snow mound and crawled swiftly to the side. That single action seemed to jolt him from his panic. He worked the bolt of his carbine, tucked himself in beside the tree and cautiously peered around the trunk, expecting the smashing oblivion of a Mosin-Nagant bullet. A Russian soldier was kneeling, partly concealed behind a tank track, firing coolly at where he had been a moment ago. Atkins aimed his carbine, exhaled and squeezed the trigger. The Russian threw out his hands and fell backwards.

Atkins felt only relief, not sorrow or anger. He had experienced something modern soldiers rarely do – that is to see the man across the line doing his best to kill him. He was calm now and he picked his targets and fired, his body under the control of long-ago training. He was hardly aware of the carbine's painful jolt against his shoulder. He fired as if he were on an Aldershot range once more, slowly, methodically, by the numbers. The shock of Radikko's death was so sudden that his mind refused to absorb it; instead, he took refuge in practised actions.

Then it was over and someone was shaking his arm to make him stop. The clearing was silent with death. The lorry burned fiercely and he saw two Finns wiring explosives to the cannon while others lashed three white-clad bodies to their skis. Five minutes later, the surviving patrol members were skiing south into the forest with their grim cargo.

The problem the Finnish general staff had foreseen from the beginning was taking effect – the critical lack of reserves was reducing the efficiency of the Finnish Army. With a population of 3.8 million, Finland could not provide enough young men to field an army to match that produced by the Russian nation of 170 million. Consequently, the Finnish infantryman was forced to remain in the front line week after week with only a day or two of rest at most.

Winter had clamped an iron fist across all of Europe. The temperature fell to fifty-five below zero Fahrenheit and at night, trees splitting in the killing frost cracked like pistol shots. Atkins shivered behind the deadfall. He wore a padded snow-suit beneath his white overalls and two pairs of felt bootees over ski-boots and still he shivered. Every few minutes, he had to clear ice away from the mouth and nostril openings of his ski mask. A soldier with an unpronounceable name passed him a cloth bag containing the day's iron ration. The cold, and the constant shivering caused them all to burn energy at prodigious rates.

They had been lying in ambush above the road for an hour. His companion was a Lapp who spoke no English and little Finnish. The man's eyes moved along the road in the rhythmic sweep of a professional hunter. It was high banked at this point and a perfect ambush site for tanks but the cold was so intense, he did not understand how any vehicle could be made to operate. The Lapp rested his Swedish-made machine pistol on a square of oil cloth to protect it from the snow and from time to time, rubbed a hand along the barrel as if in a caress. Next to the machine pistol was the slender, guardless hunting knife that all Finns seemed to carry.

Since Radikko's death, Atkins had moved from unit to unit on his own, all the while struggling to master the overwhelming fear that stalked him like a demon. In two weeks, he had worked from the northern to the southern end of the Nautsi line. He could not have said why for certain but deep inside, he suspected he stayed in the north partly as punishment, partly as atonement for his cowardice.

The Lapp beside him was little more than a boy. Another soldier had told him in laboured English that the boy's entire family had been killed in the first week of the war when Russian planes bombed and machine-gunned his small village near Petsamo. The boy wasn't really a soldier but he had attached himself to their unit and demonstrated such skill at killing Russians with carbine or knife that he was worth any ten of the rest of them.

In the two weeks that Atkins had been in the north, he had heard a dozen such stories. Rarely did a village or a settlement have any strategic or tactical value. As in Poland, the objective was only to spread terror and discontent among the civilian population and so Finnish hatred for Russians, ingrained over six hundred years of invasion and oppression, now verged on the fanatical. The Finns were outnumbered ten and more to one by the Red Army and knew it, but there was no talk of surrender or armistice, only of killing more Russians. Once a Finnish soldier had told him in laboured English that the only time the Finns welcomed Russians was over open sights. And too, he had never forgotten the fierce joy with which Erko had talked about the machine-gunning of parachutists or Radikko joking about awarding wooden crosses, second class. But then, he thought, hadn't it been the same in Warsaw? What was that Polish officer's name – Yitzak? Of course. The son of the violinist. Hadn't his only concern been to join a partisan group and go on killing Nazis?

Atkins had marvelled at the timeless patience of the Finnish soldier. As the winter wore on, Russian strength and sheer willingness to expend a hundred lives for one Finnish life began to tell. The Russians attacked isolated portions of the line in human wave assaults and were shot down in neat rows as they waded through waist-deep snow. The wounded froze to death within minutes and the sight of grotesquely twisted bodies had long since ceased to sicken him. There were even reports of Russian parachutists jumping from aircraft flying at less than fifty feet above deep snow, *without parachutes*. Casualties were said to be as high as two in five. And he wondered what drove the Russian soldier to as fanatical a determination as the Finn? Or was it all propaganda?

The Lapp stiffened, then pointed towards the far end of the cut. The last of the midday twilight was fading and the road seemed to have disappeared into a dark tunnel. Atkins concentrated all his senses and heard it, a distant rumble of engines growing louder in the iron-hard air. The first tank emerged from the gloom and Atkins closed his eyes as the panicky urge to run nearly overwhelmed him.

The driver stood in the turret, scanning the narrowing road with field glasses. Without warning, the tank's machine gun blasted the sides of the road, a tactic the Germans had used in Poland to demoralize infantrymen. Atkins ducked and when he glanced up, ashamed of himself, he saw the young Lapp grinning at him, also from beneath folded arms.

The Lapp pushed his rifle forward and caught the Russian in his sights as the tank drew closer. Atkins had seen him shoot down a running soldier at four hundred yards, in twilight. A second tank emerged from the darkness, then a third and a fourth until there were ten in all and Atkins was surprised at the efficiency of Russian maintenance crews that could keep them operating in such severe weather. That in itself boded ill for the Finns. In the first light snows of December, the Russians had been unable to operate any kind of vehicle with reliability. But intelligence had verified that the new Soviet commander, one General Semen K. Timoshenko, had assumed command of what the Russians termed the North-west Front.

Atkins' attention was drawn to a spot of movement as a white-clad soldier slid through the underbrush to within a few yards of the narrow road. For a moment, it was as if he were watching the cavalry manoeuvres of the previous autumn. When the tank rattled abreast of the soldier, he pushed a canvas pouch of explosives into the tank treads with a long stick. The driver of the following tank saw the movement and swung the tank's heavy machine gun in a flashing arc and killed the soldier, but he was too late. The Lapp fired at the same time and the lead tank commander slid down inside the turret, shot through the head, before he could warn his crew. The explosives detonated with a dull boom and the lead tank swerved in a half circle, burst into flame and halted. Simultaneously, there was another explosion at the far end of the cut as the last tank blew up and the retreat was blocked. Glass bottles flashed and spattered against the line of tanks. Flame whoofed as flammable liquid splattered and ran down inside hatches, ventilation ports and drivers' slits. The Finns were using the famed Molotov Cocktail, a bottle filled with petrol and lubricating oil, with a cloth jammed into the neck to act as a wick – the mysterious bottles of dye he had seen in that afternoon manoeuvre in November. The thrower inverted the bottle to soak the rag, lit it with a match and threw. When the bottle smashed, the flaming cloth ignited the contents and the resulting fire was impossible to extinguish with water.

The road was suddenly alive in the orange glare of flaming petrol as Russian crews erupted from their tanks. Most were shot as they emerged and the rest were picked off by sharpshooters. Two tanks backed and filled, attempting to run off the road and through the snow but the banks proved too high and, within minutes, they too had been stopped by hand grenades tossed into the treads. Bottles of petrol rained onto both. Atkins saw one tanker stand in the turret with arms raised in surrender only to be shot down instantly.

The action lasted less than five minutes. Not even the ambush of the Russian infantry battalion at the start of the war had seemed so complete a victory. Ten men had destroyed a column of ten tanks and killed thirty or more soldiers in seconds, but unlike that first time, the cost had been high – four dead. Four soldiers that Finland could ill afford to lose. He knew this raid would be accounted a failure.

*

Atkins stared at the winter-blighted landscape as the train struggled towards Helsinki. The tracks had deteriorated alarmingly under the twin onslaughts of winter and war usage and they had passed gang after gang of pinched-face Russian prisoners working under the watchful eyes of machine-pistol armed *Lotta Svard* guards. Atkins knew these Russian prisoners were immeasurably better off than Finnish POWs. Those not shot out of hand were placed in concentration camps reputed to be little more than barbed wire enclosures open to the weather. Few survived more than a day or two. Russian prisoners of war were at least fed and housed.

The telegram from the legation ordering him to return had caused a curious mixture of relief and guilt; relief that he was leaving the front, guilt at leaving the exhausted soldiers he had come to know so well. Above all was the curious light-headed feeling brought on by exhaustion that gave everything a tinge of unreality.

The Helsinki station was blacked out. Blue lights gave dim illumination and holes gaped in the roof covering the platforms. The porter signed for him to wait and guided a young soldier onto the steps. She helped him down, crooning softly in Finnish. An elderly man and woman stepped forward hesitantly. One of the boy's sleeves was pinned to the shoulder and his eyes were covered with bandages. The old woman kissed his face while her husband clutched the boy's remaining hand as tears streamed down his face. The crowd parted around the silent tableau and the porter stepped back, blotting her eyes with her coat sleeve.

The legation secretary met him inside and gaped at his face.

'My God, Atkins!'

Atkins touched one of the watery blisters on his cheek. 'The cold brings them on,' he muttered. 'They go away after a while.'

Snow filtered through the damaged roof and an icy wind swept the platform. His companion shivered. 'I say, let's get out of this damned cold.'

Atkins almost laughed; the station might have been in the south of Spain, it seemed so warm. 'All right. I need a cup of tea.'

He shouldered his pack and followed the secretary through the double-doors. The café was crowded but they found a table near the door and ordered tea.

'Good Lord, man, you're bundled for an expedition to the north pole. It really is that bad?'

Atkins had few dealings with the secretary and they had been enough to cause him to form the opinion that the man was an insufferable prig. But there was sincere sympathy in his voice and he nodded. 'Worse. I don't see how the Finns do it. Some of them have been in the line since the first of December.'

'Well, that's decided it then,' the secretary shook his head. 'When they call me up, I'm going to request duty in Singapore.'

The tea came and they drank in silence until the secretary took a buff envelope from his pocket. 'Sorry to do this to you, old man. The Minister sends his regrets as well, but there is no hope for it.'

Curious, and apprehensive at the same time, Atkins slit the envelope and extracted the single sheet. It was the standard War Department form ordering him to proceed to Stockholm and report there to the British legation at the soonest possible instant.

He glanced at the secretary who only shrugged. 'I'm only the messenger boy. But I suspect it may have something to do with the fact that the Allied Commission will not visit Finland after all. The Russians raised a stink and Germany threatened all sorts of dire consequences.'

Atkins crumpled the form and found himself struggling to breathe in his anger. Everything he had endured the past two weeks had been for nothing. The sleepless nights, the mind-wrenching fear; he knew he could never do it again.

'Easy, old son,' the secretary said softly and eased the paper from his fist.

Atkins sat motionless for a while, staring at his tea, trying not to think. 'Is there a plane tomorrow?' he muttered finally.

The secretary shook his head. 'Sorry, but it's tonight. Plane's waiting for you now. I've a car outside. Shouldn't have stopped for tea really, but you looked done up.'

'Tonight! Christ, look at me. I haven't bathed properly in two weeks nor shaved for that matter. I haven't even the proper uniform!'

'Here, here,' the secretary grinned. 'I've packed all the proper kit. There is a bag in the motor. You might even catch a few winks on the airplane and I am certain they will allow you time to clean up in Stockholm.' He glanced at his watch. 'We've no more time, I'm afraid. Something about a weather front moving in. You have to leave by midnight, otherwise the flight will be cancelled. Off we go?' The secretary dropped coins on the table and Atkins followed.

It was indicative of the extent of Finland's mobilization that no one looked twice at his worn, filthy winter uniform and his haggard, blistered face – the railroad station was filled with men and women in dirty winter uniforms. If anything might have drawn attention to him it would have been his lack of weapons. Atkins had turned his carbine in before starting south.

The secretary shook hands with him at the car and opened the back door. Atkins slid in to find another occupant.

'Welcome home, Captain Atkins,' Major Erko greeted him. 'I am sorry we must meet in such circumstances.'

'I suppose you're responsible for this bit of cloak and dagger nonsense,' Atkins growled when the car was underway. His head was beginning to clear as the strong tea made itself felt.

'To a degree. But believe me it is necessary. Germany has been making terribly threatening noises about the Allied Commission.'

Atkins nodded. The car had a heater unit in the back and the interior was fast becoming unbearable. He cracked a window and gulped the fresh air. Erko fumbled with the controls and the blast of hot air against his legs died away.

'You are going to Sweden to meet with a very important personage. The Marshal asked that these documents be given to you. Please study them before you land, then give them to the pilot. He will see that they are returned.'

Atkins nodded and slid the envelope inside his greatcoat, too tired to protest further or to ask questions.

Erko hesitated. 'I have followed your progress in the north and am impressed with your diligence. You, more than any other foreigner, now know our capabilities. In that envelope is a detailed description of our remaining resources. When the time comes, you will understand what to do with the information.'

There was a moment of silence, then Erko gripped his gloved hand. 'Finland will not forget what you have done for her. I told you once before, you are a very brave man, Captain Atkins. I am proud to call you my friend.'

Long after the Junkers trimotor of the Finnish air force was airborne, Atkins, unable to sleep in the frigid, thundering interior of the corrugated metal hull, stared into the darkness and cringed as Erko's remark repeated itself over and over in his mind. If Erko only knew how really frightened he had been, how badly his hands had shaken, how he had fought to keep from screaming. A brave man! He was nothing more than a play actor! Erika was lucky to love a man like Erko. He had no business . . . he turned his mind resolutely from the subject and opened the envelope.

Sweden 21 January 1940

Stockholm was a world away from Helsinki. The embassy car drove through snow-cleared, well-lighted streets. Posters everywhere warned of the danger of aerial bombing and large signs with arrows marked bomb shelters but the city was whole, untouched and he felt like an explorer who has stepped from jungle to civilization in a single stride.

Once clear of the city, neat farms nestled behind windbreaks of tall trees. Fields were covered with snow and unmarked and the light traffic was entirely civilian. He glanced at the special envoy from Prime Minister Chamberlain sitting beside him. The man was an austere career civil servant with the demeanour of an aristocrat that did not invite conversation and that was just as well with Atkins.

It had taken most of the flight to absorb the information in the dozen closely typed sheets and he had arrived well before dawn to find the envoy waiting. A servant at the Embassy showed him to a single room with lavatory facilities. The luxury of a hot water and soap bath was overwhelming and when the servant finally knocked on the door, his anxious tone suggested his concern that Atkins had drowned.

Bathed, the blisters reduced with a hot needle, shaved, dressed in a clean uniform, and fed, he needed only sleep to feel human again. Instead, they drove deep into the countryside and even now, three hours later, only a dim twilight was growing in the overcast sky. Atkins peered at his watch, nearly 1100 hours.

The car slowed and turned through an open gate. The envoy sat forward and surveyed the road ahead. Atkins did the same. It was little more than a lane winding into the trees and the snow looked soft and powdery. The car slid and slipped twice and once the rear wheels drifted right but the imperturbable driver managed well enough and as they rounded the last bend in the track, the lane widened into a ploughed drive that circled in front of a huge, Empire-style mansion.

Atkins got out, wondering. The envoy, who had spoken little during the drive, frowned.

'Captain Atkins, I do not approve of amateurs conducting the foreign affairs of nations. Do I make myself clear?'

Puzzled, he shook his head. 'No sir, I am afraid not.'

'You were not briefed in Helsinki?' the envoy demanded, his voice incredulous.

'No sir. I was ordered from the front, put directly on a plane and flown here.'

The man's voice shook with anger. 'This is unbelievable. In a few moments, you will meet the Prime Minister of Sweden and you have not even been told!' He took a deep breath. 'I trust you will know how to conduct yourself?'

'The Prime Minister, sir?' Atkins asked, even more mystified than before. 'I thought I was to speak to the Allied Commission.'

The envoy thrust his hands into the pockets of his overcoat and glanced at the snow-shrouded lawn and the steel-coloured skies. The aspect was forbidding.

'The Commission exists no longer. Norway and Sweden have been asked to allow the passage of arms and soldiers to the Finns from Narvik across the mountains to the Finnish border. Germany has threatened invasion and occupation should they comply. It is our position that without such aid, Finland will be forced shortly to surrender. In that event, Norway and Sweden will have Russia for a next door neighbour. For both countries, it is a choice between two evils. Do you understand the situation now?'

'Yes sir. But I fail to see the need for my presence?'

'As do I, Captain Atkins. It would seem that someone in London has been pressured by someone in Helsinki to allow you a hearing today. Therefore, you will answer any question the Prime Minister asks honestly and fully. He agreed to see you, I suspect, only to compare your information with that received from his own people.' He turned without another word and strode up the swept walk.

The Prime Minister was waiting for them in the library. Per Albin Hansson was a smallish man, dark-haired and with a hawkish visage from which two level eyes watched the world with a great care. It would take quite an actor, Atkins thought, to fool him for long.

The envoy and the Prime Minister exchanged personal remarks and then turned to him. The Prime Minister opened with a blunt statement.

'Captain Atkins, your government has requested that Sweden allow free passage of Allied arms and troops to Finland. To reinforce the importance of this request, they have asked that I receive you.' His English was excellent, with just a hint of Scandinavian lilt, and his tone told Atkins the Prime Minister did not desire his presence any more than the envoy did.

'Sir, I can only tell you that if Finland falls to the Soviets, Sweden is threatened.' Meet bluntness with bluntness, he thought. 'And Finland cannot last beyond June.' The information in the report to Marshal Mannerheim had made that very clear.

The Prime Minister nodded, neither offended nor impressed. Atkins imagined that he heard this same cant a hundred times a day.

'The Finns are holding up well enough against the Russians. There are many who doubt the Russians can win.'

'I beg your pardon sir, but anyone who holds that opinion has not visited the front.'

'And you have?'

'Twice, sir. The first time in mid-December. I returned from the second visit sixteen hours ago. I was in the line south of Nautsi.

156

As long as winter continues to hamper Russian movements, the Finns will hold their own. But in the spring, when the snow is gone and the roads dry, the Russians will overwhelm them with sheer numbers. Even now, the Russians are learning how to operate their mechanized equipment under the harshest winter conditions.'

'Until June then?'

'That is my view, sir. Without help, it is inconceivable that Finland can win. The army will never surrender. The Russians will have to occupy the entire country.'

The Prime Minister glanced at the envoy, as if to ascertain his feelings, but his craggy face remained carved from stone. Hansson touched a button on his desk and a moment later, a door opened and butler clad in black uniform brought in tea. The room was overly warm and Atkins was on the verge of falling asleep. The butler served the tea and it was all that he could do to keep from gulping his down.

'Since you have been sent by your superiors to impress me with your expertise, Captain, perhaps you would give me a first-hand account of your adventures?'

Atkins started to snarl a reply but caught himself in time. Even though it was clear the man did not want to be convinced, he took pains to describe his experiences, emphasizing the small number of Finnish soldiers who had participated in each action. He was also at great pains to describe the contrast in morale and casualties observed between the two visits.

'I think it is especially important to understand, sir, that Finland has only thirteen divisions – three more than when she was attacked – with which to face fifty Russian divisions – twice as many as *they* had when they began the war. Finland has, or had, forty tanks against three thousand and less than five hundred artillery pieces against four thousand.'

The Prime Minister was silent when he finished. Atkins cleared his throat and wished he dared pour another cup of tea.

'You speak most eloquently, Captain Atkins, and it is obvious you have taken your duty seriously. I feel, therefore, that I owe you an explanation. This is, of course, most personal and private.' He glanced at the envoy who nodded.

'I am as moved by the bravery of the Finnish people as you are, sir. However, emotional considerations have no place in responsible government. To be quite blunt, if Allied forces and supplies are allowed – and I only speak for my country you understand – to move through Sweden, we will incur the enmity of the Germans who have already stated, publicly and privately, that they will invade and occupy Norway and Sweden to protect their northern flank. We have been warned at the same time by the Soviet Union that we shall be subject to invasion when Finland falls, as she must ultimately.' He peered shrewdly at the envoy. 'Allied guarantees have been offered, but not against Russia who remains their potential ally. So you see, I can do nothing except bring war to Sweden.

'There is justice in the positions of both sides. Finland must resist any incursion of her territory by a foreign power. The Russian government, on the other hand, is charged with the task of protecting her own citizens. She cannot do so with the indefensible frontiers thirty kilometres from one of her largest cities. She has chosen to improve those borders by demands on the Baltic States and on Finland.'

The Prime Minister spread his hands. 'What can be done? Nothing. Finland is doomed to lose the war. We have studied the aid proposals from the Allied, Italian and American Governments. If all forces and supplies promised, could be delivered and distributed through Finland at the points where most needed, they would still be insufficient to repulse a full-scale Russian offensive. That is the considered assessment of my military intelligence department.'

He stood up and walked to the window to stand with his back to them. Atkins had to strain to hear him. 'Sweden has been at peace for one hundred and fifty years. Our defences are poor and our offensive capability is non-existent. We may escape destruction only by remaining staunchly neutral. It is also possible that if we interfere, Captain Atkins, the Germans and Russians will be driven to cooperate against Finland, as they did against Poland. It is a cynical game the leaders of these two nations play.'

Viiborg Front, Finland 30 January to 2 February 1940

Heavy snow whipped by a thirty kilometre an hour wind tore at Senior Lieutenant Mikhail Gregorvitch Dogorov's greatcoat as he stumbled down from the truck and crossed the clearing to the blur of tents. A half-frozen sentry challenged him and he had to remove his gloves and expose his already stiffened hands to temperatures that were far below forty degrees of frost to show the man his papers. The wind nearly tore them from the sentry's gloved hands but Dogorov managed to grab them in time. The sentry nodded without speaking and he trudged on to the command post.

Tents concealed the entrance to a large underground bunker.

Inside, flickering paraffin lanterns cast huge shadows and caused staring eyes to gleam from the tiers of bunks that lined the dirt walls. Icicles hung from every horizontal surface and the temperature was little warmer inside than out.

A crudely lettered sign directed him to the officer of the day, a fat man wrapped in two greatcoats and a fur balaclava pulled well down so that his haggard face was all but concealed. He took the orders without looking up. His only concession to Dogorov's rank was a nod toward a crate that served as a side chair.

'Welcome to the ninth circle of hell, Comrade Lieutenant. . . .'

He squinted at the papers in the bad light . . . 'Mikhail Gregorvitch Dogorov.'

'As bad as that?' Dogorov asked with an attempt at humour.

'Worse. If Dante had spent a week in Karelia, he would have chosen it for the *centre* of hell. I envy anyone doing his term in the fire.'

He cleared his throat. 'You served in Poland? Good. Then you have an idea what it's all about. This is a light artillery battalion doing the job of a medium artillery unit. We've plenty of ammunition but precious little else. You will take command of B Battery which is equipped with the Model 1933 76.2 millimetre Field Gun. I assume you are familiar with it?'

The man slapped a stamp on the orders without waiting for his answer and dropped one copy into a box. The other copy was returned to Dogorov. 'In the morning, you will assume command of your unit, a light artillery battery at map coordinates ah,' he consulted a map, 'Zed eight-three.' The man's grin was ghastly in the dim light. 'You will be only three thousand metres from Finnish lines so watch yourself. The Finns like to stick officers with their nasty little knives.' The man laughed and pushed his chair back. 'You though, you should last longer. You're a combat veteran.'

'In the morning,' Dogorov repeated. 'And how do I get there?'

'Get there, for God's sake? Like everyone else, you walk! It's only a kilometre but I hope you know how to use a compass. The Finns don't take many prisoners these days. In the meantime, find an empty bunk and get some sleep. You won't get much on the line.'

Dogorov found his duffle bag where it had been dumped by a sullen enlisted man. He searched along the bunks until he found an empty one and crawled in with the new winter weight down sleeping bag he had been issued. Poland was cold enough, he thought, but at least they had been quartered in comfortable houses with plenty of heat. Here, there were thousands of square kilometres of wood for the cutting, and yet the bunker was freezing.

In spite of his weariness, sleep was a long time in coming. His mind was still reeling with the shock of what he had seen. For two months, the country had been told by Radio Moscow, by *Pravda* and *Izvestia*, by all the propaganda organs that small Russian forces were inflicting terrible defeats on the Finns at every engagement and that only the unexpected severity of the terrible winter prevented the Red Army from smashing the fascist Finns and bringing them to heel.

The last twenty-four hours, spent mostly in the unheated cab of a truck had put the lie to that. For hours, the road, such as it was, had paralleled the Finnish-Russian border in Karelia. The snow had obliterated any trace of the track but the driver had no difficulty following the route; he had only to steer along the endless line of burned-out tanks, trucks and frozen, half buried bodies. For a few kilometres, the way had been marked by the stiffened arms of corpses pointing at the overcast sky. Some wag had even hung a blue lantern from the clawed fingers of one to mark the road. In other places, the bodies had been stacked head to foot, criss-crossed like cordwood, awaiting burial in the spring when the ground thawed enough to dig graves. And here, morale appeared non-existent and the conditions were the most primitive he had ever seen. There wasn't the slightest bit of heat in the dugout and the cold bit through the sleeping bag as if it did not exist. Dogorov got up again and put on every bit of clothing he had, including his water-proofed boots, but still he continued to shiver.

Dogorov woke slowly. Bodies moved around him in the cramped bunker. He slipped one arm from the bag and focused on the Swiss-made steel wristwatch he had bought two months before in Poland. Cold air flowed in through the opening and he drew his arm back hastily. He was not comfortable by any means but it was definitely warmer inside the bag than out. In spite of bladder pressure, he remained in the bunk for another ten minutes, dozing until someone shook his arm.

He opened his eyes reluctantly and an enlisted man grinned at him, obviously not suspecting that he was an officer.

'Up, sluggard. They'll be coming in to see who's still in bed. Those that are get the shitty details.'

Dogorov slid out of the bunk. 'Why in hell don't they light a fire in here?' he muttered.

'The Finns. They find our bunkers by the smell of smoke. And, they pick off the woodcutters. If you have to go anywhere outside when it's not snowing, stay low and move fast.'

'As bad as that?' he asked incredulously.

His unknown benefactor nodded. 'Worse. You'll see.'

Dogorov ate a cold ration and decided to start for his battery. He found the quartermaster's store and was issued snow shoes, rations and fur-lined mittens. He asked for and was refused a rifle.

'Sorry. Standing orders, Lieutenant,' the supply sergeant told him. 'No rifles for officers. Looks bad to the men.' He grimaced. 'Besides, if one of the bastards shoots at you, you'll be too dead to shoot back. And I guarantee you won't see him first.'

As he tramped out into the ice-still morning darkness, he thought about the sergeant's pessimistic comments and what he had seen so far. The truth of his statement was evident in the eyes of everyone he had met; they were deathly afraid of the Finns. But they couldn't possibly be that good. After all, they were only human. But, as he passed battery after battery, each seemingly deserted, his own fear began to grow until he unbuttoned his holster, drew his Tokarev pistol and carried it tucked under his greatcoat.

The dense forest pressed in except where the trees had been felled to provide clear fields of fire. A few sentries watched from sheltered locations that allowed an approach from the front only. None bothered to challenge him and only their eyes moved beneath the layers of blankets in which they had swathed themselves.

He saw his own battery as a deserted camp barely visible against the snow-shrouded trees. Not a soul was to be seen, including a sentry. Dogorov stopped before a tent, a high-peaked affair well-banked with snow and flaps tied securely. He glanced around the area, noting that the canvas-shrouded piles of ready ammunition near each gun were half buried in the snow.

He kicked off the snow shoes and used his hunting knife to cut the tent flap fastenings and stepped inside. The icy interior was heavy with the smell of unwashed bodies. The tent was lined with flimsy pine double bunks and a man lay on each, tightly wrapped in his sleeping bag and whatever blankets or greatcoats he could find. One man roused himself long enough to protest the damage he had done.

Dogorov ignored him and clasped his hands behind his back. 'My name is Mikhail Gregorvitch Dogorov, Senior *Lieutenant* Mikhail Gregorvitch Dogorov,' he roared. 'I have been assigned to command Battery B, Sixteenth Battalion, Fourth Regiment of Artillery. I will have every man out of his bunk, dressed and ready for duty in five minutes.'

Dogorov pulled his glove back on and stepped outside without another word. He repeated the performance in the other two tents, then went to the centre of the clearing to wait. Nothing happened for long minutes, then the first figure shuffled out, followed by another. Dogorov waited, struggling to remain impassive while all the stories of Finnish snipers he had heard, worked on him. It took seven minutes for the battery to assemble and he nodded to the sergeant to call the roll.

As the names were called, he could see the men darting glances at the trees and their fear heightened his. But he was determined to stick it out.

'This battery is a disgrace,' he began when the sergeant had made his report. He pitched his voice so that all could hear clearly above the wind. 'I walked straight into this camp without a challenge. So could the Finns as there was not a single sentry posted. I find no one about their duties even though it is past time for morning fatigue. And I find no evidence that hot food has been prepared.'

'Beg your pardon, Comrade Lieutenant,' the sergeant broke in. 'There is no hot food and no wood on which to cook it. We do not get hot food in the line.'

Dogorov stared at him and the man subsided immediately. Dogorov had never heard that peculiar whiney, petulant tone before but he was smart enough to guess that it came from a man who had all but given up hope.

'Sergeant,' he snapped, 'you will detail four men and four armed guards to return to headquarters. They will bring back hot rations for all personnel. If they encounter any difficulty in obtaining the food, they are to have the officer in charge speak to me by field telephone.'

He waited while the sergeant chose the men and started them off. 'If they do not return within one hour, they will stand sentry duty in rotation for the next three nights,' he told the sergeant, loudly. All eight dropped their shambling gait and hurried off.

'Sergeant, you will see to having the ready ammunition restacked in proper order and covered as per regulation. You will see that the main ammunition supply is not frozen together and that it is ready for use. You will detail as many men as necessary to accomplish that task in one hour. You will detail sufficient men to re-rig those tents in the centre of this clearing, well away from the trees. You will establish six sentry posts in the shape of a hexagon and each sentry will walk a beat. You will detail five men and five armed guards to cut firewood. When those tasks are underway, you will report to me in my tent.'

Without another word, he trudged across to a small tent obviously meant for the officers. Inside, frost clung to everything. He surveyed the mess. An empty sleeping bag lay on the floor of hard-packed snow and papers were frozen together on the portable field desk. A pistol belt and empty holster had been thrown into one corner. A canvas wash-basin was half full of ice and the contents of a field pack had been strewn about as if ransacked. If he had not seen it, he would not have believed that morale could have fallen so low.

Dogorov found a paraffin stove beneath the desk where it had fallen and shook it. The tank was half full and he worked the plunger to build up pressure, cleaned the orifice with a safety pin kept inside his tunic for that purpose, then loosened the cap and tipped a bit of fuel into the depression about the top of the tank. The fuel in his cigarette lighter refused to vaporize in the cold but the flint sparked and the stove fuel caught. When it had burned low, he turned the key and was rewarded by the steady hissing of escaping fumes. He adjusted the flame and went outside to fill a pan with snow. The wind was harder and the drift snatched from the surface was blowing almost head high. He cast a worried glance at the surrounding forest but knew that for the moment, there was little he could do.

The sergeant entered after knocking on the tent post, followed by a corporal. Dogorov accepted their salutes, nodded to the cot and the two men sat down side by side. He poured hot water into a pan in which he had crumbled tea leaves.

'I should have you both court-martialled for dereliction of duty,' he began without preamble. The two exchanged glances and Dogorov motioned for their canteen cups. He filled both and tapped cigarettes from a packet, then studied each in turn. Dogorov had the feeling they would welcome a court-martial, would welcome anything that would take them from the Karelian front.

The sergeant, Alexander Prokovitch Braun, was a shambling bear of a man. Several days' growth of beard and the close-drawn hood of his tunic hid most of his features, but his eyes were beaten, dumb and devoid of hope. The corporal, Yuri Alexander Yupuri, seemed more lively and intelligent. Twice, he supported Braun, even while swaying with weariness himself.

'You two are a disgrace,' Dogorov snapped. 'Not those soldiers out there. They look to you for leadership but instead you have given up, like old women ready to die. Are you merely waiting for the Finns to come and finish you off?'

Braun's fist crashed onto the table. 'You,' he choked, 'what do you know what goes on here, you from Moscow or Leningrad or wherever with your nice warm quarters, plenty of food and vodka, and women. We've seen none of that for three months. The Finns . . . Wait until you've been here a few days!' His anger was so great that he choked and fell to glaring at Dogorov. His companion's expression had not changed but Dogorov saw that he was embarrassed.

Dogorov knew the sergeant-major's type; regular army, probably a conscript during the Great War, joined the Red Guard early, fought through the Civil War and stayed in the Army, not knowing how to do anything else. Twenty-five years of service, of keeping his nose clean, of avoiding the least odour of politics had taught him to do the job strictly by the book. And then he was sent to Karelia where the book was useless and so was he.

'What happened to the former lieutenant?' he asked, ignoring the man's outburst.

The corporal answered. 'Dead, Comrade Lieutenant.'

'Dead? How?'

'Murdered by those bastards, the Finns,' Braun burst out. 'Like every other. . . .'

The corporal stopped him with a gesture. 'It was like this, Comrade Lieutenant. It was dark and he was pissing at the back of his tent. A sniper shot him through the throat. He died in the morning.'

'Damn his soul,' the sergeant burst out. 'I told him to stay. . . .'

'Sergeant Alexander Prokovitch,' Dogorov roared. 'You forget yourself.' The field telephone rang and he picked it up.

An angry voice burst over the wire. 'Are you the new commander of Battery B, Sixteenth Battalion? I have just placed eight of your men under arrest. They demanded that I give them hot food immediately. Can't you control. . . .'

'Who is this?' Dogorov interjected and he heard the voice on the other end take a deep breath.

'This is Senior Lieutenant Pytor Borganovitch Grinsky. I am in charge of the commissary.'

'Well, Senior Lieutenant Pytor Borganovitch Grinsky, this is Senior Lieutenant Mikhail Gregorvitch Dogorov and those soldiers are acting under my direct orders. You are to give them hot rations for my battery and see that they have transportation back. I want that food to arrive hot.'

'Now see here, Lieutenant, ah, Dogorov is it? You don't. . . .'

'Lieutenant,' Dogorov's voice was lazy. 'If those men are not back here in twenty minutes, with hot food, I will march my battery down there and take them at gunpoint. I will then see that you answer to a board of inquiry. Do I make myself clear, Senior Lieutenant?'

He dropped the phone back on the cradle without waiting for an answer and glanced at his watch. The two non-commissioned officers watched with ill-concealed cynicism.

He smiled. 'Do the men know how to form a skirmish line?'

The sound of a lorry engine brought them all out of their tents. Standing in the back were the eight artillerymen, grinning from ear to ear. Dogorov stood back to let the two non-commissioned officers arrange the distribution of the food and, as they ate, he fancied he could see new life flowing back into the men. Often, he knew, nothing more was needed to turn exhausted, dispirited men into first-class soldiers again than the knowledge that they had not been abandoned; that, and a hot meal.

By 1700 hours, the artillery battery was in reasonable shape. Ice had been chipped from the two new Model 1939 76.2 millimetre field pieces, the ready piles of ammunition had been cleaned and restacked and sentries paced their routes with new alertness. Depending on that fact, he ordered the stoves lit inside the tents and for the first time in weeks, the men were warm again.

Dogorov managed to snatch a few hours' sleep near midnight only to be awakened at 0300, muzzy and disoriented. He had been dreaming again of a woman's body. He sat up, trying to clear his head, overcome with the sick feeling that it had been his mother's body . . . He took the message from the enlisted man.

An opening barrage had been ordered for 0900 hours – the start of General Semen Timoshenko's long-anticipated offensive. He stumbled into icy boots, lit the stove and studied the map while the water warmed. Any activity, even violent shivering, was welcome as it took his mind away from the dream. What the devil was the matter with him? he wondered. The woman's face was never identifiable but he was certain. . . .

The orders called for a thirty-minute bombardment of the Mannerheim Line to precede an infantry attack on Finnish positions fifteen kilometres south-east of Viipuri. Listening to the wind howling through the forest, Dogorov wondered if the attack could even take place.

Viipuri had become a symbol for both sides; to the Finns it represented their indomitability; to the Russians, the end of the war. For two months, the Finns had beaten off every attack, even when outnumbered fifteen and twenty to one. Take Viipuri, it was clear from the map, and the way along the railroad to Helsinki and victory was open and Leningrad, the second city of the Soviet Union would be safe.

The sergeant came into the tent as Dogorov was laying down estimated lines of fire and plotting ranges. The objective of the infantry attack which they were to support was a narrow salient protruding from the outer-most defence line a bare three kilometres north of Lake Kuolema. By all tactical considerations, the Finns should have withdrawn from the salient to even the line. That they had not done so suggested that it was a convenient jumping-off point from which to mount terror raids.

Dogorov had been wondering how he was going to get rid of the useless Braun. He knew that it would do no good to request a replacement as they were in far too short a supply. He could make do or denounce him to the military intelligence authorities for defeatism, or . . . Dogorov nodded to himself. Of course. And that would be much better for all concerned. And his family would think him a hero.

'Sergeant Braun, I want an observation post here,' he tapped a map coordinate that lay atop a small rise facing the lake. The map showed the area as clear of trees and high enough that a spotter should be able to see the fall of shell accurately, if the snow held off.

'Good God, Comrade Senior Lieutenant, you are sentencing the observer to death.'

Dogorov stared at him. 'Explain yourself,' he snapped.

'The Finns, Comrade Senior Lieutenant. They hunt artillery observation parties.'

'Sergeant, are your orders specific enough? You will take charge of the observation post and see that the Finns do not succeed. Select one other man and see to his equipment yourself. Issue a double ration of ammunition. Be ready in,' he looked at his watch, 'ten minutes.'

Braun's face had gone deathly pale but twenty years of unquestioning discipline combined with Dogorov's forbidding expression told him that the only alternative was a firing squad. He stumbled out of the tent without saluting.

Braun was speaking earnestly to the man chosen for the detail but broke off as Dogorov approached. The two pinched faces were filled with fear and hostility as he expected they would be. The stories were familiar, had formed a part of the folklore of the Great War. An officer who asked the impossible too often usually received a bullet in the back. He would walk behind them all the way, he decided.

'Report.'

'All present and accounted for, Comrade Senior Lieutenant.' Braun's voice, shaky as it was, barely concealed his hatred. 'Rations and ammunition for two days.' He did not flinch away from Dogorov's steady gaze and he thought, at least he is not a coward.

'The barrage has been ordered for 0900,' he told the soldiers. 'Are there any questions?'

The two men exchanged sullen glances and Dogorov nodded. 'Lead out, Sergeant.'

They travelled easily at first. The snow was hard packed and the snow shoes were not needed. But after the first kilometre, the forest began to thicken and the snow was softer. Underbrush protruding through the crust caught at their snowshoe webbing and Dogorov longed for skis.

The forest ended abruptly. Broken cloud scudded past the half moon whose reflected light from the fresh snow cover was misleading in brightness. Dogorov selected a position from which the observation party would be able to verify the fall of shot, yet remain hidden from marauding Finns. Under his direction, a hollow was scooped in the snow and surrounded with cut branches for camouflage. Braun was nearly useless. He started abruptly every time Dogorov spoke to him, then questioned every word in that whiney, hopeless voice. The man was an insult to all Soviet soldiers, Dogorov thought furiously.

When the field telephone was tested, he gave Braun the spotting map clipped to the plotting board and marked their position with great care. Braun's eyes shifted constantly and his hands shook so badly that the pencil point broke.

'Damn it man,' Dogorov exploded, 'they aren't Red Indians. The Finns are human, like you and me. If you stay awake and alert how could they possibly sneak up on you?'

The sergeant's lips drew back in a snarl; Dogorov tensed, but Braun laughed instead, a sharp, bitter laugh. 'We'll be all right, Comrade Lieutenant. Never you fear.'

Dogorov had wanted to shout at them, to beat sense into their heads but it was hopeless, a waste of energy. Braun at least was convinced that he would die. Dogorov started back, paralleling their course to watch for breaks in the telephone line.

He hadn't gone a thousand metres when he heard the faint snap of rifle shots. Dogorov sidestepped away from the wire in a panic and threw himself under a deadfall.

He remained perfectly still for twenty minutes, Tokarev pistol clutched in his shaking hands, shoulders hunched against a Finnish bullet or bayonet. For the first time in his life, he experienced real fear, the kind of fear that churns the stomach into a hard lump, that twists the intestines into painful cramps and liquefies their contents and he understood what Braun had endured for so long. But it was too late to change what he had done. The metallic taste of his own fear threatened to gag him and he wanted to close his eyes and retreat inside himself. The forest was close and still in the grey twilight of dawn and nothing moved, and everything moved. The cold finally drove him to his feet and duty sent him in the direction of the observation post.

Across the snow-covered fields below the rise, the pill boxes and the fortified positions of the Mannerheim Line were still invisible in the Arctic night. He turned slowly until he was staring at the spot where the observation post had been. Churned snow surrounded it and he moved stiffly, afraid of what he knew he would find, more afraid to show himself in the open.

Both men were dead, shot and bayonetted. Their positions suggested that they had simply waited for death and done nothing to defend themselves. Their rifles were still leaning against the side of the trench. He took a deep breath and backed off, watching the trees for the least sign of movement, thinking that at least he was rid of Braun.

'I want four men detailed for observation duty.'

Corporal Yuri Alexandrovitch Yupuri stared at him in disbelief, then nodded slowly. 'Will the Comrade Senior Lieutenant permit me to volunteer?'

Dogorov nodded, relieved that he had passed that hurdle. 'They are to be issued with extra rations and ammunition. Are there any automatic weapons in the battery?'

'Two PPD submachine guns, Comrade Senior Lieutenant.'

'Issue them to men you consider best able to use them.'

The corporal was puzzled, and frightened. Two men had died merely to prove to their new commanding officer that the Finns were unbeatable. Now he wanted four more.

Dogorov waited impatiently while the four men were mustered and their field gear checked. It was already 0700 hours. They would have to hurry.

There were three Finnish soldiers and they waited patiently in the trees opposite the break in the telephone wire. In their winter white overalls they were almost invisible against the snow. Dogorov held up a hand and the men following stopped. He pointed and Corporal Yupuri grinned suddenly, showing bad teeth between frost-blackened lips. Dogorov waved the two men with the PPDs forward and they crawled silently through the trees to within thirty metres. The Finns lay quietly in the snow, each separated by ten metres, watching the track made previously. The sky had turned charcoal grey and the shadows were still and dark.

Dogorov took a rifle from one of the men, checked to make certain a round was chambered, aimed and fired. The centre man threw up his hands and convulsed and an instant later, twin volleys from the submachine guns killed his companions. He left the bodies as a warning.

This time, Dogorov had two additional trenches dug in the snow so that the position formed a rough triangle with overlapping fields of observation and fire. The Finns would have to strike at all three posts at the same moment to be effective and it was well-known that their raiding parties travelled in small groups of three or four at most. The elimination of the three snipers responsible for the death of their comrades seemed to have infused a new spirit into the men and Dogorov thought that the Finns were in for a surprise very shortly. To each man, he gave the same instructions.

'Keep your eyes open in all directions. If you see the slightest movement, fire. You have more than sufficient ammunition. If you become careless, you will die. If you stay alert, you will kill Finns.'

By the time he returned to the battery only twenty minutes before the barrage was due to begin, he was exhausted. The word had already been passed along the telephone line that the observation party was ready – and of course, that three Finnish killers were dead. The battery seemed to have come alive at the news. The remaining artillerymen had already divided themselves into makeshift crews to replace the two dead men and the four on observation duty. Dogorov checked the field telephone and Corporal Yupuri reported that they had already beaten off one attack by Finnish snipers without a loss. Dogorov congratulated him and had the word passed through the battery.

At 0900 hours exactly, his arm dropped and the first gun smashed the silence with ear-splitting violence. Their battery had been the first to open fire.

Snow cascaded from trees and they were overwhelmed by the roar as the other guns of the battalion to either side opened up. Dogorov pressed the handset to one ear and covered the other against the concussions. The first corrections came back from the observation post and he passed them to the runner. A second shell was fired on target and the remainder of the battery opened up in sequence and he was lost in a world of swirling noise, shrill voices and numbers which he saw in his mind's eye as targets three kilometres away.

Concussion hammered his head, cordite fumes sickened him and filled his lungs until he could hardly breathe. He could imagine the scene from the forward observation post as the Finnish positions disappeared behind a shroud of exploding earth and smoke. Tiny corrections flowed in as the shells marched closer and closer to the tip of the salient.

Several minutes into the bombardment, the observation post came under attack again and in one of those unexpected instants of silence that come when all guns reload together, Dogorov clearly heard the crackle of small arms fire over the wire. Then there was no longer time to worry about the four men forward.

Finnish gunners had found their range and the forest erupted with the explosions of shells walking about them. A runner slid into his trench with instructions, distracting him for a moment from his personal terror.

A blinding explosion tore the breath from his lungs and dirt and ice showered the trench. In the roar of the battery he had not even heard the Finnish shell approaching. He cowered against the frozen earth, more frightened even than he had been earlier as he waited for the Finnish snipers to find him. Splinters of steel and wood slashed overhead and he was aware of the telephone operator's shaking body pressed against his and more shells exploded and the world disintegrated into a swirling maze of noise, head-splitting concussions and choking fumes. The next explosion was further away, as was the following, and then the barrage was walking deeper into the forest. The telephone operator swore filthy curses and stared at the end of his arm where the hand used to be. He turned to Dogorov as if to share his outrage and died. Only when his body slumped against the trench wall did Dogorov see the thin splinter of steel protruding from his temple.

He never knew, Dogorov thought in shock! In the intense cold, the man had not even felt the splinter.

Dogorov could feel the power of exploding charges as the frozen earth vibrated like a machine gone mad. When he dared look above the trench wall, it was to see a gun half dismounted, barrel pointing crazily at the sky while its the crew lay dead or dying in red-stained snow. There were no more explosions and he realized that he had not only survived his first enemy barrage but had done so with his wits intact. He forgot about the radioman and grinned in stupid relief, then vaulted out of the trench to check on the surviving gun crews.

A new telephone operator waved the handset at him and then Corporal Yupuri was on, telling him they had beaten off a third Finnish attack.

'We lost only one man and there are four Finnish bodies out there,' the corporal exulted. 'Think of it, Comrade Lieutenant, only one dead for four.'

The midday was bright and clear and the sky an electric blue as the cold grew sharper. Dogorov eyed the double line of men standing at attention in the snow and felt absurdly gratified that they did so at his order. A thought unworthy of a Red Army officer, he knew, but gratifying all the same.

The morning's successful action had bolstered the morale of the battery and made the six dead and four wounded easier to bear. At least they were killing Finns in exchange for their own lives. Now, he needed to reinforce that feeling, to tell them in the simplest terms why they were fighting and dying in the depths of the

Karelian forest. It was not as clear to the common soldier as Army Command seemed to think. Such explanations, he knew, were best left to the political commissars – more than one general had disappeared in the past few years because he had mixed politics and duty, but this was wholly different, he decided. This was war and there was not time to find and then convince a commissar to visit this near the front.

In any event, he sensed that the enlisted men did not fully trust the commissars. Dogorov was a devout party member, had been so from childhood. But he suspected that the issues in this war and the war he saw coming, transcended political considerations. The very survival of Russia was at stake, as it had been in 1812 when Napoleon had led his veterans to victory at Borodino and the occupation of Moscow. He doubted if more than one or two men in all the battery were party members – but all were Russian.

He cleared his throat and walked along the double rank. So far they knew him only as one more officer. His only advantage lay in the fact that he had just shown them how to apply common sense to the task of killing Finns.

'The Union of Soviet Socialist Republics offered Finland a reasonable exchange of twice as many square kilometres of territory for two vital naval bases and some forest land on our immediate border which would have protected our second great city of Leningrad from foreign attack,' he began quietly, keeping his voice conversational. 'Such an exchange would have benefited Finland by providing her with rich, new forest lands. Instead of being reasonable, Finland chose rather to treacherously attack Soviet border positions in late November. Even so, we continued to extend the hand of friendship and offered even more concessions. But the Finns, obsessed with the self-importance of their insignificant state, refused to be reasonable.' Dogorov was himself puzzled at Finnish intransigence in the face of the obvious.

'Finland is so insignificant in the dynamics of history that not once since 1919 has the USSR sought to take back historic Russian lands in Karelia. Instead, we offered an exchange for what was rightfully ours in the first place.'

He paused to let the significance of his analysis sink in. They were attentive enough, the best that he could hope for at this juncture.

'A great war is coming. It is no secret. Our enemy will come from the west.' Vague enough, he thought, to encompass anyone. 'Earlier in this year, we defeated the Japanese and threw them back from Mongolia. Today, we must do the same to the Finns and tomorrow – ' he pivoted swiftly and pointed to the south east. 'There is Leningrad, twenty-five kilometres away. Our second city is exposed to that enemy. The governments of Lithuania, Latvia and Estonia understood and allowed the Red Army and Navy military bases within their territory. They were quick to realize that a threat to the Soviet Union was a threat to themselves as well. The Finnish government refuses to understand this simple fact.

'Now we must defeat the Finnish army. Spring is coming and we will roll forward to the Gulf of Bothnia, on Finland's west coast,' he added hurriedly realizing that many of them would never have heard of the Gulf of Bothnia, 'and that will end the foolishness of the imperialistic Finnish government who have shown themselves nothing more than the tools of the Capitalist west.

'It is the policy of the Soviet Union to be always at peace with its neighbours, and it is the duty of the Red Army, our duty, to safeguard that peace. But we also have a duty to our Soviet state to see that it is safe from attack.'

He had spoken enough, he thought. Any longer and he would begin to lose their attention. Dogorov stiffened to attention and, to the surprise of the assembled battery, saluted them.

'Today, we killed many Finns and I salute you for your bravery and disregard of personal safety. The infantry offensive which our guns supported achieved its objective. Your actions were in the best tradition of the Red Army. We have taken the offensive against the Finns and will keep it. Do your duty and earn the gratitude of your motherland.'

Standing beneath the intense blue of the windswept sky, Dogorov's weariness suddenly vanished and he was filled with elation. He could sense the tide turning against the Finns.

Salla Front 13 – 18 March 1940

Atkins pushed past the rubble blocking the entrance and stumbled up the steps from the basement shelter into the March daylight. Torsten Fredriksson followed, stumbling with fatigue. The all-clear siren wavered in the damp air as a young village boy cranked the handle. The siren had a curiously hollow sound, as if a piece of shrapnel had penetrated its vitals.

All about the two men, people emerged from the ground like troglodytes and gathered in small groups, voices full of dull anger. One man raised a fist to the sky, then dropped it and shuffled away, too tired even to curse. The war is taking its toll, Fredriksson thought. These people hardly seemed the same cheerful, self-reliant Finns who in December and January had laughed at the ineptness of the Russian bombers.

Atkins had languished in Stockholm for several days until the sudden Russian offensive in mid-February had brought War Department orders to return. Fredriksson was on the same SAS flight to Helsinki and by some mysterious exercise of influence, had been allowed to travel to the front without an escort. This was the second time Fredriksson and Atkins had encountered one another.

Atkins had gone, dreading the visits to the front. The first had been into the beleaguered city of Viipuri at the end of February. For three days he had endured the continuous bombardment by the Soviet Seventh and Eighth Armies and he began to understand what the front-line soldiers in France had meant when they wrote during the last war about the curious fatalism that overcomes one in the face of massive and continuous bombardment. The body could only absorb so much fear, he discovered. After that, the mind either retreated into itself – what had once been called shell shock – or learned to tolerate it. That first night in a forward trench, he had reached those limits and when the Russian infantry materialized in the morning mists in human waves, he was able to observe the Finns stumbling out of the deep-buried bunkers to the firing points. In places the battle reached hand-to-hand proportions yet he found that he was able to function in spite of the nausea that raged and the fear that threatened but could not quite paralyse him.

He had learned then that one could control one's own fear and curiously, that lesson stemmed from the night he had shielded Erika from the Russian bombs with his own body. He hadn't been afraid then with death and bursting steel all about them because he hadn't thought to be and therefore, he reasoned, it must be a matter of mental control. And so it had proven, for him. He was still frightened to death on the front lines, but the fear was no longer paralysing.

Atkins had seen for himself the reinforced-concrete Finnish pill-boxes knocked askew by Russian artillery so that their guns could no longer be brought to bear. He had seen soldiers stumbling back from the front lines after a three-day rotation under continual artillery bombardment and infantry attacks. Their three days of rest in Viipuri were no rest at all; the Russians weren't bombarding just the front line, their shells smashed the city as well. Since Timoshenko had assumed command, the Russian offensive had increased both in efficiency and ferocity. The days when a ten-man Finnish patrol could destroy a Red Army battalion were over. Timoshenko believed in massed artillery bombardment and successive infantry attacks until an objective was achieved.

Fredriksson had not been especially surprised to see the British military attaché on the SAS plane. He had picked up curious rumours that the Prime Minister had received a briefing regarding possible Swedish intervention in Finland from a special envoy sent by Chamberlain, who was said to have brought along an officer with experience at the front. There were few enough British officers in Finland these days and Fredriksson had immediately remembered encountering Atkins at the Helsinki reception before Christmas. Atkins had brusquely denied having been at the front then. Seeing him on the plane, returning to Finland had confirmed his suspicions.

Atkins managed to avoid him in Helsinki but they had run across each other at Viipuri, purely by accident. By the time Fredriksson had arrived in Sortavala, the fighting had wound down in this sector and there was little to see or do for the moment. But he had needed a rest, and the mixed bag of Finnish officers and enlisted men, as well as a handful of Swedish and French volunteers, had interested him, and Atkins had appeared the following day.

In spite of certain language difficulties that arose, as the level in the vodka bottle sank each evening, Fredriksson had picked up enough stories to last him for a month of columns. In the process, he had gathered some details of Atkins' sojourn among the wild Finn and inferred others, although he stubbornly remained silent on his reason for having been in Stockholm three weeks before.

Atkins and Fredriksson climbed the steps to the town hall that also doubled as army headquarters. The Finnish battalion commander turned as they hesitated in the doorway. The man's eyes were full of tears. The Finn spoke fair English, learned as a sailor on British merchant vessels, and he had taken Atkins' arrival as the signal that the long-awaited British reinforcements were on their way. In fact, even Atkins had begun to hope that the rumours of a British-French task force loading in the Scottish port of Rosyth were true.

He smoothed out a tan message form and translated its contents in a shaky voice.

ARMISTICE ARRANGED WITH SOVIET FORCES STOP ALL HOSTILITIES CEASE 1040 HOURS 13 III 1940 STOP

The rest of the telegram defined the line to which Finnish forces were to pull back immediately. Viipuri was included forward of that line as was 90 per cent of Finnish Karelia. There was nothing either could say. Atkins took the telegram, stared at the unfamiliar language as if to assure himself that it had been translated correctly, then placed it on the desk. He saw an envelope addressed to him, stuffed it in a pocket and went out without a word.

The news spread quickly and the reaction was heartbreaking. Fredriksson followed to the top of the steps and watched Atkins walk into the trees. In the street, a young soldier in dirty uniform backed away from a knot of people, shouting over and over, 'No, no!' Others cried unashamedly and one soldier had sunk to his knees in the mud and slush where he remained, staring at his hands.

Atkins sat for a long time, staring into the white and grey depths of the forest that now belonged to the Russians. He had known it would end like this one day. There was no other way. Finland might win in the early stages but eventually the vast resources of Russia would wear her down, as it had worn down all of Russia's enemies from the Mongols to Napoleon's Grand Armée.

After a while he remembered the envelope and opened it. It contained orders to return to Great Britain immediately for reassignment. He was to report to the War Plans office in London.

Atkins stared at the sheet for a long time, his mind a maze of conflicting thoughts and impressions, remembering that first morning as he stood with Johan Erko and watched the Russian bombers race across the harbour towards Helsinki; that first patrol where, huddled in the snow, he had seen a rifle pointed at him for the first time and felt the gut-wrenching spasm of fear that had never left him since. He also remembered the forest sauna and the humorous sight of naked men resting their heels against a ceiling beam. He thought about the friends he had made among these courageous people who had done what the rest of the world merely talked about – faced up to outright aggression.

There were faces of those he had seen die; the young officer who had banged on the door of his overheated sleeping compartment; the boy, one instant crouching next to him in the midst of an artillery bombardment at Viipuri, then dead the next, killed by shrapnel. He remembered the soldier who had thrust the pack of explosive into the tank tread at the exact moment, knowing he would die an instant later. And there were all the villages carved from the Karelian forest, their only camouflage the snow and the trees as Russian aircraft searched for the faintest trace of light in the darkness, or smoke in the daylight.

Atkins brushed the snow from his white ski-suit. The air had taken on a hint of softness; illusory, he knew. Spring was weeks off yet. But it was coming, inevitably, and when it did, the Soviet juggernaut gathering deep in the Russian forests, would have rolled over the nearly fictional Mannerheim Line with armour and aircraft clear to the Gulf of Bothnia. In a David and Goliath contest,

David won only if he delivered a quick knockout blow. There had never been real hope for Finland.

He sat in the office of the British Minister to Finland two afternoons later describing the effects of the armistice on the Finnish army.

'Stunned surprise, sir, as if it were the last thing they expected. No one thought the Russians would do more than repeat the old demands to the Armistice Commission.'

'They did not this time,' the Minister replied grimly. 'The Russians added a new demand as well. You are aware that Hanko Cape, the north-western shore of Lake Ladoga and the entire Karelian Isthmus were ceded? Well, in addition, the Finns are now to cede the ice-free port of Petsamo in the Arctic and another in Salla. Then, the Finns are to build a new railroad from Karelia to the Swedish border and grant the Russians unlimited transit rights.'

'I don't understand why the Finns accepted,' Atkins shook his head. 'It just. . . .'

'Doesn't make sense?' The Minister toyed with a silver pencil. 'Nothing makes sense, I'm afraid. Not Czechoslovakia, not Poland, not Finland. Intolerable, each of them. Yet what could have been done? Any action we and the French might have taken would have, not might have, but would have degenerated into another world war. We are not ready and neither are the French.'

Atkins listened but did not agree. His own study of world history had led him to believe that rarely had any nation been prepared for war. Not even France under Napoleon and certainly none of the combatants in 1914. Wars were fought and won or lost by the willingness of government to persevere and their citizens to endure. Conversely, wars were prevented by governments who refused to be intimidated by an aggressor – and were supported wholeheartedly by its citizens. Finland had the determination but she lacked the resources, and the democracies had failed her as they had Poland, Czechoslovakia and Austria. It wasn't considered expedient he thought to take the side of tiny Finland against giant Russia because Russia might be needed as an ally against Germany. Perhaps. But it seemed to him that expediency, fine for the short run, would demand severe payments in the long run. Perhaps more severe than the democracies would care to make.

The train would take him to Turku, reversing his entry to Finland just four and a half months ago. It seemed a lifetime ago, he mused as he strode after the porter trundling his bags along the platform. There had been a telephone message earlier from Erko but he had not returned it.

The porter manhandled his trunk onto the train and received his tip. Atkins started to step aboard when he saw her and his carefully constructed indifference crumpled. She was more beautiful than he remembered. The greatcoat hid her figure but Atkins could still feel her soft slimness as if it were yesterday and not three months. Her hair cascaded from under the *Lotta Svard* cap to frame her pale face and large green eyes that searched his.

Atkins took Erika's hand formally, while passengers swirled about them.

'I had to come,' she said softly. A train whistle pierced the cavern and a blast of steam swirled past. The tannoy mumbled unintelligibly. 'I knew you were to leave today. Johan said you hadn't returned his telephone call. He left for Moscow this morning, to help. . . .' Her voice trailed away.

'You are to be married in May?'

Erika nodded but said nothing. Atkins could see the train guard waving towards the engine driver and the warning gongs sounded. He stepped onto the car step and looked at her, feeling as if he were about to burst. 'All the happiness in the world,' he whispered and leaned to kiss her cheek. The train began to move and Erika lifted her hand.

'There is an old Finnish proverb,' she said and began to walk beside the train as it moved. 'One can take back a good silence, but not a bad hurry.'

Atkins felt her fingers slip away and saw that her eyes were bright with tears.

The train ran out of the station and he watched her grow smaller and smaller until the track curved and she was lost to sight.

In the country of the blind, the one-eyed man is considered a fool.

Apologies to H. G. Wells

New York 24 November 1939 to 10 January 1940

The Italian liner *Leonardo da Vinci* edged against the battered pilings of Pier Thirty-six. Mooring lines snaked down, tugs hooted, the gangplank clattered into place and Keith Thorne's journey ended.

He joined the other passengers streaming down the gangway and breathed the icy effluence of the Hudson River and Manhattan gratefully. He pushed his way through the crowds about the luggage dispersal point, reclaimed his single suitcase and waited in line for the attentions of a customs officer. As he did so, he searched the crowd beyond the barrier for a familiar face and when he saw none, wondered if his cable had penetrated the various levels of Italian censorship after all. A customs officer motioned him to open his suitcase and rummaged through it, suspicious at his lack of baggage. The case contained two shirts, a second pair of slacks, socks, underwear and shaving kit, all replaced in Bucharest or Rome. When he found nothing that even suggested contraband, the customs officer stamped his ticket and passport reluctantly and released him.

Outside the terminal, a chauffeur appeared and touched his cap. 'Mr Thorne? My name is Collins.' He took the bag and led Thorne towards a dark blue Buick. 'Your parents sent me for you, sir. They are waiting for you at home.'

Thorne acknowledged the message and stepped into the back seat, grateful for the Buick's heater. Even though the sun was bright, the November wind was biting and the puddles scattered in shadows had crusts of sooty ice. The chauffeur crossed the island on Houston and turned up Lafayette. Traffic through the Midtown Tunnel was light and Northern Boulevard took them out through Queens towards Oyster Bay. Pedestrians filled the streets along the way, heads down against the wind, coats wrapped tightly, noses red. The sight of so many well-dressed people was a shock after the depressing conditions of Europe.

Trachial bronchitis had struck him down when he reached Bucharest and required two weeks of convalescence. A further two weeks were wasted while he waited for an inquiry into the death of Deborah Thorne, while supposedly under the protection of the Romanian government. The hearing was never conducted; neither the Romanian government nor the United States Embassy in Bucharest were especially interested in what might be uncovered.

Thorne was made to understand that as Deborah's citizenship status was questionable and the position of the Romanian government was precarious, he could expect no further inquiries to be made.

He had spent a further month in Rome waiting for an exit permit. Both there and in Bucharest, he found the people sullen with the foreknowledge of war and the two fascist parties swollen with their own self-importance. Mussolini made bombastic speeches day after day that reminded him of the ravings of Adolf Hitler.

The shops in Rome were little better than in Bucharest. There was little merchandise on display and the food markets were worse. Huge posters in the heavy-handed heroic style that seemed common to despotic governments everywhere, exhorted the masses to produce more – and consume less.

Long Island was as neat and clean as he remembered. Traffic was growing heavier but the chauffeur was able to maintain an even forty miles an hour. Blocks of apartment houses alternated with neat homes and overflowed with children. Business districts came and went and the number of billboards advertising products was overwhelming. Or perhaps, he had just never noticed them before. After Europe, he was seeing it all with new eyes, it seemed. An automobile advertisement portrayed a family enjoying their first ride in a new Plymouth. Significantly, no details of the car were shown, only the happy faces of the ideal American family. The war was so distant it might not have existed.

Thorne began to pay more attention. Mothers passed on sidewalks pushing bundled children in strollers. People went in and out of stores with packages. The crowds that gathered around bus stops had the prosperous, purposeful air of people who knew what they wanted and how to get it. They would, he suddenly realized, have little patience with a war that might threaten the pursuit of the good life.

The limousine stopped on the circular gravel drive before the house. His father, as stern and self-possessed as ever, emerged to wait for his son. Thorne stepped out with his suitcase, resolved to hold his temper.

'You look well enough, Keith.'

'Well enough for what?'

Thorne cursed himself. In two sentences, they had fallen into the old pattern – the challenging statement on his father's part, the offensive reply on his. To make up for it, he gripped his father's hand a little tighter.

'Let's go in out of the cold.'

In the foyer, the coloured butler, Johnson, smiled a welcome.

'Welcome home, Mr Keith. Welcome home. We were all very worried about you.'

For a moment, emotion choked Thorne and he could only grin foolishly. Johnson nodded and smiled, understanding. 'Good to have you back. Let me take your coat.'

Glad of the excuse to turn away, Thorne surrendered his coat and Johnson picked up the bag. 'I'll just take this upstairs, Mr Keith, and draw a bath.'

Thorne followed his father into the library, contrasting the welcome given him by a servant with the coolness of his father's. Keith Thorne Senior was a largish man, over six feet with shoulders to match his height. For the first time, Thorne took a really good look at him, startled at the evidence of aging. The golden streaks in his hair were gone, leaving it an even iron grey. The skin of his face had begun to sag about his nose and mouth. There were dark pouches beneath his eyes and the definite beginnings of wattles. Even so, he stood as straight as ever. His father had always been proud of his ramrod posture, a legacy of his service in World War I as a Captain in a New York National Guard regiment.

Perhaps the changes had been there all along and he hadn't noticed. Who was it that said that a man's first intimation of his own mortality came when he noticed his father growing old?

The elder Thorne handed his son a brandy and raised his glass. 'To your safe return.' Thorne answered the toast and watched warily over the rim of his glass.

'By the way,' his father said, 'Shirley insists on a small cocktail party this evening to welcome you home. Just your own friends. We all thought you would prefer that to a large crowd at the dock. Allow you a chance to readjust.'

He nodded, keeping his expression neutral. Christ in heaven, that was the last thing he wanted! He groped for something to say.

'Mother isn't feeling well?' In spite of his resolution, he could not keep the tinge of sarcasm from his voice.

The elder Thorne ignored it. 'She asked me to apologize and say she will join us at dinner.' Both men knew that her sick headaches were only a ploy to avoid unpleasantness – or signal annoyance.

Keith Thorne automatically pulled the uncomfortable leather side-chair to the desk and sat down. As a child, he had rarely entered the library for any other reason than to receive punishment. In spite of his resolution, his temper was slipping again.

'What the devil's the matter with her this time?' he demanded.

His father affected surprise at his outburst.

'I told you, she is not. . . .'

' . . . feeling well,' Keith finished. 'As always whenever she's displeased with me. What is it this time, for Christ's sake?'

'Keith, I will not allow that kind of language in my house.'

Thorne grunted and subsided. His father was a devout Presbyterian. 'I assume you received my letter?' He had written a careful report of his experiences in Warsaw, and afterwards on the Romanian border. While he hadn't expected a hero's welcome, he certainly hadn't foreseen such a chilly reception.

His father nodded. 'Yes. I was sorry to hear about the death of Jacob Yitzak. He was a great talent. And your wife, of course. I showed parts of your letter to the editorial staff. Tompkins has suggested that you write a short book based on your experiences. Quite a demand developing for first-hand accounts. . . .'

'Showed him my letter?'

'Of course.' His father shifted in the chair. 'That young woman. . . .'

'Deborah,' Thorne supplied.

'Ah, yes, Deborah. It was a legal marriage?'

'The ceremony was performed by a Lutheran minister from the Danish legation. All the proper legalities were observed.' He could not keep the snide tone from his voice.

'I understood from your letter that it was a marriage of convenience. You thought the girl was in grave danger from the Germans?'

Thorne stared at his father in amazement. 'Thought she was in danger . . . my God, I told you in my letter she was executed by the SS!'

His father nodded uncomfortably. 'But she was an American citizen, why would the Germans have dared. . . .'

'The Nazis don't give a damn for law, international or otherwise, except of course, for the ones they make themselves.'

His father winced at the *damn*, but let it pass. 'Was she accused of a specific crime?'

'Of course! They justify every atrocity with legal trappings. She was a Jew for starters. Her husband was also Jewish and a Polish army officer. He was declared a terrorist and executed. She was killed because she was his wife, and because she was a Jew. That was more than enough reason for them and they used the same "legal" rationale to murder Jacob Yitzak.'

'Keith, I find it hard to believe that German soldiers would murder a woman and an elderly man, in fact, a world celebrity, simply because of their religion. This is the twentieth century, not the fifteenth and the Germans are a civilized people. I am aware that there is a great deal of anti-Semitism in Germany, but you are suggesting that Jews are being murdered on a large scale and for no other reason than their race.'

'Don't try to tell me about the Nazis, Dad! They damned near executed *me*. They claimed that I was a British spy. Instead of verifying my identity with the American Embassy, they tortured me. I was sentenced to death by an SS tribunal – or about to be – when I was recognized by a German army officer I had met a few weeks before. Do you know what it's like to be half-drowned in a bathtub, not once but four times? Or beaten and kicked when your hands are tied behind your back?'

Thorne found himself leaning over the desk, shouting at his father who was staring at him as if he were a madman. He muttered an apology and subsided into the chair to drain the brandy in a single gulp.

His father, he saw, had drawn on the familiar inquisitor's mask with which he struck terror into the hearts of his son, servants, editorial and accounting staffs and not a few authors who had disappointed him.

'Are you asking me to believe that you were actually tortured?' he asked in a cold voice.

'Of course! What the devil else do you think they do to spies?' Somehow, his father's reaction was not as unexpected as it might have been.

'I am sorry, Keith, but I cannot believe that. You are overwrought and in need of a good rest.'

Thorne chuckled in spite of his anger. He was twenty-nine years old but his father still treated him like a boy. His manner was exactly that of a parent who has caught his child in a lie. How many times had . . . he shifted restlessly.

'I don't care what you think,' he muttered. 'I know what happened to me.'

'Keith, there is no need to continue this senseless charade. We were told by the State Department that you were detained but that no formal charges were made. And there was certainly no mention of torture.'

Thorne swore under his breath and stood up. He unbuttoned his shirt and pulled it off. 'There, damn it. Look at that.' He pointed to a fading bruise on his rib cage, and was suddenly aware that the intervening weeks had nearly eliminated the physical signs of the torture.

'I was kicked there by the guards. What the devil would the Embassy know? The Germans closed it as soon as they occupied the city. No diplomats, including their own, were ever allowed anywhere near the prisons and concentration camps. If you want to really know what happened, write to Jim Howell. But don't be surprised if the letter never reaches him.' He drained the glass again and slammed it down on the bar.

'Maybe I should have brought you a signed affidavit from Warsaw. Dear Mr Thorne. We have tortured your son. Signed, the SS.'

The elder Thorne waited for his son's tantrum to run its course. He had hoped the experience in Europe would mature him but he was beginning to despair of that ever happening. This babbling about torture and the Lord knew what else, was as usual designed to cover up another failure.

'I think I'm beginning to understand.' Keith stared at his father. 'Mother refuses to come down because I married a Jewess.'

'Keith, don't be foolish. . . .' but the guilty start of surprise told Thorne he was right. It was now his father's turn to shift uncomfortably and he felt a vague satisfaction at this minor victory.

'You don't want to believe that people are being killed in Poland simply because they profess a certain religion. You don't want to believe it because your Christian faith would then demand that you do something about it and that poses a moral dilemma as you certainly can't be placed in the position of defending Christ-killers and money-grubbing kikes. That would be unthinkable and so you dismiss any. . . .'

'Keith!' his father thundered. 'I will not have those words spoken in this house!'

' . . . evidence that conflicts with your rationalization,' he continued relentlessly. 'The fact that I married the girl to save her life, doesn't make the slightest bit of difference to either of you. Your real concern is the damage I might have done to your social position!'

'That is just about enough, Keith. That is a cruel and foolish accusation. I have seen no proof that Jews, or anyone else for that matter, are being killed as you claim. But if they were, of course I would be upset and would do my best to stop it, whether in this country or another. As for the girl, I know only that she was the daughter-in-law of Jacob Yitzak and she would have been welcome in this house simply because she was your wife. Her religion would never have been held against her.'

He probably believed every word, Keith thought and he was convinced that he would have done his Christian duty by allowing her to enter his home. For the first time in his life, Keith Thorne felt superior to his father.

'I can see it's no good trying to talk to you about this,' he stood up. 'I'd like to take a bath and get some rest if you don't mind.'

He paused at the door and looked back across the warm room smelling of old books and polished leather. Through the open blinds, he could see that the afternoon sun had disappeared and heavy snow clouds had swept in from the Sound. He wanted to say something, anything, that would mitigate the old harshness between them but his father had already turned away to read a manuscript.

Thorne was surprised to see that his old room was much as he remembered. New blue wallpaper replaced his childish selection of airplanes and tanks but otherwise the room had changed very little. The oak desk at which he had agonized over school books, struggling with the lines of print that faded and jumped before his eyes, remained against the wall facing the window. God, how he had hated that desk.

The closet was filled with new suits and shirts. Four pairs of shoes were on the floor, everything brand new. Not a homecoming present but simply a necessity to be met. A telephone call by a servant to the tailor had taken care of it. That they might not fit perfectly never entered his mind.

He shed his clothes and relaxed in the bath. On top of the clothes hamper was a small tray with another brandy. He grinned at Johnson's thoughtfulness and sipped the liquor. The hot water eased his incipient exhaustion and he felt contentment begin to steal through him. In spite of its tensions and frustrations, this was home.

Thorne managed two hours of sleep before it was time to dress and see his mother. The nurse-companion answered his knock and stared at him with the usual mixture of hostility and jealousy reserved for anyone who sought to intrude upon her charge. His mother lay propped up in bed, a damp cloth across her forehead, and assayed a brave smile.

'That's all right, Matty. I am always well enough to visit with my son.' She patted the bed and Matty retired into another room.

His mother looked well enough, he thought. In actual fact, she was as healthy as the horses she rode summer and winter about the estate. There was nothing frail about her other than a deceptively diminutive frame that concealed enough stubbornness for ten women. He was never certain what had changed her from the carefree, effervescent woman he barely remembered from early childhood to this hypochondriacal, self-centred snob. Years before, she had convinced her husband that she was hovering on the brink of death and he, whether from fear that she was right or gratitude for the freedom it allowed, played the game.

She clasped his hand and raised it to her lips and, for a moment, Thorne hovered between love and disgust.

'You can't know how happy I am to have you home again. I never did like the idea of your going off to a foreign country. If you had to go to Europe, you should have gone to a civilized country, England or France for instance.' She smoothed the blanket. 'I must say, Keith, I was quite taken aback. Marriage is a serious decision. At the very least, you could have wired your intentions. You haven't the faintest idea how badly we felt at having to learn about it from one of your father's friends in the State Department. Why, it must have been all over Washington.'

Oh Christ! Thorne groaned to himself.

'Now, you must tell me about your adventures.' She smiled in self-satisfaction, prepared to be entertained.

He tried his best to make her understand what had happened in Poland and how bad conditions were in Warsaw. But it was so far beyond her experience that he might have been describing conditions on Mars. She asked a question now and then but he had the feeling that she was only playing the dutiful mother and waiting patiently for him to finish. In anticipation of her questions, he described Deborah in some detail. For some reason, he glossed over his own imprisonment and arrest, alluding to his treatment in general terms and it was only when he had time to think about it some days later, that he realized that embarrassment was responsible. He simply did not know his mother well enough to talk about anything so personal.

Her questions were predictable. 'Then you did not know for certain that the girl's husband was dead when you married her?'

'He was reported to have been executed by the Nazis. . . .'

'A report? Only that. Why didn't you go to the government? Surely, even in Poland they must have an office where you could have asked?'

'Mother,' he said, exasperation creeping into his voice, 'the city was a shambles. The Government had left weeks before and so many had been killed that no one could possibly have known. I married her only to make her an American citizen and get her out of the country.'

'Now, Keith, I understand all about the war. The newspapers are full of such stories. What I don't understand is how you could have allowed yourself to be taken in like that?'

'Like what, mother?' His voice took on a sullen edge and she tapped his hand.

'Now don't you take that tone with me, young man,' she said with mock severity. 'I am sure she was very pretty and in such conditions, quite appealing. It is only natural that she take advantage of you. A pretty girl will turn your head every time, dear.'

He ignored the reference to the paternity trial. 'Mother,' he forced his voice to remain even when he wanted to shout through her obstinate wall of prejudice and ignorance. 'I am not a boy any longer. Soon I'll be thirty years old. I did not marry Deborah because she was appealing or attractive; in fact, in the three weeks I knew her, I not only did not have sexual relations with her, I didn't even kiss her, for Christ's sake!'

'Keith, please, I am your mother. . . .'

'I married her because I thought it would save her life. Can you understand that, mother? To save her life. But it did not make any difference to the Nazis that she was an American citizen or that she was pregnant even. A soldier put a pistol to her head and killed her!'

His mother began to cough and he handed her the water glass. She sipped a bit and patted her throat, staring at him with widened eyes. From the corner of his eye, he saw Matty poised in the doorway.

'I am certain,' his mother said in an artificially weak voice, 'that you thought you were doing the proper thing at the time, dear boy. An act of Christian charity. . . .'

'What the devil are you talking about?'

'Why marrying that Jewish girl of course, because you thought the Germans might harm her. I am sure that because you made an emotional decision, your motives are no less valid. . . .'

'You think that. . . .'

'Now Keith, you must really stop and think. You are so impulsive. People don't shoot other people for no reason, my dear. People are executed only if they have committed crimes. . . .'

'For Christ's sake, what the hell would you know about it?' he roared. 'Here you are, safe and sound on Long Island in a huge house with five servants and a nurse. Your biggest worry is which horse to ride tomorrow morning, or which evening gown to wear to the country club.' He crossed the room in two strides and yanked the door open.

'I'll tell you what Deborah's crime was, damnit! It was her religion. A madman in Berlin decreed that Jews aren't human because they worship God a bit differently. And so they shot her, just as they did her husband and her father-in-law and God knows how many others as well.'

After the door closed, his mother turned to the nurse who had hurried in to soothe her with a cold compress.

'Matty,' she asked rhetorically, 'what do you suppose I said to make him so angry?' Instead of answering, the nurse pressed the cloth to her forehead.

'But then he always was such an unpredictable boy.'

His mother did not appear at dinner and his father did not comment on the fact. They ate in silence interrupted only by the noiseless comings and goings of the serving staff.

Keith Thorne thought his father an overbearing egotist convinced of his right to direct the lives of others, a conviction reinforced by years of authoritarian direction in the family publishing business. He still insisted on personally reading and approving any manuscript passed for publication by a select staff of editors – not one with less than fifteen years seniority. Thorne, Dorsten and Winslow published few bestsellers but by the same token very few of their books failed to earn the minimum corporate profit established at the beginning of every fiscal year and accordingly, they were considered an extremely sound, if conservative to the point of stultification, publishing firm.

From the opposite end of the table, the elder Thorne was in turn thinking about his son. During his last two years at Harvard, he had entertained the hope that the boy was at last beginning to mature. His grades had improved to a respectable level and he seemed to have taken a much greater interest in academic pursuits. But it had been an illusion of course, as so many things about Keith were. The boy had run off to join the Army! To fly! Even now, seven years later, it was enough to anger him. He had seen the crash and Keith's subsequent resignation from the Air Corps as a blessing and he had at last come into the firm.

He looked along the table to where Keith was playing idly with his food, just as he had done as a child, and bit back a caustic remark; after all, he wasn't a boy any longer.

That mercenary young woman had nearly ruined everything. The rumours had been going on for months that Keith was acting like a playboy. Certainly, there was little enough he could do about it. The boy had his salary and a sizeable trust fund from his grandparents and what he did with the money was his own business. But the scandal caused by the newspaper stories during the lengthy court battle had almost broken his heart and it had cost him fifteen thousand dollars to expose the little harridan as a fraud. Not only was she not pregnant, but she was married to the man who had planned the entire affair. To remove him from his usual crowd, who, in his opinion were the main cause of the problem, he had sent Keith to Poland. And even there, the boy had managed to create an incredible mess. And now this absurd story about executions and torture to justify marrying a Jewess! It was simply failure after failure.

The cocktail party was to begin at seven. Thorne arrived at the Case residence at six-thirty and was shown into the sitting room by a maid. Ten minutes later, Shirley, trailing Chanel, swept into the room and allowed him to kiss her cheek, then whirled away to stand by the fireplace.

'Damn you Keith,' her voice was low and deadly. 'You've made a laughing stock of me!'

Thorne gaped at her. 'I did what?'

'You made a fool of me. Did you forget that I am your fiancée?'

'What the hell are you talking about?'

'This damned marriage that you let yourself be trapped into by some scheming little bitch. Keith, sometimes I wonder if you will ever grow up.'

'Shirley, it wasn't like that at all. The Nazis were. . . .'

'Keith, I've heard all the nonsense about Nazis I care to. I don't believe any of it and I certainly wouldn't expect you to believe it either. My father told me about British propaganda during the First World War – German soldiers raping Belgian nuns and bayonetting babies.'

Thorne shook his head doggedly. Why had he expected her to sympathize? 'This time, it isn't propaganda. I was there, I saw what happened.'

'You saw what certain people wanted you to see. For God's sake Keith, your father is an influential American publisher! Do you think the Germans would dare harm you? When the Poles attacked Germany, Father was certain a new propaganda campaign would be started. He has many business contacts in Germany and is certainly in a position to know! The Jews schemed to involve you and like a fool you fell into their trap.'

'Shirley,' he broke in, 'you weren't there, and I was. You didn't see what the Germans did to Warsaw. . . .'

'I saw the newsreels,' she broke in scornfully. 'A few buildings damaged.'

He shook his head. 'Newsreels don't show everything, especially when they've been censored. They damned near levelled the city. They bombed and shelled indiscriminately to terrorize the population. God knows how many people were killed. I saw women and children killed in the streets. I worked on the barricades myself and a young girl next to me was killed by German machine-gun bullets.'

Thorne had gripped her wrist and was shaking it at each point. 'What about Deborah? Executed because she was Jewish and her husband was a Polish army officer. For God's sake, her father was a world-renowned violinist!'

Shirley yanked her wrist away. 'Keith, you can be the biggest fool sometimes! How do you really know she hadn't committed a crime? Or her husband, or her father-in-law for that matter? You hardly knew those people! My father looked into the matter when your letter came. He even spoke to some people at the State Department and they said there was a great deal more to the story

190

than even you knew. They even feel that the Germans are being quite circumspect in their treatment of the Polish people and there was no evidence that Jews were being treated any differently. There are no reports of atrocities from the American Embassy in Warsaw, nor have the newspapers or the newsreels reported the mass killings which you claim are taking place. Oh here and there, you can hear some nonsense but the source always turns out to be connected with either the British or the former Polish government.'

Thorne exploded with anger. 'I can't believe this! I can't believe that you would take the word of some damned bureaucrat over mine! I was there, damn it! I saw what was going on! What the hell is the matter with you?'

Shirley recoiled and covered her face with her hands. He heard a muffled sob and in an instant, his anger dissolved and he gathered her into his arms, muttering apologies. She clung to him, whispering, 'Keith, let's not talk about it anymore. I didn't mean to start a tiff. This is your first night at home. I'm just so glad that you're back; just so glad.'

She half turned in his arms and raised her lips to be kissed and he caressed her bare shoulders. For an instant, she pressed against him, then pushed away.

'Please Keith, not here. The servants. . . .'

The evening passed in a dreary succession of desultory conversations with people who, for some reason, he had once considered interesting or influential but who were now merely boring, ignorant or just plain inconsequential. Everyone asked perfunctory questions about his trip but barely listened to the answers. Everyone alluded to his marriage but no one dared ask a straightforward question until an old flame, assuming a position of special privilege, asked him point blank about his little Polish wife in a voice calculated to make them the centre of attention. Keith did not miss her icy smile directed at Shirley.

Here it was, he thought, the evening's entertainment. Even so, he told the story, hoping it would break through their smugness. Thorne told it as factually as possible, yet even before he finished, one or two had turned away to carry on conversations of their own. Some listened with smiles that suggested he had been victimized – as Shirley seemed to feel he had – few seemed concerned, the rest were merely politely bored. He found himself dramatizing his own treatment and Jacob Yitzak's beating and execution – and describing Deborah's death proved a mistake; it served only to confirm in their minds that he was exaggerating.

There were questions, mostly about the Nazis; what they looked like, how their officers acted, had he seen tanks and Stuka airplanes? Had he seen Hitler when he came to Warsaw? No one asked about the Yitzaks or the Polish people.

A pushy individual he did not recognize demanded to know if Roosevelt wasn't leading them all down the garden path to war, then pushed his slick hair back and answered his own question.

'Senator Borah is right. Let the damned Europeans stew in their juices this time. America has had enough of bailing the British and French out of their messes. The Poles got just what they deserved. Didn't they help the Germans carve up Czechoslovakia? I'm sure you agree.'

Thorne drew a deep breath, not quite sure how to answer, or even if he should. 'No, I don't.' A few people turned to listen. 'The Nazis are going to overrun Europe unless someone stops them. If the British and French don't, then within two years you'll see Nazi warships along our Atlantic coast demanding an end to the persecution of our *ethnic* Germans.'

The man snorted. 'Nonsense. How could they possibly carry an invasion force across three thousand miles of water? Instead of supporting the British and French, we should be doing business with the Germans. They know the value of. . . .'

'Aw, for Christ's sake!' Thorne muttered and stalked away. Shirley had watched the encounter and hurried into the hall after him.

'Keith! Where do you think you are going? You can't walk out in the middle of your own party! What will people think of me?'

'I'm leaving, damn it. That damned bunch of know-it-all bastards. Explain my bad manners any way you wish.' He snorted and yanked his coat from the closet, ignoring the stricken maid.

Shirley waved her away, started to retort, then thought better of it. She took her own coat and pushed him to the door. Outside, the night had turned bitterly cold. It had snowed most of the afternoon and the lawn was covered with a glistening, white shroud. Shirley led him to her car and got in.

Traffic was heavy but moved smoothly as they approached Manhattan, brilliant against the black sky, like a science-fiction vision of a future of graceful towers and fairy-lights. In the black canyons of Manhattan, traffic signals glowed like beacons. A policeman, muffled to the ears, watched them pass without curiosity. The garage was closed and Shirley found a parking place just off Park Avenue on Thirty-fourth.

'Come on, grouch,' she called and paced him to the glassed lobby of the apartment building. The doorman was sound asleep and Shirley held a warning finger to her lips.

The townhouse was cold and Thorne built a fire while Shirley went round to open radiators. She came back with two large whiskies and they pulled the sofa to the fireplace. The whiskey relaxed him and he kissed her long and hard. When he started to unfasten her cocktail gown, she pushed him away and went into the bedroom.

Thorne sat back in the couch, content to wait, and finished the last of the whiskey, wondering if perhaps he hadn't expected too much. Everyone could not have changed in four months, therefore he must have. The thought made him uncomfortable. He liked himself well enough the way he had been. His years in the Army Air Force as an officer had taught him the meaning of responsibility; the years following had taught him that it was easier to do without and he had been content since his resignation to drift.

The flat had warmed considerably when he heard the door open and turned to see Shirley standing in the bedroom doorway. She had wrapped a towel about her and was posed, one hand on the frame, one knee bent; demure virginity. For just an instant, he had a terrible urge to laugh. Then she let the towel slip and he got up quickly and crossed the room to her.

It was after three a.m. by the clock on the nightstand. The flat was overheated now and they lay side by side on the bed without the blankets. He had made love to her twice, the first time quickly at her urging. The second time, she had been reluctant but he persuaded her and that had been much more satisfying, for him at least. But Shirley had turned away almost immediately afterwards. Thorne lay with one hand behind his head, smoking, mind drifting.

He got up after a while to turn down the radiators and open a window. In the kitchen he found a bottle of bourbon and poured some into two glasses. On the way back, he stopped to stare down at the street, deserted in the frozen night. It would have been much more satisfying to have made love to Deborah. The unexpected thought surprised him and suddenly uncomfortable, he pressed his forehead to the cold glass. The room was dark except for glowing ashes in the fireplace. A snowplough hissed past on Park Avenue and the street was still again. A traffic signal changed in monotonous cadence from red to green to yellow to red. . . .

When he returned to the bedroom, a cigarette glowed in the dark. Shirley lay on her side and when he placed a hand on her hip, she pushed it away irritably.

'Keith, if I become pregnant, we'll be married immediately. Do you understand?'

What the hell? he thought.

'I only allowed you to do this so that you would get *her* out of your system. I don't care whether you were right or wrong and I don't wish to hear *her* name again. You are not to even think about her again. Is that understood?'

193

Having delivered her ultimatum, Shirley mashed her cigarette in the ashtray so hard that sparks flew, then drew the blankets up to form a barrier between them. Thorne finished both whiskies but they failed to help him sleep. He lay awake until five, then got up and dressed without bothering to shower. The doorman was still asleep when he went out into the frosty darkness and walked up Park Avenue to Grand Central where he caught a train for Long Island.

The newspapers were curiously lacking in solid war news. Brief stories about Finland appeared, supplemented with outraged warnings from politicians and community leaders against international communism. There were demands that the United States send funds and arms but little else. There was an abundance of glowing tributes to reviving business or the details of the latest Hollywood scandal. The country was working hard to put a decade of depression behind them and, as if to assist in that endeavour, the war seemed to have collapsed of inertia. The newsreels could show only steely-eyed French *poilus* eyeing German bunkers across the Rhine or British Tommies marching along French country lanes. At a Manhattan rally of the America First Committee, an American Bund leader lauded the Fuehrer's civilized reserve in confining the war's spread.

The press seized on the British Broadcasting Corporation's characterization of the war as the 'Sitzkrieg' and political cartoonists and pundits had a field day. The war in Europe was a joke or an annoyance depending on one's political persuasion. Republicans and democrats alike were unanimous in predicting that hell would freeze over before the United States would involve itself in a European squabble again.

After an abrasive week in the Long Island house, Thorne arranged to borrow a friend's empty Manhattan flat. His mother remained in her room the morning he left. Both of his parents, he had long ago concluded, preferred their lives uninterrupted by anyone or anything except their own interests.

Thorne returned to his office two weeks before Christmas. His father was cordial but distant whenever they met in editorial conference. Thorne plunged into the pile of manuscripts that appeared on his desk and laboured over the precise reports his father insisted on, and ignored the memos from his chief editor suggesting that he write up his experiences in Poland.

He worked long hours and took a briefcase full of manuscripts back to the Seventieth Street flat each evening. He saw Shirley only on weekends. She refused to go to his flat, claiming that too many people in New York knew her, a supposition Thorne found vaguely egotistical in a city of seven million people. Since her parents had come into the city for the pre-Christmas Season, the apartment on Park Avenue was unavailable to them.

He found that everyone he came in contact with knew at least a part of his story. Someone would stop him in the hall and ask how things were, then would test their bits of the information with questions like, 'heard you were wounded in Poland, old man. Nothing serious I hope,' or 'heard you were a guest of some German (or Polish) general. Interesting people, those Germans (Poles).' The other editors were envious and the secretaries and typists seemed to think it all very romantic.

The day before Christmas as he was poring over a particularly convoluted manuscript full of vague literary allusions, someone knocked on his door. He tossed the manuscript aside in relief.

A particularly nubile young typist slipped in, closed the door and shrank against it for a moment, then as if recalling a resolution, took a deep breath and arched her chest in imitation of Paulette Goddard. Thorne was entranced by the bobbing motion of her tight sweater.

'I just . . . I just wanted to tell you, Mr Thorne . . . that I heard what happened, in Poland . . . and to your wife.' She stopped and blushed but the effect was lost when he noticed her saddle shoes and rolled stockings. 'I think . . . I think it's all so terribly brave of you . . . and romantic. If there's ever anything I can do for you . . . anything,' she finished with a suggestive wriggle and flew out of the office before he could say a word.

What surprised him the most was the deep-seated rejection of war that had sprung up throughout the country. As a military officer, he had automatically subscribed to the belief that a major war was inevitable and that the United States would at least be engaged against the Japanese sometime in the distant future. He had been caught up in a small portion of that war – which was far worse than anything he might have imagined – and had seen at first hand, the meaning of fascism. He had read the Italian dictator's speeches which seemed carbon copies of Hitler's and had viewed with distaste the wave of fascist repression sweeping Romania. But the vast majority of Americans had not and that fact, coupled with the historical strain of pacifism in the American people – many of whose ancestors had left Europe to avoid its periodic wars – meant an automatic rejection of any part in another European squabble.

His father's Christmas Eve party for friends and associates was traditional and attendance obligatory. Shirley was the centre of attention in a daring blue gown and a dark-haired man whose name he had forgotten the moment they were introduced, hovered about her with a faintly proprietorial air.

Near midnight, he was staring through reflections in the plate glass window into the frozen garden that was his mother's pride and the gardeners' despair – she supervised them with all the ruthlessness of a Mississippi chain gang boss. He was on the verge of sneaking upstairs to bed when an abrasive voice broke his thoughts.

'Aren't you young Thorne?'

He hated being referred to as 'young Thorne', as if he were only a robotic extension of his father. He turned to see a self-assured, heavy-set man watching him speculatively. He thought he had seen him about the offices once or twice and knew vaguely that he had something to do with a bank approached by the firm to finance a new expansion. The man was short, almost squat and had a pugnacious face that one would normally have associated with a used car dealer, or some other questionable profession, and was accompanied by a stunning young woman in a black cocktail dress.

'I understand you got yourself caught in that mess in Warsaw. Damn fool Poles thinking they could stand up to tanks with horses. Tell me, what did you think of Herr Hitler's army boys, impressive?'

Thorne took an instant dislike to the man. 'Impressive?' he snapped. 'Hardly the word for thieves and murderers.'

'Murderers,' the banker boomed and peered at him. 'Seems to me I did hear that you had some personal reason for disliking them. Married a Jewish girl didn't you?'

'What else would you call someone who breaks into your house, kills your family and steals your property? And yes, she was Polish. And her religion was Judaism. That answer all your questions?' Thorne put his drink down and started to turn away.

'Break into your house . . . hardly the same thing!' The man was nettled. 'Long history of Polish provocation, young man. The Danzig Corridor for instance.'

'The Danzig Corridor was fixed by the League of Nations, if I recall correctly. If Germany wanted redress, she should have pressed her case there. As to the claim that Polish citizens of German extraction were being persecuted in Poland, *your* Herr Hitler never produced anything in the way of proof, just as he failed to do so when he made similar claims for the Sudetenland Germans.'

The banker clearly was not used to having his opinions challenged. His face reddened and he shook a finger at Keith.

'Look here, I happen to be very well-versed in current European affairs and I have numerous business contacts there. Hitler has done wonders for that country. Why, he's taken a nation prostrated by the Depression and rebuilt its economy into one of the most financially viable in the world today.'

'What's that to do with the invasion of Poland?' Thorne demanded. 'Or Czechoslovakia, or Austria for that matter? Hitler may be an economic genius but he's also a damned liar. During the siege of Warsaw, Hitler claimed that no bombs were dropped on the city. He also claimed that residential areas, hospitals, and non-military objectives were being carefully avoided. Well, the German air force must have a different definition of non-military than I do because I saw three hospitals deliberately bombed by Stukas. All had huge red crosses painted on their roofs and a blind man couldn't have missed them. What's more, most of the civilian casualties in Poland were the direct result of indiscriminate air bombing and artillery fire.'

The man, feeling himself on surer ground, now drew himself up and waved his pipe at those who had gathered to listen. 'Young man, whenever people start shooting at each other, there are bound to be a few who get hurt by accident. If you had any military training. . . .'

'I was a first lieutenant in the United States Army Air Corps and so am familiar with aerial bombing tactics.'

The banker stared at him and sucked his pipe and suddenly, Thorne felt his temper slipping. 'I can also tell you what Herr Hitler's impressive army did to me and how they murdered my wife, an American citizen.'

'You married her to get her out of the country is that it?'

'What the devil has that to do with anything?' he demanded. 'An American citizen is. . . .'

The man smiled. 'Nothing. Except the way I heard the story, she was a member of a Polish gang who fought the German occupation forces after the surrender. That makes her, and others like her, outlaws.'

The silence in the room was total for an instant, then the woman in the black cocktail dress swore. 'George, you are a damned ass. That was the cruellest, stupidest thing I have ever heard you say. You . . . you,' she choked and walked away. The man started after her, forgetting all about Thorne.

Shirley materialized beside him. 'Damn you. We had an agreement that you were not to mention her name again. Do you delight in making a fool of me?' Her eyes blazed and her colour was high and Thorne ached for her, but for only a moment.

'*You* had an agreement, Shirley. I didn't.' He caught sight of the dark-haired man hovering near the entrance to the foyer. 'I think your friend is looking for you,' he snarled and walked away, too angry to say anything further. A servant fetched his coat and he heard his father's angry voice as the front door closed, but he didn't turn back.

On Tuesday, the day after Christmas, he posted a letter of resignation to Thorne, Dorsten and Winslow. Then, he removed the telephone from the hook. He stayed in the apartment for a week, not seeing anyone nor answering the door. He went out only to eat at a cafeteria on Lexington, knowing that in the swirling masses he was unlikely to run across anyone he knew. Christmas and New Year's Days both were spent in movie houses, brooding.

In the first week of January, bored with the flat and restless, he took a train to Boston, rented a car and drove out US Twenty past Lexington to Hanscom Field, where he had learned to fly. Little had changed, he thought as he walked across the frozen, oil-splattered taxiway. The same scattering of private aircraft occupied the apron, the lone, humped hangar with its cantilever beams poking out like insect's antennae, the flat sweep of grass that served as a runway, now crisped with frost. Patches of snow were visible in the shade and across the field houses huddled, their storm windows flashing sunlight signals.

The office windows were steamed over so Harry didn't see him until he stepped inside and shut the door. The sudden heat and humidity made Thorne blink.

'Well, look who's here,' Harry shoved an iron-hard hand at him. 'Heard you was in Poland. Don't look the worse for wear.'

Harry Belden was an anachronism – a real New England yankee. One expected to see him behind a plough with a flintlock musket in one hand, reins in the other as he surveyed the boundaries of his land for Indians or red coats. Instead, he wore a one-piece overall and greasy mechanic's hat – exchanged only for a leather flying helmet when he climbed into a cockpit – and was possibly the best stunt flyer on the East Coast. He was a large man with shoulders as broad as a yardstick and a nose to match. He had ham-like hands that Joe Louis would have been proud of yet Thorne had seen him repair a lady's wristwatch with nothing more than a bent paper clip and a tiny screwdriver. Harry Belden was one of those exceptional people to whom anything mechanical was as plain as an open book.

He indicated the coffee pot and Thorne poured a cup, lacing it heavily with evaporated milk. He knew from past experience that Harry changed the grounds only on Fridays.

Thorne had last seen Harry the day before he enlisted in the Army Air Corps. Harry acknowledged that he had heard about his resignation but said nothing more. He listened without comment while Thorne talked about his Air Corps days and experiences in Poland, and finally Deborah's murder.

'So, now you want to fight the Nazis,' he commented after filling and lighting his pipe.

Thorne considered that for a moment. A week of brooding had failed to resolve his quandary. He really did not know what he wanted to do, only that he was restless and nothing held his attention. One minute he was full of confidence, the next in the throes of depression. He had a vague yearning to do something, to take some kind of useful action but in what direction and how, he could not decide.

'Yeah, maybe I do,' was his cautious reply.

'When's last time you flew?'

'The day of the crash.'

'Why?'

Thorne snorted. 'Are you asking if I'm afraid to fly?'

Harry waited.

'No,' he said after a moment. 'I don't think so. I think I stopped flying because . . . hell, I'm not sure why.'

Harry tapped his pipe in the ashtray. 'Because you are lazy.'

'What?'

'You heard me. You're lazy. You're a rich man's son. You don't have to worry about where the next meal is comin' from, so there's no need to make decisions.'

Thorne was starting to get angry. 'What the hell has that got to do with it?'

'Never had to set goals, 'cept once.'

'Oh? And when was that?'

Harry chuckled. 'Day you first come out here. Wouldn't let you in a cockpit 'til you'd memorized the book. Remember? Told you then, I wasn't gonna waste my time unless you was serious.'

'For God's sake, Harry, what the devil are you talking about?' Restless, he got up and went to the window and brushed a clear spot in the condensation.

'Simple, boy. Settin' goals and workin' hard's what life's about. Gotta do that or you drift. Driftin's okay if you're rich – and ain't too smart.'

'You think I'm not very smart?' he asked, watching his breath cloud the glass again.

Harry snorted in answer.

'So what are you suggesting?'

'Hell, Keith, it's your life. Decide what you want to do, then do it. Simple as that.'

'I guess I want to fly.'

199

Harry snorted again. 'Fly? Fly how? Everybody wants to fly. Ten dollars'n you fly for an hour. Rent by the week if you want.'

Thorne turned away from the window and stumped over to the old coal-burning stove. 'That's not what I mean?'

''Course not,' Harry grunted. 'Look here. Ain't too many jobs available flying here 'bouts. 'Specially for an ex-Army pilot quit when he was right.' He glanced at Thorne. 'Why'd you do that, Keith?'

Thorne shrugged. It was still a sore point and he had never really discussed it with anyone. He shook his head.

'Try California. Foreigners orderin' airplanes like there's no to-morrow. Canadian air force's lookin' for pilots, too. Fellow through here two weeks ago. Asked me to mention it around.'

Thorne spent two hours that afternoon in Harry's Taylorcraft, dis-covering that his skill hadn't deserted him. He was nervous as the aircraft turned into the wind and he pulled the throttle open but at the first bound on the frozen surface of the field, he knew he was going to be all right. He flew the little single-seater in a long dog-leg pattern down to Hartford, turning east over Wethersfield to avoid Pratt & Whitney's Rentschler field. There was quite a bit of snow down here and the tobacco fields were peculiar patterns of white dotted with geometrically-spaced specks – support poles for acres of cheesecloth that covered the tobacco in summer. He turned east, enjoying the sight of his favourite country, the fields and woods of eastern Connecticut before turning north for Lexing-ton and Hanscom Field. He landed at dusk, half frozen but happier and more settled than he had been in months.

He went back to Boston that night, turning down Harry's offer to put up a cot in the back of the hangar where he'd lived since his wife died. He took a room at the Angier Hotel and that evening, tracked down an old friend in Los Angeles who had left the Air Corps a few months before his crash, by long distance telephone. The connection was bad and the operator had to try three times before they got a line clear enough to understand one another. Even then he had to shout.

'Hell, Keith, there's plenty of jobs out here. I can get you on with a small air freight company near Santa Ana that needs a pilot. Pay's pretty good if you aren't too particular what you fly or where. Mexico, South America. Cash on delivery, no questions. The usual thing.'

Thorne told him to expect him in a week.

The following day, he returned to New York, packed and wrote a brief note to his parents with the promise of a letter to follow.

Half a pint of scotch helped him sleep, if fitfully. He left the apartment early and took a taxi to Penn Station. The terminal was a madhouse and he joined a ticket line. He had nearly reached the window when he changed his mind abruptly and went out onto Thirty-First Street and flagged a cab.

'Grand Central,' he told the driver. He was fussy after all.

Ottawa 10 – 25 January 1940

It snowed heavily as the train slogged through upstate New York and Quebec to Ottawa. The Canadian capital sparkled under a bright sun and two feet of fresh snow. The snow ploughs were out in force grunting as they pushed the snow into head-high barriers.

Thorne, charged with the energy of good intentions, went directly to the Royal Canadian Air Force Recruiting Centre, even before finding a hotel. The marble hallway was overheated after the five-below zero temperatures outside, but the pretty receptionist was bundled into a sweater and coat and her teeth chattered as she directed him to the proper office on the fourth floor. The room was crowded and he waited for most of the morning, dozing and reading until his name was called.

An RCAF corporal led him into a bare interview room. A few minutes later, an elderly officer with a large moustache, and paunch to match, entered. He nodded a greeting and began to question Thorne about his background. He seemed interested only in specific answers to his questions and ignored any information Thorne volunteered. When he finished, he handed Thorne an application form, told him to fill it out and leave it on the desk.

'We will contact you as soon as a decision is reached. If you haven't a local address yet, telephone the clerk as soon as you do.'

Thorne took a room at the Château Lorraine, phoned in his address as requested and spent the afternoon in the bar. The reception had been the exact opposite of what he had expected. What had he expected? A hero's welcome? Hell, and why not? He was an experienced military pilot for Christ's sake. They needn't waste time and money training him. Near midnight, he remembered that he hadn't yet written to Shirley.

A week passed slowly. Ottawa was snow-bound and in his opinion, the least exciting city he had ever visited. In desperation, he toured the Parliament Buildings, the National Gallery and the National Museum where he at least was intrigued by the Eskimo and Indian exhibits. And he went to the recruiting centre every day but was unable to get past the receptionist. Canada was at war and to reinforce that image, a beefy guard wearing a special police armband and holstered Webley pistol watched him. The remaining time he whiled away in the hotel bar.

On Thursday, he visited a bank and arranged to have additional funds transferred to Ottawa as his hotel bill was eating up his cash. He had rarely given money a second thought before. While in the Air Corps, his negligible pay had been supplemented by a generous allowance and by his trust fund from which deposits were made to his bank account twice a year, in March and September. He rarely paid attention to the balance, but was now shocked to find less than two hundred dollars remaining, and the next deposit not due for nine weeks. He almost wired his father for money before remembering Harry's comments. Instead, he decided that if he hadn't received an answer from the RCAF by the end of the following week, he would find a cheaper hotel.

On Monday, a letter arrived requesting that he present himself Wednesday morning at eight hundred hours for an interview. Tuesday night, he avoided his usual seat at the bar and went to bed early. Even so, as he shaved the following morning, he noted that his eyes were bloodshot.

Thorne was interviewed by a carefully pressed officer wearing embroidered wings on his blouse. The man had a disconcerting habit of staring directly at him, as if continually assessing his value as a human being.

Thorne's application lay open on the desk beside a slim stack of duplicated documents that Thorne guessed had come from Washington. Whatever optimism he felt concerning his application evaporated.

'You were an officer in United States Army Air Corps from 1933 to 1937, were you not, Mr Thorne? Perhaps you could tell me why you resigned.'

Thorne held up a pack of cigarettes for permission to light one. The Canadian shook his head. Surprised, he put the pack away and cleared his throat.

'I was . . . er . . . involved in an air crash in September, 1937., My co-pilot was killed and the flight engineer badly injured. I . . . I resigned after that.'

'To avoid a hearing, is that correct?'

Thorne nodded. 'Yes.'

'The official findings of the crash review board suggest the aircraft was not at fault. Pilot error is inferred. Were you at fault?'

'The consensus was yes,' he said, trying to keep the bitterness from his voice.

'I see. From your tone one senses you believe you were not.'

'There was no way to prove I was not,' he answered reluctantly. 'Regulations require that you consider the safety of the crew first. I was convinced that we were safer making an emergency landing than we would have been if we had parachuted. Neither my flight engineer nor co-pilot had jumped before.'

'I see,' the officer tapped the desk a moment. 'So instead of sticking it out and possibly being charged with pilot error, you chose to resign?'

Thorne stood and shrugged into his coat, wondering how long he would have to wait for train connections between Ottawa and Chicago.

'Mr Thorne?'

'Thanks for your consideration,' Thorne told him. 'I shouldn't have wasted your time.'

'Please sit down, Mr Thorne, and tell me your side of the story. I *am* a flying officer myself.'

Thorne hesitated but the Canadian officer's attitude seemed one of friendly curiosity. He shrugged. Why not? 'There isn't a great deal to tell. I was a pursuit pilot. The Air Corps needed bomber pilots and transferred me. I wasn't happy about it, but . . .' he shrugged again. 'I was sent to the Second Bombardment Group at Langley Field in July and in August, we received twelve aircraft, the new YIB-17s for final testing. After completing the familiarization course, I was ordered to fly one to Seattle for modifications.' Thorne took a deep breath.

'Over Kansas, the number three engine quit and number two overheated. I followed procedure and feathered both engines; the B-17 can fly on two engines. The map showed a commercial field thirty miles south and we had eight thousand feet altitude. But the political situation was a real factor; there had already been two serious B-17 crashes and the Army had cut its order back from 130 to thirty aircraft. We had all been told that one more serious crash could kill the airplane. It was suggested, unofficially you understand, that we do everything possible to avoid another crash.'

'So you decided to try for the airfield thirty miles away.'

Thorne nodded. 'It looked like a good chance at the time. Fuel was low and the aircraft was light as armament and armour hadn't been installed yet. Even the radio had been removed since that was one of the modifications to be done in Seattle. The remaining engines showed no sign of distress. Even though we were losing altitude, I knew I could stretch it to the airfield.

'As it turned out, the map was out of date. The airfield had been sold and a factory was under construction. I didn't have any choice then and I tried to put it down in a nearby field. We didn't make it. My co-pilot was killed and the flight engineer broke his back. I came out with a wrenched shoulder. By resigning, I spared the Air Corps a hearing that could have jeopardized the acquisition of more B-17s. I was finished anyway, as a pilot.' He shrugged.

The Canadian regarded him for a long moment. 'I think I would like a cup of coffee. Would you join me?'

'Ah, no thanks.'

'I insist, Mr Thorne. There is a café across the street that will do nicely.'

The café's steamy windows concealed the interior from the out-side – mercifully. The place was small and greasy and a counter ran across the back to separate the grill from the eating area. Tables and chairs and a tinny juke box swinging *Night Train* were the only furnishings and the café smelled of dishwater and burned toast. His guide was apparently a regular customer because the elderly waitress drew two coffees automatically. They exchanged a few comments in Canadian-accented French that were too fast for Thorne, and she shuffled back to the counter in her broken-down carpet slippers.

'The Royal Canadian Air Force has rejected you,' the officer began without preamble.

'Thanks for the coffee,' he nodded.

The Canadian ignored his sarcasm. 'According to your service records you were an excellent flyer. You made the transition from pursuit aircraft to bombers easily. Your fitness reports, on the other hand, suggest you may not be suitable officer material. Our flying service is very much more disciplined than the American Air Corps and discipline seemed to be your weakest point.' He sipped at the coffee. 'However, if you are still determined to fly, I am certain the British would be interested in you.'

'The British?'

The officer nodded. 'Not the Royal Air Force, and for the same reason. But there is a British company which is hiring civilian pilots to ferry aircraft from the States to Canada. The pay is only sixty-five dollars per week but this may well be the most vital flying job of the war effort. If you are interested, I'll give you an address. You go down there and they'll fix you up.'

Thorne understood why they had come out to the café. Being off the premises, absolved the Canadian government of complicity in the hiring of what might be interpreted as mercenaries. If he accepted the job it would make him a soldier-of-fortune. He recalled the evening in Warsaw when he had defined a 'free-lance' for that Swedish newspaper reporter and he grinned.

'I'll take it.'

'In the Trade of War'
Othello

William Shakespeare

Drobak Narrows 8 – 9 April 1940

Captain Friedrich Prager pushed through the crowd of army officers gathered in the wardroom and went up and out onto the main deck of the heavy cruiser *Blücher*. He breathed the chill night air in deep gulps and the pounding in his head began to lessen. He had lost track of the hours he had been cooped up in Rear Admiral Oskar Kummetz's day cabin with General Erwin Englebrecht and the staff of the 163rd Infantry Division, reviewing the final details of Operation *Weserübung*, the landings at Oslo, Kristiansand, Bergen, Trondheim and Narvik and the airborne landings at Stavanger and Fornebu, where a party from the German legation was waiting to greet them. Towards the end, it had been difficult to breathe, let alone think, in the cramped space filled with cigar and cigarette smoke.

He walked along the deck to the stairs – ladders they called them in the Navy – leading to the bridge. The armed sentry recognized him and saluted. In contrast to the rest of the crowded warship, there were only eight men on the bridge, ratings and officers combined. Two sailors stood at the immense wheel while a senior officer hovered nearby. A large metal table was strewn with charts.

The Captain stepped onto the bridge from the radio room and everyone stiffened to attention as he accepted the watch officer's salute. After a glance at the log, he crossed the bridge.

'Well, Mr Prager?' he said, using the naval style of address.

'General Englebrecht presents his compliments, sir and wishes to report his landing force ready at 0600 hours.'

The Captain nodded. 'Good. We are well into the Drobak Narrows now and will be off Oslo an hour before dawn as planned. Since our altercation with that Norwegian mine-layer, there seems to be no indication of further alarm on their part. We will pass the Oscarborg Fortress in less than thirty minutes and then we shall see whether or not they intend to accept the protection of the Reich, or fight.'

The Captain was summoned away and Prager found a quiet spot near the bridge wing. Remaining here was certainly preferable to his cramped cabin below. He would never understand, he decided, how sailors got used to breathing the same stale air over and over again. It was only up here in the fresh air that the incipient signs of sea sickness had finally left him.

The invasion fleet had sailed before dawn in a race with the British and Prager felt that same sensation of mingled excitement and apprehension he had experienced in that hour before the attack on Poland. This time the prize was Norway. The British Navy had been active all along the Norwegian coast since the war had begun but so far they had, with one exception, confined their activities to international waters. That exception, the capture of the *Altmark*, the auxiliary ship to the *Graf Spee*, had clearly shown they were not above breaching international law when it suited *their* purpose. The fact that the Norwegians had passively allowed it to happen and, even when all the facts had been made public, reacted with so mild a protest to the British as to insult their own national honour was beyond understanding. What other choice did Germany have? She could not allow Norway to fall into Allied hands.

Certainly to listen to Chamberlain on the radio, one would have thought that the state of war now existing between Germany, France and England had been entirely Germany's fault. The British had absolutely refused to understand that it was their own foolish insistence on supporting the corrupt and inept Polish government that had brought about a state of war. If Germany and Poland had been left alone to settle their differences, peace would still be the order of the day.

He shifted restlessly, resenting the fact that he was again serving in a staff capacity rather than commanding a Panzer unit as he had expected. After all, he had been promised a posting to a Panzer unit in return for six months in *Oberkommando des Heeres*, Section One.

A stray memory slipped past the barrier of professional concerns, the memory of a last day two weeks before spent with Sonja Vishenko. A smile creased his face in the darkness and he took a deep breath. How much longer before he would see her again? Probably months.

The six months since his return from Poland in mid-October had certainly not been a 'phoney war' as the British called it, for him. While the Fuehrer may have been content to let his combat units rest during the winter months, Section One, responsible for planning, had worked round the clock on one contingency plan after another, all anticipating spring operations. His only leave in six months had been cut short abruptly when OKH learned that the *Oberkommando Wehrmacht*, the High Command of the Armed Forces, had planned an invasion of Denmark, Norway and Sweden, without reference to or advice from, either the Army or the Luftwaffe.

Apparently, the *Altmark/Cossack* incident had been the last straw as the Fuehrer demanded an invasion as soon as possible. Only

Finland's unexpected armistice had eliminated Sweden from the time-table, even as it released the Anglo-French Finnish Expeditionary Force assembling in Scotland for use in Norway, most probably against the port of Narvik to cut off Germany's shipments of iron ore.

A sailor jostled him, murmured an apology and unlocked a fire hose cabinet to test the pressure valve. Prager stepped through the hatch onto the bridge wing where a lookout glanced at him and went back to scanning the far shore with night glasses. It was cold, even for early April, and an Arctic chill cut through his overcoat as he hunched in the meagre shelter of a ventilator.

If he went below, he was certain to be engaged in conversation again by those two damned Gestapo officers sharing his cabin. Since he had foolishly mentioned that he spent several weeks in Oslo in 1937 observing Norwegian Army manoeuvres, they had pestered him constantly for the addresses of the best whore houses, night clubs and other recreational spots. Damned farmers, he thought. Both of them called up from some provincial police force and making the best of it, as their custom-tailored uniforms showed. Prager's distaste for secret police, necessary as he knew they were in these times, had been heightened by what he had seen of the Gestapo in Warsaw.

The dark shore slipped past and only an occasional light showed on the steep slopes of the fjord. The *Blücher* was feeling her way up the centre of the channel, ignoring all marker buoys since it was conceivable that the Norwegians had moved them. Quisling, that pompous little man, had promised the Fuehrer that Norwegians – excepting only the Communists – would rise up as one to overthrow their morally bankrupt government. Even their king, Haakon, was supposed to favour the German cause but. . . .

The lookout drew his attention to a dark mass on the bluff off the starboard bow, perhaps two kilometres ahead.

'Oscarborg,' the man said and refocused his glasses.

The fort was strategically placed to guard the narrow approaches fifteen miles below Oslo but its cannon had been obsolete in 1914. Norway, neutral in 1914–1918, had done little since but dust them off occasionally. In fact, it seemed that the Norwegians might have forgotten how to fight a war, not having done so since 1814. Their entire army consisted of only six chronically understrength divisions.

They were coming abreast of the fortress now. In the pre-dawn darkness, it was impossible to determine more than a darkish mass against the overcast night sky. The fortress showed no lights, as was to be expected, and the waters of the fjord were calm. By leaning over the railings and peering past the stern, he could just make out the *Blücher*'s gleaming wake and beyond, the single mast-head lamp of their destroyer escort.

He straightened and as he did so, a light winked from the fort. The lookout jammed his glasses to his eyes, then sprinted for the bridge. He reached the open hatch and shouted just as Prager heard the roaring whirr of a high-velocity artillery shell pass overhead. A gun turret on the main deck whirred into motion. Prager saw the silhouettes of the long rifles begin to rise as a second shot was fired from the fort. Behind them, the pocket battleship *Lützow* opened fire. *Blücher* shuddered as her twenty-centimetre turret guns lashed out, the crack of the explosions striking Prager's eardrums with stunning force. Choking cordite fumes swirled past.

Prager saw another flash and the glowing blur of the projectile rise. An instant later, the bridge exploded into hell and the railing against which he was leaning disappeared. His last thought was of falling.

London 8 – 9 April 1940

Captain Charles Atkins hurried across Whitehall, cursing softly. Wind swept at him from the river, flapping the skirt of his overcoat and chilling him to the bone. A silent bobby watched from a doorway. The Admiralty appeared deserted from the outside, but once past the huge doors, the corridors blazed with light and activity. The porter was expecting him and a young naval officer clattered down the steps, shook hands and conducted him to the Operations Room.

It was so damned typical, he thought savagely, to plan a combined operation with no official contact between the services. When in the name of God would the Government realize they were not playing at soldiers, that this was deadly business in which people paid for mistakes with their lives. After this was over, he thought grimly, there would be a reckoning by God!

In the Operations Room, a portly, red-faced man with the gold-lace rings of Captain's rank on his uniform jacket nodded to him with ill-concealed displeasure and motioned to an aide.

'Captain Atkins? My name is Dobson, Lieutenant Rand Dobson,' the aide offered a hand. 'I understand that you've been sent over from the War Department to act as liaison?'

'That's correct, Lieutenant.' As Dobson turned to look at the situation board, he noticed the Australian shoulder flash. 'What is the latest. . . .'

'Oh, no need to worry about that, Captain. The Navy has everything well in hand.'

Atkins uttered an obscenity and the Lieutenant broke off in mid-sentence.

'Everything well in hand? You must be mad!' He took Dobson's arm and turned him so that their backs were to the room. 'Listen to me, Mr Dobson. The Navy has this so well in hand that the Germans have landed in force in at least four spots in Norway – four that we know of. And where is the Navy? Laying mines off the Leads and chasing a non-existent German fleet! A note was sent across from the War Department on the third of April warning that German troops were assembling at Kiel for a possible invasion of Norway and Denmark. It is now the eighth of April and what's been done? The Germans have been allowed to land in force, that's what, Mr Dobson. The Navy's been caught with its pants down . . . at half-mast, if you prefer, Mr Dobson, and if I hear any more talk of how the Navy has everything in hand, I will telephone my superiors in Whitehall and you can believe me when I tell you they will speak to the Prime Minister, immediately. Oh yes,' Atkins added with a malicious smile, 'I will be certain to mention your *name*. Now, once more, what is the situation, please?'

Dobson's expressions had run the gamut from outrage to apprehension and now he glanced in desperation at his chief who resolutely ignored him, having guessed the general thrust of Atkins' comments. Dobson murmured an apology, broke away and hurried across the room. Atkins swore again. German troops were landing in Norway and it was business as usual. The greater enemy was not the Germans, but the Army – and *vice-versa* he had to admit. One would have thought it appropriation time.

Atkins did not need a briefing to tell him the situation. It was plain enough from the maps – charts, he supposed they were called here – and the harried expressions of the naval officers and other ranks in the room. The large-scale table map was cluttered with models of German warships scattered about the coast while the models sporting tiny Union Jacks were well off the west coast or heading into the North Atlantic after the ghost battlefleet. *Operation Wilfred*, the long-delayed plan to mine the coastal Leads, was no longer in effect.

One ship lay on its side; sunk perhaps? He read the tiny flag attached to its mast. *Blücher*. The Norwegians must have accounted for that one themselves as there were no British ships in the area. He traced the path of the German landings west and north along the coast from Oslo. Kristiansand, Bergen and Narvik. As he watched, a rating solemnly overturned another German model, one supposed to indicate a troopship. Further south, Denmark was solidly ringed with German ships. They had word at the War Department that the country had been overrun in a matter of hours from across the border with Germany and from the sea by a landing at Copenhagen.

Lieutenant Dobson beckoned to him and Atkins moved around the table and across the room to where the senior Naval Captain stood waiting, face grim but otherwise expressionless.

'Dobson here tells me that you've been sent by the War Department and that you think very little of what the Navy has accomplished.' It wasn't a question, but a statement and Atkins started to retort sharply, but thought better of it in time.

Relations were bad enough; he did not need to add to the hostility.

'I apologize if I gave that impression, Captain. It was unintentional. Events at the moment do not permit such personal feelings.' He stared hard at the Captain, as if challenging him and the man frowned, then permitted a slight smile.

'Just so, Captain. If you will excuse me, I have duties to attend. Mr Dobson will serve as your liaison.' He nodded abruptly and went over to stand by the map table. Dobson let out a long breath.

'Clever, challenging the old man like that,' Dobson breathed in relief. 'He's certainly on edge. It was his recommendation to chase the German fleet.'

Atkins glanced at him but Dobson shook his head. 'Don't misunderstand me. On the basis of the information we had, I would have done the same. So would you.'

'Maybe,' Atkins growled. 'But in this business, heroes are made by guessing correctly. Goats by guessing wrongly.'

'Then I suspect there will be many goats and damned few heroes before this war is over,' Dobson murmured in a bleak voice.

'I daresay,' Atkins replied. 'Now, I gather, German forces have secured Oslo, Kristiansand, and Bergen and are moving on Narvik?'

'In fact, they seemed to have already taken Narvik. We can no longer make radio contact there. The last word we had was that German soldiers, hidden in a merchant vessel, had come ashore and captured the local army detachment and police force. But we've a destroyer flotilla under Warburton-Lee moving into the fjord.'

Atkins took a small notebook from his pocket and flipped through the pages. 'The War Department would like to know when the invasion force that sailed from Rosyth will be in position to go ashore?'

Dobson's face reddened with embarrassment. 'I . . . I'm afraid that Operation R-4, our own invasion, was abandoned . . . when the reconnaissance reports were received,' he stuttered, 'the Home Fleet and the Second Cruiser Squadron were ordered out to meet them. The First Cruiser Squadron sailed in support. Your troops were marched off onto the docks. . . .'

'Good God!' Atkins stared at him, horrified. 'Marched off . . . what about their equipment?'

'Still aboard, I believe. There wasn't time to unload. . . .'

'Show me to a telephone,' he demanded but Dobson spread his hands helplessly. 'We have only the one and it's in constant use. It will be at least an hour. . . .'

Atkins found a pay telephone on the first floor near the cloakroom and dug through his pockets for the proper change. The War Department switchboard answered but he was asked to wait. A moment later, the line went dead. Fuming, Atkins tried again . . . and again.

Hamburg 17 – 19 April 1940

At first he did not understand where he was as the lamp barely illuminated a long, unfamiliar room. His head ached abominably and when he moved, a blinding pain raced in waves through his skull. Captain Friedrich Prager lay still and, gradually, the pain lessened. He became aware of the breathing of others and, occasionally, heard a low murmur of pain. When he raised a hand, he saw that his arm was covered with a dressing as was his head. He was also wearing an uncomfortable gown with knots that poked him in the back and he realized that he was in a hospital.

Memory began to ebb back. The darkness, the bridge of the *Blücher*, the scream of shells from the Oscarborg Fortress. He felt the railing give way and the stunning violence of the icy fjord waters closing over him as his greatcoat and uniform dragged him down. Something had clutched at him, rolled him wildly and he was nearly torn apart as the propeller's wash thrust him down and down until, his lungs burning in agony, he passed out.

He remembered a voice, a hand hauling at his coat collar. Another shout and he was dragged painfully over the sharp gunwale of a boat, ridiculously angry at the rough handling and he remembered nothing more.

A nurse drifted past and saw that he was awake. She took his pulse, held a finger to her lips to silence his questions and left. A doctor appeared and examined Prager's pupils with a small electric torch, turning his head gently to either side.

'Well now,' his voice, though muted was full of confidence, 'you seem to be mending properly.'

Prager tried to speak but found his throat and mouth too dry to form the words. The doctor filled a glass from a carafe and helped him to drink.

'Easy now. Too much will upset your stomach.'

Even swallowing exhausted him. The doctor nodded. 'Rest now. Plenty of sleep and you'll be all right in a week or so.' He turned to go but Prager stopped him with a gesture.

'What happened . . . ?' he croaked.

'You were aboard the *Blücher* I believe?' He glanced at Prager's chart. 'She was sunk as she approached Oslo. You were extremely lucky. They say she went down with over a thousand men and officers.' He patted Prager's arm and slipped it back under the blanket. 'You were rescued by an escort ship. They brought you here to the naval hospital in Kiel because your wounds were not that serious.'

The doctor turned at the foot of his bed. 'By the way, you might be interested to know that Oslo was occupied yesterday morning in spite of the fact that the *Blücher* took most of the occupation force down with her. A young officer found a military band, assembled a few other troops and marched them through the city to accept the surrender of the garrison.'

The idea of a single officer and a military band occupying a city the size of Oslo was too ludicrous to believe and Prager eyed the doctor sceptically.

He chuckled and shrugged. 'The story was on the wireless.'

Prager was released from the hospital eight days later. He shuffled down the steps into the crisp spring air feeling very much like an old man. Rest, they had told him. Two weeks at the minimum and he would be as fit as ever.

A cold wind blew off the Kielerhafen and in spite of the weariness that dragged at him, he turned in that direction. The Naval hospital was near the University and students hurried between buildings as always, as if a full-scale war weren't going on four hundred kilometres to the north. He entered the Schlossgarten from the north end and found a bench from where he could watch the busy harbour. There was still an hour to his train and he needed a few minutes to himself. He lit a cigarette and pulled his coat about his neck. He could feel the tentative warmth in the sun but the wind had a cutting edge.

Joachim Brenner was his very good friend. They had been

inseparable as boys and he smiled, remembering summer days along the canal. Once, in 1923 before his mother died, Joachim's father had brought his mother, Joachim and he to Kiel for a short holiday. They had ridden an excursion boat through the Kiel Canal which had seemed to him to be the greatest engineering marvel of all time. Herr Brenner had described the great naval docks built in the years before the Great War to serve the Imperial German Naval Fleet.

But they were gone even then; the docks demolished, fuelling points torn up, huge cranes broken down for scrap, all part of the infamous Versailles settlement. That was the first time he had really understood the cliché phrase, *Heerlos, Wehrlos, Ehrlos*, disarmed, defenceless, dishonoured.

'What difference,' Herr Brenner had said in a bitter voice, 'that it meant life or death for Germany's foreign trade? They wanted it that way, those bitter old men who had driven so many French and English soldiers to their deaths in order to protect their grasping merchants. They meant from the start to destroy the German Reich, to reduce us to a poor agricultural nation to serve them. The Great War was fought only to protect English and French markets from German competition.'

Prager had not understood everything he had said that day, but, as he had grown and studied, it had all become clear enough. The unholy pressures on Germany brought to bear by the Allies after the armistice – first the devaluation of German currency because of grasping reparation demands and, when that did not work, the depression engendered with the connivance of Wall Street that got out of hand and swept the world.

It was only Germany's good fortune that, at the crucial time, as so often in the past, a leader had come forward. Adolf Hitler, questionable though some of his actions were, had led Germany back to prosperity and her rightful position in the world. He had wiped out the stain of the ignominious surrender of 1918 and restored to Germany her honour.

The English and French were in for a surprise this time, he thought with a grim smile. We German people are ready and waiting for them. It will not be like the last time, like 1918 when the Communists had begun the disorders right here in Kiel that had brought down the Kaiser and the Government. Now we are a disciplined, committed people.

He shivered as a cloud passed across the sun and suddenly the bright day had taken on the dreary aspect of winter. Passing up-channel was a destroyer, battle flags snapping. The ship moved past a concrete pier that showed the slight effects of a British bombing raid and off-duty sailors lounged against the stern railing, watching the city recede. The ship was painted with the broken grey of Arctic camouflage and Prager knew they were sailing for Norwegian waters. A second destroyer appeared astern and he shivered, thinking of the *Blücher*, massive, indomitable one moment, a twisted, sinking mass of rubbish the next.

The sixteenth-century castle that gave the park its name frowned across the harbour as he walked towards the tram stop. The statue of Wilhelm I, mounted on a rearing charger, was much as he remembered it from that day years before and he shook his head at the rapid passage of time. The University clock tower tolled the half hour as he walked into the Wasseralle and along to the tram stop.

Prager was dozing in the empty compartment when the door slid back and he heard a familiar laugh. He turned painfully to see Torsten Fredriksson grinning at him, suitcase in one hand, portable typewriter in the other.

'I'll be damned,' Fredriksson said in his Scandinavian-lilted German, 'I would have guessed you to be bashing about the Norwegian mountains.'

Prager stretched carefully and sat upright, adjusting his uniform jacket. Fredriksson's eyebrows went up at the care with which he moved and the way he favoured his head.

'I started in the direction,' he shrugged and regretted doing so.

Fredriksson placed his bags in the rack and dropped into the seat across from him. He slipped a silver flask from his pocket and offered it to Prager who declined, then changed his mind. 'You look as if you could do with a drop or two,' Fredriksson said with concern.

Prager took a sip from the flask and made a face. 'Schnapps! Don't you ever carry anything else?'

'It was certainly good enough for you last February!' Fredriksson said in indignation.

Prager snorted. 'I was freezing to death if you remember. I just imagined it was anti-freeze.'

In February 1939, Munich was behind and the final act in Czechoslovakia still a month away. France had followed Chamberlain's lead in December by signing a 'friendship' agreement with Germany. For a few short weeks, the possibility of war had seemed remote and it was easy not to give a damn. Both fell to silently remembering their first meeting fourteen months previously when Prager had served as Fredriksson's guide during a military demonstration at Kummersdorf. Afterwards, an official from the Propaganda Ministry had bailed them out of jail for brawling in a brothel on the Clausewitzstrasse.

'What are you doing here?' Prager asked.

Fredriksson snorted. 'Do you mean what am I doing in Germany after the invasion of Norway and Denmark? I've been summoned to Berlin by the Reich Press Director to learn why it was necessary. I was in Malmo when the invitation was received and it was easier to travel this way than to return to Stockholm. What happened? Did you get hurt?'

Prager prefaced his remarks by saying, 'Of course, you will not be able to use this story, you understand?' and when Fredriksson nodded, went on to tell him what had happened in the Drobak Narrows. 'I remember very little . . . the cannon flash and an explosion on the ship. I suffered a severe concussion, aches and a few sprains but nothing more.'

Prager reached for the flask. 'I met a mutual acquaintance,' he said to change the subject, 'in Poland last October.'

Fredriksson arched an eyebrow and Prager nodded. 'That American with you at the American Embassy cocktail party whose name I believe was Thorne?'

'Keith Thorne!' Fredriksson exclaimed. 'In October? Where, when . . . ?'

Prager was startled by Fredriksson's reaction. Had he heard anything about. . . . 'Why, in Warsaw. Seems he was accused of being a British spy and working with Polish terrorists.' Fredriksson's unexpected interest made him wish he had not raised the subject.

'I thought he had been killed.' Briefly, he told Prager about the neutral evacuation of Warsaw and what had happened at the airfield. 'He was running towards the aircraft with his wife. I tried to get the pilot to stop but it was no use.'

'Well he was injured. He hadn't a passport and the Gestapo put him in prison. There were questions about his involvement with Jewish terrorists.'

Fredriksson gave Prager an odd look. 'I believe the only Jews he knew in all Poland were the Yitzaks – Jacob Yitzak, the concert violinist? Certainly you don't believe that he was a terrorist?'

'No, I certainly don't,' Prager said, his discomfort growing as he remembered the dignity with which the old man had crossed the lawn to the gate and his execution. 'But the tribunal did. They had sentenced him to be shot when I intervened.'

Prager managed to turn the conversation aside and Fredriksson acquiesced without comment in deference to their friendship, although he tucked away a mental note to investigate the affair at a future date. There had to be more to the story than the bald facts as Prager had told them.

He was curious to hear the version of the story Thorne and his new wife would tell.

*

It was late afternoon when the train reached Hamburg and he was shaking with exhaustion as he climbed aboard the number three tram to Wandsee. It began to rain as the tram reached the suburb and he trudged up the deserted Zoll Strasse towards the old house in a downpour. Lights twinkled from windows as dusk fell and suddenly he was reminded sharply of winter nights when he had walked home from a succession of after-school jobs. The rain-spattered sheen of the Wandsee River appeared through the trees and he knew he was almost home.

The house smelled of long disuse and it suddenly occurred to him that it had been over a year since he had last been here. The winter snows and spring rains had loosened roofing shingles and water had seeped in to discolour ceilings and walls. The pantry, of course, was completely bare but the fire that he had laid the previous June before leaving for Poland was undisturbed. The fire caught only after he found an old magazine and shredded the paper beneath the damp wood. He found a bottle of cognac in the cupboard, waited until the water from the tap had emitted its quota of rust and washed a glass.

He pulled his coat about him and sat before the fire. The cognac warmed him and he closed his eyes, thinking of the years his father had spent in this very chair. The stories the old man had told him! Stories of his adventures in the Army, stories from the history of Germany as long ago as Charlemagne. He barely could recall his father before the war, when he had been a tall, powerful man with massive arms and hands – before Russian shrapnel had destroyed his strength in 1917. For all his rough barrack-room manner, he had been amazingly gentle with his delicate French wife and son – as if he stood ever in awe of these two people who had anchored his life to Germany.

Even now it seemed that he could smell the rough odour of wool, tobacco and gun oil that his father had worn like a second uniform. Prager sighed, then smiled at his nostalgia. The cognac had eliminated his headache, and the war and the world seemed far away. Tomorrow he would see Sonja. That was as far as he cared to plan ahead.

The city of Hamburg was the second largest in Germany with a population well over one million. Before the 1914–1918 war, it had been second only to London as Europe's busiest port. Nothing certain is known of its origins but as early as 811, it was thought that Charlemagne built a castle to command the Elbe river mouth. A church followed and a bishop was named shortly thereafter. Hamburg's real growth began with the Hanseatic League in the thirteenth century. The combined influences of the Reformation and the opening of trade routes to India made the League and its cities economically powerful trading centres. The arrival of the English cloth makers, the 'Merchant Adventurers', following their expulsion by the Spanish from Antwerp in 1567 set the seal on Hamburg as the foremost trading city in the north. A general business decline in the early to mid 1700s, due chiefly to the series of wars between France and England, reduced her prosperity somewhat until in 1778, the first vessel sailing direct from America arrived to begin a 150-year traffic that ceased only in 1917–1918. In the years following the Great War, trade revived slowly and it did not reach pre-war levels until 1926.

Prager stood on the Kornhaus-Brücke spanning the Zoll-Kanal and studied the hundreds of merchant vessels filling the commercial harbour. He could see no sign of the sporadic bombing raids that the British had conducted recently. From where he stood beneath the statue of Vasco da Gama, he could look east past the great basins bounded by massive quays, the Sandtor-Hafen, Grasbrook-Hafen and beyond the gas works to the Baakenhafen. The ball on the great water-tower clock at the end of the Kaiser-Kai was almost at the bottom, indicating one o'clock p.m. Hamburg time.

He was to meet Sonja for luncheon at the Rathaus at Number 1 Ness. He surveyed this indication of Germany's proud resurgence one last time and walked off the bridge and up Brandstwiete to the Reichsstrasse. The wind was fierce from the North Sea and intensely cold. He had slept badly which had surprised him as he had expected the familiar surroundings to act as a soporific.

This would be the first time they had managed to meet alone. And at Sonja's instigation. He smiled as he recalled the lectures he had endured in his studies of modern history concerning the evils of free love, supposed to be a matter of State policy in Russia. He could testify from first-hand experience that the Russians were as strait-laced as any English Victorian from the last century.

He stepped aside as a senior naval officer pushed the glass door open and allowed his young woman – so young she seemed a school girl – to precede him. He stared hard at Prager, dressed in mufti. Prager's smile was cynical. Inside, the porter bowed just enough to be polite – his civilian clothing – and accepted his coat. Prager walked towards the dining room, a round arch wreathed in potted ferns and glass windows obscured with cream-coloured curtains. The clerk's stare was haughty, as if questioning the right of a civilian his age to be there at all. A glance at the reservation book changed his manner instantly.

'Of course, Hauptmann Prager, the young lady has already

arrived.' He snapped his fingers and bade a waiter escort the 'Captain', he emphasized the rank and title, to table number eight.

Sonja was wearing a fawn dress of some soft material that gathered about her slender waist and emphasized her shoulders. The latest Parisian fashion was padded shoulders and, war or no war, the lady's clothing industry still took their cue from the French designers. Her hair was longer than he remembered and fell in waves across her shoulders. There was certainly nothing about her of the drab proletariat style her mother affected. When she saw him, her huge eyes filled with tears and Prager was not aware of the waiter holding the chair nor his soft-voiced good wishes.

His hand went automatically to hers and he clasped her fingers as if she were his anchor to sanity. Until that moment, he had not even begun to understand what the war had done to him.

'You are well?' Her soft Russian accent overwhelmed him and he could only nod.

'I was so, so frightened when we were told you had been wounded. I imagined all sorts of terrible things. . . .'

He forced a smile then. 'It was only a bump on the head.'

'How long will they . . . how long before you must return?'

'Two weeks. I'm on convalescent leave. We have two entire weeks to ourselves, Sonja.'

They ordered the waiter's suggestions, too engrossed in one another to look at the menu. Amazingly enough, Prager thought as they ate, his headache had disappeared and the tense knot in his stomach had dissolved. For the first time in years, he was preoccupied with something other than military plans and studies. This new feeling of well-being seemed to him worth more than a month of rest.

Afterwards, they walked along the Alsterdamm, oblivious to the waters of the Binnen-Alster flashing grey and gold as the sun slipped in and out of banks of gathering cloud. Swans covered the surface and gulls wheeled above, calling raucously. The promenades were thronged with pretty secretaries and soldiers idling about. Sleek, well-fed businessmen clutching briefcases fat with war contracts hurried along. At the south end where they could see the imposing edifice of the Rathaus in the next block, the wind suddenly became chill and spatters of rain lanced the streets. Sonja hugged his arm to her side and pressed against him for warmth.

As if they had discussed the next step, Prager hailed a taxi and gave the driver the address in Wandsbek. Sonja sat close to him, her thigh pressed against his, saying nothing. He cleared his throat once from nervousness and she glanced at him and smiled.

It was raining steadily when the taxi turned into the narrow lane. Sonja exclaimed at the amount of the fare but Prager laughed and added a substantial tip and they dashed for the house. The fire had gone out and the house was chill. He built a new one while Sonja used the old wood stove to boil water for tea. They sat on the floor before the fire, not touching yet, knowing they had all the time in the world.

'Your parents?' Prager asked.

'They know I am having luncheon with you. They need know nothing more.'

He laughed at her rare declaration of independence. Sonja went into the kitchen and returned, carrying the brass bedwarming pan which she had set on the stove to heat. Prager's eyes widened and Sonja blushed but lifted her chin and went up the stairs to the bedroom. Prager was surprised as much at her actions as his reaction. His previous experience with women had been limited to prostitutes, the expensive kind reserved for officers, but prostitutes nevertheless. Their only interest in the sex act was the money it earned. Previous liaisons had often been quick, sweaty affairs, passion feigned in a perfunctory manner. Pleasing the customer was not really necessary as there were plenty more waiting. Prostitutes and armament makers, he thought sourly. Only they benefited from war.

He felt Sonja's fingers on his cheek and jumped, startled and ashamed of his memories.

'Friedrich?'

He turned in the chair and drew her down on his lap and held her closely. She had removed her coat and her thin dress offered little protection from the chill that permeated the house. They sat for a time, watching the fire, preoccupied with private thoughts. It seemed to Prager that he had travelled into a world apart in which the only sensations were the firm softness of her body and her fluttery breathing. Sonja turned in his arms and he kissed her tentatively. She slipped a hand behind his head and opened her lips so that he felt the soft touch of her tongue. His hesitancy disappeared and he pulled her to him firmly. She clasped his hand in hers and pressed his fingers against a nipple. He fumbled with the buttons and his fingers slid over an unbelievably soft breast, tracing the outline of the brassiere until she, still with her lips against his, undid the clasps.

Her body was a revelation. She lay back in his arms, staring into his eyes as he moved his fingers across her pale skin until driven by sudden need, he stood swiftly and carried her up the stairs.

The cold air of the bedroom made her gasp and he removed the rest of her clothing quickly. Her smooth body, ivory in the half-light, was amazingly beautiful and he reluctantly drew the feather tick over her when she shivered. Her dark hair spread across the pillow like a halo. He undressed and slipped into bed beside her. Sonja turned to him and they made love with an urgency that startled them both. Afterwards, she lay with her head on his chest, touching his chin and lips with her tongue and he held her tightly, unable to believe the pleasure she had brought him.

The tip of his cigarette glowed and the rain gushed down again. Sonja lay pressed against him, her breathing even as she slept and he thought about how they had met in Berlin at the beginning of last year, at a reception for the officials of a Soviet Trade Association. He had been introduced to the Vishenkos as he passed through the reception line. Sonja's father was of medium height and balding. His powerful body was squat and he had all the humourlessness of a Soviet bureaucrat. Madame Vishenko was nearly a carbon copy of her husband but with peering eyes that roved restlessly, poking, probing, calculating. She took in Prager's captain's insignia and dismissed him at once as of little consequence. And Sonja had made little impression on him that first time. He remembered only her high cheek-bones and honey-blonde hair but his chief recollection was of a dowdy grey wool skirt and blouse and sturdy flat shoes, all worn like a uniform.

They met again a week later at the opera. He had escorted his commanding officer's wife, an elderly matron who had disappeared to the ladies' room during the intermission. He was standing in the lobby, smoking and wondering about the possibilities of leaving early, when he noted the Vishenkos off by themselves. Sonja was wearing an evening dress of some dark colour and her long hair flowed about her shoulders. The transformation was astounding and he quickly reintroduced himself and struggled to make small talk against the tide of her parents' obvious disapproval. Only when Frau Otteniger returned and the Vishenkos discovered that he was attached to the Army High Command had their attitude warmed. From then on, he had taken what few opportunities occurred to call on Sonja until he was sent to Poland.

In the past few months, he had begun to detect a certain desperation in her letters and guessed that her home life was becoming intolerable. Her parents were quite strict and he sensed her rebellion growing – after all, she was close to twenty-three. During the long months away from her he had thought many times about marriage and it wasn't long before he wanted more than anything else to marry this quiet Russian girl with whom he had fallen deeply in love.

But Prager was a realist; childhood years spent with a paralysed father made him so. This war was only beginning. Germany had so far won her victories quickly and with a minimum of bloodshed, a trend that could prove terribly misleading. The Rhineland, Austria and Czechoslovakia had not offered armed resistance. Poland and Norway and Denmark had, but superior planning, equipment and tactics had enabled Germany to crush them easily. That phase was ending. France would not fall so easily and the war in the west could easily bog down into years of positional warfare as had happened so quickly in 1914, unless the General Staff was willing to learn from the lessons of mechanized warfare as demonstrated in Poland.

The memories of the cruelty and rejection his French-born mother had endured in the last war while her husband was fighting on the eastern front were far too clear in his mind. Even after Sergeant-Major Gerhard Prager returned home, paralysed from the waist down by Russian shrapnel, the ill-treatment by her neighbours and former friends continued. And then, after the war, when inflation made veterans' pensions a joke, his mother had struggled to find and then hold a succession of jobs to support her family until in 1925, worn out from exhaustion and exile, she had died of tuberculosis. He would never allow that to happen to Sonja.

If he were killed, there would be no one to protect Sonja from the excesses of both State and neighbours. And even worse was the possibility that he might be mutilated like his father and be incapable of earning a living. How would they survive on the pension granted disabled officers when prices were already inflating?

The following morning, Prager watched her lonely figure trudge up the path to the three-storey block of flats in which she lived with her parents. The taxi driver was impatient to be gone but Prager ignored his restless mutterings. Sonja had not spoken of her fears and he had been loath to open the subject, knowing what it would eventually involve. When she turned to look at him, he nearly went after her. As the door closed behind her, a great weakness swept through him and he put a hand to the taxi door to steady himself.

Dombas 23–30 April 1940

The fog was rapidly being torn to shreds by the wind blowing in the Leads, that narrow, deepwater passage between the mainland of Norway and its fringe of off-shore islands. The destroyer HMS

Eskimo rolled through the choppy waters with more than half her passengers seasick, much to the delight of her crew.

During the early morning of 23 April 1940, Captain Charles Atkins stood on the bridge deck watching the village of Andalsnes emerge from the icy fog and shivered in a borrowed duffle coat as the meagre sun touched the village. Atkins was impressed by the overriding quality of blue-grey sky that predominated, blue-grey water, blue-grey cloud, blue-grey land.

The *Eskimo* tied up to the wharf amidst an air-raid staged by two Stukas flirting with the anti-aircraft protection. Working parties swarmed up from the dripping, iron-bound compartments below and Atkins shuddered to think of spending another night in the tiny cabin he shared with nine other officers.

Following his return from Finland, he had been reassigned to the staff of General Edmond Ironside, Chief of the Imperial General Staff, supposedly in recognition of his work in Finland. A stint on the Imperial Staff certainly would not hurt his career, he thought, but he had arrived at the wrong time and with the wrong background. Instead of highly visible duty as an aide, he had been assigned to War Plans to review the preparations that had been made in the event that Allied troops were sent to Finland via Norway. He could still remember how appalled he had been when he read the plan and he expressed his opinion in a succinct minute to the effect that it was fortunate the Finns had concluded an armistice when they did as the Allied plan would have been a disaster.

He had pointed out deficiencies that should have been self-evident; motor vehicles not winterized, no snow tyres and no provisions for chains. Someone had decided that each soldier should be issued one tube of light lubricating oil to keep their rifles from rusting. Atkins noted that in the temperature that prevailed during a Karelian winter, the oil would have frozen solid, rendering the weapons useless. Additionally, only the French *Chasseurs Alpins* had received winter training. The planners, he observed, seemed to have learned nothing from the Russian experience.

Atkins' memo was returned from General Ironside's office by messenger. He broke the seal with apprehension. A handwritten note on the bottom thanked him for his analysis. Only then did he remember that Ironside had commanded the Allied Expeditionary Force to North Russia in 1918 and 1919. The following day, he was ordered to revise the plan to land an entire brigade at Narvik to occupy the rail line across the mountains into Sweden and thus cut off German ore shipments.

The Germans, however, struck first and, as a result, he was at long last being granted a field command as an emergency replacement for an officer killed in action.

The town of Andalsnes was overrun with the khaki uniforms of the Fifteenth Brigade under Major-General B.T.C. Paget. Atkins had expected an interview with Paget and then assignment to a staff job but an aide apologized.

'Damn it, Captain, I'd like to oblige, but neither of you has time. Look here.' He tapped the map of the area between Namsos and Andalsnes. 'Brigadier Morgan's 148th Infantry Brigade is already in retreat from Lillehammer, 150 miles south. He's taken a fearful pounding. We know that Von Falkenhurst, the German commander in Norway, has managed to bring in major reinforcements in spite of all the Navy claim to be doing in the Skagerrak. The Fifth Norwegian Infantry Division moved north towards Trondheim a week ago. They had almost made it when they were stopped by the German 2nd Mountain Division, reinforced by elements of the 181st Division – or so we suspect. Intelligence's a bit spotty. How they did it, we aren't certain; probably simply ignored Morgan and pushed right up the rail line from Oslo. We do know that Morgan is facing the 163rd Division at Lillehammer.'

He rubbed his forehead and Atkins could see how weary the man was. 'The German has simply outmanoeuvred us. It's amazing how they move forces about, as if they'd wings. In any event, General Paget has ordered a general withdrawal on Andalsnes. What we'll do then, I really haven't a clue.'

Atkins studied the map, noting positions of opposing forces, trying to visualize the country in which they were contending. The map was intended more as a place guide than a geographic guide but it needed little imagination to decide from the wide scattering of villages and towns and the frequent lakes that the terrain must be both mountainous and heavily forested.

'What about the force at Namsos?'

'Carton de Wiart's 146th? Same story. He didn't get in either. Stopped at Steinkjer in fact. He's been reinforced by the Fifth Demi-Brigade of the French *Chasseurs Alpins* but there aren't enough of them and some fools somewhere sent the wrong bindings for their skis. That's been our problem in this whole bloody campaign!' The aide threw down his pencil. 'Too many foolish mistakes; not enough of the proper equipment, not enough heavy guns and not enough bloody ammunition – of any kind.' The aide shook his head and turned from the map. 'The Brigadier wants you to take over Company D. You'll find them about here,' he tapped the map just ahead of the red arrow signifying the head of the German line. 'They are engaged in demolition work along the railway. We need to slow the Hun if we are ever to establish a strong line. The Brigadier feels your experience in Finland would be an asset, even if this is an infantry and not an armoured command.'

Snow fell, at times heavily, making hard going for the small convoy moving desperately needed ammunition and supplies up to the Fifteenth Brigade. Atkins had hitched a ride with a young driver too exhausted to even talk. Snow swirled at the windscreen with a hypnotic effect and after the five-ton lorry ran off the road a second time, Atkins ordered the reluctant boy from behind the wheel and took over himself.

'Don't argue,' he snapped when the driver protested that he was responsible for the lorry and its contents. 'If you wreck it, no one benefits.'

He edged the lorry back onto the road and resumed the twenty mile an hour speed, all that conditions allowed. The driver saw that Atkins did indeed know how to drive and fell asleep.

The journey south took two days and it snowed constantly. In the occasional few minutes of relatively clear skies, the Luftwaffe pounced on them. Stukas from the X Fliegerkorps waited only a for a break in the weather. At Dombas and again at Otta, bombers smashed the supply points and sheds and warehouses burned fiercely in the strong winds.

On the morning of the third day, they ran across elements of the retreating Fifteenth Brigade. The convoy was directed further south towards Lillehammer and, at noon they came on the main element of Morgan's Brigade. Atkins left the convoy and sought out the Brigadier's headquarters in a village schoolhouse. Morgan welcomed him, briefed him quickly and sent him on south again to find D company.

His new command was dug in along the railway approaches to a village six miles south. The Sergeant-Major, a Flanders veteran from the first war, gave him a quick tour. The company Lieutenant had been wounded earlier that morning down the line and left behind for the Germans.

'Nothing for it, sir,' the Sergeant-Major growled in his west country accent. 'Jerry 'as the wherewithal. Alway's t'yks good care of 'em 'e does. Would'a died sure if they st'yed wi' us.'

The company's complement stood at eighty-three men, two machines guns and three two-inch mortars, two of which 'had been pinched,' the Sergeant-Major explained without expression. He went on to trace the terrain from Lillehammer to Dombas where the rail line split, one section to Andalsnes, the other to Trondheim traversed the mountains which formed Norway's spine.

The Sergeant-Major had deployed the company along a ridge overlooking the narrow valley through which the railway ran and up which the Germans *must* come. Steep, heavily forested hills rose on either side and, whenever the snow stopped, he could see scattered farms in the valley below. The village consisted of a single street with scattered houses, some stores and a post office over which the Norwegian flag still snapped. There was nothing remarkable about the town, Atkins thought, merely a country village whose only sin was that it lay directly in the path of the Nazi invasion. The civilian population had wisely left some time before – Finland all over again. The unexpected memory of Erika swept over him and he cursed himself for a fool.

Hidden at the north end of the village was an ancient engine, coal tender and two goods wagons. Smoke chuffed methodically from the high stack and Atkins shook his head.

'Got us this far, she did.' The Sergeant-Major patted the steam box. 'She'll t'yke us the rest o' the way, sir.'

'I hope to God, Sergeant-Major. I hope to God.'

The last unit of the retreating Fifteenth Brigade straggled off along the road paralleling the rail line and silence descended on the village. Atkins walked the perimeter. The cloud thinned and the sun poured long columns of molten light into the valley. He watched the rail line with field glasses until a train appeared.

''ere they comes, sir,' the Sergeant-Major observed in a non-committal voice and Atkins handed him the glasses. 'I'd best warn the lads to keep a sharp lookout.'

'Watch the trees to either side as well, Sergeant-Major.'

The first Stukas came at 1330 hours and by the time they left, half the village was in flames. The probing attacks began promptly at 1400 hours when a small party of infantry trudging ahead of the train exchanged long-range fire with British pickets.

Atkins had been dreading the moment when he would have to face his fear again. It had been growing ever since the convoy started down the road toward Dombas and now, with German infantry in sight, it began to squeeze with demoniacal strength. He held his breath to keep from choking and tried to remember the lessons learned so hard in Finland.

They could hear the German train on the freshening wind. Atkins' orders were to hold until sunset, then withdraw twenty miles up the line and re-establish the rearguard. The tracks had been mined and he gave the order to blow them up. Half a mile down the valley frozen earth erupted and dull *carumps* echoed between the valley walls. Through his field glasses, Atkins could see that a half mile of track and bed had been blasted into ruins. It would take the Germans half a day or more to lay temporary rails.

He squatted over the map, trying to sort the symbols into coherence at the same time, fighting the gagging sensation. For an officer to exhibit fear was, in his opinion, worse than cowardice; it destroyed the enlisted man's faith in all officers. And soldiers without faith in their officers, died. It had been relatively easy to hide his fear from the Finnish soldiers as he spoke little of the language. But here, he was in charge and the men depended on him.

He mumbled an excuse to the Sergeant-Major who was watching him with a curious expression. 'I'm going up the church steeple, Sergeant-Major. See that the men have facilities to prepare hot food. We may have to leave quickly.'

Inside, the church smelled of winter. He found the ladder leading into the steeple which was little more than a gabled box. Inside, it was barely six feet high and not much wider. A cast-iron bell hung from a cradle and a rickety footwalk had been constructed about the perimeter.

Slats of angled wood, to protect against snow and rain, formed the four sides and wire screening had been nailed up to keep birds out. Atkins pulled away the screening on the side facing the valley and broke away two slats. The sun was disappearing once again as the cloud cover thickened and he guessed snow would follow shortly. The extra height provided an excellent view of the railway. The Germans were already at work on the stretch of destroyed track and there was activity about the goods wagons behind the tender but the light was too poor for details. What he did see was the soldiers who had marched back along the line until they were out of sight from the village, turn and move into the trees to the left – the flanking party he had anticipated.

Mobility and surprise, he told himself as he sank down onto the catwalk. That was the Hun trademark. His small force wouldn't stand a chance if flanked during a head-on attack. A sudden cramp doubled him over. Christ in heaven, he thought as he stumbled down the ladder and ran to the outhouse he had seen behind the church. He fumbled his trousers down just in time. The violence of the cramps and the rush with which his bowels were evacuated left him limp.

What in the name of God, he thought, and pressed both fists against his abdomen to contain the hot, angry pain in his guts. Afraid! he thought. I'm frightened, like a child! And I can't control it. He rocked back and forth in mental and physical agony until the sound of aircraft engines caught his attention. 'Damn!' Two air attacks. They hadn't. . . .

He ran to the front of the church, fumbling the buttons on his trousers closed, as the first Stuka dove at the railroad depot. Atkins saw the bomb slide free and arrow down so fast the building exploded before his mind registered the fact. The roof erupted and a portion was sent spinning into the tracks. The second Stuka seemed to aim directly at him. He hurled himself into a ditch as the bomb shot at the village and exploded further up the road.

He was up and running as the two aircraft climbed for the second pass. Atkins dove head first into the first sandbagged trench he saw as the lead Stuka came in low, machine guns blazing. The Sergeant-Major had done an excellent job of siting the trenches and it was evident he had experience of Stukas. The aircraft could only approach from up or down the valley because of its narrow configuration and the slit trenches had been dug perpendicular to the walls to allow the minimum possible exposure.

He rolled over to see three soldiers with unshaven, haggard faces and mud-caked coats peering at him.

'I'm your new CO,' he drawled trying to make his voice sound casual. 'I saw these bastards at work in Poland.'

One soldier raised an eyebrow. 'You wer' in Poland . . . sir?' he added as an afterthought.

'Warsaw. Where's the Sergeant-Major?'

Machine-gun fire chewed across the trench. Someone screamed and Atkins rolled to see one of his trench mates leaning against the dirt wall holding a hand to the bloody mess at his shoulder where a bullet had blasted through the edge of a sandbag. He could hear the second Stuka following and snatched up the wounded man's SMLE rifle. The aircraft was at less than a hundred feet and beginning to climb for altitude when Atkins fired. He plunged to his feet, working the Enfield's bolt, cursing the cold-stiffened action and fired again as one wing lifted into the climb. A burst of white smoke appeared, stopped and spurted again. The pilot continued the climb, unaware, and Atkins fired a third shot, more in frustration than in the hope of hitting.

He was dragged down as the lead Stuka dove a third time. When he scrambled up again, it was to see the two unwounded soldiers staring open-mouthed at the second Stuka, well down the valley now as it struggled for altitude. Its air base was probably the airfield at Lillehammer. The smoke changed from a thin plume of white to a greasy black stream and the Stuka hesitated. Atkins saw the nose come up as the pilot fought with the controls, then the aircraft dipped and almost faster than he could follow, smashed into the trees and exploded. The two soldiers regarded him with awe but Atkins could only lean against the lip of the trench, just as astonished as they at what he had done.

'They only move at ninety miles an hour as they pull out of a dive,' he said weakly. 'If you lead them by a handspan as they start the climb . . .'

Suddenly, he felt extremely foolish. What the devil was he doing telling these men about Stukas? They had been facing them for days now.

The Sergeant-Major snorted as Atkins traced the probable route of the flanking party along the ridge. 'Aye, sor. They'll come at sunset. We've done the quick fade once too oft'n.'

'Then I think we should surprise them, Sergeant-Major.' He glanced at his watch. 'It's already 1510 hours. We'll have dusk in another hour and darkness about 1800. I suggest that we make our withdrawal earlier than they anticipate.'

'Earlier, sor?' The man was plainly dubious.

'Certainly. Get out ahead of the flankers. We'll fire off the second set of demolition charges as we go. I doubt if they will be able to repair the track before dawn and by then, we will have reached our next position.'

'It might work, sor.'

'It will, Sergeant-Major. There isn't an alternative is there?' He stood up, grunting at sore leg muscles. 'Alert the men. Have them ready to move at 1730.' He watched the middle-aged non-commissioned officer stride off. The backbone of the professional army, he thought, fighting his second war. Does the lack of fear come with experience, or is it inborn?

On 28 April, a runner brought orders to continue the retreat as far as Dombas at their best speed consistent with delaying the enemy. The decision been made to withdraw completely from Norway south of Narvik. Atkins wondered if anyone had yet told the Norwegians.

The snow stopped shortly after dawn on the third day and all morning they were harassed by Stukas. The ancient train puffed up the steep valleys and across pass after pass leading to the coast, trailing a long plume of smoke that served as an unavoidable beacon to marauding aircraft. Once, they had been able to look straight down and see two trains full of Germans following far below.

In a late afternoon full of blue shadows in another deserted village, Atkins' company set demolition charges, built barricades of railroad ties and hacked trenches from the frozen earth. Aircraft appeared at sunset, flying high enough so that the sun flashed and danced on their wings. He raced down the line, shouting to the men to get into the trees, away from the railroad. The bombs fell in rending explosions that battered the eardrums and shattered the frozen ground. The village disappeared in a maelstrom of flame and concussion.

Atkins, tired to death after three days and nights with only a few minutes' sleep snatched here and there, stood at the end of the road when the aircraft had turned south again, staring at the village being consumed by flames, at the fat pillar of greasy smoke that rose in the icy air and at the slopes of the peaks enclosing the valley. The setting sun vied with the fire to paint the snow with gold. Another cramp clutched at his gut but he held himself upright with a resolution he did not know he possessed and gave orders for the demolition of the rail line. As the train strained up the valley in the darkness, he saw his own contribution to the war; the flashes of demolition charges that completed the destruction.

Snow began again at midnight and by dawn had become a full-scale blizzard roaring out of the Arctic in waves of ice and wind. The temperature plummeted far below zero and the snow was blinding, hiding anything beyond a few yards in winter's last bid to hold the mountain fastness in thrall.

At midday, half frozen and battered in the unheated goods wagons, they reached the point south of Dombas where the rails divided. Uncommitted elements of Paget's 148th Infantry Brigade had been moved up to the rail junction and Atkins' weary company was scheduled to be withdrawn through them for a few hours' rest while a short-lived counterattack in the blizzard was mounted to convince the Germans to keep their distance.

A few miles north of Dombas, the rail line entered a long tunnel. Atkins stopped the train inside for shelter from the vicious wind. The tunnel made an excellent defensive position; they could only be ousted by direct frontal assault and the Nazis wouldn't send Stukas to seal the ends, not if they wished to continue their advance to the coast.

There was no time to search out either Morgan or Paget for orders and he dispatched his overworked switch engine up the line under cover of the blizzard with the wounded and to bring back food and ammunition.

They mined the approach to the tunnel, set off the charges and settled back into the icy interior to wait. The first probe came at noon, more by accident than design. German advance units groping up the track stumbled past the advance posts that Atkins had established a hundred yards ahead of the tunnel. In the brief firefight at the tunnel mouth, the German squad was killed to a man.

Unexpectedly, the defenders came under fire. The first explosion blasted the track and sent splinters of steel and rock slashing through the tunnel, seriously wounding two men. The Germans were using the train's 88 millimetre anti-aircraft gun to blast them out. Only then did Atkins guess that the patrol had been in communication with following units by wireless and had acted as a mobile measuring device in the blizzard. Atkins was forced to order his company well back into the tunnel to avoid the shrapnel.

Two more attacks were mounted against them during the day but they were warned in time by the lonely, half-frozen outpost in the forest south of the tunnel. As the afternoon wore on and the train did not return, Atkins began to worry. They had little ammunition left and not enough gelignite to destroy the tunnel. In the lull following the second attack, he ordered the tunnel entrance mined with the remaining explosive and the mortar bombs that were useless in the blizzard. There was not enough to do the job properly but it would at least slow the German advance by several hours.

At sunset, the snow ended and in the smokey, grey-blue twilight they could see the German train stopped, half a mile beyond where the track had been blown up. Work crews were dispersed with a volley of shots, but, with darkness, he knew the Germans would resume track repair, moving closer and closer to the tunnel mouth, their work crews sheltered behind moveable log barricades. Atkins estimated three hours.

The Sergeant-Major crouched as near to the entrance as possible, head cocked to one side, listening. Atkins knelt beside him and the Sergeant-Major shook his head.

'Coomin' nearer and nearer, sor. 'Nother hour.'

The clang of hammers on spikes carried over the wind and Atkins swore. 'Get the men to the far end of the tunnel, Sergeant-Major. Jerry's up to something.'

The old veteran gave him a quizzical look but trudged back through the tunnel, gathering the men as he went. Atkins shrugged into his own pack and picked up a rifle left behind by one of the wounded and followed to where the men were assembling. A single pressure lantern barely relieved the gloom. He saw the haggard faces – sixty left in the company. There had been eighty-three four days before. My God, had it only been four days?

'The train is overdue. Anything could have happened; avalanche, German bombers,' he shrugged. 'Therefore, we are leaving this,' he gestured about the tunnel, 'pleasant holiday spot before the next charabanc arrives.' It drew the expected laugh and he went on.

'I think that Jerry will attempt to flank us once again. So, we are going to walk out. It's fifteen miles to Dombas, uphill. And Jerry will be dogging our steps every bit of the way. But we've come this far and we can go the last bit. I don't relish the idea of a Nazi POW camp for the duration.'

There were no cheers, but no disaffected muttering either. They had sense enough to recognize that they were all in this together.

They marched out of the tunnel into the full force of the wind in proper order. Atkins had suggested that each man tie a scarf about his face for protection from the wind and those who hadn't taken his advice, now did so promptly. When they had gone a hundred yards, he stopped and waited for the end of the column to pass. The Sergeant-Major loomed in the darkness followed by the two demolition specialists. At his nod, they connected the charge wires to the accumulator pack. The Sergeant-Major growled an order and the Corporal twisted the key. The sky flared into light for an instant outlining the harsh bulk of the mountains and the concussion struck at them. Debris pattered down nearby. He hoped to God the makeshift charges had done their job and sealed the tunnel at both ends.

'Would you want me to hav' a look, Captain?'

'How much faith do you have, Sergeant-Major?'

The man chuckled. 'In them lads? All the faith in the world.'

'Then let's catch up.'

The night was one that Atkins would never forget. He was to serve in other places where the fighting was as desperate as this final rear-guard action in the Norwegian mountains, but never again would the weather serve the enemy more. Winds gusted to forty and fifty miles per hour and collected vast quantities of snow whirled from the ground into a stinging blizzard of ice crystals. The ground snow had hardened into *névé*, a crystallized intermediate product that was more than snow, but not quite ice. A close examination would have revealed that each individual flake had lost its lacy construction and compacted into the rugged substance of glaciers. It was their bad luck to have to march fifteen miles up grades as steep as 15 per cent in the midst of the final and worst blizzard of the winter of 1939-40.

Atkins plodded steadily along the snow-encrusted sleepers striving to stay even or a bit ahead of the double line of men on either side of the rails. At times the wind struck him so hard that he had to bend double to keep moving at all. At the end of the third hour he was exhausted. At the end of the next hour, he wanted to lie down in the snow's soft embrace and sleep forever. The fact that he was constantly moving up and down the line to make certain no one fell out effectively doubled the distance he had to march. The Sergeant-Major, he noted dimly, was doing the same on the other side. The lines of men lacked substance; they seemed little more than shuffling, snow-crusted phantoms and all his life seemed to have been spent plodding into swirling greyness, ears filled with the banshee ululation of wind.

A hooded lamp gleamed through the snow and he plodded on, wondering what it meant. Only the screech of airbrakes and steel on steel startled him from his daze. Strong arms helped him up. He was conscious only that the wind had stopped and there was warmth. More bodies crowded in and someone thrust a steaming mug of tea into his hands and he marvelled at its warmth. At that moment, he did not care if their rescuers were British or German.

The train banging to a stop woke Atkins. The sliding door of the goods wagon was thrown open and a soldier in an officer's great-coat leaned out. When Atkins shuffled to the door, he saw a thick column of smoke rising from a base of flames half a mile ahead.

'Jerry must be on them,' the officer muttered. 'What I'd like to know is where the bloody hell's the RAF?' He stuck out a hand to Atkins.

'You're Captain Atkins aren't you? Commanded the rear guard and all that. Heard you did a splendid job. Name's Townely, Lieutenant Paul Townely. Attached to Brigadier Morgan's staff, or was until we were separated south of here. Jerry aircraft again. Great damned Stukas diving on us, machine guns and bombs but I expect you know all about that. Heard you shot one of the bastards down with a rifle?'

Atkins was amazed. 'Where the devil did you hear that?'

Townely grinned. 'Hoped it was true. Teach the bastards a lesson. Good God man, story's all up and down the line. Men pot-shotting the buggers all the time. Makes 'em feel good and keeps the bloody Hun up, I'll tell you!' He motioned ahead. 'Petrol storage tanks. No bloody aircraft, no bloody anti-aircraft guns. We aren't retreating now, we're running, as fast as we can for the coast. I only hope we get a clear track to Andalsnes.'

They didn't. A staff officer came shouting along the train for Atkins and when he found him, ordered him to set up a defence perimeter at the north end of the railyard.

'Damn it, Colonel,' he raved. 'Those men have been in the line for two weeks straight. They've had nothing but cold rations for a week and last night they marched five miles. They've been given one cup of tea and three hours sleep, at best.'

The Colonel disengaged Atkins' fingers from his arm. 'I know how you feel Captain, believe me I do. We've all had similiar experiences. But you are the last organized force I have. I need you to hold long enough for me to get the last trains loaded, two hours at most. And I promise you, hot food will be sent up immediately.'

But the attack which came almost immediately did not allow them such luxury. A flight of Stukas, braving the intermittent snow, struck hard at the railyard, searching out the defenders. Mortar shells slammed into the area at the same time and almost before they knew it, German infantry was pouring into the yard.

As familiar with the German tactics of constant and unremitting attack as he was, Atkins was still stunned by the swiftness of this assault. His forward positions were driven in at once and one of the two machine-gun posts was isolated and destroyed. Atkins had expected a wave of assault growing in strength as the Nazis tested their disposition. Instead, they were driven back into the second line almost immediately and he realized they would have to withdraw again unless the ferocity of the attack slackened. And when that happened, there was no place for them to go except up the line until they were jammed against the rear elements of the retreating forces. He had no artillery, only three mortars and now one machine gun.

He crouched in the signal tower near the yard's centre, battling the fear that had renewed itself in the interval between the staff officer's orders to hold the yard and the attack. He wanted to break and run, to hide somewhere in the maze of buildings and sheds until the Nazis were gone and the shooting and explosions had stopped but gradually, he brought himself under control. His teeth chattered, as much with fear as with cold and his hands shook, at times so badly that he could only jam them into the pockets of his duffle coat.

A combat unit had been thrown out to his left in an attempt to flank the British positions around the signal tower on the east side of the yard. Atkins wrote a set of coordinates on a slip of paper with painstaking care to minimize his shaking hands and sent it off with one of the lightly wounded soldiers pressed into service as a runner. As he continued to watch the Germans moving quickly from cover to cover, overrunning the lightly manned defences along the perimeter, he saw the leading elements of the flanking attack appear between two sheds and slip past the line of signal lamps he had marked as the final withdrawal line. The battle was less than fifteen minutes old and the Germans had knocked out or isolated a third of his meagre force.

They were almost at the end of the alley now. If they fanned out, drawing reinforcements behind them in strength, they would surround his main positions within minutes. Atkins slammed a fist on the table. Where the hell were the mortars; and as if to answer him, the first round slammed through the roof of the shed, blowing it to pieces. A second followed and the German soldiers still on their feet pulled back quickly.

Quick reaction had saved them that time but their situation was perilous. How long to regroup? He gathered up his maps and stuffed them inside his duffle coat, took a last look through his field glasses at the darkening yard and went down the ladder. At the bottom, he paused long enough to light the fuse to the demolition charge with his cigarette lighter, then ran across the frozen cinders to the squat, brick administration building which was their final position before retreating to the last train loading half a mile north of the yard. The signal tower blew up with a tremendous roar and a flare that lit the night sky like a burst of lightning. The explosion did double duty, denying the Germans the centralized switching facility and serving his people notice that the time had come to gather in.

A runner appeared, waving one good arm furiously and fell headlong. Fear galvanized Atkins and he dove to one side and rolled into the cover of a stack of steel wheels. Bullets splattered on the cinders and screamed off the wheels. Atkins clutched both arms tightly about his stomach, fighting the urge to retch. He could see three soldiers in coal scuttle helmets approaching at a run and without thinking, he turned swiftly to kneel, pushed the Enfield's safety off, took careful aim and fired three shots as fast as he could work the bolt.

Someone shouted in English and a khaki arm appeared at a window. Atkins took a chance, broke from his sparse shelter and raced across the cinders. A frame structure held signal lamps glowing green and red against a gunmetal sky. Atkins saw two flares arc up, one after another, as he reached the illusory shelter of the building and dove for the doorway.

The inside of the brick warehouse was icy. Three men crouched by windows, watching while a fourth grinned and reached to help him. The man had a shock of reddish hair protruding from beneath his helmet and a scattering of large freckles across his cheeks. Atkins reached for the man's hand and the room exploded outwards. The red-head's face dissolved and blackness engulfed him.

Yorkshire 14 – 16 May 1940

A fine, grey rain was falling beyond the windows. The room stopped spinning and Captain Charles Atkins took a first hesitant step. The sister kept pace with him, holding one hand. For two weeks he had been confined to bed in the overcrowded ward of a

Yorkshire country hospital, recovering from a severe concussion and two operations to remove a round dozen mortar fragments.

The window was fifteen feet high and betrayed the nineteenth-century origins of the hospital as a consumption clinic at a time when fresh air, sunlight and bed rest were the only treatment available for tuberculosis and the host of related lung diseases that affected Yorkshire miners. Beyond the rain-streaked glass, the unbelievable green of spring fields sloped away to distant trees. Atkins longed to feel the rain on his face and know that he was still alive and the fear gone.

The Allies had evacuated all of Norway but Narvik on the night of 30 April 1940. All available forces had been thrown at the port in an effort to cut the Iron Road and hamper Swedish shipments of iron ore to Germany. For days, Atkins had lain in bed, listening to the wireless reports of German attacks through the Ardennes into Holland and Belgium. The nightmare of the tank as a super weapon had been verified as German Panzer units smashed all opposition as they had done in Poland, crossed the Meuse and raced towards the North Sea and the English Channel. Only the election in the House of Commons of Winston Churchill as Prime Minister to replace Chamberlain gave him any hope at all.

Atkins was allowed to leave the clinic for short walks a few days after Holland had surrendered on the fifteenth. He was weak and his numerous wounds itched and pulled as he moved. Nevertheless, he forced himself to go a bit further afield each day.

An unseasonably hot sun shone through a thin haze as he trudged along a country road, looking for a place to sit and rest. A grassy clearing shaded by an oak offered refuge and he sank down gratefully and lit a cigarette. A figure on a bicycle toiled up the sandy road towards him, a young woman making heavy going of it. Fifty yards off, the front wheel caught in a patch of sand, turned sharply and the woman fell. He dropped the cigarette and struggled to his feet but she was up quickly and yanking on the handle bars to straighten them by the time he reached her. There was a streak of blood on her forehead and her eyes were full of tears.

'Are you all right?' He tried to look at the cut but she pushed his hand away and remounted.

'No thanks to you,' she snapped, brushing at one eye furiously. 'If you were any sort of gentleman, you would have come right away instead of sauntering down the path as if you . . . oh go away.' She tried to walk the bicycle through the soft sand, then jumped off to pull it back onto firmer ground, struggling to control her tears. Atkins, astounded by her attack, was speechless and she wobbled away before he could think of anything to say.

The following day, he walked as far as the town. The doctor had pronounced him on the mend and promised he could go on leave soon. He had no place in particular to go, yet the idea of a few weeks of quiet without responsibility was appealing and he was thinking about fishing in Scotland or Ireland. His wounds were plentiful and painful but not serious and the doctor had joked that he would look like a patched-up sieve after the shrapnel wounds healed.

By the time he reached the village, he wondered if he hadn't overdone it. The sun was quite warm in the high street and he removed the old tweed jacket a doctor had lent him. His wounds itched abominably and perspiration only irritated them more. A bout of giddiness attacked and he stumbled against a railing and clung to it for support as the world suddenly darkened and a tremendous whirling roar rushed at him.

"Ere now lad, rest on me.' A strong arm encircled his shoulders to steady him. 'All done in? Come along.'

A heavyset man, a farmer by the look of him, helped him up the steps and pushed open a solid oak door. Atkins was breathing deeply, trying to hold the nausea in check, and was dimly aware of the man lifting him onto a table and slipping his folded jacket under his feet.

The world whirled into a dark fog shot through with light, closing in until only a narrow tunnel was left. He was soaking with perspiration and his teeth chattered. A blanket settled over him and the chill began to recede. When he opened his eyes impressions flooded in – a large room faced with bookcases above which was polished red oak wainscotting. The peppery odour of old paper filled the place and a craggy face with a bulbous nose above a walrus moustache peered at him. The man was dressed in dark corduroy and wore a cloth cap set squarely on his head. He seemed as broad as he was high; not fat, but solid, and immensely powerful, a man who had worked rough all his life.

'Ye're lookin' better now, lad,' the farmer observed and with the sound of his voice, the world steadied.

A young woman appeared at his shoulder and a damp cloth was laid across his forehead. Her face was familiar but his brain was too fuzzy to identify the girl until he noticed a small cut on her forehead.

'You seemed to have recovered nicely from your fall,' he mumbled and she blushed.

'I must apologize for the way I spoke to you yesterday. I had no idea you were a patient at the hospital.'

Atkins tried a grin and it seemed to work because she smiled back. 'I understand.' He took a breath. 'I . . . I might have done the same.'

239

'No, please, there was no excuse.'

'Do ye think ye can sit up naow, lad?'

She started to protest but the farmer cut her off. 'Nay, lass. Best he be up and about quick as possible.'

The dizziness and nausea had abated but he was shaking with exhaustion which confirmed his belated realization that he had indeed overestimated the extent of his recovery. The young woman brought him a cup of tea and he wrapped his cold hands around the mug with gratitude and drank. He was in a library, she explained. Her name was Wendy Hiller and she was the library staff. The farmer was introduced as Mr Thomas Fitzgerald, the owner of a small dairy farm some distance from the town and one of her best patrons. Fitzgerald nodded ponderous agreement and excused himself to finish his business. He promised to give Atkins a lift to the hospital on his return.

'I don't mean to interrupt your work, Miss Hiller,' Atkins told her 'but I would be grateful if you allowed me to sit here for a few minutes, then I'll go and wait outside for Mr Fitzgerald.'

'Nonsense! You will remain in here, away from the sun. I expect that's what gave you a turn. And please, my Christian name is Wendy. I'd be ever so grateful if you'd use it.'

Atkins felt himself colouring like a schoolboy and grinned in spite of his embarrassment. 'Only if you call me Charles.'

A sudden silence fell between them and before it grew awkward, she gathered up a stack of lending cards and went to the desk. She gave him a quick smile and began to sort them. Atkins leaned back and closed his eyes a moment, feeling exhaustion race through his body.

The aftermath of these sudden attacks was always the same, a weakness that delved to the core of his being, as if the winter's activities in Finland and Norway had extracted the last of his reserves. The doctor had assured him that he was exaggerating its effects and that with time, there was no physiological reason why he should not regain all his strength.

In the meantime, it was pleasant to sit quietly, eyes closed and listen to the rustle of her skirts as Wendy returned to her desk. It was the small, familiar sounds that he found he had missed so badly. He opened his eyes to see her reach across the desk for a pencil and a soft curve of breast and shoulder was outlined against the sun-filled window for a moment. He thought again of Erika and the spasm of pain slipped past his defences.

Atkins came to the library the following afternoon. The comfortable old building was again empty except for Wendy Hiller sitting at her massive desk like an old-fashioned school teacher. But there was little that was old-fashioned about her, he thought, as he walked between the wrought-iron bookcases. She wore her softly waved chestnut hair long and when she leaned over the desk and it fell forward, she had an enchanting way of brushing it back with both hands that caused it to sway and shimmer.

She looked up when he was half way down the aisle and her smile turned his knees to water. 'I was hoping you would come again.' Her voice was low and musical.

Atkins had agonized over doing so through most of the night. He was uncertain of whether he would be welcomed or merely tolerated as a 'wounded soldier'. In the end, he screwed up his courage, hitched a ride into town, bought a bunch of spring flowers in the market and marched to the library. As added insurance however, he wore his uniform.

He laid the assortment of larkspur, maidenhair and lilacs on the desk and gave a half bow. 'In return for your hospitality, milady.'

Wendy laughed with delight. 'You sir, are a gentleman. I'll just go and get a vase.' She hurried towards the back of the room with the flowers and Atkins found that his hands were shaking.

He remained in the library talking to her until closing time. Afterwards, they walked through the village enjoying the soft spring evening as the shadows drew across the green. Wendy told him that she had rooms at the end of the village, with a young mother whose husband had gone into the RAF and was somewhere in Belgium. His letters which had been full of complaints about the Phoney War and the boredom had stopped suddenly the week before.

'I don't like to leave her alone in the evening, after the children are in bed,' she told him with a worried frown. 'Madge is all right during the day when the children are about to keep her occupied but at night she tends to fret herself into hysterics.'

Atkins nodded. The Phoney War she had called it – as did most people in England because it had not really affected them yet. But the Finns never called it that, nor the Poles or the Norwegians or the sailors, merchant and Royal Navy, who could not escape the effects of war during those long months.

Wendy sensed his thoughts and turned quickly. 'I didn't mean to imply . . .'

Atkins laughed and tucked her arm under his. 'Of course you didn't. I just happened to be in the wrong place at the wrong time, you see. Even the French have a name for it as well, *drôle de guerre.*'

Wendy tightened her grip and he was absurdly pleased. 'I thought after Norway that the war might end. I asked myself if the Nazis hadn't got all that they wanted. I am ashamed to admit it now, but I was almost glad they had beaten us in Norway because it meant perhaps an armistice. But now they have attacked Belgium, Holland and France and, if they win, I'm so afraid that we in Britain will be next.'

Atkins kept silent. In the past few days, the country had begun to understand what he had first seen in Poland. The democracies were facing the most severe test of their right to exist in history. And beyond that, the differences involved more than political philosophies. The First World War had been fought for the control of markets; this one would be fought for the control of raw materials and land. All over the world he could sense its definitions coalescing; the Japanese in Manchuria and China and their stated designs on the East Indies; the Italians in East Africa and their designs in the Middle East; Germany snatching up everything in sight to build a twentieth-century version of Britain's empire. Oil, coal, minerals and agricultural land were to be the prizes this time.

Control of vital resources: Atkins knew that if any of the participants in this developing war lost sight of that; if they failed to subordinate every effort to achieving the *objective*, they would lose the war.

They paused at the end of the green. The Yorkshire hills ran into the gold of evening and he drew a deep breath of mild air, so different from the frozen breath of Scandinavia. He knew it would soon be like this in Finland, the woods growing alive, the ice melting from lakes, air softening. But for what? How would the Finns deal with their loss?

'I tried to read Mr Hitler's *Mein Kampf*,' Wendy told him. 'Other than the fact that it is patently unreadable, it's the work of a madman! He writes over and over again of what he calls the *untermenschen*, by which he means anyone not Aryan – his term for the racially pure German.'

Atkins glanced at her. She frowned as she spoke, as if seeing the page in her mind's eye. 'He is convinced that there are sub-species of the human race which are patently inferior and must be destroyed to prevent contamination in the rest of the human race.'

'And who are these sub-humans?' Atkins asked, half teasing but she ignored his humour.

'The Jews, gypsies, Slavs and Negroes. Those who are not Aryans. We English are acceptable because we are supposedly of the same racial stock.'

Atkins laughed. 'Then I'd say that we're safe enough.'

'It is not something to laugh about,' she said sharply. 'The man believes what he writes. One detects in his books the same fanaticism one hears in his speeches.'

They were both silent as they resumed the walk towards the house at the end of the village.

Cry Havoc

Belgium 10 – 27 May 1940

The early morning was absolutely still. Captain Friedrich Prager stood in the turret of his four-wheeled *Leichter Panzerspahwagen* 222 and drank his tea. The air held a delightful spring softness and the smell of new growth in the forest was so strong it almost overpowered the grating smell of petrol fumes. A thin mist hung in the air softening his view of the valley below. It was almost as peaceful as that late summer dawn before the invasion of Poland, he thought.

But, this isn't Poland, he told himself, and there are no cavalry squadrons with lances and carbines. The Belgian army – twenty-two divisions of 600,000 men – waited instead, their only task to hold a line running from the French–Luxembourg–Belgian border to the Meuse and along the line of the Albert Canal to Antwerp long enough for the French and British armies to move up. And, if that happened, the trench war of 1914–18 would begin afresh.

Prager had read the revised summary of *Fall Gelb*, Case Yellow, the plan for the attack in the west. It was to be a lightning-fast attack along a broad front against Dutch, Belgian, French and British fortifications and armies, all neatly lined-up and with plenty of warning they were coming. He had also reviewed *Fall Rot* – the plan to contain a French counterattack – and in his own mind, was convinced that it was totally inadequate. If the Allies should attack through the Maginot Line at Germany's western frontier, there was damned little to stop them. The Fuehrer was staking everything on the gamble that they would not do so. Why the *Oberkommando der Wehrmacht*, the High Command of the Armed Forces, had agreed, he would never understand. And he was not alone among the professional military officers of Germany.

This is madness, he told himself. We are drunk with our successes.

He recalled Sonja's agonized face when he kissed her goodbye on the train platform at Hamburg's Main Station a week ago. She had pressed her lips hard against his and for an instant the tight sexual ache for her against which he had struggled since the first and only night they had made love, nearly overwhelmed him.

'I've done the right thing,' he thought and knew it had become a litany. But it was true. If anything happened to him, she wouldn't have to bear the burden of widowhood in a foreign country. If he survived, then nothing would prevent their marriage – by autumn, if they succeeded in France. It would depend on which side moved the faster. Five kilometres a day, the planners had calculated. In 1914–18, *monthly* gains had been calculated in metres.

The radio operator tugged at Prager's trouser leg. 'Oh-five hundred sir in twenty seconds, sir.'

Prager nodded and brought his mind back to the ridge line overlooking the forested slopes of the Ardennes. A thousand metres away lay Belgium, the cockpit of Europe, the most fought-over, blood-soaked piece of ground in the world. He gave the command and the armoured car's engine started easily. All about him in the woods, the sound of engines burst forth, startling birds and men alike and, in moments, the air was hazed in blue exhaust.

The Seventh Panzer Division was commanded by General Erwin Rommel, a former infantry commander being rewarded for service on the Fuehrer's staff, and consisted of the Twenty-Fifth Panzer Regiment, the Thirty-Seventh Panzer Reconnaissance Battalion, the Sixth and Seventh Rifle Regiments (motorized), the Seventh Motorcycle Battalion and the Seventy-Eighth Field Artillery Regiment. Damned little, he thought, with which to face a combined Belgian, British, and French force of nearly double their weight of numbers in tanks and men, if the intelligence reports were correct.

Prager stood, one arm raised, eyes on his wrist-watch. At the instant the second and minute hands touched twelve, he brought his arm down sharply and the car lurched forward.

For the first twenty minutes, his scouting force met no opposition. They drove out of the trees and crossed a sloping meadow where a milk cow stared stupidly at the lines of grey vehicles clattering across its preserve. The sun cleared the ridges and he could feel its warmth cut the dawn chill. A dust cloud was already forming behind them.

Prager had spent every spare moment during the last two days studying maps of this section of the Ardennes. Some of them dated to before the 1914–18 war, others had been recently updated. Even a Michelin road map had been included. Even so, Prager lacked confidence in them and he knew it was because he had not verified their information himself, as he had in Poland.

There were few roads through the thickly forested mountains that defined the border between Belgium and Germany. In 1914, a revision of the Schlieffen Plan had directed the German armed forces south of this rugged area in the belief that a large force could not move through it without losing coherence. That theory had held until past years when surveying parties had secretly mapped routes that took advantage of the terrain for concealment and speed. If German armoured forces were to succeed against the overwhelming might of France, they stood their best chance here. If they could move through the Ardennes quickly enough, they could outflank the Maginot Line. A big if. France was known to have more and better tanks and the four allies – France, Belgium, Holland and Great Britain – could between them field a total of 149 divisions to Germany's 136. And the defender always held the advantage.

He halted the column where the track turned onto a dirt road shown on the map as leading out of the Ardennes and heavily marked in red. He studied the road in either direction through the Zeiss field glasses his father had taken from a dead Russian officer in 1915.

The roadblock was five hundred metres ahead, sited where the road began a sharp curve. Trees had been felled and a lorry was parked behind the barrier. Prager could see an officer watching him through field glasses. A machine gun had been placed to cover the approaches. Very professional, he thought admiringly, and his first real test against a modern enemy.

Other than the steady rumbling of engines, the morning was still. Am I privileged to fire the first shot? he wondered.

He gave instructions for his second-in-command to move up beside him and for the radio vehicle to signal headquarters. Did they have an anti-tank weapon? he wondered. Sparks winked about the sandbags and something wanged off the hull. The privilege of the first shot had been claimed by the other side.

The armoured car mounted a twenty millimetre cannon and a 7.92 millimetre machine gun. Prager pumped three cannon shells at the log barrier and at the same time, the commander of the other vehicle swept the undergrowth on either side of the road with his machine gun. The fire from the barrier ceased immediately and a moment later, the lorry reversed back down the road at high speed. Prager encouraged the driver with another burst and drove forward.

The position was deserted. The cannon had shattered the logs throwing splinters everywhere. He noted with surprise that the defenders had run so fast they had left their machine gun behind. He led the column around the barrier and they resumed speed as he ordered the radio vehicle to notify the Fifty-eighth Engineering Battalion following that a road block needed to be dismantled. They marked the correct route with the small signs which had been painted with 'DG-7', an innovation of Rommel's designed to clearly indicate the route and prevent units from going astray. Prager thought it an excellent idea, if unofficial, but he knew there was a great deal of resistance within the division and could imagine what it would be like when the high command found out.

Twice more they came upon barricades and both times their light cannon and machine guns were sufficient to disperse the defenders. Prager had studied the action reports of tank commanders in Poland and concluded that the combination of high speed and blanket machine-gun fire to either side of the road at the first sign of resistance could be depended on to panic enemy infantry. If the Belgians thought to apply some of those lessons by building road blocks, they had seriously underestimated the Panzers. To be successful, a roadblock had to be backed by well-handled, carefully sited anti-tank guns. The flimsy barricades with machine guns for support they had encountered so far were suitable only for stopping automobiles.

By mid-afternoon, they were encountering fewer barricades and Prager wondered if the Belgians might not be pulling back. Perhaps they had begun to think that if the terrain of the Ardennes was insufficient to slow the Panzers, then piecemeal resistance was equally futile which suggested in turn that they might be falling back to the formidable river and canal defences in the lowlands.

The following day, Saturday, 11 May, was much the same; push ahead as quickly as possible and don't worry about the ability of the infantry to keep up. The armoured cars of Company A, Thirty-Seventh Reconnaissance Battalion, Seventh Panzer Division kept to a steady thirty kilometre per hour pace and used their machine guns liberally. Already they were beginning to see the first sign of what would soon become the outstanding phenomenon of the campaign; soldiers standing beside the road, hands in the air, surrendering in the face of Germany's overwhelming firepower and mobility.

On Sunday, Prager's column came up with the leading elements of the Twenty-Fifth Regiment which had reached the Meuse an hour before. General Erwin Rommel was standing beside his eight-wheeled *Schwerer Panzerspahwagen* studying the far bank through field glasses while enemy artillery fire slashed at their position. The air was filled with the acrid-sweet smell of high-explosive.

An aide took Prager's report as they crouched beside the rear bogey wheel of a Panzer IV which in turn was sheltered by a rise of ground. Prager studied the situation map as the aide marked in Prager's information. They had reached Bouvignes, a point on the Meuse half way between the villages of Dinant and Houx with only sporadic resistance. On the map the bridges in either town had been X'd out but the bridge at Bouvignes was so far intact. The aide corrected the map gleefully. One-hundred-and-twenty metres across the river, elements of the French Sixty-Sixth Rifle Regiment were serving as a rear guard and they seemed determined to hold – their heavy artillery had stopped the Seventh Division's advance cold.

Intelligence reported reinforcements from the French Fourth Cavalry approaching and if they arrived before the crossing was completed, Allied strategy would pay off handsomely and the German drive would be halted on the Meuse. A shell slammed into the earth close by and the concussion smacked Prager's head painfully against the tyre. Shouts and screams rose and a medical corpsman raced across an open area.

A concentrated barrage struck at their position and suddenly, the contrast between the green spring day and the murderous artillery fire spewing across the river was astonishing. The din was continuous – like cast-iron plates being slammed to concrete floors. The tanks began to return fire with their fifty and seventy-five millimetre cannons.

Rommel ran towards them, bent low against the sleet of shrapnel. He threw himself down in the shelter of the tank, panting and grinning, nodded at Prager and began to shout into his aide's ear as he sketched with a finger on the map what it was he wanted. The aide nodded and ran back through the line of trenches towards the rear and Rommel leaned back against the bogey beside Prager.

'*Ein Riesensauerei*, one hell of a mess, heh Prager. But we've broken across at Houx with some motorcyclists and a few riflemen from the Seventh Rifle Regiment. They crossed on one of the locks, it seems. But we have to get them reinforcements and remove the pressure. Can you bring your cars up at dawn and lay down a barrage on the far bank?'

Prager nodded, impressed at Rommel's coolness and informality, even as he traced a route upstream.

'Good. Then I want you to drive to the village of Leffe here,' Rommel pointed to a collection of houses on the map that were little more than a suburb of Dinant, 'where you will be well screened. Lay out your firing positions and at 0430 exactly, I want you to open fire. As our boats approach the bank, lift your fire inland. I'm having some anti-aircraft guns brought up to concentrate on the French artillery.'

He clapped Prager on the shoulder and moved on. Prager checked his notes, shoved the tablet in his pocket and when a lull in the firing occurred, ran through the trees towards his unit.

By midnight, he had his cars in laager in a small park and had scouted the far bank through field glasses. There was little to be seen in the darkness; thick brush grew down to the swift river which was twenty metres wide on the average and the current, swift enough to undercut the banks, would make it dangerous to cross under shellfire. French snipers had positioned themselves in the trees and an occasional shot whistled across to make it amply clear that the Sixty-sixth Regiment was waiting for them.

It was difficult to snatch more than a few minutes' sleep with the French guns active all night. The booming roll of artillery and the sudden, sharp explosions of shells forward of their positions continually jolted him awake and he was grateful when at 0330, it was time to move into position.

Prager gave orders to open fire at 0430 and for twenty minutes, they poured twenty millimetre shells and machine-gun fire across the river while a company of riflemen raced across the top of the lock. He could see the water curling ankle high about their boots, but all managed to cross without mishap. Far in the rear, he could hear the sharp crack of an eighty-eight millimetre anti-aircraft cannon searching out French artillery beyond the river.

Without warning, murderous French artillery shells whirled onto them. Four in succession smashed the bank not twenty metres from where Prager crouched in the shelter of a gnarled oak. As the third shell exploded, he felt the tree quiver against his back and saw a half-metre of metal vibrating in the trunk just above his head. He shouted for the armoured cars to pull back and they backed straight down the slope. A shell exploded behind one car, flipping it over like a child's toy. The three crewmen popped out and ran. His radioman handed him a message from Rommel, ordering them back to support the infantry crossing with machine-gun fire and as they reached the road and hurried south, he was suddenly weak with the delayed fear of the shell splinter.

It took them nearly an hour to drive the four kilometres through the tangle of traffic and refugees. A waiting staff officer shouted them into position above the river and in among the trees. Prager went forward to the edge of the bank where he could look straight down to the river's edge at the assault boats loading with riflemen. With only a few centimetres of freeboard showing, paddles stirred the water and the craft lumbered away from the bank. One, caught in the current, spun lazily until its paddlers got it under control. Each boat described a diagonal from bank to bank as it struggled through columns of water thrown up by artillery shells. Smaller spurts showed that rifle and machine-gun fire from the far bank was heavy.

Across the river, clusters of grey uniforms huddled along the water's edge. One or two figures could be seen trying to climb the clay bank and an explosion on the crest trailed a geyser of smoke

251

lazily in the still air. There were four boats in the stream now, all blundering towards the same area. A single mortar round dropped between them with a tremendous splash but failed to explode.

The crossing had become a shambles. Several of the inflatable boats had been hit and were whirling downsteam as tangled masses of rubberized canvas. Bodies were sprawled along the water's edge or were being carried away by the current. Enemy fire was too intense and too close to permit the establishment of a bridgehead and the height of the banks made it impossible for the attackers to clear the crest or the area just behind. As he watched, a machine gun stuttered and water spurted around the lead boat. Prager saw a disturbance in the brush across the river and the machine gun racketed again.

I'll be damned, he thought, they have moved right to the edge.

Machine-gun fire raked the bank and Prager ducked. A branch fell across his back and he jumped spasmodically, then stared sheepishly at the green, half formed leaves. A bullet had clipped it as neatly as a gardener's pruning shears.

When he was certain that the French machine gunner was searching elsewhere for a target, he raced down the slope towards the village where infantry reserves filled the back gardens of every house, out of sight of the occasional French Potez observer aircraft. The civilians had disappeared during the night after closing shutters and hiding such valuables as they could not carry away. Headquarters had issued strict instructions concerning looting and the houses were out of bounds to everyone, including officers.

Something heavier than the machine guns and twenty millimetre cannon of his armoured cars was needed and Prager found four Panzer IIIs parked beneath trees on the village green. The senior tank commander grinned when he explained what was needed and invited him aboard. They rumbled out of the village towards the river, keeping to the cover of the trees to avoid the attention of the French gunners.

Prager found himself grinning with delight. This was the war his father had described to him, before trenches had turned the Galician fields to abattoirs. The kind of war where men strove against one another in honourable combat and all depended on skill and that imponderable the French called *élan*.

The river flashed in the morning sun. Prager hastily arranged simple hand signals with the four tank commanders, then wormed his way to the top of the bank.

The scene was madness and eliminated his enthusiasm instantly. The huddle of men on the far bank had been reduced by half and the number of bodies doubled. Machine-gun fire slashed at their flanks and infantrymen who should have been across the river by now, were crouching behind whatever bit of cover they could find. Further upstream, the bridge was under concentrated fire as the French sought desperately to bring it down.

At his hand signal, the four tanks lumbered forward, grinding saplings and underbrush beneath their treads. As they came hull down onto the crest, their powerful fifty millimetre cannons whip-cracked and the vegetation on the far bank shivered under the onslaught.

The surviving infantrymen took heart from the unexpected support and Prager heard a Sergeant shout at them to get into the boats. In moments, it seemed the Meuse was full of the flimsy craft. Across the river one soldier slithered to the top of the bank, and then another. The tanks were firing furiously now, lifting their sights to carry the shells into the trees as the infantry gained a foothold. The volume of French artillery fire slackened and a Panzer tank appeared on the bridge. Prager held his breath as it rumbled across. A single shell exploded in the upper works of the structure but the tank had already driven into the trees on the far side.

General Rommel appeared suddenly and slid down the bank. Prager saw his grin when a Sergeant roared at him to get back but Rommel ignored him and splashed into a boat. As they slid out into the current, Rommel found a seat in the stern and urged the paddlers on. As soon as the inflatable boat touched the far shore, Rommel was first out to disappear up a tiny gully.

Prager swore softly to himself, remembering that Rommel had done something similar in Poland. A column of tanks had been tied down by enemy fire and Rommel had taken his own armoured car in a wide circle and attacked the anti-tank gun from the flank, destroying it with machine-gun fire before it could turn on him.

By nightfall, a secure foothold had been established across the west bank of the Meuse and the French rear guard driven far enough back for the decimated Seventh Infantry to stand a chance of surviving a counterattack. Casualties had been heavy but morale had risen as the artillery fire slackened. The clearing in which Rommel had established his *Gefechsstaffel*, headquarters group, was filled with officers, each as weary as Prager, their uniforms as rumpled and filthy. He accepted a cup of coffee and was delighted to find that it was the real thing and not ersatz.

'Found a tin in the village,' the steward grinned at his exclamation. 'It was sitting on the ground. So it wasn't looting, you see.'

Rommel, wearing a fresh uniform, was talking with two other officers as Prager wandered up. He nodded to Lieutenant Haufer, whose company had knocked out the pillbox on the bridge ramp with hand grenades that morning. Haufer's answering nod was barely perceptible, which suited Prager. The man was a party member and an arrogant fanatic and quite unpopular. Fortunately, he was also an excellent soldier.

When they were all assembled, Rommel called for their attention. 'Gentlemen, tonight we move in force across the Meuse which means that we will have done in three weeks what Berlin said couldn't be done in three weeks. Now, I want as much equipment as possible across before dawn. Other elements of the Seventh Panzer will be crossing at Montherme and Sedan and we will begin a three-pronged sweep that will clear the French and Belgians all the way to the Channel. Are there any questions?'

Prager spent a sleepless night manoeuvring his unit through the narrow streets of Dinant and along the shell-torn roads bordering the Meuse. An occasional artillery shell whistled over but, in general, they were able to get their forces moving with little more than darkness and poor roads with which to contend.

The bridge had been badly damaged by the French bombardment and the engineers were hampered by darkness – the merest pinprick of light brought a sniper's bullet from the west bank. The incessant grinding of treads and revving engines coupled with petrol exhaust gave Prager a raging headache that at times made it difficult to think.

Towards 0130 hours, the engineers had shored up the bridge structure sufficiently to permit one tank at a time to cross. The first behemoth, a Panzer IV, eased onto the bridge. One man walked ahead, shouting orders to the driver as anxious engineers hovered about. The bridge surface had been torn and splintered by shrapnel and, in midspan, the iron supports had buckled, thrusting the decking upward. A large, bite-shaped piece of the bridge and railing had been carried away and the remaining road bed, barely the width of a tank, groaned and creaked as the heavy vehicle approached. The left tread ground up onto the buckled portion and the tank tipped sharply so that for a moment, it seemed suspended over the missing chunk of bridge. No one had expected the tank to lay over at such an acute angle and the engineer, standing on the bridge railing, saw the panic start on the driver's face as he looked straight into the black river twenty metres below.

'Go!' he shouted. 'Go, go go!'

If the tank lost momentum, gravity would snatch it straight down but the engineer's shouting galvanized the driver and the Panzer IV surged forward off the hump to crash down onto the bridge decking.

It required fifteen minutes each to move the fifteen tanks across the bridge. Prager's armoured cars followed without difficulty and drove immediately into their forward positions. He saw to the placement of each car and established a two-hour sentry-go, then sent his own crew for a few hours' sleep. He climbed back into the cupola of his car and lit a cigarette but immediately crushed it out. His throat was too raw from tobacco, fumes and shouting. He found his blanket, wrapped it about him and stretched out on the steel deck between the seats. Even so, nervous tension kept him awake for some time before he fell into a fitful doze.

'Prager, I've work for you.' Major Karl Erdmann, his Commanding Officer, spread a map on the fender skirt and tapped an area circled in red pencil.

'We've had a wireless message from Colonel von Bülow. He has surrounded the village of Onhaye, five kilometres west of here but is receiving heavy fire from the French. I want you to take five cars to his assistance.'

Prager compared his map to Erdmann's and five minutes later, they were bowling along the dusty road towards Onhaye, past Mark IVs from Rothernburg's Twenty-fifth Panzer Regiment and plodding infantry who shouted and cursed both the armoured cars and tanks for the dust boiling in their wake. At a point a kilometre or so east of Onhaye, Prager sent two cars curling east about the village as a precautionary measure and led the rest straight up the road.

The village of Onhaye consisted of a few houses and two or three shops that straggled along the single road. A column of thick black smoke showed where the battle was being fought beyond the town. They flashed through the village and turned off into a field where the sound of cannon fire was loudest in the trees. The French gunners saw them coming and managed to turn one gun and get off a single shot that damaged the last car in line. A merciless barrage of twenty millimetre shells silenced it almost at once. As they turned to run in towards the trapped Panzers, an unsuspected second anti-tank gun fired and the car behind Prager's exploded with a loud, flat bang. He shouted to his driver and they bore right and ran down a slope to plough through a stand of young saplings as a second shell exploded in their wake. A sharp exchange of cannon fire behind them culminated in a blast that sent hot metal whizzing viciously through the trees.

The French gunners had done an incredible amount of damage. Prager counted five of von Bülow's tanks burning furiously. One of his own cars was destroyed completely and her crew dead, a second badly damaged and her driver killed. The French had chosen their locations well. The Panzers were forced into single file as they left the meadow and the track funnelled through a draw on either side of which stood ancient oaks. The anti-tank gunners had a field day picking the Panzers off, one by one as they tried to escape from the trap.

And if I hadn't sent the two cars in a flanking movement, I'd be dead as well, Prager thought. The two had broken through the trees, directly behind the hidden gun and their first shots had struck the stacked ammunition and turned the gully into a blackened wasteland where metal and flesh had fused into a single mass. The stench of burned meat was horrible and he turned away as his stomach heaved. He bent over, hands on knees, and strove to control himself while several others vomited at the sight and smell.

He found Colonel von Bülow beside one of the damaged tanks, helping a medic tend a German officer whose arm had been blown off. The man was lying on a stretcher, breathing noisily. His face was pasty white, his eyes closed and lips thinned. The medic cut away the man's tunic sleeve to expose the raw stump, squirted an ointment onto a pad and slipped it over it. The officer began to grunt, 'uhn, uhn, uhn,' weakly between clenched teeth and the medic gave him a worried look, searched through his kit until he found a second ampule of morphine and injected it quickly. Von Bülow caught his eye and the medic gave his head a slight shake, as if to say, 'I've done all I can.'

The Colonel watched as the stretcher was carried to a lorry, then staggered to his feet like an old man and wiped his own sweating face. He stared at the bloody map in his other hand, drew a deep breath and straightened his shoulders. He tugged his campaign cap straight and motioned to Prager.

'We must clear these woods, quickly before the French bring up more anti-tank guns. If they stop us here, we lose our momentum. I want you to drive in a wide circle, pivoting on the bridgehead, before dusk.'

The wounded man shouted as his stretcher was being lifted into the lorry. The medic tried to persuade him to lie still, but the young officer's voice, filled with wonder and shock, interrupted to say quite clearly, 'I'm going to die now.'

Startled, Prager turned to see him smile and close his eyes. The medic fumbled for a pulse, shook his head and drew the blanket over the dead officer's face.

Panzers fanned out from the bridgehead across the Meuse and drove at top speed along the dusty roads, deeper into the west, covering in hours distances that had taken the Army days and even weeks in 1914. Events blurred in Prager's mind; roads jammed with civilians fleeing ahead of the advancing hordes only to be overtaken by the tanks and left behind. Villages seemed draped in white bed sheets as their inhabitants watched from behind parted curtains while the tanks roared past. Top-hatted village officials stared after them open-mouthed, wondering to whom they should surrender.

Only occasionally now did they encounter organized resistance in the countryside. For the most part, the Belgian and French soldiers mingled with civilians by the roadsides, some with hands raised, but all with expressions that seemed to Prager to contain as much embarrassment as resignation. Most tried to surrender but the exhausted tankers no longer even bothered to acknowledge them. Turning once to watch as they passed a concentration of French infantry, Prager saw them exchange shrugs of resignation, shoulder their weapons and continue their march along the road to meet the motorized infantry coming up behind and who in turn would pass them on to the regular infantry who were often a full day or more in the rear. Thank God they are demoralized, he thought, otherwise we might well find ourselves attacked from the rear and swallowed up.

At other times, especially to the west of sizeable towns, the highways were so packed with refugees that only machine guns fired over their heads could clear the road. Outside one nameless village, they had passed a grotesque pile of bodies, smashed carts, torn mattresses and furniture jumbled helter-skelter along the road.

The Stukas had been at them, machine gunning them from the air to impede the movement of French troops. Regrettable that civilians should die this way, but necessary. Civilian terror could only hasten the war's end, and thus ensure that more would survive. The bodies were jumbled in a most democratic manner; the men were mostly old, women of all ages and children. The children, of course, were the worst. Studying the faces of his men, Prager knew they had reached the same conclusion.

Dunkirk 24 – 28 May 1940

They had been driving for hours over dusty back roads clogged with troops grown oblivious to the raucous warning of horns. Torsten Fredrikkson marvelled that these exhausted, unshaven and filthy men were the same that he had seen only four days earlier marching east in long khaki lines, many of them singing the old marching tunes of 1914–1918. They even looked like the soldiers in pictures he had seen as a boy in their funny tin helmets that looked more like the soup bowls his mother set out on the supper table every evening.

The driver's burst of profanity startled him from his daydream. A horse-drawn artillery piece had slewed across the road, one carriage wheel broken. A sergeant-major in a dusty but parade-neat uniform was barking precise orders as enlisted men struggled to lift the axle high enough for a spare wheel to be slipped on. The driver shook his head, muttered in a Seven Dials accent and re-versed the lorry so suddenly they banged the one behind. As that lorry's driver began to shout, they lumbered out of the line and towards the field. The lorry dipped into the ditch but the driver pressed harder on the accelerator and the vehicle lurched and staggered up.

Grinning now, the driver wrestled the wheel across the uneven ground still soft from spring rains. At any moment, Fredriksson expected the lorry to bog down, but they passed the dismounted artillery piece and nosed back onto the road some hundred yards further on.

No one seemed to know what was happening and depending on which road you took there were an equal number of troops moving up to the front as marching to the coast. No one had received orders to retreat but a sense of self-preservation seemed to have taken hold of large portions of the French, British and Belgian Armies. And no one knew the whereabouts of the British Expeditionary Force headquarters.

It had taken Fredriksson four weeks to get himself accredited as a press correspondent and eligible to visit the front. He had landed at Calais on Monday 20 May and had learned damned little since, had, in fact, spent the last two days searching for the front with the driver of this ammunition lorry, a short, stubby cockney with a perpetual cigarette and an accent so heavy as to be unintelligible.

It had seemed an easy enough task at the time. On Monday, the front was somewhere east of Arras. He would go there, report in and attach himself to a combat unit, then arrange telegraphic or long-distance telephone facilities to transmit his stories to Stockholm.

Nothing particularly difficult about it. He had done it before in Abyssinia in 1937, China in 1938 and Spain earlier that year. But he had not reckoned with the chaos that marked everything the Allies touched.

He had long ago learned that if you want to find the front lines, follow the ammunition drivers. But this front was so fluid it changed hourly and thus gave rise to the most incredible rumours. He had already drafted a column about them, banging out the pages while the lorry-full of two-pounder anti-tank ammunition inched across the Belgian landscape searching for the unit designated to receive it.

At midafternoon, they ran across an anti-tank unit camped beside a country lane. They had the exhausted air of men who had seen more combat than was humanly endurable, Fredriksson thought. It was most obvious in their eyes – a peculiar, hooded and distrustful gaze – and in the way their weapons were never far from hand. The driver grunted and stopped the lorry. A young officer in filthy battle dress strolled towards them and Fredriksson stepped down from the cab and stretched.

The soldiers stared at him with mild interest, taking in his heavy denim pants, stout hiking boots and his light jacket. *Civilian*. He could almost feel their contempt and he grinned. Three weeks ago, he doubted if one in fifty had heard a gun fired in anger.

The young officer, to Fredriksson's relief, seemed to be having as much trouble understanding the driver as he had.

'We can certainly use the ammunition,' the officer replied finally. 'As to the whereabouts of the 143rd Battalion, I haven't the faintest idea. Have only the vaguest idea where I am.' The officer shouted for a working party and the driver ambled off to untie the canvas flap.

The officer offered his hand. 'Name's Wilton, Harold Wilton, Lieutenant, Fifth Border Regiment.'

Fredriksson shook his hand. 'My name is Torsten Fredriksson. I am a Swedish journalist accredited to the *Daily Mail*.'

The Lieutenant's expression changed instantly to one of suspicion as Fredriksson had learned to expect whenever a combatant discovered he was a foreign journalist. He handed Wilton his War Office press credentials. 'I've been looking for Lord Gort's headquarters for two days now. I've been accredited to his staff but no one knows where he might be.'

The officer read the papers carefully and examined the ID photograph. 'I see,' he said, still with a trace of suspicion. 'Suppose it is a bit of a problem for you.' He glanced towards the lorry where a line of men were already humping the crates of anti-tank shells towards their own transport.

'BEF headquarters moved to Premesques two days ago. Damned Stukas, you know. I'll have a word with your driver.'

They drove southwest this time as the sky clouded over. The driver observed that it might rain, or so Fredriksson interpreted and nodded.

'Friar Tuck the Charley 'astard!' the driver shouted and swerved off the road as an ear-splitting howl slashed overhead. The lorry slewed across the verge and smashed through a rail fence.

Fredriksson had the barest glimpse of an aircraft slicing into the failing light, one wing already drooping into a tight turn. The lorry bounced to a stop beneath a large oak and the driver was out and running before the engine quit. Fredriksson wasn't far behind. They had been strafed twice already and he knew the drill perfectly, had in fact learned it in Spain.

The aircraft banked, lined up and came in low again along the road, swaying from side to side as the pilot searched for the lorry, its engine's howl unnerving. Fredriksson crouched at the base of a tree, fascinated by the power represented in the slim shape. This was the first time he had managed a good look at the new German pursuit aircraft, the Me.109, in action. As it pulled into a steep climb without appreciably slackening speed, he whistled soundlessly. Compact and graceful, it was no wonder the British and French were taking such a beating in the air. The Messerschmitt 109 disappeared into the gathering clouds and the driver emerged from the woods, rolled a cigarette and stared after the aircraft thoughtfully and muttered something that sounded like 'Tom Tit.'

Lieutenant Harold Wilton's estimate of the distance involved was a bit off and it took another day of driving before they ran across a military police detachment who were able to provide specific directions. Field Headquarters turned out to be an ancient château at the end of a tree-shaded lane. Only after a staff aide arrived did the suspicious sentry relax and re-sling his rifle.

An enlisted man followed with his canvas travel bag and portable typewriter as the staff officer led him into the château. 'I'm afraid that General Gort is unavailable at the moment, Mr Fredriksson, but I would be most happy to arrange an interview for tomorrow.'

Fredriksson had long ago observed that one specific condition must exist for an aide to be helpful – the Commanding Officer must be about to lose a battle.

'Did you have much trouble finding us?' the aide asked anxiously as they entered a sitting room. The walls were hung with numerous canvases, most badly in need of cleaning.

'As a matter of fact, I've been searching for several days,' he couldn't resist saying. The aide winced. 'It's been a most interesting experience, I can assure you.'

'I see, well, I do apologize. One needs to . . .' The aide stopped, gave Fredriksson a searching glance, folded his hands on the desk and prepared to be frank. Fredriksson raised an eyebrow to indicate interest in the game.

'There is no need to beat about the bush, Mr Fredriksson. We, that is the BEF, are in a bad way. The Dutch, in spite of all the evidence to the contrary, relied on their neutral status and refused to cooperate with us. Even so, the enemy's lightning conquest of

Holland was a shock. Now, the German forces engaged in that duty have been released and are placing great pressure on the French and Belgian positions on our northern flank. The Belgian lines have not held as expected and the French field commands are in chaos. They appear to have committed only second line troops north of the Maginot Line. I do think, however, that we will be able to hold and possibly even roll back the tide.'

Fredriksson did not bother with notes. When they began to blame their Allies and talk about 'possibly', the end was near. The man was merely putting on a brave front in the hope that he would write that the BEF under Lord Gort was confident and ready. Fredriksson let him ramble for a few moments, then interjected a few personal questions about Lord John Gort, as if fleshing out the background for an article, learning in the process that it was the General's unvarying routine to walk in the afternoon.

Ten minutes later, Fredriksson was ambling along a wooded path after the aide had been called away for a telephone message. Several hundred metres from the château, he came upon a solitary figure seated on a log. Smoke curled from a large pipe while the man stirred the past winter's dead leaves with his walking stick.

'Lord Gort?'

The General turned and smiled. 'Good afternoon, young man. Lovely time of day isn't it.'

Fredriksson introduced himself and quickly reminded the General that they had met once before, at a weekend party in 1936. Gort screwed up his face, trying to remember, then nodded.

'Ah, yes. I recall the circumstances now. You were the young man who rode so well but declined to take part in the fox hunt. But aren't you Swedish? What are you doing in a war zone?'

Fredriksson showed him his press credentials and they talked for a few moments in general terms about the war. 'Well, young man, it seems you are quite well informed. Have you seen anything of the German side yet?'

Fredriksson shook his head. 'No, sir.' He let the answer speak for itself.

Lord Gort nodded. 'Of course. Shouldn't have asked.'

He chewed the stem a moment, then tapped the pipe against the stump and scuffed earth over the ashes. 'Walk back with me, Mr Fredriksson. You might as well be the first to hear. I've decided that our position is entirely untenable. The BEF will withdraw from Belgium.'

The gathering darkness made it difficult to read the General's features. 'No secret about it. Any fool can see that it is necessary. The Germans are moving far too quickly. Our forces never had a chance to reach their forward positions and I'm not sure it would have done us that much good in any event. The German has shown a masterful use of tanks and aircraft, I must say. Masterful. One can always count on the Hun for a new twist.'

Gort was silent a moment, as if reviewing the events that led to his decision one last time to make certain he had not overlooked anything, then murmured, 'The Belgians will surrender soon. They must. Their King is young, inexperienced. The Germans are pressing him hard from Holland as well as from the east. The French are quite paralysed. Can't even communicate with their commanders most of the time. The final battle will not be fought here or in France, but on England's shores. Therefore we must conserve as much of our army as possible. It is inconceivable to me that Hitler will stop at the Channel.'

'Are you saying, sir, that the war is lost?'

Gort gave him a sharp look. 'Don't put words into my mouth, young man. I said nothing of the kind. The battle is lost, not the war. Belgium will go soon and then France. Before summer's end.'

'But General Gort, the entire French army stands between the Germans and Paris. How?'

The old man chuckled. 'So it would seem. But just this morning I had word that the first German Panzer units had reached the Aa canal, only twelve miles from Dunkirk.'

They had reached the château and as they stood in the garden, looking up at the dour sky, Lord Gort stuffed and lit his pipe. Fredriksson was bursting to ask a thousand questions and the General must have sensed it for he held up a hand.

'I am sorry that I can say no more at this time. I would appreciate it very much if you would keep the news to yourself for the next day or two. An announcement will be made soon and you will be free to publish the information then.'

He peered hard at Fredriksson. 'I feel safe enough in having told you that, sir, as the only communication facilities to the outside world are controlled by my staff.' He chuckled and walked off to his dinner. Fredriksson watched him go, admiring his erect carriage and air of confidence in spite of the fact that he was on the verge of losing a battle of epic proportions. His decision might well lose the war, might decide the world's fate for centuries to come. Fredriksson shuddered at the thought of having to bear such responsibility.

Fredriksson muttered a curse in Swedish as the lorry hit an especially deep pothole. The new driver, a red-headed Englishman with an infectious grin, laughed and swerved to miss another.

'Worst road ever,' he commented. The lorry banged down again and Fredriksson was grateful he wasn't riding with high-explosive ammunition this time.

He had left BEF Headquarters early that morning, convinced after his talk with Lord Gort that the story had shifted to the coast where the British Expeditionary Force was to be re-embarked. That feeling had been further strengthened later the previous evening after overhearing a conversation in which he had learned that Panzers had finally broken through at Lille and were pouring through the Allied lines. The Germans were now charging north across the river Lys in an attempt to cut the BEF in two. If true, Belgium was lost as Gort had said it would be – and possibly the entire BEF with it.

The roads were all but impassable. What even the day before had been a disciplined trickle had now become a flood. There was no panic that Fredriksson could see and even the units detailed to act as rear guards seemed confident enough as they dug trenches and sited automatic weapons. But a retreat was definitely on and rumours were wilder than before.

Nearing the coast, the terrain changed from flat farmland to rolling, sandy hills. Fredriksson saw more and more French and Belgian units mixed in with British and he wondered how long Allied cooperation would fare when the boats were full. Some ten kilometres from the coast the crush became so great that everything came to a standstill on the narrow road. Tanks, lorries, staff cars, troops on foot, field guns, refugees and their carts and automobiles had become entangled in a massive traffic jam that stretched as far ahead as Fredriksson could see.

The driver left the road as soon as the ditching on either side allowed. Fredriksson wrestled rails from a fence and they drove into a field. The driver grinned at the journalist and pointed at the countryside.

'O'm from Chattisham, Suffolk. Country here, 'tisn't all that different from home. Be plenty o' country lanes about. We'll go this way. Avoid the canals.'

They reached Ostend late in the evening of 25 May after struggling through a final mile or so of jammed traffic. The rumours had become both worse and more precise as they often do and Fredriksson was now convinced that the Germans were mounting a concerted pincer movement to squeeze the BEF in a vice and close them off from the coast. The rumour most extant concerned surrendering soldiers being shot out of hand by fast-moving German tank crews who couldn't be bothered with prisoners.

He said goodbye to the red-haired lorry driver and made his way through the town towards the docks. Air-raid sirens wailed and he searched the empty evening sky flaming with sunset. The clock tower and the many church steeples were blood red in the failing light and he repressed a shudder. A military police barricade had been thrown up well above the docks and troops were being organized into long lines. Fredriksson showed the Sergeant commanding a special police detachment his papers but the man shook his head.

'Sorry sir, but my orders are to keep everyone out until they've been processed. Can't myke no exceptions, sir.'

In the morning, the streets were full of rumours that Dunkirk had fallen. Fredriksson ate the last ration he had picked up at Lord Gort's headquarters and went in search of anything that would pass as military headquarters. He found it shortly after nine o'clock, full of scurrying clerks and angry officers demanding to know the whereabouts of this unit or that. Dunkirk had not fallen after all and German tanks had indeed stopped on the Aa canal three days before, although no one knew why. All Allied forces were retreating into an arc-shaped sector extending from Ostend south to Dunkirk. Ships of all types, military and civilian, were pouring across the Channel to take off the BEF and were being harassed by long-range guns and the Luftwaffe, which latter, because of the weather, had failed to mount a concerted attack.

He dug out his Baedeker's Guide to Belgium and studied the front map, mentally ticking off the cities and forts that had fallen to the Germans; Maastricht, Liege, Huy, Hasselt, Namur, Dinant – where the first crossing of the Meuse had been made – Gilly, Louvain, Brussels, Mons, Tournai, Renaix, Ghent, Courtrai and Lille in France, bypassed but not taken. Ironically, the British and French had fought for possession of these same forts for ten years at the beginning of the eighteenth century.

God only knew how thin German infantry support really was across Belgium. And the Germans might very well have got themselves into a box if their tank divisions were pushed so far ahead of the infantry as to be unsupported. Was that why the tanks had been stopped? he wondered. But even so, it made no sense. Destroy or capture Allied forces in the Dunkirk perimeter and England must leave the war.

Intrigued, Fredriksson made up his mind quickly and hiked towards the southern limits of the city, wondering what chance he stood of crossing to German lines. His excitement rose as he thought of the coup he might pull off. If the entire BEF were bagged, it could end the war! Certainly with major forces committed to the Continent, Britain had very little in reserve and a German victory here could force her to sue for peace. Now, if he were able to report both sides of the surrender!

He had walked, he judged, five kilometres along a country lane leading generally east and had seen but one or two farmers working their fields. There was no sign of an Allied defence perimeter and, surprisingly, no sign of the German forces pushing into the vacuum. The sun had reached midpoint and the day seemed to him as hot as anything he had ever experienced in Africa. Late spring flowers grew in profusion along the roadside and birdsong was constant and he had been lulled into thinking that the countryside was deserted when two British soldiers stepped from a stand of trees and signalled to him to raise his hands. One tried terrible French and when he answered in English, instead of being relieved, they became even warier.

"Ands behoind yer 'ead, mate, and start walkin',' one told him in heavy Irish accents.

They turned a deaf ear to his claims of neutrality and marched him through the trees to a command post tucked into a small clearing. A middle-aged Captain eyed him with curiosity and told him to sit down. When Fredriksson asked if he could put his hands down, he was ignored. When he started to do so anyway, one soldier released his rifle safety with a deliberate click. Fredriksson decided to endure his aching arms.

He was only beginning to realize the extent of his foolishness. This wasn't Abyssinia, where everything was so disorganized that men came and went with ease across the front lines, nor was it Spain where both sides did everything possible to accommodate neutral journalists in that curious public relations war. These men were professional soldiers and, to them, a spy was more dangerous than an armed soldier. He certainly could not tell them that he was walking east to find the German lines! He could be shot as a spy, newspaper correspondent or not, if they thought his accent German and no one would ever know what happened to him. He called to the British officer who turned to. . . .

Fredriksson stood up slowly, trying to understand what had happened. His head was filled with a terrible roaring noise and the trees that hemmed the clearing were twisted and torn. He wiped at his nose and saw a smear of blood on his sleeve and only then was he aware of the stench of high-explosive that filled the clearing. The soldier guarding him lay face down, his back blown half away. Other bodies were tossed about and his mind refused to credit the smoking, blackened hole near where the tent had stood.

In response to some atavistic instinct, he scrambled into the trees and began to run as fast as the undergrowth permitted. Behind, more explosions shook the ground like jelly. There had been no warning, no high-velocity scream and he knew it had to be one of the terrible new eighty-eight millimetre shells that travelled faster than sound and he had survived only because he had been sitting.

The explosions became one continuous roar and the soft ground bounced and jigged so that it was hard to keep his footing. The underbrush, full of new spring growth, slowed his progress to a crawl and the woods became a living nightmare. A flash in the trees to his left, something ripped past his face to shred tree limbs and shower him with new leaves; there was an odour of white-hot metal and explosives. Then the trees were gone and he stumbled onto the road.

Fredriksson reached the first checkpoint on the outskirts of Dunkirk that evening. A low bank of cloud had moved across the sky and condensed along the western horizon. The sun was just going down and the sky had flamed the orange and golds of a Turner sunset. He showed his press credentials at the barrier and was allowed through.

He had been thoroughly chastened by the morning's experience – neither combat soldier nor artillery shell could be expected to honour one's neutrality in this war, he had learned. A miasma of dust, petrol fumes and exhaustion hung over the Ostend–Dunkirk Road which was lined with soldiers walking or sitting or sleeping and, whenever the road ran close to the beach, bathing naked in the Channel.

He slept uneasily that night in the open and shivered awake when the morning fog crept in. He was not in Dunkirk proper he discovered, but at a place called Bray Dunes. In the thinning fog, he could see two men in naval uniforms standing in the surf directing lines of other men into small boats which plied back and forth to an odd collection of vessels swept, he guessed, from every port in the south of England. Around him, thousands waited patiently for their turn to board. Abandoned vehicles were everywhere, some even being used as living quarters. Artillery pieces had been left where their transport had stopped. Officers seemed as bewildered as enlisted men and he saw rifles everywhere, some neatly stacked, others thrown into piles. French, Belgian and British soldiers mixed indiscriminately and Special Police with red arm and cap bands guarded houses or vehicles or crossroads, sometimes for no reason that he could see. There did not seem to be any organization nor any of the usual services of a field army. There were no field kitchens, no field hospitals, not even a first aid tent. There were no motor pools, no repair depots and no ammunition dumps. This wasn't an army any longer, he thought, but a mob, no matter how well-behaved.

The dawn air was chill and the Channel waters sullen under a flat bank of grey cloud. He gritted his teeth and went down to the water's edge, stripped off his clothes and waded out into the icy water and washed. Afterwards, he dried himself with his shirt and cursed the loss of his jacket, knapsack and rations.

Dunkirk proper was a shock. The dull orange glow he had seen on the horizon the night before must have emanated from the town, or what was left of it. The waterfront was a shambles. Its eight kilometres of docks had been rendered useless by aerial bombing and artillery fire. Giant unloading cranes had been reduced to twisted wrecks and only the East Quay remained at all serviceable. Houses and shops fronting the beach were battered shells. Anti-aircraft, cannon and machine gun emplacements were surrounded by sandbags and the soldiers manning them waited patiently for the fog to lift and the Luftwaffe to come. A destroyer picking its way towards the dock reminded him of an old maid holding her skirts above the mud. Offshore, more ships waited in the overcast.

But what surprised him the most were the artificial quays. As he trudged nearer, he wondered how the engineers had managed to build them so quickly. And then he saw that they were composed of abandoned lorries, staff cars, ammunition tins; anything in fact that would not float, and were filled with immense lines of soldiers, some chest deep in water by the time they reached their ends.

Fredriksson found what passed for army headquarters by following two staff officers to a line of tents raised in the meagre shelter of the mole. A harassed junior officer grunted at the sight of his pass and shrugged.

'Sorry, sir. All military personnel have first claim to shipping space. I can only suggest you join a queue.'

He began to argue that, as a neutral, he was entitled to preferred treatment but the contemptuous look on the officer's face stopped him and he turned away, half angry, half ashamed and found a line that at least was no longer than any other.

The sun began to break through the dense haze in early afternoon and, as it did, the day's heat increased and so did his appreciation of what was happening at Dunkirk. Fredriksson estimated that perhaps 90 per cent of the BEF were already on the beaches waiting to be loaded onto boats and ships. And not only the BEF but French and Belgian troops as well. He was very surprised when he did not detect any attempt to discriminate by nationality. Even so, he was certain that only a fraction of the entire force would be got away before the Germans captured the port.

The Germans carried on a desultory artillery bombardment that was more nuisance than effective. Shells fell with monotonous regularity but the smothering effect of the beach sand reduced their effectiveness. The smoke pall mixing with the summer haze was clearly a factor that hampered the German air force although a few craft did appear, flashing through the cloud to race along the beach, shooting indiscriminately while the anti-aircraft guns banged away with surprising effectiveness. But everywhere he heard the same complaint - 'where the bloody hell is the RAF?'

By late afternoon, Fredriksson's queue reached the stone quay. Two destroyers were tied alongside and the explosions of their five- and six-inch guns firing steadily inland, were deafening. Exhausted pioneers worked to load and unload while thousands of bored soldiers looked on and Fredriksson wondered what had happened to the marvellous British penchant for improvisation in this instance.

As twilight settled in, a wind came up to blow the pall of smoke inland and the Luftwaffe appeared instantly. Anti-aircraft guns on the beaches and quays, supplemented by those of the warships, opened fire. As the soldiers about him watched the aircraft ducking about overhead and racing along the beach, machine guns blazing, the muttered curses about the 'useless RAF' were renewed.

A Messerschmitt tore along the beach at less than two hundred feet altitude; the port wing dipped and it turned on the quay so quickly that there was no time to duck for cover. A bomb hurtled at the leading destroyer and Fredriksson had a vague impression of wing edges blazing as machine gun and cannon shells pumped across the dock. The bomb exploded just short of the ship's side and the concussion slammed the destroyer against the quay with a bang that sounded like the gates of hell closing. A soldier a few steps away, a young man with a freckled face and ready grin, clapped a hand to his forehead and swayed. Someone reached to steady him but his knees buckled and he collapsed like a limp cloth. A stray bullet had shattered his skull.

The Luftwaffe disappeared as the sun set in a burst of colour. Footsore and exhausted, Fredriksson stepped aboard the minesweeper, HMS *Catalon*, which had taken the place of the battered destroyer. Visibility was surprisingly good for the late hour and looking along the beach from the deck Fredriksson realized that this would be one of those sights that, for no apparent reason, would imprint itself on his mind forever.

In the last traces of light, he saw a sandbagged gun emplacement manned by two British and one French soldier; half a kilometre on, a black strand of soldiers crawled across the beach to wade out to the small collection of civilian yachts – sloops, ketches and yawls. Not far from them a cabin cruiser burned fiercely and sent a streamer of black, oily smoke inland.

Shouts and the roar of an aircraft engine caused him to turn. The minesweeper's twenty millimetre Oerlikons opened fire but the Messerschmitt flew straight on, lifting disdainfully only at the last moment as it released its bomb. Fredriksson glimpsed the black shape just before it slammed into the water aside *Catalon*'s bow and exploded, flinging him against a gunmount. He felt the ship shudder like a wounded animal as he lost consciousness.

It was pitch dark and someone had covered him with a blanket. Fredriksson raised a hand to touch his aching head and felt the bandage. He lay still, nauseated by the effects of the blow and the ship's irregular rolling motion. When he woke again, the sky had begun to lighten and the nausea had abated, even if the pain was worse.

After a while, he managed to stand. The sky and sea wheeled abruptly and Fredriksson closed his eyes and clung to the rail. The pale blur of the Dover cliffs was parading past so close that he could see an occasional house along the tops. The monument to sailors killed in the First World War blinked as the sunlight strengthened. A child stood on the grassy edge and waved.

Berlin – Hamburg 2 – 4 June 1940

The Friedrichstrasse Bahnhof was jammed with people – far too many of whom were young men in civilian clothing and, for a moment, Prager was reminded of his return from Poland when he had seen huge numbers of troops pouring into the Berlin railway stations. Nearly all had dashed off to the lavatories immediately to change into civilian clothing bought or looted in Poland. The 'war-is-over' feeling that had swept Germany at the time had accelerated the demobilization of entire divisions; divisions that would have been useful in France. But if the civil population was expecting a repeat of that performance, he thought, they were in for a surprise this time. France was far from being beaten.

Captain Friedrich Prager stood on the sidewalk outside the Friedrichstrasse station and watched traffic swarm on the Georgenstrasse. The sun was warm but without the dust and petrol fumes that made it so unbearable in France. He started to walk to the end of the taxi line but a porter grabbed his bag.

'Here!'

The porter trotted to the head of the line and roughly shouldered an elderly man aside. The displaced passenger shouted angrily in protest, then when he spotted Prager's worn and dusty uniform, smiled suddenly and insisted that Prager take the cab.

The taxi went south on the Friedrichstrasse to the Unter der Linden. Prager had booked a room at the Adlon Hotel, not really expecting to get one but his rank and regiment had apparently done the trick. The taxi driver bubbled with enthusiasm for the campaign in France and pressed him for details.

He was exhausted. Near Lille, Major Erdman had been killed and Prager had been named to command the battalion. The increased responsibility and four solid weeks of campaigning had taken their toll. He knew he had not recovered entirely from the head wound and the pace of their advance through France and Belgium had left him on the verge of a physical breakdown. The divisional medical officer had been firm in his assessment and had ordered him off for a short leave while the division laid up for rest and refit. He had gone with only the barest twinge of guilt.

Berlin's shops were jammed with goods and people in spite of rationing and he supposed that French and Belgian goods were already flowing into Germany to supplement those from Poland and Norway. The Home Area, they called it and he snorted angrily. Uniforms were everywhere, most of them sporting the insignia of units that had not been within a hundred miles of any front. Young girls in this season's short skirts fluttered in the spring sunshine. Money and food were plentiful; you had to give Hitler his due. He had put Germany back on its feet in short order. Seven years ago, the country had been bankrupt, the people demoralized and her industry paralysed. Today, she was the most powerful nation in the world. But, in spite of the deference shown his uniform and the driver's questions, he had so far detected no great enthusiasm for the war. The Party paper's headlines blared but there was no great rush to buy. Propaganda posters were everywhere and universally ignored. Eavesdropping on conversations on the train, he had heard little discussion of the war and constant complaining about the rationing imposed the previous autumn.

The taxi deposited him under the portico of the Adlon. At the registration desk, the clerk left a civilian businessman, to wait on him. The foreigner, an American according to the passport on the counter, eyed his uniform and then the fawning clerk with a sardonic expression.

'Finish with the gentleman,' Prager snapped. 'He is a guest in our country.'

The clerk, a pinched-faced little man with hunched shoulders and an air of persecution, effected not to notice Prager's protest and arranged a registration card and pen before him with a flourish. It seemed that everyone recognized the colours of his *waffenfarbe* and the Roman numeral thirty-seven on the shoulder boards. Prager shrugged an apology to the American who nodded with amusement.

The bellman insisted on demonstrating the windows, taps and the bath. But he was not sufficiently overawed to resist the *trinkgeld*. Even though tips were included in the bill, Prager had long ago learned that it never hurt to have a reputation for generosity.

He filled the bath with the hottest water he could stand, stripped off his filthy field uniform and lowered himself into the tub. He slouched down until he was covered to his chin and wallowed in pleasure.

After an early dinner in his room, he sat at the window and watched the crowds on the boulevard, feeling no desire to join them. The evening paper the waiter had brought was full of war news but said little about the evacuations at Dunkirk. How much of the British Army had been captured? he wondered. There were rumours but no factual accounts and that in itself was strange. Even *Signal*, the government's propaganda journal, spoke only in generalities.

Prager tossed and turned into the morning hours. The boisterous sounds of the city grew louder in spite of the blackout and towards midnight, reached a crescendo. When he did finally sleep, a succession of ugly nightmares left him depressed and barely rested.

He spent the morning walking, treated himself to luncheon at Hocher's which was filled with elderly generals in brass-studded uniforms glimpsed behind the curtains of *chambres séparées* with women young enough to be their granddaughters and walked again, this time in the Tiergarten where he avoided the zoo and other populated areas. The sun disappeared in mid-afternoon and the air grew chill. Back in his room at the Adlon, he stared at the streets below, grown curiously sullen. Rain began with a mad rush that sent people scurrying in every direction and snarled traffic.

He needed Sonja. He had come to Berlin rather than home to Hamburg, because he knew that he might not have the strength *not* to see her. He telephoned the desk to ask the time of the next train to Hamburg and sent her a wire.

The house stood against the backdrop of the river. Towering thunderheads in the west combined with the humid, flat air to promise a storm of huge proportions. The paint was peeling badly on the siding; he hadn't noticed it in April but now he would have to make arrangements for it to be scraped and painted before he left again.

To his surprise, the house had been aired and cleaned thoroughly. The rear windows were open to the river breeze and flowers graced every room. As he set his bag down in the parlour, the door to the kitchen flew open and Sonja ran into his arms. They walked along the river that afternoon and the grass was incredibly green beneath a brilliant sun that poured golden columns through high-piled thunderheads. The willows were in full leaf and their branches swept the current. The apple orchard, neglected now that Herr Meyer, his father's old friend had gone, was overgrown.

Prager could well recall long summer evenings when the two veterans, both crippled in the service of their country, had sat in the garden drinking Meyer's home-made cider. Meyer had been a regular also. And, like his father, had literally given of himself – in his case, his right eye and right arm – for Germany. Like his father, Meyer also held the Iron Cross First Class. But even so, he had heard that Nazis had called him a Jew-traitor and taken . . . Prager shied away from such thoughts. They served no useful purpose. Today he was concerned only with the woman he loved.

'It's so still,' Sonja murmured.

'A storm, before evening. You'll see.'

'Mmnn. I'd like that. Remember the last storm we spent together?'

Prager chuckled. 'How could I forget?' His resolve was beginning to slip already.

That afternoon the storm did break in spectacular fashion. They stood at the parlour window and watched the clouds darken and felt the atmosphere grow oppressive. Thunder cannoned and lightning flickered like a night-time artillery barrage and Sonja felt his sudden fear, until the rain came with a roar of wind that shook the house. A bolt of lightning stabbed the earth nearby and the sudden smell of ozone rankled. The river disappeared behind a blurred curtain of rain and the garden path became a river. She held him tightly, suddenly frightened of all he had endured, which she could never share and, therefore, would never understand. For his part, he felt absurdly comforted, as if he were a child and safe from the terrors of the night again.

'I do want to marry you, Sonja.'

She lay beside him, staring into the darkness and listening to the rain beat on the roof. They had covered themselves with a sheet against the cool breeze flowing in through the open windows. She turned and pressed her lips to his gently, not kissing but making contact.

'I want to marry you when the campaign in France is finished.'

'Why not now?' she murmured.

Prager was tempted, almost beyond endurance. He had given in

272

to his emotions by coming to Hamburg. Now, the iron-discipline had reasserted itself and he shook his head in the darkness, haunted by the memory of his mother's ill-treatment and deterioration.

'I must return to my unit the day after tomorrow, Sonja. When we marry, we must have time to begin as we should. The campaign is exceeding all expectations. France must ask for an armistice in the autumn. We can be married in the winter. There will be plenty of time then to plan, to post banns.'

'A church wedding?'

'Church or civil, whichever suits you.'

She pushed away and sat up against the headboard, clutching the sheet to her chin, all business now. 'Must you leave again, so soon?'

'Certainly. It is my duty.'

'Duty,' she snorted. 'Duty is a man's excuse for doing what he wishes to do. Why not marry now, before you return?'

Prager made a grab for her but she evaded his hands. 'Nothing more until this is settled. I know what soldiers are like. Once you have what you want from a girl, no promise is too great to make in order to get a second helping.'

'Or a third, or fourth or. . . .'

'No more, Herr Hauptmann Prager. Now tell me why we cannot be married now.'

Prager pushed himself up beside her. 'Because,' he said, 'you are a foreigner and I am an Army officer. I must obtain the permission of my Commanding Officer which must then be forwarded to Berlin. All that will take weeks.'

'Berlin? Why should . . .' Sonja's voice contained a hint of fear and he laughed.

'There is nothing to worry about. A matter of routine only. Our two countries are friendly. Information concerning your background will be requested from the Soviet Embassy. Just because your parents are Communists does not mean that you are too.' He stopped abruptly when she gasped.

'But I am, Friedrich,' Sonja whispered. 'When I was sixteen, my father arranged it. I am not a political person. It made it easier . . . the Party has never meant. . . .'

Prager exploded from the bed. 'Damn it all, why didn't you tell me!'

Sonja cowered back against the headboard, terrified that he might strike her and never so frightened in her life. This wasn't the man she knew, the man who had made such gentle love to her. He was suddenly a stranger, a soldier, a raving maniac like the White counter-revolutionaries she had learned about in school who had raged across Russia during the Civil War committing terrible atrocities. In that instant, she understood that the terrible reality of war is quite simply a human being gone berserk. She knew in that instant that their relationship had changed in some subtle manner she would never understand. Would she ever have complete faith and trust in him again? she wondered.

Prager leaned his head against the cold window glass and waited for the anger to drain. What did it matter, he asked himself, if she were a Communist? To him, nothing! But it would to the Government, and to his career. Did that matter?

He stared into the wild darkness. Did it matter? If he married her, it might end his career. He might have to resign his commission, become a common soldier. Startled by his own perception, he caught himself as he started to shout that nothing made any difference to them. A sixth sense told him that if he wasn't careful, he might lose her forever. Sonja must never suspect that he had even considered his career ahead of her.

He sank down on the edge of the bed weary, frightened and confused and reached for her hand, cupped her unresisting fingers and kissed them.

'Sonja, you will have to renounce both party membership and Russian citizenship. You must declare that you wish to become a citizen of the Reich. Can you do that?' He wanted to add, 'for me', but stopped himself in time.

Sonja nodded without hesitation. Some of her fear was beginning to dissipate but she knew it would never disappear entirely.

France 5 – 12 June 1940

Prager returned to the Thirty-seventh Reconnaissance Battalion on the fourth of June, 1940 to find that he had been promoted to Major. Artillery rumbled on the horizon, growing louder as the convoy in which he had found a ride, approached the front. His own command was fourteen kilometres north of the Somme and the countryside seemed as tranquil as if the war did not exist, until one spotted the camouflaged grey and tan tanks and armoured cars, the motorcycles and tents and clusters of soldiers under the trees. Farmers worked in the fields, paying no attention to the soldiers. Life must go on, he thought, even in a world turned upside down.

*

June fifth dawned hot and clear. *Fall Rot*, the attack across the Somme, was about to open. Prager strode along the line of tanks and armoured cars. He had been awake until well past midnight reviewing maintenance records, appalled that so little repair work had been accomplished because spares were unavailable. His two companies were down to an effective strength of 48 per cent over this same date in May. The maintenance crews had been reduced to cannibalizing otherwise repairable tanks but, even so, the twin lines of rumbling monsters spewing exhaust gases boded well for their success.

They moved out at 0500. The approach to the Somme river which had been canalized in this area, had to be made across bogland which offered excellent defensive possibilities. General Rommel expected the French to make a firm stand and had promised heavy fighting at the staff meeting the evening before. The ground on the north-eastern side of the canal-river was marshy and would force the vehicles to travel on the two roads elevated above the surrounding terrain in plain view of French anti-tank gunners until they were just short of the two railroad bridges that crossed the Somme river-canal.

To complicate the situation still further, almost a kilometre beyond, two additional bridges crossed the road from Hangest to Longpré. The bridges had been reported standing at sunset and Rommel guessed the French were delaying their demolition to the last moment to permit as many trapped Allied units as possible to escape.

Prager was ordered to capture the bridges before the French could react. His armoured cars, supported by two Panzer IIs, raced along the road above the bog towards the bridges. Infantry had fanned out on either side to sweep for snipers and artillery observers but were quickly left behind. The marshy nature of the terrain was evident in the glint of water and the presence of thousands of birds clinging to marsh grasses. But all Prager could think about was what perfect cover the trees and tangles of bushes and briars made for snipers.

As they came in sight of the bridges, Prager studied them through his glasses and saw French soldiers running up the road approach from the opposite direction. He shouted for machine-gun fire; the range was extremely long but the storm of lead drove the demolition parties to cover. Enemy artillery fire erupted about the bridge approach and Prager knew there was nothing he could do now but run the gauntlet.

The road dipped unexpectedly before mounting the dyke edging the canal. This feature hadn't shown up on the map and Prager shouted in delight. He fanned the armoured cars into the marshy hollow below the banks, out of view from the other side, and ordered the two companies of Armoured Engineers up. The Panzer IIs caught up to them and Prager sent one and an armoured car forward until they had the bridge decking in sight from turret and cupola and could keep the bridge clear with machine-gun fire. The engineers raced onto the bridge under an umbrella of white tracer flashes, swarmed over the sides and moments later, one reappeared waving his arms. Prager led three armoured cars onto the bridge at full speed. The rails and sleepers caught at their tyres and the cars careened from side to side but two of them made it across. The French, trapped between the two bridges, were caught in a devastating cross-fire and either surrendered or leapt into the river and swam downstream. The first bridge across the Somme was in German hands.

Prager clambered down from his *Panzerspahwagen* and went back to survey the bridge decking. One of the armoured cars had torn a tyre and the Panzer IIs found it impossible to cross as their treads slipped from the rails and jammed in the sleepers. The engineers removed several hastily placed demolition charges then began to tear up the tracks. Prager was able to drive three more armoured cars across with the loss of another tyre, and fan them out in combination to form a bridgehead just as a flurry of French artillery shells struck along the northern approaches.

He climbed into the iron girders and studied the terrain to the south-west. The two cars that had followed him across were still engaged about the bridge over the highway but that too was winding down. There was now no sign of the French except for occasional artillery fire. Beyond the bridge, he could see where the river diverged from the canal to take a more southerly course. A church steeple in the village of Hangest three or four kilometres beyond was just visible above the trees and he guessed the French artillery was being directed from there.

The drawn-out whistle of an in-coming round caught him before he could climb down. The shell exploded in the river and doused him thoroughly. The engineers roared with laughter as spluttering and dripping, his dignity offended, he retired stiffly to his armoured car.

Their objective that first day across the Somme was Hornoy, a small town eight kilometres distant, which they entered in early evening. They had spent more than twelve hours constantly moving, most of the time under French artillery fire, and all were looking forward to a few hours' rest. But, at 1925, orders reached him from Rommel's staff directing that the attack be continued in the direction of Cap Amienois. In spite of their weariness, morale among the Thirty-seventh was extremely high due to the day's outstanding success and they raced on with less grumbling than usual from the crews. As they neared Bois de Riencourt, they were held up briefly by a large concentration of French troops who resisted fiercely with rifle and machine-gun fire and one anti-tank gun, until the tanks overran their positions.

They finally halted for the night at 2130 and Prager leaned wearily on the driving step and stared across the plain. To the west, a giant pillar of dark smoke rolled into the pale sky where it spread into a curious mushroom shape. A petrol dump, he decided. To either side of him stretched a line of tanks and armoured cars looking, in the gathering dusk, like a scene from that English film, *The Shape of Things to Come*. In the twilight, they seemed dark monsters crouching to rest. To add to the air of surreal fantasy, a riderless horse galloped across the plain under a sky that was turning a peculiar coppery colour.

For a moment, he was confused, time seemed to have undergone a curious juxtaposition and he did not know whether he was in France or Poland. The warm summer night was filled with the smells and sounds of war; high explosive and burning petrol and sweat and fear; of the sound of distant guns, laughing men and screaming horses shocked with pain and noise. Firefly flashes in quick succession and artillery shells crashed among the Panzers. A tank exploded in a white blaze. Behind them, German guns boomed like distant thunder and the western horizon flickered with devil light. Then darkness was complete and the fighting stopped as if by mutual agreement.

They had driven twelve kilometres beyond the Somme bridges and Rommel had ordered the halt only because he feared they might be bombed by their own aircraft.

Italy declared war on France on the tenth of June and Paris fell four days later. On June sixteenth, General Pétain became premier of France and requested an armistice. Astonishingly, the war seemed to be ending! The French armies melted before them and each day became a race to see how many kilometres could be covered. Even though men and equipment were wearing out, morale continued high and the drive across the French countryside in the midst of the nicest summer in human memory, might have seemed more like a lark if they all hadn't been so tired.

British troops had landed at Cherbourg as late as June fourteenth. To trap the last remnants of the British Expeditionary Force in Brittany and the Cherbourg Peninsula, Hoth's Panzers were ordered to turn north-westward on the same day that Pétain asked for the armistice. To Prager, it seemed as if the French had simply given up. Until a week or so ago, the contrast in attitude between captured French field forces and staff personnel was phenomenal. The former had been full of fight, cursing the Germans as they surrendered, proving uncooperative on the long marches to the POW collection points and in general acting as good soldiers should when captured. Staff officers on the other hand surrendered readily, babbled about satisfying their honour and turned their backs on the lower ranks to fraternize. Prager was quick to sense that the rot of discontent and defeatism had spread outward from the military staffs.

Even so, Prager and other field officers were nervous about Rommel's latest order. He had ordered the drive on Cherbourg as quickly as possible and armoured units were sent off well in advance of infantry and artillery support. If the French decided to stand after all and the Luftwaffe's Stuka failed them, they could very well be annihilated.

But Berlin, at long last, was more than willing to accept the challenge. The stakes were high; a few reconnaissance units and a regiment or two of tanks against the accelerated surrender of France weeks before anyone would have thought it possible.

They moved at 1840 hours, taking advantage of the summer evening light and used the main roads whenever possible to drive at top speed, headlights full on, now that the enemy air forces had been knocked from the skies. Farm fields fled past on either side, the scent of fresh earth and growing things heavy in the warm night. Occasionally a light would spring up in a cottage near the road and they would see the faces of astonished French farmers and their families, ghostly white in the glare of headlights. Even more occasionally, they heard cheers as they were mistaken for French or British forces.

Only once that night did they encounter resistance; a roadblock of two trees across the road. Prager did not allow the French defenders a chance to open fire. He himself manned the machine gun and had the satisfaction of seeing the French run into the fields. The trees were nosed aside and the column raced on.

They drove all night without stopping except to refuel and shortly after mid-morning, the Thirty-seventh Armoured Reconnaissance Battalion approached another of the tiny villages that stretched along the Cherbourg road. All road and name signs had been removed and there was no time to ascertain the correct name of the village. The whitewashed walls of the village were blinding in the hot sun. A knot of soldiers and civilians had gathered on the outskirts.

He waved at the soldiers as his car approached and pointed to a lone oak tree to indicate they were to assemble there. One soldier, an officer, broke away and ran towards the road. Prager saw the pistol in his hand just as he gained the road and instinctively yanked the machine gun around. The officer dropped to one knee, pistol pointing straight at him. They fired together. The pistol bullet wanged off the car's turret and whined away past his head. His machine-gun burst stitched the Frenchman's body and flung him away.

Prager's car was in the village before he fully realized what had happened. Machine-gun fire from the following cars and the Panzer IIs accompanying swept the field and echoed between the houses and he saw a woman throw her hands to her face and scream. As the column streamed out of the eastern end of the village he looked back to see bodies in the field. Prager held himself rigid in the turret, hands gripping the coaming, fighting nausea and revulsion. The damned fool, he thought, over and over.

Elements of the Seventh Panzer Division had driven 240 kilometres in twenty-four hours, the greatest single day's advance in the history of warfare. And they were exhausted but exultant. Rather than risk the Thirty-seventh's lightly armed units in the dark this near the last concentration of British and French troops in the Cherbourg Peninsula, Prager's command had been halted for the night in the village of La Haye-du-Puits. The crews serviced their vehicles as best they could without their maintenance units. A company of motorized infantry, looking just as dirty and worn as the tankers, arrived and were dispersed into a defensive perimeter. The villagers were sullen and uncooperative but Prager learned after patient questioning that units of the British Army were in the area. A town official admitted that less than an hour before, a British tank column had gone through the village. The small garrison of French troops had gone with them and he pointed sadly to the empty house at the end of the village where they had been billeted.

Tired as he was, Prager was alert enough to realize that the official was really bemoaning the village's loss of a traditional source of revenue. In his halting French, he assured the man that German infantry with plenty of money to spend would arrive the following day.

The official perked up immediately. 'How else shall we live?' he asked and shrugged as if to excuse his concern with economic realities while his country was dying.

'The soil is too poor for good farming. We have only the traffic on the road and the army garrison. A man must be practical.'

Darkness fell as Prager completed his inspection of perimeter defences. Auto headlights flashed on the west road and he started for the barricade. The sentries moved into the shadows on either side and the machine-gun crew watched the approaching car.

They could hear singing and Prager strained to identify the words. The car stopped and in a burst of laughter the driver opened the door and waved at the shadowy figures of the sentries to open the barricade.

'Damn it all, man, we're overdue in Cherbourg.'

English! Prager grinned and stepped into the headlights, motioning the sentries to close in. The doors were wrenched open and the occupants dragged out as the driver wailed, 'Oh my God, the Hun!'

Prager saluted the four men, all British Army officers, as they were searched for weapons. 'Gentlemen, I am Major Friedrich Prager, Seventh Panzer Division,' he said in French. 'I am sorry to have to inform you that you are now my prisoners.'

The senior officer, a Lieutenant-Colonel by his shoulder pips, returned the salute with reluctance. 'How in the devil did . . . we had . . . you were reported more than a hundred miles. . . .'

Prager smiled. 'As you can see, your reports were,' he struggled for the French word, 'erroneous. May I ask where you are coming from?'

The Colonel braced himself stiffly. 'I am sorry, uh Major is it? I am required to give you only my name, rank and serial number. I am Lieutenant-Colonel Richard Whytly and my serial number is. . . .'

'Please, Colonel, I do not wish to interrogate you, only to know if we can expect other visitors. I would rather there be no killing. We are in the area in strength you know.'

The Colonel looked at him doubtfully, then shrugged. 'I suppose it doesn't make any difference now. We were at the sea, bathing. We expected there would be plenty of time to return to Cherbourg before your lot appeared. There may be one or two more behind us.' He shrugged.

A grinning sentry hurried up at that moment clutching a newspaper-wrapped bundle of wet bathing suits. Prager had the British officers taken to the abandoned French barracks for the night and started towards the house he had appropriated as his headquarters, relishing the idea of sleeping in a real bed, when a sentry ran up with the message that another car was approaching, but from the opposite direction. Swearing, Prager hurried through the village to the barricade on the northern side.

The automobile, an ancient Citroën, displayed the markings of a Cherbourg taxi service and contained a French Army officer who was persuaded at gunpoint to leave the taxi and speak to Prager. The Army officer introduced himself as Captain André Durwood.

In stiff tones that indicated his extreme displeasure, he told Prager that he had been sent to organize roadblocks against the German advance. He had intended to drive another eighty kilometres west.

'I am afraid, Captain Durwood,' Prager chuckled, 'that you've left it too late. We are already *here.*'

Durwood, a slim man of medium height and with a wisp of a moustache, looked about him with a bewildered expression. The blackout Prager had imposed on the village prevented him from seeing much but the presence of a German officer, two armed sentries and the shadowy bulk of tanks and armoured cars were apparently sufficient to convince him.

He shrugged helplessly.

'Captain Durwood, I suggest you return to Cherbourg and tell your Commanding Officer that we will be on the city outskirts by tomorrow evening. I would suggest that he seriously consider surrendering his garrison to prevent further bloodshed.'

Durwood struggled to compose himself. 'Are you suggesting that negotiations be opened?'

'Nothing of the sort. I am just stating a fact that any intelligent man can see for himself.'

Prager motioned to the sentries. 'See that the Captain,' he said in German, 'is started safely back to Cherbourg.'

They came within sight of Cherbourg's church spires in the early afternoon and Prager stopped the column below the crest of a hill for a look. Farmland divided by hedgerows stretched across a valley and all he could see of the city were the church spires and a tethered artillery observation balloon.

This is damned uncomfortable, he thought as they continued up the road in extended order. We are too far ahead of our support and the hedgerows make perfect defensive positions. He could envision dozens of anti-tank guns hidden behind the impenetrable hedges. Prager passed the word back along the column to keep a sharp eye out for snipers, then checked the machine gun to make certain that the belt ran freely into the breechblock.

They had gone less than two kilometres when the first artillery shells screamed down. The fields on either side erupted in geysers of dirt and stones and a sickening pall of HE filled the humid air. The observation balloon, he thought. He ordered the column to seek cover and radioed a report to staff headquarters and requested artillery and air support.

The French barrage continued for the next hour as naval cannon from the ships in the harbour combined forces with the heavy artillery of the defending forts to lay down accurate fire on their positions. The flinty soil threw up secondary shrapnel and kept them sweltering inside the armoured cars and tanks. Prager twice repeated his request for both artillery and air support and cursed the fools in the rear who had only to sit in comfort and play God.

He even considered withdrawing but the pressure of traffic coming up behind made that impossible. All they could do was keep their collective heads down and wait. The ground vibrated to the constant explosions and the air was hot and biting with fumes.

A lone aircraft appeared two hours after his first request. It slashed along the column as the tank crews cheered and disappeared behind a hill. Prager caught sight of it a few moments later, climbing at a steep angle towards the balloon. At almost the same moment, a counterbarrage against the port facility began. The observer must have spotted the German aircraft as a parachute blossomed and moments later, the balloon wavered, collapsed on itself and began to drop. The aircraft did a victory roll, turned north and disappeared into the haze. Moments later, the skies were torn with the screeching sound of German artillery shells. Dull explosions rumbled from the city and columns of black smoke began to climb above the harbour.

Under the counterbarrage and without their observation balloon, the French bombardment became sporadic and inaccurate and soon stopped altogether as darkness closed in. Prager studied the map, made up his mind and gave armoured car and tank crews the word to settle in for the night.

After he had seen to the posting of sentries and the seemingly endless succession of problems and decisions, Prager dragged his sleeping bag from the back of the car and while his orderly was off seeing about hot food, spread it on top of a rubber poncho and two blankets. He stripped off his tunic, boots and trousers, checked the magazine and safety on his Walther P.38 and slipped the pistol under the small feather pillow he had long ago decided was worth its weight in gold.

Prager was so tired after the succession of sleepless nights that even the thought of food was nauseating. But as tired as he was, he could only doze, cursing an insomnia that grew worse the more tired he became. But merely the opportunity to stretch out on solid ground that did not jolt and move provided a measure of rest. The constant headache that affected all of them began to lessen and for minutes at a time, he was unaware of the painful pounding.

The night passed with ludicrous slowness and he tried every trick he knew to fall asleep; counting backwards from one hundred, relaxing his body muscle by muscle or attempting to blank his mind of all thought. Nothing worked and when a dawn breeze from the Atlantic stirred the trees and swept a damp mist across his face, he gave up and struggled out of the sleeping bag. His supper tray was still on the ground beside him, its contents, mashed potatoes and some unrecognizible type of potted meat, congealed into a solid mess. A sentry acknowledged his presence and he found the coffee pot.

Coffee, he thought. I live on coffee these days. He stared at his hands in the growing light, surprised to see they were shaking. Coffee nerves, he snorted. Isn't that what the advertisements always told you. But that was nonsense because the coffee was ersatz for the most part and contained almost no caffeine. His nervous condition was compounded of worry over Sonja – and, always in the recesses of his mind, the effect their marriage would have on his career. It was easy enough to dismiss such concerns when he was with her, but in the cold light of a sleepless dawn, the stark reality of her foreign birth and membership of the Communist Party confronted him and was not so easily denied. Time after time, he had resolved to end it, only to see within minutes how foolish the decision was.

The R/T operator jumped down from the radio car and hurried across with a message. They were being ordered to move west about the city and seal off all roads to prevent the garrison's escape. To business, he thought gratefully and began to issue orders.

But the roads over which he had to move were clogged with civilian refugees fleeing from the city and his column slowed to a crawl. Engines began to overheat and tempers soared. They did not reach the main highway until 0700 and he immediately stationed a Panzer III and two armoured cars at the first crossroads to block all further traffic of any kind. The refugees dammed up behind the road block and, as they left, the tank's commander was shouting at the crowd to return home.

By noon, Prager had closed all major roads leading west and south out of Cherbourg. French artillery fire had been sporadic all day, as if afraid of hitting French refugees, but now they began to lay down a steady barrage. Prager had gained an idea of the town's defences from questioning refugees and from maps and knew that most of the artillery was concentrated within the port area and comprised two naval forts, the Army garrison at French headquarters in Fort Central and the few British and French naval craft remaining in the harbour. A motorcycle dispatch rider brought word that the main elements of the Seventh Panzer had isolated the city during the night. High up, glinting in the sun, German bombers passed over the city to bomb the docks and British ships that were trying to evacuate the last of the British troops. A counterbarrage began against Fort Central, then shifted to the naval forts until at 1700, all firing ceased as the French garrisons surrendered.

The actual occupation of the city seemed anticlimactic. Little damage had been done to the civilian sections of the town, Prager saw as he led his column through narrow streets towards the harbour. People stood along the roads or watched mutely from windows as they passed.

The dock area was another matter. Here the damage was extensive and bodies were strewn about. Whole buildings had fallen in on themselves or cascaded into the narrow streets. A stray dog watched suspiciously, ready to bolt at the least sign of hostility.

The oily waters of the harbour were visible between two warehouses when they met the first sizeable cluster of French soldiers. They were in company strength and had been drawn up at parade rest under the command of a portly, red-faced non-commissioned officer who saluted gravely as Prager drove by. By contrast, in the next block, a dozen or so soldiers formed a drunken, disorderly rabble. Several sat in the gutter like American hoboes, drinking looted wine and whisky while others staggered about, cursing and shaking fists at the German armoured cars. A lorry appeared and disgorged a load of German grenadiers who began to round them up.

The diffident sun sat level across the harbour and the burned and damaged buildings seemed uncaring in the flat light, like ancient ruins. Prager could see a last vessel already well out of the harbour and felt no elation in having reached the sea, or in having taken part in the greatest advance in military history. He was simply too exhausted. His insides quivered with lack of sleep and proper food and he knew he was operating on nervous tension alone.

Sonja passed across his mind and, unconsciously, he touched the pocket where he kept her letters. The fears of the morning were submerged in a sense of longing for her, tempered only by the knowledge that they could be married in the autumn, his favourite time of year. France was finished. And the British had no alternative now but to sue for peace. They could never hope to stand alone against a Germany controlling the resources of half the European continent.

Lieutenant Rand Dobson, Royal Australian Navy, took the fresh mug of coffee from the mess steward with one hand and gave the new sailing orders to Captain Peter Boles, Royal Navy, who had just bustled onto the bridge of HMS *Catalon*. Boles was a short, rotund man who exuded energy, a Battle of Jutland veteran aboard the old *Queen Elizabeth*, an officer who had avoided the Geddes axe in the twenties and, in spite of the odds, had reached the rank of full commander at the beginning of 1939.

While Boles read through the new instructions, Dobson stared out at the thinning fog shrouding Dover harbour. Dobson had long heard stories of the political struggles that had raged in every military establishment in the Commonwealth in the 1920s and early 1930s. The various Governments that had come to power during the Depression had sought for ways to reduce their multimillion pound and dollar national debts by reducing the military services to useless skeletons while turning a blind eye to developments in Germany. Officers and non-commissioned officers with years of seniority were turned out. Pay was reduced and military expenditures trimmed to the bone – and the country was now paying the price across the Channel in France. Not even the Naval mutiny – or strike, the preferred term, as if that somehow made them more acceptable – at Cromarty Firth over pay cuts, had deterred the Government for long.

Australia's own military establishment, never large to begin with, had been severely reduced after 1918 and so had suffered more than that of Great Britain. There had been times when he wondered why he had chosen the Navy as a career. In peacetime, a duller, more boring existence in one shore posting after another could hardly be imagined. He had been in the Navy six years before being granted his first sea duty assignment, a three-month training cruise.

When the war broke out, Great Britain sought experienced regular officers from the Commonwealth to supplement her own reduced establishment and he had been transferred to London. He had eagerly looked forward to sea duty; instead, he had languished at the Admiralty, planning convoying procedures, then Arctic operations pertaining to the aborted Finnish and Norwegian operations. He had discovered that for all its vaunted superiority, the Royal Navy was no more efficient nor intelligent than the Royal Australian Navy. He had quickly learned that a too-large percentage of ranking staff officers responsible for planning and deployment, had reached their positions solely on their ability to read the political winds and act accordingly. The knowledge and expertise required to run a vast military organization was, in spite of Winston Churchill's vigorous efforts to the contrary during his short tenure as First Lord of the Admiralty, sadly lacking. Since he had observed the same conditions in the Royal Australian Navy, he supposed it to be a problem common to all peacetime navies.

Captain Boles slapped him on the shoulder, startling him. 'Didn't hear a word I said, did you, Rand? Look here, get your head down for an hour or two.'

He held up a hand when Dobson started to protest. 'No good to me as a zombie. We've orders to go across again. Leave as soon as the decks are clear and the medicos load their supplies. Won't need you for at least two hours.

'And that's an order,' he added as an afterthought.

Dobson went, thankfully. He had been awake for thirty hours and on duty for twenty-six.

He woke to the soft slurring of fans and the feel of a ship at sea. His head ached and his mouth was dry and filthy-tasting. As executive officer, he rated a cabin by himself, for which he was profoundly grateful. He brushed his teeth and made a mental note to have the converters checked again – he didn't care what the tests showed, the damned water still tasted salty.

With ten minutes to go, he stripped off his underwear, wrapped a towel about his middle and padded along the narrow corridor to the shower, marvelling at how empty the ship seemed with only its normal complement aboard. He showered quickly, rinsed with the fresh water piped aboard from the city mains and returned to his cabin.

Dobson stepped onto the bridge at 1600 exactly, in a fresh uniform and feeling somewhat better. Captain Boles grinned at his wet hair.

'Made the best of it I see. Ought to be good for another thirty hours then.'

Dobson gave a mock groan and glanced at the compass repeater. 'Le Havre again?'

'None other. We go at 1800 hours.'

The late morning sun blazed on the white cliffs edging the horizon to starboard. A flight of single-engined aircraft appeared high up in a tight vee, heading for the French coast. In the clear summer air, France was quite visible. They had paralleled the coast nearly to Brighton during the night, then dashed south-east for the Bay of the Seine and Le Havre in an effort to dodge the marauding Luftwaffe as long as possible. The return trip would also be made during darkness and then the German E-boats would be the biggest threat. HMS *Catalon* was an elderly minesweeper mounting a single three-point-five-inch gun, two Bofors and four twenty-millimetre twin machine guns, and was barely a match for the torpedoes of a fast E-boat.

It was 13 June. Dobson sipped his coffee and leaned on the bridge rail while the cold breeze cleared away his muzziness.

When his transfer had come through in early May, it was not to the Home Fleet as he had expected but to Minesweeper Flotilla, Ms4, berthed at Harwich. When he reported in, he found to his surprise that he had been assigned as Executive officer in HMS *Catalon*. Even before he had unpacked properly, they sailed to cover Allied landings at Mo in Norway and for a week patrolled along the coast, sweeping for German mines dropped by aircraft and U-boat. On 10 May, as German paratroopers landed at The Hague and Rotterdam, HMS *Catalon* was ordered south into the North Sea where she patrolled the east coast from the North Foreland to Felixstowe. In the last week of May, *Catalon* had been detached from sweeping duties to spend six days and nights plying back and forth across the Dover Straits loaded to the gunwales with British and French evacuees. She had been bombed and strafed twice, incurring rather heavy damage to her bow plates which had been hastily shored up at Harwich.

By mid-morning, the smoke pall from the burning oil storage tanks at Le Havre was visible. Far off on their starboard bow, a trawler ran in towards the coast and, through his glasses, he saw that it sported a large red cross. German or British? he wondered. They had orders to leave the German rescue ships alone if in mid-Channel, but to pursue and sink if near the British coast on the assumption they were spying. The trawler answered his unspoken question by running up a red ensign and the *Catalon* answered with two sharp blasts of her siren.

There were numerous British, and come to that German, pilots who owed their lives to those unarmed trawlers that spent days on end stooging around in mid-Channel, waiting for the sight of a parachute.

German coastal guns at Fecamp were too distant to bother them but Dobson ordered a small course change that would shift them out of range of any new installations that might have been established closer to Le Havre. As an afterthought, he sent additional lookouts aloft to watch for derelicts or ships sunk since their last visit. The bright sun glaring off the choppy waters made for difficult visibility although not as bad as an early morning approach with the sun directly in one's eyes, he thought. Coastal guns were not the big danger; on this last leg of the course paralleling the coast, it was the Luftwaffe that made it so bad.

Searching the skies above the battered harbour through his glasses, he spotted only a few German aircraft, all single-engined fighter types. Further out to sea, an air battle raged along the horizon. On every run back to England, he heard the soldiers cursing the RAF for inactivity while the Luftwaffe massacred them on the beaches. But, as at Dunkirk, the RAF had, in fact, taken heavy casualties; most of the air battles were fought either well out to sea or miles inland. Either way, they were largely invisible to the troops on the evacuation beaches.

Le Havre had been battered to a pulp. Buildings and warehouses lining the piers had been devastated and here and there whole blocks had been burned out, like teeth rotted to stumps. The fairway was jammed with vessels and the Mole was in operation once again but the lines of soldiers seemed just as endless even after three days of evacuation.

Tea was distributed among the watches and Dobson drank his on the bridge. Two messages had been signalled; the first directing them to tie up to the Mole, the second, arriving moments later, ordered them to stand by to tow off damaged ships. Dobson and Boles exchanged glances; that signal had become the standard prelude to a bombing attack. They were already at full action stations but Boles activated the ship's loudspeakers and told the men to look sharp. He had no sooner clicked off than the first wave of bombers appeared at ten thousand feet. Instantly, every anti-aircraft weapon in the harbour opened fire.

The bombers passed over the Fortress of Saint Andresse, a relic of the Napoleonic days when a three-mile territorial limit was the most that thirty-two-pounder cannon could command. Dobson counted at least fourteen bombers as the first strings of bombs began to fall across the docks.

'I'll take the conn, Mr Dobson,' Boles shouted. 'Hard to starboard, two-thirds ahead.' The Captain's voice was terse but controlled. The fairway was broad enough for manoeuvring although the congested shipping made it dangerous. The *Catalon*'s anti-aircraft batteries encased the ship in a solid wall of noise. Tracers rocketed upward in thick curtains but the bombers, Heinkels, he had identified them now, flew on unharmed.

Bomb explosions raced along the docks. A three-storey shipping crane crumpled like a child's toy and an elderly four-stack destroyer, a relic of the First War called back into service, received a direct hit on the fantail. The destroyer, fully loaded, had been turning away from the Mole and its decks were solid with men. He counted at least three separate explosions on or about the ship which was suddenly wreathed in smoke. A secondary explosion blew the smoke away and he saw that the entire stern section was gone.

Boles shouted directions at the quartermaster and *Catalon* veered in her direction. Dobson grabbed the bridge messenger and sent him racing off to have boarding nets rigged and boats crews told off.

A second and then a third wave of Heinkels appeared over the harbour to subject it to a merciless bombing. The *Catalon* churned her way towards the oil-saturated water around the destroyer which was now a seething mass of struggling sailors and soldiers. *Catalon* rounded to as her boarding nets went down. Her boats were lowered and soldiers and sailors began dragging themselves up the netting or clung to the gunwales of the whaler and lifeboats. *Catalon* took aboard two hundred survivors as boats from several other evacuation ships criss-crossed the area, their crews ignoring floating bodies as they pulled the still living aboard.

The Heinkels disappeared as suddenly as they came, leaving three ships badly damaged and two sunk. *Catalon* suffered two near misses, one of which had jammed her rudder momentarily so that the port bow had sheered past the Mole and ripped a gaping hole in her plate at the waterline. They stood out into the fairway at 1900 hours.

One scene remained fixed in Dobson's mind as *Catalon* slipped out of the harbour. The setting sun illuminated the ruined waterfront buildings with golden summer light and turned the towering smoke clouds to celebratory plumes as German soldiers moved cautiously onto the docks. A French infantry officer, pulled from the water, stood wrapped in a blanket on the fantail. When he caught sight of the distant enemy soldiers he went berserk. Screaming Gallic obscenities, he pulled the trigger of his service pistol over and over again but it refused to fire. With a final curse, the officer threw the wretched weapon towards the docks, then put his face in his hands and wept. A British sailor took him gently by the shoulders and led him below.

Dobson came onto the bridge again at midnight. The night was utterly black under a thick cloud cover which had moved across the sky with sunset. On the bridge, only red night lamps reflecting from the glass distinguished interior from exterior. He relieved the second officer and logged the fact and they talked for a few minutes before the man left to snatch a few hours' sleep. Dobson filled his coffee cup and walked over to the new radio-direction-finding console that had been installed the week before he had joined the ship.

He was familiar with the principle of radio-direction finding – a beam of high frequency radio waves transmitted in a specific direction. If they struck against something solid, a percentage were reflected back towards the source. A sensitive receiver measured their signal strength and from that, a skilled operator could deduce the direction and range to the object and its approximate size.

This particular set was experimental and, of course, temperamental. Theoretically, it could detect an object as small as a submarine periscope at a distance of six miles. In actual fact, they had been lucky to spot the Dover cliffs while in harbour. The set must be giving trouble tonight, Dobson thought. He could hear the operator muttering curses under his breath as he fiddled with the dials. The greenish screen with its sweeping line of white light was empty – as usual.

The watch passed slowly and Dobson drank coffee until his stomach protested. They had taken aboard over four hundred soldiers, including those rescued from the bombed destroyer, and they were jammed everywhere there was a bit of room, in passageways, under and on top of mess tables, even in the officers' wardroom. After a month's worth of such rescue operations, he no longer thought it odd.

At 0300, the RDF operator reported a target bearing twelve degrees north, northwest. Dobson heaved himself from the high chair and hurried to the console. The sweep arm flickered past a point of light which brightened, then faded until it came around again.

'What do you think?'

The operator frowned. 'It's a firm sighting, sir. No fluke. Course bearing 282 degrees true. Probably a small boat, MTB or E-boat, sir.'

Dobson watched it a moment longer. By turning ten degrees to port for thirty minutes, they would intercept at half-speed. He took down the pilot book to make certain. There was no reason for a British MTB to be in that particular area and the rescue trawlers normally did not work at night. Captain Boles had chosen their present roundabout course in the hope of avoiding German aircraft at dawn. British MTBs striking across the channel at the occupied French coast or running in to lift their share of trapped Allied soldiers would have used a more direct route. But German E-boats could be about anywhere.

E-boats, like the British Motor Torpedo Boats, were fast and heavily armed with torpedos, light cannon and machine guns. And there were over four hundred soldiers aboard *Catalon* who would be exposed to the E-boat's fire if she turned to fight it out. And there was that hole in the bow – it had been shored up but it would not take much pounding. The seas were calm now, but the overcast sky and the latest report of a storm front moving in could change that in minutes. Dobson stared at the glowing screen as the sweep toured round and round, literally in a dither. What would Boles do? he asked himself. But he knew the answer to that.

The two craft were on diverging courses and the range was opening rapidly. In another few moments, they would lose sight of the E-boat. Dobson cursed his indecision. He could summon Boles and let him decide. But he knew if he did that, Boles would be extremely unhappy with him; he had made clear the boundaries of his executive officer's authority when on watch and initiating an action of this kind was clearly within that authority. The only other alternative was to delay another few minutes by which time the E-boat would either disappear or be out of range. The RDF operator cleared his throat, as if urging a decision. Dobson glared at him but it worked.

'Come port, ten degrees at twelve knots,' he snapped at the Quartermaster, then sent the messenger to wake the Captain and returned to the radio-direction-finding console. Boles arrived a few moments later, still buttoning his shirt, and peered over Dobson's shoulder.

'Possibly an E-boat, Captain, on a shipping raid. There's a coastal convoy moving round for the Nore. I've set an intercept course that should bring us within range in thirty minutes. It should be light enough in twenty-five to open fire.'

'Quite right,' Boles murmured. 'Be nice to bag one of the bastards.'

'I'll turn the watch over . . .'

'Carry on, Mr Dobson.' Boles grinned and leaned against the console.

Dobson's acknowledging smile was strained. He gave the order for battle stations and the bugle blared through the ship, cheating the watch below of their last ten minutes' sleep before dawn stations were called. He fully appreciated the trust Boles displayed in letting him conn the ship during an action, even if he was apprehensive about his ability to do so. If successful, Boles would be bound to mention in his report that Dobson had conducted the action and a successful ship-to-ship engagement could lead to his own command. At the same time, he was also aware that the lives of over four hundred and fifty men now depended on his skill. Once *Catalon* opened fire, if the E-boat was not quickly sunk or at least badly damaged, the engagement would be considered a failure. If *Catalon* sustained heavy damage and numerous casualties, he, as well as Boles, could say goodbye to naval careers at sea. It would be shore-based desk assignments for the duration. If only he had more sea time. Damn that RDF set, he thought. Why now, of all times, must it work?

While on one level he wondered about his fitness as an officer, on another, his mind struggled with the complex problem of the E-boat's interception. The E-boat showed no sign that it had been observed, confirming the opinion that the German Navy had not yet placed RDF sets aboard such small craft, either because they did not have enough or because their sets were not capable of sorting through the hash of spurious signals encountered so close to the surface. He ordered *Catalon*'s speed increased slightly and stared anxiously at the eastern horizon for the first trace of dawn.

'Estimated range 29,000 yards, sir.'

They were still far beyond the range of the *Catalon*'s single three-point-five-inch gun and would have to close to within 10,000 yards to be so, with all the risks that implied of alerting the E-boat. In spite of their larger size, the two would be evenly matched at best. The E-boat had at least fifteen knots more speed and her torpedo tubes balanced the *Catalon*'s main armament. He chewed his lip a moment, on the verge of asking Boles' advice, but rejected the idea.

'We will close to within 9,500 yards. RDF, advise at five thousand yard intervals. Quartermaster, come starboard two degrees.' He hoped that the slight margin might be just the edge his gunners would need in the uncertain dawn light.

He risked a quick look across the dimly lit bridge at Boles, but the Captain was staring at the RDF screen with no sign of either approval or disapproval. Dobson found himself tapping his fingers on the chair arm and forced himself to stop, to sit rigidly in the high chair, visualizing the complex array of courses, speeds and positions.

The minutes dragged. The sky had grown perceptibly lighter in the east while the range closed with maddening deliberation. There was enough light now to see the deck where the Master-at-Arms and a hastily organized gang were herding the last of the soldiers below, cramming them in anywhere they would not interfere with the operation of the ship. The three-point-five-inch gun's muzzle cap was knocked off with a ramrod and the stubby barrel rose smoothly and the turret rotated in both directions as the gun crew tested the mounting. Ammunition would now be in the hoist and the first shell would be sliding into the breech. The gun captain would be listening over his headset while the gunnery officer fed him the initial set of coordinates – there! The muzzle rose towards maximum elevation and the turret swung questingly. Only the command to open fire remained to be given. The night's coffee lay like a pool of acid in his stomach. Christ, if it should be a British boat and not German.

Dobson leaned forward to grip the rail, to get himself under control. The urge to turn the ship over to Boles was irresistible. He started to do so when the RDF operator spoke calmly.

'Eleven thousand yards, sir. Target turning eight degrees to starboard. He is now on a course for Southampton.'

Christ! What next, he groaned to himself. The chance that it was a British vessel had just increased. An MTB flotilla was based at Southampton. If he fired on a British boat, his career would be ruined. He would never be officially blamed, of course, as the boat was where it should not have been. But even so, the rumours and whispers would follow him, would destroy his naval career as effectively as a court-martial verdict of guilty – that's Dobson, Australian you know. Sank a British MTB one night off Southampton. Couldn't be helped, I suppose. Still, the beggar should have known. . . .

'Range 10,500 yards.'

If he waited to verify its nationality and the E-boat escaped, he would be finished just as certainly. Damn it all, he raged at himself, let Boles take over. It's his ship. Let him assume the risk. The bastard's left you to it so he won't have to make the decision.

'Range 10,000 yards.'

Dobson blinked. Visibility had grown to at least a thousand yards. The next few minutes would be crucial as the sun mounted the horizon. He must be ready to give the order to fire on the instant the first light rolled across the sea, he told himself. The ranging shots must be on the way before the E-boat's lookouts saw *Catalon*. Split second timing was required and he knew that he was not capable. . . .The sun would be across their starboard quarter, the dazzle would hamper the E-boat lookouts – but suppose the sun was too bright, suppose the German E-boat was indistinguishable at that distance from a British MTB; he tried desperately to recall the details of the recognition silhouettes he had spent so many hours memorizing. Why hadn't he called for the book before this to refresh his memory? Damn it, he thought, he always managed to leave something undone.

'Range 9,500 yards.'

Light swept across the heaving sea without warning. He had seen it happen many times before, had always enjoyed the phenomenon of the sunrise line racing across the planet's surface at a thousand miles an hour. He heard the gunnery officer's tinny voice tense with new data, saw the cannon muzzle moving just the tiniest fraction as the range was corrected. Then he had the boat in his glasses. For a moment, the image swung wildly before years of practice took over and eye and image met in the circular field. The boat was long, too long for an MTB and the mounting of her torpedo tubes was all wrong. Even as his mind registered these facts, he shouted, 'Fire!'

Confirmation poured in from the lookouts but the deck gun had already smashed the dawn silence. The concussion slashed them and the bridge windows shivered. Dobson's earlier fears were now occupied with the gun crew's shooting ability, sadly neglected these past weeks.

He found the shell, a tiny glowing dot visible for an instant as it passed high enough to catch the sun. He didn't see where it fell but the gunnery officer's calm voice was feeding new data and the gun crashed out again. This time, he saw a white splash close alongside. The E-boat had turned to starboard, into the sun to aid her lookouts but the gunnery officer had anticipated the move. The third shell fell even closer astern and the fourth burst in smoke and Dobson was certain it was a hit. The E-boat turned back onto its original course to present the smallest possible target but the relentless gun followed, pouring round after round about the E-boat until a wild explosion blasted against the still dark north-western sky and the E-boat was gone.

Five minutes later they ran over the area where the E-boat had been. Only bits of wooden wreckage, a life vest and two bodies rocking gently in the oil slick, remained.

United States 15 January – 15 March 1940

The mid-west was caught in the grip of winter and snow was deep along the right of way as the Super Chief ran into New Mexico. Even so, the towns they passed gave the impression of returning prosperity. One small Kansas town had even proclaimed itself the 'New Utopia'. Keith Thorne spent most of his time in the club car nursing a drink until darkness swept the prairie.

Los Angeles and San Diego were drenched with rain from pregnant clouds squatting over the coast. The streets were awash and a copy of a Los Angeles paper picked up at Union Station, contained page after page of photographs showing houses and hillsides sliding into one another. In one, a grinning city policeman rowed a boat up Washington Boulevard. The Los Angeles River was out of its banks wherever the new channel had not been finished and block after block in the residential area bordering the river looked like Johnstown during the flood. The train ran south along the coast to San Diego and the Pacific was as grey and stormy as the sky.

Southwest Aviation, in spite of its grand name, was a rundown hangar with an elderly Waco biplane crouched inside, reeking of the same disuse and neglect that had overcome most aviation-associated small businesses during the Depression. The hangar was a leftover from the Great War, a squat, flat-roofed building with the company name painted in sun-faded block letters. Inside, Thorne found a small space sectioned off with plywood panels to form an office. A short, fat man in greasy overalls dozed in front of an electric heater, a mash of black cigar crunched in his mouth.

'You don't sound like a limey,' the man squinted suspiciously when Thorne woke him and explained what he wanted. 'You ain't one of them Federal boys?'

'Not me, friend. I'm just a ferry pilot.'

'What's the guy's name what sent you?'

'Charles Napier. Had an accent, London, I think.'

'Wouldn't know about that. Never met the geezer.' He struggled out of the chair. 'Name's Percy Daggenheim.' He stuck out an unwashed hand, cast a sad look at the glowing heater and motioned Thorne to follow.

They dodged streams of water pouring through the battered roof and walked to the shadowy back where a twin-engined Lockheed Model C-14 transport waited. In contrast to its surroundings the aircraft gleamed with care.

'This's the one. Little wet, but it won't hurt her. Gi'me the hundred bucks and she's yours.'

'A hundred dollars? That aircraft costs a hell of a lot more than that,' Thorne protested. 'I'm not flying any stolen airplane for anyone!'

The fat man laughed and hitched up his overalls. 'You new, boy?' He removed the cigar stub, glanced at it and tossed it into a puddle. 'The Limey's already paid. The hundred bucks is for getting her ready, everthin' 'cept gas and oil. That's extra.'

Thorne climbed inside with misgivings. The mechanic's sloppy appearance was certainly no testimonial to his skills but the aircraft was in first class shape. The Lockheed C-14 was especially desirable, he had been told in Ottawa, as it had the range to fly itself across the North Atlantic.

He made arrangements with Percy to have the aircraft gassed and oiled at dawn, phoned for a taxi and directed the driver to take him to the Coronado Hotel. The old hotel was exactly as he remembered it from a visit in 1936 when as part of the Third Pursuit Squadron, he had flown to Lindbergh Field to take part in combined manoeuvres. Then, as now, the bar had been full of uniformed naval officers. Thorne sat by himself and the drone of conversation full of references to aviation, the war in China and occasionally in Europe, made him feel at least a part of it all again. He also heard unreserved approval for the President's December 'fireside chat' during which he had declared the United States 'the great arsenal of democracy'.

It was raining again the following morning when he arrived at the Southwest Aviation hangar and Percy was just scrambling off the wing with the fuel hose. A strong wind blew in from the ocean to remind him of storms on Cape Cod. Rain lashed the field in sudden fury and they retreated to the hangar office and the electric heater.

'Gonna cost you $278.00 for the gas and oil, boy. Plus the hundred dollars for my time.'

Thorne did a rapid calculation in his head and found that Percy Daggenheim had charged him honestly for the gasoline. He paid the money, then borrowed Percy's car, for another two dollars, and drove across to the commercial terminal to file a flight and studied the latest weather information.

The rain was the result of a typical winter Pacific storm. A series of rain cells were sweeping in from the Hawaiian Islands via the Gulf of Alaska. A low pressure area prevailed inland over Nevada and Utah and the storm cells drifted southwards along the coast until they piled up against the Sierra Nevada and San Gabriel mountain ranges. Occasionally, one storm cell would have sufficient strength to force its way across and lash the desert as far east as the Nevada–Utah line. Thorne had thought to make his first leg from San Diego to Las Vegas, Nevada as a check flight but it was already raining in the tiny Nevada town and the ceiling was less than five hundred feet. He revised his flight plan for San Diego–Tucson–Denver and drove back to the hangar.

The rain was as hard as ever but Thorne decided to chance it. Percy had warmed up the engines for him and he dropped his bag in the cabin and settled into the hard leather-covered plywood chair. It had been almost two years since he had flown a twin-engined aircraft and gingerly, he eased the throttles forward and the engines responded with a satisfying roar. He fastened his seat belt and opened the flight manual to the last page on which he had written down a pre-flight checklist. The checklist was a new procedure instituted in the Air Corps in 1937 after a B-17 pilot had forgotten to unlock the horizontal stabilizers and crashed. That accident had started the witch hunt that had nearly ruined the plane and influenced his resignation.

The checklist completed, he slid back the window and waved at

Percy who, clad in a black slicker, dashed from the hangar, ducked under the wings from behind and yanked away the chocks.

The aircraft tugged and bounced against the brakes. The wipers were barely able to cope with the rain and he had to open the side panel and lean out to see the taxiway. When he released the brakes, the aircraft rolled forward eagerly. Chill water ran off his hair and down his collar and he wished that he had had sense enough to steal a hotel towel.

At the end of the taxiway, Thorne took a deep breath and wheeled the aircraft onto the runway. He ran the engines up twice and they responded smoothly – the oil pressure and ammeter needles shivering in the white. The cockpit was full of shuddering, racketing noise and he was aware of the familiar tang of lubricating oil, aviation gasoline, plastic and leather. The tower light winked green, and he shouted happily and released the brakes.

The Lockheed fled down the runway. He held her back, riding the pedals gently, correcting her deviations as the ground speed built. It was coming back now; he didn't have to think about his next response; feet and hands worked independently and his eyes roved instruments, blocking out anything but a deviation from normal.

The plane bounced and was airborne. The two 1,100 horsepower Wright Cyclone radial engines pulled her up smoothly and, at a thousand feet, he throttled back and banked south. The wing fell away and through the rain he could see the choppy Pacific and its broken lines of whitecaps marching shoreward. San Diego came into view, huddled against the storm, and to the south was the naval yard and the blurred outlines of the Pacific Fleet – massive battleships and cruisers.

The city passed beneath, half shrouded in rain and low cloud, and he climbed for altitude and broke through the cloud into brilliant sunshine at twelve thousand feet. Happier than he had been in years, he rested his hands on the wheel and drank in the sublime view of endless cloud mountains and azure sky.

'I should never have resigned,' he said aloud. Then grinning, he switched on the cabin heater and began putting the Lockheed through her paces.

During the winter, Thorne shifted aircraft between the United States and Canada and, once, even slipped across the Mexican border to fly one out of a lonely strip in Baja California. At first the work was enough to satisfy him but as the weeks dragged on and the empty nights spent in small hotels and dingy motor courts began to pall, he found that a bottle of scotch and occasionally a bar-room pickup helped him to sleep. He was at a loss to explain this nagging restlessness and after a while, gave up trying.

The armistice in Finland depressed him. The Democracies once again had lacked the courage to stand against a dictatorship. The Bund leaders and the America Firsters renewed their cries for non-involvement. Charles Lindbergh stumped the country warning against German military might and the price the United States would pay for intervention.

In early March, he spent three days in New York while an aircraft was repaired at Flushing Meadows. The transfer of American aircraft had been reported in the press and the America First Committee was waging a vociferous campaign against the practice as were other isolationist organizations. His father guessed that he was involved but said little directly, rather made plain his sympathy with the aims of the America First Committee. He was not only a member of a business advisory group, but an active campaigner as well. This was Keith Thorne's first visit home since his precipitous departure in December and the atmosphere was even more strained than he expected.

'You mark my words, Keith, that madman in the White House will draw us into a war yet. Damned fool said as much in that ridiculous speech before New Year's. If he would mind his own business, it would all be settled by spring. But he insists on encouraging France and Britain even though they've shown time after time they don't want to fight – and with good reason. They have the Maginot Line. Hitler will never dare to attack so strong a position. Why, the war is practically over.'

'What about the North Atlantic? And China?'

His father chuckled while the maid removed his dinner plate. His mother had been looking from one to the other, seeming to follow the conversation but Thorne doubted she was listening. She had the trick of seeming to pay close attention while, in fact, hearing almost nothing of what was being said.

'Exactly my point. In the last war, German submarines nearly starved England. She is even more dependent now on imported food than she was twenty-five years ago. Chamberlain knows that. He also knows that it is going to take Hitler a few years to digest everything he has gobbled up since the beginning of last year. And Hitler knows it as well. You mark my words – both sides will conclude an armistice soon.

'But you may be correct about China,' he went on in a thoughtful voice. 'The Japanese have been insufferable for years. With our interests and markets in Asia, we dare not allow them to gobble up China. If they do, it will be only a matter of time before they strike out for the rest of Asia.'

Thorne remembered the Japanese naval officer's comments about American *insufferability* in the Pacific that night in Warsaw. He was tempted to point out that Japan viewed the United States in exactly the same manner as the United States viewed the Japanese but decided that it wasn't worth the argument.

Dessert was his favourite, baked Alaska, but Thorne only picked at it. His mother noticed his lack of appetite and remarked on how lean he had become. 'And your eyes are so bloodshot, Keith.'

He wanted another drink but his father's abstemious ways prevented that. One drink before dinner, perhaps another before bed and never wine on the table. He'd have to find some excuse to go to his room.

He telephoned Shirley that evening and was made to wait. When she came to the phone, her voice was distinctly frosty. No, she could not see him tonight, nor tomorrow afternoon. She had other plans and she couldn't be expected to drop everything whenever he decided to make an appearance. She would be in Manhattan tomorrow evening and they could have dinner together at the Plaza.

He spent most of the following day trying to resolve the dilemma of Shirley Case. He knew that he did not love her; in fact, doubted that he ever had. They had known each other since childhood and a marriage had always been taken for granted by both families. Why? he wondered. They had almost nothing in common. And, as long as he could remember, Shirley had ordered him around as if he were a servant. And the hell of it was, he usually complied. He wasn't certain he wanted to break off their engagement, perhaps because she did represent a certain stability in his life that had always been lacking.

And too, it would devastate her. In spite of her exterior self-assurance, Shirley lacked confidence in herself. Such a rejection would hurt her terribly and he did not want to subject her to such an ordeal. By late afternoon and train time, he had talked himself into patching things up once more. He packed, showered and said goodbye to his mother – interrupting one of her interminable phone calls – and was driven to the railroad station.

In Manhattan the following evening, he paid the taxi driver and sprinted through the evening traffic on Central Park South. Wreaths of vapour issued from mouths and exhaust pipes in the evening cold. He paused on the hotel steps and glanced up and down the street, breathing winter New York – damp air, gasoline fumes and grill food. New York in winter smelled distinctly different from New York in summer – at least about the park – no horses. Lights were preternaturally bright in the crystal air and lines of red slithered into Central Park. Looking west, the sky glowed saffron above Seventh Avenue, darkening rapidly as the sun settled behind the Palisades.

Shirley was waiting impatiently in the lobby, full-length mink wrapped tightly about her against the icy draught and face glowing with the cold. She had never looked more beautiful, he thought, as she offered her cheek to his kiss.

They began on the wrong note as soon as they were seated and he ordered cocktails. Shirley was snappish and demanded an explanation for his childish and unheeding actions in disappearing God only knew where to do God only knew what, all without a word of explanation. Half way through her salad, she pushed it away and lit a cigarette. Smoke wreathed her carefully-done hair and she brushed at it nervously. Shirley wore a simple, black dinner dress that reeked of the understated elegance so many designers claimed and so few produced. A smart pillbox hat was tipped rakishly on her glowing hair and to accent the dress she wore a five-strand pearl choker with matching earrings. And her engagement ring.

'Perhaps,' he said mildly, 'you can tell me why you were so busy last night and today that you could not make time to see me?' In the back of his mind was the sudden picture of the man who had hovered about her at the Christmas Party. 'I telephoned you at least a dozen times from around the country. Either you weren't in or you weren't taking calls.'

'Don't change the subject, Keith,' she snapped. 'I am not asking for an explanation of *your* actions. As your fiancée, I am demanding one. I want to know why you chose to disappear to Canada or God only knows where without even consulting me. Your behaviour the night of the Christmas Eve party was simply abominable. The man you insulted. . . .'

'I insulted?' he raised an eyebrow. 'I insulted him?'

'You certainly did. That man is . . . never mind him now. Ever since you came back from Poland, you've been different, even more thoughtless than before, if that's possible.'

The last of Thorne's appetite disappeared and he laid his fork down. 'Look Shirley, I think both of us have been rather thoughtless with one another. Perhaps we've spent too much time together, taken each other too much for granted. I have a complaint or two myself. For instance, I would still like to know what was so damned important that you couldn't see me before tonight, especially after I told you I was leaving in the morning.'

'Keith, you are changing the subject again. You always do that when you don't want to answer my questions. Now. . . .'

He cut her off. 'I asked you, what was so important that you couldn't see me before tonight?'

Shirley stared at him, her eyes as cool as her expression; as if she were calculating his mood and weighing various alternatives.

'Keith, perhaps this isn't the place to discuss this.' Her voice was suddenly soft, intimate. 'My parents are in Florida and the town house is empty.'

He recognized the ploy; she was dangling sex to keep him in line. It occurred to him then that Shirley rationed it carefully, never so little that he might begin to lose interest, or too much so that he took her for granted. Watching her as she sat forward, shoulders back to emphasize her enticing bust, the idea of being bullied and manoeuvred for a lifetime revolted him. For the first time, he recognized the depths of her selfishness and his hard-won intentions evaporated instantly.

'I want to break the engagement, Shirley.'

His words stunned her and she gaped at him, mouth open.

'You can make the announcement any way you like. Keep the ring if you wish. I've just realized that we are about as wrong for one another as two people can be.'

'You bastard,' she hissed. 'You Goddamned bastard. What will everybody. . . .' She tugged the ring off and flung it at him, stood quickly and whirled out of the restaurant.

Thorne looked after her for a moment, then dropped the ring into his pocket and left a ten-dollar bill on the table and went out. He found a quiet bar on Fifty-fourth Street and, as he nursed a drink, wondered if he really had seen relief in her eyes just before she flounced out.

The following day, he flew north from Flushing Meadows to Montreal and turned the aircraft over to an RCAF pilot and managed to catch a train for Chicago. He changed there and arrived in Kansas City the following morning. The Beechcraft he was to pick up had a cracked cylinder head and repairs would not be finished until late the following day and so he took a hotel room downtown.

The temperature was in the low twenties and late winter snowfall had jammed the city to a halt. Tired by the long train ride and disgusted with the way his engagement to Shirley had ended, he avoided the crowded restaurant and ordered a club sandwich in the bar. He nursed drinks for most of the evening, balancing carefully on a mild euphoria that banished the need to think yet would leave him able to fly in the morning.

Nearing eleven p.m., the bar began to empty but a man in a nattily cut grey suit took the stool beside his anyway. After a moment, he remarked on Thorne's choice of scotch and introduced himself as a sales representative for Seagrams Distillers.

They made small talk for a few minutes, the salesman doing most of the talking, mostly amusing complaints about the amount of travel his job required. 'All this damned snow sure as hell doesn't make it any easier.' He contemplated his drink for a moment. 'What do you do? You travel much?'

Thorne shook his head and reached for his wallet. Tonight was not a night he wanted to spend conversing with a total stranger. 'Not a lot. I work for a publishing company in New York. Editor. If you'll excuse me, I've a meeting with my boss.' He dropped a few bills on the bar. 'Let me get your drink too,' he offered when the man seemed disappointed.

He went up to his room, undressed and washed. The bed was old and sagged in the middle but he was used to that. He had just settled under the blankets when someone knocked on the door. He swore and ignored it. A key slid stealthily into the lock. For a moment, he lay rigid with fear, then as the first surge of panic subsided, he slipped out of bed and crossed the room. The door opened and a figure started to edge into the room.

Thorne hit the door hard with his shoulder, slamming it on the man's face and shoulder, yanked it open and struck hard with a straight right to the face as a second figure fled down the hall. Thorne started after him only to realize that he was naked. He jumped back inside and dragged the dazed burglar into the room just as an elderly woman across the hall peeked out and gasped. He kicked the door shut, grabbed his robe from the suitcase and turned on the lamp. The burglar was the liquor salesman from the bar. He telephoned the front desk.

The police arrived within ten minutes. Two patrolmen muffled in heavy overcoats handcuffed and searched the man, then one examined his wallet while the younger man took down Thorne's story. The older policeman was sorting the papers in the man's wallet when he sighed.

'Take the cuffs off him, Charlie.'

'Take the cuffs off, hell,' Thorne yelped. 'I want this bastard arrested for breaking and entering.'

'Easy, Mac,' the cop said and went to the telephone. 'You'd better sit down and be quiet.'

An uneasy ten minutes passed before a man in a rumpled business suit arrived. He glanced at the man Thorne had hit and shook his head.

'Doctor looked at him?'

'Not yet. Thought it best to wait 'til you got here.' The man nodded and turned to Thorne.

302

'What's your name, buddy?'

'I'd like to see a badge, if you don't mind?'

'Not at all.' He flashed a gold-plated shield. 'Name's Hayes. Satisfied? Good, 'cause I'm not gonna ask you again, fella. What's your name?'

Puzzled, Thorne glanced at the burglar lying on his bed, a cold towel pressed against the side of his head. His pasty colour was beginning to disappear and he glared now and then at Thorne as he answered the detective's question.

'What's your business in Kansas City, Mister, ah Thorne?' He tossed the wallet on the desk.

'Sorry, officer, my business is private.' Thorne cast a quick glance at the man in the chair. 'Look here, what's going on? This idiot breaks into my room and you put *me* through the third degree!'

'Ease up, bub. Ain't no evidence of breaking and entering that I can see. Looks to me like he had a key.'

'So, go down and ask the desk how he got it. I sure as hell didn't give it to him.'

The detective shrugged. 'We'll get around to it. Now, I asked you a question, what are you doing in Kansas City?'

Thorne stared at him. 'Are you arresting me?'

'Why should I do that?'

'Then you haven't any right to ask me that question. I'm the one who made the complaint, remember?'

The detective pushed his hat back on his head and nodded. 'You get smart with me, asshole, and you go to jail. Got that? I got plenty of charges that'll do nicely.'

Thorne smiled. 'My father is Charles Thorne of Thorne, Dorsten and Winslow, the New York publishers. Put me in jail and there'll be a dozen lawyers handing out lawsuits in the morning. Starting with those two,' he indicated the uniformed officers, 'and working up through you, your boss, the local D.A. and the mayor.'

The detective studied him with scepticism. 'Make a phone call to New York,' Thorne prompted.

The detective swore. 'All right, you two. Get him the hell out of here. Take him home.' He ignored Thorne's protest and walked over to the bed and glared at the burglar.

'You tell your boss I'm gonna call him first thing in the morning. He better have a damned good explanation or I'm coming after you. Got me?'

The man nodded and the cops helped him from the room. The detective shut the door after them and motioned to Thorne's travel flask. 'Help yourself,' Thorne muttered. The detective poured two measures, handed one to Thorne and sat down with a sigh. He drank off half the glass and nodded.

303

'Better.' He leaned back and regarded Thorne. 'I am going to make that call, boy. If you lied to me, you better not be in Missouri when I find out.' Thorne snorted.

The detective, having made the call, seemed satisfied and eased his position in the chair. 'Now look here. I would appreciate it if you'd leave Kansas City by tomorrow night.'

'The hell I will!' The detective held up a hand.

'Hold on, bub. This is all unofficial, and for your own good. That boy was the chief assistant to Congressman Haight. Walter Haight. Name ring a bell?'

'Haight? Why should it. . . .' Thorne nodded. 'Yeah, I guess it does.'

Walter Haight had been in the newspapers quite a lot lately. He was the Congressional spokesman for the America First Committee and it was rumoured that he had close connections to the American Bund.

'I thought it might.'

Thorne nodded. 'Look, I. . . .'

Again the detective held up a hand to stop him. 'Don't tell me any more. Just call the police station and tell them everything has been resolved amicably. Guy got the wrong room or something. But not a word about my being here, understand. What I don't know, won't hurt either of us. One of these days Haight and his storm troopers will get their come-uppance, but now ain't the time.'

The detective tossed off the last of the scotch, nodded to Thorne and left.

Thorne sat in the spacious suite of offices Charles Napier had rented at the Savoy Hotel in Ottawa and told the story carefully. Napier's clothes were impeccably tailored – those of a very rich, very well positioned Englishman and he had that elegance that comes only from a lifetime of doing the right thing, attending the right school and knowing the right people. Thorne had been born with a silver spoon in his mouth, so to speak, and recognized the breed instantly.

When Thorne finished, the Englishman nodded thoughtfully. 'Fortunately, that police detective was clever enough to keep his mouth closed.' He smoothed his moustache unconsciously. 'Unfortunately, your usefulness to us has now ended.'

'For Christ's sake, Napier,' Thorne protested. 'What's the problem? I'm not afraid of a few Bundists.'

'Look here, Thorne, this is not a game. There are far too many people who wish to stop us and do not care how they go about it. Please remember that the man who broke into your room was employed by a member of the House of Representatives. We know

304

for a fact that there are quite a number of people in your government who sympathize with the Nazi regime. We have identified more than a few who have done more than merely express their sympathies.'

Thorne nodded, reluctantly. 'All right, I understand. So what do I do now? Pick up my paycheque?'

Napier smiled. 'I certainly hope not.' He selected a white index card. 'Have you ever flown across the Atlantic, Thorne?'

England 16 May – 25 June 1940

It was raining when Keith Thorne touched the Lockheed Hudson onto the wet runway at Croydon Airport, south of London. The Royal Canadian Air Force pilot in the co-pilot's seat muttered in his sleep as he had been doing for the last hour while snoring happily enough in the cramped position.

As he taxied onto the apron in response to the flagman's directions, he nudged the Canadian awake. The man stretched and yawned and peered out at the rain.

'Want me to take over for a while?'

Thorne shook his head and jerked a thumb at the administration building a few yards away. 'Thanks.'

The Canadian yawned and leaned forward for a better look. 'I'll be damned! Landed already!' He unbuckled his seat belt. 'Sorry. I wasn't much help was I?'

'You surely weren't,' Thorne muttered. They had taken a three-hour break in Aldergrove and he had tried to snatch a little sleep in the back while the plane was being refuelled and checked by RAF fitters. But the drumming of hard rain on the fuselage and the noise of petrol bowsers – trucks, for Christ's sake; he was even beginning to talk like an Englishman – had prevented much of that. The Canadian pilot, who was supposed to have flown the final leg, had disappeared into the terminal and Thorne didn't see him again until a car full of WAAFs careened to a stop and he stumbled out, too drunk to fly.

Thorne shut down both engines and wrote up the log. The hatch banged open and he saw the Canadian trotting across the tarmac and shrugged in exasperation. The cool air had a fresh rain-scrubbed smell and he inhaled deeply as he jumped down and and walked towards the administration building. There was no sign of the Canadian inside and he stopped at the flight counter and gave the log book to the severe, middle-aged woman who responded with her usual stiff nod, entered the flight particulars on a sheet, handed the log back and thanked him, as she had done on each of his previous sixteen flights during the past two months. He winked, as he always did and grinned when she ignored him.

In the locker room, Thorne stowed his parachute and harness. The dingy room was full of steam and the smell of sweaty clothing. He was peeling off the leather flying suit when an airman called his name.

'I beg your pardon, Mr Thorne, but the Admin. officer wishes to speak to you before you change.'

Thorne followed him along a corridor to a door marked Administration. The airman knocked and opened it for him. The Administration officer looked up over a desk piled high with paper, forms and requisitions of the kind that drive even hardened veterans of military red tape to the wall.

'Ah yes, Mr Thorne.' The officer gave him a harried smile. His blue RAF uniform looked slept in and there was a sheen of perspiration across his forehead and his skin had the pasty look of a man kept too long in darkness.

'Please sit down. Cigarette?' Thorne produced his own pack of Camels and offered him one instead. The Administration officer declined and lit an Oval. 'Mr Thorne, I know you are tired after your flight so I will make this brief.' He assessed Thorne's physical condition with a sharp glance and tapped his cigarette against the overflowing ashtray.

'Look here, I need a man to fly that Lockheed of yours across to France. Place called Abbeville. Big military airfield there. The BEF is taking a pasting further north at Lille and need immediate tactical support. That Hudson's just the ticket. Short a pilot. Be a large bonus in it for you. Quick flight over and back. What do you say?'

The need must be serious for him to ask a civilian and a neutral, he thought. But why not? His only plans for the evening had been to see the film, *Queen's Heart*. Abbeville was a long way from the fighting. The British were supposed to be using it as a major staging base and it would be well-defended. And there was the bonus – Napier's usual practice was twice flight pay.

'All right,' he agreed. 'When do you want me to leave?'

The Administration officer looked relieved. 'Good show. As soon as possible, if you don't mind. The need is urgent. You'll be flying in company with two other Hudsons. Both are Royal Air Force pilots who have made the flight a number of times. Miss Stillson will fix you up.' He gave Thorne a perfunctory handshake and led him to the door.

*

The skies cleared over the Channel and the coast of France was a thin white fringe that separated blue water and green land. After crossing the coast, the terrain became a patchwork of farms in various shades of brown and green. Vehicles could be seen on the roads, moving steadily along as if their occupants hadn't a care in the world. Only a single smoke plume on the northern horizon suggested this wasn't a normal spring day.

It reminded him of another flight, across the Atlantic a month or so earlier. West of Ireland, he had spotted another plume of smoke, from a merchant vessel listing badly to port. He had circled once and seen exhausted sailors stop work to watch and then wave as they identified the British roundels on the wings. But there had been nothing he could do for them except to waggle his wings and let them know they were not completely alone; that and report their position as soon as he landed. He never did find out what happened to that ship. Classified information, they told him.

The leading Hudson began to lose altitude and Thorne followed down, watching the farms and fields grow larger. A woman hung washing behind her house and, in a field, an ancient tractor chugged towards a gate. A small boy walked along a road, returning from school, Thorne decided. The airfield was ahead now and he could see fighter aircraft in sand-bagged revetments – and three more like sharks, lined up for takeoff.

The windshield shattered. Plexiglass slashed his face and a piece of steel bounced off the head rest and he banged his face hard against the cabin window as the Hudson dipped onto its right wing, engines screaming in protest. Dazed, acting solely by reflex, Thorne jammed the port engine throttle forward, chopped the starboard engine, kicked the rudder pedal hard and yanked the wheel to lift the wing. As the Hudson righted itself, he struggled to clear his eyes of the blood pouring from the gash in his forehead and glimpsed the leading Hudson explode as it touched down.

The pain in his head was intolerable. A shadow plunged past as he fought to raise the aircraft. The Hudson shuddered badly, veered, and the starboard engine oil pressure went to zero. The port engine laboured, its oil pressure was dropping as well. The needle shivered against the pin; a moment later smoke poured from the nacelle and the propeller windmilled.

Something hammered at the fuselage, stopped and banged again and the co-pilot's seat and right side of the instrument panel disintegrated. Thorne kicked the nose down and yawed right, searching the ground. The airfield was too far away now and in any event he could see more aircraft swooping and darting about the runway and hangars like angry insects.

Below him were trees, endless trees. The Hudson tried to stall and he held the nose up by sheer will power. A ploughed field appeared and the Hudson struck hard and skidded, throwing him against the control panel as flame blossomed from the full tanks – 'saves having to send more fuel over, you know' – the flight line officer had told him. His mind was clear enough now but he could not make his fingers work nor would the seat belt open. In an agony of frustration he beat at the buckle with his fist, forgetting that he must lift the tab. A dull explosion seared his neck and flames were reflected in the rear-view mirror. A finger caught the tab and the belt fell away and he lunged upward and through the smashed windshield, unmindful of the shards of plexiglass that caught and tore his flight suit and hands. The plane's broken nose was slippery and he fell. Another explosion rocked the aircraft and flames roared around him as he staggered up and ran, stumbling in the soft dirt of the freshly ploughed field until he was a hundred feet away. Thorne sank down then, panting and sobbing at the same time. The Hudson was a pyre; black, thick smoke rolling into the spring sky.

So much worse, he thought, so much worse than the B-17 crash which he had also walked away from. His heart was racing and the adrenaline pain of utter terror held him; was this what his co-pilot had felt? Had he died like this?

An engine screamed and a shape flashed over the trees. Thorne flinched as the German aircraft raced towards him and before he could move, twin lines of tracer flashed and the freshly turned earth exploded.

Galvanized by a fresh eruption of fear, Thorne scrambled towards the trees. The German pilot yanked his aircraft around in a tight, climbing turn to lose speed, and dropped the nose. As Thorne ran, he heard the machine guns firing in quick bursts sounding exactly like the guns that had killed the Polish girl. A rock flew up to glance off his shoulder and the dirt boiled as the woods loomed darkly, twenty yards, fifteen, ten, five; the aircraft was diving and he jinked to the right and raced parallel to the trees before throwing himself into their cover. It worked; the pilot caught by surprise, was unable to correct his aim and the sleet of copper-jacketed lead slashed the trees where he should have been instead of where he was.

Thorne lay beneath a fallen tree well inside the tree-line. His face and hands burned from cuts inflicted by the exploding windshield and by brambles and branches. He lit a cigarette with hands that were shaking so badly that he had to strike three matches. The tobacco smoke began to calm him and with half-closed eyes, he listened to the sounds of the forest. Mingled with the smell of growing things was the scorched leather of his own jacket and the odour of burned petrol from his aircraft.

In the years of the mid-1930s when another great war was still unthinkable after the devastation of the last, it had all seemed a great game. If someone were injured in the string-and-cloth kites they flew, that too was just a part of the game. Men died playing football, or driving race cars.

The first intimation of war's new horror had come the first time he climbed into the B-17 cockpit. A bewildering bank of switches and dials surrounded him and he sensed that a nation's ability to make war would now be linked directly to its technological and productive capacity and not the bravery of its soldiers nor the genius of its leaders. War had been dehumanized and man the individual would count for nothing more than a pair of hands and a conditioned brain to direct the machine, which would do all the killing.

'Don't think,' the flight instructor had thundered at him a hundred times. 'React! Kill the bastard! Practise until you can do it in your sleep! Practise until it becomes as much a part of you as breathing, because, if you don't, in a week, a month, or a year, he will return in another machine to kill *you*.' Obviously the Germans taught their pilots the same way.

It was raining as the train left Croydon but had stopped by the time Thorne reached London. Victoria was crowded and he pushed his way through the queues and went out into the soft spring air and walked up Elizabeth Street to Kings Road, busy with traffic in spite of petrol rationing. The flat he rented in Cadogan Lane with three other pilots was cold and empty and a half-empty whisky bottle stood on the side bar. Thorne poured a drink, then pushed the blackout curtains aside and opened a window. The hissing roar of London came in with a trace of coal smoke; like some pensioner he thought, still feeling the chill of winter. Britain was already on Summer Time, had been since February, and in spite of the late hour, the sky was not yet completely dark. Restless, he turned away from the window and gulped the whisky. He was drinking too damned much lately and he needed a woman, badly.

Shirley slipped into his mind and he was surprised that he should think of her. He hadn't heard a word from or about her since that night at the Plaza. His father though was incredibly angry. A single letter had contained the same dreary accusations of irresponsibility and undisciplined behaviour and he had thrown it away without finishing it. There had been none since. But he had not dismissed the charges quite so easily. His father was partly right, perhaps not as far as Shirley was concerned, but there had been enough other incidents to warrant his father's accusations. That damned girl, for instance. She may not have been pregnant, but he sure as hell had slept with her.

Thorne was surprised that he had finished the whisky. There were plenty of empties in the wastebasket – what did the British call them, dustbins – but not another drop in the flat. He wanted to get squiffed, he decided. Another Britishism, 'squiff'. Squiffed hell, he wanted to get falling-down drunk.

The bar of the hotel on Draycott Place was crowded for a Tuesday evening. Tuesday, for Christ's sake! He had flown the Hudson to France on Sunday! The bartender brought him a double scotch and he drank it slowly, determined to make it last. One drink per twenty minutes, he decided, and he would have the barman leave the glasses so that he could check his progress by the clock.

'Playin' soldier?'

The woman smiled at him. She wore a red slash of lipstick and her makeup was applied in layers to conceal a mild case of acne. Her hair was done in the latest rolled pompadour style and her sheath dress was cut low. She had applied makeup to her breasts as well – the white lace edging of her bodice was tinted orange – but for all that, she was pretty enough.

He nodded at the glasses. 'Sure am.'

'May I help?'

Thorne patted the stool beside him and summoned the barman. The next twenty minutes weren't up yet, but what the hell, he had company hadn't he?

He bought her drinks until she was giggly. By the fifth round, she had draped an arm around his shoulder and moved closer so that one breast was pressed against his arm. 'My name is Mona,' she confided. 'Me Mum always liked the Mona Lisa. Dad took her to Paris once and they went to the Louvre.' She pronounced it *Loover*.

The hotel bar closed at midnight and Thorne paid the tab and added a generous tip. Outside, it was raining again. The misty quality of the night was sensuous and Mona invited herself to his flat. Glimmer lights were few, just enough to show mud-splashed white paint on the curbs. Mona wore one of the luminous plastic flowers the street vendors sold for a sixpence but it was barely visible as she had broken two petals off.

They were soaked by the time they reached the flat. Thorne lit the gas jet in the fireplace and sat down unexpectedly on the carpet. His expression was so comical that Mona burst into laughter.

'You ought to get out of those wet clothes,' he said slyly, 'before you catch cold.'

She agreed readily and turned so that he could undo the buttons. He fumbled at each one, making a production of it, helped her slide the dress down and quickly undid her bra.

'Oh, but you're the quick one,' she murmured, nestling against him as he cupped her breasts and buried his lips against her neck. 'You're all wet too. Fair's fair.'

The fire cast an orange glow that obscured her makeup and youth. She knelt before him, lips parted, eyes wide, waiting, and he thought, she is probably a lot more experienced than he had been at that age. The hell with how old she is – so long as she's not jail bait.

'What a horrible bruise,' she murmured, drawing a finger along his ribs. 'How. . . .?'

'Never mind.' He drew her to him so that they were kneeling facing one another and kissed her as her distended nipples brushed his chest. She stood and removed her slip and panties and he nuzzled the soft flesh of her thighs, ignoring the odour of perspiration and cheap perfume. The area before the fireplace was warm and he laid her back on the rug with a sofa pillow beneath her hips but when he knelt between her legs, he was astonished to discover that he was limp.

Mona pushed against him but there was no response and he sat back on his heels, staring at himself then at her.

'For God's sake!' Mona raised herself on one elbow and laughed. 'Damn you! Are you a Nancy boy?'

She reached but he knocked her hand away.

Mona grabbed at him again. 'Can't get the poor soldier to stand to attention, can you? You let Mona help.'

Thorne pushed himself up and staggered against the couch, revolted. She was an underage tart, little better than a whore, and drunk as well and she smelled as if she hadn't had a bath in a week, but had doused herself in cheap perfume and half a pound of face powder and lipstick instead. And he was even worse, so drunk that he couldn't even. . . . Thorne staggered into the bathroom and vomited. Twice, three times, his stomach heaved and regurgitated two days' worth of steady drinking that had begun in the officers' mess at Abbeville.

When the spasm subsided, he washed his face and brushed his teeth to remove the foul, acid taste. With a towel wrapped about his waist, he went into the living room, holding on to walls and furniture to steady objects that tended to spin away. Mona was sprawled on her back in front of the fire. Passed out, he supposed.

311

Saliva trickled down her cheek and he knelt shakily and used his shirt to wipe it away.

She was pretty enough. The severely rolled pompadour that made her look like a cartoonist's version of a movie starlet, had come undone and her brown hair was spread about her shoulders. One knee was lifted and turned slightly inward and one hand lay across her stomach. For a moment, she looked like a sleeping child; but only for a moment. Her lipstick-smeared mouth and full breasts destroyed the illusion.

God, but he was drunk. He closed his eyes and lost his balance. He couldn't leave her here. She would catch pneumonia, and he never knew when one of the others might come in. Thorne got one hand under her back, the other under her knees and struggled to his feet, grunting with her weight. By leaning against the couch with his hip, he managed to steady himself. He gained a firm grip but the room stretched away so that the door to the bedrooms appeared miles off. The worst stretch, he thought; nothing to lean against. One step at a time, like a tightrope walker – instead of a pole he carried a naked girl. The thought made him giggle. The hall was easier; there were walls to lean against and he made it into his room.

Mona disappeared before he woke. Thorne staggered into the bathroom shortly after ten. Ten pounds was gone from his wallet – expensive, he thought ruefully, for nothing, and he was embarrassed all over again at his lack of performance.

The flat smelled of damp and old whisky and rain fell steadily. Four aspirins and two cups of coffee made him feel human again. The flat's chief attraction had been the fact that from the kitchen, sitting-room and his bedroom, one could look out over a nicely kept garden which was alive again after the long winter.

He sat in his room and ignored the arrival of another pilot who banged on his door. Thorne was humiliated by his failure with the girl; nothing like that had ever happened to him before and now that it had, he was reminded that he was thirty years old and time was slipping past quickly. Too damned quickly.

He had experienced periods of depression before. But this time, it ran much deeper. Twice the Nazis had tried to kill him and he thought of the fat general behind the table in the Warsaw garden, and of the SS officer smiling as he motioned for the soldiers to shoot Deborah. Now a German pilot had not been content with merely shooting down his aircraft, but had wanted to make certain that he was dead as well.

An opalescent light spread though the rain cloud and everything below was clearly, but softly, delineated. The new green of leaves

312

glowed vividly and tree trunks were solid bars of dark colour. A bus slipped past a break in the trees, a placard advertising Typhoo Tea and Littlewoods glowing on its orange-red side.

His father's accusations of indifference and indiscipline were on the mark. He was, of course, referring to the family business, but they applied to his life in general. And Harry was right as well, he decided. He was a rich man's son with no need to worry about anything. The image of Deborah's body lying beside the tracks in a Polish village – 'Vengeance is mine saith the Lord' – all he remembered from years of enforced Sunday school. Why should God have all the fun?

The following morning was clear and fresh. Thorne stopped outside the RAF recruiting office on Curzon Street, stubbed out his cigarette, straightened his tie and went inside. Twenty minutes later, he sat before a young officer who took constant notes as he described his previous training, his reasons for resigning from the United States Air Corps, the nearly five months spent ferrying aircraft to Canada or Great Britain, and his present desire to join the Royal Air Force.

The officer excused himself and a few minutes later, Thorne was escorted along a gloomy corridor to an unmarked office. Inside, an elderly man in RAF uniform with an insignia that he later would recognize as belonging to a Group Captain, read through the sheaf of notes while the young officer stood impassively to one side. The Group Captain glanced keenly at Thorne, then nodded. Ten minutes later, he was sworn in as a Pilot-Officer Candidate in the RAF Volunteer Reserve.

The desperate battles in France and the loss of Norway and Holland had caused the British to be a little less choosy, he decided.

On Thursday in the third week of May 1940, Keith Thorne stepped from the train in Cambridge with forty other recruits. They stood about the platform in the spring sunshine wondering what to do next. Some speculated about their training, others discussed the war. The attack on France had galvanized the country into a renewed war fever – the real thing this time, as a newspaper headline had proclaimed gleefully.

A Warrant Officer in blue battle dress stamped along the platform towards them.

'You will form two lines, tallest men to the ends,' he barked by way of greeting and Thorne, at five foot ten inches found himself near the end of the line. There was a great deal of laughter and horseplay as everyone found their place which the Warrant Officer watched without comment.

'Right!' he shouted when the two lines had formed. 'You are now in His Majesty's Royal Air Force. This country is at war. You can, and will, be shot for cowardice, desertion, or dereliction of duty.'

A sudden silence enveloped the recruits. The Warrant Officer went on briskly. 'Government can and will do things in wartime that would never be allowed in peace-time. Serious business, war. Therefore, no more larking about.' He peered at each man, as if to memorize his face in case of escape.

'Right, then. On my command, you will all turn to the left,' he pointed, 'and on the next command, you will march forward, left foot first. If I say, right turn, you will take exactly two further paces and change direction to your right,' he pointed again. 'If I say left turn, you will take two further paces and change direction to your left. If I say halt, you will take exactly two further paces and stop.'

They marched off the platform in reasonable order and the Warrant Officer paced them through the town, calling the cadence in a steady voice until he was certain they were into the rhythm. Parties of this sort had apparently become a familiar sight in Cambridge as they only attracted the attention of a few small children who ran to the curb, yelling with excitement.

Thorne had expected a week or two to pass before receiving orders to report but they had arrived in the afternoon post the day after he volunteered. He was given twelve hours to report to an RAF base near Cambridge called Marshalls. He had also expected a week's classroom work at most, to familiarize him with RAF practices and procedures, followed by a week or so of brush-up flying before he was sent to an operational unit. Yet day after day, in spite of his protests, he was forced to plod along at the same rate as the rawest recruit who had ever set foot inside an aircraft.

He held his temper until the morning they were introduced to an ancient biplane trainer known as the Tiger Moth. Thorne grimly requested permission to speak.

The flight instructor, an ageing, balding officer who had flown in World War I when the RAF was known as the Royal Flying Corps, nodded.

'Sir, I served four and a half years in the USAAC. I am a trained pilot and have qualified in both pursuit and bomber aircraft. It is a waste of time and money to have me start all over from the beginning in this . . . this kite,' he gestured at the Tiger Moth. 'I should be sent on to advanced training so as not to waste your time nor that of the rest of these men.'

'Mr Thorne,' the instructor peered at the name tag sewn to Thorne's overalls. We are most familiar with your "service record".

However, this is not the USAAC but the Royal Air Force. Resume your place in line.'

Thorne's face reddened and sniggers sounded behind him.

The instructor went on as if there had been no interruption. 'Gentlemen, this is an aeroplane. This is the wing. This. . . .'

The amused tolerance shown him because of his age and nationality by the other pilot candidates evaporated with that incident. They saw his demand for advanced training as a plea for special favours but Thorne did not care, wanting to finish this ridiculous charade.

He made two flights with the instructor, listening carelessly to what he was told. After the second flight, the instructor climbed out of the cockpit.

'Make one circuit of the field at five hundred feet, Mr Thorne. Fly the standard approach.'

The Tiger Moth was amazingly responsive for a trainer and Thorne experienced the natural pilot's affinity for a good aircraft. Irritated at the attitude of the RAF in general, and the instructors' in particular, he took off as instructed, flew the requisite leg around the field, then yanked the nose up and climbed to ten thousand feet, winged over and dropped, laughing like a madman at the sudden surge of freedom that came with the sharp whistle of air past the tiny plexiglass windscreen.

He pulled out of the dive at five hundred feet and swooped upward again, rolled once, twice and a third time to a thousand feet and completed with a wing-over that dropped him within touching distance of the ground. He flew the Tiger Moth sedately around the field again, amused to see that red-crash trucks were racing out to meet him. His landing was a perfect three point within the turnaround zone and he taxied towards the hangar where his instructor was waiting with folded arms. A few of his squadron mates were standing beside the hangar door waiting for their turn and as he brought the aircraft to a stop and switched off, they surprised him by turning their backs.

'Mr Thorne,' the instructor said without inflection when Thorne climbed down, 'can you repeat the instructions I gave you?'

Thorne pulled the leather flying helmet off and ran fingers though his hair, still grinning. 'Yes sir. Fly one circuit around the field and make a standard approach.'

'Then you disobeyed orders, did you not?'

'Yes, sir!'

'You are confined to your quarters, except for duty and instruction, for ten days. You will sign in and out with the squadron clerk and you will hold yourself ready for extra duty at all times.'

Thorne took a deep breath. He had expected to be chewed out, not treated like a raw recruit. 'Sir, may I emphasize that I. . . .'

'You may not,' the instructor said calmly. He hesitated, then stepped forward so that he could speak without being overheard by the other trainees.

'Mr Thorne, what you did was worse than foolish; it was dangerous. As an experienced officer, you know as well as I the need for discipline at all times. The RAF is well aware that you are a trained pilot. It was not necessary to demonstrate that fact in a training aircraft.'

'It seems it is, sir. I'm trying to show that the RAF is wasting time and money on me. There must be hundreds like me.'

The instructor snorted in exasperation. 'I am sure there are, Mr Thorne. Just as I am sure you are an excellent pilot, perhaps a better pilot than I. But your childish attitude, Mr Thorne, only demonstrates your lack of maturity. Not only did you jeopardize a scarce war resource, but your display of flying bravado in an aircraft not suitable for such manoeuvres could very well encourage other trainees to attempt the same, with disastrous results. I do not know the philosophy of the USAAC, Mr Thorne, but in the RAF we train pilots who, as officers, are leaders and not foolhardy exhibitionists. That, Mr Thorne, requires discipline. You are dismissed to your quarters, sir.'

The restrictive discipline of flight training school did have one positive benefit; his drinking diminished to a reasonable level. It wasn't until his permanent headache began to ease and then disappeared that it even occurred to him that he had been drinking excessively.

In spite of his constant complaints, his training was accelerated so that in mid-June, Thorne finished training at Marshalls and was transferred to Sealand, near Chester for advanced training. Eight weeks had been enough to turn the war into a disaster for France and Great Britain. Germany had overrun Norway and Denmark, the Netherlands and Belgium. France was on the verge of capitulation as German tanks converged on Paris. Nazi U-boats were moving into new ports along the Atlantic coasts of the newly occupied countries and the Battle of the North Atlantic had begun in earnest as shipping losses sky-rocketed.

The Allied retreat at Dunkirk started an invasion scare. All during the summer of 1940, farmers armed with shotguns and even ancient smooth-bore muzzle loaders, patrolled fields twenty-four hours a day, watching for parachutists. An appeal to the United States for weapons to arm the Local Defence Volunteers to repulse the anticipated invasion resulted in the collection of millions of privately-owned rifles, shotguns, pistols and revolvers – 99 per cent of which were never used and would eventually be melted down for scrap. Convoys of ill-armed LDVs in oversized denim overalls careened along the roads, a greater menace to themselves than to any potential invader.

On a particularly boring cross-country training flight one day, Thorne amused himself by flying low over a party of schoolboys digging an anti-tank ditch across a cricket-pitch. On his second pass, the groundsman ran out and fired a shotgun at him. A twelve-bore shotgun has an effective range of less than thirty yards; even so, Thorne climbed quickly for altitude as the schoolboys cheered and threw stones. The groundsman let go a final blast.

The training squadrons gathered each evening in the mess to hear the BBC news read by Alvar Liddell at nine o'clock. The war news seemed to worsen each night but afterwards, J. B. Priestley, with a turn of phrase to match Churchill's, narrated homey bits of gossip gathered about the country, and managed to put it all in perspective. The entire experience reminded Thorne of the spirit he had seen develop in Warsaw. Aggression, he began to suspect, promoted defiance rather than fear.

At Sealand, Thorne's reputation as a trouble-maker dogged him. His constant complaints and demands for abbreviated training alienated everyone but, by now, frustration had taken him past the point of caring. Luftwaffe attacks on coastal shipping and on operational bases in south-east England had increased in ferocity and the frustration of not being able to hunt the killers, as he thought of them, was unbearable.

He had been scheduled for the first of three cross-country night flights during the last week of June and the night flying instructor placed him last in retaliation for the manner in which he had corrected a blackboard navigational calculation in class. They were barely civil to one another as the lorry drove them along the flight line to where the Miles Master was warming up.

After a derogatory comment about the training schedule, the instructor snarled, 'Thorne, I'm fed up with you. You are within inches of being washed out.'

Thorne laughed at him. 'For Christ's sake, I'm not some dumb kid you can push around with that kind of nonsense. If you think the RAF is going to let a trained military pilot fly a desk you're crazy. Wash me out and I'll demand a hearing so you can explain why you are wasting time and government money by retraining a trained pilot. Hell, I've probably made as many night cross-country flights as you have.'

'Damn it all, Thorne, that's not the point!'

'Then what the devil is? The British Army has been kicked out of every country in Europe. The Luftwaffe has a free ride over England because there aren't enough pilots and you keep me stewing in this hole, practising routines I can do in my sleep. Hell, I flew the North Atlantic sixteen times this winter! All I need is a familiarization. . . .'

' . . . course on a Spitfire and I'm ready.' The instructor finished wearily. 'The point, Mr Thorne, is that you lack discipline! Do you really expect us to trust you with an aeroplane worth ten thousand pounds if we cannot even depend on you to keep your mouth shut and do what you are told? There is a definite way of doing things in the Royal Air Force, just as in any military organization. You must learn to do it that way.'

Thorne was scheduled for a 2200 takeoff during the last of a long summer twilight. The past few days had been humid and quite hot and the air was full of moisture. A westerly wind mixed Liverpool soot with the haze and visibility at sunset had been less than two miles. Thorne knew that conditions were marginal at best and the flight should have been cancelled, but the instructor was too angry to do so. And Thorne was not about to ask.

The tower flashed a green light and he opened the throttle. The little single-wing trainer bounced along the grassy strip and was airborne. As he climbed for altitude, the landing field lights faded quickly into the haze even before they were turned off.

The murk was almost solid. He had been cleared to eight thousand feet and he climbed on, wondering where the ceiling really was. Not that it mattered as he was supposed to make an instrument flight. The simple rectangular course that had been outlined was a piece of cake under any circumstance.

Ten minutes after takeoff, he encountered freak winds. For several minutes, he was shaken and jolted from side to side and tossed up and down. A strong gust caught him broadside, flipping a wing up sharply so that he fell into a wild spin. Thorne grinned and dragged the stick back against his chest; he had plenty of altitude and this was the sort of flying he liked.

He came out of the spin at three thousand and decided to forgo another attempt to climb above the cloud. Thorne checked the compass heading; he had turned onto the westerly and shortest leg moments before the winds caught him. The compass gave a southerly heading now and he corrected, wondering just how far he had been pushed by the winds. Ahead were the Clwydian Mountains – hardly mountains, he thought. More like hills. They hardly constituted a danger under normal circumstances.

He dragged his eyes from the murk beyond the canopy and concentrated on the comforting saffron glow of the red-lit instrument panel. For God's sake, he was making every novice mistake in the book. Keep your eyes inside, watch the instruments, ignore the seat of your pants. As soon as the thought formed, he felt the aircraft dip to port and fall off one wing, even though the horizon indicator remained rock steady. Thorne brushed a hand across his forehead and clenched and unclenched the muscles of his legs to drive blood to the brain for increased alertness.

The 715-horsepower Kestrel engine skipped a beat. Oil pressure, air speed, horizon indicator, temperature, fuel indicators all remained steady. He swore at his sudden nervousness and forced himself to relax as he studied the map clipped to his kneeboard. He had been airborne for twenty minutes – hell, the entire flight was supposed to last only twenty minutes! The west leg was to be the shortest as he was flying what amounted to a long rectangle. He must have been caught in the winds for close to nine minutes which at his cruising speed of 175 miles an hour meant that he could be anywhere within a circle roughly twenty-six miles in diameter. Commonsense suggested that deviations caused by the southerly winds would drive him several miles north of his course. So, he could be as far as fourteen miles further west than the farthest limit of his flight plan, or conversely, fourteen miles short. That's what he got for playing around instead of tending to business.

He could be as far north and west as Liverpool Bay, the River Dee mouth or even over the coast from north of Mold. Thorne made careful note of the time, 2223, and began a gentle turn north while losing altitude at the rate of four hundred feet per minute. If he was correct, he should come out of the overcast at six hundred feet, somewhere over the peninsula jutting into Liverpool Bay between the Dee and Merseyside.

At 2231, the overcast began to break up and suddenly, a dark span of countryside was below, and Thorne cursed. He had forgotten about the blackout. The countryside was as featureless as the murk.

Well off his port wing, he spotted the gleam of water – Dee or Liverpool Bay? He altered course and dropped lower to cross the coast at three hundred feet. The horizon was hidden by the haze and he could not tell which body of water it was.

The River Dee flowed out to the Irish Sea through a narrow corridor formed by Wales to the south and England to the north. Without lights to distinguish the sprawl of Liverpool, he was little better off – except he now had a place to ditch the aircraft, if necessary. The memory of the B-17 and the Lockheed Hudson crashes intruded and he shook his head in exasperation, and fear. He had two strikes against him already.

He glanced at the map again; the principal difference between the Dee and the Mersey was their shape. The Dee ran arrow straight nearly to Chester while the Mersey's course was roughly crescent in shape.

Thorne laughed at the simple solution and turned to follow the coast. After minutes he knew he was entering the River Dee as the shoreline tended straightaway south-south-east. Feeble traces of moonlight penetrated the haze and provided just enough light for him to pick out gross objects. He turned onto a more easterly heading. The empty spaces below became an industrial complex of factories and gasworks and he climbed to avoid smokestacks. The river had narrowed to a thin line now and on the south bank the sprawl of Connah's Quay and Shotney were barely visible. Thorne relaxed. He had a choice of two landing fields now, Hawarden to the south or Sealands across the river.

He began a gentle turn to the north-east after passing the bridge at Queensferry and the familiar buildings of Waterloo Farm. A few moments later, the flare path blazed on as listening devices picked up the sound of his engine.

Thorne was sitting on the grass some distance from the Miles Master, smoking when the old Ford belonging to the night flying instructor roared up and he and two other instructors got out and ran to him. Thorne stubbed the cigarette out and in response to their nervous questions, told the entire story, holding nothing back, including his momentary panic.

When he finished, he looked at the three men in the strengthening moonlight. 'I think,' he said quietly, 'I should apologize for my behaviour these past few weeks. I'm not as ready as I thought I was.'

A la guerre les trois quarts sont des affaires morales

Napoleon to St Cloud

Occupied France 15 – 18 July 1940

Travelling west from Berlin, Torsten Fredriksson felt that he had crossed into another world. Except for an abundance of uniforms aboard the train, there was no other evidence that the world had been turned upside down by Nazi tanks and soldiers who had swept across western Europe in six weeks.

No military convoys patrolled the roads in either Germany or France and the customs officials had been no more difficult than in peacetime. The stores in Berlin were as full of goods as those in Stockholm – a decided contrast to London in early June when the first signs of severe rationing were becoming apparent. A shopkeeper had asked for the cardboard packet when he bought cigarettes, to use again. The statue of Eros had been removed from Piccadilly for safekeeping and, at night, the huge junction seemed to belong to a desolated planet without its blazing lights. In England, armed troops were everywhere and contingents of ageing men had been organized into a Local Defence Force and stumped about the countryside armed with a motley collection of weaponry.

In contrast to what he saw on the continent now that the fighting was over, England had been gripped by war hysteria. The Government seemed to be arresting anyone who disagreed in the slightest with their policies – on either the right or the left – he had been told. Fascists, Communists and even a farmer who had cursed Local Defence Volunteers for trampling his grain had been imprisoned. Just the week previously, the British merchant ship *Arandora Star* had been sunk off the coast of Ireland with the loss of eight hundred people, many of them enemy aliens being deported to Canada. Some of those enemy aliens had been Jewish refugees from Germany and Austria.

France had fallen in six weeks, finally, utterly, ingloriously and now German soldiers idled about Paris unarmed, hands in pockets and gawking like the tourists whose places they had taken. They wandered past the stalls of Montmartre, clogged the halls of the Louvre, the Tuileries in Vincennes and the elevators and restaurants of the Eiffel Tower and the parks and walks along the Seine. Like the healthy young men they were, they eyed the girls swinging along the boulevards in short cotton or rayon summer dresses and were examined carefully in exchange.

He took a table at a sidewalk café on the Boulevard des Capucines to enjoy the cool morning. He had slept late, bathed, dressed and gone for a morning walk in search of breakfast and impressions and found Paris little changed.

A somnambulant waiter brought him an exquisite omelet and a small glass of red wine. The pleasing aroma of chestnut trees was strong now that the Occupation had ended private motor traffic and the stench of petrol fumes had disappeared. German soldiers strolled past, boys really, with short cropped hair and bare necks. Their uniforms seemed a bit too big and they acted with the false bravado of adolescents, unaware as yet of how overpowering Paris was and that the Parisians were well-versed in the art of putting foreigners in their place. One soldier called to him, obviously mistaking his blond hair and square face for that of a fellow countryman. Fredriksson shrugged and waved a hand at his ear, a very Parisian gesture indicating that he did not understand, or did not wish to understand.

'*Boche merde,*' he muttered for the hovering waiter's benefit, and added a few choice French obscenities.

The German boys did not understand French nor had they yet learned the implication of the gesture as they grinned good-naturedly and strolled on.

He finished the omelet and checked the train schedule issued by the Occupation authorities. With their usual efficiency, the Germans had revised all French railway schedules to assist in the movement of German troops, even before the invasion.

The invitation from the German Embassy in Stockholm had been a surprise and invited him to call at his convenience. He had tossed it into the wastebasket, thinking that he hadn't the time to waste kicking his heels outside some bureaucrat's office just for another propaganda handout.

Then a week later the Embassy press attaché telephoned personally to invite him to lunch. Reluctantly, he had agreed and they had met that afternoon at the Grand Hotel.

'We have read with interest your stories about your experiences in France and England, Herr Fredriksson,' the press attaché had begun immediately. 'We in Germany are concerned that you are presenting an unfair picture of the war by reporting only the side of the Allied powers.'

Fredriksson shrugged. 'That's not my fault. I've applied several times to your Government for press credentials and each time, they've been refused.'

The attaché nodded. 'A regrettable mistake. Actually, a clerical error.'

Fredriksson touched his lips with the napkin. 'Herr Doctor Kann, I am very busy these days and the Allied Governments have been most cooperative. My reports have been censored certainly, but only to eliminate information that would have had tactical value to their enemy. In each case, I have been given the opportunity to remove the offending portions voluntarily.'

He held up a hand to forestall Kann's protest. 'I know full well why your people have refused to grant me press credentials. Last summer I wrote several articles about troop build-ups along the Polish border. Even though Germany did not bother to disguise those troop movements, when the first article appeared I was approached by a member of your Embassy and asked to stop writing "inflammatory and inaccurate propaganda". Of course I refused.' Fredriksson gave Kann a thin smile.

'I'm afraid that your Government's policy is in conflict with my belief in a free press. Perhaps you could find someone more sympathetic to your views?'

Kann twisted the wine-glass stem between his fingers. Fredriksson had first met him five years before in Berlin, when Kann had been a stringer for a Munich daily. Now he was the press attaché in the Stockholm Embassy. In the interval, he had acquired thirty kilogrammes of excess weight, a smooth personality and a fanatical devotion to the Nazi Party. He wore a gold Party badge in his lapel and a red and black armband on the sleeve of his expensive, and no doubt, English tailored, summer suit. And he looked exactly like what he was: the embodiment of the self-satisfied German bureaucrat riding the crest.

'My dear Fredriksson, I do not dispute what you say for one moment. I also know that any protest I might make about concealing military intentions was, in our eyes, justified, if not in yours. I suppose if I were still on your side of the fence, I would feel as you do.' He smiled candidly.

'Times are changing. Germany has been successful beyond our wildest dreams. A new order has arisen in Europe and there is no longer a need for such secrecy. You will see. Germany, the Greater German Reich, will become an open book to qualified journalists such as yourself. It is now time to show the world what we have accomplished and to prove that we are not nearly so bad as English propaganda portrays us.'

'Am I to assume that I am being invited to tour Occupied Europe?'

Kann feigned distress at the question. 'Please, my dear Fredriksson, the Occupation is a temporary expedient. When the war is settled, German troops will be withdrawn. So yes, you are being invited to tour the Reich and our new allies, France and Belgium.' Even though they were speaking Swedish, Fredriksson was amused to note that Kann used the German names, *Frankreich* and *Belgien*.

'The invitation will be issued by Herr Minister Goebbel's office and will carry his personal signature – your guarantee of access to anything you wish to see. The Ministry will arrange an escorted tour in first-class comfort,' he eyed Fredriksson, barely concealing his smirk. 'Of course, the Reich will assume all costs.'

Fredriksson shook his head. 'If I accept your invitation, I travel alone and pay my own costs. That way, there can never be any accusation of undue influence. If I go, I will be free to travel when and where I wish. I will submit my stories for military censorship only.' Fredriksson stood. 'I will need such an agreement in writing from your people. When I have it, I must then see what, if any, interest there would be in such a story.'

Kann's disappointment was swiftly concealed with a strained smile. He had obviously expected him to jump at the chance. Good, Fredriksson thought. Let them understand they were doing him no favours. It had been the same with the British.

'I will relay your conditions to Berlin immediately.' Kann stood up and faced him across the table. 'I would advise you not to wait too long, Herr Fredriksson. Herr Goebbels is not a patient man, even for a journalist of your reputation.'

Of course he had accepted, as they had known he would. But he had won his concessions. His reputation for strictly neutral reporting was well-known and they needed him as much as he needed them. Virtually the only news from Occupied Europe came from Germany's various propaganda organs or from Italian news services whose objectivity was questionable. In the United States, the New York *Times* jumped at the story as did the Hearst syndicate. His readership in Sweden, North America and Great Britain tripled within three days to more than four hundred subscribers. No other European journalist had ever managed such a wide readership. He even picked up a Japanese newspaper, the Tokyo *Ashai Shimbun*.

A traffic policeman darted into the road, blowing his shrill whistle. The sparse traffic stopped and Fredriksson heard the whoop-whoop of a siren. A moment later, two black Mercedes automobiles wheeled around the corner and accelerated along the boulevard. People rushed to the sidewalks to stare and Fredriksson followed. As the last car passed he saw a man in black uniform inside, studying a sheaf of papers. Expressions of anger were on every French face and the four young soldiers who had followed everyone else to the curb, were suddenly isolated. Several people went out of their way to walk around them in an elaborate manner.

325

Fredriksson returned to his table as the waiter cleared away the omelet dish. He dropped a ten-franc note on the table and picked up his paper.

'What was that about?' The waiter slipped the note into his pocket quickly and glanced at the street. His mouth twisted into one bitter word.

'Gestapo.'

Fredriksson paused outside the well-kept mansion at 8, rue Balny Auricourt that had been subdivided into flats before the turn of the century. Everything looked normal enough, he thought, but so did all Paris for that matter. He pushed into a well-scrubbed lobby that smelled of disinfectant and polishing wax and pushed the buzzer above the engraved calling card marked 'Mme Jeanette Rodale'.

'Who is it?'

'Torsten Fredriksson.'

'Torsten!' the speaker squealed and the buzzer sounded instantly. He went up three flights of stairs to find Jeanette waiting for him at the door. She hugged and kissed him soundly.

'That damned climb,' he wheezed when she let him go, half suffocated. 'Why don't you move to a building with an elevator?'

Jeanette laughed and drew him into the living-room decorated in the Bauhaus style, a severely modern room but amazingly comfortable. A bright Finnish rug of red and blue wools covered half the polished wood floor and the walls were hung with her paintings. Fredriksson had once told her that by starting at the door to the flat and touring in a clockwise fashion, it was possible to view her development as an artist – from the severe realism of her artschool days through the various periods of the last hundred years to her present pre-occupation with surrealism.

'I see you are still painting watches that drip and ladies engaged in sexual conduct with geese and snakes,' he observed sourly.

Jeanette laughed and pushed him into a Barcelona chair and disappeared into the kitchen. Her parents had been extremely wealthy and, when they died in a train accident several years before, she, as the only child, had inherited everything – which included several large companies, extensive real estate holdings in Metropolitan France and North Africa as well as a good deal of land in the United States. She had once told Fredriksson that her income amounted to eighty million francs a year – or more. She wasn't really sure. 'But I will find out, of course, once you promise to marry me.'

She returned with a tray of sliced cheeses and a bottle of wine and knelt at a small table beside the chair and poured. Torsten raised his glass to her in silent toast.

Four years ago, they had been lovers. He had worked for Reuter's then and was stationed in Paris. They had met at a showing of her work. Fredriksson had panned the exhibition and when they next met, at a party, she had ignored him completely, refusing even to be introduced.

Challenged, he had sent a dozen roses in apology and wrote an article for *Paris Soir* praising her earlier work. Still no response and so he sent two dozen roses and a bottle of champagne. In turn, he received a telephone call late one evening to thank him. Before being transferred to Tokyo six months later, they had come within a hair's breadth of marriage. Only at the last moment had both decided that their respective styles of living were totally incompatible.

Jeanette was the archetypal free spirit. She required total independence which, fortunately enough, her wealth and talent provided. Fredriksson, likewise, was incapable of giving up his nomadic way of life and even, he suspected, of remaining faithful to one woman for long. In the end, they had agreed to remain lovers but without claim on one another – he would appear at her flat in Paris or she would fly to Stockholm when the need demanded. It had become a satisfactory relationship for both.

'How long will you be staying?'

'I'm not certain. I've been cajoled by your new masters into doing a review of their occupation policies. It could take a few days or a few months. I have the impression I'm to stay until I get the story right.'

'Our new masters? Is that the way you see the Boche?'

Fredriksson chuckled. 'What would you call them?'

Jeanette glared at him. 'France signed an armistice. We have retained our own Government. . . .'

'Hah! You retain that Government as long as it meets with Berlin's approval.' He tilted her chin. 'Darling, let's not talk about the Germans. Let's talk about us instead.' He kissed her again and she slipped onto his lap.

The bedroom was shrouded in twilight and Fredriksson guessed it was early evening. He could have raised his head to look at the clock's luminous dial but he didn't. Instead, he settled deeper into the feather mattress and thought about the warm softness of the woman beside him and the story she had told of her escapades during the two weeks Paris was in danger of becoming a war zone.

Jeanette, like many of her fellow citizens, had not believed that Germany could possibly win, until the disaster at Dunkirk. Even then, she, in company with the majority of her fellow citizens, had not become truly alarmed until the thirteenth of June, the day Paris was declared an open city.

By the fifteenth, the city was practically empty.

Her friends had been urging her to go for days but Jeanette had refused, confident that the French army would hold. 'Socialism,' she told them stoutly, 'is stronger than Fascism. When the Army and the Government realize that they are on the brink of destruction and that socialism in France is doomed, they will fight like lions!'

Fredriksson grinned into the twilight. For one so rich to be such an ardent socialist – and to see no contradiction in her position! She was fond of explaining that it was her inherited wealth that allowed her to live in ease, to paint and do whatever she wished.

'So, you see,' she would explain seriously, 'when the last vestiges of capitalism are disposed of, all people everywhere will enjoy the same benefits as I. The State will supply everything to everyone, rather than the stock market to a few.'

She greatly admired Lenin and was forever extolling the strides made by Russia in the past twenty years – quoting, of course, from the latest Communist publication – and she dismissed the purges as nothing more than capitalist propaganda. Fredriksson had made it a practice never to contradict political or religious beliefs in others and he certainly was not about to begin with her. In any event, discounting her interpretations, Jeanette's political philosophy matched his own closely, although he liked to think of himself as being far too sceptical to be taken in by left-wing rhetoric.

Jeanette had finally succumbed to the general panic that emptied Paris of four-fifths of its population.

Rumours of German rape and pillage were racing through the city and the ease with which the enemy had penetrated the Maginot Line was the deciding factor. She packed her jewellery, a large sheaf of francs, a portable easel, paint box, several canvasses and sketch book, two changes of casual clothing, underwear and a single evening gown and slippers and set out with a girl friend in her Peugeot. They got as far as Chartres by midnight where they spent the night in the car in the midst of a refugee encampment.

'I must admit, Torsten,' she said ruefully, 'it was my first experience with, well, people. Real people. The common people as they have been termed. I had no idea they were so noisy, and unwashed.'

'Darling, most of them had been walking all day, probably carrying children or belongings. Anyone would be unwashed in those circumstances.'

'Perhaps,' she said doubtfully. 'But they kept staring at us, as we drove past. As if they hated us.'

Fredriksson chuckled. 'Reverse the circumstances, Jeanette. How would you feel if two young ladies in a very large and expensive automobile rode past while you pushed your belongings in a cart, your wife carried a child and probably a suitcase as well and you hadn't the least idea where to spend the night or even how to find something for your family to eat.'

The question went unanswered as another incident occurred to her. 'An airplane shot at us and killed some people. It was horrible. There was no need. The people were not soldiers and we were running away. Yet, every time the airplanes came, they killed people with machine guns and bombs.'

Fredriksson glanced at her; Jeanette's expression was a mixture of puzzlement and anger. Why, she really doesn't understand, he thought.

'They shoot at people to create confusion,' he tried to explain.

Jeanette muttered an expletive and pushed herself into a kneeling position. Fredriksson knew that other than a few Communist tracts or pamphlets on socialism, her only reading matter was a steady diet of books describing the real and imagined ills of French society and government. Jeanette knew almost nothing of the world outside her severely restricted circle of artists, actors and hangers-on and they were hardly the type of people to encourage hard, unemotional thinking.

'The object of war is to dispose of the enemy as efficiently as possible,' he tried anyway. 'When they shoot and bomb civilian refugees, the German pilots are merely aiding *their* war effort by spreading panic and terror which hampers the fighting forces and the productive capacity of French industry. The idea is to end the war as quickly as possible and thus save lives.'

'How horrible,' she said softly. 'How horrible that one human being could treat another so. And why? What has France ever done to Germany?'

Fredriksson laughed and took one of her hands, surprised to find how cold it was. He kissed her fingers. 'Ignoring a hundred years or more of historical imperatives, it comes down to this: France occupies land Germany needs for expansion. French industry turns out goods that compete with German goods. France does not agree that Germany should dominate the European continent simply because France believes she should do so. Just as France and England fought for a thousand years to dominate this continent, now France and Germany struggle against one another. In 1871, Germany was victorious and imposed a humiliating settlement on France. In 1918, France was victorious and imposed a humiliating settlement on Germany. Now, it is Germany's turn once again.'

Jeanette's expression was sad, as if she had discovered something very disappointing in Fredriksson. He laughed and reached for her but she eluded his hands.

'Now wait, darling,' he protested. 'Just because I understand the modern military mind does not mean I agree with it. War is a horrible business. I know, as I've probably seen more war than most soldiers and certainly more than the politicians who send the young men off to die.'

'Then why do you defend them? Why do you defend the pilots who fly the airplanes who shoot down innocent civilians?'

'I am not defending them. I am merely trying to explain to you why they do so. It is not the fault of the soldier. He is given an order which must be obeyed on pain of death.'

She shook her head stubbornly. 'No. You defend them! They may be soldiers but they are also rational, thinking human beings and as such they will know that it is wrong to murder unarmed civilians! Can they not make a choice? Can they not refuse to obey an order that is clearly wrong?

'Look here, Jeanette, I understand that you are upset over what happened on the roads. I've seen it myself, in China, in Spain and Poland. But you cannot blame a soldier for the actions and decisions of his leaders! A soldier is told to kill the enemy and knows that if he refuses, he will be shot and so he follows orders. If the situation were reversed, if those pilots had been French and flying over German roads, they would do the same. The soldier is not the murderer; it is his military and political leaders who give such orders, that are.'

'Torsten, that is ridiculous!' she scorned him. 'If one follows your line of argument to a logical conclusion, one sees that only Hitler is guilty of criminal conduct as he claims to be the ultimate authority in Germany. Everyone below him is therefore guiltless, no matter their crimes.'

He nodded. 'Just so, Jeanette. The ancient Romans executed defeated generals on that premise. In the Middle Ages, captured military leaders were ransomed, the excuse being that a payment of money was reparation for their crime. In 1918, there was great pressure in France to execute the Kaiser as the source of Germany's guilt.'

'Quoting historical precedent does not make it any more correct,' she snapped. 'It is wrong to kill unarmed civilians no matter how you may rationalize it. And all those soldiers who obey Hitler's orders do, by their very acquiescence, maintain him in office and by doing so they agree and participate in his decisions and, therefore, are as guilty as he. And besides, no Frenchman, pilot or not, would kill an unarmed civilian, I am certain!'

He rubbed both hands across his face in humorous exasperation. *'Galen kvinna!'*

'Que'est-ce que c'est?'

'C'est le Suedois. Peu importe. . . .' he lunged, caught her off guard and smothered her protests with kisses and caresses until she stopped struggling. Jeanette held her political and moral views – as fuzzy as they were – very deeply. But, first and foremost, she was still the most sensual little minx he had ever encountered.

The weather that first summer of the war was the finest in human memory. For days on end, warm sun beat down on the farmlands and cities of Europe – Fuehrer weather with a vengeance. Rain fell intermittently in gentle showers and the harvests across the continent exceeded all expectations.

Paris in July, 1940 could have been the Paris of July, 1904. Food was still relatively plentiful, the restaurants and shops were open and the Germans obtrusive only by their ubiquitous presence. And French soldiers were beginning to trickle home as they were released from prisoner-of-war camps. After the surrender of France, it seemed to Fredriksson that the war – with the exception of scattered instances of aerial combat and U-boat torpedoings – had ended. Speculation was rife concerning the final attack on Great Britain even as Prime Minister Churchill asserted over and over that they would never surrender. But the opinion in Berlin and Paris was that he would now have to negotiate.

Fredriksson spent two days in Paris with Jeanette. They made love in her apartment, walked along the Seine and talked about her coming to live with him in Stockholm. At first she abolutely refused to hear of it but by the time he was ready to leave, she had almost been persuaded.

He saw these two days as a healing time for her, though he tended to dismiss the real depth of her experiences during the 'evacuation'. Gradually, the entire story was told and he was able to visualize the masses of exhausted people clogging the roads and dispirited soldiers without weapons, a few armed men who took advantage of the chaos, the marauding Stukas. But perhaps the most vivid of all her impressions was that of a French officer in the turret of his Renault tank, leather crash helmet askew and pistol in one hand, weeping as he begged the refugees to get off the road and allow his column to pass.

'But the people no longer cared. He was nothing to them. France was nothing.' Apparently the war, he decided, had wakened some long-dormant strain of patriotism in her. But he doubted if it ran very deep.

He left the flat on Thursday morning, promising to return before

Sunday at the latest. He did not say anything to Jeanettte but the previous afternoon he had spoken with the Swedish consul and been assured that there would be no problem in obtaining a Swedish visa for her. He planned to spend the next few days marshalling his final arguments but he was confident enough of success to book two seats on the Monday train to Berlin.

Guines 20 – 30 July 1940

As the train ran swiftly out of Paris, Fredriksson was not surprised to see that it was filled with more German soldiers than French civilians. Most were enlisted men, many little more than boys, although scattered among them and wearing NCO's or officer's insignias were hard-eyed veterans with ribbons representing campaigns in the Rhineland, Austria, Czechoslovakia, Poland, Norway, Denmark, Belgium and Holland. Eight countries since 1936 – two countries per year. At this rate, Hitler would gobble up the entire world by 1986. Would Germany and Italy have fallen out before then? And the other dictatorship: Spain, the Soviet Union, Romania, Japan – a military dictatorship even if it pretended to a parliamentary system? Would they resist or join? The democracies were done for, he thought. They had been defeated or, like his native Sweden, cowed absolutely and the only remaining democracy that counted, the United States, was a joke. Their President huffed and puffed about neutrality while their Congress withdrew farther from reality with each month.

He had been granted permission to visit a forward Luftwaffe airbase where a few men of the German armed forces still engaged the enemy daily. Such a precedent was unheard of for a neutral reporter but then he had been selected for this junket because of his large following in the United States.

Somehow, he had developed the ability to explain the intricate, seemingly contradictory and implausible standards of European politics to Americans who, lacking the experience of existing cheek-by-jowl with quarrelsome neighbours for a thousand years, tended to be far less flexible in their approach to others.

When two European leaders met at Munich and agreed to divide up a sovereign country, Europe hailed it as a masterpiece of diplomacy. When one of those statesmen went home to declare 'peace in our time' he hoped for a breathing space of a year or two. The agreement was perfectly understandable to Europeans who had experienced at first hand the horrors of countless wars, the latest of which had devasted most of the continent only twenty years before. But Americans had only sniggered at one more example of European self-delusion. They knew Czechoslovakia was just more evidence of Hitler's ambitions. Europeans knew it as well but remained silent – and began to prepare for war. Great Britain increased her military budget and began to organize the civilian population. The French Government reviewed plans, purchased new aircraft from the United States and increased the size of the army. Europeans knew that to claim a war was inevitable only accelerated its juggernaut approach. Americans could say anything they wished as it would not be their land that would be devastated or their families that would be killed by the bombs and bullets. In fact, Fredriksson had written with a certain cynicism, Americans stood to gain from a European war. They would sell arms and munitions in vast quantities as they had done in 1914–16. Then in the last few months of the war, they might again send a token force to Europe and claim the lion's share of the victory after the other participants had bled themselves white for three years.

Fredriksson was met at the train station by a young officer wearing a Luftwaffe uniform without flying insignia who introduced himself as Oberleutnant Kurt Mahr, the public information officer. It was a very warm afternoon and the wind blowing through the open windows of the confiscated Renault was refreshing as they rattled along a dusty road. There wasn't a sign of war. Farmers worked their fields, children on school holiday played in the woods or yards or helped about the barns and kerchiefed women fed chickens, worked in gardens or hung glaring white clothes to dry. A somnambulant stillness lay over the countryside and nostalgia surged through Fredriksson as he was reminded of childhood summers spent on his grandparents' farm near Strängnäs.

The airfield at Guines was another matter and the contrasting reality of war was jolting. A massive Panzer IV tank painted Luftwaffe blue guarded the main gate. Armed sentries were everywhere. Their credentials were checked while they waited inside a guard house and the soldiers were polite, but distant. Driving onto the base, he was amazed at the quantity of anti-aircraft weapons in sandbagged emplacements and on the roofs of sturdier buildings.

'Yes,' the young officer smiled. 'We learn from British mistakes. We have two or three times as many anti-aircraft guns as they did and, consequently, they cannot strike at us as effectively as we did them.'

Fredriksson raised an eyebrow but the officer smiled. 'Please use that information in any article you write. It may discourage the English from attacking Guines – and save lives, on both sides.'

The Renault stopped before a white-washed building which Mahr told him was the operations room. 'Here, we have the headquarters of III *Gruppe*, *Jagdgeschwader 54*.'

All the windows were open but it was still quite warm inside the building. Fredriksson followed Lieutenant Mahr along a narrow corridor past opaque glass doors on which the previous occupant's names and titles, in French, had been covered over by hand-lettered signs in German. Fredriksson was led into an empty operations room. A large easel supported a map, covered with a white sheet, and rows of folding chairs were neatly aligned, each with a clean ashtray on the floor beneath.

'I believe a patrol from 3 *Staffel* will be returning shortly,' the officer remarked, glancing at his watch.

'*Staffel*? I'm not familiar with that term.'

'Perhaps it will be easier to explain the organization of our air forces by the use of a diagram,' Mahr said as he stepped to the blackboard. 'The air force is divided into four main air fleets – *Luftflotten*, in English, air fleets. Each fleet has an administrative branch – the *Luftgau*, and an operational branch – the *Fliergercorps*. There are usually two *Fliergercorps* associated with each fleet. A *Fliergercorps* is in turn divided into three *Geshwader* which can have as many as 120 aircraft. The *Geshwader* is further subdivided into *Gruppes* of between thirty and forty aircraft and each *Gruppe* consists of three *Staffeln*. If the *Staffel's* job is bombing, then it is composed of two *Rotes* of five or more aircraft each. A fighter *Staffel* is divided into four *Schwarm* of four aircraft each. It is a very logical subdivision that allows the commander at each level the maximum flexibility. On the tactical level, each *Schwarm* operates as a unit and flies so as to have complete visibility and still provide protection to one another. The British still insist on flying in large concentrations, very closely together and their pilots must spend as much time looking out for one another as for our fighters.'

Fredriksson nodded. 'I take it that 3 *Staffel* is part of III *Gruppe* then, which is equipped with fighter aircraft?'

'Yes. With the BF109E Messerschmitt aircraft, our best, in fact. The pilots have nicknamed it the Emile.' He peeked beneath a map cover, then a second and flipped the sheet back. 'Perhaps you would care to see where they have been?'

'You are allowed to tell me this?'

The officer nodded seriously. 'I have been instructed to show you anything you wish to see, short of those matters which are highly classified. My instructions are from the very highest authority.'

Was Goebbels keeping his word after all? he wondered. 'In that case, I would be very interested.'

The map showed the entire southern coast of England from Lands End around to the North Foreland. Numerous crayon marks indicated what he took to be airfields and coloured strings had been stretched between Guines and locations off the coast. A number was written in blue pencil on a square of paper pinned beside each string.

'These are the approximate positions of English coastal convoys, with estimated flying times. Such convoys are our main target today. The pilots look on them as great sport. You might say, as a way to keep their hands in.'

'For what? An invasion?' he asked sharply.

Mahr smiled. 'I understand you were in England last month. Surely you must have seen the defences they are erecting along their beaches.'

Fredriksson gave him a cold stare and Mahr hastened to apologize.

'I meant that only as a comment. Please do not assume I am trying to elicit information from you.'

The man was good, Fredriksson thought. Very good. He had never paid much attention to German intelligence methods; perhaps it was time he began. He fingered a strand of red wool.

'This coloured string tells me that a convoy south of Ramsgate is being watched. I assume that it will be attacked before it comes under the protection of British anti-aircraft guns?'

'That is correct. It is the hope of the German Armed Forces that by interdicting England's shipping, sufficient pressure will be placed on their economy to force the Government to sue for peace. The Greater German Reich will offer most generous terms, I can assure you. We are not a vindictive people.

'After all, how can she possibly resist to the end of the year?' Mahr's voice had the oily smoothness of an experienced salesman. 'The Commonwealth has proven reluctant to furnish more than token military support and the Americans won't have anything to do with propping up a decrepit British Empire.

'There are factions in the British Government that will soon kick Churchill out,' Mahr leaned close and all but whispered, subjecting Fredriksson to a blast of bad breath. 'They have powerful support, perhaps even as high as Buckingham Palace. After all, isn't the Royal Family of German extraction? Our most prominent *volks-deutsch*,' he laughed. 'You will see. This nonsense with Churchill will end soon. He must now recognize that Germany has conquered more territory in a shorter time than ever before in human history.' Beaming and hugely pleased with himself, Mahr ticked them off: 'Poland, twenty-seven days; Denmark, one; Norway, twenty-three; Holland, five; Belgium in eighteen; and France in thirty-nine.'

Fredriksson recognized Mahr's speech for what it was. He had heard it before in a slightly different guise while in Berlin. Yet, he wondered, how much truth was there to it? Germany's ability to insert, maintain and use fifth columnists had been well demonstrated in Czechoslovakia, Austria and Poland. There could be no doubt that Great Britain, all along Hitler's main target, was riddled with spies and saboteurs. Did they really possess strong support high in the Government? Had that been the reason behind Britain's massive sweep of arrests during the past month? Then too, there had been the disturbing wisps of rumour concerning the embittered Duke of Windsor. Hadn't he remained at La Croe, in the south of France, until it was almost too late. Certain of the rumours had it that the British Secret Service kidnapped him when he refused an order from his brother the King to leave.

Mahr cocked his head. 'I hear aircraft.'

They stepped out into the brilliant sunshine of late afternoon. The clear sky was deep blue, shading to browns near the horizon where summer dust was apparent. There was a wood on the far side of the airfield with hedgerows running at right angles to the trees. A sun glint caught his eye and he saw the barrel of an anti-aircraft gun protruding above the hedge. The space before the grassy flight line was filling with people who had also heard the familiar buzz of returning aircraft.

'There!' Mahr pointed and Fredriksson shaded his eyes. Four aircraft were descending from the sun, tiny black specks making an inordinate amount of noise, one lagging far behind the others. Wheels were down now and one after the other, three of the aircraft bumped onto the hard-packed surface and raced along the grassy strip. They turned just past the flight line and lumbered, tail down, towards their parking revetments – head-high open rectangles of sandbags.

Aircraft fitters raced to the three aircraft. Fredriksson saw the cockpit of the leading aircraft, identified by a red number "1" painted ahead of the national insignia – the *Staffelkapitan*, he supposed, pop open as soon as it had come to a halt. The pilot vaulted out clutching a pair of binoculars. Fredriksson heard him shout to another pilot.

The man pointed. Fredriksson squinted against the sun's glare and made out a thin trail of smoke from the last aircraft. An alarm bell rang at that instant and the fire trucks roared to life.

The aircraft was low, very low, Fredriksson thought. Thick white smoke abruptly spurted from the nose and he heard the word *glycol*, but it meant nothing to him. The firetrucks turned as the Messerschmitt crossed the end of the runway and raced after it.

Fredriksson held his breath. There wasn't a sound to be heard other than the strident fire bells and the rattling, uneven roar of the aircraft's engine and, incongruously, a lark. The aircraft wobbled. The pilot was clearly visible through the metal-barred canopy – a pale face beneath the brownish blob of the leather flying helmet.

Less than fifty feet above the runway, the engine began to howl and the propeller lurched to a stop. Instantly, the aircraft nosed down as if swatted by an invisible hand, cartwheeled and exploded.

The three pilots ran across the grass, lifejackets oddly cheerful against the red mass of flame shot through with smoke. They reached the burning aircraft just ahead of the fire trucks and one of the pilots had to be dragged away by two firemen. Foam poured from a nozzle to drench the wreckage and the fire was out in seconds. The foam, Fredriksson thought, with a journalist's perception, looked like a shroud.

Fredriksson was invited to the *Gruppe* mess that evening for dinner. The sun was low on the horizon and the French countryside glowed as the staff car drove away from his hotel.

They passed through a small village where an old man sat on a bench outside the local post office and smoked. Children, freed from onerous chores, dashed about the square. He saw one German soldier, cap off and tunic unbuttoned, sitting comfortably by himself at a roadside café, drinking a glass of wine and reading a newspaper. Again, Fredriksson had that strong impression that the war was over – until he remembered the young pilot who had died less than four hours ago.

The *Gruppe* had taken over a local 'great' house, two kilometres from the airfield. It was not a château by any means but a sprawling, whitewashed building constructed a hundred years ago in imitation of a country manor house.

The III *Gruppenkommandeur*, a thin man of medium height with a wide moustache and etched lines about his eyes, came to meet him. He had a pleasant voice and the manner of a professional politician.

'Herr Fredriksson, I am Oberstleutnant Franz Botha, at your service.' He clicked his heels and bowed slightly as he shook hands and Fredriksson did the same.

'It is a pleasure to have a distinguished Swedish journalist to visit.'

'A fellow Aryan, you mean?' Fredriksson probed as they strode up the path.

Botha laughed. 'Please. I leave that nonsense to the Party. I am a soldier.'

They went into the three-storey house and Fredriksson was impressed with the immaculate condition of the interior, not at all what he would have expected in a house commandeered by rowdy young men. He commented on the fact and Botha nodded.

'I enforce certain rules strictly. If damage is done to the house or its contents, the culprit's pay is docked until the item is repaired or replaced. We are, after all, guests in this country, and certainly in this house.'

Botha threw wide two carved walnut doors and ushered Fredriksson into a bright room filled with young men in summer white or dress blue Luftwaffe uniform. Someone shouted '*Achtung!*' The silence was instant and all eyes turned to the door.

'Gentlemen,' Botha announced, 'we have a dinner guest this evening, Herr Torsten Fredriksson, a distinguished journalist from Stockholm. We have been instructed to provide Herr Fredriksson our fullest cooperation. Our Government wishes the neutral nations of the world to see that we are not the two-headed monsters our British enemy have proclaimed us.'

A polite laugh rolled through the room just as a bell jangled. Botha rubbed his hands. 'Ah, dinner!' He bowed and escorted Fredriksson to the head of the long table and seated him on his right. The rest of the *Gruppe* pilots selected seats according to a precedence Fredriksson failed to detect. A door opened at the end of the room and a line of German enlisted men filed in, each with a tray holding a tureen of soup which Fredriksson found to be excellent.

The meal proceeded quickly. Apparently, it was the practice to eat in silence as no one spoke. Huge candle holders marched the length of the table and lent a distinctly medieval tone to the room, further heightened by dusty banners and weaponry decorating the walls. A carved sideboard dominated one side of the room while glass doors opened onto a wide sweep of lawn on the other.

He counted thirty-four men at the dining table. Near the centre, one place had been set but remained empty, and Fredriksson's eyes were drawn again and again to the empty chair. When the apple compôte desert was served, Botha leaned towards him.

'I see you are wondering about the empty chair. It belonged to the pilot who was killed today, Leutnant Otto Hans. It is our practice to set a place for dinner the day an aviator dies, out of respect.'

Fredriksson nodded. 'I saw the crash. Until the last moment, I was certain he would land safely.'

Botha nodded.

'May I ask what happened?'

The Oberstleutnant put his napkin down. 'Certainly, I myself led the flight this afternoon. We found two English coal ships, I believe they call them colliers, off Beachy Head and attacked. We had sunk one and were reforming for another attack when six Hurricanes came at us out of the sun at a crucial moment. Hans had not yet completed his pass and did not break off soon enough. His aircraft was hit but he was able to keep up with us. At first, I thought he was unhurt but a bullet had smashed his leg. He did not want to bail out into the *scheisskanal*, which is what we call the English Channel, in that condition and thought he could nurse the aircraft back. He almost did. A very brave fellow, Hans.'

Botha shrugged. 'He had four confirmed kills to his credit, all English, since he joined III *Gruppe* in May. He was a fine pilot.'

Brandy was served in a library converted to a common room. The pilots were friendly enough and regaled him with sufficient stories for several columns. He was surprised to note that there was little or none of the horseplay of the kind he was used to seeing among young professional soldiers. In fact, the evening ended early with Botha explaining that most were scheduled for early flights.

After returning to the hotel where he had been quartered, Fredriksson spent an hour outlining four columns that dealt with his observations to date, including the crash of the returning fighter aircraft. That would certainly be a test of the Propaganda Ministry's unusual forbearance, he thought. Afterwards, he stepped out into the cool night. The sky was filled with millions of stars and the blackout made them seem even brighter. The sound of an aircraft high up and heading west caught his attention. He searched for the navigation lights, then laughed at himself. Neither friend nor foe was likely to show such lights for a long time to come.

The pilots' behaviour that evening bothered him. Why? Certainly German soldiers he had met in the past were no different from any other young men their age. At first he had attributed it to the death of their fellow pilot, but it went beyond that. As the evening had lengthened, he had begun to suspect that the pilots were exhausted. And why not? he thought. They had been continuously in combat since the beginning of May. And now they were flying sorties against convoys, to keep their hand in, as Mahr had put it. What was the range of the Messerschmitt fighter? Not more than 700 kilometres, he suspected. Which meant they did a great deal of their flying over water and, if damaged, like that young boy this afternoon, their choice lay in parachuting into those waters, frigid even in summer, or trying to make it back.

He recalled something else. One of the fighter pilots had spoken of the difficulties involved in escorting bombers and of trying to guess what they would do next. A senior pilot had frowned at him and quickly changed the subject. The junior pilot mumbled about sleep and wandered away. He hadn't thought much of it at the time but now. . . . Of course a fighter pilot would resent being tied to a slow-moving bomber when it kept him from his natural task of engaging other fighters. But did it go beyond that? Did it suggest that the fighter pilot had no means of communicating with the bomber pilot in flight? If not, why talk about having to outguess them?

Was that possible? Hadn't Colonel-General Milch, the Luftwaffe Commander, made such a fuss about equipping his fighter aircraft with radio sets a few years ago that the news leaked out publicly? And hadn't the Germans made a big propaganda play out of that fact during the Polish invasion, claiming their successes were due to superior tactics in which radio communications played such an important part?

The unexpected bit of information posed a problem as he would not be able to make use of it without compromising his neutrality. If the British were to find out – from him – that German fighter aircraft had no direct means of communication with the bombers they were escorting, it could be of inestimable tactical value. And he would become *persona-non-grata* with the Axis powers.

An even greater danger lay in the fact that one side or the other might be tempted to use him as a conduit for false or misleading information. And this could very well be just such an attempt. He sighed with regret. It would have made a fine reporting coup.

Fredriksson boarded the train the following morning for the trip to Antwerp, lost in thought over the implications of his quick visit to the Luftwaffe aerodrome. He had seen, or at least inferred, much more than Goebbel's propaganda machinery had meant him to. What struck him most was the desultory nature of it all; as if tired by six weeks of lightning war, the entire German armed forces had sat down to rest and think about what they would do next, if anything. Only once on the outward trip from Paris had he seen any indication that the war might continue – a convoy moving west along a dusty road carrying canvas-shrouded loads which were clearly flat-bottomed boats.

He steadied the typewriter against the train's sway and began to draft a column, slowly at first, gearing his speed to his thinking.

From Across the World, Torsten Fredriksson, Vichy France, 21 July 1940 – For Immediate Release: The old order is finished. France has passed from the world stage and Great Britain is about to succumb. Who is left to challenge the *new order?* The British Commonwealth? Canada, Australia, New Zealand and South Africa, the principal components of the British Empire, have shown little enthusiasm for war to date and if the mother country falls, it is doubtful they will press on.

Alone among the surviving democracies, only the United States remain. And she is too far away and too complacent in an isolation made viable by self-sufficiency to care about European squabbles.

The Soviet Union? Eventually, of course, the sleeping bear will be kicked awake but, by then, the Third Reich will have consolidated all its holdings into a united empire. Germany will be immeasurably stronger than a Russian state weakened by endless rounds of internal dissension and purges. When Germany sends her tanks and aircraft against the Soviet Union, half of her population will welcome the Nazis as liberators.

Japan? She will soon surge into the Pacific basin or south towards Australia or both, and perhaps that may finally move the United States to fight to protect her own interests. Will she find herself allied with Nazi Germany in classic confrontation between East and West

– he backspaced and struck that out and typed –

classic confrontation between Oriental and Caucasian, a duel that has been gathering momentum since the yellow race discovered at Tushima Straits in 1905 that its inferiority to the white race is a colonialist's myth?

He read what he had written, surprised at how far afield he had strayed from his original theme of France's fall and Britain's final days. But then, it was all part and parcel of the *change*.

The Caucasian discovered the scientific method and in doing so built a rigid frame of reference for his view of the world. Because the scientific method deals supposedly with fact, the Caucasian ruthlessly strips away the mythology into which the human mind scurries whenever expectation and reality refuse to mesh. As a result, western man depends on technology to improve his world while Oriental man takes refuge in the mind. In the short run, the harsh realities of physical force will always prove superior – i.e., the Mongol Invasion of

China, the Opium Wars, the Boxer Rebellion and so on. But in the long run – and the Oriental prefers that view – the strength of the human mind triumphs and conquerors always melt into their ancient fabric.

But the Japanese are infected with western ways. Beginning in the mid-1800s, faced with the spectre of dwindling resources and living space, they were forced to combine the Oriental's spiritualistic approach to problem-solving with the pragmatic techniques of the Caucasian and they chose to model themselves on another island nation of limited natural resources, Great Britain. Japan saw that Great Britain had built a vast overseas empire to provide markets for her industrial output in return for agricultural products and raw materials and saw no reason why she should not follow her example. The vast, underused area of South-east Asia and China lay on her doorstep, closer even and more amenable to control than the far-flung empire of Great Britain.

The Sino-Japanese war of the early 1890s gave her confidence that she was superior to the best of Asia. In 1905, she tested her new strength against the massive Russian Empire and evicted its armies from Korea and Manchuria and destroyed the Imperial Russian Grand Fleet sent round the world from St Petersburg.

From that moment on, Japan was convinced of her invincibility. That victory also made inevitable the greatest conflict in all human history – the war that must now develop between the white and yellow races for control of the entire planet. How much of all this do the Party leaders in Berlin or Moscow suspect? Only time will tell.

It is this correspondent's position that the defeat of France was the end of the opening round. The fall of Great Britain, in view of Germany's methodical preparations seems assured. Will round two then involve Germany and Russia? And will the winner of that holocaust face Japan?

Jeanette's flat was dark. He used his key to let himself in. As soon as he closed the door, he knew she was gone. She must have left recently as very little dust had settled on the polished wood furniture and Jeanette was a meticulous housekeeper. The note was uncharacteristically brief and to the point.

'Dearest Torsten, I know that if I am here when you return, I will not be able to resist your demand that I go to Sweden. I cannot do so. I cannot abandon my country. Please do not try to find me. You will be unable to as new friends are assisting me. Only since the Boche destroyed my country have I come to understand that everything I own comes to me from her. Now it is my turn to give something back. I love you. Jeanette.

It was only after he had read the note for the third time that Fredriksson came to grips with the unsatisfactory nature of their affair. The essence of a caring relationship, it occurred to him, was the knowledge of the other's constant support. Had either of them had that from the other? As if to emphasize that they had not, he realized that her admonition not to search for her was totally unnecessary. He had no idea who her friends were. In fact, everything about her life that did not immediately concern him was blank. He had only the sketchiest idea of how she lived, who she saw and where she went in the weeks and months between his visits. He supposed he might telephone the two or three art galleries where she regularly displayed and he went so far as to open the telephone book before realizing that he was unlikely to learn anything that way. What Parisian would tell a foreigner who looked and sounded like a German, anything about another French citizen these days?

Ave Caesar, Morituri te Salutant!

Claudius 21

Westhampnett 3 July – 13 August 1940

Pilot Officer Keith Thorne had reported to 142 Squadron at Westhampnett Airfield an hour before, had a brief interview with the squadron CO, received his room assignment from the squadron clerk and was unpacking when the alarm went.

The CO had shouted down the corridor, 'Stick on me, Thorne.'

Thorne caught up with him as the squadron pilots were boarding the Bedford lorry that would take them to the flight line. The CO tossed him a woollen flying jacket.

'Don't do anything else, unless I tell you to. Understand?'

The lorry stopped at a battered Hurricane. 'This one is yours, old man. Be careful.'

An RAF fitter throttled the engine back and slid out of the cockpit as Thorne struggled into the parachute harness. The engine's backwash set him coughing as he stumbled up the wing. The fitter helped shoehorn him into the alloy seat in the cramped cockpit. Thorne checked the transmitter/receiver, flipped the oxygen mask switch and scanned the control panel as the first aircraft wheeled onto the taxiway.

Everything happened with such bewildering rapidity that there wasn't time for apprehension. His earphones crackled and incomprehensible voices roared and buzzed. He eased the throttle, feeling the engine respond immediately. A green light flashed at the corner of his vision – the all clear – and he released the brakes.

The Hurricane lurched, bucked when he overbraked and his tailplane swung dangerously close to his wingmate's aircraft but Thorne was far too busy to worry about that. The squadron CO moved directly onto the runway and Thorne saw the sudden blur of his propeller and, in reflex, pulled his own throttle open. The two aircraft leapt down the runway as if they were Siamese twins. The tiny strip of concrete he could see between wing and fuselage fled and the Hurricane bounced once and was airborne. He retracted the gear and, in the rear-view mirror, saw another Hurricane climbing after him.

When 142 Squadron was airborne, they formed up in echelon, turned south across the city of Portsmouth then east to parallel the coast while climbing for altitude. Fifteen minutes into the flight, the squadron leader advised that it had been a false alarm. The bandit was a naval training aircraft gone astray.

'But, as long as we are up, we'll continue our regular patrol. I've already advised 601 Squadron and they are going in early.'

Far below, he saw a similiar echelon formation looking like a school of tiny fish slipping past towards the coast. Thorne did a quick survey of the instrument panel and readjusted his oxygen mask to ease the pressure of the nose clip. Damn, it was cold, he thought. The wool flying jacket wasn't enough for this altitude and when he played with the cockpit heater, nothing happened.

The map showed a section of coast from Southampton to Beachy Head. Off his port wing, the green of forest and farmland came right down to the English Channel, separated only by a very narrow strip of tan beach and white breakers. Ahead, he could see where the cliffs began, bluffs really, marked with numerous cuts and defiles above rocky beaches.

Thorne liked the heavy, but responsive Hurricane. He had fallen in love with the aircraft the first time he had flown one. Perhaps he was conditioned by the fact that he had literally stepped from a Fairey Battle used as an advanced trainer, right into the Hurricane – like going from a Plymouth sedan to a Buick roadster. Or a Morris Minor to a Bentley, he corrected himself. He had taken enough kidding lately about his American accent and usages. The rivalry between Spitfire and Hurricane pilots had already spread to the civilian population and the laboured poem –

The Hurricane pilot is something that other pilots are not.
When most other pilots are pissing about, the poor bugger's put on the spot.
The Spit may be handsome and luvverly,
Like a better class cabriolet,
But when it comes down to shifting the shit,
Which bugger carries the day?

– was as familiar to every schoolboy as to the pilots themselves.

They levelled off at ninety-five hundred feet and moved a bit farther out from the coast. The squadron leader was keeping to the glare of the sun while they watched for intruders approaching from the east or south.

'Everyone. Sharp lookout. Mr Thorne, are you there?'

His name over the R/T surprised him. 'Ah, yes sir.'

'Welcome to 142 Squadron, Mr Thorne. The usual introductions will have to wait until we return. Must apologize for the haste in dragging you up here, but no time like the present. Certain rules, Mr Thorne. Inflexible. Eyes open at all times. Search the sky in every direction. Excellent habit to cultivate. All directions in terms of the clock. Got that?'

'Yes sir.'

'One other rule. Newcomer always stands the squadron a round of drinks.'

'Ah . . . my pleasure.'

'Everyone now, look sharp.'

Standing at the window of the squadron mess two weeks later, Thorne swore wearily at the incessant recording of 'White Cliffs of Dover' and contemplated the rolling hills touched with sunset. The radio never seemed to play anything else but Vera Lynn or that horrible organ piece, 'Bells Across the Meadows', and if the radio didn't then the gramophone did. He sipped at his drink – the single one he allowed himself each evening – and thought about how tired he had become in just the two weeks. He had found it far easier to adjust here than he had in training. Perhaps it was because he was accepted as a professional, even if he was the new boy and a foreigner as well, but mostly because discipline was less formal and what mattered was doing the job properly. Doing it improperly carried its own penalties.

But he was exhausted and very bored with the constant patrolling – two and three flights a day. He had yet to see, let alone engage, a single German aircraft. The other members of the squadron encountered action but every patrol he flew was as uneventful as a Sunday drive. The other members of the squadron had begun to joke about it and talked of arranging to join those patrols to which he was assigned.

'Goering has given his pilots strict instructions to stay away from Americans,' was the standard joke. Thorne tried to take it in good humour but, as the days wore on, it became harder and harder to maintain his equanimity. And harder and harder to limit his drinking. The only positive aspect of the situation was that his skill with the Hurricane continued to improve to the extent that the squadron leader had stopped offering unsolicited advice.

The following day saw heavy rain sweep over most of England soon after dawn. The steady drumming on the tin roof woke him and he lay quietly for some time, listening. The room was pitch dark and close due to the heavy blackout curtains and he could see nothing but the luminous dial of his watch. Most of the pilots scorned the ancient barracks which one wag claimed had been built during the Marlborough Wars. After a while, he got up, shivering slightly in the damp air, dressed and stepped outside under the eaves to light a cigarette. The night sky was greying in the east but the airfield remained shrouded in darkness, intense, all encompassing darkness that lacked form or substance. The rain slanted heavily and a mild wind whipped spray at him. The air was fresh and almost cold, a welcome relief after the past few days' heat and humidity.

His mind was a turmoil of thoughts, formed and unformed. He shifted nervously, aware that he had shredded the butt end of the cigarette by constantly flicking the ash. He tossed it away and watched the spark die, jammed his hands into his pockets and strode up and down the narrow corridor protected from the rain.

He had become a loner. He liked the others well enough and often joined them in the mess in the evenings. Perhaps it was their ages, he thought, as most were still boys, some in their teens, the rest in their early twenties. Their most popular reading matter was a comic book hero, Rockfist Rogan, heavyweight boxing champ and fighter ace. The accent in Fighter Command was on youth. At twenty-six they kicked squadron leaders upstairs and replaced them with a younger man. And he was thirty.

Then too, their impromptu horseplay – the same kind in which he indulged in the USAAC – now set his teeth on edge and he even found it difficult to join in the songs and other activities that so often reminded him of the boy scouts. The curse of growing old, he thought.

But more than anything else, he knew, it was the constant tension that was driving him nuts. Since Poland, nothing suited him anymore. He was too easily bored and hadn't the patience to stick with anything – the publishing house, Shirley, ferrying aircraft, flight training, whatever. Most of his problems with flight instruction had stemmed from boredom, he now realized. He seemed to be always looking forward to the next step and could never summon the patience to see through what he was doing at the moment.

A sudden gust swirled the rain and drove him back inside where he lay on the bunk, staring into the darkness, trying to ignore the close-packed bodies and the stuffy atmosphere. If this was the first war, in France, he thought, I could drink as much as I liked. Harry told him once how all the fliers drank gin to offset the effects of the castor oil used as an engine lubricant. 'We were always half-smashed,' he had said. 'Made the dying easier.'

'B' section of 142 Squadron took off at five-thirty to relieve the dawn patrol from Tangmere. The oxygen system in Thorne's aircraft was giving him intermittent trouble as they crossed the coast and he was tempted to turn back. Only the thought of the long hours with nothing to do made him press on. They tested their guns with the usual jokes about no activity because he was with them and settled down.

Visibility was generally poor. The rain continued and twice they were vectored onto suspected enemy reconnaissance aircraft but saw nothing, and returned to base two hours later. Thorne stalked off the flight line and avoiding the mess flung himself on his bunk to glare at the ceiling, wrapped in frustration. In total, he had more flying time in single-engine pursuit aircraft than anyone else in the squadron, including the CO. If he added all of his multi-engine time, there were no two pilots in the squadron combined who could equal him.

At one-thirty, the alarm bell rang in the ready room. A convoy steaming south west through the Straits of Dover escorted by six Hurricanes of 32 Squadron out of Biggin Hill were being attacked by several squadrons of fighters and bombers. 142 Squadron flew an easterly course across the rainstreaked landscape of south eastern England and crossed the coast south of Romney. The Channel lay below, grey and cold in the fitful sun, and the broken cloud was dull grey on the underside and blinding white above.

'Look sharp, chaps,' the squadron leader's voice buzzed in his earphones. 'I've just been told that additional help is on the way from Gosport. Looks like a big one.'

A wave of excitement and fear swept Thorne and a peculiar tightness crept into his throat. Someone began the old Congregational prayer,

Oh Lord, from whom all blessings flow, Bless these thy children. . . .

'Close up and shut up!'

The squadron leader's emotionless voice reminded him of his task and he swivelled his head to scan the sky; nothing but broken cloud with sun streaming through the gaps. For a moment, he was intrigued by the surface of the English Channel. Wherever the sunlight touched, the colour was a deep, deep blue, but in the cloud shadow it was dark and metallic grey, like the North Atlantic in February.

Five minutes later, they spotted the convoy and above them the escorting Biggin Hill squadron, six faint specks against a towering thunderhead.

Someone swore. 'Bogeys one o'clock high.'

A mass of dark specks paced the RAF escort several thousand feet higher. As they flew on, the shapes resolved into twin-engined Dorniers and above them, dozens of Me.109E fighters flying in groups of four.

'Up lads, angels-one five,' the squadron leader barked and immediately, the Hurricanes began to climb at full throttle.

Thorne spotted another group of fighters approaching from the west – the supporting Gosport RAF squadron – and he counted twelve planes.

The scene had a surrealistic quality. The British aircraft were badly outnumbered yet the Germans had not moved to engage them. What could they possibly be waiting for? Thorne wondered. Twisting his neck, he saw the approaching British squadrons dive straight at the concentration of enemy bombers who, anticipating the attack, had already begun to form themselves into a circle.

'Follow me!' the squadron leader snapped and his nose dropped immediately. Thorne followed suit and they flashed towards the circling Dorniers while the Me.109s moved in to protect their charges. Thorne rechecked that his firing button safety ring was off and tried to force himself to relax as the G-forces built up. The bombers began to grow in size; he picked one and eased it into his reflector sight. He scanned the sky automatically with a quick twist of his neck and spotted three more fighters dropping towards them. Above, he had the impression of more specks of what he hoped were other British aircraft but there wasn't time to be certain. The Dornier slid away from his gunsight; a tap of right rudder brought it floating back. He was approaching from above and slightly to the left. The Dornier's slim pencil shape slipped through a fringe of cloud and for a moment, a panicky feeling shot through him at the thought of losing it. But the Dornier emerged once more, foolishly still moving in the same direction. The huge glassed cockpit flashed sunlight at him then winked with red. The gunner in the cockpit rear was firing at him. Something clattered against the wing but he didn't dare look.

'Don't hurry,' Thorne muttered over and over, unconsciously echoing years of flight instructors, both American and British. Sure kills were made at fifty yards or less. Another stream of tracers flicked past his cockpit – he was being fired on by another aircraft in the circle. Time slowed; there was an instant to wonder at the defensive circle the German bombers had taken up while the fighters fought off the attackers, time to make certain that the ice-sharp image of the Dornier was squarely in his gunsight and that the twin black crosses on either wing were inside the gunsight ring before he pressed the firing button. The Hurricane shuddered and streams of white smoke whipped away in the slipstream. Tracers curved towards the Dornier and passed beyond the starboard wing. He corrected and fired again, a short burst. The tracers chewed into the wing root behind the cockpit and short spurts of red flame danced back across the fuselage. He gave the Hurricane a bit of left rudder to push the nose up and fired again and saw the cockpit glass explode and then he was past. He had a brief impression of the Dornier's starboard wing lifting violently, so close it seemed he could touch it and then there was only the grey, sunstreaked Channel below.

351

Thorne pulled out of the dive, jinking hard right and left as he struggled to regain altitude. He gave the sky a careful look and found it empty. Startled, he swung the Hurricane into a tight circle – nothing. Even the Channel was empty but for the grey line of England on his left. He climbed to fifteen thousand feet. Abrupt snatches of conversation, a pilot's yell of pain, terror, or exultation, he could not tell which and the radio channel was silent. He tried the other frequencies but they all remained maddeningly empty.

The sky was full of cloud that hung in massive columns of white and grey marble. They had flown eighty miles to reach the convoy and the needle in the fuel gauge was past the half full mark. He glanced at his elapsed time chronometer and was surprised to find that the action which had seemed to happen so quickly had in fact consumed twenty minutes. He decided to give it ten more minutes before turning for home.

The sky remained empty. He had experienced this phenomenon before in manoeuvres. Aircraft moved so swiftly that if one were pursuing another at an acute angle to the mainstream, five minutes sufficed to open twenty-five or more miles of sky. What's more, the air battle could easily be hidden in the masses of broken cloud. He topped out at fifteen thousand feet. Still nothing. Five minutes remaining. He flew on steadily towards the English coast and when the remaining minutes expired, he reluctantly turned onto a heading for Westhampnett.

Thorne was the first in. His ground crew were waiting with the usual thermos of tea and he could see them shading their eyes to study his wings as he turned off the runway. An unjustified surge of anger went through him – they were looking to see whether or not the streamlining patches over his guns had been shot away. They hurried up with the low blue trailer with the mysterious warning emblazoned on its side: 'Use with 24 volt system only.'

'Trouble is it?' the chief asked when he eased out of the cockpit.

'Nothing except the radio,' he snapped and stepped down from the wing. He glanced at the other two and saw their apprehension.

'We intercepted a German bomber group escorted by Me.109s. We got above them. I took a shot at a Dornier. By the time I recovered and got back to altitude, I was all alone. So, I stooged around for ten minutes then came on home when I couldn't find anyone else.'

'Get to it, lads!' the chief barked as if suddenly aware of the tension. 'Why are you standin' gawkin'?'

Thorne knew they were wondering if he hadn't contrived an excuse to return while the rest of the squadron went on. Too angry to speak, he tossed the thermos to the chief and started to stalk off. The airframe mechanic pointed to the fin and called over his shoulder, 'Look here, sir,' and pointed to the vertical stabilizer.

There was the reason why he had been unable to raise anyone on the R/T. The leading edge of the rudder had been badly chewed and the radio antenna anchor shot away. The chief suddenly looked abashed.

'You must excuse the lads, sir,' he whispered. 'They've taken a great deal of ragging.'

Thorne's anger evaporated all at once. 'That's all right, sergeant. I understand.'

The squadron CO walked into the debriefing room later and clapped him on the shoulder. 'Fine shooting, Thorne. Couldn't have done better myself. Knocked the bastard right into the drink.'

'I did?' Thorne yelped in surprise.

The CO laughed. 'You mean you didn't know?'

'No sir. By the time I recovered, I was completely alone.'

'Well that's luck, old chap. I'd say you've been blooded. Let me be the first whom you buy a whisky.'

Later, Thorne stood in the fading twilight and watched as his rigger painted the first swastika below the cockpit canopy. After all the years of training for this moment, he still wasn't ready for the fierce surge of exultation. He wondered for a moment why he felt no regret at having ended the lives of the German aircrew – but only until he recalled Deborah's face watching him so calmly from the circle of arc-light until the pistol went off. Retribution had only begun, he thought.

That evening, Thorne stood the required round of drinks for a first kill in the mess bar. The spell had broken, the hilarity was high and, for once, it seemed to him the usual British reticence as well as his own stand-offishness that had always stood as a barrier between him and the rest of the squadron had disappeared. He had proved himself their equal. Several of the others tried to press further drinks on him but he managed to turn them away easily enough until a young replacement named Peter Simpson insisted. Simpson had already had too much to drink and Thorne knew that it would be no good trying to explain, so he thanked him and refused. Simpson was too young and too drunk and his manner went frigid. The boy shrugged at several other pilots and, in that instant, Thorne realized he was being tested.

He was suddenly reminded of an incident, years before at Love Field in Texas. A young lieutenant had joined the squadron, a nice enough young guy but one who refused to socialize with the other members of the squadron, preferring to keep to himself. He was, however, a very fine pilot. Thorne, serving as temporary CO during combined manoeuvres with the infantry, had requested the pilot be assigned to his squadron. Due to his efforts, the squadron accumulated a surprising points total and won. A week later, Thorne was surprised to learn that the Wing CO had transferred the boy. When he asked for an explanation, the Colonel shut the door and told him to sit down.

'Thorne, this comes under the heading of a "judgement call". It's a part of the process of command they don't tell you about in the books. Peterson is a fine pilot. Damned fine. But, he had to go. No, don't interrupt, just listen.

'An air squadron is a team. Just like a baseball or football team, each member has to know every other member's foibles, prejudices and characteristics to the point where an almost telepathic awareness exists between them. You only develop that awareness and trust through personal interaction. You don't have to like another team member, just *know* him. Peterson does not belong in the Air Corps because he won't allow anyone to know him, nor will he make an attempt to know anyone else. I don't want someone in my command killed because one man insists on being a hermit. Understand?'

Thorne hadn't until a year later when he learned that Peterson had been killed when his wingman had turned inside a shade too sharply.

Leaning against the bar in the officers' mess at the present moment, conscious of the mixture of hurt and anger in Simpson's eyes, he suddenly realized that he was becoming another Peterson.

'On second thoughts,' he said and clapped the young pilot on the arm, 'I will have another drink.'

On 23 July, a routine dawn patrol took B flight west along the coast towards Portland and Thorne was flying as wingman to the patrol leader. It had rained during the night and the sky was filled with huge blackish-grey clouds. A small convoy was making its way around the coast from Plymouth to the Nore and they were flying high cover at twelve thousand feet. Attacks on convoys had become increasingly frequent and the Germans were pressing them home with great determination.

They made the turn-around off Portland Bill and were returning through patchy cloud cover. Five minutes after the turn, they made visual contact with a Coastal Command escort of Gladiators from Plymouth. Below them, the five ships in the convoy were moving in ragged formation shepherded by a destroyer and an armed trawler, the convoy's position well marked by a column of smoke trailing from one of the merchant vessels. Thorne heard the exchange of recognition signals and the Gladiators began the turn for home. As 142 Squadron formed up over the convoy the patrol leader shouted, 'Break right, go!'

He kicked his Hurricane over one wing and dropped like a stone. A tracer greased past the cockpit and Thorne glimpsed the Me.109E in his rear-view mirror. He half-rolled, kicked the rudder hard, jinked right then left, brought the nose up sharply and gave the Hurricane full throttle. The engine screamed and he rocketed into a near vertical dive for a moment, chopped the power and kicked the plane into a spin. The manoeuvre worked. The Me.109E pilot, confused by his unorthodox tactic, was above and slightly ahead. Thorne rolled upward and fired a long burst as the German slid through his gunsight. Three distinct flashes showed near the wing root and the plane faltered, then recovered. There wasn't time to watch any longer. He twisted his neck, grimacing at his sore muscles, and saw another Messerschmitt pursuing the patrol leader. He followed, twisting and jigging to shake anyone trying to lock on him. It became a three-aircraft race that spiralled over the coast at ten thousand feet. The German fired several bursts and Thorne was certain the patrol leader was struck at least once. The Me.109E was faster than the Hurricane and he had trouble closing at the slight angle.

Thorne was certain the German was so intent on his kill that he did not realize he was being followed – yet. His choice was a gamble – fire a burst at extreme range and hope, or wait until he closed the distance to make the kill a certainty, and chance detection. The Messerschmitt fired again and that resolved his dilemma. If he waited the patrol leader was a dead man. For just a moment, he was tempted still to wait to score another kill, then with a gesture of disgust, he shouted, 'Foxtrot leader, break left, go.'

When the Hurricane cut left, out of his line of fire, he pressed the trigger button. Tracers curved past the Messerschmitt which jinked up and away as if scalded.

The patrol leader ordered them to break off combat with the fighters and attack the bombers. Distracted for an instant, Thorne banked sharply and saw through a gap in the cloud, bombers swarming in on the convoy. Tiny white puffs showed that the destroyer's anti-aircraft guns were in action. He swept the skies with a quick glance and spotted the Me.109E he had chased away. The German pilot had completed a tight circle and was coming up on his tail. An instant later, machine gun bullets punched through the fuselage with metallic clangs. Twice, he jinked in the same direction, hoping to throw his pursuer off, but the German pilot hung on.

A twin-engined bomber swam into his sights and without

thinking, he eased his nose up. The bomber ballooned in the front panel and he fired. He went past so close that he could see the rear gunner duck. He pulled out of the dive beneath and twisted the Hurricane up and at right angles to the bomber but the Me.109E had disappeared.

Two ships in the convoy were burning now. The destroyer and the armed trawler had churned the sea to a froth as they raced back and forth to protect their charges. The German bombers had turned back after completing their run and their fighter escort broke off and raced after them.

When the squadron reformed, they discovered one Hurricane missing. They completed the patrol in tense silence and when aircraft from 143 Squadron, Tangmere arrived they were only too glad to head for Westhampnett.

Southampton 15 – 18 August 1940

The summer of 1940 was a blur in later memory. Attacks against convoys and coastal shipping, as well as targets of opportunity anywhere along the coast were almost constant. Swarms of bombers protected by fighters built up over Occupied French airfields. Alarms, relayed from the Chain-Home radio-detection stations located along the coast, came one after another. Their predictions as to direction, altitude and strength, only partially correct at first, began to improve and the RAF was soon able to meet the invaders at altitude. 'Hun Kill' pools became a daily feature in the evening mess following the nine o'clock news.

Thorne's first break in the exhausting routine of constant flying came in the first week of August. The squadron commander called him in one morning and handed him a three-day pass.

'Get out of here, Thorne. Go up to London or take a holiday in Wales. I don't want to see you again until Sunday evening. And that,' he added, 'is an order.'

Thorne stared at the slip of paper in his hand while his brain slowly absorbed its implication. He showered, shaved and watched by envious squadron mates packed a single suitcase and left the base in less than an hour. A lorry driver gave him a lift to the tiny halt that served Westhampnett.

Thorne sat on the weathered bench in the warm sunshine and waited for the train. The distant growl of aircraft engines was muted and for long periods of time was replaced by the lazy drone of bees and blissful silence. He fell asleep waiting for the train and the guard had to step down and wake him.

Southampton and its docks were choice targets for the single German raiders who liked to sneak across the Channel from airfields in the Cherbourg Peninsula or the coastal area between Le Havre and Abbeville. As the train ran into the city, he noticed that an entire block might appear normal until suddenly a pile of rubble marking the remains of a shop or a house was revealed for a moment. Anti-aircraft guns were scattered everywhere and behind their sandbagged revetments, bored gunners drank tea and played cards until the alert sounded, under hoardings for Reckitt's Blue or Robin Starch.

Thorne hesitated outside Central Station, suddenly at a loss. London was the usual magnet that drew servicemen on leave but he had no wish to visit the city. He still paid his share of the Chelsea flat but the idea of going there repelled him for now. He thought of renting a car to drive into the countryside where he could find an inn but the hire-car office was closed and he remembered that petrol was now rationed.

He was too tired to go far and what he wanted more than anything else was sleep, hours and hours of sleep uninterrupted by the alert bell. He'd take his chance with the German bombers, he decided. He obtained directions to a good hotel, the Dolphin, in the High Street from a porter and walked through small, pleasant streets. The Dolphin, an old hotel, was easy to find and as he started up the steps, a horn honked and someone shouted his name.

A red MG sports car slipped to a stop beside the curb and Peter Simpson waved to him.

'Thought it was you, by God. All you Americans walk like gangsters. Come and meet my sister.'

Simpson hopped out of the MG and shook Thorne's hand. He was quite a bit younger – Thorne tended to think of him as a boy like a good many of the pilots he flew with. He was rather short and thin and affected a wispy moustache that curled at the ends. His face was pale beneath a thatch of dark blond hair and his eyes were pale blue, giving the misleading impression of vacancy. Although Thorne did not know him well, Simpson had a reputation for brains that belied his looks. He had been posted to 142 Squadron a few days after Thorne and since then had been credited with two kills and a possible, matching his own record.

'Charlotte,' he said, turning easily to the woman in the other seat, 'I want you to meet the mysterious American. We understand his family is very rich. Not only that but he was an American Air Corps flyer as well.' He held a hand to shield his mouth and whispered *sotto voce*, 'There are tales of beautiful women and dark deeds done in Poland. A very mysterious fellow.'

'Peter, do stop embarrassing the man.' Charlotte held up a hand. 'How do you do, Mr Thorne, is it? My name is Charlotte. Please forgive Peter. He really shouldn't be allowed out.'

'He's not much different when kept in,' Thorne grinned and shook her hand, noticing that she was rather attractive. Her long hair was tied back with a pale blue ribbon and her colouring was similar to Peter's but there the resemblance ended. Her eyes were darker making her face seem more forceful and she had a smaller, firmer chin. Whereas Peter had what he tended to think of as Norman features, Charlotte's bone structure was quite a bit finer, almost delicate, and lacked the angularity of many English women.

'What are you up to, old boy?' Simpson demanded.

'Not a great deal, I'm afraid. The CO called me in this morning, gave me this three day and told me to get out. I thought I'd start with some sleep.'

'Sleep!' Simpson pretended to be aghast. 'Waste seventy-two hours' leave on sleep. Good God in heaven! Is that how Americans do things? Nonsense. We must see that. . . .'

Thorne broke in. 'I really am fagged.' He grimaced at his unconscious use of RAF slang.

'Of course! But that doesn't mean that you have to waste all seventy-two hours sleeping.' He turned to his sister. 'Look here, Charlotte,' he appealed, 'surely there's room for one more at the party tonight?'

'No, look, Peter,' Thorne began.

'Of course. If Mr Thorne would like to come, that is.' She smiled and her expression of reserve disappeared. 'In fact, Mr Thorne would be a refreshing change from Daddy's usual clique.'

'All settled then. Look here, old man. Get your sleep. Plenty of it. I'll come around sevenish to pick you up. Don't expect a smashing good time. Old Dad tends to the slow side and his friends are the same. But the food is good and there's always plenty of liquor. We'll make our own party if need be.'

He got back into the MG and they roared off leaving Thorne standing bemused on the steps of the hotel.

He had expected trouble obtaining a room but discovered that his RAF uniform with its embroidered wings were all the passport needed in Southampton. He was given a room immediately and the bell boy even refused a tip when he took the bags up.

'Thanks anyway, guv, but you lads are doin' plenty for us.'

Absurdly pleased, he unlaced his shoes, shrugged out of his jacket and lay back on the bed to plan the day.

A cool breeze blowing in through the open window brought him awake with a bout of sneezing and he sat up, trying to think where he was. The hotel had given him a room on the fourth floor and from the bed, he could see through the window into the harbour. The sun was low in the west and his wrist watch read six-thirty.

He had slept all day! My God, he thought, I couldn't have been that tired? The lassitude he remembered from the morning was still with him but less pronounced. Something nagged at him, something he was supposed to do. He lit a cigarette, wincing at its harsh taste and stared blankly at the window. Smoke curling into his eyes brought him awake again and he stubbed the cigarette out and unpacked his bag. His spare uniform was a bit rumpled and he hung it up near the window, then undressed. He'd call the porter in the morning and have both cleaned and pressed. Thorne went along to the bathroom, filled the tub to the regulation three inches with lukewarm water and washed as thoroughly as the hard soap allowed.

He remembered then. He was supposed to attend a party this evening. What had Simpson said? Something about picking him up at seven. Thorne groaned. He wasn't up to a party tonight. He'd telephone when he got back to the room. The idea of sleeping straight through the night without the anticipation of a patrol at 0330 was too good to be true.

He propped his shaving mirror on the side of the tub, lathered his face and shaved carefully, enjoying the smooth feel of the Rolls razor over his face. If there was one invention, he thought, that should receive a Nobel prize, it was the clever self-sharpening Rolls in its little kit.

He walked back down the musty corridor to his room and found the door ajar. Charlotte Simpson was sitting in the chair watching the harbour.

'Hallo. I thought you must be down having a bath. That's the first thing Peter wants whenever he shows up. I'll just wait in the foyer until you are ready.' She flashed him a smile, gathered up her gas mask bag and slipped past before he could say a word.

Damn, he muttered, closing the door, not sure whether to be annoyed or pleased that she had come, and early as well. Then he looked down at the ragged old robe he had worn for so many years and grunted. Wonderful. He rang down to the porter to see if he could have the uniform pressed immediately. A few minutes later, the bell boy knocked on the door, took the uniform and skipped off.

He found the lobby, when he entered fifteen minutes later, to resemble a Hollywood version of a Victorian room complete with potted palms, overstuffed mohair chairs and innumerable knick-knacks. Two elderly ladies drinking tea smiled at him.

'Young man,' one called. 'If you are looking for your young lady, she wished me to say that she is waiting in the bar.'

Thorne thanked her and went along the walnut-panelled corridor to where a discreet sign marked the bar, wondering at how war seemed to change people's moral perceptions.

The nearly-empty bar was lit with yellowish shaded lamps and the colour, and odour, of well-oiled and polished wood was pronounced. The barman, middle-aged and in a white shirt and black jacket, read a newspaper. Charlotte waved to him from a table near the far wall and he slid into the chair across from her.

'I ordered you a drink, a whisky,' she indicated the glass. 'I'm told you Americans call it scotch.'

'Those who don't know any better, do,' he smiled.

A nervous silence fell between them and he found himself appraising her. When he had walked into his room he hadn't recognized her immediately. Even now, she seemed different from the girl in the red MG. Her hair was much lighter than her brother's, almost honey blonde in colour and her eyes, at least in this light, did not appear blue, but brown. In the strong sunlight he had thought her very pale and perhaps the flattering light helped here, but her skin was really a delicate golden, as if she spent a great deal of time in the mild, northern sun.

She was wearing a suit – a three-piece Chanel design. The waistcoat fitted very well and outlined rather than concealed a nicely proportioned bosom. The material was a brownish tweed that matched her hair perfectly. He studied her face as she talked about her brother, noting the thin, straight and very English nose that tipped slightly at the end. Her lips were rather full and she had used a light shade of red lip colouring to balance her hair which fell in soft cascades to her shoulders.

'What were you smiling at when you came in?' she asked.

The abrupt question surprised him and he had to think a moment. 'The two elderly ladies in the lobby.'

'In the foyer,' she corrected and he grinned.

'No one will ever make an Englishman out of me. Okay. In the foyer. A year ago if you had asked them to pass on that message about waiting in the bar, they would probably have gone looking for a cop. Do you know the little one winked at me.'

Charlotte's laughter was genuine. The barman looked up and Thorne signalled for two more drinks. He could afford them tonight, he decided, since he did not have to fly tomorrow.

'Like all Americans, you think we English are incredibly stuffy. I must tell you, Mr Thorne. . . .'

'Keith,' he corrected and she smiled.

'Only if you call me Charlotte.'

'All right,' he agreed. 'Charlotte.'

'As I was saying, Queen Victoria has been dead for some forty years and even when she was alive, we weren't all that bad. In fact, some of the worst or, depending on how you view such things, the most explicit pornographic literature ever was written at the height of her reign, in the 1880s.'

'Pornography!' Thorne sat back in astonishment.

'See, now I have surprised you, haven't I.'

'I just never thought I would be sitting in the bar of a perfectly proper English hotel discussing pornography with a perfectly proper young English woman.'

Her laughter pleased him and he began to relax. 'Well, I don't think you could categorize me as a "proper young English woman". Certainly my father doesn't think so. He is quite certain that I'm a lost soul. But then he still refers to most young women as flappers.'

They laughed, sharing the superiority of the young at the shortcomings of their elders and a few minutes later, they went out to where she had left the MG. She handled the car very well, he thought as they shot through nearly empty streets. Here and there a boarded-up window or a scorched or damaged building showed the effects of hit and run raids. Several shops bore signs reading, 'Jerry, do your worst, we are open for business anyway', or similar sentiments. The sun was closing on the horizon but the sky was perfectly clear. Southampton would certainly be a target tonight, he thought. The house, she told him, was twelve miles north and west of the city in the direction of the New Forest.

'Where the devil do you get gasoline – petrol,' he corrected himself, 'to run this thing?'

She gave him an impish grin and took a tight curve up and out of the valley without slackening speed. 'I've done a deal with Peter. He gives me his petrol coupons and, in return, I let him have it whenever he goes on leave. And I often drive out to pick him up. Daddy says that's not in the spirit of the thing, but then I really don't waste the petrol. He does have to get home somehow.'

The evening was surprisingly cool in the open car and the trees closed in to edge the road with dark massy shadows. Charlotte changed down abruptly and swung into a narrow drive that led through the trees and widened to a gravel lane before a large three-storey, white house. Several automobiles were parked there, mostly Austins and one or two Fords, certainly not the Rolls and Bentleys he had expected.

Inside, the house was cool and dim. The windows were open to the evening and the blackout curtains drawn aside as the lights had not been turned on. Peter was at the door to meet them. He shook Thorne's hand vigorously and led him into the house while Charlotte drove off to the garage.

'I want you to meet my father,' Peter told him, indicating a large man in a rumpled business suit clutching a glass of whisky and holding forth to a group of similarly dressed friends. He spotted them half across the room, broke off his oration and came over to them. Thorne's hand was gripped hard and he winced.

'I understand from Peter,' the elder Simpson rumbled, 'that you were a pilot in the American Air Corps. Come and have a drink.'

'There is one thing I neglected to tell you, Dad,' Peter Simpson said when the whisky was poured. 'Keith has seen more of this war than even we have.' He gave them a brief sketch of Thorne's experiences in Poland and flying aircraft between the United States and Canada and across the North Atlantic.

Again, Thorne was surprised and then annoyed. 'How the devil did you find out all that?' he demanded but Peter Simpson only grinned. 'Everyone in the squadron knows, Keith old boy. Everyone.'

'That's quite a history, young man. I suppose then you must see the Nazis as a menace to the entire civilized world, one that must be stamped into the dust?'

Thorne shifted his glance to the elder Simpson. Several of the other men were watching closely, waiting for his answer.

'I suppose I do,' he answered carefully.

But no one seemed content to let it rest there. 'Don't you think that Great Britain should reach an accommodation with Germany, as Russia has done? Accept the inevitable as it were?' one of the other guests asked.

Surprised, Thorne hesitated. 'Don't you mean surrender?'

'Now see here!' the elder Simpson began but Peter chuckled. 'You asked for it, Dad. Let him finish.'

'I didn't mean that quite like it sounded,' Thorne said hastily. 'I suppose I mean that the two forms of government, as well as your national aims, are so far apart that I don't see how any arrangement short of surrender could work.'

'The Russian and the German systems are even further apart,' someone else broke in, 'but that arrangement looks to be going strong.'

'Maybe,' Thorne muttered, his voice dubious. Damn it, he thought, I didn't come here to argue politics.

'Look here, young man,' the elder Simpson said. 'I fought Jerry in the last war. Did my stint in the trenches and all that. When all was said and done, who won? The result was ruinous worldwide inflation, culminating in a disastrous depression that brought this Hitler fellow to power. Now I don't hold with Fascism mind you and, in fact, I've spoken against Mosley many times but when you step back and examine the total picture, perhaps it is all for the best. Germany has gobbled up so much territory that she will be a century digesting it. And in the meantime, the opportunities for business are immense. Could put this country back on its feet. Let the damned Nazis finance our recovery. I say that Russia is the far greater menace. In alliance with Germany, we can eliminate Communism for all time.'

Thorne resisted the effort to deny the fuzzy logic.

'The Soviets know that,' Simpson went on, 'and they, being realists, have chosen accommodation. They aren't prepared to fight a major war any more than we are but if you contrast the present condition of the two countries, you find the Soviet Union reaping a grand harvest selling goods and services to Germany while we bankrupt ourselves fighting a foolish war that's none of our business.

'Why, the strategic and political thinking has hardly changed since the days of Marlborough. Chamberlain let himself be pushed into that Polish treaty by Churchill and his clique, damned warmongers all.

'It is common knowledge that Hitler is assembling invasion fleets all along the coast from Holland to France. How ever are we going to stop him? The BEF came back empty-handed. I say reach an agreement with Hitler. Allow ourselves time to build up. Then, if still necessary, we can face the Germans. But when the time comes, I think we will find Herr Hitler ready to come to terms and better still, to keep them. He said so himself not more than two weeks ago.'

The elder Simpson's remarks finally provoked him to reply. 'From first-hand experience I doubt that. There are two Germanys involved, it seems to me. One is the old, rational Germany of Bismarck and the Kaisers, who in spite of a conservative, militaristic tradition introduced workable social legislation of the kind that Marx was only dreaming about, and did so within a capitalistic framework and who went to war in 1914 as a miscalculation. That was the Germany you fought in the first war. That Germany was led by an officer corps dedicated to the betterment of the nation. Today's Germany is led by fanatics of the worst kind. Violence is the only method they know and Hitler has said so on every possible occasion.

'The SS are now Germany's guardians and they are fanatics; mental and moral weaklings who police the Nazi Party and the nation ideologically. How can you deal honestly with people like that? Sign an armistice agreement today and be trampled by jackboots tomorrow. Remember Czechoslovakia?'

One or two in the group were smiling but all were listening, if with polite tolerance – and closed minds. Thorne realized that he was wasting his breath. They reminded him too much of the people he had sparred with in New York. He turned to Peter and held out his glass.

'All this talking is making me thirsty. I think I need a refill.'

Simpson waved his son to the bar and took Thorne's arm. 'But you must admit, Mr Thorne, Hitler has waged a different campaign against us.'

He ticked off points on his fingers. 'He stopped his tanks about Dunkirk to allow the BEF to escape. He's confined air raids to coastal areas, military installations and convoys at sea. He even apologized for the sinking of the *Athenia* last September. Now suppose for the moment we do win this war. What will we have accomplished but the bankruptcy of ourselves and the jeopardization of the Empire? Why, we never did fully recover from the last war. And with your government demanding cash for everything we buy from the States, we'll soon deplete our hard currency reserves and overseas holdings.'

Thorne was saved by a burst of laughter and the entrance of the ladies. Charlotte came across to claim him and not a moment too soon.

'I can just imagine how you all have been badgering poor Mr Thorne. He's supposed to be on holiday and I mean to see that he enjoys himself.' And she whisked him away.

'Oh God,' she breathed and led him out to the garden. 'Daddy's dinner affairs are all so boringly alike. Even if you had two heads and warts, I would have done anything to get you here tonight, just for relief.'

'Nice to feel wanted,' he murmured and she grinned impishly.

'If you are fishing for compliments sir, you come to the wrong pond.'

The sun had set and the luminous darkness of a British summer evening had fled inland as starlight caused the high haze to glow. The garden pressed about them, warm, moist, breathing a heady mixture of humidity and life and he was surprised to see plants he had always considered tropical.

'Oh they do well enough in the summer,' Charlotte explained, 'but we have to take them indoors in winter. Come up here.'

At the end of the garden, steps had been cut into a hillside. At the top, the trees fell away to the south east and they could look down a long, shallow slope to the English Channel. As they watched, a red line shot up soundlessly.

'A raid,' Charlotte whispered. 'Watch.'

A searchlight beam sprang into existence and even at this distance they could see the pale cone and the ovoid top when it swept the base of a cloud. Another beam joined it, then a third and fourth, all moving restlessly through short arcs. An almost sub-audible thrumming began and the red lines increased in number until they were a slashing tangle against the sky, each terminating in a bright flash from which tiny shockwaves flickered outwards. Brighter flashes and concussions appeared at the line where land met water and twice, he saw flames leap upward.

'It happens nearly every night when the weather is clear,' Charlotte said quietly. 'Sometimes I'm ashamed of myself when I come up here to watch. It has such a . . . a . . . different beauty. I don't know any other way to describe it.' She turned restlessly and crossed her arms across her breasts and shivered.

'Perhaps Daddy should see this,' Charlotte murmured. 'I've tried to get him to come up but he only smiles and tells me that emotions are mankind's greatest enemy.'

The anti-aircraft fire disappeared and Thorne shook off the spell cast by the unholy spectacle. 'Perhaps he's right. If humans thought logically about their politics or religion, we wouldn't fight wars.' Then he cursed his banal comment. What the devil was the matter with him anyway. He was acting like a tongue-tied schoolboy.

'Perhaps.' She turned before he could amend his statement. 'Peter has told me a little of what happened to you in Poland. Not much really, as he pretends to know more than he does. Will you tell me?'

He took out a packet of cigarettes, offered her one, took one himself, and made a deliberate show of lighting them to gain time to think. His initial reaction had been to tell her to mind her own business. But as the match illuminated her face, he realized that it was not just a case of some witless girl seeking vicarious thrills. Charlotte's eyes were full of concern.

'It's a long story,' he warned but she took his arm and led him to a garden bench from where they had a wide view of the dark, glistening Channel. The moon was just beginning to edge over the eastern horizon.

The moon was well up by the time he finished and Thorne was surprised to discover that it was nearly ten-thirty.

'I think we've missed dinner,' he said but Charlotte shook her head. 'Tonight, they won't serve until eleven. A late supper. I'm sorry, I should have warned you.'

His story had a strangely unnerving effect on her. It was so different hearing it from him, the person who had lived those horrible events rather than hearing it from someone else or reading it in a newspaper or magazine. It would have lacked the intensity that unwittingly crept into the narration, even though he had spoken in a quiet, unemotional voice. And then too, he was so unlike what she had been led to expect of Americans who were always pictured as loud, aggressive and tall and spoke like the cowboys in the cinema.

As he had talked, Charlotte constructed a mental image of Deborah that would have surprised her with its accuracy. He said little about what happened to him inside the SS prison but she had read enough to guess; this time her guess fell far short of reality as she had no basis for understanding the pain, both physical and mental that could be induced by one human being in another.

His story had all the facets of a romantic adventure with him as the troubled hero – like the character Anthony Adverse, in the novel she was reading that summer.

They returned to the party a few minutes later and exchanged mutual glances of congratulations that their absence had not been remarked. But Peter sidled up to Thorne a few moments later.

'Are your intentions honourable?' he murmured. He chuckled at Thorne's startled glance. 'Watch yourself, old man. Charlotte isn't quite the innocent she appears.'

Following the late supper, the Simpsons prevailed upon him to remain for the rest of his leave. Peter pointed out that Charlotte would be driving him back to Westhampnett on Friday afternoon and he could ride along as well. 'Makes better use of the petrol, you see.'

At her encouraging nod, he agreed. A guest room was made up for him and he lay awake in a pair of borrowed pyjamas for some time, listening to the utter stillness of the countryside. The absence of aircraft engines being run up, men shouting, lorries roaring about and sirens going off, all characteristic of war-time airfields, was unnerving.

Charlotte phoned the hotel to have his bag sent up on the morning bus. The skies had turned overcast and a vague rain storm threatened. The day was warm and quite humid as they walked down the curving drive to meet the bus. Trees and bushes grew so thick in this coastal area that it seemed a jungle a few steps off the road. Lichens and moss sprouted everywhere in startling displays of muted colour. The absence of war was unsettling and, at odd moments, Thorne was jolted aware of it by the sudden appearance of something so normal he would not have noticed it another time.

In the afternoon, Charlotte prevailed on him to ride with her. The stables had been reduced to three horses because of the war.

'You see,' Charlotte told him, stroking the nose of her mare, 'when the war began, a fat old cavalry officer and the district veterinary made the rounds of all the farms and estates to requisition horses. What they intend doing with them, I don't know,' she told him as they mounted. 'The better ones in all likelihood wound up in someone's polo string while the rest will be ground into chopped meat if rationing gets any worse.'

Charlotte led him along a closely grown trail that mounted into the hills. Thunder muttered in the distance like gunfire, the atmosphere was oppressive and they had tied rain slickers to the saddles. They crested the hill and immediately, the dense foliage gave way to open parkland and scattered stands of trees. The slope flowed into a natural bowl through which a small stream ran. Beyond, Charlotte told him, the ancient lands of the New Forest began and explained that in spite of the name, the New Forest was almost nine hundred years old, having been established by William the Conqueror as a royal hunting preserve. Even today, the government maintained strict control of the major part of the preserve.

'A bit like your national park system begun by President Teddy Roosevelt. Wasn't he the father of Franklin Roosevelt?'

Thorne grinned. 'Some kind of cousin, I believe.'

A light rain began as they entered the forest proper. For several minutes, they heard it pattering on the leaves high above until it penetrated and they pulled on the slickers. An unexpected peal of thunder announced a burst of heavy rain and Charlotte laughed and shouted at him to follow. She set her horse at a quick trot along the path and Thorne urged his elderly gelding after her.

They sighted a hut, little more than a tar paper shack, with a fading public works sign above the door. Charlotte led them under a shed overhang at the back and they removed the saddles and stacked them under the eaves.

'You seek shelter!'

She stood before him, one hand poised on her right hip. Her eyes were darker than ever in the soft light, with tiny gold flecks around large deep irises. She watched him with amusement and challenge.

A challenge Thorne could not resist and he kissed her. Charlotte responded immediately and he felt her tongue touch his. Peter was right, he thought. She is dangerous. But what would Peter say about the man who took liberties with his sister? Charlotte nestled into his arms and even through the rain slickers, he could feel her firm body pressing against his. She put a hand behind his neck and leaned against him so that her breasts pushed against his chest. The action startled him and he realized that she was planning to seduce him.

367

A sudden flurry of rain drove in under the shed roof and Charlotte stepped away. 'We had better go inside,' she murmured.

Thorne nodded, realizing what that would lead to and the sudden memory of his failure with the girl in London shot panic through him. Charlotte pushed the door open, eyes laughing and head turned to say something to him.

'Good day. Wet enough for 'e?'

An elderly man dressed in baggy corduroy trousers, tweed jacket and cap was seated on a pile of weed-killer bags smoking a particularly foul pipe. 'Ducked in 'ere meself.' He grinned at Charlotte who was regarding him with dismay.

'Who are you?' she blurted.

The old man laughed. 'Sorry, mizz,' he pronounced with the buzz that marked him as a Devon native. 'Groundskeeper. Was down along in the coombe when she started in to rain.'

On Friday, 16 August, Charlotte drove the two pilots back to Westhampnett. Simpson sat up on the boot deck, wearing an old pair of flying goggles and his helmet against the windblast as Charlotte sped along the empty country road. They sang campaign songs and the sun shone brightly after the rain and the countryside was as clean as a newly minted coin.

Thorne found that he liked the Simpson family. Mrs Simpson, like her daughter, was far from the caricature English matron he had first taken her for. She had a ready laugh and was addicted to mild practical jokes. The elder Simpson wasn't as stuffy as first impressions had led him to believe. The evening before, he had dragged Thorne off for a tour of the greenhouses, his special hobby, and they discussed politics and world affairs until after midnight. He was crusty and self-opinionated, but not above according others a full airing of their views. Thorne could not help contrasting Simpson *père* with his own father, equally opinionated, but impatient with the views of others.

Thorne tried not to think about what he was returning to during the forty-minute ride as the war had belonged to another place and time the past two days. Charlotte, wearing a blue jumper and a peasant scarf which quickly blew off to free her long hair, was distraction enough.

At the gate, a red cap flagged the car to a stop and saluted. 'Sorry sirs, but the airfield is now closed to all civilian traffic. All flight officers are to report. . . .'

A flight of four Hurricanes blasting into the afternoon sky drowned the rest of the sentence. Thorne and Peter exchanged glances, then Peter kissed Charlotte quickly and hopped out.

Thorne stooped awkwardly and Charlotte accepted his formal kiss, then threw her arms about his neck and kissed him fiercely, opening her lips and thrusting her tongue against his. 'Next time,' she barely whispered.

'Telephone me when you get leave again,' she said in a normal voice as he straightened and wiped away the smear of lipstick. Charlotte laughed, slipped the MG into gear and the tiny engine screamed as she shot around the guard post in a tight circle and roared back along the lane to the road. The SP shook his head, grinning and Peter guffawed. Thorne, aware that his face was bright red, started to curse under his breath when the air raid alert went.

'Lorry, sirs,' the SP pointed and they ran towards the vehicle.

The flight of Messerschmitt 110s appeared low over the field as the lorry disgorged them on the flight line. Bombs fell in a diagonal path across the field towards the administration complex. The pilots and driver dove for a slit trench as the first aircraft passed over their heads.

There were four of the sleek, twin-engined bombers and the roar of their unsynchronized engines coupled with the continual snarling of anti-aircraft cannon and machine guns and the explosions of their bombs was deafening. When the bombers were past, they vaulted from the trench and ran for the flight line. For some reason the German aircraft had ignored the Hurricanes and concentrated on the hangars and administration buildings. As they ran, Thorne saw, low in the south over the distant hills, black specks of more attackers.

He and Peter reached their aircraft well ahead of the others. The engines were already warm and the ground crew buckled them into parachute harnesses and life jackets and literally tossed them onto the wings. Thorne slid down into the cockpit and the straps were fastened as he completed a fast pre-flight check. The senior NCO dashed his signature onto the 700 form and waved the airframe mechanic to snatch away the wheel chocks.

The Hurricane bounded forward. The breeze was light and he raced straight across the field towards the trees edging the far side. As the Hurricane lifted, he risked a glance behind and saw Simpson coming after him. They climbed for altitude as the new swarm of bombers swept over the edge of the field. There would be fighters above, he knew, waiting for them, and he keyed his microphone.

'Foxtrot Three to any other Foxtrot. Form on me. Ignore the fighter cover. Get the bombers!'

Two more aircraft clawed their way into the air. A fifth faltered as its wheels came off the ground, cartwheeled and exploded in flames. Peter's Hurricane wheeled into position on his starboard side and Thorne waved an arm and pointed at the 110s, proposing to attack head on into the fearsome concentration of four 7.92 machine guns and two twenty-millimetre MG FF cannons grouped about the nose of each aircraft as they completed their turn around the field. Foxtrot two and five acknowledged.

Thorne concentrated on the Me.110 growing in the reflector sight. The German gunner, who also doubled as bomb aimer, had not seen him yet and Thorne fired at fifty yards. The Hurricane jerked in the familiar way and red lights winked in the nose and canopy of the Me.110 where the explosive De Wilde bullets struck. There wasn't time to see more and he rolled violently as they shot past one another at a combined speed in excess of six hundred miles an hour.

A second line of bombers appeared. This time the pilot was more alert and Thorne heard a metallic cracking as bullets whanged into the fuselage and wings. He touched the rudder pedal slightly to bring the tail around and pressed the trigger button. Chunks of debris erupted around the Me.110's cockpit and he yanked the Hurricane hard into a wing-over, gritting his teeth against the G-forces that drew a red haze over his vision.

He came out of the turn directly behind the fighter-bombers. They were clear of the field now and the Me.110s were turning for the coast while the Me.109Es stooped on them like killer hawks.

'Bandits, two o'clock high,' he said calmly into the microphone. 'Foxtrot two and five engage. Peter, follow me.'

Behind, he sensed as much as glimpsed the two Hurricanes climbing to meet the approaching fighters. He wanted to join them but killing bombers was more important. There was no time to calculate the odds against the two left behind or even to wonder if other aircraft had made it off or where the flight of four Hurricanes that had taken off moments before the warning had got to.

They were over the Channel now, closing at an angle as the two remaining bombers raced for home. The sun was brilliant on the azure water and Portsmouth, shining like a Mediterranean coastal city, lay off his right wing tip. Curiously, there were no columns of smoke there. The Germans had concentrated solely on the air-field. Had Tangmere been hit as hard? If not, where the devil were her aircraft? Red flashes fluttered at the rear of the Me.110 cockpit and he declined to jink to throw the gunner off. He was two hundred yards distant, too far for accurate shooting. The head-phones were silent and the sky was empty except for the two bombers and Simpson's Hurricane. The glowing red dot on the illuminated gunsight clarified. The Me.110 was faster than his Hurricane but the angle of closure was making up the difference. He held his fire, waiting. Eighty yards, seventy. White tracers drifted past – Simpson had fired; too impatient. . . .

At fifty yards, the Me.110 he had chosen was centred perfectly and he pressed the firing button. The lines of tracer arced into the wing root. He pressed the firing button again and lifted the nose a touch and saw the tracer rounds chew across the cockpit. The rear gunner fired a short burst at him; Thorne was now in the suicide position, attacking from directly astern, but the long chase had left him no other choice.

The bomber bucked suddenly and a long streamer of smoke burst from the starboard engine. The Me.110 banked gently to the right and fell into a shallow dive and he knew the pilot had been hit. As he went past, he saw the rear section of the cockpit tear away in the slipstream and the gunner struggled out as a wing folded. He watched the man plummet and was curiously relieved when the parachute appeared. Then he cursed himself and turned back to the business at hand.

There was one more Me.110 still out of range ahead and he looked around for Simpson and saw instead a lone Me.109E. He pulled the stick in tight and pressed the rudder bar to tighten the turn. The Messerschmitt stuck and his vision began to redden as the curve drew in. The Hurricane Mark I was 20 miles an hour slower than the Me.109E but they were nearly evenly matched in turning ability; but the other pilot was wearing full flying gear and he was not and there was no way he could win this one.

Thorne half-rolled to prevent the engine stalling and fell off into a dive. The German pilot's reflexes proved exceptionally good and he hung on, waiting for a clear shot. Thorne swept out of the dive into a high roll, winged over at the top and sideslipped. He kicked the rudder hard to open the distance between them, then yanked the nose up and chopped the throttle. He had used that manoeuvre to win a regional combat final in 1936. As he pulled the throttle open, he prayed that the Hurricane would recover from the stall fast enough. The German shot past and Thorne corrected with a bit of rudder to turn onto the German's tail and fired two quick bursts to keep him off balance. The German jinked hard and dove and Thorne followed him down. Again, they flattened out at less than a hundred feet above the waves, only this time, their positions were reversed. The Me.109E shuddered as red lights danced on the after fuselage. A solid mass of tracers blew a chunk of metal off the vertical stabilizer and Thorne's guns stopped abruptly. The Messerschmitt recovered altitude and fled. Cursing, Thorne yanked the Hurricane up and around in a tight circle for Westhampnett.

The German bombers had wreaked havoc among the administration buildings and hangars. Fire raged everywhere and the grassy runway was pocked with bomb craters. Thorne was waved into a new parking area where sweating soldiers were busy throwing up new sandbagged revetments. His rigger slung a last sandbag into position and Thorne saw him shout for the others and come trotting towards the aircraft. The three looked exhausted.

The chief poured a mug of tea from his thermos. 'Get this inside. Make you feel a 'undred times better, sir.'

Thorne sipped at the scalding, sweet liquid while the fitter described the raid.

'Heard the sirens go and they were on us. Went for the buildings first, the stupid sods. Left the aircraft all sitting in a row like ducks on a pond. PO Farely was killed when his plane crashed. Took off right behind you, he did. Heard on the R/T just before you come in that Jerry's plastering all the airfields in the south counties.'

'Have you heard anything about PO Simpson?'

The chief fitter shook his head. 'Sorry, sir. Not a word. Several of the lads is overdue.'

Thorne walked slowly towards the remains of the barracks while his Hurricane was being serviced, unable to rid himself of the sick feeling that Simpson had bought it. The two wooden frame buildings that served as pilots' quarters showed light bomb damage and one wall was scorched. Inside, the room smelled of scorched paint, cordite and death.

142 Squadron lost five pilots, including Pilot Officer Peter Simpson, that afternoon, the worst one-day toll in its history. Thorne's section was scrambled twice more before dark. He knocked down another bomber and damaged a fighter and the following day was posted with two kills and three possibles. There had been no one to confirm the second Me.110 shot down as Simpson disappeared.

A piece of slate salvaged from the Ops. Room had been set up in a corner of a canvas tent and the names of missing pilots lined through as each was accounted for. Simpson's name remained until the following day. Thorne had just come in from his second patrol when the operations officer waved him over.

'They've found Peter's aircraft,' he said in a voice hoarse with exhaustion. He motioned to the board where a fresh chalk line had been drawn through his name.

'An army patrol found his Hurricane washed up on the beach this morning. Simpson was still at the controls. He must have been damaged and tried to make it to the coast.'

Thorne nodded slowly.

'His family have been notified. A chaplain from the naval base took the news.'

The air battles increased in frequency and fury. Invasion rumours swept both Britain and Germany and vied with daily aircraft kill totals for public attention. But for the ground crews and pilots on both sides there was only the next patrol and the next raid to be survived.

Canvas tents were erected about aircraft and work went on all night while night raiders prowled the skies over southern England or the French coast, searching for the faintest sign of light at which to aim a bomb or a machine gun. Men on both sides lost track of meals and stumbled about half-asleep. Some developed such an aversion to tea and coffee which were consumed by the gallon that they never drank another drop for the rest of their lives. Few pilots on either side became inured to the strain of not knowing if they would survive the coming day. Some broke under the strain but the majority endured and died or lived as much by luck as skill.

Pilot Officer Keith Thorne survived. He could feel the tension in his gut as a constant, never varying ache. His stomach was a mass of churning acid and he slept fitfully, if at all. Pilots on both sides had been on the thin edge of exhaustion for weeks even before the air battles intensified; now they developed in common a haggard, smudged appearance, as if their features had been drawn by indifferent artists.

When they looked back on those six weeks, the surviving pilots of 142 Squadron would be able to recall only isolated moments or specific scenes. The rest was buried far too deeply by exhaustion and fear to ever be recalled as a coherent whole. Instead, those suppressed memories became the catalyst for life-long nightmares.

A scene that remained in Thorne's memory was of standing outside a Nissen hut one September morning, just at dawn because he could not stand to have the siren jolt him from sleep one more time. The sun was rising in glory behind low-lying clouds and the old rhyme

Red at night, sailor's delight,
Red in the morning, sailor's warning.

passed through his mind. He prayed that it would prove correct, that it would rain and so allow them to rest.

On the first day of September, Thorne was promoted to Flight Lieutenant and made acting squadron leader – the fourth since May – when his predecessor was killed in a mid-air collision with a Heinkel bomber. Just the night before, he had nailed a cigarette packet dated 2 March 1940, over the bar.

RAF fighter aircraft strength had reached a peak of 740 including 63 Blenheims, 23 Defiants and 6 Gladiators on 24 August but had declined badly since. On 3 September, Fighter Command operational strength stood at 707, only 621 of which were Hurricanes and Spitfires. The older Blenheims, Gladiators and Defiants were no match for the sophisticated Me.109Es and Me.110s.

Thorne often thought how different the actuality of war was from what he had expected in the palmier days of the mid-1930s. Military pilots formed a select club in the United States as, of course, they had in the rest of the world. Thorne, like all professional soldiers, had often protested that he never wanted war. But it simply hadn't been true. In the first place, he and his comrades were not professional soldiers; not one had ever participated in combat. They were too young to have served in the First World War and those who had were now upper echelon officers as remote from them as they were from the enlisted ranks. War had then seemed the entire *raison d'être*.

Their ideas of combat had been shaped by the novels of Nordoff and Hall and the movies of Howard Hughes. Combat flying was considered the ultimate experience for any military pilot but my God he thought, how different was reality from remembered dreams.

Thorne now knew the physical and mental aspects of terror first hand. The fear he had experienced the day he crashed the B-17 had been too transitory to have left a deep impression. He had been terrified in the SS prison and at the moment Deborah was executed but that had been quickly transmuted into anger and hatred. But the kind of fear he was now experiencing did not fade but was reinforced daily and continued week after week. It occupied the depths of his mind, it waited for the unguarded moment to burst forth; it caused adrenalin to spurt and his heart to race and his throat to constrict so that he felt he was always on the verge of choking. Hormones flooded his body and a burning, sinking feeling – physical as well as mental – was a constant. He could not force food past his convulsing throat. What sleep he managed was fitful and full of horrible images of death.

The fear tore his insides to pieces, reduced him to a mass of quivering nerves, a tub of guts filled with diarrhoeic jelly that did more to erode his self-confidence and ability to think coherently than the thought of death or maiming. His strength had gone and, like the others, he was content to doze in a lawn chair between alarm bells, clad in flying boots, jacket and life jacket to save time, face turned to the sun, mind blank, existing. He hated the fear more than he hated the faceless enemy who was only a leather-clad, oxygen-masked blob behind a sun-glinting canopy.

At first, Thorne wondered if he was a coward. But then he began to see the same uncontrolled tics, the moody stares, the sudden tears in his fellow pilots, and as all combat soldiers do sooner or later, came to realize that he was no different and no more a coward than they. And finally, he understood that even the concept of cowardice was meaningless. Sooner or later, everyone reached an intolerable limit of fear and when they could contain no more, broke. Only fools, the insane or the safe thought otherwise.

London 5 – 8 September 1940

On September fifth, bad weather brought a lull and Thorne sat in his office reading Charlotte's letter for the fifteenth time.

> . . . and so darling, if you can get away anywhere even for a day, please, please tell me. I'll meet you wherever it is! I still get very angry when I think of that damned little man in the forest shelter! If only you knew the pains with which I arranged that rendezvous without rousing Mummy's and Daddy's suspicions. . . .

Since Peter's death he had received two invitations from her parents to spend a few days' leave with them. But there had been no opportunity, even if he had been so inclined; he had no wish to become the substitute for their son.

The Wing Commander stepped through the open office door and rummaged through his pockets for his stubby pipe.

'It's no good you know.'

'Sir?'

'Killing yourself with overwork. The Hun will do it for you quick enough. Now the Air Marshal has directed that all pilots with excessive flying hours be rotated to Group Ten for a rest.' He lit the pipe and stared at Thorne through the clouds of smoke for his reaction. 'Hate to lose you. Lasted longer than most, so I'll give you a choice. Two days' leave in London or rotation.'

'Two days,' he said promptly.

Thorne telephoned the estate agent in London and learned that the flat was empty. He arranged to have food and whatever liquor was procurable sent over. Then he stared at the phone for several minutes, feeling his resolve begin to ebb. He swore at himself and dialled.

Charlotte answered and he took a deep breath, told her about his sudden leave, described how to find the key and, in spite of her letters, was surprised when she readily agreed.

The flat had been closed for so long that the interior was damp and smelled of mildew. Thorne threw open all the windows and checked the kitchen, then wandered disconsolately into the sitting room, wishing to God he dared have a drink, and sat down to wait. The loud ticking of the Westminster clock was the only sound in the afternoon silence. He remembered his last fiasco in these rooms. Would it happen again? Angrily, he tried to think of something else.

Charlotte arrived in late afternoon. She had missed the first train because it was full and had to take a later one and her chagrin was evident. She wore a one-piece dress that gathered sharply at the waist to emphasize her bust. Her hair was as long and honey coloured as he remembered and fell softly across one side of her face, like a movie star's. It was incredible, he thought. He had only met her once before and yet he still felt perfectly comfortable.

She smiled at his quizzical stare. 'Yes?'

'Nothing, just . . .' he stopped the banal flow of words in time. Charlotte laughed and swept into his arms.

'Don't talk. Just kiss me, then take me to bed.'

Maybe it was the lengthy period of abstinence, or perhaps Charlotte's eagerness. In any case, his fears proved groundless and the result was satisfying, for both of them. He lay beside her later, one hand thrown across his eyes, relaxed for the first time in weeks and all thoughts of the war banished.

'Pangs of remorse?' she asked softly.

'My God, no!' He rolled over. The twilight was fading and the room was in dusk. 'Why would you ask that?'

'You were so silent. I wondered if it was because I was a virgin.'

Thorne grinned. 'Surprise, I suppose.'

'Surprise?'

'That a virgin over age sixteen exists – existed. You are over sixteen aren't you?'

Charlotte sat up abruptly. 'I like that, you bloody monster. I'll. . . .'

Laughing, Thorne pulled her down and she snuggled against his chest. With his free hand, he drew the blanket over them both.

'This is perfect,' she murmured. 'If only it could last forever.'

'It might, if you don't talk about it.'

After she had fallen asleep, he lay thinking about her. She was so different. There was none of the subdued friction that had always existed with Shirley. And unlike Shirley, Charlotte, after the first, brief hesitation, was amazingly responsive, enthusiastically so. She did not just go through the motions as so many women did. His feelings for her were, were what? he wondered. Protectiveness was uppermost – a strange feeling about someone so independent. He had the uncomfortable feeling that her strength of character far surpassed his. Then too, he had somehow expected her to be pale and withdrawn, still in mourning for her brother, dead less than a month. Had it been that long? he thought. A month? More than once he had found himself watching her in an unguarded moment. Her expression would take on a certain blankness sometimes and he guessed that she was enduring in those moments, waiting simply for the pain to abate.

He nuzzled her tousled hair and ran his fingers lightly over the subtle curve of her back. Why, of all the men, of all the pilots she had known when her brother was alive, had she picked him? He could not believe his incredibly good fortune.

After a quiet lunch at his favourite London restaurant, La Petite Estelle, they walked along the Thames Embankment under the barrage balloons the Londoners had nick-named Dumbos. It was late on Saturday afternoon and the streets were flooded with people and motor cars in spite of the petrol rationing scheme. They were nearly to the Vauxhall Bridge when air-raid sirens began to wail. Londoners were no strangers to air-raid warnings – the first had sounded on 3 September 1939, within an hour of Prime Minister Chamberlain's announcement that a state of war existed between Germany and Great Britain – but after twelve months of mostly false alarms, most people regarded them as more a nuisance. A few bombs had fallen on civilian property, especially around the airfields at Croydon and Biggin Hill, but even so few people bothered to go to the shelters any longer, much to the chagrin of the Air Raid Precautions wardens.

They heard the bombers before they saw them; countless silvery specks flashing in the sun as they approached in perfect formation looking much as he had seen them dozens of times from the air. He had never seen so many bombers massed in one fleet before and decided that there must be close to three hundred aircraft all told. The first explosions were low rumbles to the east and south – the docks in the East End. Dense pillars of smoke began to roll skyward. Distant anti-aircraft guns began to fire, the heavier ones sounding like sacks of rock being dropped on iron sheets and the smaller ones like bacon fat as it snapped and sizzled.

The rumble grew and merged with the peculiar noise of hundreds of desynchronized engines until the city vibrated to a vast, sub-sonic roar. They stood hand-in-hand on the bridge approach, watching with thousands of other Londoners as the Blitz began on 7 September 1940.

English Channel 8 September 1940

Three hours later, Thorne fought his way through the crowds at Victoria and, because of his uniform and pilot's wings, was given two tickets on the night train for Southampton. Charlotte slept most of the way against his shoulder and he quickly kissed her goodbye at the station where military police were gathering up military personnel and sorting them out to their destinations. Thorne's last glimpse of Charlotte came as the ancient bus ground out of the station square. She was standing on tiptoe, trying to catch a glimpse of him. He knew she did not see his wave.

He discovered that two new replacements had come in during his absence, one of them a cocky Australian named Jennings. He was a short, dark-haired pilot with an excess of energy who had completed the conversion course to single-seaters. Thorne saw a good bit of himself in the boy and sensed he would make an excellent fighter pilot if he could be taught to maintain discipline in the heady environment of fighter aircraft. The other man, Flight Lieutenant Vincent Mathers, also a bomber pilot, was nearer his age and seemed steady enough. Thorne took Jennings on as his wingmate.

'Check out the new boy, hey?' Jennings laughed as they climbed out of the lorry when it stopped on the flight line. It was just dawn and alerts were going out all over England and Scotland. There was a feeling of tense expectation about the day; everyone sensed that the bombing of London the previous evening had changed the rules of the game. The morning raids would tell them whether the bombers intended to switch targets or would instead resume their aerodrome-raiding techniques which were on the verge of destroying the RAF as an effective fighting force.

'That's right,' he murmured.

He gathered the squadron pilots about him. 'I know you are all tired. Tired hell, if you feel like I do, you are half dead and I had a full day's rest. The rules are the same. Save your life and the wingman's and bring those aircraft back. Ignore the fighters and knock down any Hun bomber you can, but the object is to get back, alive and whole.'

He turned to the new pilots. 'We fly in three sections, fingers four formation. Weave constantly and keep your head swivelling. I'm sure you've both heard the phrase, "Beware the Hun in the sun." Pay attention to it. Other than that, there are only three fixed rules in this squadron and they are never, never broken. Number one, stick on your wingman like glue, no matter what. You must protect him. Number two, keep radio silence unless I speak to you or you spot bandits. And number three, newcomers buy the first round. Remember,' he repeated for emphasis. 'Stick to your wingman.'

Jennings' grin was just a bit too easy and Thorne felt compelled to add, 'You won't be protecting just me. The aircraft is every bit as important.'

Iceberg masses of clouds filed across the sky and his flight slid through sunlit corridors. Where are the Germans? he wondered as the controllers remained silent until forty-five minutes into the patrol.

'Red Indian One, this is Punjab,' he heard them calling other patrols. 'Box building over Calais. Estimated sixty-five aircraft at angels twelve. China Two this is Phoenix, estimated thirty-five aircraft moving towards Dutch coast, vicinity of Zeeland. Sabre One this is. . . .'

Fact began to replace guesswork as the volume of enemy activity built. Thorne switched frequencies and warned his flight to be on the alert.

At 0830 hours, Punjab Control called his code name. 'Foxtrot One, this is Punjab calling. Box moving your way, estimated contact in six minutes. Appear to be bombers sixty plus at angels ten. Escorted by fighters at angels thirteen. Vector thirty.'

Thorne acknowledged and passed the information to the squadron and turned onto the heading ten degrees in excess of that given him by the controller to bring the sun at their backs. They were cruising at eleven thousand feet on the return leg of their patrol, two thousand below the German fighter canopy and a thousand above the bombers and so would attack from the east – in the same direction as the bombers were moving. Perfect position he thought, sandwiched between with only a short run out of the sun to be made. They flew towards the distant coast at the interception angle, shadows flickering on the sides of thunderheads towering another fifteen thousand feet above them.

'Bandits, eight o'clock low.'

Thorne picked them out instantly; seventy plus, he estimated, Heinkels and Dorniers in tightly bunched formation that allowed each aircraft to protect another. He found the fighters above, three flights of four each – *rotas* the Germans called them – so far, unaware of their presence.

'Wait, boys,' he murmured into the microphone. Their course was converging steadily; in less than a minute the bombers would be below them – the familiar gamble again. Wait for the perfect position and chance discovery or attack now and possibly miss?

'What are we waiting for?' Jennings demanded and Thorne glanced quickly at the aircraft behind his starboard wing.

'Jennings, shut up,' he snapped. 'And close up.'

Jennings' Hurricane edged up and Thorne caught his sardonic wave. But there wasn't time to worry about him. The bomber stream was almost directly below now.

'Safeties off,' he said into the microphone quietly, as if afraid the Germans might hear. 'Pick your target. Stay on it and stick together. I'll count down. Four . . . three . . . two . . . one. Go!'

Thorne nosed the Hurricane over. Jennings had anticipated his count and was slightly ahead but the short dive did not allow time for adjustments and he kept still, concentrating instead on keeping one Heinkel bomber in his gunsight. He fastened onto the leader. There was the usual burst of panicky fear that the aircraft were too tightly packed to fly through – he had seen three mid-air collisions – but he knew that it was largely an optical illusion caused by the ice-clear air and the angle of approach.

The Heinkel's wings filled the reflector sight from edge to edge and he pressed the trigger twice in short ranging bursts and red flares danced across the fuselage. He touched the rudder pedal gently to increase the angle and fired a long burst. The Heinkel's port wing disappeared abruptly and the bomber rolled starboard and began to tumble and then he was past and pulling the stick back hard against his stomach to drag the Hurricane out of the dive and back into the swarm for another run. A reddish-grey haze filmed his vision at the bottom of the arc. A Dornier swam past, floating against a blinding white cloud as he climbed again. Thorne blinked hard to squeeze out tears. The Dornier was growing in the gunsight reflector and he risked a quick scan. Nothing. Not even Jennings. The Dornier was less than sixty yards ahead and above. His approach was perfect, right through the gunner's blind spot, and he fired two short bursts and saw them hit dead on. Flame blossomed from the Dornier's port engine and he was past. Where the hell was Jennings?

'Jennings,' he shouted into the microphone, 'close on me!'

A voice laughed and someone else was speaking, shouting rather. 'There, straight on, after him,' he recognized the voices of Welby and Harrison. 'I can't at the moment, Squadron Leader,' Jennings' voice broke in. 'I'm in the midst of pranging a bloody great Heinkel.'

Thorne cursed and jinked sideways. He jinked again and the

sound of rattling scrap iron filled the cockpit. A hole appeared in his windscreen and the Hurricane shuddered. He rolled off one wing, turned left and in the mirror caught a glimpse of a yellow spinner hard on his tail. The scrap iron sound again and the cockpit was full of choking white smoke. Glycol, he thought in fury and fear. Something exploded and slammed his head against the rest. The German was going to follow him right down and make certain. His mind churned furiously as the Hurricane shuddered and dropped into a spin. He kicked the pedals and thrust the stick in every direction to no avail.

Hardly aware of what he was doing, he punched the quick release on his seat belt and dragged himself up against the centrifugal force of the spin. The cockpit canopy refused to slide back and he battered at it with his fist in frustration, but it had jammed solidly in the track. He hunched his shoulders against the frame and pushed with his knees in one convulsive heave. The alloy seat distorted but the canopy slammed back and for an instant, he hung half over the side of the cockpit coaming, his boot caught in the broken seat. A shadow sliced past, the tailplane, and he was tumbling end over end. Sky, cloud and water blurred as he fought for the ripcord with his left hand. His right arm refused to function and the fingers of his left were stiff with the terrible cold and the wind sucked at him. A finger hooked the ring by accident and the shock of the opening chute snatched him hard and jounced him twice.

He hung quiescent in the shrouds. The canopy was a white cloud above him and there was no sense of falling. Far below, something struck the sea and exploded. After a while, he realized that it was his own Hurricane.

The chill brought him to consciousness. Thorne coughed and choked water from his lungs and struggled to lift his head. A wave broke and forced him under and he panicked and struggled for the surface. The parachute billowed and filled like a great balloon and dragged him up. He remembered what had happened, what he had to do to survive. The quick-release. He struggled to find the buckle with his left arm. He pushed it and the harness went slack. He screamed in agony as a belt caught on his right arm. It broke away, dragging his arm up and he saw that the sleeve of his Irvin jacket was scorched and torn to ribbons. The Mae West, his training prompted, but he hadn't the strength to find the tube and blow it up. The kapok filling would have to serve. A shadow passed over and his ears were assaulted by a scream. Something struck the water not far away and he saw an Me.109, throttled down, pass above him. Twenty or more yards away bobbed a yellow package. The engine's roar made him realize that the package was a life raft and without it, he was dead. He began to stroke with his left arm and kick feebly. The Mae West hampered him and his sodden flying suit weighed him down and he was too weak to try and remove it underwater.

The package bobbed away and he redoubled his effort, swearing at every stroke, mouthing water and coughing and retching as the chop slapped his face. The water was very cold and what little strength he had left was slipping away. His arm struck something and his fingers clutched slippery rubber, sought and found a trailing strap. Acting by instinct, he yanked and the raft hissed and began to unfold. Somehow, he dragged himself in and sprawled on the flexing, dancing bottom, too exhausted to do more. Above him the Messerschmitt made a final pass and disappeared.

What had made the German pilot drop him his life-raft? Thorne wondered. The man was his enemy. German pilots sometimes shot RAF pilots to death as they floated earthward in their parachutes and the RAF pilots retaliated against Luftwaffe pilots in the same manner over the Channel – curiously, a German pilot descending over British soil was safe, already considered a prisoner.

A cup or so of water sloshed back and forth past his mouth and nose and he hadn't even the strength left to move his head.

His mind veered away from the unknown German pilot to Jennings. The boy had disobeyed the rule to stick to one's wingmate. He hadn't followed procedure. Thorne tried to laugh. Jennings had seen an opportunity and taken it and perhaps he had shot down his Heinkel. Thorne had also seen an opportunity one day and turned a damaged B-17 towards a distant airfield that wasn't there. Both actions had seemed right at the time and both would have been, except that fate was prone to playing nasty tricks.

Funny, he thought. The flying instructors could have made it so easy for him if they had only taken the time to explain. But then, Thorne knew, he would have paid no more attention to them than Jennings had to him. It was so funny that he was going to die.

On 8 September 1940, one RAF pilot was killed, five went missing and five were wounded in action. One RAF pilot was rescued by the Life Boat Service from a yellow Luftwaffe life raft. Two British aircraft were lost as against fifteen German. The tide had begun to turn.

My sentence is for open war

Paradise Lost
Milton

Libya 13 – 21 September 1940

On 13 September 1940, Lieutenant Alfredo Marchetti stepped out of his tent and stood looking east into the brilliant North African dawn. He drew a deep breath and clenched his hands, still trembling with the nervous apprehension that had kept him awake most of the night. His batman appeared with a cup of coffee and Marchetti gulped the steaming liquid.

'Is everything packed?'

The batman took the empty cup. 'Yes sir.'

Marchetti strode towards the neat line of tents before which his company was assembling on the stretch of sand that constituted their parade ground. Captain Giulio Maroni arrived at the same moment and the senior non-commissioned officer called the company to attention. Marchetti fastened his hands behind his back, assumed a stern expression and followed the captain along the line.

His demi-company was the best in the crack Sixty-Third Cirene Division. They had taken honours twice for drilling although that had been in Italy, months before he had joined the Division. But certainly, they looked like soldiers. Their uniforms were smart, boots shined and rifles glistening with oil. The Sixty-Third was new to the desert and Marchetti had joined them only two weeks ago himself. He could still remember his first sight of the town of Bardia with its gleaming white houses and buildings in the midday sun. What a contrast it had been to the incredible squalor and seediness he found when he stepped ashore. He thought with disdain that Arabs lived like pigs.

Whistles blew and the divisional band struck up a stirring march. Orders were shouted and working parties began to strike the tents. A crowd of civilians had gathered on the edge of the camp in spite of the early hour and their cheering rolled across the scrub. The Italian population had turned out *en masse* to see them off. To one side, though, he noted a group of sullen Arabs watching silently.

The column was two kilometres long and as the sun rose and the plume of dust scuffed up by thousands of feet cloaked the marching men, their smartness quickly disappeared. Boots became caked with the penetrating dust, faces went yellow with it and uniforms assumed a sandy tint. All had been issued desert goggles but the blazing heat made them uncomfortable to wear and many preferred to suffer with the dust. Even so, they were a stirring sight and pride swelled in him. The British Army would break and run before them as they had done before the Germans, by God!

The column was halted briefly every hour, and at noon for thirty minutes. The endless kilometres of desert and dust were made worse by lorries and tanks that went clanking past and added petrol and diesel fumes to the air and even more of the insufferable dust. This was Marchetti's first real taste of the desert and he did not like it. The pervasive sand got into one's eyes, caked one's throat and covered one's skin with a fine, even coat which itched terribly when one perspired.

He recalled his feeling of dismay the day he had arrived and the elderly corporal who introduced himself as his batman, showed him a hard cot inside an overheated tent which he was expected to share with another officer. Why, the cot hadn't even sheets and the blankets were filthy. He had ordered the corporal to have them washed immediately.

'How can you possibly allow such conditions in an officer's....'

'Ah, good morning, Lieutenant. You must be the new replacement. Allow me to introduce myself. I am Lieutenant Carlo Cremoritti.' He held out a grimy hand and Marchetti took it gingerly. The man was a Sicilian – his voice was too loud, his manner too hearty and his skin too greasy for his liking.

'You must forgive our poor housekeeping,' he said, dismissing the corporal with a wave. 'Unfortunately, it is not possible to wash your bedding as there is no water to spare. In fact, you will find that fresh water is very limited. I would advise you to conserve your allotment intended for washing in order to drink it. With the entire Mediterranean less than a kilometre away there is plenty for such other purposes. We are allowed six litres of fresh water per day and that is barely sufficient in this heat.' He wiped his streaming face with a filthy, sweat-stained handkerchief and Marchetti cringed.

He smiled wryly at the horror with which he had greeted Cremoritti's suggestions. But he soon overcame his civilized scruples. In fact, after less than a week, he had begun to take pride in the fact that his lips were cracked and his skin already taking on the leathery appearance of a veteran. He was beginning to discover that a real soldier considered it more important to do one's job well than worry how one looked.

At 1500 hours, when the heat was at its worst, the column halted for the day and the men were allowed an hour's rest before fatigue detail. Marchetti checked his demi-company and collapsed onto his camp stool while his batman raised the tent. He crawled inside then and lay panting in the heat, trying to remember when he had ever been so exhausted. Thank God, he didn't have to carry a pack but even the weight of his Beretta pistol and holster had begun to drag in these last hours and his cavalry boots were twin cylinders of sweat, and pinched his feet besides. They looked very military, but had obviously not been designed for marching.

The column had covered the twenty-five required kilometres that day and the senior officers were pleased with their progress, Marchetti discovered when he dragged himself to headquarters to attend the evening briefing. Everything was brisk and businesslike for once. All of the rancour and wrangling of past meetings was absent now that they were on the move. The officers present had been in the desert at least a month and the regiment had been blooded in combat against the French in June and a number of the officers and men were veterans of the Abyssinian Campaign as well.

By contrast, this was not only Marchetti's first combat assignment but his first assignment to a field regiment. Heretofore, he had served in staff positions or as military attaché in Warsaw and before that in Madrid. Only his father's timely warning had enabled him to request a field assignment in the nick of time. To have missed campaigning against the British in Egypt would have been devastating and a detriment to his career as well.

He returned exhausted to his tent, undressed and lay down on his cot. The heat was stifling and fine grit chaffed and burned in every body crevice. When he could not stand it any longer, he got up, removed his underwear, wrapped a towel around his waist and went out.

All during the long day, the marching columns of perspiring, parched men had been tantalized by the Mediterranean. They had turned inland only in the last few hundred metres of the march and the sea lay half a kilometre away, mercifully hidden by low sand dunes. The western sky still glowed with the final moments of sunset and reds and oranges fading to blues and magentas. The air was clear in spite of the heat, and when he looked back, white tents were sharply outlined against the darkening sky. He passed a sentry who only stared after him.

To his surprise the beach was deserted. He had expected other officers and even enlisted men to be bathing. Perhaps they had done so earlier. As he strode into the delightfully cool water, he was reminded of that evening in June when he and . . . now what was her name, that daughter of the Chilean diplomat who had gone with him for a midnight swim at Cadiz and afterwards made love until dawn. There were, he thought with a smile, some compensations after all for the boring duties of a military attaché.

Marchetti slid into a crawl, enjoying the sensual feel of the water washing the dirt and perspiration away. The High Command should arrange for every soldier to bathe at the end of a day, he thought and resolved to march his men *en masse* to the sea whenever the opportunity presented.

He dried himself with the towel and started back. As he struggled over the dunes and started down onto the graveled hardpan, cursing because he hadn't worn his bedroom slippers, something off to his left clinked against a stone. He stopped, uncertain. The last light had gone from the day with the abruptness characteristic of the desert, the moon had not yet risen and a high haze obscured all but the brightest stars. Marchetti knelt and drew the towel higher to conceal the gleam of his white skin.

A voice muttered nearby. Arabic? A torch beam sprang out and Marchetti held his breath. Who were they? What were they looking for? Suddenly, he was deathly afraid; he was unarmed and alone and half a kilometre from camp and safety. All the tales he had heard about the Arabs and their hatred for his fellow-countrymen since he had arrived in Cyrenaica rattled through his mind.

The urge to run, shouting for the sentry, was overwhelming but he held himself rigidly in check, knowing they would be on him before he had gone three steps. The light flicked past and he steeled himself for a shout and rush of feet, but the beam went out and the voices moved on towards the beach. When Marchetti was certain they were out of earshot, he began to run.

For three more days, they followed the coast road and the outline of the great offensive began to take positive shape in Marchetti's mind as he studied the situation map each evening. They had crossed the Libyan border the previous day into Egypt. However, the high spirits of the first days seemed to give way to reluctance on the part of the staff to press forward. Only the most vigorous prompting from Rome kept them moving.

There were already signs that supply lines were beginning to break down. The heat and the terrible roads took a vicious toll of the motorized transport and consequently food, and even water, was often delayed. Even so, General Annible Bergonzoli, commanding the XXIII Corps, of which the Sixty-third Cirene Division was a part, now stood less than one day's march from their first objective inside Egypt, the coastal town of Sidi Barrani.

The General spoke for thirty minutes that evening regarding its vital importance to both sides. 'Sidi Barrani is only the first objective,' he told them in a voice grown hoarse from the irritating effects of the dust.

'The loss of all Egypt will be a mortal blow to England as it will close the Suez Canal to her shipping. Her holdings in the Middle

East will wither. Communications with India, Burma, Singapore and Malaya will collapse. Nothing will stand in our way to the oil fields of the Middle East. We are supported every step of the way by the Duce's example and courage. The Mediterranean Sea is now an Italian lake, our *Mare Nostrum*, as the world's four most powerful battleships, *Littorio*, *Vittorio Veneto*, *Caio Diulio*, and *Andrea Doria*, have now joined our magnificent naval fleet! Italy is invincible!' he roared.

'Tomorrow, we attack Sidi Barrani. Return to your commands and make certain your soldiers know exactly why we are here and what they are expected to do.'

Bergonzoli stepped back and saluted and the officers filed out of the stifling tent. The Mediterranean gleamed in the dull moonlight and Marchetti left the others to their cynical commentary on the General's speech and started towards his tent. He removed his pith helmet and massaged his brow where the hat band had begun to chafe.

His demi-company would have returned from their bathe by now, which always seemed to improve their morale a hundred-fold. He had been teased by his fellow officers, of course. And Captain Maroni had gone so far as to hint that such concern for enlisted men smacked of Bolshevik tendencies. But then Maroni was a stupid man. He had sharply pointed out to the captain that the senior Marchetti owned three manufacturing plants in Milan and had been one of Mussolini's earliest supporters, had in fact stood by him with moral support and *cash* while the Duce languished in prison!

Marchetti had been an officer for six years now, and even though all of his previous postings had been in staff positions and this was his first line command, he was already shocked at the blindness and contempt for the enlisted men among his fellow officers and the staff of the XXIII Corps. But perhaps it, like the Navy's inefficiency, would resolve itself with experience. But to accuse a fellow officer of Bolshevik tendencies because he was concerned with the well-being of the enlisted men! How could a soldier respect an officer who considered him of less value than a pig or a cow? And if an officer was not respected no soldier would follow him in battle.

Marchetti stood shivering in the dawn cold while his batman heated his morning coffee on a bulky alcohol stove and the non-commissioned officers oversaw the distribution of rations to each company. The men seemed in excellent spirits this morning, he thought. Perhaps it was due to the expectation of reaching their positions around Sidi Barrani and an end to this damnable marching.

No one thought the Tommies would offer serious opposition. Hadn't they refused to honour their agreement with Poland, hadn't they run home from Norway and France as quickly as possible? That, no doubt, was the result of allowing their socialist labour unions to elect socialist governments. No, they would have little trouble with the British. Unconsciously, he tightened his hands clasped behind his back and that caused his baton to switch nervously, like a tail. He smiled back at the grinning soldiers, unaware of the source of their amusement.

Again, they marched all morning and the powdered eggs, toasted bread and bitter, unsweetened coffee rolled in his stomach. The route led due east now having turned in that direction after leaving the sea. They were to intersect the coast again at midday and when the azure of the Mediterranean actually did come into view, he felt his spirits lift. No smudge of smoke or sail impaired the incomparable view.

The pace slowed now, until several times the line came to a complete halt and the men stood about gossiping idly, smoking and complaining of the heat, the flies and the *Commando Supremo*, the high command. At this rate, he began to doubt they would reach the city before nightfall. When they moved forward the second time, a drawn-out booming which he mistook for thunder at first, began and swelled rapidly in volume. Sharper explosions sounded every now and then and an artillery officer told him they were British land mines being exploded by Italian cannon fire. 'Much quicker than using sappers.'

There was little transport in evidence now. A few tanks – inadequate M-11s – ground past at intervals raising vast clouds of dust and followed by curses. Orders came along the line to extend into open formation. They completed the manoeuvre and tramped on. Marchetti wanted badly to send a party inland to keep an eye on the tanks which were supposed to protect them against a British flanking move. He had been listening for fifteen minutes and, during that time, had not heard a single engine. In addition, the terrain was changing from relatively open, sandy waste to a hard-packed flinty surface, that rose in successive waves towards a rugged escarpment. In those hills, he thought, you could hide a regiment. But no orders came to do so.

The sun blazed out of a coppery sky and the atmosphere grew oppressive. The temperature was well over fifty centigrade and the men dragged along, thumbs thrust into pack straps to ease aching shoulders.

An aircraft appeared, little more than a black speck barely visible in the sun's glare. Marchetti held out his hand and his batman ran up with his field glasses.

Through the powerful lenses, the dot resolved into a bi-plane. He studied it carefully wondering if it wasn't one of their own Iman Ro. 37s scouting the line of march. The aircraft cruised into the sun then forcing him to look away. When he found it again, it was much lower and he could hear the engine clearly. It was still too high for positive identification but even so his apprehension began to grow. It seemed to be diving rather steeply towards them. Someone shouted a warning and the aircraft's twin machine guns laced spurts of dust across the road and the soldiers ran in every direction. As the aircraft roared above them, British blue, white and red roundels were clearly visible on both wings.

It banked steeply for a second pass and came on, lower this time, to be met by a fusillade of rifle fire. Watching through the glasses, Marchetti was certain he saw holes appear in the wings and fuselage as the aircraft jinked, climbed quickly and disappeared over the escarpment while the soldiers cheered.

They moved into their designated position on the outskirts of Sidi Barrani late in the afternoon. Military policemen were everywhere, shouting and cursing the shuffling, dusty soldiers who responded with insults. They dug trenches in the flinty soil, sweating in the heat but, since the air attack, the need was clear and they needed no urging to dig deep. There had been no other sign of the enemy and Marchetti wondered with some disappointment if the English would refuse to give battle altogether. Even the artillery had stopped firing.

Rumours had it that the British had already withdrawn from the Western Desert and were in headlong flight towards Cairo, disconcerted by the strength of the Italian advance. If true, Marchetti thought, all the discomforts of the long, swift march would be worthwhile.

A new thought occurred to him. If the British were that badly demoralized by this first Italian thrust, then might they not abandon western Egypt entirely? Perhaps even the whole of Egypt and the Middle East? With the Germans poised on the English Channel, they might want every English soldier at home. Perhaps Sidi Barrani was the first indication of major retreat.

He recalled with some excitement the rumours making the rounds at *Commando Supremo* in Rome that Italian forces would soon march into Albania and Greece. If true, then the reconstruction of the Roman Empire was underway.

In their Rome apartment, his father had long maintained a separate room filled with books and maps and thousands of lead soldiers, all organized into modern regiments and armies that man-oeuvred across realistic dioramas. In this favourite room, the two of them had often discussed the strategic implications of the con-quest of North Africa and the Middle East and its immense benefit to Italy. The key to all was the Suez Canal; without that back door to the Mediterranean, Italy would remain forever caged in a land-locked sea; her second-rate status forever ensured by England's naval might.

He pictured the great map board he had seen at *Commando Supremo*, with its glass overlay and grease pencil markings that traced the flow of armies from Abyssinia into British East Africa, then north to strike at the canal, while a second army marched east out of Libya. They would squeeze the British from Egypt like pips from a grape. Palestine would tumble next, and Trans-jordan, and the way to the oil fields of Iraq and Persia would be open.

Marchetti had studied oil geology at the university in Florence. In his thesis, he had proposed that the fields of the Arabian pen-insula possessed an amount of oil equal to the world's total known reserves. He had then applied that theory directly to the national well-being of Italy. To control the future oil production centre of the world was to secure the Empire. But to do so, the British must first be driven from all of Africa above the equatorial regions, else they remained a constant threat.

His thesis had been read quite widely within *Commando Supremo* at the instigation of his father and, only this previous spring, he had been asked to amplify it in the light of the German-Polish campaign and the likelihood that the war would spread into west-ern Europe. He had done so, going far beyond to the almost certain assumption that Germany and Russia would declare war on one another within the next three to five years. Germany would win, he predicted, and a conquered Russia would provide her with raw materials and food, the need for which had been the cornerstone of her foreign policy since the 1840s. If events did follow the course he laid out, Italy might well become a useless appendage to Ger-many, if not an outright competitor.

The Marchettis saw, as did others well-placed in industry and government, a growing world dependence on oil as the means to control Germany. Let her have her *lebensraum*, living space in Rus-sia. If Italy controlled the Middle East and its oil, she would remain an equal partner.

As the night shadows reached towards them from the escarp-ment, Marchetti was suddenly filled with a boundless enthusiasm for the future. Today, they had taken the first step. Mersa Matruh, the next town, would fall in a few days and the way to Alexandria and Cairo would be open.

At the evening briefing, General Bergonzoli read out a telegram from Mussolini who expressed his delight at the blow struck against the vile English and wished the advance to continue as soon as practicable while the English reeled under Italian hammer blows. The officers cheered the sentiments but Bergonzoli immediately dashed cold water on their expectations – and Marchetti's expectations.

'Gentlemen, I have communicated with Marshal Graziani and we are in agreement that before our advance can continue, we must consolidate our position and repair our supply lines. We are seriously lacking in fresh water and our vehicles badly need maintenance. In addition, reserves of ammunition and fuel must be strengthened.'

General Bergonzoli paced on the small stage that had been set up in the staff tent. 'You should view the desert as an ocean,' he told them. 'Provision must be made to support one against all eventualities, as when one is at sea. Only the greatest possible independence is effective – a lesson the Navy would do well to learn.'

The assembled officers smiled in appreciation. The Navy often bore the brunt of jokes these days and, if not the Navy, then the Air Force.

'I may tell you, gentlemen,' the General continued, 'that the English are not retreating in headlong panic as has been rumoured, but are conducting a careful withdrawal. Their intention is obviously to entice us into over-extending ourselves, at which point they will turn and, with their supply lines shortened, attack. We must prevent that by making our dispositions carefully to guard our supply lines as we would our very lives, for they are one and the same.'

For the next two days, the army idled about the makeshift camp set up behind the trenches. The men grew bored with complaining about the fleas and the Arabs who sold food, bad water, and old French pornography at outrageous prices. The quartermaster system, overextended by the long march and the lack of adequate, dependable motor transport, had broken down badly and Marchetti, at first angry over what he saw as a lost opportunity, grudgingly came to admit that perhaps General Bergonzoli had made the correct decision after all. To have continued the advance without adequate and dependable supplies of food, water and ammunition would have been to court disaster.

The following evening after he had instructed his sergeant-major to march the demi-company to the beach for their evening bathe, he was summoned to the captain's tent. Maroni's rubbery Etruscan features settled into a glare as he stooped through the entrance and saluted. The captain touched his forehead in return but did not ask Marchetti to sit down nor did he offer to pour him a glass of wine from the bottle at his elbow. Puzzled, Marchetti waited. He had little respect for the man but thought he had always managed to conceal it well. Maroni had been a store clerk before joining the army, and a Blackshirt and he was fanatically devoted to the Duce. A captain's commission was his reward for some no doubt distasteful and illegal action on behalf of the Party. Marchetti had seen the type before; a political and a small man of no consequence in civilian life, the Party's blaring self-confidence and bullying tactics had appealed to him. Maroni exhibited all of the weakling's lack of self-confidence and, to cover his inadequacies, he had become a martinet.

The tent was stifling and the odour of dirty clothes and the captain's unwashed body was rank. Raised to be fastidious in personal habits and dress, it was all Marchetti could do to keep from wrinkling his nose.

'About this business of taking your men to bathe every evening,' the captain began. 'It must stop. It is bad for the morale of the other companies. What is more, sea-bathing is not permitted in the regulations.'

Marchetti was too surprised for a moment to answer. Maroni started to dismiss him, thinking he had overawed his subordinate but Marchetti's face suddenly went red with anger. Maroni flinched.

'If the morale of other demi-companies,' Marchetti grated, 'has suffered, then arrange for their officers to bathe them daily. As for regulations, may I also point out that there is nothing forbidding sea-bathing . . . sir.'

Marchetti knew he was wrong to challenge the man but he could not help himself. Maroni was everything he detested in the lower classes and he knew the feeling was reciprocated in the other direction. Maroni hated him for his wealth, his father's social and political position and God only knew what else.

'That is not possible,' Maroni snapped.

'Bathing is good for the health and well-being of the men,' Marchetti persisted. 'It also gives them something to look forward to and that makes for more efficient and enthusiastic soldiers.'

'That is only your opinion, Lieutenant Marchetti. You will obey my order.'

Marchetti regarded him without bothering to conceal his dislike.

'Certainly, Captain. I would like that order in writing, if you please.'

Maroni's face paled. He started to say something then, obviously remembering Marchetti's connections, thought better of it. 'Dismissed!' he snapped.

Sofafi 22 September – 22 October 1940

Three days later, on 22 September, Marchetti was ordered to march his demi-company sixty kilometres south to occupy a newly fortified position in the desert. The location was the westernmost of a series of fortified camps about Sofafi, some fifteen kilometres south and east of Bir Enba near the Egyptian border. Even though they would be leaving the milder climate of the coast, Marchetti saw it as a small blessing putting him beyond the immediate supervision, and harassment, of Captain Maroni. His fellow officers were all content enough to sit about all day in the shade, waited upon hand and foot by their batmen while the non-commissioned officers drilled the men endlessly and kept them busy with useless and degrading make-work chores, but he was not.

General Bergonzoli's pause to repair supply lines had begun to petrify and Marchetti was convinced that their best chance to defeat the British Army easily was ebbing away. While the British regrouped, the Italian Army sat. He had twice made himself unpopular in the evening staff meetings by raising that question, an unheard of liberty for a junior officer.

They reached the position indicated at sundown on the third day. The flat, level rays shone across the rocky escarpment above and cast long shadows over the desolation of scrub bush, gravel and broken scree. The camp site was marked only by heaps of supplies trucked in earlier. The plain below the escarpment ran down a nominal slope to a depression a kilometre or so in diameter and it was here that the camp was to be constructed. Marchetti swore. The position was ill-chosen and indefensible as anyone with the slightest conception of military tactics would have seen instantly had they bothered to select the site other than from a map. He kicked at the only evidence of construction, a surveyor's marker stake, then gave the sergeant-major orders to shift the supplies onto the escarpment where the folded rock offered admirable cover.

The sergeant-major protested that their orders were very specific and Marchetti lost his temper. 'Sergeant-Major Lucretti, you will carry out your orders,' he roared, 'or I will send you back under arrest.'

It was long after midnight before the last of the supplies – great rolls of barbed wire, crates of mines, tins of food and rations and nearly one thousand twenty-litre cans of fresh water – were in place and rudimentary trenches dug. Only then did Marchetti allow the exhausted men to turn in.

The following morning, while working parties began to widen and lengthen the trenches, string barbed wire and lay mines according to pattern, Marchetti sat in the comfort of his tent, shaded from the worst of the early autumn sun, and studied the map and drank his morning coffee under the flapping awning. He had pencilled in the defence line as discussed in the staff conferences and stared at it with scepticism. What Marshal Graziani was attempting was obvious and, because of that, Marchetti knew that something was wrong.

The Libyan Army's mission had been modified to allow the development of static positions along the border to contain a possible British counter-attack. At the same time, supply dumps and additional forces were to be built up. When all was ready, the Libyan Army would then march forward to overwhelm the British with superior force. The carefully prepared supply lines would make it possible for them to continue the push all the way to Cairo and the Suez. Marchetti's misgivings lay in the fact that the defence line lacked depth, and the entire army lacked the resources to accomplish both tasks in the short time available before the British began to recover, and a quick look at the map told him that the distance between fortified positions was too great to be effectively patrolled on foot or to allow the forts to be mutually reinforcing. Marchetti suspected that *Commando Supremo* in Rome was relying on the German invasion of England to hand them Egypt.

By the morning of their third day in the desert, he was satisfied with the quality of his defences. The final supply lorries had departed, the officer in charge still grumbling about the need to manoeuvre up the rugged slopes of the escarpment. The last of the barbed wire had been strung the ten kilometres north to meet the wire of the next outpost and the first patrols had already been sent out under the sullen sergeant-major, Lucretti.

The man was a political, of that he was certain. One of the lower class, a mechanic, a street-sweeper, someone of that ilk who had joined the Party and accumulated enough support to arrange a sergeant-major's post. There were more than a few such in the Army, he knew, nearly all impressed with the power of their position and knowing nothing of military affairs. Perhaps that had been acceptable when the Army had nothing better to fight than naked black savages in Abyssinia, but they were a weak-link now that Italy was fighting a war in earnest.

The following week the first of the season's *khamsins*, the great sandstorms of the North African desert, began to blow. For hours, visibility was near zero and all those off-duty hunched in tents or trenches, goggles snugged across eyes, handkerchiefs tied across mouths and noses, cursing. The fine sand penetrated everything. Mucous membranes became inflamed and the sand made its way into the folds of skin and in a matter of hours produced abrasions so painful that movement was torture. The heat was overpowering and even inside his tent the sand worked its way through the slightest crack or tear and covered everything with a thick, gritty layer.

Between storms, there was the monotony of the desert. From their vantage point on the escarpment, Marchetti had a clear view for nearly forty kilometres in a fan-shaped half-circle north to south. It was evident that eons ago an ancient river had drained the area. The meanders cut along the base of the sandstone cliffs and the multi-coloured layers of rock were unmistakable as was the triangular depression below, the remains of a long vanished river delta. What had this desolation looked like millions of years before, he wondered, when the land was green with grass and trees and water ran as freely in rivers and streams as it did in Italy?

Marchetti felt that he had done everything he could to create a defensible position. Twice now, they had seen dust clouds in the east that could only have been British scouting forces. It was clear to him that sooner or later the British had to probe. His mortars and machine guns had already been sighted in on unobtrusive markers which identified the various ranges and he had also increased the frequency of patrols. Marchetti was confident and ready for anything.

At the end of the second week, Maroni arrived with a sour-faced staff colonel. They toured the compound and Marchetti gave a demonstration of mortar and machine gun fire that left both officers visibly unimpressed. After lunch in Marchetti's tent, Maroni loosened his belt and regarded his subordinate with ill-concealed distaste.

'Lieutenant Marchetti, you have moved this compound without permission. May one ask why?'

Marchetti had been expecting the question but the presence of the senior officer made him cautious. 'This position on the escarpment provides a better field of fire and visibility. It is also a superior defensive position. I am conscious that. . . .'

'Yes, I am certain you are, Lieutenant,' Maroni waved a negligent hand. 'The point is that you moved the compound without asking permission to do so, without in fact informing anyone that you had done so. There *are* procedures to be followed, as you well know. There are definite rules governing the siting of defensive positions, unlike those for bathing troops in the sea.' He said this last with a perfectly straight face and the staff colonel did not even raise an eyebrow.

'I beg your pardon, Captain Maroni. But I instructed the officer-in-charge of the supply convoy to inform you that I had. . . .'

'You took it upon yourself to move the camp, in direct defiance of orders and then entrusted the news you had done so to another? Did you think that would absolve you?'

Marchetti stared at the supercilious little captain with distaste. 'Not at all, Captain. We have only the single telephone line linking all camps to the coast. It could not possibly have been secure. Our radio has only just arrived. My garrison is too small to have sent a messenger sixty kilometres.'

'Never mind your excuses, Lieutenant,' Maroni waved a hand. 'The fact remains that you disobeyed your orders. Unfortunately, proper disciplinary measures will have to wait for another time. You will return this camp immediately to its original site. Is that clear?'

The colonel rumbled his assent, glared and stalked out to the lorry.

A series of petty annoyances began instigated, he was certain, by Captain Maroni. At the end of the month, the wine ran out and the weekly supply column failed to bring a fresh supply. Their mortar ammunition was recalled without explanation, leaving him only a ready reserve of twenty rounds. When new supplies did arrive, they were the wrong calibre. These foolish evidences of disfavour, coupled with the exhausting work of re-establishing the camp, dampened the morale of his demi-company. Sergeant-Major Lucretti had received the instructions to reestablish the camp with ill-concealed triumph And from then on began to gather about him a small coterie of party members and just plain trouble-makers. Twice, Marchetti requested that the man be replaced and twice Maroni refused. Only then did it occur to Marchetti that the sergeant-major was serving as Maroni's spy. His refusal to comply with Maroni's demand that he stop bathing the men each evening had not only earned him this exile, but had festered in Maroni's small mind.

In the first week of October, Marchetti led a patrol himself. They marched all morning in intense heat. The air was dead. Not a breath of wind stirred. The sullen heaviness he had come to associate with the *khamsin* hung over the desert and by noon, a brownish pall was growing in the west. Within an hour, it had become a vast curtain that towered thousands of metres and filled the horizon as shifting curtains of yellow, ochre and tan mounted one above another. The whispering began with the first touch of wind. Grains of sand tumbled over one another as if possessed until the desert surface had become a flowing sea.

He called a halt and the soldiers dug in while the desert smoked. Except for the heat and abrasiveness, they might have been standing in a river. The whispering became a hissing and the full fury of the sandstorm struck. Hair, ears, mouth, uniform and boots filled instantly with sand. The wind battered them at velocities of seventy and eighty kilometres an hour. The heat grew. Sweat dried instantly and skin cracked.

He crouched in the crumbling trench, back to the wind with the others and endured hour on hour. All night, the weird hissing of sand particles fleeing one another went on and conjured phantoms and shapes in the brownish darkness.

In the morning, when visibility had expanded to a hundred metres, Marchetti took a compass bearing and marshalled his soldiers. There would be no relief in camp but at least there was water and some shelter in the tents.

'Sir! sir!'

Marchetti grunted and rolled over. The air was cold but the insistent voice was accompanied by a muscular hand shaking his shoulder.

He struggled into a sitting position, swearing but the voice commanded him to be quiet. As he started to protest the insubordination, a single word penetrated his sleep-sodden brain – 'English.'

He drew on his trousers and shirt while the sentry spoke quickly. 'Something is moving on the plain and I am certain I heard an engine.'

Marchetti followed the sentry into the pitch blackness of the desert night. The dawn overcast had moved in and only the vaguest sky glow – star and moonlight filtering through the cloud – was evident.

He followed the sentry to his post and took the night glasses handed him.

'The movement was in the east, sir. I am quite certain I saw it.'

Marchetti sensed the man was beginning to doubt what he had seen and for a moment, anger at his impudence in wakening him after the sergeant-major had sent him packing almost erupted. But then caution slowed him.

'Where is the sergeant-major?'

'He would not come, sir.'

The night was cold and gritty sand and dust were everywhere. By God, he thought, he would have the sergeant-major court-martialled for this.

Something clanked faintly. Marchetti steadied himself on the edge of the parapet and stared through the glasses, shifting his eyes from side to side to catch movement in his peripheral vision – much more effective at night. But there was the vaguest sense of something.

'Fire a flare.'

In the rocket's eye-searing white light, Marchetti saw humped figures at the wire. Beyond and waiting, were the vague outlines of two vehicles. As the flare swayed earthward, the nearest raked the perimeter with machine-gun fire. Marchetti blew his whistle and emptied his Beretta pistol at the approaching British soldiers who, having been discovered, had rushed the wire. The pistol was too small to do any damage but it served as an excellent reinforcement to the whistle.

The mines they had so laboriously placed failed to work. He trained his glasses on one British soldier bent over, probing the sand with his bayonet. In the flare's weird light, the desert surface was pocked with shallow dimples. The soldier probed into one, knelt and brushed the sand away. He fiddled with something, then went on and Marchetti cursed. The soldier had just disarmed the mine. The firing-pin contacts had been so badly corroded that in order to make certain they went off, the mines were buried in shallow holes. Apparently, the wind had blown the sand away, exposing them.

Soldiers clattered into the trench around him and a mortar bomb exploded beyond the camp, a second landed equally distant in front. The machine guns began to fire in unison, sweeping the open spaces before the wire. Marchetti saw red flashes against the vehicle silhouettes and heard the hammering of Bren guns.

He fired another flare and scrambled out of the trench and ran to their mortar emplacement to find it empty. Working like a mad-man, he tore open the ammunition carrier, checked to make certain the mortar was set securely on its base plate, then peered through the range finder, straining to make out one of the British vehicles. It was too dark to do more than approximate. He grabbed a heavy bomb, turned the fuse setting and locked it in place, checked to make certain the fuse igniter was clear, dropped it into the tube and ducked. The mortar barked and he saw the faint red trail as the bomb slammed up and out. Marchetti waited tensely for the explosion and when it came, several hundred metres beyond his target, he cursed and halved the distance.

He saw this one very clearly, far too short and increased the distance one half. This time the bomb exploded near the vehicle which jerked to life as if electrocuted and shot away. He now had seventeen mortar bombs left; the rest were the wrong calibre he suspected Maroni of having sent down to teach him a lesson.

The slope beyond the wire was lit with sputtering flares fired from both sides and Italian soldiers fired coolly at the British, driving them back from the wire. Twin explosions blasted the fence and sand and wire sprayed upwards. British mortars had found the range and bombs began to fall inside the compound. Marchetti pushed along the trench complex shoving riflemen into positions to fill gaps. The two vehicles with their Bren guns had taken up positions on either quarter to send a sheet of bullets whistling across the trenches. A soldier kneeling beside him was struck squarely in the head; his body flopped against the back wall of the trench and slid into a sitting position, rifle across its lap and hands turned palms-up. Marchetti gagged and stumbled into a side trench where he vomited. Until that moment, he had been too preoccupied to remember that this was his first experience of combat. The soldier was the first human being he had ever seen killed.

He wiped his mouth and stumbled out of the trench, thankful that no one had seen his moment of weakness. His mouth was bitter with bile and, angry at himself, he started for his tent and his canteen, then veered towards the wireless tent as he saw a shadow move across the entrance.

He entered to see Sergeant-Major Lucretti slapping the operator and screaming hysterically at him to send for help. Marchetti dragged the man back. 'You coward!' he shouted. 'Get into the trenches where you belong and attend to your duties or I'll shoot you myself!'

Lucretti stared at the flare-lit expanse of desert beyond the wire, eyes wide with terror, and hesitated. Marchetti unbuttoned his holster flap and he scuttled out, whimpering. When he turned to the wireless operator – a boy only, skinny and shock-haired with issue wire-rimmed glasses, one lens of which was cracked – the soldier cringed away from him.

'Have you made contact yet?' Marchetti forced his voice to a normal tone.

'No . . . no, sir. Atmospherics. I had Bardi for a moment only.'

'The telephone?' he asked, knowing the answer.

'The wire has been cut, sir.'

Marchetti swallowed his frustration. 'When you do get through, send this.' He scribbled a message requesting air support at dawn and a relief convoy with additional supplies of ammunition. He turned away, then a thought struck him and he snatched the pad and pencil from the table and quickly wrote a note describing the sergeant-major's cowardice and requesting his court-martial. If anything happened to him, the man would still face punishment.

'Send this as well. Over my name.'

The boy read it quickly, tipping the note towards the shielded candle. His eyes grew wide and he nodded vigorously. 'Yes sir!'

Twice that night, they drove the British back with fierce counter-attacks. A mortar shell damaged one of the tracked vehicles and it withdrew, but still the British persisted.

At dawn, the camp came under air attack. Three Gladiators droned in to bomb and machine-gun their position and there was little they could do as their machine-gun ammunition was too precious to waste on futile potshots. During a third air attack at dusk, the British succeeded in pushing through the outer wire and, supported by the remaining Bren carrier, nearly burst through the inner wire before they were driven back.

Radio contact was finally established after midnight by the exhausted operator who had remained in the airless tent through the blazing day. Headquarters in Sidi Barrani at first refused to believe the report and the wireless operator tapped out a furious stream of sentences detailing the British force arrayed against them, the aircraft attack and the state of their supplies and ammunition. The details must have been convincing as headquarters finally began to respond. A convoy of lorries was promised. Aircraft would be dispatched at first light with emergency supplies of ammunition and water.

It was also suggested that Marchetti maintain his perspective and composure as it was probable that he had overestimated the enemy force and faced no more than a small patrol probing the nature of his defences. The British, he was told, had no way to exploit the capture of territory. Therefore, the situation could not be as serious as he portrayed. Marchetti detected Captain Maroni's hand in that final statement and stormed out of the tent without making a reply.

At dawn on the second morning, a single aircraft appeared far to the east and dropped several parachutes onto empty desert. When he turned his glasses on the descending cargoes, he saw the Bren carrier already darting after them.

An hour later, he was summoned to the eastern perimeter and squinting into the sun, he made out a white flag held aloft by a British soldier. He nodded to one of his own men who waved a shirt in reply. Stretcher bearers went forward from the British lines.

Sergeant-Major Lucretti, who had kept well-clear of Marchetti since the first night, shook his fist and began to spew a stream of obscenities. Without warning, he grabbed up a rifle and aimed before three soldiers overpowered him. Marchetti raced to the trench where Lucretti was struggling like a madman.

'Tie and gag him. You three keep an eye on him.'

The sun had faded behind the escarpment and long shadows reached towards the camp. Glints of light where the sun reflected on British guns or equipment mocked him. They had taken more than 50 per cent casualties, all the mortar ammunition was gone and only a few belts of machine-gun ammunition remained. The promised convoy had never appeared nor had any air support and Marchetti doubted that either would.

He reflected bitterly that if he had been allowed to maintain his original position on the escarpment, he could have held it forever. The enemy would have had to attack over broken ground, uphill and his machine guns could have commanded the slopes for twice the distance. He trudged back to the wireless tent knowing he had only two choices; remain and be chopped to pieces in the morning or abandon his position and retreat to the next fortified compound twenty kilometres northeast.

They marched at midnight. Marchetti had supervised the wiring together of all the wrong calibre mortar bombs and set them to destroy as much equipment as possible. When the last of the column had disappeared into the night, he waited another five minutes, then gingerly set the makeshift time fuse he had assembled from his wrist watch and the wireless batteries. He screwed the last terminal nut down and left. At the wire, he checked to make certain of his path through the useless minefield and began to run. Ten minutes later, the night was shattered by a brilliant flash of light and a thudding concussion.

Impossible Loyalties

Taranto 11 – 13 November 1940

For eight endless hours, Torsten Fredriksson had not dared stir from his compartment. Lake Como shimmered as the train wound through the pine forests dusted with winter snows, the Swiss border was only thirty minutes away and Fredriksson had toyed with the idea of leaving the train and crossing the border on foot but had finally discarded the idea. Whether caught or not, it would be a clear admission of guilt. Better to take his chances with a legal exit.

In Berlin the week previously three pretty air hostesses had welcomed him aboard the tri-engined Marchetti S.M. 75. The rest of the party had consisted of two French journalists well-known for their fascist sympathies, a fierce anti-communist Spaniard and an ex-patriate American author whom he had met previously and knew to be a close friend of Joseph Kennedy, the American Ambassador to Great Britain. Fredriksson had known immediately which way everyone's copy would be slanted. In fact, the composition of the entire party was so pro-Axis that he was sorry that he had accepted the invitation. A neutral journalist had, like Caesar's wife, to avoid even the appearance of sin if he wished to retain his effectiveness as a neutral. Had the fact that the Italians had tried to taint him helped rationalize the breaking of his strongest self-imposed rule – never to report anything that might be of the slightest tactical value to the host's opponent? The story, when published, would certainly prove that he was no tout for the Axis.

In Rome the week before, they had been feted with banquets, granted a private audience with Mussolini and subjected to endless briefings at the *Supermarina*, the Ministry of Marine. There had been parties every night in their honour, and women were abundantly available. The overriding impression he carried away from Rome was one of great enthusiasm for anything military – in spite of the fact that the Italian army was unable to subdue tiny Albania – in everyone but the majority of the civilian population who had to endure the hardship.

From Rome, they travelled to the fleet base at Taranto in a train specially laid on for them. Their first view of the fleet in harbour made amply clear the reason for the *Supermarina*'s claim to superiority. Three new battleships lay at anchor, *Littorio, Caio Diulio* and *Cavour*. Three more cruisers, two of the *Trento*- and one of the

Bolzano-class were also moored in the harbour and three *Zara*-class cruisers were tied at the dockside while numerous destroyers, mine sweepers and patrol craft scurried about. The following day they were given an exhaustive escorted tour of the harbour defences which consisted, they were told proudly, of more than twenty one-hundred millimetre and two hundred light anti-aircraft guns hooked into a complex ultra-modern sound detection and search-light system. Swarms of barrage balloons bobbed above the harbour – to prevent torpedo bomber attacks, which were impossible any-way, a naval officer smugly admitted, as it was too shallow to permit the effective employment of aircraft-dropped torpedoes.

The day, though brisk, was filled with sunshine and surprisingly mild for November. The fleet admiral's gig took them past the endless bulk of *Littorio*, the premier battleship of the Italian fleet. She seemed as long as a city and was painted in shades of grey and blue camouflage that emphasized her silent menace. Standing in the gig's bow as it slid past *Littorio*'s 38,000 tons, she seemed the offspring of a greyhound mated to a panther. Nine thirty-five centimetre guns in three main batteries gave her fearsome claws. Fredriksson divided rapidly in his head for the English equivalent – fifteen inch guns – necessary for his transatlantic readers.

The American author sauntered up and they watched in silence until the man shook his head and said in bad German, 'Such a waste of manpower and money.'

Fredriksson glanced at him. 'Why do you say that?'

The American shrugged. 'Why not? Just look at her. She's mag-nificent. Death slipping through the heaviest seas, the worst storms. Yet her day is past. The battleship died twenty-four years ago at Jutland.'

At Fredriksson's snort of amusement, the man became serious. 'Think of what will happen when a fifteen inch shell crashes down on her decks. Is there any amount of armour that can withstand such a destructive force? Of course not. She will go into battle to face another battleship with fifteen inch guns and in two salvos it will be over. Every battleship captain knows his first salvo must strike and destroy.'

The American leaned towards him with the air of a conspirator. 'The British have radio direction-finding and the Italians do not. I know.' He nodded confidently.

Fredriksson regarded the American author with surprise. How did he know anything about radio direction-finding? He himself had only discovered its military use by accident – an overheard conversation in a pub near Dover in June. He thought of the massive aerials rearing above the British coast. Was it possible to make such antennae small enough to place aboard a ship? The theory was well-enough known; radio waves reflected from a solid body could be detected and displayed on a cathode ray tube. He had even written a popular science article on radio direction-finding some years before.

'But in all likelihood, it will never come to that,' the American went on. "Aircraft will destroy the battleships once and for all. It was an American flyer, Billy Mitchell, who proved years ago that aircraft can sink battleships. A year ago in Japan, I watched a fleet exercise. They've built huge carrier ships from which they fly off swarms of aircraft which have no other purpose than to find the enemy fleet and sink it a hundred, two hundred miles away! The Japanese have built more of these ships than the rest of the world combined.

'The Italian admirals are not fools. They know this as well as I and so they remain in harbour. They wait patiently, hoping to lure the British fleet within range of their own aircraft. And when they do, that will be the end of the British Navy in the Mediterranean.'

Fredriksson had laughed at the man's predictions but then naval affairs had never held much interest for him.

During the night a violent storm blew up and woke him. He watched the trees thrashing in the gale and the rain pound the courtyard for a few moments, before going back to sleep. The following day, he endured another tour in the storm's fitful after-math and another heavy meal and too much wine. That afternoon they were taken to watch crews repairing damaged barrage balloons blown down by the storm during the night and that was the final straw. Immediately afterwards, he informed the distracted naval official in-charge of the tour that he would be leaving the following morning. After a short argument, arrangements were made for him to return to Rome early the next morning. That evening, he declined an invitation to dine a second time with the fleet admiral and retired early.

A bumping noise woke him and at first he thought someone was moving furniture on the floor above. Subsonic vibrations ran through the room and flickers of light played about the edges of the blackout curtains. Fully awake now, Fredriksson stumbled to the window.

Fire slashed into a sky gone mad with searchlights and he stood transfixed, reminded of the biblical description of Armageddon. Every anti-aircraft gun surrounding the vast harbour was in action and visible concussions rippled from the heavy guns. In the dark pool of the harbour proper, strings of multicoloured fire soared up-wards as three battleships, three cruisers and dozens of destroyers, minesweepers and auxiliary craft added their batteries to the fray and the scene reminded him of New Year's fireworks.

Above the grinding roar of guns, he heard the scream of an aircraft engine and, for an instant, saw it pinned in the confluence of searchlight beams. It trundled so slowly towards one of the warships that he thought it would be swatted, like an insect. Flashes and streaks of tracer shells criss-crossed on all sides. It dipped suddenly and the searchlights stabbed vainly, catching it just as a black dot fell away and the aircraft lifted from a shallow dive. A torpedo airplane, by God!

A veritable roman candle of light blew skywards. The grey immensity of a battleship was starkly outlined for an instant as she heeled to a mortal blow and then the flare subsided to angry flames sheathing the forward part of the huge ship. God in heaven! he thought.

The officers' quarters was a madhouse. The guards had disappeared and no one paid any attention to him as he pushed through the excited crowd and ran outside. A car crammed with naval officers started up; he shouted and it halted long enough for him to leap onto the running board. They raced through streets lit by the eerie glare of parachute flares and star shells, searchlights and bursting artillery rounds. Pieces of shrapnel pelted the car twice and one struck his shoulder painfully just as they roared through the unguarded gates of the dockyard proper and slid to a stop half along a pier. The officers ran to a launch. Fredriksson started to follow, but stopped.

Whatever was happening, he would see it better from here. If he were discovered, he would probably be locked away for security reasons. Even at that moment, Fredriksson had no illusions as to how tightly the naval censors would clamp down on this story.

The cold wind from the harbour carried the smell of diesel oil, cordite and burning ships and equipment. He counted four major fires in the harbour and at least fifteen more on the surrounding docks. The British had attacked the Italian Mediterranean Fleet inside its own harbour – the one thought to be too shallow to permit such an attack!

If only one of the great battleships and one or two of the cruisers were put out of commission for a few weeks, the naval balance in the Mediterranean would tip to the British. If that happened British supply convoys would swarm through the Straits of Gibraltar to Egypt and Italian convoys would be immobilized, cutting off the North African armies.

Fredriksson prowled the docks until dawn, avoiding the few sentries who had remained at their posts until finally it was light enough to see three immense shapes riding low in the water. Far out in the harbour, nearly to the entrance, only the masts and upper works of a great battleship were visible. Fredriksson could not believe his eyes; *Littorio* had sunk at her moorings!

The officers' quarters was deserted when he returned. Not even the officer of the day was to be seen. He packed quickly and took an automobile from the car park, one of the ubiquitous Fiat staff cars. The guard at the gate saw only the official card pasted to the windscreen and waved him through with the ambulances and rescue lorries. He managed to reach the train station with minutes to spare and boarded without incident.

In Rome, he studied the connections board, then bought a ticket to Lugano, in Switzerland. He spent the two-hour wait wandering about the station, watching for security police but saw only the usual number of Carabinieri and nothing at all out of the ordinary. The Italian papers were full of war news but not a word about the events of the previous night, as expected.

The train ran north through rain-lashed farmlands. The weather changed gradually to sleet and then snow after they left Milan and wound into the Alps. Station after station passed without incident but as they drew nearer to the Swiss border, Fredriksson's apprehension increased until it was painful and he thought he understood how a spy must feel. For a spy he was, in effect, or so the Italians would see it.

He committed nothing to paper even though he wrote and rewrote the story a dozen times in his head. If stopped, he would claim he was only doing what he had been given permission to do – leave Italy.

The implications of what had happened at Taranto were immense. Even now, the British must be announcing the results of the raid. The Italians would, of course, deny 99 per cent of Great Britain's 50 per cent exaggeration and in another day or two, newspapers around the world would clamour for his column. This one story could, at a single stroke, make him the most sought-after syndicated columnist in history.

Personal considerations aside, the balance of power in the Mediterranean had changed seemingly beyond repair. He had picked up rumours of a new German plan of invasion in Berlin and again in Rome; one code-named *Operation Felix* and aimed at an occupation of Gibraltar, the Canary and Cape Verde Islands to deny Great Britain all access to the Mediterranean from the west. General Franco would now certainly balk at further Axis pressure to bring Spain into the war and Greece and Albania would be heartened in their resistance. And, most importantly, Great Britain now was effectively confirmed in her rule of the entire Mediterranean and could interfere at will with Italian resupply efforts in the Adriatic Sea. Yugoslavia and Bulgaria might also be emboldened to resist German influence. The great unknown was the effect of all this on the Italian position in North Africa. General Wavell would not be long in mounting a massive counter-attack unless the British completely underestimated what they had accomplished.

The British had added a new twist to naval warfare. Never again would a naval fleet be safe from aircraft, even in its own harbour. Perhaps the American had been right after all; domination *had* passed from the battleship to the airplane.

The train stopped for customs at Como, on the end of the lake and only minutes from the border. Fredriksson forced himself to smile politely and respond to the talkative customs official who, with an armed border guard, entered his compartment. His passport was stamped and, a few minutes later, the train was allowed to proceed. The tension had been so great that Fredriksson vomited into the wash basin and afterwards, sat staring out as the choppy grey expanse of Lake Lugano came into view and tried to regain his composure.

In Lugano, he went directly to the local post office and telephoned through to his secretary in Stockholm. He dictated the story quickly and gave her instructions to send it as a substitute for his column to all regular subscribers, then as a special news feature to all non-subscribing wire services, Allied, Axis, and neutral alike. The temptation to auction the story among the various press agencies had been strong, but the effect would be even more devastating if it appeared as just another of his routine columns.

Darkness over the land of Egypt
Exodus 10:21

Cairo 15 July – 9 December 1940

Cairo was an oven.

Captain Charles Atkins dodged across the boulevard amidst the incessant flow of battered taxis and military vehicles. The noise was incredible, even to one used to London's vibrating streets; honking horns, shouting street vendors, the roar of military lorries and motorcycles, the voices of a million people raised in daily commerce. Dust hung over the city and the stench of rotting animals and dung mingled with petrol fumes. The sun glared with a white light more intense even than on the Riviera coast.

Three weeks ago he had been safely, if restlessly, ensconced at Aldershot. Several long talks with a private psychiatrist in London had helped him to understand that a certain amount of fear was perfectly normal, and even healthy, but he was not anxious to test himself again in a combat situation. He would have been content with a staff position in England – would even have endured the boredom of further attaché duty somewhere. And there was also Wendy.

In the weeks of his convalescence she, more than the hospital staff, had done the most to put him back together. Her common sense approach to everything and her perpetually sunny disposition had been his anchor as he struggled to come to terms with the overwhelming fear of combat. The psychiatrist had pointed the way but it was Wendy who gently, and without knowing, led him through the maze of his own creation to self-respect.

He turned into the narrow street that led to Shepheards and paused on the curb, looked back to Sinclair's English Pharmacy and watched with amusement as the doorman, clad in a flowing *djelabia* and white and brown wingtips, nodded to a pretty young woman in a thin print dress that flicked about her silk-clad legs. She was followed by two laughing officers with staff colonel's pips on their shoulders. Both were tipsy and it wasn't even 1000 hours.

Perhaps Wendy and he had become a bit too involved. That last night of his leave had been a disaster, he now recognized. Returning from Hemsley after dinner, they had driven slowly across the moor. Wendy hadn't demurred when he parked on a ridge crest that gave a sweeping view down the valley. It was nine-thirty and dusk was gathering. He had only meant to compliment her on her dress when she came into his arms. Her lips had been sweet and soft against his.

She leaned back against the seat then and brushed a lock of hair back from her face. Without looking at him, she murmured, 'I will, if you like.'

The temptation was almost too great but finally he shook his head and started the engine.

'It wouldn't be fair, to either of us,' he muttered, uncertain of himself and whether she actually meant it or not. He did not see her nod, reluctantly.

He had seen her to the door, fearing yet hoping that she would ask him in. They had kissed but everything that could be said had been – the invitation extended and refused. The door closed with a certain finality and he had driven back to the hospital with a feeling of loss mixed with relief.

The feeling had persisted during the long journey out to Egypt. Why, he was at a loss to say. He had known her two months. Yet when he thought about it, he realized that because of her, he hadn't thought about Erika in some time. He had watched the flat Egyptian coastline shimmer into view under the flat African sun with something approaching relief.

Shepheards' lobby was a madhouse. He stood in line at the reception desk for what seemed hours, shifting from foot to foot and occasionally kicking his duffle bag ahead and thinking that he hadn't seen so many different uniforms at one time since that last embassy cocktail party in Warsaw.

'The hotel is filled to capacity, my dear Captain Atkins,' the head clerk, a soft-spoken Egyptian with a glint of steel in his eyes told Atkins. 'But not to worry. We maintain a certain number of rooms at various hotels.' He selected a card. 'Ah, here we are, Brownings? Do you know it?'

Atkins didn't, but he wasn't about to admit it to the blandly smiling Egyptian. It had taken him less than ten minutes to realize how thoroughly detested the British were. The Egyptians were waiting anxiously for complete independence, which they thought would appear magically when the Germans swarmed across the English Channel and the Italians entered Cairo. In the meantime, they contented themselves with superior smiles, smug remarks and the refusal to participate in any way in the war effort.

Brownings was an ancient hotel, built not too long after Napoleon was chased from Egypt, he decided. The desk clerk studied the Shepheards referral slip and nodded grudgingly.

'Very good, Captain.' He frowned, 'The room has not been made up yet. With the number of guests . . .' he sighed. 'If you would care to wait in the bar, I would be most happy to send a boy for you. Ten minutes at most?'

An hour, more likely, Atkins thought as he thrust his way into the overcrowded bar filled with officers, none of whom ranked higher than himself, and he understood immediately. Shepheards was not for company grade officers without connections. He ordered a gin and tonic and drank it straight off. It was warmish but badly needed. 'Again,' he shouted at the harried barman.

His orders had been marked *most urgent* and he had flown out of England in mufti on a Pan American clipper to Lisbon, then travelled on a neutral Mexican steamer to Greece. HQ in Athens was apologetic but there was absolutely no possibility of early transport across to Egypt. And so, he had taken a hotel room near Piraeus and spent two days lying on the beach. Then, bored to distraction, he had rented a car and driven down to Marathon where he fell in with a party of British dependants and three Anglican bishops, all on a last holiday before going home.

For a while that evening, they had re-created a small bit of England near the historic battlefield. Someone produced a packet of Darjeeling tea and a broad-hipped Scots woman bullied the inn-keeper into the use of his kitchen and baked the finest wheaten scones he had ever tasted. Greek brandy and Metaxa appeared and, by midnight, all, including the bishops, were tipsy and singing 'There'll Always be an England' and 'The White Cliffs of Dover'.

The next day, in spite of a stubborn hangover, he had driven north to Larisa intending to go on to the border the following day.

The weather had been excellent and he found a room in a small inn. Larisa swarmed with rumours of an Italian offensive but the following morning as he watched the sun rise over the rugged terrain of northern Greece, he doubted if he had ever seen territory so perfect for defensive warfare, even in Norway.

After a brisk morning hike, as much to test his recovered strength as to view the countryside, he returned to the inn for lunch. The sun filtered through a plane tree that shaded the court and four British soldiers, part of a training contingent to the Greek Army, he supposed, sat several tables away and took no notice of him, even though he was wearing his uniform. He was just finishing when five German soldiers turned the corner. One of them nudged a companion and pointed to the British uniforms. At almost the same moment, the British soldiers saw the Germans.

An old man sunning himself in a rickety chair tipped against the whitewashed front of a building, eased to his feet and shuffled away. A housewife pushing a pram stopped abruptly. A traffic policeman in the nearby square hurried to a corner shop and darted inside.

Which way the Greek government under General Joannis Metaxas would jump was a constant topic of conversation in the British community. Some claimed that Metaxas was just another fascist and would slip under the Axis wing at Mussolini's urging, while an equal body of opinion claimed that his fascist pose was only anti-communism. The British Embassy seemed to feel that Greece would sooner or later have to ask Great Britain for help to curb the Duce's designs. Either way, there were both British and German training units presently in the country. Usually, the government saw to it that they were kept well apart.

The British soldiers stood at the sight of the German uniforms. Something was said and they all laughed. The Germans started forward and Atkins rose but before he could intervene, one of the Tommies shouted and instantly, bodies collided. Atkins shouted for attention in English and German. The two groups separated, reluctantly, leaving Atkins at a loss; he could not very well order the British soldiers to retire and he had no business giving orders to enemy soldiers, nor they accepting them. To his vast relief, a German staff car roared up and an officer jumped out. He adjusted his gloves, surveyed the situtation quickly and ordered his soldiers to move on. A police lorry rounded the corner at that instant but Atkins waved back the policemen who got out. The German officer nodded his agreement.

'All right, you lot, back to your tables,' Atkins said to the Tommies, trying to keep the relief from his voice. The German officer bowed and Atkins nodded no more than was necessary. After the car had driven away, he took a deep breath, surprised at the depths of his hatred for someone he did not even know. It was enough that he was the enemy.

When the Greek police had also departed, Atkins paused at the Tommies' table. 'Look here,' he grinned. 'The next time you feel like a jerry bashing, don't do it when an officer is about.'

The four laughed. 'Right, Captain. And don't worry. We'll get another chance. The place is lousy with them.'

Atkins had played cricket at school and was good enough that, while stationed near London in 1934, he had been invited to play county cricket. As soon as his CO learned of this, he was drafted into the Gezira Sporting Club which, with hanging about the club pool drinking John Collins in the evenings, was not the most unpleasant way to spend a war and a vast improvement over his experiences to date, he decided. Like all good things, he knew it wouldn't last but in the meantime, there were still reserves of French wines, steaks, cigarettes, beer and whisky available to those in on the fix, all brought in in anticipation of the usual influx of

American tourists which never materialized due to the war. The Turf Club was thronged in the afternoons as were the dozen open-air cinemas in the evening, and Madame Bodius' Cabaret in the Pont des Anglais where the most exquiste belly-dancers performed proved a curative for recurring regrets over Wendy.

In mid-September, he received orders to proceed to a map-reference point in the desert, code-named Piccadilly, and assume command of a mechanized squadron in his old regiment, the 4th Hussars, of the Seventh Armoured Division. After ten years, he was finally going to have a chance to do what he had trained to do at the Royal Military Academy.

Atkins had accumulated a desert kit of clothing and articles recommended to him by desert veterans and hitched a ride with three war correspondents who had rented a car. They were wearing battle dress with the green and gold shoulder tabs of the war correspondent. During the months he had languished comfortably in Cairo, he had discovered that befriending war correspondents paid off handsomely as they all had generous expense accounts.

The car was an ancient, black Chevrolet and it was jammed with the four of them plus the driver, a middle-aged Egyptian dressed in a spotless white shirt and a black, vested suit so old the material had taken on a brassy sheen. Their luggage was roped to the top, a metal ice chest full of beer and sandwiches was placed in the boot and they left at dawn.

The landscape changed swiftly from the poverty-ridden city suburbs to a narrow belt of well-tended farms that ended abruptly in sand. At one moment, the car was driving between green fields of cotton sparkling in a rainbow mist of irrigation sprinklers; the next, the desert overflowed the road to the horizon. There was no other traffic on the road and nothing to see but scrubby bushes and knee-high banks of sand left by road graders and, in the shimmering distance, a low range of hills. The correspondents were grousing about the new censorship rules and the fact that the Royal Navy and the Army had established censorship offices so far apart that a fifteen-mile round trip through the city's impossible traffic was required. And then the staffs were frequently playing golf or in their clubs and so unavailable. After an hour, he drifted off to sleep.

A choking cloud of dust and sand pouring into the interior woke Atkins. He coughed and swore as they struggled to roll up the windows. The haze shimmered and he had the vague impression of other vehicles passing. The heat shot up and perspiration ran down his neck, his chest and under the constricting binding of belt and trousers.

'Convoy,' the Australian journalist who had introduced himself as Alan Whitehead, shouted over the noise.

The dust storm disappeared as they passed the head of the column and the windows were hurriedly rolled down again. Behind stretched an endless column of lorries with trailered tanks, all enveloped in the horrible dust.

Whitehead chuckled. 'You'll get used to it. It's certainly not as bad as a sandstorm.'

Atkins closed his eyes at the Australian's prediction and eased his legs into a more comfortable position. He had already decided that he hated the desert.

At mid-afternoon, they passed the turn-off to Alexandria some twenty miles north on the coast. The Chevrolet stopped long enough to drop off one of the correspondents, a BBC-type wearing khaki bush clothing who promptly upended his suitcase and sat down. As they drove away, he was already typing assiduously on his portable typewriter while waiting for a ride.

The heat moderated slightly near the coast. For a while, a fitful sea-breeze blew inland but, as the afternoon waned, it stopped. Atkins had related the encounter between the British and German soldiers in Greece to Whitehead and he responded with a description of his visit to the Sudan and the start of hostilities against the Italians there. The air began to take on a breathless quality that Atkins found harder to endure than the dust. For two more hours they drove through small towns that lined the coast, Daba, Fuka, Bagush. White Mediterranean-style villas overlooked the beaches and everything seemed so peaceful that it was hard to believe that a quarter of a million Italian troops menaced Egypt.

As they neared Mersa Matruh, the afternoon heat drew to its height and a sense of impending doom seemed to surround him. Atkins twisted nervously on the seat and cursed the heat, the war and the fact that he had anything to do with it.

Short of Mersa Matruh, the driver growled, 'khamsin'. He pronounced the word as he might an obscenity and pointed to the south where a dirty-brown line had formed on the horizon. Atkins had heard tales of the khamsin, the hot wind which blew in from the desert and down through the mountain passes where it was compressed and heated and accelerated onto the plains to gather up untold millions of tons of sand.

'Bloody damned nuisance,' Whitehead growled. 'Blows up so much sand that the particles rub together and create static electrical charges. Makes you feel as if you are going mad.' He shifted uncomfortably. 'If the khamsin blows for more than five days, it is considered legal for an Arab to murder his wife if she annoys him.'

There was a peculiar fascination in watching the storm front grow, Atkins discovered. It reminded him of a summer thunderstorm approaching. But rather than grey and cooling, the *khamsin* was a sickly yellow-tan and unbearably hot. The first whisper of sand against the windscreen caused them to roll up the windows again. The main force of the storm struck five minutes later but by then Atkins was already covered with a gritty, flour-like dust. The driver reduced speed to search for the scraped road and Atkins clamped his lips together and tied his handkerchief over his nose as the others were doing.

Because of the storm, they did not reach Mersa Matruh until after nightfall. The shuttered villa that served as bachelor officers' quarters was as hot as the exterior, and almost as dusty. He was too exhausted by the long day's cramped ride in the overwhelming heat to do more than report, eat a gritty, bully beef sandwich in the mess and fall onto a hard cot. In spite of the wind's howl, he was asleep in minutes.

A servant woke him to a yellowish dawn. The *khamsin* blew as strongly as ever and he put on his sweat-stained uniform and went in for breakfast. Afterwards, he braved the wind and heat and trudged across to headquarters where a totally unsympathetic officer signed him on to the battalion roll and shouted for the orderly to find him a ride to his company area.

It was late in the day before a lorry going in the proper direction was found. Atkins had been dozing, his head shrouded in his tunic when the lorry wobbled across a succession of ruts and stopped. Atkins climbed down stiffly into a wilderness of swirling sand and hot wind. He adjusted the goggles Whitehead had given him as a parting gift and squinted at a huddle of flapping tents that seemed to comprise the assembly point. Gradually, other shapes resolved into American jeeps, lorries and Matilda tanks shrouded in sand-covered canvas. The light was failing and he was exhausted by the endless journey. He found his tent and fell asleep almost immediately.

A foot thudded against his sleeping bag. 'Up, up, up!'

Atkins was conscious of a peculiar wail wobbling across the desert and a rush of feet past his tent. He struggled out of the tent to find the area deserted. His sleep-fogged mind registered only the heat and sun-glare before the snarl of an aircraft engine and the sudden *carump* of a bomb galvanized him into action. He dove out of the tent into a slit-trench. A single explosion dominated all others and he cowered, hands over his head, mouth open to ease the concussion. Anti-aircraft guns smashed away at the sky; more bombs fell then the AA fire stopped as suddenly as it had begun.

He looked up to see a sunburned and very thin young man clad only in shorts and desert boots grinning at him. He tossed Atkins a packet of Egyptian cigarettes. 'You'll get used to it. Seems worse in the desert for some reason. Can't think why.'

Atkins discovered that his benefactor and trenchmate was Captain Peter Bowen, who also shared his tent. The all-clear sounded and they climbed out of the trench; only then did Atkins discover that he was naked. Grinning, Bowen called after him, 'No need to worry. There isn't a woman within seventy-five miles – damn it!'

Bowen volunteered to show him around after a gritty breakfast and they strolled through the camp to the vehicle park.

'Not much to tell, I'm afraid. Piccadilly's the concentration point, but for what I'm sure I don't know. Been here a month now. A few longer than that. The Eyties are pretty good fighters in spite of the nonsense you read in the newspapers. Their problem is lack of decent leadership, and transport. The poor devils have to *march* all over this damned desert. Good thing for us, or we'd be evacuating Egypt. Wavell's been trying to make them think there are three or four times more of us than there are but I suspect that's wearing a bit thin. That Italian bomber for instance. He comes over pretty much on schedule and so far, the only thing he has to worry about is a lucky shot.' Bowen shrugged. 'But then he doesn't do much damage either. His bombs are small and he doesn't have many of them.

'But don't let the propaganda fool you. The Italian is a first-class fighting man when he's evenly matched.'

Atkins was given command of a troop in C Squadron consisting of eight Valentine Mark III tanks, eight fifteen-hundredweight lorries, four universal carriers – known colloquially as Bren Gun carriers, and one quarter-ton American vehicle which for some reason was called a 'jeep'. All had seen harder usage than their designers had intended and only three of the Valentines and the jeep were fully operational.

During the next several weeks, Atkins learned to live in the desert where life seemed to centre on two items of overriding concern – water and spare parts. They were allowed, in theory, three-quarters of a gallon per day per man, except that half this allotment went directly to the cookhouse. So Atkins learned to leave his morning washing and shaving water in the canvas basin all day, scrape the suds off in the evening before washing up, then pour it into a petrol tin until he had accumulated enough to wash his clothes. After the sand had settled out, a corporal came to collect it for use in vehicle radiators.

The struggle for spare parts, he quickly learned, was the Desert Army's greatest problem as he struggled to bring his squadron to full operational status. He became extremely unpopular in the quartermaster's tent where he spent endless hours arguing for spare parts.

But the weeks of monotonous manoeuvres interspersed with constant patrolling gave Atkins the opportunity to train his people into an effective fighting force. Once the Valentines were all operational, he kept them at squadron manoeuvres as often as fuel allowed until they all thought and acted as a single organism. In spite of the hardships associated with the hostile desert, Atkins enjoyed these months more than any in a long while. For one thing, he was among other professional military men of his own nationality and with whom he could talk freely for the first time since 1935. And he listened avidly and learned.

The desert took a harsh physical toll on them all. Bowen had warned him that it would and they often discussed the ways various individuals reacted, before Bowen was unexpectedly transferred to East Africa in November.

'Some merely wither away to nothing,' Bowen said one breathless afternoon as they sprawled in the shade of a Valentine. 'You see them staring at nothing for hours. Let it go on long enough and they become useless vegetables. Others retreat into themselves but do not lose their mental anchor and they are the ones who seem to come to terms with the desert. Some even come to love it, like the Arab. They make the best officers if there is something absolutely bloody impossible to be done but are useless for anything else as discipline means nothing to them. They become fanatics, like Lawrence. I met him once. Came down to lecture to our class at Camberley on guerrilla warfare, 1930, I think it was. Ireland, Palestine, India, you see. Strange man.

'Then there is my type who hates the desert. Keeps you sane, I suppose. Worst terrain in the world for fighting a war. See the bloody enemy coming for miles. Biggest guns, stoutest armour and best supply line will always win. So the Eytie will lose this one as he hasn't the equipment nor the weapons. Look at what we've captured, for God's sake. Maxim-type machine guns from the first war. Damned things cook-off when they get too hot. Artillery from the 1890s for God's sake. And no transport.

'That's why the Eytie soldier surrenders so quickly. Knows that he doesn't have the weapons and, worst of all, the transport. He knows he will die if cut off from his base.'

*

It was clear enough that something was building up. Rumours had become so absurd by the middle of November, no one paid them more than passing attention. The heat broke and, for a week or so, the desert was almost pleasant as the daytime temperatures hovered in the low eighties, the insidious flies disappeared and the winds stopped. Atkins woke one morning to find the sky heavily overcast and was cheered by the gloom. Two days later the temperature dropped and a cold rain began and the compound changed to a sea of mud. By the end of the week, he found himself longing for the heat again.

In the last week of November, Atkins was summoned to Alexandria. The Brigade Major initialled his pass and sent him off with a quizzical expression. Atkins hitched a ride with a returning supply convoy and was dropped at a large hotel overlooking the sea. He went straight to the bar and drank his fill of water, then went up to his room and bathed completely for the first time in three months.

'Captain Atkins, you were Military Attaché in Finland during the Winter War, I believe?'

Puzzled, Atkins acknowledged that he had been and waited for the brigadier, an incredibly fit man in his late fifties, to continue.

'Good. Thought so. I was at the War Office then and read a report you wrote about a Finnish technique for dealing with tanks. Your report impressed me at the time, young man.' He stared at Atkins for a moment, then resumed. 'I presume you have heard of the Long Range Desert Group?'

Atkins had; a small force, primarily New Zealanders, who ranged far behind enemy lines gathering intelligence and establishing supply and ammunition dumps. 'Yes sir.'

'Good. It should be obvious now that something is building in the desert. Old Musso has taken it on the chin in Albania and Greece and has divided his reinforcements between North Africa and the Balkans. We, on the other hand, have never been in better shape. Since the Red Sea has been cleared out, equipment and reinforcements are coming in through the Suez Canal. So we are about to begin a raid in depth against Italian positions on a line from Sidi Barrani to Bir Enba. One brigade under General Selby will attack west along the coast road to Maktila and, if they are lucky, on to Sidi Barrani while the Fourth Indian Division and your own Seventh Armoured Division will attack north and west from Piccadilly.

'Now, elements of the LRDG have been scouting about the Sofafi fortified camps and north from there across the escarpment towards the coast for some weeks and they've given us a very good idea of what we can expect. I want you to take your squadron and with an LRDG acting as your guide, probe ahead of the main body.'

The brigadier went to a map board and pulled back the green baize curtain. 'The Seventh Division will curl north from Piccadilly through a gap that has been discovered in the Italian fortifications at the southern end. Now I want you to proceed in advance and drive north to the coast road here, between Alam el Dab and Buqbuq. If the route is clear, the Seventh will follow and that should force the Italians to pull back into Cyrenaica. You will receive operational orders when you return but I wanted the opportunity of impressing upon you the importance of this assignment. Do you have any questions?'

Atkins had listened with a mixture of apprehension and excitement. 'Yes sir. Only one. I don't have a great deal of desert experience and North Africa is not Finland. There must be other suitable officers with far more desert experience?'

'The LRDG will supply the desert experience. GHQ thinks we need someone with ah, well, you might term it, experience of unconventional operations. Apply some of the tricks the Finns used against the Russians if the occasion arises.'

The brigadier studied him thoughtfully. 'I will admit frankly, Captain, that for all our years in the Middle East, the British Army does not have a great deal of experience in desert operations and the Italians do.'

At 2100 hours on 8 December 1940, a soul-freezing wind flapped the tent as Atkins stepped outside. The sky was crystal clear and stars blazed unhindered. The engines of five Bren carriers, three Valentine tanks, four troop and two repair lorries gasped to life. Atkins buttoned his overcoat and, without ceremony, gave the order to move out.

Since returning from Alexandria a week before, he had been so involved in preparations that he had barely had a full night's sleep. How in the name of God, he wondered, did they expect him to take a few tanks and lorries right around fortified Italian positions and on to their single most important supply route without being detected?

Everything he was being asked to do depended on the success of other units like the Fourth Indian Division and Selby's makeshift forces. And if he did reach the coast, the Seventh must be directly behind or his meagre command would be swatted with no more thought than a fly in spite of the brigadier's optimism. The whole thing was insane; the entire British force in Egypt was only 36,000 troops, 57 tanks and 156 Bren carriers and armoured cars; what the devil could they accomplish against 200,000 or more well-dug-in Italian troops?

They rendezvoused at dawn with their LRDG guides who were waiting for them in two ten-ton lorries well south of Sofafi. Other than small arms, the only weaponry the LRDG possessed were the Bren guns mounted atop each cab.

Atkins spent an hour conferring with the young New Zealand lieutenant, Brian O'Shea, in charge of the LRDG group and afterwards managed a few hours' sleep as the convoy continued north in broad daylight, depending on the fierce opening battle far to the east to fix the Italians' attention.

The equipment performed credibly, to his surprise. Breakdowns were minor and did not delay them unduly. The sky was overcast and lowering and aircraft would have found it difficult to detect the small convoy as they tacked north-northwest towards the distant escarpment, like a squadron of frigates in the trackless Atlantic.

The LRDG force had scouted a way up the escarpment and although the Bren carriers lurched from side to side, tracks slipping on the gravel and slabs of rock thrusting through the sand, they managed it and were followed by the stolid Valentines. Once atop the escarpment, the convoy had a tendency to string out and, looking back, Atkins saw one of the LRDG lorries grind up and down the column, chivying laggards as a sheepdog might.

Their first casualty occurred at midnight. A Valentine threw a track and clattered to a stop and Atkins hurried back to assess the damage. A link had fractured straight across; the maintenance sergeant was certain he could have the track replaced inside an hour and Atkins pressed on, leaving one of the Brens to guard the tank and repair lorry.

To his surprise they reached the northern edge of the escarpment without further incident as dawn flooded the rocky terrain running down to the road, and beyond that, to the Mediterranean a mile or so away. They had not seen a single Italian patrol nor heard so much as an aircraft, Italian or British. While they stopped to make contact with Piccadilly base, eat and carry out minor maintenance, the repaired Valentine clanked in escorted by the Bren carrier and repair lorry.

They were ahead of schedule, no mean feat in the desert, and the news was good. The massive raid had been more successful than anyone had hoped. Maktila had fallen and Selby's force was moving on Sidi Barrani. The Fourth Indian Division had taken Nibeiwa and Tummar West. Tummar East was expected to surrender at any moment and they would then push on to Sidi Barrani from the south. The Seventh had been delayed at the Sofafi complex but

423

was breaking through. It was believed that the entire Italian XXI Corps had been ordered to pull back. The Sixty-third Cirene Division had already passed Buq Buq some fifteen miles west from his present position but, according to reconnaissance aircraft, the Sixty-fourth Catanzaro Division, east of the salt flats, was beginning to move west towards him. He was instructed to do everything possible to hold his position astride the road.

The grey dawn made Lieutenant O'Shea seem thin to the point of emaciation and nearly as brown as his leather pistol belt. He folded the message sheet, glanced at the map, and whistled softly.

Atkins tapped the map. 'I make us here, twenty-two miles west of Sidi Barrani. We might just be able to delay the Sixty-fourth Division long enough for our main body to come up if we are quick about it.'

The New Zealander shook his head. 'You're the boss,' he said in a morose voice.

Intelligence had placed the main bulk of the Sixty-fourth Catanzaro Division at Alam el Dab as late as three days ago. The Sixty-third Cirene Division had moved much faster than anyone had anticipated and the question was now how fast the Sixty-fourth would follow suit. They scouted the road for several miles in both directions until Atkins found the site he wanted. The best he could hope to do with his meagre resources would be to delay the leading elements and hopefully cause confusion.

The sharp ridge through which the road bed had been blasted sloped towards the sea quite steeply for half a mile before petering out above the beach. The approach from the east sloped upwards for more than a mile, he judged, and the descending side was even longer.

He divided his force into two parties, one to dig in and hold positions above the road, the other to serve as the mobile striking arm. One of the tanks was sent south of the road towards the beach with orders to conceal itself hull down. A second was dug in on the ridgecrest and he held the third back as a mobile reserve. One Bren carrier was sent west to watch for any sign that the Catanzaro Division might return. Two more were used to support the tanks and the fourth was sent with the two LRDG lorries to a point two miles up the road to keep watch. His dispositions made, there was little else Atkins could do except smoke and worry and watch some of the soldiers prepare a desert brew.

A cut-off petrol tin was filled with sand and petrol syphoned into it from a lorry. A soldier tossed a match into the tin and a pot of water was placed on the burning sand when the flames had died down. The water boiled rapidly and a few handfuls of tea, sugar and powdered milk were thrown in. They all squatted down to watch avidly as the brew strengthened and Atkins discovered that he was watching just as closely. Just as anyone who had come out to the desert, he had become an addict and he inched closer so as not to be forgotten. The tea when it was poured had a muted flavour of petrol but it was hot and bracing for all that.

The overcast persisted and the wind grew steadily colder until he wondered if it ever snowed on the North African coast. The road remained ominously empty until at mid-afternoon, an LRDG lorry appeared in the distance. As it drew closer they could see that it was followed by a Fiat 508c field car. The lorry humped up to the crest with the staff car clattering in its wake like a puppy on a leash because a young New Zealander sat behind the driver with the muzzle of his Tommy gun pressed against the man's neck, a dead officer in the passenger's seat. The frightened driver clenched his hands on the wheel and closed his eyes tightly, plainly expecting to be shot.

O'Shea spoke to the driver in bad Italian but he only shook his head. O'Shea grinned and drew his side arm, an American Colt forty-five. He chambered a round and let the slide run forward with an ominous clatter. The Italian sighed and began to talk.

'He says the Sixty-fourth Division is evacuating,' the New Zealander translated, 'and can't be more than an hour behind. He was driving this officer to Solem. The officer panicked when he saw my men and started shooting. It's a miracle the driver wasn't killed as well.'

An hour! A shaft of fear went through him unexpectedly and he grunted in surprise. The New Zealander took it for a sign of annoyance and nodded.

Atkins turned away, struggling to regain his composure. He hated this. He hated the fear, and the lack of self-control it brought. He hated the weakness of watery muscles, of churning bowels. After a moment, he cleared his throat loudly and coughed, clamped both hands behind his back to conceal their trembling and began to pace. Atkins forced himself to concentrate on the problem. It would be at least four hours before the leading elements of the Seventh reached the road, he thought. He had to hold up an entire division for at least three hours, with a handful of men, three tanks and four Bren carriers. He glanced around at the site he had chosen. It was good, but not up to this. Nothing was.

O'Shea, his face growing longer by the minute, waited. The pacing had at least helped to clear his mind, Atkins thought and he realized with surprise that he had misled the others into believing that he was totally in control as was evident from the calm way in which they waited for his orders.

'There might be one or two things we can do to ease the odds,' he said more firmly than he had intended. 'Look here,' he squatted down and began sketching rapidly. The lieutenant's expression changed to outright despair.

The first mechanized elements of the Catanzaro Division appeared far down the road not quite two hours later. The LRDG sergeant on point duty watched its progress through his field glasses. The motorcycle scouts passed at, he judged, some forty miles an hour. The plan had been explained to him by the pommy captain who seemed confident enough. But then he wasn't out here, was he? A few moments later, the leading elements of the divisional convoy appeared, heavy lorries crammed with soldiers and equipment led by a single Autoblinda 40 armoured car. He counted fifteen and estimated that each carried thirty men; 450 armed soldiers. He did not like it at all, he decided.

When the lorries had disappeared over the hill, he stood and scanned the road east with his glasses. Far on the horizon he thought he could see more dust but otherwise the road was empty. He waved to the Bren carrier and they bumped down onto the road and paused. The driver, a thickset sheepherder from near Invercargill, glanced at him.

The sergeant shrugged. 'Let's get on with it.'

They turned onto the road and set off after the Italian lorries at the same speed, forty miles an hour. The Bren, with a top speed of thirty, began to drop behind but they had only two miles to go and the Bren would only be a few minutes later.

Atkins saw the dust trail first. His shout brought the others running and he heard the reserve Valentine's engine cough into life. A moment later, following his instructions, it clanked off to the south and the ridge of rock that would screen it from the road while allowing its two-pounder cannon and machine guns an ample field of fire. Through the glasses, he could see the tank commander check his machine gun, then lean forward on the turret, waiting for the flare.

The Italian motorcycle escort roared past unsuspecting. The Bren carrier stationed to the west would take care of them if they turned back. Atkins held himself rigidly erect, exerting every bit of self-control he possessed. He had observed in Finland that a correct disposition of forces was only part of winning a battle against overwhelming odds. Timing was the other cornerstone. Even so his trembling was so great that he had to lower the glasses and wait for the tremors to subside.

The lorries were plainly visible now, strung out in close order, too close, he thought and behind them, just cresting the hill, was the first of the LRDG lorries. The Bren and lorries would be, at best, half a mile behind. The advance guard passed the marker he had chosen, a concrete pillar erected to commemorate Mussolini's genius in ordering the construction of the highway, and he raised the heavy, brass-barrelled flare gun. Across the road a quarter mile away, he saw the tiny figure of the tank commander stoop into the turret, then pop out again and knew he had given the order to load. Atkins fired and the flare arced up, crimson against the darkening sky and burst. A Valentine's distant rumble changed to a clattering roar as it crunched up the slope to its chosen fire point and the flat crash of the two-pounder slammed back from the rocky hills. The lead armoured car was slammed sideways, rolled twice and erupted into flame. The tank fired again and the following lorry smashed into the burning armoured car and exploded. Troops jumped and fell from the backs and scattered into the scrub. Atkins shifted his glasses east and saw the two LRDG lorries turn off into positions on either side of the road. Behind them, the Bren carrier came straight on.

The Valentine on the ridge was firing now, working its way methodically down the stalled column. The Bren carrier behind had opened up with its fifty-five calibre Boys Anti-Tank Rifle at the last lorry in the line which was backing in an effort to turn around. In his panic, the driver rammed the vehicle into the soft sand. He abandoned the lorry and scuttled away towards the beach.

Mortar rounds fired from the other Bren carriers exploded along the line. The Italians tried to take up defensive positions on the edge of the escarpment but Atkins had instructed his fitters and spare drivers to concentrate their rifle fire on anyone, officer or enlisted man, who tried to rally the soldiers.

The road was now blocked completely at both ends and five lorries were in flames. The sandy verge served the same purpose as had the deep snow along the forest tracks in Finland. The difference lay in the fact that with his armoured force, as meagre as it was, he was incomparably better equipped than the Finns had ever been.

It was over in five minutes. When Atkins was satisfied that the smoke column would be visible for miles against the setting sun, he fired a green flare and they withdrew two miles west to a similar position and dug in. Atkins was satisfied for the moment. One lorry had been allowed to escape east and hopefully, it would reach the main body of the division and warn them. If not, the plume of black smoke should cause the desired confusion. The action had been carried out with only one casualty on their side, a hand accidentally caught in the closing breech of a two-pounder.

They kept close watch on the road but the main body of the Sixty-fourth Catanzaro did not appear. At midnight, long past the expected arrival time, leading elements of the Seventh Armoured Division found them and Atkins gratefully withdrew his meagre, but victorious force.

Cyrenaica January 1941

Lieutenant Alfredo Marchetti marshalled the remnants of his command and filtered them back in the fading light. The men moved like zombies and stumbled over the slightest obstruction. He himself hadn't slept since the British broke through the meagre line thrown up around Fort Capuzzo thirty-six hours before. All that remained now of his demi-company were the twenty-two men following; the rest had been killed or captured. And somewhere behind them, or in front of them or on either side, were more British soldiers. Marchetti was certain of only one thing – unless they kept moving towards Bardia, they too were dead men.

A vicious wind sprang up and Marchetti did not believe it was possible to be so cold in the desert. Part of it was the fact that they were so badly dehydrated they had little resistance left. Water was their biggest problem and mocking them as they stumbled along was the steely expanse of the Mediterranean.

They had been falling back steadily for more than a week, pursued by British tanks and armoured cars. Marshal Graziani had waited too long. All the months in which they had prepared for the final, overwhelming offensive that would carry them to Alexandria and Cairo had been wasted when the British moved first and not with overwhelming force, he had quickly discovered, but simply with armour and mechanized units that allowed them to concentrate their inferior forces at weak points and punch through. High mobility had done the rest. The Libyan Army had at first attempted to fall back and regroup but their tactical retreats had quickly become panicked routs when the British appeared unexpectedly far behind their lines and the army collapsed onto the Bardia–Sollum–Sidi Omar line with devastating losses. Now it was doubtful that even that could be held.

Since their escape from the Buqbuq trap, Marchetti had led his dwindling command inland, climbing high onto the coastal escarpment to bypass British pickets. For three days they had plodded through empty desert until they were able to edge back towards the coast. He had lost five men killed the night before and two missing in an engagement with a British Bren carrier before it suddenly disappeared into the darkness. They reached Sollum early that afternoon, barely ahead of the British advance guard.

Sollum, a small coastal village, was under continuous bombardment by the Royal Air Force. The Second Blackshirt Division had mounted a rear guard south of the town but its main elements had already pulled out, intending to make a stand at Bardia further north, in combination with the First Blackshirt Division. The terrain was said to be more defensible and there the possibility existed of being supplied from the sea if the enemy should cut their supply routes west to Benghazi.

Marchetti had reported to headquarters where, instead of being fed and rested, they were ordered to join the rear guard. Marchetti protested that his men were exhausted and sick but the harried Second Blackshirt Division commander threatened to have him shot if he did not obey. They would be given water and food when they reached their positions, he was told. Marchetti had been so angry that only the presence of the general's staff prevented him from shooting the man on the spot and he stormed out to comply.

But, before they could reach their assigned position, the British spearheads attacked and Marchetti, knowing what the outcome would be, pushed the remains of his demi-company west into the desert again and struck north.

The sun squatted like an obscene bug on the horizon, badly distended and blood red. Marchetti stumbled along in the fading light, barely aware of the curious buzzing that had been audible for some moments; some deep-seated reflex penetrated his exhaustion and he shouted a warning. Men threw themselves away from the line of march as the stuttering of airborne machine guns kicked stinging sand and stones about and the RAF Tomahawk snarled into the night sky to the east barely having missed killing them all.

Marchetti lay with his face pressed against the icy soil and knew he was close to the end of his strength. There was nothing more he could do and he wanted only to lie here forever on the gravelled hardpan. They had a few handfuls of dried beans and less than 500ccs of water left per man – a minimum drinking supply was considered four litres per day. Some of his soldiers had thrown their greatcoats away during the headlong retreat from Buqbuq and now suffered terribly in the nights. Boots and leg wraps were worn to shreds and a few might as well have been barefoot. And there had been talk today of surrender.

The thought galvanized him to one last effort and he struggled to his feet and went down the line kicking and tugging the others up and got them started north again. No surrender! No surrender! It became a kind of litany with him. Not until every last avenue of escape had been exhausted. Tomorrow night with luck they would reach Bardia. With luck! He thought he could hold them in check that long.

The sea was dark away on their right to the east. Where, Palestine? Yes, to Palestine. How certain they had been in September. Cairo by December; then Haifa, Damascus and Beirut in the spring! He laughed without mirth. They would certainly lose Bardia. Even Benghazi far to the west, a thousand miles distant from the fabled Cedars of Lebanon. Now he doubted that he would be alive in the spring.

'Lieutenant Marchetti,' a voice hissed. 'Look there, along the beach.'

Something bulked against the paler shade of land, perhaps half a kilometre on. A gleam of light shone briefly as if a door had opened and closed. Beyond, surf creamed against the beach.

Slowly, so as to think through each move, Marchetti gave orders to form an extended skirmish line and move forward one step at a time, probing with bayonets for mines.

As they made the transition from hardpan to beach sand, he saw the building for what it was, an Italian fort erected years before as part of a line of pickets to shelter settlers against Arab attack. A hundred metres short of its absurd, crenellated walls, they stopped.

The fort was occupied. Italian, British, Arab? In Sollum, they had heard rumours of Arab men arming themselves with weapons found on the various battlefields to pay off old scores, real or imagined. Remote farm families had been horribly massacred and even nearer the towns, Italian settlers had been killed.

A chilling thought occurred; if the British held the fort, how could he prevent his men surrendering? It would only need the promise of food and water and they would do so without reference to him. They would not think of the miles of desert to be crossed on foot to reach the concentration camps, nor that the camps would be far worse than anything they had endured until now.

Again, a flash of light and then the strains of a gramophone record welled into the night and the words were Italian.

Marchetti was almost lightheaded with relief as he stumbed forward, forgetting about the minefield. The tinny words were unintelligible but they promised food, water and shelter. Then remembering who and where he was, he snapped an order to be still. They complied immediately; no one wished to be greeted by a burst of machine-gun fire.

Marchetti walked towards the fort, shouting his name in Italian and pronouncing it carefully so that no trigger-happy guard would think him an Arab or a British soldier. He removed his greatcoat as a searchlight snapped on and swept across the gravel. When it centred on him, he raised his hands, conscious that he was shivering in the night cold, so that his rank could be seen on his *sahariana* tunic.

'The password?' a voice shouted.

Sudden anger flared in him at the stupidity of the demand and in spite of their predicament, he heard a shout of laughter from his men.

'How the devil would I know, you fool!' he screamed at the fort. 'We have been separated from our division for a week. I am Lieutenant Alfredo Marchetti of the Sixty-third Cirene Division. Open those damned doors before I kick them in!'

'Lieutenant Marchetti?' a new voice called. 'Come forward to the gate.'

The searchlight followed him until it could be depressed no further and he halted. A judas hole opened in the gate and a torch flashed across his face and uniform. Someone grunted and the gate was opened just enough for him to step in.

A hissing pressure lamp threw a whitish light and Marchetti squinted at the slender officer before him. He was unshaven and wore a dirty but tailored uniform with the insignia of a full colonel.

'The name of your commanding officer?' the colonel demanded.

'Captain Giulio Maroni. His immediate superior is. . . .'

'That is sufficient, Lieutenant. I know the Captain. I am Colonel Vincente Osano of the First Blackshirt Division and I am in command of this fort. How many of you are there?'

'Twenty-two men remain from my demi-company. We have no rations left and less than half a litre of water per man. I would appreciate. . . .'

'I am certain you would, Lieutenant. Our own rations are very short, but we have sufficient water.' The officer gave orders to allow the others to be admitted and given water and food.

Marchetti's eyes adjusted slowly to the light. Apparently, Colonel Osano had no fear of night attacks as the place was well lit with pressure lamps. The Parade was cluttered with equipment thrown everywhere, rifles were leaned carelessly against the walls and several cookfires were scattered about the small courtyard where a dozen or so soldiers watched sullenly.

'Corporal Sangini,' Marchetti called to the single non-commisioned officer left in the demi-company. 'See that everyone has enough to drink, a chance to wash and that the water bottles are filled.'

The corporal, a regular and disdainful of the Blackshirts' poor showing, replied with a parade ground salute and issued orders in a concise manner.

Marchetti followed Osano to his quarters and sank gratefully into the chair indicated. There was an open bottle of wine on the desk but the Colonel did not offer him any; instead, he stared in a sardonic manner, yawned elaborately at Marchetti and clasped his hands on the desk.

'You must leave in the morning.'

Marchetti raised an eyebrow at the petulant tone in the Colonel's voice. '*Must* leave?'

'I do not have enough food to feed my own men, Lieutenant, let alone yours as well.' He shrugged as if Marchetti should understand. 'So, you must leave for Bardia in the morning. You may carry dispatches.'

'You do not receive regular supply deliveries?' Marchetti countered.

'No. Not for a week now.' Osano's eyes shifted evasively. The lantern above the desk served to emphasize the man's insignificant appearance. To compensate, the Colonel had a habit of thrusting his lower lip forward, as if that made him appear tough, like an American movie star, but the intent was foiled by a receding chin that reduced the pose to sulkiness.

'Have you been attacked by the British?'

Osano shook his head. 'No. Only their aircraft, a fighter or two. But we expect them at any moment.'

Do you really? Marchetti wondered. Then why had they approached undetected? And why hadn't they encountered mines as they approached the fort? Wind stirred outside and brushed a tree branch against the window. The room was cold. The meagre fire had burned down but Osano made no move to replenish it. The Colonel was concealing something but what, and why?

'I *intended* to take my men on to Bardia in any event, Colonel. I would be grateful for any food you could share with us.'

Osano scowled. 'I will see what can be done.' He rose, but Marchetti interposed smoothly.

'Have your patrols encountered any sign of the English between here and Bardia, Colonel Osano?'

Osano stepped around the desk. 'No, Lieutenant, none at all. If you will excuse me now, I have much to do.'

Marchetti marched his men out as a cold dawn turned the Mediterranean to steel grey. The food and water and a night's rest had done them all good. Marchetti had been able to induce Osano to part with a ration tin of British bully beef per man and that put them in relatively good humour again. The prospect of Bardia before midnight was an extra incentive. Marchetti had begun to sense that trained soldiers will endure nearly anything if they have sufficient food, water and rest and are treated with respect. The ordeal of the last week had not only driven that lesson home but was also welding the survivors into a tightly disciplined team. Talk of surrender had ended and he could sense that the men were on the verge of accepting him as their commander without reservation. Almost, but not quite.

They moved north along the hardpan edging the beach in extended order. There was some skylarking at first which he wisely refrained from noticing but the wind was cold off the sea and it soon sobered the lighter spirits.

Their first inkling that the British had pushed between them and Bardia came at mid-morning when the corporal taking the point, suddenly threw himself flat as he reached the crest of a ridge. His frantic signals to halt brought Marchetti on the run. Together, they wormed their way through the bitter scrub until they could look down into a shallow valley that ran north and west away from the beach where four British tanks, a dozen lorries and several armoured cars were laagered.

Marchetti repressed a shudder. Except for the corporal, they would have walked right into them.

They could only retreat now, he knew, as they hadn't the food and water to attempt to circle into the desert. Had Osano lied when he said they had seen no British forces or was he simply not sending out routine patrols?

They reached the fort at noon. Colonel Osano appeared on the walls and Marchetti thought for a moment he was going to refuse them entry.

'I gave you specific orders, Lieutenant!' Osano shouted as he came through the gate. 'You were to march to Bardia. I demand to know why you have disobeyed me?' Osano's nervousness told Marchetti that he indeed knew about the British tank squadron to the north.

Marchetti checked his first inclination, which was to challenge Osano. Instead, he reported the disposition and strength of the British force. 'They are getting ready to move,' he told Osano. 'You can expect an attack near sundown.'

'The mine fields will stop them,' Osano sneered. 'Do not be afraid, Lieutenant. You will probably not be called upon to fight.'

Marchetti's hands twitched and he eyed the Colonel's scrawny throat. 'There are no mines, Colonel,' he grated between clenched teeth. 'My men and I walked to the gates last night without encountering a single one. And this morning, you did not even bother to give us a map or a guide. I also doubt that you have been sending out the proper patrols or you would have known about the British laager.'

Osano took a shaky breath, as if realizing the danger of their position for the first time. 'Lieutenant, please come with me.' All his pomposity had fled like air from a burst balloon.

His quarters still held the night's chill and Marchetti shivered. Osano poked up the fire and poured two glasses of wine.

'I suspected the British were there, but I hoped you would break through,' Osano said, avoiding his eyes.

Marchetti knew he was lying and said so. 'You do expect to leave here safely,' Marchetti snapped. 'But for some reason you do not include us.' He hesitated, then asked softly. 'Or are you planning to surrender?'

Osano stiffened. 'Surrender! I am a Fascist! I will never surrender.'

Marchetti nodded. 'All right, then I withdraw the accusation.' He was surprised at how quickly the tables had turned. Osano was now the supplicant.

The Colonel slumped behind the desk. 'My men are on the point of mutiny. They have cleared the mines so as not to anger the British when they come. They also refuse to go on patrol. Five days ago, I had word that tonight a submarine comes for us. When they heard, they were at first afraid the submarine would be too late. Now they are afraid that if your people stay, there will not be sufficient room for all.' He shrugged helplessly.

'Marshal Graziani is abandoning eastern Cyrenaica and there is talk of German aid. Greece and Albania have drawn away our strength.' Osano slammed a fist on the desk. 'Those damned fools in Rome do not understand what is happening here!' he shouted. 'We could have won, could have taken Egypt in September. But no, Graziani had to sit and rest while the British gathered strength. They have bombed our fleet at Taranto and forced us from the Red Sea. The British can resupply their forces at will from either direction, while we can barely get our ships across from Italy.'

Osano stared at him, his eyes pleading. 'I am not a professional soldier like you, Lieutenant. I have not had the benefit of fine schools and the best regiments. But I can read history and I know that if you give up the offensive before your objective is obtained, you will fail.' He subsided into the chair and Marchetti thought he would burst into tears.

God in heaven! he thought. If it was obvious to a fool like Osano, why could they not see it in Benghazi or Rome? The invasion of

Egypt had been announced in June yet it had taken three months actually to get underway. In the summer, there had been only 36,000 British in all of North Africa against 250,000 Italian soldiers. But we wasted our superiority with poor leadership, poor equipment, poorer treatment of our soldiers and a refusal to see reality.

'I no longer control my men,' Osano admitted in a wretched voice. 'They threatened to kill me if I allowed you to stay.'

Marchetti left the room and strode across the Parade, gathering up his soldiers with a nod. They followed him reluctantly, sensing a confrontation.

The garrison soldiers muttered and began to stir as Marchetti approached. It was obvious that they had worked themselves into a state of fear in which the menace of the British was horribly exaggerated. He could also sense the uncertainty in his own men and knew that it would take very little now to reduce them to the same state.

He stopped so that he was between the two groups, knowing that he was taking a dangerous gamble. But there was nothing else he could do.

'A submarine comes tonight to take away the garrison of this fort,' he told his men without looking around. 'The garrison did not wish us to know of this.'

One of his soldiers swore in surprise and they pushed forward angrily. A sergeant of the garrison, a huge man in a filthy, sweat-stained uniform, shouted and jumped to his feet. He grabbed a bayonet-mounted rifle from the man beside him and rushed at Marchetti. Marchetti, expecting something like this to happen, pivoted swiftly and as the sergeant lunged past off balance, he drew and fired his pistol into the man's neck.

The sudden pop was almost ludicrous in the still afternoon but the sergeant was dead before he touched the ground. Marchetti suddenly wanted to be violently sick but from somewhere he gathered sufficient discipline to control himself.

He straightened and holstered the pistol. The stunned garrison troops stared at the body and Marchetti waved a hand.

'Disarm them,' he ordered and walked away, knowing that he would be obeyed now, without question.

Colonel Vincente Osano of the First Blackshirt Division and a brave man crushed by fear and fatigue, shot himself at sunset, an hour before the submarine winked the prearranged code from a point a thousand metres off the Libyan beach. Marchetti heard the muffled bang and only by exerting the utmost willpower did he force himself to enter the office. Osano had not trusted the 9 millimetre Corto Beretta pistol, the officer's side-arm. Instead, he had propped

435

a Carcano service rifle on the desktop, knelt down and taken the muzzle into his mouth. It was an easy matter to push the trigger with a pencil and the high-velocity 6.5 millimetre bullet had nearly torn the back of his head away.

They buried the Colonel before the submarine arrived.

The pity of war distilled

Anthem for Doomed Youth
Wilfred Owen

North Atlantic 10 January – 15 February 1941

Lieutenant Commander Rand Dobson, Royal Australian Navy, was passed through the gate by the Royal Marine sentry and found Liverpool's Canada Docks bustling with activity even at 2100 hours. The blackout was only relieved by blue lights and he walked carefully past the huge Graving Dock where a phantom ship bulked against the black sky. Rain spattered fitfully and a cold wind blew off St George's Channel. He had been transferred from HMS *Catalon*, MS4 Flotilla at Harwich less than fourteen hours before. His orders had been marked IMMEDIATE, and there hadn't even been time for the traditional going-away party among the junior officers.

An overcrowded train had carried him west to Plymouth and his only comfort was the thought of his own command as the long-delayed reward for his successful sinking of a German E-boat off Southampton six months before. It had been raining in Plymouth as well, typical January weather for the Devon coast. There were no taxis and he had to queue for the bus. He reported to Admiral Dunbar-Naismith's office at Western Approaches Command directly, in spite of the hour, and a succession of clerks had shuttled him along to the dispositions officer who stunned him with the news that instead of his own ship, he was being sent to HMS *Adelaide* as a replacement for a First Officer who had gone down sick with pneumonia. Angry but resigned, he endured another train ride north to Liverpool where *Adelaide* was refuelling.

It was hard to make out details in the rain and darkness, he thought, as he stood at the foot of the gangway and peered at the soaked, hand-lettered cardboard sign that read H.M.S. *Adelaide*, then up at the gloomy mass of the ship. He had last been in Liverpool aboard a Royal Australian Navy destroyer during a three-month training cruise, virtually his only sea time in a major vessel before the war. Then the docks had glowed at night with light and across the Basin switch engines puffed clouds of smoke and tugs manoeuvred cargo vessels through the channels. It had been early summer at the time and not mid-winter, as now, and the air had been English soft and the sky more blue than black as he stood his watch that first night in harbour, blind to the industrial grime of the Liverpool docks.

The officer of the watch, a gangling young midshipman seconded from the Royal Naval College at Dartmouth, informed him that the captain was on the bridge. Dobson sent his dunnage below and went up, stumbling over an unexpected coaming in the dark so that his arrival on the bridge was rather inauspicious.

Peters was a spare man, white-haired but with a round, placid face that completely belied his personality, as Dobson discovered immediately. Apparently, the ship had been waiting only on his arrival.

'Expected you this morning, Mr Dobson.' He shook hands perfunctorily and snapped an order to get underway. The captain paid no further attention to him and Dobson stepped back out of the way. The bosun's pipe whistled through the loudspeaker and the ship was suddenly alive with the shadowy figures of men scurrying on deck, rain slickers glistening.

Peters backed the *Adelaide* neatly away from the quay and out into the channel without waiting for the tug which Dobson could see churning furiously down channel towards them. Warehouses, docks, cranes, ships, all the paraphernalia of a great port moved past in an eerie silence, broken only by the muted thumping of the engine.

'The last time I was in Liverpool, these docks were a fairyland of lights,' Dobson observed to Captain Peters. 'I was here in. . . .'

'No idle chatter on the bridge,' Peters snapped without turning his head.

Dobson was stunned, then a wave of embarrassment, followed by savage anger, swept over him. How dare Peters speak to him as if he were the rawest recruit. He choked back his temper and fixed his stare on the bridge window, conscious of the quartermaster at the wheel and the bridge messenger, both studiously ignoring the officers.

As the *Adelaide* passed into St George's Channel, the short chop gave way to the hard wave action of the shallow channel. The rain was heavier now, beating against the bridge windows with unremitting fury. The clear-view screen spun madly but there was nothing beyond but stygian blackness.

'Come,' Peters snapped, causing him to jump. Dobson followed him into the chartroom where the captain unrolled an Admiralty chart and pinned it to the map table. The chart showed the southern portion of St George's Channel lying between Wales and Ireland, and the North Atlantic approaches beyond. Peters indicated a rough parallelogram marked in black pencil.

'I assume they taught you to read a chart in Australia, Mr Dobson?'

For a moment, Dobson thought the captain was joking to make

up for his sharp comment on the bridge. He started to make a like reply but Peters' expression indicated anything but levity.

'Yes sir!'

'How long have you served with the Royal Navy, Mr Dobson?'

'Sixteen months, sir. Staff duty at the Admiralty followed by sea duty aboard HMS *Catalon*, MS4 at Harwich. I served as Executive Officer, sir.'

Peters might not have heard a word; before Dobson finished speaking, he was tapping the chart. 'Our assigned sector, Mr Dobson. We are short of our normal complement of officers and I expect you to do the work of two. I do not encourage familiarity among my officers, with each other or with me, Mr Dobson. You will take the next watch. See that you. . . .'

He droned on with detailed instructions concerning station keeping, course deviation, general quarters, dawn stations and general housekeeping routines. His instructions were little different from those laid down in the manuals and Dobson's mind began to wander as he speculated about Captain Peters. He knew virtually nothing about him other than the brief resumé of his naval career as it had been given to him in Plymouth. On first impression, Peters seemed a distant and harsh old man and his personal history suggested a reason. Commander John Peters had first gone to sea as a boy in sailing ships before the turn of the century. During the First War he had joined the Royal Navy and had served in mine sweepers and destroyers. He had remained in the Navy until his retirement in 1937 and retired at the rank of Commander, rather than Captain. Apparently the Royal Navy had not thought enough of him to give the courtesy promotion at the end of his service. Desperate as the Navy was for trained sea-going officers, he had been called out of retirement in September 1939.

The captain dismissed him a few moments later and Dobson returned to the bridge where he introduced himself to the quartermaster and the two ratings. Both acknowledged him with reserve; due no doubt to Peters' orders concerning familiarity. But then, the man had been called out of retirement. Perhaps that accounted for it. Dobson had been in the Navy long enough to know that no matter how harsh a commanding officer seemed on first acquaintance, if one did one's job properly, the crankiest officer was bound to unbend.

Dobson settled quickly into the new routine. In spite of, or perhaps because of Peters' acidic personality, the *Adelaide* was a tightly disciplined ship. She might not be happy, but she was efficient. His duties as executive officer, in charge of ship's operations, were thus considerably lightened.

There was no need to find work for the crew; their routine at sea – dawn and evening stations, the general alerts between sundown and dawn and the endless hours of sweeping the southern end of St George's Channel – saw to that. Peters kept his word concerning the work he expected from his officers and he refused to spare himself as well. On their second day at sea, Dobson requested routine gunnery practice and was turned down abruptly and without explanation. Gunnery was Dobson's great love and Peters' refusal to allow practice in time of war was a great surprise to him.

The two other officers were a volunteer reserve junior lieutenant and the midshipman. At first, he took their reticence for loyalty to the captain but as the days passed and the *Adelaide* churned back and forth, he began to suspect their unwillingness to talk was due more to fear. The sub-lieutenant, William Engster, was engineering officer. He was a tall, cadaverous Londoner in his mid-fifties with a thick cockney accent Dobson found difficult to understand. He had spent most of his life in a coastal collier plying between Newcastle and assorted east and south coast ports. He was a self-contained individual who neither invited nor sought company and Dobson rarely saw him off duty except at dinner.

Midshipman Harold Wesley was simply frightened to death of Peters. He was a short, dumpy boy of seventeen with traces of acne clinging to his chin and cheeks and he was deathly afraid of a bad fitness report. Not surprisingly, the majority of Peters' invective was directed at the boy.

The *Adelaide* herself was an old ship, dating from the final days of the First War. She was wooden-hulled and years at sea had taken their toll. The rumour was that the Navy had sent her down for scrapping when the outbreak of war reprieved her. She was an exceptionally wet ship and the pumps ran twenty-four hours a day in all but the deadest seas. Every compartment below the main deck was damp and rust and mildew were continual problems. Her overall length was eighty feet and she was powered by a single diesel engine. Her armament was laughable, consisting as it did of a single six-pounder gun forward and two two-pounder guns – forty-millimetre Bofors added prior to her last cruise. The two-pounders occupied jury-rigged wings one on either side of the bridge. She was expected to double as convoy escort on occasion and so had been fitted with a single depth-charge launcher and an ancient Asdic apparatus, both pieces of equipment dating from the late 1920s.

On the seventh day of the ten-day patrol, a cheerless sun glared at the *Adelaide*'s crew as they struggled with the huge paravanes streaming on either side of the bow. For once, the entrance to St

George's was relatively calm. The crew, grateful for the sun's meagre warmth, were as relaxed as Dobson had yet seen them.

He stared round the horizon with a pair of binoculars in an effort to keep awake. This was the third straight watch and he was exhausted. The glare on the oil-smooth waters hurt his eyes and he closed and rubbed them.

'Mr Dobson!' The petty officer's shout startled him into full wakefulness.

A sailor pointed along the line to a tangle of cable. 'All Stop!' he shouted. 'Booms!'

Men came running with long timbers to fend off the mine that had tangled in the cables. It bobbed erratically as the ship lost way, swinging ever closer to the hull. The damned cutters hadn't worked properly, he thought with a groan. A long cable extending to the sea bed moored mines of this type in place. Apparently the mine's cable had broken and was now entangled in the sweeping gear. As it bobbed closer, he could see that it was a double-purpose mine, designed to knock out wooden-hulled fishing, commercial and mine-sweeping vessels by concussion and steel-hulled military or merchant ships by magnetic triggers. The mine's movement was erratic due to the cable and there was a damned good chance they would be blown to hell and gone if one of the trigger horns banged against the hull. Dobson hesitated, undecided. If he cut the paravane away, they would lose a half day rigging and streaming a new one. But a surge of wind, a rogue wave. . . .

'Cut the cable and have a rifleman stand by to explode the mine,' he shouted down to the main deck. The petty officer supervising seemed about to argue, then snapped his mouth closed and relayed the orders. The cable splashed into the sea and Dobson took the *Adelaide* slow ahead. When they were a hundred yards off, he nodded to the sailor who had come onto the bridge with a Lee-Enfield Number One, Mark III rifle. He leaned against the bridge railing to steady his aim, waited for a slight roll to pass and fired. The bullet splashed behind the mine. The sailor fiddled with the sight, aimed and fired again. The mine went off with a dull boom and a geyser fountained into the air, glistening in the sunlight and shedding rainbows. The sailors on deck cheered and the petty officer took a party below for the new cable.

'Just what the devil do you think you're about, Mr Dobson?'

The captain had left his cabin so quickly that he was still wrapping his bathrobe over his nightgown and his feet were bare. Thinking that Peters was angry at having been awakened by the noise, he started to apologize.

'I'm sorry, Captain. I didn't think the explosion would wake you.'

'You cut away a perfectly good cable, Mr Dobson. A perfectly good cable,' Peters shouted and Dobson knew the sailors on deck were watching yet.

'Captain, a mine. . . .'

'I don't care what you thought, Mr Dobson. You throw away King's property at a time like this? I've a good mind to indent your pay. You've committed an act of sabotage, Mr Dobson. I can promise you a most negative entry in your fitness report, sir. A most negative entry. Have a new cable rigged and this ship underway in two hours, Mr Dobson. Two hours!'

The captain whirled away and, shaken, Dobson glanced down at the deck where the petty officer had just returned with a new cable. He had heard Peters' last order and was staring at Dobson in dismay.

The General Quarters alarm roused him from a dreamless sleep on their last day at sea. Dobson lay, without opening his eyes, his mind seeking to place him in time and space; then memories of the ship, the crew and long, sleepless days and nights came seeping back. The compartment was icy; he shuddered as his feet touched the bare deck plates and he dragged on the heavy woollen socks he had worn for three straight days because the boiler was broken down again and there was no hot water.

Dobson came onto the bridge as the eastern horizon was beginning to show the first faint flush of dawn. It was just after 0645 and he had slept less than two hours. The Malayan steward silently offered him coffee and he stood drinking it as Midshipman Wesley fussed about the chart table, conscious of his executive officer's presence. Dobson felt sorry that the boy had to serve in his first ship under such an unremitting bastard as Commander Peters.

The captain stamped onto the bridge and Dobson nodded a good morning which Peters affected not to see. Wesley handed him the yellow flimsy and for once Peters did not rail at him but contented himself with a nod. The captain then surprised Dobson by bringing his coffee cup over to the bridge window.

'Action, Mr Dobson.' Dobson could almost believe he detected a trace of friendliness in Peters' voice. 'Orders from Western Approaches Command at Plymouth. A slow convoy is coming in from Halifax, badly shot up. We've been detached and ordered to serve as escort. I want a course to intercept at the earliest possible moment.'

'Very good, sir.' Dobson tried to conceal his disappointment at not returning to Plymouth and at the same time, put warmth into his voice without sounding obsequious. For a moment, both men stared through the bridge window at the magnificent dawn flooding the sky with reddish pink, the colour of ripening strawberries. The deck was visible now and both were conscious of the six-pounder popgun below on the deck behind its canvas spray shield.

They ran up to the convoy in mid-afternoon under an unusually blue sky. The sea was just choppy enough to ruffle white caps on the long Atlantic swells and the air contained a false hint of spring.

'Bloody U-boat weather,' Dobson heard one lookout mutter to another as the watches changed. And it was. Visibility was twenty miles in the limpid air; the sea just rough enough to hide a periscope. *Adelaide* was not equipped with the new radio detection gear and her rudimentary Asdic unit was sixteen years old. Of the two hydrophones she mounted, one had been damaged two months before when *Adelaide* had fouled a fishing net off the Irish coast. She had been scheduled for dry dock twice to repair it but both times something had intervened.

The *Adelaide* made her number and the destroyer responded. 'The old *Decoy*,' the quartermaster murmured and when Dobson glanced at him, he nodded to where the destroyer was just visible off the port bow. ' 'D' Class. Served in her in thirty-seven, sir, China Station.'

The *Adelaide* was instructed to take up position on the convoy's port quarter. The convoy was six ragged lines of merchant vessels with a thin column of smoke marking the rear where a ship, too distant to be identified, limped after the rest. Dobson counted six escort vessels, two of them armed trawlers, and shook his head. The gaps in the lines were quite obvious as they came round on their new course; eight vessels missing from the total of twenty-two ships that had started from Halifax; 36 per cent of the convoy lost in the 'Black Gap,' the area in mid-Atlantic beyond the effective range of escorting aircraft, and a ninth ship on fire and lagging badly. And they were still a night and two days from the relative safety of coastal waters. With their single depth-charge launcher, light weaponry, cranky Asdic gear and ineffective hydrophones, *Adelaide* would be of little help to the hard-pressed and exhausted escorts.

The fine weather held steady all morning and, at noon, Dobson surrendered the watch to the captain who nodded curtly and sent him from the bridge. It was evident that whatever had moved him to a moment's comradeship at dawn had now disappeared. The cook, at Dobson's request, had set out a large pan of sea water to warm in the sun and he gathered up his underwear and socks and went to the stern where under the eyes of grinning seamen, he washed them in the harsh salt-water soap, used some of his meagre ration of fresh water to rinse the salt away and hung everything to dry on a line rigged along the railing. Dobson then went below for some badly needed sleep.

The sun was a flattened disc squatting above the horizon when General Quarters woke him for the second time that day. He had slept fitfully, filled with apprehension. Now, with two hours before his watch resumed, he sat up on the edge of the bunk, shivering. It was no use trying to sleep again, he decided. He could feel his nerves sharpening to a fine edge. Dobson took a hurried sponge bath, certain it would lead to pneumonia, then shaved and for the first time in days, dressed in the fresh underwear, socks and shirt which the steward brought down. He went on deck just as the sea was turning orange and gold.

The bulk of the convoy was between *Adelaide* and the sun which meant that the attack *when*, not if, it came would be from astern or to port. As it was not yet dark, he went to the rail and lit a cigarette. These English Players seemed harsher than he was used to. Far astern, he could just make out a faint tinge of smoke that marked the position of that damned burning freighter, like a beacon to every damned U-boat in the North Atlantic. The sun disappeared and moments later, as if a light had been switched off, the twilight vanished.

Dobson stepped onto the bridge at 2000 hours to find Peters slumped in the high seat, staring through the bridge windows. In the dim reddish console lights, his face was tight and drawn, a spectre's face. Dobson had to speak to him twice before Peters roused enough to acknowledge his relief. Then it was another twenty minutes before the steward could persuade Peters to lie down on the cot in the tiny chart room behind the bridge. Funny, Dobson thought, the only person the captain treats with unfailing courtesy is the Malayan.

The first explosion came at 0100 exactly, as if the U-boat commander had been waiting for that exact moment. Far off to starboard, on the opposite edge of the convoy, a brilliant fireball lit the night sky. Aldis lights winked on the horizon and the *Adelaide* was ordered to maintain station. He made out the numbers of the two armed trawlers as the *Decoy* sent them to scour the waters but the submarine would be long gone before they arrived.

Nine ships gone. The burning freighter, still with them at sunset, would probably go before dawn also. The edgy air increased on the *Adelaide* and Dobson debated waking the captain, but decided against it. It was his watch.

The Asdic operator's voice was full of suppressed excitement. 'Contact bearing oh-nine-three, range estimated at. . . .'

He didn't finish. Less than two miles ahead, another flash silhouetted a ship. Dobson found her in his glasses. She was a modern cargo vessel, American, and less than two years old. Red flames were bursting from her decks and she shuddered to a halt and immediately began to develop a list. Abruptly, a second explosion blew her bow away. In moments, she was down by the head. Without waiting for instructions from *Decoy*, Dobson shouted for full ahead. The Asdic operator called bearing and range and it was clear that the U-boat was running in on the convoy – as if she knew the *Adelaide* posed little threat.

The gap had closed to two thousand yards when the Asdic operator yelped and swore. 'Gone, sir. Just disappeared. Think she's turned.'

Dobson hesitated. His mind whirled as he tried to cope with masses of unexpected and conflicting information. The merchant ship was burning furiously on his starboard quarter and he could see figures tumbling into the sea; had the submarine turned away to attack another ship, or had she detected the approach of the *Adelaide*? If the latter, they might be on the receiving end of a torpedo in seconds. Prophetic thought – the next instant, the lookouts sighted another torpedo track. Dobson shouted for an emergency turn to port and with all the insane inevitability of a ponderous avalanche, the whitish wake ran past their bow a hundred yards ahead. The intended victim, an ancient high-pooped freighter with heavy trucks and tanks lashed to her decks, began a sharp turn to starboard, much too late. At the same instant, her mate inboard of the convoy, confused by the explosions, the star-shells bursting overhead and the luminescent night in which shadows were more substantial than shadows had a right to be, turned to port. The two ships came together with the tearing scream of fingernails on a chalkboard and the torpedo struck the outboard freighter squarely behind the bows.

Dobson shouted orders for the rescue party to assemble on the fantail and ran out onto the bridge wing. The *Adelaide* was two hundred yards from the burning freighter as it rebounded from the vicious contact. He couldn't see the other ship for the freighter's bulk. The weight of the cargo on her deck in combination with the gaping hole in her hull tilted the dying ship towards the slathering waves, her bow dipped and the single screw lifted partly above the surface, still turning with enough speed and bite to drive her ahead, a flaming beacon marking the convoy's course. The *Adelaide*'s rescue party worked furiously to swing out a boat. Burning oil lit the area brightly enough for Dobson to see the freighter's crew as a weaving, bobbing cluster of heads in the cold waters. Apparently they had panicked and gone overboard as soon as the ship was struck and the fire erupted. There were no life rafts or Carely floats in evidence.

He shouted 'all stop' just as someone pushed him away from the speaking tube. Dobson fetched up against the window and swung around furiously to hear Peters order a resumption of speed and the quartermaster to come hard to port. He looked back down at the red glare to see *Adelaide* veer abruptly and charge away in another direction leaving the men in the water to shout and scream after them.

'Captain, those men will die in minutes in that water.'

'I've taken the conn, Mr Dobson,' Peters growled. 'Kindly get off the bridge and take your station aft.'

'The crew of that ship . . .' Dobson realized he was shouting '. . . they'll freeze to death!'

'Mr Dobson!' Peters thundered. 'I'll not tell you again to leave this bridge! Go to your duty station immediately!'

Dobson could not believe that Peters was deliberately throwing away lives to hunt for a submarine that would have withdrawn by now; not with a ship full of rudimentary Asdic gear and a single hydrophone that for all intents and purposes was useless. Ten days of frustration, of discourtesy, of fault finding and nitpicking suddenly overwhelmed him.

'Captain,' he shouted, 'the job of a convoy escort is to assist the crew of damaged or sunken ships as a second priority. The U-boat is gone. I will register a protest in the strongest possible terms!'

Peters slammed his fist on the ledge. 'Then do so, Mr Dobson!' he screamed. 'And in writing, if you please! But in the meantime, take yourself off my bridge!'

Dobson stared at him for a moment, then spun on his heel and left.

The *Adelaide* came into Plymouth Harbour three days later. She had been ordered to remain with the convoy to the Nore and had anchored in the Thames overnight while hospital cutters took badly wounded survivors from the merchant ships.

As soon as the ship was secured, Commander Peters left with a portfolio of reports tucked under one arm. Dobson leaned on the bridge railing and thought of the report to Admiral Dunbar-Naismith that he had sent off in the mail bag as soon as they docked. He had anxiously weighed the pros and cons of sending the report and had gone over and over the single, neatly handwritten sheet of paper to make certain that it contained nothing but emotionless fact. He quoted no witnesses, named no names, not even Peters – referring to him only as ship's commanding officer.

The callous disregard shown by Peters when he left those men in the water to die made it imperative that he be removed from command, Dobson knew. There hadn't been a hope in hell of catching that U-boat and their duty had clearly been to act as a rescue ship. The incident was merely the culmination of a sequence of events that showed that Peters was clearly not fit to command. My God! He was past sixty! No man his age should be required to endure the winter North Atlantic in wartime. The lack of sleep alone, not to mention the pressures and tensions of minesweeping combined with convoy escort duty in a ship sadly under-equipped for the job, might well have destroyed a better and younger man.

But guilt nagged him. If he were to remain honest with himself, he had to wonder if jealousy did not play a role here. After all, he had expected to command *Adelaide*. No, he thought sharply and dismissed the idea. That was a secondary consideration.

The envelope had been marked URGENT, for Dunbar-Naismith's personal attention and the admiral might even now be reading the report and Peters would be in his office within the hour. The one thing that Dobson feared, yet at the same time half-hoped for, was that Peters would be relieved of command immediately and that he would be promoted to command of *Adelaide*. To distract himself, he spent the long morning watch considering what changes he would make to the duty schedule.

Peters returned late that evening and stumped wearily up the gangway. He came straight onto the bridge where Dobson had just assumed the watch. Midshipman Wesley saw Peters as he topped the ladder, saluted Dobson hastily and disappeared like a puff of smoke.

Peters glanced at the log. 'Mr Dobson, we've been ordered to sea immediately. We are to rendezvous with convoy HX One-Eleven from Halifax, south of Iceland at fourteen degrees west. I wish to be underway as soon as possible.'

Without another word, he shuffled off the bridge.

The *Adelaide* left Plymouth shortly after 2300 hours and steamed down the Hamoaze to the Sound and out into the Channel. Before dawn, she had passed Lands End into the choppy North Atlantic and set course to round Mizzen Head to meet the convoy as it left the protection of air cover provided from Iceland.

Dobson stepped out onto the bridge wing and stood with his back to the forty-millimetre Bofors anti-aircraft gun and its crew to clear the musty ship's air from his lungs with a breath of cold wind. He had given up wondering what had passed between the Admiral Commanding and Peters. The captain was certainly acting no differently towards him, but then his mood at the best of times was sullen. Most probably Admiral Dunbar-Naismith hadn't read the report before Peters presented himself. In any event, Dobson had resigned himself to suffering through another patrol with a captain he suspected was fast going mad. If there had been a surgeon on board, he would have sounded him out about the captain's condition but *Adelaide* was too small to rate more than a pharmacist's mate.

For two days, *Adelaide* plunged back and forth in the miserable waters south of Iceland waiting for the convoy, delayed by unexpectedly heavy seas. According to reports from London, the convoy had lost only one ship between Halifax and Iceland – an oil tanker which had disappeared shortly before dawn two days before they raised Iceland. The U-boat, if that was the cause, had not struck again and the overworked escort had found no further trace. Dobson suspected she had struck a mine and gone down so quickly that there hadn't even been time for a distress call or rocket.

Adelaide's crew had shown streaks of resentment when they put out to sea within hours of completing the previous cruise. Dobson found he could hardly blame them; leave was badly overdue and everywhere he looked, he saw signs of exhaustion – black shadows beneath eyes, haggard expressions, the tendency to snap and snarl and an increase in bickering and fights. The master-at-arms and his mates were kept busy day and night and like the rest of the crew, were becoming increasingly hard to handle themselves.

The North Atlantic in winter is subject to storms of epic proportions. Greenland is the weather-maker; her massive, mile and more thick, icecap acts as a refrigeration unit. A low pressure area forming anywhere in the vast expanse between her eastern shore and a line bounded by Spitzbergen north and the Scandinavian peninsula east and south is certain to cause a massive katabatic storm – the North Atlantic's version of the hurricane. Air cooled by its passage across hundreds of miles of ice sinks to the icecap's surface by the time it reaches Greenland's east coast. This dense mass of air then rolls down the long glacial slopes and pours out through the coastal ice canyons onto the relatively warm waters of the Atlantic with winds that often exceed ninety knots. It was Convoy HX One-Eleven's and *Adelaide*'s luck to encounter just such a storm in late January 1941.

The storm announced its intentions early on the morning of 25 January. At dawn, the sun appeared as a milky disc resting on the horizon. As the day grew older, its light was dimmed increasingly by thickening cloud pouring out of the north-west and rain and sleet slashed the decks at intervals. At noon, the convoy suddenly loomed off the port bow as sleet shredded the fog.

Peters ordered a signal made to the escort commander's flagship, an armed merchantman in command of two overage British destroyers. They, together with the *Adelaide*, constituted the total escort for the sixteen ships strung out in four disorderly ranks to the horizon. Both destroyers were engaged in charging about the convoy, flags and Aldis lamps signalling furiously. *Adelaide* was ordered to work ahead of the convoy.

At 1600 hours, a message came in from London reporting an unusual amount of German R/T traffic along the line of their projected course. U-boats appeared to be converging on a point that lay across the convoy's tracks. Peters, summoned by Dobson, read the flimsy through again and stared at the chart. An hour later, a second message confirmed that the convoy would arrive at the suspected concentration point in the early morning hours. Dobson wondered if this were not the new U-boat tactic which the Germans were calling *die Rudeltaktik*, the wolf pack, and which had been used with some success in the autumn. It made sense. As many as eight to twenty U-boats spread a fan-shaped ambush along the convoy's projected track. The first U-boat to spot the convoy reported its course and speed to Admiral Doenitz's headquarters at Lorient on the Normandy coast who, knowing exactly where each of his U-boats was, issued orders for selected ones to converge on the convoy. If they missed, the U-boat that first made contact strove to keep the convoy in sight until the others could regroup.

Evidently, Peters had reached the same conclusion because his face reflected the bemusement Dobson felt.

As he went off watch, Dobson detoured by ship's stores to replenish his shaving soap. Passing the open hatch leading into the dingy medical bay, he noticed the pharmacist's mate listening with a stethoscope at the bare back of a scrawny seaman while the man coughed on cue. When he finished, the pharmacist's mate counted out tablets into a box. 'One ever' two hours, without fail,' he told him.

The seaman mumbled his thanks and went out, nodding a careful greeting to Dobson. 'What's the matter with him?' he asked.

The pharmacist's mate gave him a furtive look and reached past to close the hatch.

'Consumption, sir.'

'Tuberculosis? For Christ's sake, how in the world did he get past the medical board?'

'Didn't 'ave it when 'e come aboard, sir. Developed it 'ere.'

'Here! On board *Adelaide*?'

''Course, sir. Old girl's a wet ship, wooden 'ull an' all. Allus damp 'low decks. No 'ot food most times, nuffin' but bully beef and cold at that, no more than three 'ours sleep straight. Then all the worry about their families in the Blitz. Can't expect nuthin' else, sir. The men needs rest, a fortnight or more at 'ome. Real rest, sir. 'E's the third case this month.'

'My God man, have you reported this to the captain?'

'Of course, sir,' he responded with a hint of reproach in his voice. 'Not much 'e can do is there, sir?'

The sun dipped towards the steel horizon and the wind seemed to increase in velocity so that spume blew off wave tops in long streamers. An iron cold clamped the thermometer at ten below zero and with the wind gusting to fifty knots and more, the wind chill factor was seventy below zero, Fahrenheit. Peters had given orders that the lookouts were to be changed every ten minutes and the galley boiled gallons of coffee, tea and cocoa.

The spate of messages flowing in from London had increased tensions to unbearable proportions. The two destroyers dashed about the convoy like sheep dogs, Aldis lamps snapping at the heels of any fat merchant ship which showed the least tendency to yaw out of line or lag. Peters maintained his vigil in the chart room which only increased the apprehension on the bridge and to escape, Dobson paced the ship from one end to the other, checking, watching, measuring the men's attitudes, worrying about the meagre supply of ammunition for the guns if it came to surface action, worried about the paper-thin wooden hull and the pumps straining at top rpms to keep up with the water pouring in through seams loosened by the heavy seas. *Adelaide* was never designed for this kind of heavy work. She had been intended for sheltered coastal waters. If wind and sea conditions worsened, she might well be forced to run before the storm, regardless of the convoy's fate.

On deck again, the wind pummelled and tore at him and waves towered thirty and forty feet high. *Adelaide* staggered suddenly as she dipped over the crest of one wave. Looking forward past the bow, Dobson saw a long, greenish-black slope fall away and felt the ship accelerate. He had the sudden impression that they were sliding into a bowl. As he grabbed for a stanchion, he caught a glimpse of the following mountain of water which the wind had exaggerated. The freak wave plunged down on them as *Adelaide* reached the bottom of the trough and Dobson knew for a certainty that the wave was going to smash them under, would poop the ship and drive her straight to the bottom.

Evil glints of light and dark swelled around him as the bowl deepened. They were far below the rim now and Dobson was frozen with terror. The silence was worst of all; the eerie, almost noiseless passage of the ship through the slick, green-black water. There should have been an overwhelming roar, the sound of a thousand express trains, not just a faint hissing as the hull sliced green water.

The bow plunged deep as *Adelaide* came into the bottom of the trough, and reared, shedding a veil of foam; Dobson cringed and cursed and prayed simultaneously. Then *Adelaide* was rising, struggling up the far side. The bulge of water had subsided, had been absorbed somehow by the witless ocean. Shaking with fear and released adrenalin, Dobson painfully unwound his arms and legs from the stanchion and stumbled forward.

For another twenty-four hours, the convoy and its exhausted escorts were pounded by the storm and the heavier, more sea-worthy merchant vessels were grateful as no effective U-boat attack could be made in such seas. But their escorts were required by regulation and common sense to maintain their vigil. Their work was made doubly hard by pounding seas that scattered the convoy and at the same time made passage so much more difficult. Sleep was impossible and pumps were beginning to lose the battle with the ever-widening seams. Dobson recalled the pharmacist's mate's comment about lack of hot food and spent an hour in the galley rigging electric light bulbs over a metal washtub so that the men could at least have warmed soup and bully beef sandwiches.

The morning of their third day with the convoy dawned brilliantly. A low band of cloud above the horizon glowed in magnificent blues and reds and the heaving ocean turned from black to copper to blue-green. They were still two hundred miles north of Ireland as the convoy had been forced to reduce speed during the storm. Scanning the horizon through his glasses, Dobson could see only two ships, both well down to the south. He gave the quartermaster orders and *Adelaide* heeled over and ran towards them at her best speed in the still massive seas, signal lamp first chattering orders to form up on her and then angry expostulations when they steamed blithely on.

By late afternoon, the convoy had been reassembled. No major damage had occurred although Dobson saw more than one battered deckhouse or lifeboat damaged in its davits. The wind had nearly disappeared but the iron cold remained and black and purple storm clouds marched in serried ranks across the horizon. Dobson had again assumed the watch from Peters. The old man made his final notation in the log with a shaky hand and stumbled off the bridge to his cot in the chart room without a word. At the door, he turned to Dobson, as if to say something, then shook his head and disappeared.

Dobson swore at Admiral Dunbar-Naismith for leaving an obviously incompetent and sick old man in charge of seventy-four lives and God alone knew how many more in the convoy assigned to their charge. Staring at the ships spread across the glittering sea as the sun dropped below the horizon, he ached to take *Adelaide* into his own hands. My God, there was so much to be done! This nonsense of riding close aboard the convoy was insane; their station should be farther out by at least three thousand more yards to minimize interference with their sonar gear and hydrophones and to allow them to charge down on an attacking U-boat from behind, rather than to chase after her.

It seemed to him that the lessons won at the cost of men like his own father, between 1914 and 1918, had all been thrown away. Why were Coastal Command aircraft confined strictly to coastal waters? Bombers based in Ulster would have reached them already and could force the U-boats to keep their heads down. Not enough aircraft the RAF maintained, yet Bomber Command would waste them on useless propaganda leaflet raids over Occupied Europe while the ships that carried Britain's very life went down at an ever accelerating rate.

The radio man handed him a flimsy and a cold chill swept him as he read,

Suspect U-boats assembling for concerted attack. R/T traffic Norway and in vicinity eleven degrees west, sixty-two degrees north suggests base direction, estimated five U-boats.

They hadn't outrun them during the storm after all. The U-boats had only withdrawn further east along the convoy's track, leaving a submarine to shadow them so closely that even when the convoy was scattered by the storm, she had not been shaken off.

Dobson went into the chart room and woke Peters. The captain sat up slowly and peered at the paper a long time, as if it made no sense, then nodded slowly. His face was haggard with exhaustion and Dobson was certain he hadn't left the bridge or the chartroom in days.

When he asked if he felt all right, Peters only grimaced and waved him out, growling in a thick voice, 'Wake me in one hour, Mr Dobson.'

Once outside, he felt a moment's pity for the overmatched old man. Any competent medical board would have ruled him past it long ago.

A tanker in the second file exploded with astounding ferocity. For an instant, the incomplete night seemed as bright as noon. Every pair of eyes, every set of binoculars in the convoy automatically turned to the ship in her death throes. A pillar of white, almost transparent flame shot upward with a sound like a welding torch gone mad. For thirty seconds it flared, then quenched instantly as the broken ship plunged to the bottom so quickly that there were no survivors.

Dobson shouted to the steward to wake the captain and jumped to the pelorus for a sighting, then dashed to the chart table to work out the reciprocal bearing for the location of the U-boat – or where she had been four minutes before when the torpedo was launched.

For an instant, he stared at the chart, uncertain, then extended the bearing parallel to the convoy, but against its line of travel. Everything was happening too fast for conscious thought but for once, he sensed instinctively that he was making the correct decision. He roared orders into the speaking tube for full speed, then to the quartermaster for a hard turn to port. The quartermaster goggled at him, but spun the wheel. The vibration of the ship's single diesel engine increased and *Adelaide* leaned into the turn. The deck dipped but Dobson was too busy shouting the U-boat's expected coordinates to gunnery control to notice either that or the steward trying to attract his attention.

Adelaide raced back along the line of the convoy, bow wave curling almost to deck height, stern deep in the water. The Asdic operator called a contact bearing and Dobson, elated, dashed to the console and translated bearing and range to steering directions as fast as he could scribble them on his pad. The U-boat was less than two thousand yards off the starboard bow, running easily in towards the convoy, again picking her next target.

He had done it, he exulted. The U-boat commander had tried to trick them with a reverse run and failed. Dobson snapped on the ship's loudspeakers and gave the lookouts the bearing. He was almost certain she was running on the surface in spite of the weather.

There it was, the lengthening ping as the U-boat spotted them and began to turn away and dive. He had her now! The U-boat's underwater speed was five or six knots and *Adelaide* was capable of three times that.

The steward was at his elbow. 'The captain, he will not wake up, sir. He only mumbles to me words I cannot. . . .'

'Damn it, man, get off the bridge . . . !' he shouted before the steward's words penetrated. He was halfway to the Asdic console when he abruptly switched directions and ran across the bridge to the chartroom. Thirty seconds, he had just thirty seconds. Inside, the red night light made Peters' face into that of a gargoyle. His mouth was open and twisted and his eyes darted madly here and there, seeing nothing. Dobson felt his forehead – cold and clammy and his breathing was shallow and uneven. His pulse was thready and there was a peculiar tenseness to the captain's face, no, just to one part of it. But there wasn't time to do more. As he straightened, the realization that Peters was too sick to function struck him. He was in command of *Adelaide*! Panic swept him as it had that afternoon the ship had nearly died under the rogue wave. He stood frozen above the cot, holding Peters' wrist, staring at the wasted, red-washed form, knowing that he had to move, had to act but his mind refused to translate the knowledge into motion.

Someone was shaking him – the Asdic operator! The quartermaster was cursing fluently and Dobson rushed out of the chartroom. The Asdic operator had left his console . . . somehow, somewhere, another ship was on fire, burning fiercely, lighting up half the convoy. His mind was mired in a peculiarly viscous glue. The Asdic operator bent over his console again and began shouting coordinates which the quartermaster struggled to translate into bearings himself.

The Asdic operator swore violently and slumped in his chair. 'We've lost the bloody bastard! Lost him, damn it to hell!'

Dobson made a superhuman effort to break the thrall of panic. He staggered with an unexpected roll and fetched up painfully against the chart table as he shouted for the steward to fetch the pharmacist's mate and ran to the Asdic console.

'Give me the last bearing,' he demanded in a thick voice. His mind was still slow, still refused to work properly; the responsibility for the lives of the ship's crew, the ship itself and for the countless other seamen in the convoy was a crushing realization he had not come to terms with before; it had been easy enough to criticize when others bore the load, now he had it himself.

The Asdic operator's voice broke his thoughts again and he jotted down the coordinates, suddenly aware that his few moments of panic that had distracted the Asdic operator had been enough for the U-boat to escape.

The sky flashed on the starboard bow – another ship. In despair, he slammed a fist on the chart table and jerked around to stare through the bridge windows into the darkening night. A merchant vessel burned furiously two hundred yards away. Inspiration struck through his despair; he shouted for a hard turn to starboard.

His mind struggled with complex estimates of positions, seeing the relative locations of the three vessels involved as an exercise in trigonometry. *Adelaide* and the burning merchant ship were the knowns, the position of the U-boat the unknown. At the same time, a part of his mind fought the panic that still festered about the edge of his consciousness.

The U-boat had two likely courses of action, he realized intuitively; her captain might decide that two kills were sufficient and withdraw; in which case she would have turned about the instant her torpedo struck. Or, he might once more be unaware of *Adelaide*'s exact location – the torpedo explosion could have caused him to lose the bearing – if so, the U-boat would likely attempt the same manoeuvre once more and parallel the reverse direction of the convoy while searching for another kill.

As *Adelaide* tore back along her own wake, Aldis lamps around the convoy winked as the merchant ships panicked and only one or two ships were actually *visible* in the deepening twilight. Only now did Dobson realize that he had seen crewmen leaping into oil-scummed water from the burning ship. He had abandoned them just as Peters had done!

The pharmacist's mate was at his shoulder. 'Captain . . . stroke . . . dying . . . permission . . . below.' Words in meaningless snatches, eyes on the Asdic operator crouched over his console, headphones pressed hard against his ears. A meaningless sound the pharmacist's mate took to be assent.

'Target bearing oh-eight-one degrees, range three thousand yards, converging.'

The minutes passed with agonizing slowness; on the far side of the convoy, a flare went up and he knew another ship had been torpedoed and for an instant, doubt assailed him. Were they tracking an echo?

'Range 1500 hundred yards.' The Asdic operator's measured chant was interrupted by a whistle in the voice pipe and the calm, tinny voice of the masthead lookout reported the conning tower of a submarine on the surface.

The intense moment of jubilation passed swiftly as a new problem was posed – the same one he had faced six months before when tracking the E-boat – to open fire at long range in a bad sea, or hope that they could approach the U-boat close enough to destroy her with depth charges. There could be no thought of ramming, Dobson knew. *Adelaide*'s wooden hull would crumple like a paper box. But if he fired now, the ranging shots would warn her; she would be ready for an instant dive, thirty seconds and no more for the seas to close over her. They were a minute and a half from her position, ninety seconds, ninety seconds during which she would surely see them and dive. A minute would take her to two hundred feet in a crash dive . . . it would be a matter of luck for *Adelaide*'s depth charges to . . . he gave orders for the six-pounder to track the target as soon as she was visible but not to open fire except on his command.

'Range one thousand yards and closing.' Had he made the right decision? Dobson started to give the command to fire just as the bridge lookout shouted. Dobson saw the enemy then, a dark shadow without substance – still time for her to dive. A wave lifted her against the sky and the U-boat took on substance. A number was painted on the conning tower side but the light was too dim to read it.

'Range eight hundred yards and closing.'

Now! Now, before she sees us and even as the thought formed, the conning tower began to change shape as she turned away.

'Fire!' he screamed and the gun crashed out. He pressed the glasses to his eyes, willing himself to see the splashes around and about the U-boat but there were none. They were firing too high and now the two 40-millimetre Bofors joined in.

'Range six hundred yards, no longer closing.'

The sub had turned away presenting her stern, a difficult shot under the best of conditions and was running for it . . . stern! My God, he screamed silently.

'Torpedo fired, closing rapidly.'

But he had already shouted for the quartermaster to come right ten degrees.

Adelaide lunged and behind, he heard muttered curses as the stretcher bearers lost their footing and stumbled into a bulkhead. 'Come left ten degrees!' Ten degrees was the smallest correction that could be made to jink them out of the torpedo's path and still keep the U-boat in sight. Even so, they had lost distance.

'Range to target seven hundred yards and opening.'

Dobson raced to the port bridge wing. The phosphorescence of the torpedo's wake was clear against the black sea. The *Adelaide* hadn't turned quickly enough, his mind screamed silently. A moment later, the torpedo rushed by fine on the port bow and disappeared. The hard, ear-drum splitting bark of the six pounder hammered the sea but the U-boat was gone. Angrily, he ordered the gun to cease-fire and the depth-charge crew to stand by and as they ran over the spot where he estimated the U-boat to have dived, he gave the order to commence firing. A single splash marked the path of the high-explosive barrel. He waited, counting the seconds to detonation, praying that the charges would explode, that the U-boat would be smashed to oblivion. Moments later, there was a dull boom and the seas heaved astern as the roiling gases breached the surface. The gun fired again as the operator announced they had lost contact. Dobson kept *Adelaide* at it for twenty minutes until the convoy escort commander's angry Aldis message forced him to break off the search.

They lost five more ships that night until at dawn, a Coastal Command Anson appeared and frightened the pack off. Dobson stood haggard and exhausted on the bridge wing and stared at the heaving sea and the distant speck of the aircraft and the misty outline of Northern Ireland.

The ambulance was waiting for HMS *Adelaide*. It was a civilian vehicle and its white paint was in stark contrast to the iron grey and khaki colours that predominated on the sun-splashed Plymouth docks. The stretcher bearers juggled the blanket-wrapped form of Captain Peters down the wobbly gangway and the ambulance drove off, warning bell clanging imperiously.

A sober Dobson came down the gangway a few minutes later, turned left along the wharf and trudged towards the drear building that housed the Western Approaches Command Headquarters. A fierce joy struggled with the depression that had settled over him after the U-boat's escape. He supposed he would take command of *Adelaide* now. Trained officers were in exceptionally short supply and he had received his final initiation in the toughest possible manner. Dobson suppressed the feeling that he might not yet be equal to command – the time for such thoughts was long past.

The docks were working to capacity, he noticed absently. Welding torches dripped molten blue sparks and denim-clad workers were everywhere. Since the end of the so-called 'Phoney war', he had observed a different aspect of the British working man. There was a new pride of workmanship, a feeling of equality, of teamwork. As an Australian, what had astonished him most during his months in Great Britain was the class-structure that smacked of the kind of medieval influence he thought had disappeared with the beginning of the nineteenth century. In Australia, no one would ever admit, or even think himself another's inferior, socially or otherwise.

A sharp-faced commander on the Admiral's staff conducted his debriefing and paid special attention to the U-boat chase Dobson had conducted. 'You say you anticipated that the U-boat would turn to parallel the course of the convoy in reverse, Mr Dobson? Why not the other way about? His attack time was shortened appreciably.'

Dobson nodded. 'All signs were that he had been shadowing the convoy for some time. The seas were very high and he could do so on the surface, with a fair degree of safety. Since his surface speed was faster than the twelve knots the convoy was making, I supposed that he had overhauled us. The first ship torpedoed was ahead of us. One escort destroyer was at point and could hardly have failed to detect her. So, if the U-boat had in fact approached from astern, it seemed logical that she would turn and run back along the length of the convoy, having already identified her victims.'

'I see.' The commander nodded and made several meticulous notes. 'A shrewd guess on your part, Mr Dobson. You do realize of course, how lucky you were. Such a course of action was contrary to stated policy. If you had guessed wrong, you would have been in a great deal of trouble.' He peered intently at Dobson. 'Captain Peters suffered a stroke at about the time you engaged the U-boat. Is that correct?'

Dobson nodded.

'Thank you very much, Lieutenant-Commander Dobson. You may have given us some helpful information.'

Outside, the clerk told him that Admiral Dunbar-Naismith himself wished to see him. With some trepidation, Dobson found his office, was asked to wait and perched himself on a hard chair. Beyond the broad windows criss-crossed with white adhesive tape, the dockyard seemed crowded to capacity with its fleet of over-aged destroyers, mine-sweepers and -layers, armed trawlers and sloops and converted colliers. Nor was the sunshine in keeping with the grim scene of war nor with his memories of ships turned into torches, or of men dying in oil-choked, flaming waters. The report. It could only be about the report that the Admiral wished to see him. He certainly could not be faulted for what he said in light of subsequent events. He would get the *Adelaide* now, he knew. A new command always brought an audience with . . .

'Would you come in now, sir?' The junior officer who served as the admiral's secretary held the door to the inner office. Inside, Dunbar-Naismith motioned to a chair and Dobson sat down feeling very awkward and ill-at-ease and not a little overawed. The Admiral wore the discreet violet ribbon of the Victoria Cross on his tunic, earned for a submarine action during the First War.

'Sorry to have kept you waiting, Mr Dobson. Things are in a bit of a mess at the moment as we are moving Western Approaches Command to Liverpool next week. But I did want to read your action report. Does you credit, I must say. In most respects.'

Dobson was surprised at the last remark but managed to keep his face immobile. 'Thank you, sir.'

'Very interesting bit of deduction on your part. Shows quick presence of mind. Hmm.' He slid the action report into his out-tray and opened another folder.

'I have another report of yours, sent before *Adelaide*'s departure. Very interesting.' He turned a page.

'I am sure you will be pleased to know that the crewmen of that sinking tanker were picked up by a neutral Spanish vessel and were repatriated at Gibraltar two days ago. Rather not have that

459

word get about though. The Spanish, as neutrals, are not supposed to release combatants, but then it's a moot point whether or not merchant seamen can be classified as such. In any event, several of the men needed medical attention.'

He smiled at Dobson and sat back in his chair, fingering a single sheet of paper that Dobson realized was the report he had made earlier in the month.

'I would like you to give me your impression of Captain Peters, if you don't mind. Not for the record, you understand. Just between us.'

Dobson coughed to cover his embarrassment. The past three days had taught him a great deal and he wasn't certain where to start. He began by describing Peters' morose attitude and his neglect of such vital ship functions as gunnery practice and the incidence of tuberculosis in the lower decks. But as he talked, the things that had troubled him before now lacked the importance he had once attached to them.

'I felt, sir,' he finished somewhat lamely, 'that although Commander Peters was a very fine officer, the abrupt onset of combat after his retirement might have proven too much for him.'

The Admiral nodded and swivelled his chair away. 'I thought that might be your attitude, Mr Dobson. I am certain you had the good of your ship and the Navy in mind when you made this report and I am certain you gave it a great deal of thought. I would like to say a few things that might be of interest, if I may.

'Commander Peters retired from the Navy in 1937 and accepted a position with the Brownell Lines as Master. His wife had died some years earlier and his only son was in the forces, serving in the Far East. He retired two years sooner than necessary as he was aware that the Navy list was overfull and he was standing in the way of younger officers. As he had private means and did not need to depend on his navy pension, he refused a promotion to the rank of Captain before he left the service in order to make room for a serving officer.'

A sinking feeling began in the pit of Dobson's stomach.

'In mid-September last, his ship was torpedoed off the coast of Sierra Leone and went down with the loss of three crew members. The day he returned to London, he phoned me up to ask for reinstatement. I was only to happy to oblige as you know how desperate for trained officers we were and in fact, still are. *Adelaide* was his second command. You may not know that he was in command of the destroyer HMS *Delta* when she was bombed and sunk with the loss of forty-three men off Norway last May. Commander Peters spent two weeks in hospital, then requested another command. I had only *Adelaide* at the time but he was perfectly

460

happy with her. He took a raw crew of former merchant sailors, landsmen, a volunteer reserve officer and a naval cadet and made her into a first class mine-sweeper and escort vessel, in spite of her many and serious deficiencies.

'You mention his inordinate anger at the loss of the sweeping gear and I agree; it may well have been excessive. But if the strain he had endured for so long is considered, one can understand. As for the lack of firing practice and his refusal to allow any, I might point out that the ammunition situation for the obsolete six-pounder mounted by *Adelaide* is very serious. As you know, her magazine holds ninety-one shells. When those are gone there will be no more. *Adelaide* is scheduled for dry dock at which time her hull will be reinforced and new, more modern weapons mounted. But I cannot afford to lose the services of *Adelaide* until the new series of minelayers comes into service. Until then, she must conserve her ammunition and herself.'

Dobson's guilt was deepening with every word. He steeled himself to remain upright in the chair but inwardly he quailed under each of the Admiral's points, as the Admiral clearly meant him to.

'Finally, I must say a personal word about Commander Peters himself. I served under him myself in 1917. He was one of the finest sea officers I have ever known. He knew his duty and did it, unstintingly. Commander Peters was a hard man, but hard only on himself and his officers. He knew about the tuberculosis problem and had reported it to me. But again, there was nothing to do but endure. *Adelaide* is a wet ship and the North Atlantic makes no allowances, nor do the U-boats.

'Your complaint that he abandoned the crew of the torpedoed tanker has no merit. Knowing John Peters as I did, I am certain that leaving those men was the hardest decision he ever had to make. It is a hard thing to say, but at this time, the preservation of *Adelaide* was far more important than the lives of those men.'

He swivelled back and looked at Dobson who managed to return his gaze without flinching, but just barely. He was thinking that he too had abandoned men in the sea, but out of carelessness and not a conscious decision.

'Commander Peters died two hours ago. The cause was listed as cerebral haemorrhage. But I know it was overwork which killed him.'

Dobson nodded, then stood and picked up the report. He glanced at it, then tore it slowly in half and dropped it in the Admiral's waste-basket.

Dunbar-Naismith watched him leave, then called his secretary in and gave him instructions to notify the Admiralty in London that Lieutenant-Commander Rand Dobson was available for reassignment, as an executive officer. He stared at Dobson's service record for a long minute, arranging the words in his mind before making an entry to the effect that while Dobson made an excellent executive officer, he was in need of further seasoning before he could be granted a command of his own.

Report

Cyrenaica 8 April 1941

Torsten Fredriksson watched as General Michael O'Moore Creagh, commanding the British Seventh Armoured Division, took the town's surrender from its fat, little mayor. Behind him the chief of the carabinieri and the town council beamed incongruously. On the fifth, Generals Cona and Babini had been captured and General Tellera killed twenty or so miles to the south at Beda Fomm. Two hundred thousand Italian prisoners had been captured, along with enough equipment, it was said, to outfit an entire army. So, he thought, in less than three months, General Archibald Wavell, long castigated for inertia, had defeated a force ten times his superior.

Fredriksson had obtained accreditation to the British Eighth Army in North Africa, he suspected, on the strength of his Battle of Taranto story, which had balanced, in the British mind, the retreat from Dunkirk column. He had arrived in the desert the day the 'limited' offensive had begun and had managed to keep up as it progressed far beyond its original 'raid-in-force' status into a complete rout of Italian forces. Between December and March, the Italian–British positions were entirely reversed and the Italian collapse in Libya was completed. The British had gone on to capture El Aghelia, the gateway to Tripoli, and the fortress of Tobruk was expected to fall within the next few days.

Contempt for the Italian soldier was strong among the Empire troops but Fredriksson knew it was misplaced. The Italian soldier was as courageous as the Norwegian or Finn but, like the French and the Belgian, he had no confidence in his leaders, political or military. Mussolini failed to provide his Libyan and Balkan armies with anything but high-flown words, and the *Commando Supremo* seemed more interested in internal politics than fighting.

During the autumn of 1940, the Empire soldier had endured daily bombing raids by the Italian air force and the Italian navy had shipped in vast amounts of supplies – every man had at least two complete uniforms while his British counterpart often wore the same shorts, shirt, wool socks and boots for months on end. Nearly every Italian encampment, no matter how small, had arrangements for laundry; the British soldier cleaned his clothes in petrol, if available, or salt water if near the sea.

Every Italian soldier carried his own little espresso machine, a marvellous contraption so dear to every man that even in the midst of an all-out rout, Fredriksson rarely saw one thrown away. Italian rations were quite good and each unit had its own cook. The British soldier ate bully beef and was allowed – in theory – a gallon of water a day. In practice it often worked out to less than two quarts; for drinking, washing, and cooking.

The Italian soldier's personal equipment was of the highest quality and his uniforms marvels of cotton drill. Shoes were carefully crafted, as were sleeping bags, cots and even bed lamps for reading at night. The most popular piece of captured equipment was a sleeveless cotton jerkin full of pockets which was called the *Sahariana*. But, in contrast, major pieces of equipment were often shoddily designed and manufactured. The huge Italian ten-ton transport lorries were equipped only with solid tyres which quickly shook them to pieces in the desert terrain. Italian aircraft were better suited to raids against primitive Abyssinians or desert Arabs. And the medium M13 tank was nicknamed the 'mobile coffin' because its light armour was proof against a rifle bullet, and little else. Their infantry rifles, while beautifully made, were outmoded and of too light a calibre for the long-distance shooting required in the desert.

There was another difference between the Finn or Norwegian and the Italian; the former had been fighting on their home ground against an aggressor; Italian troops were the aggressors and their poor morale spoke volumes for Mussolini's failure to instil an aggressive fervour in such a highly individualistic people.

Fredriksson tired of the flowery speeches and turned back into the room where he had claimed space for his typewriter and sleeping bag. He lit an Italian cigarette and sat down. The room was quiet; the other correspondents were down in the square hoping to pick up a hint of what was coming next. He rolled a sheet of expensive Italian bond into the carriage and sat for a moment, staring through the window at the intense blue of the spring sky. A cooling breeze brought the scent of the salt water and flowers.

From Across the World, Torsten Fredriksson, Benghazi, 8 April 1941 – For Immediate Release: The campaign in North Africa is over, at least for the time being. The Italian army has been thrown back into Tripoli and the British Empire army has halted at El Aghelia to overhaul and replace its battered equipment. It is supposed here that the next phase will somehow involve the Germans. Even the most pessimistic sources doubt that the famed Panzer General, Erwin Rommel, will be able to regain the ground lost by Marshal Graziani's Libyan Army this winter even though it is rumoured that London has ordered all-out support for Greece and the only Empire forces available must come from North Africa.

The British Navy rules the Mediterranean. That is a statement of fact. So, if Germany does comes in, what can she offer other than moral support to a badly beaten ally here, in Albania and Greece. How can Berlin supply and more importantly, resupply sufficient forces to do otherwise? As both sides have discovered, supply is the controlling factor in desert warfare. Every bullet, every litre of petrol and water, every kilogramme of food must be carried to the front from supply bases often three and four hundred kilometres in the rear where they are secure against air attack. And this must be done over roads that are often no more than camel tracks. The great Via Balbia, the only paved road in all of Cyrenaica and one constructed at immense cost, was torn to pieces in a week.

The value of such places as Sidi Barrani, Tobruk and Benghazi, mere villages, lie only in their port facilities. Along a coast where any kind of sheltered water is rare, they are the keys to holding Cyrenaica and thus, all of Libya. The control of such a port means that an offensive may run another one hundred kilometres before the supply lines fail and the offensive once again comes to a halt. Thus Alexandria served to recapture Sidi Barrani which made possible the capture of Bardia which in turn brought about the capture of Tobruk which made possible the capture of Derna which ended with the capture of Benghazi.

Such a victory is made all the more remarkable when one realizes that at no time could General Wavell dispose more than two divisions at the front. At the battle of Beda Fomm two days ago, the 11th Hussars of the Seventh Armoured Division slashed across some of the worst desert terrain in the world in thirty-three hours. They had timed their attack to that of the Sixth Australian Division north of Benghazi and the result was the capture of 113,000 prisoners. A victory of this magnitude says as much for the fighting spirit of the winning side as the losing side.

If the rumours are true, if Germany does enter the North African fray, they will face stiff opposition from the Empire forces who have now had a year's experience of desert warfare. And they will face even stiffer opposition from General Distance and Colonels Terrain and Supply. . . .

Even in the stripped down and very lean Desert Army, it has been found that five men are needed in a line stretching a thousand kilometres to Cairo to supply just one fighting man at the front with bullets, food, water and petrol – the four elements of desert warfare.

War, war is still the cry

Childe Harold's Pilgrimage
Lord Byron

Hamburg 5 – 12 April 1941

An April rain fell steadily as Major Friedrich Prager left the Hamburg Main Station. He stopped under the portico to breathe the damp air blowing off the river, thinking, as he did every time he returned, that this mix of coal, river, petrol smells and occasional bursts of country air, was the first real sign of home.

It was, of course, impossible to find a taxi – because of the rain, not petrol rationing. He hurried across the square to the Kirchen-Allee and ducked under the shelter to wait for the tram. Two boys of about fourteen eyed his army greatcoat and field service cap with interest.

Prager was surprised at the evidence of bomb damage. He knew that Hamburg and Altona had been raided several times but the press had reported minor damage only to the oil refineries and dockyards. But it was evident that the damage was much more extensive. Office buildings and shop fronts were spattered with the characteristic shrapnel pits and here and there windows had been boarded up with plywood. Two sections of the street were blocked off as workmen laboured in the downpour to complete repairs. Pinpricks, he thought. A pitiful attempt by the British that certainly could not compare with the devastation visited on English cities every night by the Luftwaffe. Distance was against them. The Royal Air Force must fly up to a thousand kilometres and back again to deliver their bombs while the Luftwaffe had merely to jump across the English Channel from bases in France and the Low Countries.

The tram clanged across the square and stopped and he got on, followed by the boys. Because of the rain the tram was nearly empty. Dusk had edged into the city and the usual Sunday night stillness had taken hold. He could see that the boys wanted to talk to him but he was too tired and he leaned his head against the window and pretended to sleep until they got off.

The house seemed damp and quite cold. He had half-expected that Sonja would have been round. He had not been home since his summer leave but she had written that she often went out to look after the house and had even arranged to have it painted. He stood in the middle of the clean but cheerless parlour, suddenly at a loss. Why the devil had he come? he wondered.

Sonja's father answered the telephone and his heavy accent made him seem even more hostile. The phone was put down with a thump and Prager heard him call to Sonja. There was a muffled exchange and then her voice came over the wire, breathless with anticipation. They both started to speak at once, laughed and began again. Her relief was palpable; with the exception of a single December day in Berlin, chaperoned by her mother, they had not seen each other since his sick leave had ended the previous August. And then to have seen her and not be able to touch her, to even tell her that he loved her, had been exquisite torture. But her mother had hovered about them like an eagle guarding her chick.

They arranged to meet for lunch the following day and hung up, reluctantly. She had said nothing about the letter, nor had he asked. Yet it was a subject that must be faced.

That night, Prager lay awake a long time remembering how they had made love for the first time in this same bed. It had rained that night as well. All during the long months in Berlin, he had wanted her so badly; once he had even started a letter to tell her to come to Berlin so that they could be married.

Over and over again he had struggled with the thought of what would happen to her if he should be killed or crippled as his father had been. Sonja would be treated no differently by the neighbours or by the government than his mother had been – an alien, an enemy. To make it worse, Sonja was also a member of the Communist Party. The fact that she had no real political convictions would certainly be lost on the government. And even if she renounced her party membership, even if she joined the National Socialist Party. . . .

As he had done so many times before, he balanced the negative aspects of their relationship against his love for her. Last June, he had been hopeful that the war was at an end and it would no longer matter. But, against all expectations, England had defied Germany, even though teetering on the edge of surrender under the Luftwaffe onslaught.

Prager's return to Section One of the Supply and Administration Office of the Army High Command after the French campaign provided him with ample opportunity to know what was going on at any time and what operations were projected for the future. He had been assigned the task of coordinating lines of communication between those Panzer forces allotted to the invasion of England and the Army High Command. During the winter, he had worked to refine plans for the revamped *Operation Sea Lion*, due in the spring. May or early June had been selected as the optimum conjunction of tide and weather. According to intelligence estimates pouring in every day, England was stretched to the breaking point in North Africa and now, the damned fools, as a result of *Operations*

Alpine Violet in Albania and *Marita* in Greece, that was not all. She had lost every battle against German forces and had only a rather poor showing against the Italians in East Africa and Cyrenaica to her credit.

Germany's planning, therefore, had assumed that, in spite of intensive training, in which the remnants of the British Army must be engaged, Britain would have little in the way of heavy weaponry to oppose German troops who would sweep inland from the invasion beaches in even greater numbers than had been planned the previous September.

But two weeks ago, he had been switched abruptly to a new project and from the moment he had reported for duty, he had known that the war was farther from being over than ever before. And the problem of Sonja had taken on a terrible dimension.

They met in the Alster Pavilion at one o'clock. Prager watched her hurrying towards him, short blue skirt whisking about silk-stockinged knees. She wore a pale blue blouse under her open coat and a hair ribbon to match her skirt and she looked more German than most of the girls promenading the walk. Her eyes sparkled as she hugged, then kissed him fiercely. Prager held her tightly, aware of every curve even through their overcoats.

The sun was attempting to penetrate the rain's aftermath and the wind had dropped but so had the temperature. Sonja's breath steamed as she laughed at his compliments. She pulled his hand into her coat pocket and pressed it against her hip as they walked.

'I've reserved a table in the Pavilion,' she said. 'But we won't be alone.'

'Oh?'

'My father and mother insisted on coming. They wish to talk to you.'

Prager stopped abruptly and Sonja was tugged off balance. 'Talk to me? What about?'

Sonja released his hand and turned to the rail. He went to stand beside her and she shivered as a gust of wind rippled the lake.

'My parents have been ordered to return home, to Smolensk. My father expected me to go with them of course, but I refused. I told them that I wished to remain here, with you. He called me a traitor and ordered me to go home with them but as I am of age, they cannot force me to do so. My father even tried to have my passport revoked by the Soviet authorities but I threatened to ask for political asylum if he did so.' She turned quickly before he could say anything. 'Please, do not be angry. I know your feelings about marriage until the war is ended but I will stay here in any event, whether you wish me to or not.' She shrugged and fell silent and Prager closed his eyes against her pain.

Nicholas Mikhailovitch Vishenko had chosen a table near a window that looked over the choppy expanse of the Alster-Bassin. Both parents were exactly as he remembered them; her father squat and beefy with a no-nonsense expression and not the least trace of humour about him. And again he was struck by how much her mother was the exact physical opposite of Sonja. Also short and dumpy with the harsh, reddened complexion of a peasant, she always wore tight black dresses which served to emphasize her weight and rural background. Her hair was jet black and drawn tightly into a bun at the back of her neck. How two such shapeless, unattractive individuals could possibly have produced as graceful and slender a creature as Sonja was a mystery to him.

Her father extended a grudging hand and Prager seated Sonja and sat down across the table from her. The waiter brought the menus and although a schnapps would have helped to relax them all, he shook his head at the wine steward, knowing the Vishenkos' prejudices. Prager strained to make himself cordial and they discussed the beating the English were taking in Greece and North Africa. He tried to amuse them with anecdotes about General Erwin Rommel, the hero of the moment, but Nicholas Mikhailovitch dismissed it all with a muttered comment about the natural superiority of Russian tanks and commanders. Only Sonja's smiled encouragement made the luncheon bearable. When the table was cleared and coffee brought, Sonja's father pushed his chair back and settled hands on knees.

'We return to the Soviet Union in three days. Sonja must come.'

A cold wash of fear went through him. Do the Russians know what the Fuehrer is planning? Was he being tested? But how? He had never even told Sonja what kind of work he did in Berlin. She thought he was only a Panzer officer. Perhaps the invasion of Yugoslavia had frightened them? But that had only begun a few days ago; according to Sonja, they had known since March that they would be recalled.

'Sonja and I intend to marry when the war is over,' he said in desperation and managed to keep his fear from showing. 'Perhaps she has other desires.'

'Intent is not the same as marriage,' the old man pointed out, 'nor is the war likely to end for another year or two. Sonja's desires are unimportant. She is unmarried and cannot remain alone in a foreign country.' His tone made it plain there would be no argument. 'She will return with us to Moscow.'

Her mother's face was impassive and Sonja was plainly distressed. Prager took a deep breath. 'Sonja has told you of my reasons for not wanting to marry until the war ends?'

Both nodded. 'Commendable sentiments.' Vishenko's harsh expression softened for a moment. 'We thank you for them.' Then his face tightened again and Prager was aware of the sunken little eyes watching him shrewdly. The fatherly concern was gone and he had not been offered an alternative.

There did not seem to be anything else to say. Vishenko insisted on paying the bill and left a minuscule tip. Prager added to it surreptitiously and earned the waiter's arch acknowledgement.

Outside, the sun was beginning to warm the air to a semblance of spring. Sonja spoke firmly to her parents in Russian and they nodded reluctantly. Prager shook hands with both of them and they stumped across the promenade to the tram stop, looking more than ever like two peasants lost in the city. Sonja linked her arm in his and they walked in the opposite direction.

'I apologize for them,' she murmured. 'I did not know they would come until I was leaving the flat. Then there was nothing I could do.'

Prager nodded and they walked in silence. The breeze had lost a bit of its chill and the sun was pleasant. Even so, he was having difficulty ordering his thoughts. First and foremost, he did not want Sonja to leave Germany. His troubled memories of the night before rose again. He remembered the three Panzer Divisions he had detached from France and the Low Countries with a stroke of a pen and moved across the continent to Poland only the week before to be garrisoned fifteen kilometres from the Bug river frontier. During the next thirty days they were to be re-equipped with Panzer IVs and sufficient ammunition and supplies for a six-month campaign, codenamed *Operation Barbarossa* – the attack on the Soviet Union.

He had always suspected that Russia was the Fuehrer's main target, yet the actual start of preparations had come as a shock. He, like everyone else, had always thought of it as something for the future, after the disposal of England. Communism and National Socialism were opposite ends of the political and economic spectrum and mortal enemies but it seemed worse than foolish to attack Russia before they were finished with England.

His dilemma lay in the fact that he could not possibly allow Sonja to return; he could not tell her parents why nor could he marry her. Even though Russia would collapse like a rotten melon, he remembered what had happened in Poland and knew it would be much worse in Russia. Nor did he personally think it would be the walkover his fellow-planners anticipated. He had read and reread General Ludendorff's operational plans drawn up in 1913 and

472

compared them to actual events in 1914–1917. He had studied the accounts of Napoleon's campaign in 1812 and had dug out as much information as he could on the campaigns of Charles XII, Frederick Barbarossa and even the Knights Templar. Not one had ever suceeded in winning a war against the Russians and occupying historical Russian lands for long. All had been defeated by the nation's vastness and by the Russians' greatest ally, *General Winter*. Even so, Prager knew it could be done because Germany had what Charles XII, Frederick Barbarossa and Napoleon had lacked – mobility. The key was swift movement across the vast plains and the capture of Moscow before winter. But everything must go like clockwork. A delay of even a month could be fatal.

There would be no safety in Russia for Sonja; he could not let her face that. But, over and over again, his mother's face, aged twenty years beyond her time, remained before him. But then he had never once heard her complain or even suspect that there had never been anything but love and affection between her and his incredibly gruff father. He loved Sonja too much to subject her to the coming war storm.

Sonja walked beside him with her chin tucked into the fur collar of her coat. A stray wisp of chestnut hair, turned to gold by the sun, lay against her forehead. What alternative was there? he wondered.

'Marry me,' he said quietly. 'This week, before I return to Berlin.'

The wedding was a simple affair held on Friday in the imposing sandstone Rathaus registry office. His boyhood friend, Joachim Brenner, summoned from Berlin the day before, served as best man. Sonja arrived escorted by her parents, both as grim-faced as if they were attending a funeral. Sonja herself was radiant in a simple white dress and shoes. She dimpled at Brenner's enthusiastic compliments and clasped Prager's hand so tightly he could feel her fine trembling. Both Brenner and Prager were in uniform and the Vishenkos looked even more out of place than usual in their carelessly made and worn clothes and overcoats. The registry official was impatient to have the brief ceremony over and he had begun to hurry through the text when Brenner cleared his throat sharply. A handful of clerks had paused to watch and applauded when Prager kissed the bride and the official glared at them. Brenner and Sonja's parents signed the register as witnesses.

Vishenko shook hands briefly with Prager but declined the wedding breakfast, claiming too much to do before leaving the following day. He hesitated and peered keenly at Prager, as if to say something more, but turned away without doing so. He kissed his daughter perfunctorily. Madame Vishenka clasped Sonja for a moment and closed her eyes – the only sign of emotion shown by either parent. The abruptness of their departure left them all feeling awkward.

Brenner had a taxicab waiting and they drove to the Atlantic Hotel on An der Alster where Prager had reserved a private dining room. There were no other guests, and for a moment, Prager felt the loneliness of being an exile in his own city. He had been away so long he had lost touch with even close boyhood friends – all except Brenner.

Joachim Brenner made up for the lack of guests by entertaining them with an inexhaustible fund of stories from his occupation duties in Holland. He had been attached to General Rudolph Schmidt's XXXIX Panzer Corps at the start of the western campaign and afterwards, had been transferred to Holland for occupation duty.

As the shock of the marriage ceremony wore off, Prager began to wonder why he had resisted for so long and a surprising optimism filled him. Sonja was his wife now and he would see that nothing happened to her. He would make the proper provisions, even take her to Berlin as soon as he could find suitable quarters. That had been his father's mistake – leaving his mother behind in so provincial a town as Hamburg. Berliners were much more sophisticated and it often seemed there were as many foreigners in the city as good Germans.

He glanced at Sonja across the table and thought her stunningly beautiful in the shimmering light of the crystal chandeliers. She laughed gaily at Brenner's jokes and stories and they were soon treating one another as if they were old friends. Suddenly, Prager wanted her so badly that it required all his willpower to remain seated.

'I remember this Dutchman,' Brenner was saying, 'who owned several bakeries but had shut them all, rather than accept a contract from us. He was in his seventies and he simply refused. Told us to arrest him, confiscate his bakeries, whatever, but he simply would not bake bread.

'Well, we couldn't spare enough personnel to operate the bakeries and we were unable to locate any of his former employees immediately because he had burned all the records. But we had to have that bread and the colonel was at his wits' end. So he called in the Gestapo and explained the problem to them and they took me along to make the introductions. The old man wasn't impressed. In fact, he was actually quite rude. The Gestapo officer was a young man, younger than us, in fact and he was trying very hard to be reasonable but it was no use.' He paused to pour more champagne for Sonja and grinned at Prager's barely touched glass.

'Friedrich,' Brenner laughed suddenly, 'you simply must stop acting like you've been sentenced to prison for life. Drink up!'

Sonja turned stricken eyes on him and Prager drained the glass quickly. 'Now fill it up again,' he demanded loudly to cover Brenner's unwittingly cruel remark, and toasted Sonja at length. Never did he ever want Sonja to think that she had forced him into marriage.

'Well,' Brenner went on, pleased that he had brought Prager out of himself, 'the Gestapo officer was pretty smart. He simply arrested the old man's son and family. The whole bunch, husband, wife and children, and threw them into prison. After three days, when he was sure the old man had discovered they were missing, he sent a car for him. The stubborn fool was taken to the prison and shown his son, his daughter-in-law and his grandchildren jammed into a tiny cell. None of them had been fed since their arrest. The next day the bakery was back in business.'

Brenner and Prager laughed. Stories like that were common among anyone who had spent time on occupation duty. There was always initial resistance from the locals but as soon as a little pressure was applied – enough to prick consciences – everyone cooperated easily enough. There had been dire predictions of sabotage and extensive undergrounds springing into existence but the policy of incarcerating all former members of the armed forces and releasing them slowly back to civilian life was paying great dividends.

Last month, Brenner had told him privately, there had been a strike in Holland over the arrests of some Jews and a few labourers intended for Germany. But the swift trial and execution of eighteen leaders had put an end to it quickly enough.

Even in Poland there was relatively little unrest. And a great many captured soldiers had been skilled workers and would prove useful as labourers. It was no longer unusual to see dispirited French or Belgian or Norwegian workers and even a few Poles being herded to and from factories and farms under guard. It was a regrettable way to treat brave enemies but necessary as lives would be saved in the long run. Prager noticed that Sonja had fallen silent and guessed that she was a bit overwhelmed by the wedding and all the champagne.

Joachim Brenner was Prager's oldest friend. They had attended Gross-Lichterfielde Cadet School together, two frightened youngsters trying desperately to conceal their fear. A deep friendship had sprung from that experience and with it a shared determination to excel in everything they did – on the sports field, in the school room and on military exercises.

We are much alike, Prager thought as Brenner whirled Sonja

475

around the room to a waltz played on a gramophone. We even look alike – with our height and our blond, square faces, thin mouths and long, straight noses. Prager had always considered himself the more intellectual and Brenner the more athletic. Brenner was also political and had been an active Party member from the first. Only a month before, during one of their increasingly rare meetings in Berlin, Brenner had confided to Prager that he had requested a transfer to the Waffen SS, the military arm of the Nazi Party.

'I have made some good contacts,' Brenner said over beer and sausages in the officers' mess. 'I will receive an early promotion if I do. Just think,' he punched Prager's arm lightly. 'I won't have to salute you any longer.'

Certainly, Brenner would do better in the Waffen SS, he thought. Since the end of the Polish campaign, they had expanded from four regiments to several divisions and Brenner was everything the SS recruiters were looking for, pure Aryan ancestry, Nordic appearance, intelligent, military training and best of all, from their standpoint, an almost fanatical devotion to the Party.

Brenner's train left at noon and Prager and Sonja saw him off. As the cars clattered out of the busy station, Sonja slipped an arm through his and he felt a slight shiver pass through her body. He understood exactly what she was feeling; the chill wind from the Baltic was sweeping them into the future. They boarded the tram across the street from a discreetly boarded-up building where a British bomb had blown out all the windows a week before.

Bella, horrida bella

Aeneid
Virgil

Crete 18 – 28/29 May 1941

The coastline of Crete was green and confident in the May sunshine when Captain Charles Atkins came on deck. Off to starboard, he could see the single armed trawler that had escorted them from Alexandria and, beyond, the sleepy harbour at Canae. The infinitely softer tones of the Mediterranean after the harsh desert were especially gratifying. The transition had been so abrupt that, even now, Atkins was still conscious of an air of unreality.

In January, he had been transferred to command of a squadron in the 11th Hussars under Colonel Combe. He hadn't liked changing regiments like that. It seemed a betrayal somehow but the exigencies of war, he supposed and, in any event, it was becoming more and more common. His squadron had participated in the mad dash across the desert to Beda Fomm on 4 and 5 February to smash Rommel's record, set in June, by advancing 170 miles in thirty-three hours.

Three days ago, the last tank in that squadron had thrown a tread during the retreat from Sidi Omar. A bogie wheel was smashed and nothing short of a major repair depot would ever put the Stuart back into action. They had drained the petrol tank and set fire to her with reluctance. She was the last of the original complement of American Stuarts they had received in January. With her gone, his squadron had ceased to exist as a fighting force.

There had been dozens of columns of black smoke rising from burning Stuarts and not a few from Rommel's Mark III and IV Panzers as well. *Operation Battleaxe* was supposed to have forced Rommel to relinquish his surprise gains of March and April after the departure of the British Expeditionary Force to Greece. But somehow, it had turned into a series of devastating defeats instead. Atkins had received orders to report to Alexandria for reassignment soonest and he went gratefully. With the exception of a quick trip to Alexandria the previous December, he had been continuously at the front since September.

Once in Alexandria he went first to the Officers' Club and ate an immense breakfast of fresh bacon, eggs and American ham and drank nearly a quart of fresh orange juice and coffee. Only then did he present himself at Seventh Division headquarters only to be sent quickly along to Army headquarters where, as he expected, no one knew why he had been summoned.

He sat in the crowded waiting room in his filthy shorts and blouse, the single Captain's pip he could find attached to one shoulder strap with string, self-conscious among the immaculate staff officers and replacements. No one said a word to him; in fact, all seemed embarrassed at his presence, but there was nothing he could do about it. His kit, tied to the Stuart's rear deck, had been shot away a week before, leaving him only the clothing he wore then and his pistol and holster, his wallet with ten Egyptian pounds and his driving licence. Nothing more. He remembered falling asleep while savouring the various replies he intended to make to the first rear-echelon type who dared say a word to him.

The *Endicott Royal* docked at midmorning. The air raid sirens went as Atkins stepped off the gangway, duffle bag in hand, onto the dock. A sentry shouted and Atkins sprinted towards him as the first Stuka tipped into a dive. The sentry ducked into the protection of a stone wall and Atkins dove after him as the first bombs exploded.

The Stukas took turns diving at the battered quay. Bombs fell about the ship and sprayed gouts of water and stone splinters but their aim wasn't particularly good and the ship came through unscathed. Two Gladiators appeared after ten minutes and the Stukas left, having set fire to a single warehouse.

The sentry, an Australian by his shoulder patch and accent, stood up warily, then climbed over the wall and resumed his post.

'Papers, sir,' he said as if they hadn't just spent ten minutes huddled side by side.

Major-General Bernard Freyberg, VC, sixth commander of Empire forces on Crete, had established his headquarters in a pleasant villa overlooking the harbour. The place had a purposeful air about it; Atkins supposed that the staff, those who had survived, had shaken down into a rather efficient group. The GSO1, a major, to whom he reported, wore his left arm in a sling as a result of a bombing raid.

'Took us a while to believe that Jerry'd press on here,' the major told him, 'as we certainly can't do him all that much harm from here. Unless, of course, he intends to move on Palestine. In any event, glad to have you with us. You will assume command of a tank squadron at Heraklion, one of the three airfields on the island. The other two are at Maleme near by and along the coast at Rethimnon. New Zealanders and some Greeks. Mixed lot but awfully keen.'

The major lit a cigarette and exhaled with relish. 'Just came this morning. First I've had in a week. Very short on just about anything you can name.' Awkwardly, he unrolled a map on his desk.

'Now then, you will have a scratch squad of six infantry tanks, Matilda Mark IIs. Afraid it's the best we can do. Brought them out of Greece a bit the worse for wear. I'm afraid. Intelligence suggests that Jerry will try to blitz us again using parachutists to establish an initial landing with sea-borne troops to follow. Lot of nonsense, parachutists, but then for all we know, they might be tunnelling across from Greece.'

In spite of his feigned cheerfulness, GSO-1 rubbed a hand across his face in the gesture of utter weariness and resignation Atkins had seen countless times before. A chill ran through him; it usually presaged defeat.

'We have about 28,000 men available. Twenty-one thousand of them were evacuated from Greece and are short of equipment, not in the best of health and bone tired. But they will be sufficient to hold defensive positions if the Royal Navy will see to the invasion fleet.'

A rickety motor car converted for carrying cargo by the simple expedient of having its roof and sides cut away drove him along the coast. The air was cool and fresh with the scent of spring and the sky cloudless and as perfect a blue as he had ever seen over a Devon moor.

He had left GHQ with the feeling of unreality growing stronger by the minute. What was the matter with these people? he wondered. They'd faced the German in Greece. Hadn't they learned yet that he doesn't bluff? The signs were very plain. There would be an invasion of Crete and, when it was over, the Germans would threaten the entire British presence in the Middle East. They could bomb Palestine, the Suez Canal and Cairo from Crete and invasions mounted from here and the Greek mainland would allow them to flank any defensive position the Empire forces might establish. In conjunction with a renewed Italian–German drive, supported by Rommel, in Cyrenaica, the Axis powers could easily burst through to the Middle Eastern oilfields and beyond, to India. There was absolutely nothing else to occupy Hitler's attention now. Greece and the Balkans had been conquered and the Romanian oilfields were secure. Only a small part of the German army was employed at the moment and here they were, proposing to defend a vital island in the eastern Mediterranean with a handful of exhausted, ill-equipped men. It was beyond belief. For the first time, Atkins began to seriously doubt that Great Britain could survive this war.

The driver was a dour Welshman in one of the British support companies and he responded to Atkins' questions with one-syllable answers until Atkins gave it up. The road wound along the coast above virgin beaches and tumbling cliffs. The cultivated fields gave way to pastures dotted with sheep and goats and the occasional figure of a herdsman. Olives and oaks and numerous other trees he could not identify were dotted here and there about the slopes that ran up into quite respectable mountains. There were nearly two hundred miles of coast on the northern shore alone to defend and Atkins did not dismiss the threat of parachutists as easily as the staff officer had.

The town of Heraklion seemed to consist of neatly whitewashed cottages along a central road and the airfield was only a relatively flat area of grass with a few rickety buildings beyond, its landing strip marked out with rags tied to stakes. He found his squadron in a bombed-out warehouse nearby.

Atkins stood at the entrance and struggled with something approaching despair. There were five, rather than six, tanks and two were total wrecks. The two-pounder gun on the third drooped and the engine hatch covers had been removed. One track had been stripped and laid on the concrete floor while two fitters bashed at it with sledge hammers and a welder stood nearby waiting. My God, he thought, not even a replacement track?

When he walked into the warehouse, a sergeant-major shouted for attention. The two fitters stopped bashing and others scattered about the hangar on various chores stopped what they were doing and sauntered over. The sergeant-major saluted.

One tread link had been twisted at right angles to its normal position, he saw. The welder brought the link to red heat and the fitters worked it with the sledge hammers to straighten it. But, even if they succeeded, it would not hold for long, Atkins realized. The link had to be properly heat treated and it could not be done with only a welding torch and the can of motor oil that stood ready.

He raised an interrogative eyebrow at the sergeant.

'Sergeant-Major Timothy O'Brien, sir. We only need to move the tank a short way.'

Atkins nodded. 'I see. Carry on.'

Sergeant-Major O'Brien introduced the men of the squadron and Atkins discovered they were indeed a mixed bag – British, New Zealanders and Greeks. But they were all tank men and the Greeks had sufficient English to understand orders.

By the end of the afternoon, Atkins was reeling with the paucity of resources in men and equipment. He had two operational tanks and one that could perhaps be used as a gun platform. They also had one American jeep, one breakdown lorry missing most of its equipment, including the forge and power lathe and only sufficient ammunition for two days' normal usage. Atkins quickly approved O'Brien's suggestion that they send out two of the Greek soldiers to forage for supplies as they had rations remaining for only one more day.

The resourceful O'Brien seemed to be the one saving feature in a disastrous situation. Even so, Atkins slept badly that night, mind buzzing with a thousand tasks that needed doing.

At dawn on 19 May, the last two Hurricanes left Heraklion for Egypt. O'Brien told him that since the first of the month, RAF strength on Crete had dwindled from thirty-five operational aircraft to four Hurricanes and three Gladiators. And now, even they had been withdrawn.

The fitters had succeeded in repairing the tank tread and, by working late into the previous night, had remounted it. The shrapnel-splintered fuel lines had been replaced and just enough scarce petrol measured out to move the tank into position. Atkins watched Sergeant-Major O'Brien ease the behemoth around obstacles and sharp stones that might break the weak link. By 0900, the tank reached the pit that had been dug, reversed and eased down into the hole. They all breathed a sigh of relief when the engine shut down.

The bombing raids began in earnest that afternoon. Heinkel 111 and Junkers 52 aircraft attacked at will, concentrating on the airfields. The anti-aircraft guns fired sparingly, conscious of their limited ammunition. No damage was done except to the grassy surface of the airfield and that was repairable quickly enough. When one bomber dropped out of formation trailing smoke across the sky and exploded in the hills, Atkins cheered as fiercely as the rest.

The bombing continued all during the night of 19/20 May and, shortly after dawn, the anti-aircraft guns, which had been silent during darkness, opened up. Atkins came awake slowly in the trench with the dank smell of wet earth in his nostrils and the shuddering jar of guns racking his body. Gradually, it penetrated his sleep-fogged mind that no bombs were falling. He sat up carefully and peered over the edge.

Countless patches of white drifted across the airfield while above droned low-flying aircraft. The anti-aircraft gunners were having a field day. Atkins saw a line of parachutists stream from a Junkers that disentegrated moments later. Shrapnel ripped through the figures and several plummeted straight down.

They could hear the parachutists shouting to one another as they descended. There was little enough cover on the airfield and in spite of the fact that they managed to get a machine gun into action, the New Zealanders mopped them up by the end of the first hour, killing more than a hundred in the air or on the ground.

Atkins watched and understood for the first time the Finnish officer's, Captain Johan Erko, hatred for parachutists. Above, more tri-engined Junkers aircraft circled through the meagre anti-aircraft fire.

Atkins sat beside the dug-in Matilda trying to think through the implications of the parachute landings. Was this the start of the invasion or a diversion? The telephone exchange was out of action and the airfield commander had sent a messenger off immediately by motorcycle. But it might be hours before he returned. One of the Greek enlisted men brought him a mug of tea and a ration tin of bully beef and he ate it methodically. He was not hungry but he had learned in Finland to eat whenever and however the opportunity offered.

There was the perplexing problem of his standing orders; at the first indication of attack, he was to send two tanks along the coast road five miles to support an infantry brigade waiting there to repel a coastal invasion. But he had only two operational tanks. Even if he split them up, it would be a useless gesture. Experience in the desert had taught him over and over to concentrate his strength, not disperse it. If they refused to play that game in Crete, Atkins told himself, if they refused to panic, if they held their ground and brought as much firepower to bear against the invaders as possible, they might defeat the parachutists at their weakest point – supply and reinforcements.

The sound of more aircraft droning in from the sea rumbled over the airfield. Three German prisoners in floppy camouflage-striped overalls, two leading a man with a bandage about his eyes, paused with their guards to listen. Atkins watched them, noting the set, sullen expressions that never seemed to change. He had seen German prisoners in Norway, in England, in the desert and now in Crete. He remembered the four German soldiers in Greece – boys loose for a summer holiday until they had encountered the British soldiers. They had changed instantly into the same sullen, hating men one saw at railway termini under guard or staring through the barbed wire of desert enclosures. Hating, always hating. Did we look like that to them, he wondered, when the roles were reversed? God knew that there were far more British prisoners in this war than German.

The second wave of parachutists was much larger. Twelve tri-engined aircraft flew over so low that Atkins fancied he could see the pilots wincing as anti-aircraft fire racketed about them. The aircraft were so low that the soldiers fired at them even as furious NCOs raced from trench to trench shouting at them to stop wasting ammunition.

As they approached in the clear morning light, he could see the black ovals of open hatches in the sides and suddenly, the air beneath each aircraft was full of aerial seeds wisping silk. Each blossomed into a white canopy seconds before their burdens would have been dashed against the ground. Another flight passed over and other bundles plummeted out. A vagrant breeze caught at the parachutes and several drifted beyond the confines of the airfield.

Atkins counted the parachutists as they emerged from the last aircraft – twenty-two. How many aircraft had there been so far today? Thirty, forty, fifty? More than a thousand German parachutists had landed and most of them killed. A surge of optimism ran through him. The Nazis could not continue to sustain such losses much longer.

He climbed onto the hull-down Matilda and sat behind the machine gunner, watching the tracers lick across the field, every fifth bullet a glowing dot of phosphorus streaking towards the enemy so that the gunner could correct his aim and 'walk' his gun onto the target. The stick figures at this distance were not real, merely gallery targets.

A spatter of bullets clanged against the turret and one whipped through the leg of his trousers. Atkins dove behind the protection of the turret and the New Zealand gunner grinned.

'Bastards is playing for keeps, sir.'

At dawn on 21 May, Atkins watched a glider sweep in from the sea and sail majestically inland. At first sight, he supposed it to be a Junkers transport with engine trouble. A Very flare shot up and the anti-aircraft gun crews opened fire. The pilot banked but with his limited manoeuvring ability, the guns merely walked onto him. The glider blew up and rained bits and pieces over the beach.

The second glider barely avoided the same fate and as it slid down in a steep approach directly across the beach, head on to the guns, Atkins was certain it would crash. Instead, the pilot flared the craft at the last moment and it bounced to a stop and slewed to the right. Immediately men and equipment erupted as mortar shells began to fall about the craft.

Through his field glasses he saw three men tug a bundle on a wheeled pallet away from the glider. He shouted the range and the Matilda's two-pounder gun bellowed. A flash went up just beyond the downed glider and the gunner made a slight correction. The next shell was on but a bit wide. One of the three men was down but the other two dragged the pallet away, using it as a shield from rifle fire. The third shell smashed the glider to kindling and it began to burn.

Fifteen minutes later, a howitzer shell exploded forty yards in front of the Matilda. The glider had brought in an artillery piece, probably a mountain howitzer or a 75 millimetre light infantry gun, he thought. Atkins saw a flash beyond the burning glider and a solid wall of concussion nearly knocked him from the turret.

He clutched at a handhold and hung on, shaking his head to clear it, too stunned to be frightened. He saw the gunner sprawled half-in, half-out and clawed his way up the curving side and down into the turret. The man was still alive, retching feebly, but there was no time for him. Everything seemed to waver, as if he were under water and each motion required conscious effort.

His feet found the turret control pedal and he forced his weight down. The turret bumped to the right; he pressed the left pedal and it bounced back in over-correction. He tried again and got it positioned.

'Load!' he rasped and instantly felt the driver's hand smack his leg. He eased the cannon muzzle up a bit and pressed the firing pedal. The gun went off with a crack and the barrel recoiled smoothly. The shell exploded beyond the glider but he had lost his field glasses and could not tell how close he had come to the German gun.

Another shell ploughed into the ground to his left as he corrected, but it failed to go off. The hand smacked his leg again and he fired immediately. Twice more, as fast as the gun could be loaded, he fired. The German field gun had their range and the next shell would be on target.

Smoke from the last shell drifted past the position and he bumped the muzzle up, swearing at the recalcitrant mount. A piece of shrapnel had struck the rim bending it partway into the track. He fired and a cloud of flame and dirt blotted out the German gun. He bumped the muzzle up a bit more and fired a fifth round and a brilliant flash banished the dawn shadows for an instant as the ready ammunition blew up.

The Greek gunner was dead. A shell splinter had torn his throat and shoulder open and he had bled to death in seconds. Atkins knew he could have done nothing for the man but the combination of the horrible wound, the near concussion he had suffered plus nearly forty sleepless hours combined to make him sick to his stomach. He slithered down the side of the tank and vomited.

The driver, another Greek who could speak no English, led him to a slit trench where he lay back and closed his eyes, seeking time to absorb everything. After a while, he noticed that his sleeve was wet with blood. His upper arm began to burn and he saw that a shell splinter had ripped away the cloth and sliced through the muscle just beneath the skin. He knew he ought to put a dressing on the cut but he hadn't the strength to do so. Strangely enough he thought, he hadn't been afraid.

Bombing raids were intermingled with parachute drops all during the 21st and on into the night. Flares of one side or the other blazed through the dark hours and Atkins was astounded by the audacity shown by the parachutists and glider pilots, and by the casualties they suffered.

The parachutists were shot in their hundreds as they dangled beneath white silk canopies which made excellent targets in the darkness. One Junkers pilot tried a low-level pass across the airfield but misjudged and none of the parachutes had time to open. Twenty-two men were smashed to death on the airfield. But the worst casualties occurred among the glider troops.

Crete is a mountainous island, rugged and strewn with huge boulders and clumps of low-growing trees while thick stands of brush covered the few flat areas. One pilot made a great low sweep inland from the west, a marvel of powerless flying, and saw the wall too late. He tried to lift the nose but his speed was gone and the glider stalled, dropped like a stone onto the stone wall and blew up with astounding ferocity. Atkins guessed it had been carrying ammunition.

Other gliders smashed into trees, or fouled in clumps of bushes, or were shot down by the weakening anti-aircraft fire. Disregarding their insane casualties, the German invaders came on in ever-increasing numbers and at dawn, Atkins knew that the battle for the airfield was lost.

Junkers bombers, turned into troop-carriers, began to land in sequence. The first aircraft brought in a small bull-dozer to push damaged aircraft and other equipment from the runway. More 75 millimetre field guns were brought and, by late afternoon, the German barrage was turning the tide. Atkins lost one of the two operable tanks remaining to him. Only the news that the Royal Navy had finally cornered and sunk the German battleship, *Bismarck*, cheered the hard-pressed defenders.

The Germans were in complete control of the airfield by that evening and Atkins, crouching in the lee of a rock ledge on a slope well inland was reminded strongly of Norway. Only the snow and cold were missing. The Stukas were the same, stooping out of the sky like birds of prey, as was the line of grey figures moving inexorably towards him like the beaters in old hunting prints. And the fear was the same, a solid lump in his gut, an acid that poured along every nerve fibre and twisted and caught in his throat so that he had to consciously suppress the gag reflex.

Atkins could see it in the faces of the others with him as the Stukas pounded them and mortar shells searched out their hiding places. They were running again. Why? In Finland, in Norway, in France, North Africa, Greece and now Crete. Another day, at most, before they would have to surrender. Surrender? Go into the bag with all the thousands of other Empire soldiers from Norway to Greece? Why not? he wondered. The war was almost over now. With Greece and Cyprus safely under his thumb, Hitler had only to step across to North Africa and provide Rommel with all the supplies and reinforcements needed. A final sweep into Egypt and Palestine and the Suez and the Middle East oilfields were his. The Empire was finished.

'Captain Charles Atkins!'

He hadn't been aware of the body sliding in beside him as a new flurry of mortar bombs exploded.

'Yes,' he shouted above the roar. 'I'm Captain Atkins.'

'Orders from HQ, sir.' The runner drew out a tattered map. 'You're to take any tanks you have left to this pass,' he marked a cut through the hills leading down to the south coast and handed the map to Atkins. 'You're to dig in and hold the Hun as long as possible. When your position becomes untenable, get away as best you can.'

Atkins stared at the map, visualizing the lines of German infantry sweeping into the hills with their mortars and field guns, with their close order air support from marauding Stukas and Me.109Es, and he thought about what he had seen in Cyrenaica and recalled that momentary surge of hope when so few of them had bested the entire Libyan Army of the Italian Empire. Hell, it didn't make any difference now.

It was Dombas all over again, Atkins thought bitterly as the last of the New Zealanders straggled through the shallow gap in the hills and disappeared into the sparse forest. Beyond, in the waning evening twilight, he could see the deep blue of the Mediterranean. In an hour, it would be dark and a British destroyer would run the blockade of Italian submarines and German E-boats towards shore. Already he could see the first faint smudges of smoke as Empire troops began burning their equipment.

The Boche were just beyond the next ridge and his position had been bombed twice by Stukas flying from the three captured airfields. Now they could land, refuel and rearm and be back over the target in less than thirty minutes.

They had hidden the tank in a defile overlooking the approach to the pass. The pass itself was hardly deserving of the name, being little more than a gap in the ridge. Yet it was the logical route south to the sea. Atkins had no illusions that he could hold them off for long. At the first sign of resistance, the Nazis would send out flanking parties west and east into the hills and he didn't have the troops to counter such a move and the Nazis knew it. But Atkins had learned a few things in Norway.

All that day, he and Sergeant O'Brien had scouted the lines of retreat to within a few miles of the beach. The route they had chosen was chancy but provided some shelter from air attack, especially if made at night. His rearguard was composed of twelve riflemen, a tank crew and the sergeant. They had the one Matilda, two two-inch mortars and the one breakdown lorry emptied of its remaining equipment. His orders were simple enough; hold the enemy as long as possible to permit the escape of the maximum number of fighting troops.

If successful, would they take their place in the Empire's pantheon of heroes beside Alfred the Great at White Horse Hill, Drake at his bowling, Marlborough at Blenheim, Wellington at Waterloo or Gordon at Khartoum? What nonsense, he thought bitterly. It no longer seemed heroic when you were the one at the sharp end.

It was sunset before the first lines of grey appeared on the ridge below. The Stukas had done their work and gone, leaving for a few moments a silence so intense as to seem solid. He brushed the spatters of dirt from his battle dress and nodded to Sergeant O'Brien who wriggled away and he heard the sound of the Matilda's engine start. She heaved ponderously across the bomb-blasted landscape like a fat matron on Blackpool beach, into position and the engine noise faded to muted rumblings. Atkins turned back to the slope. The Germans had reached the bottom now and, in the fading light, he could see three-man parties humping off to the side to set up their mortars. The rest came on fully confident that they could brush aside the remaining defenders. The problem was, Atkins thought wryly, that he shared their confidence.

A rifleman slithered to him with the news that he had seen a large Boche party form up and move east, obviously intending to cross the ridge and take them in the flank. Alternatively, they would be in a position to cut them off from the beach if they should escape.

How many times had the Germans performed that same manoeuvre in Norway? he thought. They were brilliant tacticians but at the same time unimaginative. If it worked well, why change, seemed to be their attitude.

O'Brien was beside him again. 'Tank crew's ready and the explosive charges are set, Captain.'

Atkins grunted acknowledgement. He was concentrating on the lead elements. The slope was steep enough that it was beginning

488

to force the wings into the centre, bunching the soldiers as they passed the first marker. The choking sensation made it difficult to speak, to breathe. Everything depended on his getting off the first shots before their mortars went into action. If Jerry acted contrary to his usual practice, they were finished.

The last line passed the marker and he breathed a bit easier. 'Sergeant O'Brien,' he said trying to make his voice sound formal and not succeeding, 'you may open fire.'

O'Brien shouted and the Matilda's two-pounder gun banged, followed by the thunking of the mortars. The 50-calibre machine gun rattled and four hundred yards below on the slope, men fell or ducked and ran. Atkins counted the seconds on his stopwatch. At thirty, the first enemy ranging shots began to fall. He waited fifteen more seconds and waved at O'Brien who jumped onto the tank and banged his rifle butt against the tank turret.

The tank engine roared and the two mortar crews leapt aboard as it bumped around in a circle. Atkins struck a match, shielded it with both hands until it was well alight and touched it to the fuse.

A mortar shell burst twenty feet to his right and he ducked involuntarily and banged his head on a rock outcropping. For a moment, the pain almost overpowered him. He staggered blindly to his feet, fear overriding the pain and stumbled after the Matilda. The tank is moving too fast. He stumbled and lost more ground against the uncaring monstrous shape belching petrol fumes. The pain in his skull was so great that he was half-blind and his limbs refused to function properly. And then O'Brien was beside him, urging him to run. A moment later his hand found a metal bar and he felt himself being pulled onto the rear deck.

The first charge went off just as the Matilda veered sharply to the right and began to descend. Darkness was almost complete now. His vision had cleared although the pain still had the intensity of a red-hot needle. They were well below the crest now and following the sheep track found earlier in the day. The path was narrow and the trees overhung it closely. Behind, Atkins heard the dull boom of mortar bombs interspersed with the sharper cracks of the gelignite they had brought from the airfield at Heraklion and which now sounded as if they were still defending the pass. It wouldn't fool the Nazis long, but perhaps enough to allow them to escape.

The Matilda nosed out of the pine forest above a steep gully. A dry water course wandered through it for half a mile to a dense stand of pines. The coast was less than four miles away but they had one last task to perform. The hills behind gleamed with the last traces of skyglow as the tank engine idled down and the mortar crews dispersed to either side. O'Brien spoke to the tank commander in a low voice and the turret revolved and the gun depressed with a dull whine. The 50-calibre was charged with a fresh belt and the sound of the breech latch closing was loud against the distant sounds of the one-sided fire fight.

O'Brien materialized. 'All set . . . look there, sir. At the edge of the trees.'

In the pale light that was more imagination than substance, Atkins thought he saw movement. But his head ached so badly that it was difficult to concentrate and every few seconds, his vision blurred.

Soldiers moved out of the trees half a mile away and down into the gully, bunched together and confident their quarry was pinned down in the pass. He waited until the last man had left the trees and added another few seconds for luck. The light was too dim in the shadows for an accurate count but he estimated close to sixty men in the party, half a company – more of them than he expected. They would have at least three light machine guns and two mortars.

An unexpected surge of fear choked him. He must let them go; they were clearly heading up into the pass, still an hour of climbing away for them. They had not turned down to the coast so they clearly had no idea that the defenders had broken out. What in the name of God had possessed them to send such a large force? How many men and tanks did they think were opposing them? What would it hurt? Not them surely. They would make it to the beach before the Germans discovered they had been tricked. If he let them go, he might be accused of cowardice, of failing to do his duty which was to kill Germans. Atkins took a deep breath. Perhaps. But there were times when it made more sense to ignore one's duty and save one's life.

'We will withdraw as quietly as possible,' he whispered to O'Brien. The New Zealander let out a sigh of relief and waved the two mortar crews in. A moment later, the tank engine rumbled softly and they backed away from the gully and down onto the sheep track.

Christ in Heaven, but I'm weak, Atkins thought. He lay back against the turret ring, one wrist locked through a hand hold and gave himself up to pain and exhaustion.

They did not teach you about fear at Sandhurst, he thought. Nor did anyone talk of it. Stiff upper lip syndrome, he supposed. Fear was not supposed to exist for soldiers; therefore, why would one speak of it. Instead, you learned of it first hand, in Finland for instance, and in Norway and in the desert and in Crete.

The majority of soldiers learn to cope but for the minority, the fear increases slowly, inexorably until one is crushed entirely. And

490

not all the soft-spoken words of a clinical psychiatrist in London, nor all the examples of brave men about you made much difference. Every combat soldier learned that there were only four ways out of combat – death, a severe wound, madness – what was once called shell shock – and survival.

'Are you all right, sir?'

Atkins heard O'Brien's voice from a great distance and felt hands fumble at his battledress. His blouse was wet and he became aware of a throbbing pain below his shoulder. He touched his battle jacket and felt the torn edge of cloth where the shrapnel had struck him. The fear was going away. He felt warm and comfortable and he was in his old room again with the familiar books and toys on the shelf, the radio set his aunt and uncle had given him one Christmas, a picture of the mother he barely remembered and the father he never knew on the mantel. Snow was falling beyond the window but a good fire burned in the grate and the room was warm and full of security. Captain Charles Atkins, Fourth Hussars, Royal Tank Regiment, His Majesty's Forces, died peacefully.

Epilogue

Vasteras, Sweden 2 January 1947

Torsten Fredriksson paused on the porch to button his old loden coat against the morning chill. He stepped down and crossed the yard, noting that the debris from the New Year's fireworks were coated with a thin rind of white. Snowed a bit during the night, he thought.

He edged between the two fence posts that formed the passage into the lower fields and followed the path through the woodlot, bare and stark now against the grey sky. The day was filled with the pearl-like luminescence that only exists in wintery sub-arctic latitudes. In the distance, a crow cawed harshly, warning of his approach. A stream, crusted with ice, ran along the bottom of the fields on its way to the Svartdn and ultimately to Lake Malaren. The crow tired of sentry duty at last and the silence took on a life of its own.

In 1942, in the first flush of monetary success from his daily column, he had bought the old farm as a retreat. But, during the war, there had been little time to visit and if it hadn't been for the American pilot he had hired from the internment camp at Korsnas, the place would have fallen to ruin.

The four months since his return from Berlin in late August was the longest he had ever spent at the farm. And the book had occupied so much of his time that he hadn't come down here since October when the woods had been a blaze of colour. Thinking about it now, he could hardly believe that he had completed the entire draft of the first volume in so short a time. And the second volume was already taking shape in his mind.

He thought of the draft waiting on his desk for editing and was struck again by the parallels between the war's first two years and the first two of peace. The dictatorships had seemed unstoppable: Germany had smashed Poland in three weeks; the Soviet Union had followed suit in the Baltic States and the Balkans; Japan had occupied China, Manchuria and Indochina as fast as she could ship troops. The Soviet Union, under the guise of national security, had continued the pattern at the war's end. Strange, he thought, how national security always went hand-in-hand with a paranoiac national need for expansion.

The European democracies, prostrated by the war, seemed powerless to intervene as Poland, Hungary, Eastern Germany and

Romania were drawn into the Soviet maw while the Americans underwent another of their periodic pacifist convulsions – as in 1939–41. They had yet to realize that their ocean barriers were no longer effective, thanks to a development of their own, the atomic bomb.

Fredriksson remembered Yalta and Churchill's barely concealed despair when he failed to persuade Roosevelt that Soviet demands were based as much on the need to acquire resources, manpower and Western Europe's industrial bases which – however war-damaged – were still far greater than their own, as on the need to secure their western borders. Somehow Roosevelt had been persuaded, or had persuaded himself, that the only motivating factor in Stalin's apparent intransigence was the need to secure Russian borders.

In 1940, Russia's ability to expand had been limited by a powerful Germany and a determined Adolf Hitler. After Stalingrad, Nazi Germany was only a factor to be dispensed with as rapidly as possible in her march to European hegemony. Today, only a disinterested America stood in her way. How far would she go before the western democracies rallied to the danger? Yugoslavia and Bulgaria were teetering and Czechoslovakia was marked. Denmark and Greece had been saved, but barely. France and Italy teetered on the brink of Communist-elected governments. And in Asia, the Chinese Communists under Mao Tse-Tung had launched a total civil war against the Nationalist Government after the apparent collapse of talks arranged by the American, General George C. Marshall.

He recalled a discussion he had with Keith Thorne the day they had met by chance in London in 1940. He had told an incredulous Thorne then that America was the greatest stumbling block to an Allied victory and might possibly cause the Allies to lose the war. 'You Americans will again wait until the last minute before you join in. In 1917, the Germans miscalculated and there was still time for your armies to make a difference. This time, they will not make the same mistake and when you do decide, it will be too late.'

He had been nearly right. Germany had stood at the very gates of Moscow when Japan's ill-timed attack had pushed the Americans into the conflict. Their resulting aid had barely tipped the scales in Russia and North Africa in 1942.

But this time? He shook his head as a combination of disgust and weariness ran through him. The Americans will watch all of Eastern Europe disappear and God alone knows how much of Western Europe as well. Berlin was all but surrounded now and daily, Allied prerogatives were being eliminated. The Russians maintained a stout foothold in eastern Austria and only a handful of Allied troops held them back.

It seemed to him that the world had learned no more from the Second World War than it had from the First, or the Napoleonic wars or any of the previous cataclysms of history. What mechanism of inertia ensured that aggression was rarely resisted until the alternative was war?

'My, how your ideas and ideals have changed,' Fredriksson mocked himself aloud. The socialism and liberal thinking of his younger days seemed to have disappeared in the depths of a Russian winter and a Gestapo prison.

So, was he in fact looking at it from the wrong perspective? Was the Soviet Union right to commit aggression against smaller nations to ensure her own security? Or was the ancient dream of secure borders and non-interference still valid in an age of long-range bombers, rockets and atomic bombs?

He could understand now why only victors wrote history. It was so much easier to think in black and white terms than to bother sorting out the conflicting needs and requirements of sovereign peoples and their self-serving leaders.